CLOAKING
FATE

CLOAKING FATE
Copyright © 2025 by N. A. Walker.

For information contact :
www.nawalkerauthor.com

Publisher : The Pegasus Publishing LLC - Star Mount Press
Edited by Emma Williams at Scott Editorial
Book and Cover design by Ruxandra Tudorica at Methyss Art
Author Photograph by Nicole Walker

ISBNs:
979-8-9923980-1-4 (Hardcover), 979-8-9923980-0-7 (Paperback)

First Edition: February 2025

10 9 8 7 6 5 4 3 2 1

To those who dare give life to dreams.
You are never too old.
It is never too late.

Dear Reader,

Thank you for chancing this tale. *Cloaking Fate* began as a tentative whisp in the depths of my unconscious imagination. I dreamt of a young woman in a dark dungeon bearing the impossible burden of fate.

I did not know her name, her story, why she trembled in the shadows, nor even who thrust that responsibility upon her. I only knew that she carried it with grim resignation, accepting the sacrifice it demanded, wanting more than anything to cloak herself in the illusion of freedom.

This is that story. Welcome to Ilistaar.

N. A. Walker

P.S. If you enjoy this story, please leave me a review!

To keep up with writing news, you can subscribe to my newsletter here:

www.nawalkerauthor.com

CLOAKING FATE

A CURSE OF FATE
BOOK ONE

N. A. WALKER

Prologue

As Written in the Godscripts

WHEN THE GODKING FIRST FOUND her, she appeared as a burst of blinding light in the nothingness. There were no stars, there was no universe. No planets or creatures. No air to breathe, no truths to hear, no time by which to mark one's passing. There was only *he*. Even his solitude did not have a name, for there was no company with which to compare it.

And then, suddenly, gloriously, there was *her*.

The moment he beheld her, the Godking knew their meeting signified something of paramount importance. He recognized a hollowness within himself, a thing he'd previously not believed could exist—a void now filled by her presence.

She was his.

His match. His mate. His Goddess.

That first clash of their powers created the cosmos as they are known today. Stars were born in the wake of their connection. Suns spun outward from their touch. Planets, moons, and entire galaxies surged and spiraled, filling the universe as the Godking and Goddess explored one another. As they loved and raged, radiating their passion across the worlds.

When the Godking gazed upon her, he became aware of that which he had been missing. What he first came to understand and then grew to cherish.

Joy. Desire. Love.

And so it was between them.

For a time.

CLOAKING FATE

After an unnamed eternity, the Goddess and the Godking yearned for more. They wove a new world and populated it with various beasts—things that flew, swam, crawled, slithered, and ran. Their planet held vast deserts, forests, jungles, seas, mountains, and plains. It was blanketed with flora and given all manner of weather. Day was separated from night.

They descended to the world they had created, each fashioning for themselves a physical form.

The Goddess's chosen form was humanoid and graceful, with ripples of gilded hair that glowed like the sun and fell in dazzling tendrils to her feet. Her eyes were pure starlight and shone like two moonbeams. Her fiery spirit, with its effervescent temperaments, was contained in a small womanly shape that danced, sang, and laughed.

The Godking, as her counterpart, fashioned himself a predator's body. A blend of man and beast capable of prowling on all fours or walking upright as he chose. He was lithe and powerful at once, with broad hands tipped in vicious claws and razor-sharp teeth set in a jaw that could crush bone. Sleek, black hair clothed him, with a longer hackled ridge that traveled the length of his spine from head to his powerful furred tail.

The Godking was strong in all the ways the Goddess was delicate. Where she was soft, he was hard. Where she could be underestimated, he was overwhelming.

They stood together on the planet they made and found themselves wanting. Their world was good, but the yearning remained. The Goddess looked up at her mate. Her light eyes met the dark of his own, and they knew.

They wanted something born of their flesh, infused with their life, and endowed with both forms. Two halves made whole. So, together, they created the first race of beings, the shurii, and gifted them the new world.

They called it Ilistaar.

Being of both gods, the shurii could take either form and shifted between the two at will. Their first form was humanoid, like that of the Goddess, while their second form was similar to the one the Godking chose.

For a long time, the Goddess and the Godking were pleased with what they'd done. They watched from afar as the beings they created grew and flourished. The shurii multiplied in their world, bearing children and forming families, which made the Goddess happy and the Godking proud. So much so that the gods decided to live among them.

Their reception by the shurii was as they had hoped. They were worshiped and adored.

The Goddess spent her days in the fields, giving life to the soil and blessing the shurii's harvests. She helped the people plant their crops, brought rain to the landscape, and took joy in delivering an abundance of food to the families. The Autumn Reaping became her holiday, and feasts were held each fall in her honor.

The Godking found himself drawn to the children, entertaining them with stories, playing games, and hiding from them in the forests. He taught the young to develop the heightened senses of their second forms by letting them hunt him through the wood. As the young shurii grew from children to adults, the Godking was given the honor of that transition. Celebrations were held for young reaching maturity and the Godking attended each of them, his pride overflowing.

At the end of each day, the Goddess and Godking stood together, happy, and reflected on the beauty of their creation.

But beauty does not equal goodness. For the gods also bestowed upon their race the freedom of will. And the wills of mortals are fickle things.

One day, a day that has since been wiped from the histories, a female shurii dared to seduce the Godking.

The Goddess was away in the fields, and the Godking was visiting the children of a small village. There were countless villages throughout the lands of Ilistaar by now, and he made a point to choose settlements to visit at random, acquainting himself with the shurii who lived in each.

When he arrived, the youngest child ran to him and threw her tiny arms around one of his legs. The Godking picked up the child, claws gentle as he clutched her. She giggled and squirmed, and her delight warmed him. The child's mother, Seren, came looking for her young.

She approached the Godking in her second form, and he was surprised. All the other female shurii in the village favored the Goddess's form.

"Is there danger?" demanded the Godking, clutching the child close to his powerful body.

Seren laughed gaily. "There is no danger," she said. "I simply like the form you gave best." She liked how fast she could run, her improved sight and sense of smell, her sharp claws, and the ability to defend herself. She claimed these things were lacking in the Goddess's form. She liked to hunt and climb and use her teeth, and she could not do these things as well in her first form. Seren explained that her child's father had died the previous year, and she found she could do many things herself, which she had previously relied upon him to do.

"The form you gave is superior, Godking," she said. "If you would forgive my candor."

The Godking was flattered, despite himself. The Goddess was renowned for her beauty and gracious heart. While the Godking was loved, the form he had given was seldom preferred by the female shurii.

He said this to Seren, who smiled at him, showing small, sharp teeth. She reached out, taking her lovely child from him, and sent her to play with the other children.

"Do you know what else is far superior in this form?" Seren asked him, leaning in close.

"I know all things," the Godking replied. "Though I should like to hear your thoughts."

"The giving and taking of pleasure," she said.

"Is that so?" the Godking mused, and Seren nodded eagerly. He found he was curious. Gods were all-powerful beings, but because they lived among their mortal creations, they were also subjected to their temptations and scheming. The Godking considered Seren's words. He'd been faithfully devoted to the Goddess for a long time and found great pleasure in her form. He liked the way she felt, her skin soft and supple beneath him. He liked her smallness and how she trusted him with her delicate body. And yet, he had never been with a female that shared his form. Was it different? Were there pleasures to be found that he had not yet discovered?

The Godking left the village and returned home. When he made love to the Goddess later under the stars they'd created, he found himself wondering if there might be something he was missing.

The Godking visited Seren's village again. And then again, and soon every day. He spent time with the children. He walked among the shurii, spoke with them, ate and drank with them, yet found himself distracted by Seren's flitting presence. Sometimes he saw her, and other times she was not there, but each day the Godking looked for her. Each morning, he bid farewell to the Goddess, kissed her mouth, ran his clawed fingers through her sunlight hair, and then went to the village and looked for Seren.

Weeks, and then months, passed in this way. Gods are patient beings, with time in abundance, so the Godking waited. Eventually, he was bound to see Seren undistracted, and she would speak with him again.

To occupy himself, the Godking spent time wandering the lands of Ilistaar. He prowled the dense forests, thick, spongy mosses tickling the pads of his feet. He napped on grassy plains, basking in the warmth of the sun. He climbed mountains, his black coat blending in with the shadows of the deep caverns and canyons. Sometimes, the Goddess would leave her fields and join him. Together, they would walk on the white, sandy beaches of the coast and play in the turquoise surf. The Godking even traveled as far as the great desert, a hot, rocky blister of land with an endless sky.

Yet he always returned to the little village nestled in the hills near a quiet wood.

After another month of only catching glimpses of the female, the Godking decided she must be intentionally baiting him. He was tired of her games. That morning, he arrived at the village earlier than usual. He'd woken before the sun, slipped out of bed without waking the Goddess, and went directly to find Seren.

He found her sharpening her claws with a rough stone a short distance inside the edge of the wood. Her dark head rose when she sensed his approach, but she did not seem surprised.

"Are you not going to try to sneak away this time?" he asked.

She smiled. "Of course not, my god," she said. "I only wondered how long it would take you to find me at the right time."

"I am a god," he bristled. "I am always here at the right time. It is you who has not been here. For months, I have visited, and for months, you've avoided me."

She dropped the stone and stood to her full height, prowling closer to him. He could smell her female scent, different from the Goddess, but it was not unpleasant to him. The Goddess smelled of sunlight, herbs, and morning dew. The smell of Seren's mortal body reminded him of a twilight cave, mysterious and earthy.

"You're right," she said. "But I couldn't continue our previous discussion with the rest of the village watching. And not in front of the children."

"The village is not watching now," the Godking said, his patience having run thin. "The children are asleep."

Seren smiled widely and reached out a clawed hand to touch him. He allowed it, curious to see what she would do. She dragged a single claw down his pectoral, not hard enough to break the skin beneath his fur but firm enough to feel the prick of discomfort.

"You wish to continue our previous discussion?"

"That is why I have come," the Godking said.

"Of course," Seren said, her voice dropping low like the path of her hand. "I mentioned pleasure."

The Godking's nostrils flared as her scent shifted. He knew that scent. Lust.

Seren's hand paused below his stomach. She looked up at him. "I can give you more pleasure than you've ever known with the gentle Goddess," she said.

The Goddess was much more than a gentle lover, but Seren would not know that, and he did not say it. He was still curious.

"You gave me this form," she continued. "Let me show you what it can do."

Without warning, Seren gripped all of his length. Her claws scraped the delicate skin beneath his sack, and she dropped to her haunches before him. The scent of her arousal saturated the air. The Godking sucked in a breath, caught between pleasure and pain. He wondered if he might have made a mistake trusting himself to the claws of this creature, but Seren looked up at him with wide, awe-filled eyes hazed by desire.

Then something hit the side of her head, and blood sprayed the God-king's stomach.

He snapped his head around, searching for an attacker as Seren's body crumpled and did not move. The hilt of a dagger protruded from her temple.

The Godking snarled in challenge, the sound menacing. "Show yourself!" he boomed.

His Goddess stepped forward between the trees. Her usual gossamer gown sheathed her delicate form, and her golden hair was woven back from her face. Her serene appearance was at odds with the bloodlust in her gaze. The Godking could only stare at her, his eyes wide with shock. Then he looked at Seren's dead body before him, and the seriousness of his mistake was like the weight of a world settling on his chest.

The Goddess pointed to him, a second dagger fisted in her hand, twin to the one at his feet.

"You will pay for what you have done," she said, voice shaking with emotion. Furious tears spilled from her beautiful eyes. "Everyone will pay."

And then she vanished.

The Godking exploded out of the wood. He had to find her. He had to explain before—

No.

He froze on the fringe of the forest.

The village was gone. The shurii who lived there, the children asleep in their beds, all of them had vanished as if they'd never been. There was no destruction. No smoking ruin. It had simply disappeared as if it had never existed, the land as if it had never been touched by the life of their creation. An entire village filled with shurii. Gone.

Rage and shame warred within the Godking. *She* had done this. But his betrayal had been the catalyst.

Determined to stop her before other innocent lives were destroyed, the Godking returned home. He found her there, waiting for him just outside.

Home. The place they had built together, for each other, which had known love, peace, and passion and would know none of it again.

"The village," he demanded. "What did you do? Where are the children?" He knew. But he needed to hear it from her lips.

"They are gone. I unmade them."

He looked at her. His beautiful Goddess. His fierce, lovely, impassioned counterpart. There wasn't a drop of blood on her, but he saw it everywhere. In his mind, he saw it staining her neck, chest, hands, and hair, marring her perfect complexion.

"You killed them," he said.

Twin moonbeams landed on him. "Yes."

Rage punched him, and he snarled. The wind stilled. "You killed the children! Young, innocent life!" A vision of Seren's daughter flashed in his mind, arms outstretched toward him, a radiant smile on her face.

A flicker of something like grief passed over the Goddess's features, a slight pinch of her brow, almost too brief to catch, but the Godking saw. "Yes," she said. "I do regret the children."

"Fix it," he commanded. "You took their life, but you can return it." He was a god, equal to the Goddess in power, but he could not give back a life she had taken, just as she could not recreate that which he destroyed. Life existed because their powers were balanced. And as much as he currently wanted to, there were certain lines that even he could not cross.

"No," she said, expression hardening. "You loved them. You let your love for them overshadow your love for me. I took them from you, and I will not give them back."

The Godking drew himself to his full height, hackles stiffly raised, black lips curling back over fangs, and faced her. He towered over her, and yet she stood her ground. "I did not love her," he growled. "Not in that way."

She nodded. "I know. But you chose her."

The Godking held her gaze, and he could say nothing because he knew she was right.

"I loved you," she whispered. "All that I did was for you. And you chose her. Did you think I would not notice? That I would not see your distraction? I saw you visit the village. I saw your obsession with her. I watched you watch her." Her voice dropped again. "Then you came to me each night. I was in your heart while she was in your head."

His heart squeezed, but he was so angry.

"Then you snuck away when you believed me asleep. I watched you let her *touch you.*"

The blades of grass beneath their feet quivered.

The Godking exhaled slowly. He may be angry, but she was enraged. He had betrayed his Goddess, had placed another female above her when none in existence could ever equal what she meant to him. He had done this, and he would own it. The Godking was no coward. He would not run, not even from his own wreckage.

"I was wrong," he said. "I am sorry."

"There must be recompense."

He spread his arms. "Recompense? You slaughtered an entire village, but only one female wronged you. Only *I* wronged you."

"I told you," she said. "*Everyone* will pay."

"There has been payment enough," the Godking urged, trying to temper her emotion with his reason. "Now, let me fix this."

"I place a curse on this race," the Goddess said. Her voice changed, suffused with power, and the Godking recoiled.

Overhead, the cheerful morning sun flickered and turned mournful. The grasses and other plant life nearby no longer quivered, they quaked. Little beasts that frequented their hilly home fled in terror.

"All shurii will be affected by your choice, Godking."

The sky overhead darkened unnaturally. A storm churning to mirror her internal tempest.

"No," he said, instincts flaring. "Stop."

The Goddess's eyes burned like twin coals of sunfire. **"The curse shall be twofold."**

He thought of the people. Families. Children living now. The children that had yet to be born. Lives they hadn't even touched, that had yet to bloom. Countless generations of shurii they didn't yet know in physical form. All would feel her curse. He couldn't let this happen.

"My love, stop. Do not do this!"

But the Goddess did not stop. Her voice was otherworldly, her gaze unfocused. She was beautiful and terrible in her rage and hurt, and he was horrified.

"I am binding all shurii male's fertility to their second forms. As of this moment, their first forms will be sterile."

A ripple went through the world, and the Godking stiffened.

"You liked your form best, did you not?"

He ignored the slight.

"Female shurii shall retain their fertility in both forms, unaffected. For now."

He narrowed his black, pupilless eyes. This meant any shurii wanting to produce a child would now be forced to do so in second form. So, this was her punishment? To rub his nose in his slight for all eternity? Fine. He would willingly accept her terms. And yet… "For now?"

The Goddess smiled, her expression raising the fur on the back of his neck. **"One day, a day not yet decided, a female will be born who will lack a second form."**

The Godking started. She would remove his mark from one of their creations? A child born having no piece of him with which to identify? It was unthinkable.

"She will be called the Prima, and her birth will signal the second phase of this curse."

"It is enough!" he implored.

"She will be the last shurii born in Ilistaar capable of bearing children. All born after her, male and female, first and second forms alike, will be sterile. They will bear the seal of this curse as a mark upon their flesh."

She had gone too far. "My love, no! Please, do not do this!"

But the Goddess looked upon him without warmth.

"You cannot do this! You are sentencing an entire race of innocent people to die!"

"There is a way to break this curse, Godking—one way. A male shall be born sometime before my Prima. One set apart from the others, from your strongest line. The Primordial Male. They will be a

mated pair. Their fruitful coupling will be the only way to undo what I have done. What *you* have done. Balance, after all."

But the Prima…She would not be capable of shifting. Because of the curse, the Primordial Male could only give her a child in second form. The shurii were mortal. Breakable. Such a pairing was exceedingly dangerous.

"The Prima will be the people's sole hope for salvation," he said. "If she does not bear a child by the Primordial Male, the shurii will die. Our creation will face extinction."

"Yes," the Goddess said.

"You cannot do this," he said again. "I will not let you."

Lightning flashed overhead. **"You cannot stop it. You will suffer here as you watch. As you wait for them."**

He had pushed her too far. He'd burned the warmth and kindness from her and left a ruin of hate and cruelty. "Is it not enough for a child to be cut off from me? You would place the fate of all people on one female's shoulders? With the only way to safeguard that future being her demise? If the Primordial Male tries to mate with her in second form, he could kill her. My form is too strong. She will be too fragile. You would curse a male to kill the female he loves?"

The Goddess lifted her eyes in defiance, and they bore a hole straight through the Godking's heart. "As you have killed your love for me," she said, her voice leeched of power at last.

And it was done.

Chapter 1

Feline

THE PRIMA, THE GODDESS'S CHOSEN female, heir to the throne, and future of all shurii people, was dying.

Felíne glanced down briefly. The polished tiles under the cushion where she knelt were pristine. She could picture her life's blood seeping over those creamy tiles. Imagined her body failing, folding, slain by an insidious foe.

Goddess above, the boredom was killing her.

The elder's voice was a rasping lull in her ears as she paced the length of floor just beyond where Felíne's gaze had landed. On the female's next turn, Felíne stifled a yawn. To say the elder droned would have been rude, and rudeness was not tolerated from the Prima. Then again, neither was dishonesty.

Despite her thoughts, Felíne was the picture of elegance. Her thick, dark hair adorned her head in elaborate braids. Sparkling jeweled strands dangled delicately from the plaits, catching the light with each subtle shift. Her pale amber eyes, more gold than green in the late morning light, held nothing but rapt interest in the elder's lecture. The sloping curves of her figure were wrapped in the finest silks. The garment was modest yet breathable enough to offer some respite from the stifling heat of the late Asterosian summer.

Any passerby, if passersby were permitted within the Royal Villas' high walls, would see the future of the shurii people. The Prima, poised and polished.

Felíne flicked her eyes toward the clock that ticked quietly on the wall to her right. It took physical effort to prevent a dejected sigh from escaping her lips. Only forty minutes had passed. This lecture was scheduled for two hours. Two hours of listening to the elder explain how the curse was born from love. How the Godking was the ultimate betrayer, the weakness of the race. How the Goddess, in her perfect mercy, provided the people a way to rectify the wrongs of that black day.

Two. Hours.

The time Felíne had spent perched on her cushioned seat, legs folded gracefully beneath her, felt like ages.

To her left, high archways opened to a private courtyard, home to a quiet trickling fountain and serene greenery. If she looked, she would see several seating areas where she'd spent countless hours reading or sketching. She could hear birds twitter and splash their delicate wings in the crystal water. The gauzy, sheer curtains that hung from the archways rippled in the slight breeze that cut through the warm morning.

The tranquil garden tempted Felíne, testing her resolve. She sat so close yet remained unable to enjoy it with the elder pacing slowly in front of her, stopping now and then to explain a point in greater detail with grand hand gestures. She dared not divert her attention for fear of appearing disinterested, which was exactly what she was.

In all fairness, Felíne should be grateful for these lectures. For the pains the elders took to ensure she was adequately prepared to fulfill her purpose, please the Goddess, and service the Primordial Male. It was her duty to bear the Godking's strongest male an heir and thus ensure the continuation of the shurii people, breaking the curse.

Generations of elders had died waiting for Felíne's birth so that they could help prepare her for this pivotal moment. It was no wonder they were all so eager to teach. And teach they did. For nearly twenty-five years Felíne had been groomed and tutored, primed and perfected. She'd had a tutor for etiquette, for math and history, for composition and language. Elders that taught movement, dancing, and song-making. Ones that taught her how to hold her dinnerware, how to hold a conversation, and even how to bathe! Everything that a female of her station could be instructed in, Felíne was. All except for one thing. That final coupling, upon which all of her success hinged.

Felíne's birth had been a long-anticipated signal of great change. The moment she was born, lightning struck at the Temple of the Rising Dawn, lighting the Goddess's scepter with an undying flame. The Prima had come at last. The one they'd been waiting two thousand years for. The only one who could break the Goddess's curse. The only shurii in all of history to have been born without a second form.

And therein lay the snake in the grass.

In a few short months, her presentation to the Primordial Male was set to occur. Together, they would solidify their destinies, join the two godly lines, and secure a future for all the shurii people. If not, the stipulations of the Goddess's curse, the second phase of which had been triggered by Felíne's birth, would continue to bleed into the people. The shurii would suffer a slow, inevitable decline in population until every last one of them was dead and gone.

This is what the *godscripts*, the sacred texts that detailed the shurii histories, foretold.

Felíne knew her life's purpose exposed her to a very real and terrible danger. While she had never met him, she was told the Primordial Male was the most fearsome shurii male to have been born in two millennia. He was supposedly larger, more cunning, and more ruthless than others of their kind. She supposed it was to be expected, considering he'd been handpicked from the Godking's strongest line. It made sense that he would be the apex of the species.

Ironic that he was a mated match to the single most fragile female in all existence.

For all her enviable attributes, Felíne's lack of a second form proved an undeniable shortcoming. That knowledge sent her stomach churning with a complicated mixture of excitement, anticipation, and absolute terror when she considered her rapidly approaching presentation and the intimate event that would follow. In those moments, she was grateful for the people in her life who worked tirelessly to ensure she would survive that encounter.

First, however, she needed to survive the next forty-five minutes.

"And that is where you alone have been blessed, Prima," the elder continued. "For the Goddess gave you her most perfect design. Purity made mortal. Freedom from the sinful nature of the Betrayer's second form."

Purity indeed. And weakness.

The elders recognized her lack of a second form for what it meant to the people: the manifestation of the second phase of the Goddess's curse. Felíne saw it for what it meant to her: a significant disadvantage.

She shoved the thought down before bitterness could fester. No positivity would grow from a negative seed.

Felíne refocused on her mentor, simultaneously burying her impatience and holding fast to the gratitude she was expected to possess and portray.

Roughly an hour later, Felíne was alive, her only affliction a mild drowsiness as she was escorted back to her chambers. Polished ivory tiles passed under her slippered feet as she followed her escort—a masked male shurii armed to the teeth and whose name she did not know—down the halls to her room.

Like the elders, any armed guards that were tasked with guarding Felíne did so with absolute dedication. It was their only role, and the few who held it took it very seriously. They did not speak to her or look at her—from what she could tell, anyway. They were always masked, so she never saw their faces. She believed there to be at least four, though she couldn't know for certain. Try as she might to identify unique features between them, they were so similar in mannerisms and movement that she wondered if the king and queen hadn't found some way to create a shurii that did not eat, sleep, speak, or smile to guard her twenty-four hours a day for the rest of her life. For all she truly knew, there could be a hundred or only one.

They were like wraiths, and Felíne thought of them as black-clad ghosts that haunted her from place to place, ready to spook any perceived threat. Of course, there were none. Not here, anyway. The palace grounds were so heavily guarded and sealed off to the rest of Asteros that even the radicals who worshipped the Godking had little chance of reaching her. And she was not permitted to leave. Felíne's only real threat was her own imagination, which tried desperately to get her into trouble on more occasions than she'd ever admit.

She suddenly wondered what her guards would do with themselves once she serviced the Primordial Male. If *he* tried to hurt her, would they react?

Would they intervene on her behalf to protect her from harm? Would they be there for her presentation in the first place? The idea mortified her, and she felt her cheeks heat at the thought of her guards seeing her exposed and served to the Primordial Male. For some reason, the image of her lying naked on a silver serving tray while the Primordial Male approached with a knife and fork in hand to feast upon her flesh entered her mind. And then her face really *was* flaming.

In truth, she had no idea what the presentation actually entailed. She knew how children were created. She knew the mechanisms involved, though obviously not through direct experience, nor having witnessed it firsthand. She also understood the reason procreation presented a danger to her specifically. However, this one thing hadn't been thoroughly explained to her. Felíne had been assured she would be safe, that her protection would be ensured as she fulfilled her duty, but the *hows* of that protection had not been disclosed. Preparations were underway, they told her.

Perhaps the Primordial Male would be the one on the serving tray. Bound and restrained so that Felíne could, what, impregnate herself upon him? She nearly choked on a very un-Prima-like laugh.

Felíne glanced up at her current guard as they neared the heavy wooden door to her chambers. He gave no inkling that he was aware of her mind's unhelpful speculations, only disregarded her as thoroughly as always and moved forward in silence to grasp the thick woven iron handle. He pulled the door open so she could pass inside, and she left him to his silent vigil.

Felíne entered the plush chamber that she knew more intimately than any other room in the palace. A massive stone-faced fireplace occupied the right corner of the expansive main room. No fire crackled in its mouth, nor would there for months, until the weather once again began to chill. Regardless of its current disuse, aromatic stacks of freshly cut wood sat inside, untouched as though waiting patiently for a lit match.

Two heavily cushioned chairs were situated in front of the fireplace, which Felíne had come to find entertaining, considering she was the only one who ever sat there; she never had company. When her mother or father visited her chambers, they did not stay and so did not sit. The elders who attended her were not her friends and did not hold comfortable seated conversations with her. Her faithful wraiths were not permitted in her private rooms.

Beyond the fireplace stood the arched entrance to her bathing chamber. It housed a large porcelain tub, deep enough for her to fully submerge if she wished, that was fed by fresh water—warmed by the sun in the summer and by a furnace in the winter. Cooler water, stored in a reservoir beneath the palace, flowed from a separate faucet if desired.

Grand, floor-to-ceiling windows lit the main space of her bedroom and overlooked the palace gardens. An enormous bed occupied the center of the room. It had been decorated with an abundance of pillows expertly displayed in the pattern of a blooming rose. Felíne scattered them each evening, preferring her bed to appear thoroughly slept in, as though faithfully serving its purpose of ensuring she woke well rested. Each time she left, she returned to find her pillows once again artfully arranged.

Beyond the bed, to the left, was a dressing chamber. Countless shelves bursting with colorful garments and shoes lined the walls. A seven-foot gilded mirror stood to one side, and Felíne remembered playing dress up as a small child, parading back and forth, twirling her skirts, and pointing her toed shoes toward the mirror as she pretended to be admired by her future mate. If only her presentation involved her displaying a lovely set of clothes rather than her skin.

Felíne slipped out of her shoes and curled her toes in the fur rug beneath her feet. For a few brief moments, solitude and silence welcomed her, ensconcing her in bliss. She relaxed her shoulders, craned her neck to one side and then the other, releasing a knot of tension, and took a deep breath of clean summer air. In a short while, she would be required to meet with the queen for a light luncheon, welcome another elder, and attend another lesson. Right now, however, there was nothing required of her, and she required nothing. Felíne plopped into a chair, kicked up her feet, closed her eyes, and emptied her mind.

Chapter 2

Elder Imogen

FELÍNE'S REPRIEVE FROM HER DAILY duties ended abruptly. Not fifteen minutes after she'd sunk into the cushions, Queen Serebine swept into her chambers, two of her attendants in her wake.

Felíne's spine snapped straight on instinct. "Mother," she said, dipping her chin in reverence. "Forgive me, I did not expect you."

The Queen of Asteros was everything one would expect a queen to be. She was regal in every sense of the word. She stood about Felíne's height, taller than the average shurii in first form, but where Felíne had full breasts and ample hips, her mother was slender, her feminine curves gentler. She was famously beautiful. Serebine and her daughter shared the same dark hair, though the queen's had gone silver at both temples. Her large emerald eyes were fringed in thick lashes.

The queen glided forward, the skirt of her turquoise gown flowing behind her like the cascade of a jeweled waterfall. She opened the curtains, allowing bright light into the chamber. Felíne squinted her eyes at the sudden afternoon glare.

"My intrusion is well warranted, daughter," she said, turning to face Felíne, her lovely lips turned up in a smile. "I have someone exciting to introduce to you."

For a brief moment, Felíne imagined the Primordial Male striding into her bed chamber in all his masculine ferocity, and her heart stuttered in sudden panic. She had the urge to clutch a nearby pillow to her chest as a shield, as if that would do anything to dissuade the male's advance. What could she expect to do? Smother him with goose down?

Feline realized belatedly that the closer she got to her presentation, the more her imagination seemed to conjure images of the Primordial Male as a soulless monster that wished to shred her to pieces and delight in her eternal torment. It was a little disturbing, considering she'd be bonded to the male for the rest of her life.

"This elder is one with whom you have not yet been acquainted."

What?

Feline's mind took a moment to catch up. When it finally did, she swallowed her sigh of relief. An elder. Of course. Who else? It wasn't as though she were permitted to associate with anyone else. Too much depended on her. Shouldering the fate of an entire race of people wasn't just difficult; it was impossible. If Feline hadn't lived with the awareness of her importance since she was old enough to understand spoken language, the thought alone would have made her physically sick with dread.

She'd long ago found ways to deal with that crushing weight.

When Feline was eight years old, she began to have anxiety attacks at night, consumed by a fear of her failure. For months, she panicked in solitude, unable to breathe, tears clogging her throat, limbs clammy and trembling, until she finally slipped into an exhausted unconsciousness. The attacks lasted longer and longer until she wasn't sleeping at all, just panicking at night and then spending the early hours of the morning reeling herself back in, fitting the mask of the Prima onto her features in time for her morning appointments.

She couldn't keep it up forever, though. The elders took notice. Feline's attention span deteriorated. She couldn't focus during her lectures, and her work became sloppy. She lost her appetite and dropped an alarming amount of weight. Before long, word reached the king and queen that something was amiss, which set off a completely different type of panic. Just imagine the scandal! To let the Goddess's favored female wither away before she grew up and saved them all? That simply could not be allowed!

The king and queen called in the most renowned physician in all the land to personally evaluate young Feline in hopes of curing whatever ailment she endured.

Save her!

CLOAKING FATE

Felíne had seen her mother on her knees only once in her life, and it had been at the feet of Mender Alcuin.

He'd taken one look at her shrunken, nearly nine-year-old self with his intensely intuitive blue eyes and seemed to know exactly how to help. Felíne hadn't had another anxiety attack since the ancient mender, with his wiry strength and eccentric brilliance, had entered her life. He'd saved her in more ways than one.

Mender Alcuin had equipped her with techniques her younger self hadn't known. She now knew how to shift that terrible weight off her chest and recenter herself. She focused on those things over which she had control and released the rest. Felíne learned how to trust in the divine rather than her own imperfection. The mender had become more than just her physician; he'd become a friend and confidant, both things she'd been forbidden as the Prima. He didn't see her status. Mender Alcuin was possibly the only shurii alive who viewed her as more than her purpose to the people, and she loved him for it.

"A new elder?" Felíne asked with polite interest she didn't fully feel. She wanted to close her eyes again, Goddess forgive her. The day felt long already, and it was barely half concluded.

The queen extended an elegant arm toward the door, which swung inward as though by her mother's invitation. A tall, striking young woman entered the room and stopped before the queen, head bowed.

Felíne looked at the door expectantly and then at her mother in question when no one else came through.

"Allow me to introduce Elder Imogen," the queen announced.

Felíne's attention went to the female dipped into a shallow bow. This was the new elder? She couldn't have been much older than Felíne herself. All of her other elders were at least twice her age, sometimes greatly beyond that.

She recovered her surprise quickly and dipped her head to the female. "I am so pleased to meet you, Elder Imogen," she said. "I look forward to being under your instruction." The words were automatic; she'd said them so many times.

The queen clasped her hands in front of her, practically vibrating with anticipation. Felíne couldn't remember ever seeing her mother so visibly excited. She suddenly had an inexplicable sense of unease.

It wasn't exactly rude to pose questions to an elder without invitation, but it also wasn't an encouraged behavior. However, as Felíne surveyed this elder before her, she couldn't help voicing her intrigue about what exactly Imogen planned to teach her.

Possibly how to attain perfection.

The female was stunning. Her skin glowed a lovely, warm brown. Her long black curls were individually crocheted into beautiful distressed coils that hung down to her lower back. She had deep, intelligent eyes set under thick arched eyebrows and a full, sensual mouth. A spattering of darker freckles peppered the bridge of her nose and both cheeks.

"It's all truly happening, Felíne," her mother said, moving forward to place her jeweled hands on either side of Felíne's face.

"Yes," Felíne said because she could think of nothing else to say.

"Imogen will be the one to teach you quite possibly the greatest lesson you have yet to learn."

Felíne nodded, her unease growing.

"You must listen closely, do as she does, exactly as she instructs."

"Of course, mother."

"She is the best, the most skilled female, I've been assured. I have hand-selected her myself, just for you, darling. For this important task."

Felíne looked beyond her mother toward Imogen, who waited with patient elegance.

"Task?" Felíne whispered.

Her mother nodded, a radiant smile transforming her features. "Elder Imogen is here to personally instruct you in the act of servicing the Primordial Male. Isn't that wonderful!"

Imogen bowed deeply at the waist. "It will be my greatest pleasure to teach you the art of intimacy, Prima."

All the blood drained from Felíne's face, and her stomach dropped to her toes. She pulled her lips into a strained smile, hoping desperately that it masked her apprehension. Then she did the only thing she could think to do: she prayed.

Chapter 3

A Friend

FELÍNE WAS MOMENTARILY SPEECHLESS AND thought seriously that she might be suffering a stroke, considering that her brain had sudden difficulty finding words.

Queen Serebine clutched Felíne to her in a brief embrace and moved toward the door, her attending females close behind, the train of her gown swishing.

She turned back as the door was opened for her. "I leave you in Elder Imogen's capable company. Your lessons will begin immediately. Elder Imogen will dine with you today in my stead. She has been briefed on your new schedule and will advise you."

Felíne thought her mouth parted, but still, there were no words.

The queen had already turned to address Imogen. "I expect a detailed report of her progress each day, Elder. You know well what depends on this. Do not fail us."

The threat that settled in the air of her bed chambers finally snapped Felíne out of her apoplexy. She glanced at Imogen. The female did not seem disturbed by the queen's words, and Felíne thought she was either an exceptional actress or truly had that much faith in her abilities. She hoped it was the latter.

That's all I need, Felíne thought. *To have the fate of another person resting on my shoulders.*

Then again, if she failed to service the Primordial Male to the Goddess's satisfaction, the entire race was doomed anyway, so she supposed it was a non-issue.

Imogen smiled politely and bowed to the departing queen. "I will personally deliver a report each evening, Your Majesty. Your trust in me will not be misemployed."

With one last nod of approval, Queen Serebine left Felíne alone with her new instructor. The sound of the door sealing shut left a sense of foreboding hanging in the air.

Occasionally, Felíne had premonitions. Not specific ones like a prophet might, but just an overall sense of things, as if she could somehow anticipate changes preparing to take place. She'd had it when she was eight and had met Mender Alcuin. His introduction had greatly affected certain aspects of her life, and his influence had led Felíne to find a manner of purpose outside of her purpose to the shurii. Something for which she would be forever grateful.

It happened again when she was seventeen. She'd been walking through the palace gardens at the edge of the orchard with one of her elders, having decided to take their lesson outside on account of the amiable spring weather. Elder Bonn had been teaching Felíne how to identify specific varieties of herbs and what properties each contributed to one's health, nutrition, or mental affect. She'd been listening to Elder Bonn explain the properties of *starpetal* when they stopped by an elevated stone planter. The sounds of the orchard had seemed suddenly off; birds abruptly quieted their chirping, and the buzz of insects gained a too-loud drone that grated on Felíne's ears. An oblivious Elder Bonn reached forward to pluck an herb from the overflowing planter. Without thinking, Felíne had snapped out her hand and pulled back the elder's arm. Elder Bonn had started at Felíne's audacity, something obviously unlike her. Then, the triangular head of a viper emerged from the herb bed where Elder Bonn's fingers had been extended.

The older woman had turned wide eyes to Felíne, who watched, mesmerized, as the viper descended from the planter into the mulch at its base. At Felíne's request, one of the palace attendants arrived to capture the serpent and deliver it to Mender Alcuin. He'd surely have some medicinal use of the creature's venom, she'd explained. Elder Bonn, who was simply happy to still be alive, had told Felíne at least six times that it was a sign the Goddess was pleased with her progress. They'd taken the remainder of their lesson inside.

That same sense of premonition settled over Felíne again as she stood with her new elder. She had the distinct feeling that this was a turning point in her life, and the notion filled her with a strange combination of anticipation and apprehension.

"You're the youngest elder I've had," said Felíne.

Imogen smiled, revealing a narrow space between two straight white teeth. Somehow, the imperfection made her even more lovely. "I will admit, Prima, the distinction 'elder' seems to belong to one who's experienced many more years than my thirty. It is a title that will take some getting used to."

"You're newly appointed?" Felíne asked, wide-eyed. The only elders that she'd ever had, had always been elders. They were born to elders, raised by elders, and taught by elders how to be elders. It was an entire priory of elders overseen by one Grand Elder, the eldest among them. Felíne's head spun. So many *elders*.

And then there was Imogen, apparently.

"How is that possible?"

Imogen gestured to the cushioned chairs before the hearth. "Do you mind if we sit, Prima?"

Felíne nodded and settled herself into the cushions. Imogen took the chair next to hers, smoothing her vestments, which were ivory with amethyst lapels and stitched with what Felíne was sure was spun gold thread in an intricate, flowing pattern. She had the odd thought that Imogen looked unaccustomed to the weight of the fabric and belonged draped in something airy and loose-fitting.

Imogen looked down at her lap as though trying to decide how to begin the conversation. Felíne wished to reassure her but had no idea what to say.

Normally, her instructors possessed the kind of aplomb that could only be obtained from years of dedicating oneself to a specific task. Elders who taught her arithmetic had sequenced numbers from the time they could count. Those who instructed her in music were adept musicians and some of the most skilled composers to have ever lived. The elder who taught her language was well versed in even the dead languages and had written his own account of the ancient *godscripts*, which he'd translated by hand from a withered scroll. They all knew exactly what was expected of them and passed on their trove of knowledge to Felíne with organized confidence.

She didn't know what to do with an elder who seemed to have no idea how to *be* an elder.

When unsure of what to say, Felíne found it most effective to replace her indecision with tactful civility.

"Would you like something to drink?"

Imogen offered a small smile and seemed to relax a fraction. "Yes, whatever you have is perfect. Thank you."

Felíne strode to a walnut drink cart set against the wall, which remained stocked with refreshments and supplies to make an assortment of elixirs and tonics. She pulled a decanter toward her and poured fragrant lime water into two glasses. She then selected one small ceramic container from an identical set of seven. Each contained a different powder that Felíne had ground herself. She dipped a tiny silver spoon into the dish she'd chosen, added a dose of the green powder to each glass of water, and stirred to dissolve the additive. The liquid turned a muted shade of chartreuse.

She returned to the chairs before the fireplace and handed a glass to Imogen.

The young elder eyed the mixture and raised her eyes to Felíne before giving it a sniff. Felíne sat and took a sip of her own drink. She closed her eyes as she swallowed, resting the back of her head against the chair's crest, and let the concoction settle.

"I'm terribly sorry for asking so plainspokenly, but what is this?"

Felíne opened her eyes and took another drink. The *maruchi* powder was already working to settle her nerves. "It's water infused with fresh lime. I added crushed leaves from the *maruchi* plant. Just a small dose. It helps clear the mind and soothe nervousness. Forgive my assumptions, but I thought both of us could benefit."

Imogen took a tentative sip. Her eyes widened. "It's delicious."

Felíne smiled. "*Maruchi* is quite sweet on its own. The bitterness of the lime helps to tame the flavor. I'm glad you like it."

"So far, it seems you are the one teaching me, Prima."

Felíne sat forward. "Please, Elder, call me Felíne."

Imogen regarded her for a moment before appearing to decide something. "Felíne. I know the rules. I was briefed on the basics, at least. I've known of you since you were born. All of Ilistaar has. I have a…unique level of experience that Queen Serebine felt strongly would benefit you before your presentation to the Primordial Male. But I will admit, I know very little about being an elder." Imogen drained her glass and set it aside. "Perhaps it's best if you referred to me as 'Elder' when we are in the company of others. However, when it is just us, I prefer simply Imogen. Or Gen," she added almost as an afterthought. "My friends call me Gen."

Felíne blinked. Friends? "May I be candid?"

Imogen nodded. "Please."

"You really *don't* know the rules."

Imogen offered a sheepish smile and a shrug. "I'm not doing a very good job so far, am I?"

Felíne opted for honesty and hoped it wouldn't boomerang back to smack her in the face. "No, not really."

The two shurii females stared at each other for several seconds before Imogen laughed in a sudden gush. Felíne cracked a smile and then laughed herself when she saw the look of surprise on Imogen's face as though affronted at her own lack of control. Then, they both laughed harder.

"You drugged me," Imogen said, wiping her eyes. "It's the only explanation for this outburst."

Felíne caught her breath, a hand over her middle. "Clearly, I drugged us both. But you asked for honesty. I should have warned you it's one of my worst traits."

"Well, one of my worst traits is that I deeply appreciate honesty, even the bad sort. Goddess above, my first official day as an elder is not going how I anticipated."

Felíne nearly dropped her glass. "You've been an elder only a *day?*"

Imogen held up a finger. One.

She couldn't believe it. The elders had selected a shurii female who had been an elder all of *one day* to be the one that would bestow this final lesson? The most important lesson? Because if Felíne was being honest, the rest of her preparation was entirely pointless if she couldn't effectively service the Primordial Male. Everything she'd learned growing up, all of her focus, early mornings, and countless lessons amounted to absolutely nothing if she failed at this one final thing. It simply did not make sense.

Why Imogen?

"Alright," Felíne said. "I think it's best if you start from the beginning."

Imogen folded graceful hands in her lap. "From what I was told, the elders are a reclusive sort."

Felíne settled back in her chair with a nod. "Reclusive is one way to put it. They live together in a colony, several days' ride outside Asteros in a remote section of the desert. Their city, Doceo, is in the heart of an enormous canyon and nearly impossible to reach if you don't know the way. It's well protected by the natural terrain, and outsiders are strictly forbidden. The elders know who they are and what their path in life entails from the time they are born. There's no questioning it, no veering from it. They were born to do one thing: to teach me. They learn from elders before them and from the scrolls that were kept from the time of the first elders." She crossed a leg over her knee. "They have the original *godscripts*. Once an elder is considered a master in their craft, he or she leaves the city and journeys to Asteros. They are presented to the king and queen and then enter into service until their lesson has been taught. Their knowledge and culture are a well-guarded secret."

Imogen nodded and took a breath. "As you learned today, I was not born an elder. I've never been to Doceo, I have never read their scrolls, and I have not spent my entire life preparing to instruct you. Essentially, I am an outsider. I grew up here, in Asteros. I attended school, but my education was basic. I understand that I am the first of my kind. An adult shurii has never been inducted into the elder society."

It wasn't said with arrogance. Imogen simply stated factual information.

Imogen's obvious underqualification piqued Felíne's curiosity. What could make her so special that the queen, the one person whose seriousness regarding the Prima's instruction rivaled that of the elders, would appoint her? And what would make the elders agree? Felíne had expected a new elder for this final instruction—the last crucial piece of her training before her presentation. The *godscripts*, up until this point, had provided the elders with very clear direction as to the content of her education. What Felíne *hadn't* expected was to receive her most important lesson from, well, what Imogen had said herself: an outsider.

"Three days ago, I was approached by an elder named Frest," Imogen continued. "He told me that my services were required by the crown. That it was a matter of urgency and that Queen Serebine had requested me specifically to instruct the Prima." Imogen inclined her head to Felíne. She paused, her eyes gaining a faraway look. "Of course, I couldn't dream of refusing. After meeting with the queen, I was moved into the palace and given a crash course in what is expected of me and my instruction to you. Yesterday, I received a thorough yet condensed history of the elders. Just last night, I was honored with my appointment and formal title and handed the customary vestments. It's all happened very fast."

Imogen sank back into the cushions and let out a breath, the mask of propriety slipping. Felíne thought she looked somewhat overwhelmed by the turn her life had taken in the last thirty-six hours, and she felt a pang of empathy for the woman. She had no doubt the appointment wasn't something that could be reversed. It was a title Imogen would carry for the rest of her life. Felíne didn't know if the female *wanted* to be an elder, but it was clear she'd had no choice in the matter. As Imogen had insinuated, refusing the king and queen hadn't been an option. It wasn't that she *wouldn't* refuse them. Imogen said she *couldn't*. Felíne noted the distinction. Even she, as their daughter, knew better than to disobey the wishes of the crown.

Imogen must have had a life before all of this. Did she have a husband? Children? A family that she left to be here in service to the Goddess and the royal family? The thought squeezed Felíne's heart. Even if Imogen hadn't left anyone behind, it was impossibly unfair if she'd been employed against her wishes. The fact that there was nothing to be done about it went unsaid. Bringing it up wouldn't change anything. It would only place more focus on the situation, making it more difficult to deal with, and the future more daunting to face.

When Felíne found herself worn from the constraints of being the Prima, she tried to look at her position from a different perspective, to find joy in her circumstances. She'd come to learn that her attitude was one of the few things in life over which she had control. Life had an interminable tendency to throw obstacles at the beings who lived it. Those obstacles became either molehills or mountains, and the thing that determined which form they took was the perspective of the person facing them. Felíne found it easier to climb the molehill.

She looked at the female before her and felt a sense of kinship. Felíne saw how she'd been thrust out of her comfort zone and forced to tread water, the depths of which were unknown and the expanse of which uncharted. She didn't know Imogen, but Mender Alcuin had taught her to see people for more than the words they spoke. She studied Imogen. She saw how her shoulders sagged slightly under an invisible weight, how she clasped her hands in her lap to stop fidgeting with her clothes, how relieved she appeared at the bit of kindness Felíne extended in contrast to the rigid formality she'd displayed to the queen.

They'd only just met, but she instinctively liked Imogen. She could picture herself sharing things with her, allowing the mask of the Prima to drop a little in her presence, believing Imogen would appreciate what lay behind it. It was a dangerous thing that she was considering, impossibly foolish, certainly reckless.

Felíne wasn't supposed to have friends.

They were a distraction. An unnecessary attachment that would only detract from her focus.

Friends were forbidden.

There was so much at stake. Too much.

And in a matter of weeks, the rest of her life would be tied to a male she'd never met. Friendship was just one more thing that she'd never experience, never claim as her own. In a lifetime of giving, was it really so horrible to want some things for herself? Her feelings, the secret desires of her heart, had never truly mattered. If they impeded the course of her path, they were strictly prohibited. It seemed Imogen's wants, whatever they may be, were also a casualty on the road to Felíne's intendment.

And why should someone else suffer for her sake?

She knew the answer to that. *They shouldn't.*

She leaned forward and smiled a small, genuine smile. "Gen," she said, and Imogen's dark eyes widened. "I don't know you. I don't know what you left to become an elder. I don't even know *why* you were chosen for this position, but I would like to, not because you're obligated to share, but because you choose to. You know *of* me, but I am equally a stranger. The people of Asteros, of the rest of Ilistaar, know I exist, whether they believe in my purpose or not. But they don't know my face. They don't know *me.*"

Imogen watched her and listened.

Felíne looked down at her hands, hoping what she said would be received as she intended. "I propose we make a bargain."

"A bargain?"

Felíne placed a hand on her chest. "I know the elders. They're *all* I know. They've been my sole caretakers and, for the most part, my only source of company since before I can remember. I can help you learn what it means to be an elder, help you navigate the unknowns of what that entails, and maybe, hopefully, you can find some reward in it. It may not be the life you chose, but you don't have to be alone in it. If you would like, I can be a…friend."

Imogen regarded her for a moment. "I would like that," she said finally, her voice small. "But what do you ask in return?"

"In return, I'd like you to teach me."

Imogen's full brows pinched. "That's not much of a bargain," she said. "It's already my job to teach you."

Felíne's lips tipped up. "I want you to teach me *more* than what's required of you as my elder."

Imogen tilted her head. "More?"

She dipped her chin. "You grew up in the city? Outside the palace of Asteros?"

Imogen nodded. Her eyes cut briefly toward the door. "Yes."

Felíne hesitated. She suddenly felt as though she stood on the edge of a cliff, looking down at a dizzying height. Had she already revealed too much? If she continued, she risked Imogen reporting everything she said to her mother, and the queen would be more than displeased. She would be livid. There would be dire consequences for Felíne's curiosity, for her disregard of the boundaries surrounding her status. What little freedoms she possessed would be irrevocably abrogated. Her time spent with Mender Alcuin would be a thing of the past. The only place she'd help another person ever again would be the Primordial Male's bed.

Imogen reached out and took Felíne's hand in her own. The act was simple, genuine. No elder had ever reached out to her in such a way. It said, *I am a friend; you can trust me.*

A tentative light crept into Felíne's honey-green eyes, and her voice dropped to a conspiratorial hush. In for a crumb, in for a loaf. "Beyond the palace is forbidden to me. In my almost twenty-five years I have never walked through the streets of Asteros." It was mostly true. "The elders have taught me everything they deemed I should know as the Prima, and they taught me well. I know numbers, language, music, and literature. I know about the cosmos and the histories of the gods and our people. I learned herbology and how to tend a garden." Her mother refused to have an uneducated broodmare for a daughter. Thankfully, the elders believed a well-rounded, well-educated Prima would please the Goddess. "I even know some medicine and principles of healing." That last bit wasn't common knowledge, but she'd already committed. She paused, suddenly excited. "But I know nothing about life outside of the palace. I have had countless elders teach me how to be the Prima. I want *you* to teach me everything else."

Chapter 4

Lessons

A KNOCK SOUNDED ON THE door of Felíne's chambers, abruptly snapping the females back to formality.

"Enter," Felíne called.

A middle-aged shurii female with graying hair and a lightly lined face entered the room and stopped inside the door. She was clothed in a plain pale-gray sleeveless gown from chin to floor, her eyes cast down as she dropped into a shallow bow. One of the queen's attendants.

"Prima. Elder," she said. "Your meal is ready and will be served in the terrace hall."

Felíne and Imogen both stood.

"Thank you," Felíne said. "We will be present shortly."

The attendant nodded, dipped again briefly, and left.

Imogen reached for her empty glass. Felíne stopped her with a gentle hand on her arm.

"First lesson," she instructed. "As an elder, though you are in service of the Goddess and the crown, you're not a servant. I'm not allowed to clean up after myself, and neither are you. Leave it. The palace staff aren't permitted to interact with me but they tend my chambers when I leave. I'm told they get cranky if they don't have something to take care of. Apparently, I'm too neat."

Imogen left the glass on the table. "Who told you they get cranky?"

Felíne smiled and whispered, "Mender Alcuin."

Imogen stopped, looking as if she'd been struck.

Felíne frowned, concerned. "Are you alright?"

The young elder shook herself. "I—yes. Sorry. I'm fine."

Felíne watched her a moment before moving toward the door. Her mother's attendant would wait with a guard and promptly inquire if they didn't make their way. Appointments ruled her life. Tardiness wasn't tolerated, and time was a precious commodity not to be wasted. If Imogen said she was fine, Felíne would have to take her word for it.

Imogen joined her, and together they left Felíne's chambers. As expected, the queen's attendant waited for them to enter the hallway. When she saw them, the female bowed again and departed, leaving them in the company of Felíne's wraith, who provided a silent escort.

They made their way through the palace, a sprawling expanse of blonde adobe, stone, and red-tiled roofing. Felíne knew the 200,000 square foot villa and its forty acres intimately, like a map written on her heart. The sheer desert cliff that bordered the palace's north side rose up like a colossal stone guardian, looking down on them as they walked. In the evenings, when the sun hung low on the horizon, golden rays bathed the mountain, casting shadows on the rugged outcroppings of red rock and hardy plant life. Just then, the afternoon light fully illuminated the rocky façade. Felíne was grateful for the shade of the walkway, which offered a significant reprieve from the blistering heat of the late summer sun.

The women turned a corner, and Felíne could make out a distant section of the towering stone wall that surrounded areas of the complex not already guarded by the precipitous face of the great alp.

She had learned of palaces built into summits with towers and spires that reached into the clouds, elaborate staircases that wound up and up, and rooms stacked one on top of another with grand balconies overlooking the castle from fantastic heights. Theirs was not one of those. The royal villa of Asteros was as dilatant as those historic castles were altitudinous. Instead, miles of winding hallways, courtyards, and covered walkways spread over an expanse of land, mostly one story but with a few structures that held nondescript stone stairwells leading to an upper level.

An immense garden lawn occupied the heart of the palace courtyard, complete with a blue-tiled swimming pool and a private orchard of various fruit trees that bordered the outer rooms. There were walking paths and hidden fountains set into secret alcoves dripping with greenery everywhere on the grounds, which were some of Felíne's favorite places. When she was a girl, she'd often squirrel herself into these small nooks, pretending she could hide from the elders, wraiths, her parents, and the world. She found moments of peace within those little verdant kingdoms, and even now, as an adult, the presence of greenery put her at ease.

Inside the palace, it was almost easy to forget that they lived in the middle of a desert. The lawns were manicured to perfection, towering palms rose everywhere you looked, and artfully arranged rocky berms filled with varying native species of cacti and flowering shrubs dotted the property.

Felíne and Imogen continued along the open, tiled hallways to the terrace hall, a smaller rectangular dining area overlooking a section of garden filled with individual raised planter beds that were staggered and crowded with foliage in bloom. How the palace staff managed to keep the flowers vibrant even through the sweltering heat of summer mystified Felíne, but they made for a lovely view, and the heady aroma enticed her senses. She breathed deeply, filling her lungs with the floral scent, and sighed.

Felíne made her way to the dining table set before a large, arched window. Light bathed the room, and despite the sun's intensity, the villa's interior remained comfortable.

She took a seat, Imogen following her lead. Felíne's stomach rumbled. The table had been laden with pitchers of cool water and black tea, platters of crunchy wafers, meats thinly sliced and folded into lovely little rosettes, pickled vegetables, and clusters of grapes from the palace vineyard. Felíne spotted her favorite soft cheese nestled next to a tiny jar of fig jam.

She nodded discreetly to Imogen, indicating that she should fill a plate. An attendant had already sampled the food before them and deemed it safe to serve.

Imogen reached forward and plucked a few grapes, some cheese, a hard crust of bread slathered in rich honey butter, and a few pieces of red meat onto a plate. She popped a grape into her mouth and appeared to hold back a moan. "I swear I will never get used to the food."

Felíne smirked. Imogen noticed her watching and stopped with a piece of cheese halfway to her mouth.

"Why aren't you eating?" she murmured.

Felíne leaned forward, thankful they were alone save for the guard, who had positioned himself against the far wall. "Before I tell you, I think I've decided I prefer an oblivious elder. It's quite fun for me to play the teacher."

Imogen set the cheese down. "What did I do wrong?"

"It's expected that you serve me when we dine alone together. If my mother were here, she'd be served first. When you dine with the other elders, you take your food at your leisure. Unless you're dining with the Grand Elder, who would eat before all others." Felíne started piling a plate, enjoying the uncustomary freedom of choosing her own delights. "As I said, though, I prefer this opportunity to forego formality. I only mention it so that you're prepared when we have other company."

Imogen sighed and sat back, then glanced at the guard, seeming to remember he was there. "Do I need to worry about him? Them? I assume he isn't the only one of his kind."

Felíne cut her head to the side. "No. Their job—and I say 'their' because I can only assume the same as you, even though I've no evidence to support that assumption—is to protect, not inform."

"That's a relief," Imogen breathed, then added, "Though I'm surprised there aren't more guards within the royal villa. The city is teeming with them."

This, at least, was something Felíne did know. Before her birth, the Asterosian military was modest, mainly focused on resolving minor conflicts within the city. After she was born, and news of the Prima's arrival spread, many people began to panic as the second phase of the Goddess's curse manifested. A whole society of people woke up to find a blissfully forgotten deadline had been stamped onto their lives and the lives of their loved ones. Felíne's father, King Domitan, was forced to control the masses by military means, and he fully dedicated himself to strengthening his army. It was an obsession he maintained to this day, decades later. Asteros was now likely the most well-guarded shurii civilization to exist.

"There were," Felíne replied, remembering. "The king's guards were once a constant presence within these walls."

"What changed?"

"When I was a girl, one of the soldiers touched my hair as I passed him. My mother saw and told my father he tried to grab me." Felíne swallowed.

"I don't know if he even meant me harm, but I never saw common guards after that. Only them." She thumbed in the wraith's direction.

Imogen's gaze slid to the black-clad guard against the wall, considering. "If not them," she said, returning to their original topic of conversation. "Is there anyone I *do* need to worry about?"

Felíne thought for a moment while chewing on a piece of soft, pungent cheese, then took a long swallow of tea. "The female that called upon us earlier is one of my mother's attendants. They are the queen's creatures, loyal only to her. I would be mindful of your words and actions while in their presence. Whatever transpires in their company inevitably makes it back to the queen. The wraiths—sorry, the guards," she amended at Imogen's confused expression, "are loyal to the Goddess. They took a vow to safeguard the Prima. As long as I don't do anything dangerous, they don't interfere."

"Do you typically do dangerous things?"

Felíne smirked. "When I was twelve, I had a fascination with discovering how long I could hold my breath underwater. I practically lived in the pools. Mender Alcuin said he was surprised I didn't sprout fins."

Imogen focused on her plate. "That doesn't sound all that dangerous."

"After two weeks of successfully diving to the bottom of the deepest pool, I decided I needed more of a challenge. I scaled the outer wall one night and jumped into the moat. It's very deep."

Imogen's wide eyes snapped to Felíne's face.

"I thought I was a sneaky twelve-year-old, but in my excitement, I left my cloak and shoes in a very obvious pile near one of the turrets. Good thing, too. It took them about twenty minutes to find me. I was very good at holding my breath by that time, and an adept swimmer, but you'd be surprised how quickly you tire treading water in the dark."

"Dear Gods," Imogen breathed. "What happened?"

"The wraith on duty that night found me barely keeping my nose above water. I got pneumonia and had to listen to Mender Alcuin's lectures for three weeks while I recovered."

"Goddess above. I'm glad it wasn't more serious."

Felíne hummed her agreement and reached for another slice of marbled meat.

Imogen sipped her tea, her features assuming a carefully casual expression. "Mender Alcuin, you know him well?"

Feline glanced over. "Yes."

"Is he good at what he does?" Her voice was quiet, tentative. As though she almost didn't want to let the words pass her lips, but couldn't help asking.

"He is the best physician there is," Feline said without hesitation. "My frame of reference is limited on account of my complete lack of comparative experience, but I have never once seen him encounter an ailment or injury he couldn't treat. Shurii travel from very far away to seek his expertise. He's been offered numerous opportunities to leave his practice and teach, but he's declined, turning down riches beyond imagination and choosing instead to stay here and heal those in Asteros."

Feline wondered if any of that had to do with her. Mender Alcuin had already traveled to places of the world that Feline hadn't even known existed, seen countless lands, encountered many shurii, and learned so much. She had listened in rapture to many stories of his travels and thought he had a wanderer's soul, but he'd been in Asteros since she met him sixteen years ago. If he ever yearned to leave, he never mentioned it. Selfishly, she was glad. The palace of Asteros would be a somber place indeed without Mender Alcuin's wit and wisdom. *She* would be somber without him.

Imogen didn't respond. Her gaze fixed on the remaining bits of food on her plate, and Feline thought she looked for a moment like she'd gone somewhere else. She wasn't sure what the rules were between tentative friends, but her curiosity probably wasn't a welcome addition. Trust was one thing that she didn't get to cultivate with people often, and she thought that if she pried, it might undermine any fragile credence that she and Imogen had developed.

Feline used a napkin to dab her mouth and folded it neatly on her empty plate. "Well, Elder Imogen, I have spent most of our time together selfishly hoarding the attention. The afternoon is waning, and you need something to report to the queen other than my confession to you of my adventurous endeavors." She leaned forward. "Actually, I sincerely hope you neglect to report that. My mother doesn't approve and firmly believes the intrigues of youth are behind me."

Imogen cracked a smile. "Don't worry, Prima. Tales of your reckless streak are safe with me."

Felíne smiled back.

"But you're right," Imogen said. "I do need something to report. Queen Serebine expected your lessons with me to begin immediately. There is a lot for me to teach you and not much time."

Felíne swallowed the knot that tried to form in her throat. "You mentioned earlier that you had a unique set of experiences that qualified you to teach me."

Imogen nodded seriously. "Yes. I imagine you're curious as to what those qualifications entail."

Of course, she was, and she admitted as much. Why Imogen? What equipped her to teach this branch of material when other elders proved unfit?

Imogen took a deep breath. "I was one of the Fates."

Felíne visibly started, and her jaw dropped. She couldn't help it. Some small part of her was immensely grateful they were in relative privacy because she wouldn't have been able to contain her surprise. The rest of her—the majority—was dumbfounded.

Imogen was a Fate!

The Fated Mothers, more commonly referred to as the Fates, were a select group of females Felíne had never met, only heard whispers of. She had a limited understanding of their origins based solely on what she'd been able to glean on her own.

One of the byproducts of King Domitan strengthening the military presence in Asteros was a distinct difference in male to female population ratio. The soldiers, when they weren't fighting, required an outlet. At first, that mostly manifested in the forms of brawls, gambling, and drunken disorder, but quickly escalated to a spike in violence and homicides. The army began to deteriorate from within. King Domitan's generals had a fit over the resulting chaos. They petitioned the king to allow the formation of public pleasure houses inside Asteros city limits, which had previously been decreed illegal. The queen objected, but King Domitan relented to the wishes of his generals. The change was nearly immediate. Disorderly conduct among the military rapidly declined.

When the queen's advisors got wind of how successful these pleasure houses were within Asteros, it led to some creative speculation. Why not take the opportunity to devise a solution to the shurii's greatest looming problem: the Prima's pairing with the Primordial Male? Many females in the city took no issue with sharing a male's bed, as long as they were fairly compensated. The idea was proposed to take the act of pleasure a step further and select volunteer females to procreate, allowing the crown to explore methods within a controlled environment that would ensure the Prima's survival during her servicing. After receiving approval from the crown, the Fated Mothers were created.

Felíne did not know the details regarding how successful the experiment became, as they were established when she was still young. She'd only been told that the venture "held promise," and that "she needn't concern herself." It was a polite way of reminding her that even if she did have an opinion, which she most certainly did, it was of little consequence. Her persistent curiosities refused to be quelled through submissive obligation, however, and she'd spent no small amount of time over the years trying to discover details surrounding the Fated Mothers' history without her mother's knowledge. It had been no easy task, considering the only people who could answer her questions were the same ones she couldn't ask. The Fates' identities were well-guarded, as were their endeavors. All she'd been able to discern was that the females were paid handsomely for their services.

And Imogen was one of them! Here! Sitting right in front of her!

Felíne managed to pick her jaw up off the floor.

Imogen huffed a laugh. "I suppose I should be grateful you didn't pass out."

"I'm sorry, I just … A *Fate!* I'd begun to believe they were a myth. I want to know everything." Felíne reached out and grasped Imogen's forearm. "Truly. As much as you are willing to share."

Imogen offered a small smile, but her eyes dimmed.

"Very well, Prima," she said. "Tonight, after last meal, you will have your first lesson."

Chapter 5

Mender Alcuin

FELÍNE BID FAREWELL TO IMOGEN a short while later. Gen assured Felíne she would inform the queen of her plans to begin their lessons that evening. Why Imogen preferred to wait until after nightfall, she didn't say, and it left Felíne with a sense of wary anticipation. Whatever her reasoning, she hoped Gen was successful in securing the queen's approval. Felíne didn't want to lose Gen when she'd only just gained the beginnings of a friendship, something she had thought just mere hours ago that she would never have.

At just after four in the afternoon, Felíne made her way to the southwestern wing of the villa with her trusty wraith in tow. Imogen had left the terrace hall without a guard. Elders weren't required to have them, and Felíne suspected Imogen was accustomed to moving about on her own anyway.

She glanced over her shoulder at her current companion. While his features were completely obscured by a dark mask, he was undeniably male. She took in his tall, muscular body that moved with sure, silent steps. Black leather armor wrapped his frame, a thicker stitched plate over his chest, abdomen, and thighs. His feet and calves were clad in soft boots that laced up the sides. Dark leather bracers covered his forearms, and his hands were protected with flexible gloves the same color. A matching cloak with a deep hood draped his shoulders and fell below his waist. Two wicked-looking blades hung from either hip, completing the ensemble.

Felíne wondered why her wraiths even bothered with the weapons. The shurii were lethal without any tools of war, especially ones well-trained, as she was certain her guards were. It took a split second for a shurii to shift into second form. All physical appearances of humanity would disappear in a blink to be replaced with a set of vicious claws and a mouth full of teeth more deadly than any blade.

Then again, the crown expressly prohibited use of the second form, save for very specific situations. The Faithful Cursed—their religious faction—deemed it permissible only when strictly necessary, such as during the act of procreation.

Her guard wouldn't be doing any of *that* on duty.

The wraith gave no indication that he noticed her scrutiny as they left the main body of the palace and turned down a long, open breezeway. He simply glided by her, making no noise whatsoever. Felíne only knew he was breathing because he remained upright. She had long given up trying to converse with the guards. They never responded. She made up her mind that they'd all taken a vow of silence upon entering into her service. It made her feel better than believing they simply did not wish to speak with her.

Felíne witnessed a male and a female shift into second form for the first time when she was six. The demonstration had been performed by two of the younger elders in their late fifties, both likely still a century from the inevitable touch of age.

The lesson had been on shurii history. The elders were thorough with their teachings, and while the king and queen preferred they focus on the blessings bestowed by the Goddess, their instruction could not entirely neglect to teach the Godking's hand in the creation of their race. He was the one, after all, who provided the second form.

When the two elders shifted, Felíne remembered being in absolute awe. She'd seen pictures and paintings and thought she knew what to expect, but witnessing an adult shurii transform up close stole her breath. She wasn't like other shurii children, who shifted even in infancy and grew up knowing that second piece of themselves as intimately as she knew her own reflection. Even if it was a piece that children were taught from a young age to suppress and control, it was still one they had. One which she lacked.

Felíne hadn't been intimidated by the slightly jutting muzzles, elongated canines, or powerful, deadly jaws. Nor the hands suddenly tipped with four-inch-long talons that curved slightly toward the tip. The elders were magnificent. Muscle corded their bodies—the female being leaner than her male counterpart—and the fibers rippled under short pelts of sleek hair with each movement. The male had a longer ridge of hair that jutted out from the base of his head and traveled down his spine before tapering off at his hindquarters. The elder male had crouched down to where she stood, feeling impossibly small in comparison, and let her run her hands along the stiffer charcoal-colored strands. His powerful tail had swished back and forth, and he'd watched her with intelligent green eyes. The female elder held out a clawed hand, took Felíne's smaller one with surprising gentleness, and led her back to her seat.

The elders had continued their lesson in second form. Their words came out slightly distorted, their voices having to accommodate the difference in dentition. Felíne kept getting distracted by the click of claws on the tile floor as the female elder paced back and forth, offering her input. Felíne had been enraptured by the female's beauty, her movements lithe and graceful. The elder's dark blue eyes seemed somehow more expressive in her second form, and her dainty ears twitched and turned with her attention.

In that moment, Felíne wanted nothing more in the entire world than to be able to shift into a creature so exceptional. To have that creature as *part* of herself, waiting inside of her. The second half of her whole, the other side of her coin. She could not even recall the details of that particular lecture, but the awe she felt at the elders' second forms, the way they looked and moved, and the desire that blossomed within her heart remained planted, rooted in place.

That was the only teaching Felíne received from an elder in second form. If it hadn't been for Mender Alcuin, it would have remained her only time witnessing it. She'd never even seen her mother or father's second forms.

"We worship the Goddess for a reason, Felíne," the queen had told her in the days after that lesson, when she'd expressed her yearning for the ability to shift. "Her form exists as the purest part of us. The part that reasons and loves and learns. It is the form we choose when we wake each day, the same way we choose to be the best version of ourselves, which brings us closest to the Mother of our people. She blessed you, Felíne. She gave you *only* of herself. You are the best version of all of us and you don't even have to choose it. You simply are."

What could she say to that? How could she express the deep pit of yearning that had opened within her? She couldn't. A young child's curiosities were one thing, but there were those who went against the crown and the Faithful Cursed. They were the Cozened. A radical group of fanatics who worshipped the Godking. Any association with the Cozened carried a charge of treason, the penalty of which was death. Her father had spent the better part of a decade eradicating their ilk from the city. The king regulated the use of second forms with an iron fist.

"Good for fucking and fighting." Felíne had overheard the soldiers outside her father's council room not long after that lesson with the elders, before her wraiths had been assigned. Apparently, even fighting in second form was prohibited. Not a week later, that foolish guard had touched her hair, and the soldiers were removed from the palace. Even King Domitan's generals were forbidden. When the king had business with them, which was often and for extended periods, he left the palace and sought them beyond the wall.

Felíne rounded a final corner and stepped out from under the awning into the sun. The hottest part of the day had arrived, and the heat was a thick blanket that settled over the city and surrounding landscape. The slight breeze that swept down from between the mountain buttes offered no relief. The scorching air made Felíne feel like she was breathing in the blast of a blazing furnace. Sweat beaded along the back of her neck and curled the dampened strands of hair coming loose along her nape. Her wraith had to be suffocating under all that dark leather, but he showed no sign of discomfort.

She picked up her pace, moving swiftly along the stone pathway that led to another adobe building. This one was painted reddish-brown, with a dark ash-gray tiled roof and lovely multicolored ledger stone decorating the entrance. Two well-manicured hedges boasting waxy green leaves and a plethora of tiny white five-petaled flowers bordered the steps leading to the front doors. The structure was separate from the main body of the villa and situated closer to the perimeter wall, near the exit.

It was arguably her favorite place in the entire palace, its only rival being the gardens.

CLOAKING FATE

Felíne grasped the handles of the simple wooden door, painted to match the color of the roof, and pulled. The cooler air inside the building flooded the exterior, bathing her in a wash of crisp relief.

Felíne stepped into the spacious vestibule of the royal infirmary. Potted plants sat tucked into corners between the plush seats and benches that dotted the space. The muted, mossy-green walls supported a number of paintings depicting various landscapes of lush jade forests, turquoise seas with towering white cliffs, and rolling golden plains. The desert outside had no place in this room. It was like traipsing into a different clime. A desk to her right held a neat stack of papers, quill pens with a stoppered pot of ink, and a vibrant cerulean ivy that dripped its tendrils over the edge to the floor. The room was empty.

Felíne's wraith took up the usual position to the left of the entrance, his back to the wall. This allowed him to see the doors on either side of the room: the front they'd just come through and a rear set that had been left open. She moved toward the far entryway.

"I won't be more than an hour today," she advised. No response. She hadn't expected one, but he wouldn't follow. Aside from her personal chambers, this was the only other place the guards were forbidden to shadow her.

The rear doors of the vestibule opened to a hallway that wound up and back, leading deeper into the building in a sort of horizontal zig-zag pattern. Doors lined the walls, all shut, numbered, and vacant. Patients in the royal infirmary were a rarity. The general public didn't have access to the palace grounds. The wall and the moat remained heavily guarded at all times. The only potential patients at this clinic were the visiting elders, the queen's attendants, and the royal family, which essentially consisted of Felíne and the queen. The king had his own private physicians in the city, where he spent the majority of his time. Other palace staff were sent out into Asteros for treatment in the case of an injury or illness.

Felíne was frequently the only visitor here. She knew that one of the reasons her parents agreed to her spending as much time with Mender Alcuin as she did was that they believed *all* of her time with him was spent here.

Mender Alcuin was as brilliant as any elder and likely much older than most of them, with more life experience than several combined. After he'd saved her from her crippling anxiety as a child, he'd advised the king and queen that the Prima would require ongoing therapies that even the elders of Doceo couldn't provide. When he offered himself as her personal therapist under the strict condition that no guards or other persons were to interfere, they'd agreed without hesitation.

Elders had expressed concern over the years that the amount of time dedicated to these therapies was substantial and might detract from her other studies. Mender Alcuin had asked the queen if she preferred an over-educated Prima with an unmistakable disability that may or may not impact her ability to perform the responsibilities required of her, or a still well-educated Prima with no disability. The choice was obvious, and the elders did not question Felíne's time spent at the clinic again. The crown was indebted to him.

And so was she.

Of course, she didn't have any disability to speak of.

And not all of her time was spent at the clinic.

Today, though, it would be.

She found Mender Alcuin at the end of the twisting hallway, through another set of doors, and down a flight of stairs in a hidden basement. He stood hunched over a mess of papers that lay scattered on a long, pale stone counter in the center of the room. An army of glass flasks and beakers filled with liquids of varying colors and viscosities littered the tabletop. The mender's wiry white hair clouded around the crown of his head like a fuzzy halo, more disheveled than normal. Spectacles perched precariously on the thin bridge of his nose, and the deep lines around his mouth—a result of many years of easy smiles—stretched as he muttered angrily to himself. The skin of his neck had long ago lost the elasticity of youth, and it wobbled slightly when he looked back and forth between the array of papers in front of him.

Felíne approached the desk. "Preoccupied with something important?"

He didn't look up. "Anything with which one would become preoccupied is by definition a thing of importance."

Felíne smiled. She dialed down the burner of a flame that was happily throwing heat and threatening to melt the skin off her left arm. The contents of the beaker that sat atop it bubbled dangerously and had turned an ominous shade of blackish purple. The syrupy liquid smelled disturbingly like burnt hair.

"What are you looking for?"

"Notes on a rare wasting condition that I penned some forty-odd years ago while in the Faresian Jungle." He shuffled through more papers.

Felíne stepped closer to his bent form and scanned several of the pages. She reached for a weathered notebook, the corner of which peeked out from under a discarded stack of parchment. "Is this it?"

Mender Alcuin pushed his glasses back into place and peered at the notebook. When he saw Felíne, he scanned her styled hair, diaphanous lavender gown with its delicate lace bodice, and her slippered feet. He frowned, disapproving. "Why are you dressed like that?"

Normally, when she visited for any length of time, she changed into a navy-blue homespun gown after she left her wraith in the lobby, an exact copy of the ones that the mender's assistants wore. The change in clothes was necessary because Mender Alcuin shared Felíne's best-kept secret.

She might enter this building as the Prima, but she became someone else entirely during her stay. Her "therapy" visits usually entailed smuggling her into Mender Alcuin's other infirmaries to care for the many patients he saw. While she'd never been permitted to venture into the city of Asteros, her parents would be aghast to discover that she had in fact been beyond the walls of the royal villa. Mender Alcuin had an entire network of tunnels under the city that led to several other facilities. He was very cautious, and they never entered the city proper. This was his condition of her. They visited *only* the infirmaries, and she went *only* under his supervision. It was more than she could ask for, and she'd chew off her foot before she betrayed the mender's trust.

Felíne had been going on these outings with him for years now, learning from him, watching him work. She didn't bother with hiding her face since none of the citizens knew what she looked like. To them, she was simply another assistant. She took vitals, did assessments, assisted in surgical procedures, and comforted ailing patients. Felíne loved it. Helping Mender Alcuin with his practice gave her a sense of belonging and purpose that had nothing to do with being the Prima. It was wonderfully liberating. This was the only place where she could truly be herself without the fear of disapproval or condemnation. Mender Alcuin encouraged her curiosity and challenged her intellect. He saw potential in her that had nothing to do with the salvation of the shurii people, and she loved him for it.

She handed the notebook to him, and he flipped through it. "I can't stay today. I only have an hour."

"Why? That is not enough time. I have a patient I want you to see." He paused, the scowl leaving his bushy brows. "Ah, here it is. Well done, my girl." He tapped the page containing the elusive notes and tucked the book into his jacket.

"One with a wasting condition?"

He regarded her with eyes the color of a cloudless summer sky, brimming with brilliance. "Yes. I haven't seen the likes of this illness among the shurii in over four decades. Female, fifty-two, otherwise healthy, has lived in Asteros her whole life. Good nutritional status, voiding appropriately, and vitals all within normal limits. Emaciated like she hasn't eaten in weeks."

"What did her bloodwork show?"

"Nothing terribly out of the ordinary. Her inflammatory cells are slightly elevated, but she had sustained a superficial injury prior to entering my care, which could account for that."

Felíne pondered it. "What have you tried so far?"

"Fluid therapy, rest, change in diet, *honeyleaf* teas. No change in the three days she's been in my care. She appears to have been deteriorating for some time."

"Did you try *wormwood*?"

Mender Alcuin gave her a look over his spectacles. Ok, he tried wormwood. Hmm.

"This would be a good case for you to see," he said. "I can use your young mind. Come. It is early enough to get you home by a decent hour. I'll have word sent to the queen that you'll take last meal with me." He began reorganizing his notes.

"I can't today," Felíne said. "I have a new elder. Our first lesson is this evening."

"Astronomy again? The stars have nothing left to teach you, Felíne."

She shook her head and helped collect and stack his papers, mindful of the dates on each note. "She is a *new* elder. Newly appointed. Her name is Imogen. Mender, she is a Fate!"

Mender Alcuin gave her a sharp look. He was well acquainted with Felíne's hunger for information about the Fates. She'd asked him several times, but he'd refused to provide any substantial information. "A Fate, you say? Imogen is her name?"

"Yes." Felíne studied the ancient, lined face. "Do you know something that you're not telling me?"

The mender watched her for a moment before he removed his glasses and rubbed his eyes. "I do know some things, though I doubt I should share them with you. Especially if this new elder has firsthand experience with things she may not want you privy to. Things that could compromise her association with you."

"You're saying I should ask Imogen?"

"I'm saying you should be careful what information you seek and mindful of how you seek it. I am always in favor of your curiosities, Felíne. However, when they put you in danger, I will advocate for your safety over your quest for answers."

Felíne tilted her head. "You realize that telling me this does absolutely nothing to discourage my curiosity. Is there anything you *can* tell me?"

Mender Alcuin sighed. "The Fated Mothers were established before I came to Asteros. There were some practices that I, as a physician honor-bound to my oath, did not agree with. Females died. Others were damaged. The mender who oversaw the operation was not an ethical man. I was asked to become involved upon my arrival. After learning what transpired and what would be expected of me, I felt obligated to decline. I did see several of the females after."

Her eyes went wide. Had Imogen suffered harm? Gods, and she'd basically demanded the female tell her everything. How could she be so obtuse? Alcuin's sense of morality ran deep. If he had personal aversions to whatever practices were taking place, it couldn't have been good.

"Do the king and queen know about this?" she asked.

Mender Alcuin replaced his glasses. "I don't think I need to tell you that there is little that happens within Asteros of which your father and mother are unaware. Serebine especially, was directly involved with the establishment of the Fated Mothers, and all reports of their progress went to her, but I do not know if either she or Domitan were cognizant of the mistreatment that transpired.

Felíne's head spun, and her stomach soured. She'd had no idea. And these females, however many there had been or still were, had gone through all of this on account of her? Females were put in harm's way because the elders wanted to ensure *her* safety? She felt sick.

Mender Alcuin reached out and gripped Felíne's hand with surprising strength despite his feeble appearance. The older elders that she had seen had hands that were gnarled with age, with knobby joints and twisted vessels that bulged under thin skin. Mender Alcuin's hands were elegant with long, slender fingers. His skin was soft and wrinkled like worn parchment, but his grip was steady and sure. She'd watched those hands perform incredible healing and skilled surgeries. When he took a patient's hand, he imparted compassion and understanding and delivered hope. He held her hand now, and his touch gave her reassurance.

"I know what you are thinking," he said. "And you are not to blame. Go and see your new elder. Learn what she has to teach you. Be empathetic, but be mindful. The logical mind can easily drown in the wave of powerful feelings. You have a good heart, Felíne, but remember, the heart is a deceptive organ. Do not be afraid to use it, but also do not let it have its way with you."

"Don't let my emotion cloud my judgment?"

He squeezed her hand. "I am comforted to know you retain some of my lessons at least."

She squeezed back, smiling. "A few. I'll be cautious."

He nodded, satisfied, and released her. "Good. Come back tomorrow at a decent hour. We have a medical conundrum to construe."

Chapter 6

Sacrifices

IMOGEN STRODE DOWN THE LONG hallway with a purpose in her gait that she didn't feel in her bones.

Fatigue pressed on her.

She could admit that her meeting with the Prima had gone better than she hoped. Felíne surprised her, and she wasn't often surprised. Imogen had had plenty of practice throughout her life reading the subtleties of shurii. Studying body language, noticing small mannerisms, and identifying slight inflections in tone. She considered herself an accurate judge when it came to discerning another's character. In her estimation, the female was genuine, intellectually sharp, and cared a great deal about the responsibility she bore to the people. All good traits. All things that Imogen valued herself. She liked Felíne. And she would do what she could to help her succeed. Not just because of what was on the line, or more accurately, *who*, but because she wanted to. This female, who had been sequestered and hidden away from the rest of the world, clearly had aspirations that could not be bound by these palace walls. She deserved to succeed. Whether Imogen could help her find happiness in that success was yet to be seen, but she would try.

A crepuscular light filtered in through the high windows of the hall, gilding the red runner under her feet a glowing crimson, making it appear as though she walked on a line of fire. Sconces on the wall flickered to life, the flames ignited by a timed mechanism set to discharge at dusk. The first time she'd seen such a contraption was in the palace. She'd started, convinced that the spirits of her ancestors were back from the next life to deliver an omen. She could have told them they were wasting their time; she was already living her own special brand of torture. She felt foolish when Elder Frest explained the technology, but she had seen nothing like it in the city. The flickering flames were no longer a surprise, but she hadn't completely grown accustomed to them. There were likely many things inside these palace walls that had the potential to unbalance her. After living a life of relative instability, one would think that being given a set objective would steady her, but she found the opposite to be true.

She had one job now. One destination. And suddenly, she was adrift. It took effort to maintain her course, and she was so damned tired.

Imogen neared the end of the hallway, which stopped abruptly before two massive doors. Their surfaces were carved with lifelike renditions of native cacti in bloom, one towering plant per side. Their arms stretched up to the ceiling, blooms as big as her head, and the detail of each needle chiseled into the wood was inconceivable. The amount of time it must have taken the carver to construct each piece made Imogen's head spin. She hoped the artist was well compensated for having such masterpieces hidden away in a palace hall. They belonged in a gallery or someplace public where everyone could admire their grandeur.

Twin armed guards stood before the doors. Like Felíne's guard, they were masked and covered from glove to boot. Somehow, the two of them seemed more menacing at the entrance to the queen's receiving chambers than the one who had followed Felíne earlier that day.

Imogen stopped before the guards. "I'm here to see Queen Serebine. She is expecting my report."

Neither guard moved. They didn't speak. They didn't so much as twitch.

"My name is Imo—er, Elder Imogen." The title felt strange on her tongue when tied to her name. Like it didn't belong.

Nothing.

Umm? She glanced behind her. Surely, this was the correct place. The queen's attendant had given her specific instruct—

One weighty door heaved inward. An attendant appeared, the same female who had called upon the Prima for their earlier meal. She dipped her head to Imogen. "Welcome, Elder," she said. "Her Majesty will see you." She swept a hand aside, beckoning Imogen into the suite. Imogen bowed her head and moved past the guards. The female led Imogen to the center of the room and departed through a side exit.

The queen's receiving chambers were as opulent as she expected any royal rooms to be. Thick amethyst curtains adorned the floor-to-ceiling windows to her right. Purple cushioned benches with elaborately carved armrests were situated between the windows. A plush divan upholstered in a rich blue-green velvet sat against another wall. A fireplace with a polished soft-gray marble face and mantle was to her left, not as large as the one in the Prima's chambers, but more extravagant. She expected the remnants of ash to have stained the crystalline stone from last winter's fires, but it was spotless, as if no tinder had ever burned in its mouth. A massive mirror with a heavy, decorative gold frame sat directly opposite the entrance, which made the room feel infinitely larger than it was. The floor was laid with the same ivory tile as the rest of the palace. Dense, expensive lavender and cream carpets in varying patterns blanketed the tiles. Imogen wanted to remove her shoes so she could dig her toes into the piles. She wondered if Felíne ever had.

The most elaborate piece in the room, however, was Queen Serebine herself. The reigning female monarch of Asteros sat at a small round table, the legs of which were fashioned into the likeness of three desert foxes, their tails splayed into a spiral at their base, little paws uplifted to carry the substantial weight of the glass tabletop. Imogen wondered where the queen found these pieces. She likely had the woodworker on staff, capable of crafting new and exceptional household items at a moment's notice. *See here! Look at my fancy new chamber pot. It's shaped like the gaping mouth of a lion! Do mind the teeth when you sit.*

Imogen dropped into a deep bow. "Majesty."

Queen Serebine placed her teacup into its saucer with a delicate *clink* and smiled. "Elder Imogen, welcome. Join me, won't you."

It wasn't posed as a question, and Imogen didn't treat it as one. She rose from her obeisance and sat in the only empty chair across from the queen. An attendant arrived swiftly and poured steaming liquid from the kettle into a fresh cup. Imogen thanked the female and sipped, resisting the urge to sniff the drink before sampling it. They were again left alone, and Imogen wondered how the queen's attendants knew when to appear when they received no discernable summons.

The queen watched her with big emerald eyes that reminded Imogen of a jungle cat. She imagined the female possessed a terrifying second form. Queen Serebine wore a different gown than the one she'd been in when accompanying Imogen to Felíne's room. This was a dark pine green floor-length piece made of a sheer, reflective fabric that had been layered several times over. The effect made the wearer appear sensual rather than salacious. Silver threads wove into the deep vee between the queen's breasts where the material crossed and along the hem of wide sleeves that flared out at her wrists. The dress cinched at the waist, and a delicate silver chain hung off one hip. The intimate piece of clothing reminded Imogen of the fancier attire worn by the women she'd grown up amongst. The garment put Imogen instinctually at ease, and she wondered if the queen had worn it intentionally to lower her guard.

"I looked forward to this visit, Elder Imogen. Elder Frest has monopolized your time since your appointment, and we have precious little as is. I trust your accommodations are to your liking?"

The rooms Imogen had been given at the palace were more elegant than any she had ever occupied. Too elegant. They felt entirely foreign. Like she was sleeping in a stranger's chambers. "Yes, majesty. They are perfect."

The queen nodded approvingly and took another sip of her tea. "Excellent. You have everything that you need?"

What she really needed was a generous shot of *mezahl* to burn away the knot of worry that had attached itself to the wall of her chest. She'd already searched the refreshment cart in her room. No liquor to speak of. "Yes, majesty. I have been provided with every comfort."

"I am so glad." The queen set her tea to the side, and Imogen braced herself. Pleasantries had been exchanged. Now the real conversation would undoubtedly commence. "And what of my daughter? Please, I am so eager to hear how your first lesson went. I will admit I expected it to last longer. Did the Prima exceed expectation?"

Imogen set down her cup. She was an elder now. She had authority. She was allowed to set her own schedule within reason. So why did she feel like a child about to be scolded for not completing her coursework?

"Our first lesson is to take place this evening, majesty," she said. She'd spent the last few hours since leaving Felíne in the terrace hall modifying her instruction plan and sending the required correspondence to her contact in the city. Now, she just needed to convince the queen that her methods were trustworthy and that interruptions couldn't be permitted.

An unmistakable flash of disappointment crossed the queen's features. "Oh?"

Imogen forced a steady breath. "The lessons I intend to teach the Prima are best demonstrated at a later hour, majesty. When certain attendees are more easily acquired."

The queen's eyebrows rose. "Attendees?"

"Yes, majesty. To be as thorough as possible in my instruction, I will require an assistant. The demonstrations are imperative to the Prima's understanding and future application."

"I see. And did you think to attain permission before you acquired this assistant? Citizens are not permitted within the palace walls. The safety of the Prima must be everyone's primary concern at all times. Outsiders are strictly prohibited. Surely Elder Frest explained this to you?"

Imogen feigned surprise. "Forgive me, Your Majesty. I would not presume to overstep my jurisdiction. Elder Frest had expressed that I should be provided with any materials I deemed necessary for my instruction. It was my mistake that I extended that approval to a female trained in servicing. I only sought to provide the Prima with the best possible education. There is so much depending on her success."

The queen sat back and raised a perfectly sculpted brow. "Are you not confident in your abilities to teach, Elder? I fail to understand why *another* trained female is required. Are your skills not sufficient?"

This was a delicate dance indeed. "I shall need to provide demonstration. I would never presume to dishonor the Prima by besmirching her vestal nature, majesty. It is my intent that the Primordial Male be presented with a chaste Prima, but one that has knowledge and skills in servicing beyond her own first-hand experience. To accomplish this, I need to *show* her."

Understanding lit the queen's eyes. Imogen thought she looked predatory.

She pressed. Just a little. "I believe it truly is the only way."

"One female," the queen ceded after a moment of tense silence, and Imogen felt a modicum of relief. "One of your choosing. No outside males. I do not trust the soldiers of Asteros."

Imogen didn't point out that not all males in Asteros were soldiers. She bowed her head. "Of course, majesty. Thank you."

The queen nodded, waving her hand dismissively. "If you require anything else, Elder Frest can assist you. He will know what is permissible." As in, this thing that you've asked for is not, but I've magnanimously granted a one-time exception, so don't ask for any more favors. Ugh. Royalty.

Imogen nodded, the picture of appreciation. "I will make all necessary preparations for this evening. It would be...prudent to avoid interruption during my lessons with the Prima, do you not agree, majesty? The Prima is the embodiment of modest femininity. I would hate to compromise that attribute with an untimely visit by any of the palace residents, especially during such sensitive instruction."

"Yes, yes, of course," the queen agreed. "I shall ensure that you are undisturbed during your lessons."

"Thank you, majesty."

Queen Serebine rose and glided to a window, one graceful hand on a curtain. She looked out contemplatively. Imogen took that as her cue to depart. She stood.

"I shall inquire after your mother, Elder," the queen said, and Imogen froze. "All of your time is dedicated to such an important task now. I am sure she understands that few moments are afforded to indulge in leisurely visits."

Imogen fought the welling panic and anger that surged to the surface from where she'd buried it inside herself. Not deeply enough, it seemed. The queen watched her closely, eyes slightly narrowed.

"I imagine having the burden of caring for her removed so abruptly is an equal source of respite and woe. It is fortunate you understand the importance of your new position and the necessary sacrifices that must be made on behalf of the Goddess and the shurii people."

Sacrifices. *Sacrifices.* She hadn't seen her mother in four days. *Four days.* After taking care of her every single day for three and a half years, not being allowed to visit her was slowly killing parts of Imogen's soul. She hadn't heard a peep. Not a whisper of an update as to her mother's condition since relinquishing her to the queen's people and Mender Alcuin's care. Imogen never had the chance to meet the physician, and while Felíne's endorsement of his skill did manage to lessen her worry, she desperately wanted to see for herself how her mother fared. She would even be grateful for an update. But she knew better than to believe that's what the queen was offering her. Imogen could read between the lines. She knew exactly what Queen Serebine implied. *The person most precious to you is in my clutches. Her life rests in my hands. Fail me, and you will lose more than your head; you'll lose your heart and soul.*

"I...Thank you for asking after my mother, Your Majesty," Imogen forced out. Her hands shook, and she fisted them behind her, dropping into a bow to disguise the tremor. Queen Serebine hadn't outright forbidden her to visit her mother, but the implication that such things should remain exceedingly low on her priority list was apparent.

The queen said nothing, so Imogen stayed like that, bent at the waist, fighting the fear and fury that trembled through her.

Finally, what seemed a small eternity later, the queen spoke. "I imagine you have much to prepare, Elder." An attendant appeared again and brushed past Imogen, heading for the door. She heard it open a moment later. "I will receive your report tomorrow. I very much look forward to learning of your first demonstration's success."

Imogen murmured, "Majesty," and backed toward the exit. She couldn't get out of the room fast enough.

When she finally made her way hastily down the hallway, free from listening ears and seeing eyes the color of malachite, she released a shaky breath. Belatedly, she realized the interior doors to the queen's receiving chambers were carved with a great, prowling jungle cat. One with glowing emeralds the size of her fists for eyes.

Chapter 7

Secrets

FELÍNE LEFT HER ROOMS SHORTLY before sundown and made her way to a small lounge room just down the corridor from the grand banquet hall. The room was closer to the southern entrance to the villa and situated in a wing that also housed the kitchens, old servants' quarters, several garderobes and pantries, as well as other storage chambers. She rarely frequented this portion of the palace, considering it usually bustled with staff with which she was prohibited from interacting. According to the missive she'd received earlier that evening, the wing would be vacant in preparation for her lesson.

Felíne had expected Imogen to commence her instruction in one of the larger tutor rooms, where most elders preferred to hold their lectures. Those were in the rear of the villa, closer to her rooms and the elders' annex, which extended off the eastern edge of the grounds. Imogen's quarters were located there, and Felíne wondered why she'd chosen this modest lounge room for their lesson.

She and her guard for the evening arrived at the appointed door, and she found Imogen waiting for her. Felíne had done her best to allay the flutter of nerves that had taken up residence in her stomach on the walk over. She'd returned from Mender Alcuin's infirmary with slightly more than thirty minutes to prepare for her lesson when she'd found Imogen's instructions waiting for her. She had bathed and released her hair from its many pins and adornments, letting it fall to the middle of her back in a ripple of dark waves. She had dressed in a simple cream gown and switched out her normal light slippers for heavier-soled shoes, which currently hid beneath the hem of her dress.

Imogen smiled when she saw her. "Good evening, Prima."

Felíne returned the smile. "Elder."

Imogen looked toward the guard. "We shall be occupied for the better part of the evening. I am expecting an assistant; the queen should have informed you. Please show her in when she arrives and then ensure we are not disturbed."

The guard inclined his head in understanding, and Felíne's eyes popped. She felt a pang of envy at the minute acknowledgment. It was brief, however, and quickly replaced with curiosity. Imogen expected an assistant? From *outside?* And her mother allowed it?

Imogen turned, her elder's vestments swishing with her movement, and opened the door to the lounge room. The guard did not follow them inside.

Felíne had considered the sitting room small, but she supposed that was a matter of perspective. The rectangular space was large enough to fit fifty people comfortably, with room to move about unobstructed. The ceilings were high, though not as vaulted as the entry foyer, ballroom, or banquet hall. A long table—supporting a platter of fruit, sweetbreads, and pitchers of tea—had been pushed up against the far wall under the shuttered windows, its accompanying chairs set to the side as though unwanted. A number of heavier lounges took up the main body of the room, their cheerfully designed cushions adorned with pillows of varying shapes and cozy blankets. To her right, a huge wooden armoire occupied most of the wall, one door slightly ajar, displaying several shelves lined with stacked dishes, serving platters, dinnerware, and neatly folded tablecloths.

She turned to Imogen. "I have questions."

Imogen smirked. "I'm beginning to think that shouldn't surprise me." She walked to the table and poured two glasses of tea. She handed one to Felíne. The other she raised to her nose, inhaled, and then took a long sip.

All of her previous inquiries momentarily left her head. "Why do you do that?"

Imogen raised a brow. "Do what?"

"Sniff your drink before you drink. You did it earlier when I gave you the *maruchi* tea and again just now."

Imogen looked down at her glass like she didn't know how it got into her hand. She seemed subtly surprised by Felíne's observance. "Did I?"

Felíne nodded.

Imogen shrugged. "Force of habit, I suppose."

Felíne took a sip from her glass without smelling the contents. "That much I gathered, but it doesn't exactly answer my question."

Imogen regarded her. "I'm not going to get away with being evasive, I see." She set her drink on the table. "The short answer is this: I didn't brew the tea myself."

"And the long answer?"

Imogen sighed. "You were raised here and have spent your entire life inside these palace grounds, yes?"

Felíne nodded.

"I will be blunt. You have grown up in significant comfort and relative safety. While there have been murmurs of threats against you in the past, the chances of you facing actual danger are very low. You live in a heavily guarded home, protected on one side by a perilous mountain range and on the other by the largest shurii army ever to exist. You have personal guards watching your every movement. You don't have to worry about someone slitting your throat while you sleep, poisoning your evening meal, or accosting you on your way home to steal your day's wages. I did not grow up with that kind of security. Your elders taught you history, math, and language. I was taught from a young age to closely inspect any food or drink that I did not prepare myself before consuming it. I am an elder now, but I was not raised one. No matter my title, I am still a product of my upbringing."

Felíne tilted her glass, the dark liquid swirling. "If it was poisoned, you could smell it?"

"Mostly, yes. Most poisons favored by the common criminal have a subtle scent, like sour fruit, which is relatively easy to detect if you know what to look for. I lose some of my sensitivity in first form, though. In second, I could tell if *your* drink had been poisoned without having to place it under my nose."

Felíne grinned. "Not if it was poisoned with *crypt-bloom*."

Imogen gave her a questioning look.

"The plant itself is harmless except for the pollen on a mature blossom. It's completely tasteless and has no discernible smell. A significant dose will paralyze the muscles necessary for movement in about sixty seconds, shut down vital organs in two minutes, and stop the heart completely in five."

Imogen's eyes widened, an entirely different look crossing her features.

Felíne laughed heartily at her expression. "Don't worry. I've never poisoned anyone. And I doubt even the typical apothecary would know of *crypt-bloom*. The plant is common enough, but its properties are not widely known. Most would think it a weed."

"I have a distinct feeling the elders didn't teach you this."

"Your feelings would be correct." Felíne continued when Imogen's raised brow indicated her interest. "Mender Alcuin uses *crypt-bloom*. In small controlled doses, it produces temporary paralysis, which can be useful during certain surgical procedures. It's completely reversible with the antidote."

Imogen appeared doubtful. "And Mender Alcuin grows these deadly plants?"

"He does have many medicinal herbs in his nursery, but not *crypt-bloom*. It grows abundantly about ninety miles north of here. He makes the trip to collect what he needs. The pollen can be stored easily as long as it's sealed and kept dry."

Imogen frowned. "I'd hate to be the poor bee that tried to pollinate that murderous plant."

Felíne's eyes lit up. "The flower produces a pseudo-pollen, which contains the toxin. The flower bees that pollinate the *crypt-bloom* have learned that the plant's true pollen is contained in small pods on the undersides of their leaf stems. The pseudo-pollen exists as a deterrent for eagle wasps, which are the flower bees' natural predators. The eagle wasps land on the blossoms while hunting for the bees and pick up the pseudo-pollen, which paralyzes them, allowing the flower bees to collect the real pollen without being harmed. The wasps wake up after a few minutes and fly off."

Imogen stared at her. "Wow."

"Fascinating, isn't it?"

Imogen's eyebrows raised suggestively. "Riveting. And you secretly use it to paralyze people."

Felíne huffed a laugh and rolled her eyes. "Drink your tea."

60

The elder raised her glass. "You surprise me yet again, Prima."

Imogen reached into the folds of her gown and pulled out a small time-piece. She checked the time and frowned slightly.

Felíne stepped closer to her, and Imogen turned a hand to show her the face of the watch.

Nearly eight at night. Felíne suddenly remembered her earlier questions, and they spilled out of her. "Why the lounge room instead of a lecture hall closer to our quarters? Also, how in the world did you get the queen to permit you an assistant for this lesson? And what do you *need* an assistant for in the first place?" That last one made her nervous all over again.

Imogen looked smug, like a fox that had spent the last hour terrorizing chickens in the coop, and the farmer had yet to realize. "Your first and third questions will be answered shortly. Your second is my secret to keep. To-night, you will learn and see much, both what you need to as the Prima and hopefully some of what you hoped to as yourself."

She swallowed.

Imogen seemed to sense her growing apprehension because she said, "Don't worry, Felíne. I know I have yet to earn it, but you can trust me."

A yawning chasm of anxiety opened inside of her, threatening to devour her carefully constructed exterior and leave her at the mercy of a young girl's emotional chaos. Because that's what slumbered inside of her. Beneath the poise and propriety, the temperance and abnegation, existed a young woman scared to death of her own future.

Felíne needed to get a grip. Why was she so nervous? It felt as though her insides had come untethered, and everything floated about out of place. She had mentally prepared herself for these lessons for years, ever since she was old enough to learn what servicing a male entailed. She knew the sensitive nature of the subject material. The intimacy that would eventually require her participation. Her imagination had conjured what she'd thought to be every possible case scenario, good and bad, constructive and damning, enticing and terrifying. She'd had plenty of time to process the emotions that accompanied those thoughts. So why did it feel as though she was contemplating all of it for the first time? She needed some form of concrete expectation. A line in the sand that she could see and clearly adjust to. All of this unknown was making her tense. And crazy.

She opened her mouth to ask Imogen—

A knock thudded on the door, and Felíne nearly jumped out of her skin.

"Finally," Imogen breathed and moved to the entrance.

A hooded figure several inches shorter than Felíne ducked inside the room and unceremoniously unslung a canvas tote from its shoulders, dropping the bag on the rug. The door shut, and Imogen sealed the deadbolt.

The elder turned and regarded the newcomer, hands on her hips. "You're late."

The figure threw back her hood. "Oh, piss right off, Gen," she retorted in exasperation. "You're lucky I came at all. Do you know how hard it was to convince Madame last minute that I needed the night off? I canceled a whole night of clients. She'll expect repayment for the loss."

Felíne watched the sassy little female with wide, disbelieving eyes. She was short, with curly yellow-blonde hair, fair, freckled skin, large blue eyes heavily lined with a smudge of dark kohl, and a small but expressive mouth that seemed set in a perpetual pout. The female walked farther into the room, curvy hips swishing, and plopped into a chair. Her posture was preposterous. Her attitude, irreverent. She shrugged out of her cloak, and Felíne's eyes nearly bugged out of her head.

Her garment was…was positively scandalous. The shurii wore a thin sort of wrapped tunic. The ivory material crossed over her full breasts and cinched underneath with an excess curtain of fabric that fell down to her knees in varying layers, shorter in front and longer in the back. A loose skirt of the same cut and fabric pooled to the floor. The effect made it appear as though a number of cresting, frothy white waves covered the woman from waist to feet.

Well, maybe *covered* was the wrong word. The material was almost completely translucent. If she turned just so, Felíne could make out every intimate curve and contour, shade and shadow of the female's body. She couldn't believe it. The woman sat there, slouched in the chair, without a care in the world, while Felíne gawked at the clearly visible silhouettes of pink nipples that were pierced with delicate golden hoops.

Imogen strode to the female and tossed a tied cloth pouch into her lap. The female caught it, peeked inside, and dumped a handful of coins into her palm. The female looked up with wide eyes.

Imogen smirked. "That should satisfy Madame."

"And then some," the female said. "How?"

Imogen tsked. "You know better than to ask how."

"Are you sure you want me to have all of this? It's just one night, Gen. What about your mo—"

Imogen cut her off. "It's for you, Vee. Consider it an advance. I may need you again."

Vee eyed her as though she were about to argue, but then she jutted her chin at Felíne. "Who's your friend?"

Felíne glanced at Imogen questioningly. Wasn't this her assistant? Surely, the female knew who she was. Knew why she was here.

Imogen answered smoothly. "Apologies. This is Wren, a member of the palace staff. We met when I started my new assignment." She turned to Felíne. "Wren, this is Veely. A former colleague."

Vee snorted. "So professional since you left us, Gen." She waved a hand above her head in a mock wave, and her golden rings bounced. "Nice to meet you, Wren." And then to Imogen, "Is there food?"

Imogen indicated the table against the wall and said, "Help yourself." Veely's eyes widened with excitement. She rose and bounced to the table, gold hoops dancing.

"Did you bring what I asked?" Imogen crouched by the canvas bag that Veely had brought with her.

Veely nodded, her mouth already filled with something she clearly found delicious. "Gods, this is good," she mumbled. "How long will you be gone?"

"The night," said Imogen as she inspected the bag's contents. She seemed satisfied. "You remember my instructions?"

Veely gave another nod. She swallowed. "Don't unlock the door. Don't try to leave the room. Make occasional noises." She waggled blonde eyebrows at Felíne. "Trust no one. I got it."

Imogen stood, the bag over her shoulder. "I'm serious, Vee. Rules are different here. It'll be your hide and ours if you don't do exactly as I said."

Veely waved her off. "Gen. I said I got it. You gave me a night off, fed *and* paid me. I'm not going to screw you over. Go. I'll cover your exit."

Imogen gave the female one more glance before motioning Felíne over to the boudoir at the far end of the room. "Ready for your first lesson?"

CLOAKING FATE

Felíne's mind whirled, completely lost. Imogen didn't wait for an answer before pulling the boudoir doors wide. The shelves on the right were crammed with dishes, linens, and the like. The shelves on the left held a few pieces of cutlery, a somewhat sloppily folded tablecloth, and a pair of candlesticks. Imogen removed the few items from the left shelves and set them on the floor. She then inspected the inside ledge on the lefthand side of the divider between the two halves. Her eyes lit as her fingers stilled on the lip. She pried some sort of hidden lever and shoved.

Felíne gawked for a second time that evening as she watched one half of the boudoir swing inward on invisible hinges, revealing a narrow staircase that descended into darkness.

"I...how..." She had a hard time formulating thoughts, let alone complete sentences.

Imogen reached out and took her hand, pulling her forward through the false door and onto the landing that shouldn't exist. Felíne balked. A hidden passage in the palace? How was this possible? How did *Imogen* know it was here? Did the king and queen know? The elders? Where did it lead, and who used it? The only person she knew of who utilized any type of tunnel system was Mender Alcuin, and as far as she was aware, they led exclusively to his infirmaries in the city. She looked at Imogen, this woman she'd known all of one day, and realized she was a total stranger.

"Veely is not your assistant, is she?"

Imogen answered but did not let go of her hand. "No. She's a stand-in. She is here to ensure our absence is not discovered."

Felíne pulled her hand back and hugged herself. Imogen had said she could be trusted. But she was right; she hadn't earned it. What if this was some sort of trap? A lure to get her away from the safety of her guards. If she followed Imogen down that staircase into the darkness, there was no telling where she would end up. If she would return. And yet, the elders trusted Imogen with her care. Surely, they would not allow just anyone to be welcomed into their fold. And the queen? She had dedicated her life to ensuring Felíne had the preparation and instruction necessary to fulfill her duty. She would not have hand-selected Imogen for this task if she suspected treachery. But the queen couldn't know *everything*, contrary to her childhood belief of the opposite.

Felíne fingered the heavy gold coin that hung on a matching rope chain around her neck, indecision clouding her. She could feel the familiar engraving of her name on one side, worn smooth from years of her fiddling. It had been a gift from Mender Alcuin when she'd turned thirteen. She hadn't taken it off since. How she wished he were here to offer his input. Would he go into the darkness? She stared into it, momentarily losing herself in her deliberation.

Moments passed.

She glanced up at Imogen. There were so many things she wanted to ask.

"It's my job to provide your lessons, Felíne," Imogen said softly. "The only way for me to effectively do that is to show you things that do not exist within these walls. The night will not last forever. If you come with me now, I promise to answer all of your questions on the way. But we cannot linger. Time is not an ally."

She looked again into the darkness. Mender Alcuin wouldn't stand here plagued with uncertainty. He would weigh the odds and take action. He'd be deep in the tunnel by now.

She had a job to do, and nothing in her life had ever afforded her the luxury of choice. And here Imogen was offering it to her. The woman wanted her to follow, but she was *asking* Felíne to trust her. If she really did not want to go, Imogen would not force her.

"Okay," Felíne said, and Imogen gave her a small, relieved smile.

Together, they descended into darkness.

Chapter 8

Kalevar

KALEVAR KAINE SLUNK THROUGH THE city like a ghost in the night. If any were to see him, they would think that level of stealth impossible for a male his size. He stood about six feet, four inches, his frame corded with slabs of muscle—the kind one developed only from years of physical demand—and he'd perfected a scowl that made most intelligent people scramble to get out of his way when they saw him coming.

No one saw him coming tonight. He stuck to the shadows. A dark cloak concealed his formidable frame, its deep hood hiding his glower. His boots were virtually silent on the cobbled streets of Asteros. Not even the soldiers, groups of whom wandered about the city, moving from tavern to pub, brothel to bar again, noticed him slipping through the alleyways, around various establishments.

He passed one such soldier in one such alleyway leaning against the brick side of a building, grunting in satisfaction as he relieved himself on the ground, splashing on his own boots. Kal passed behind him, and the stench of ale piss filled his nostrils. Another lovely night in the capital of Ilistaar. Gods, he hated this city.

As he rounded the corner, his destination almost in sight, he caught a glimpse of the sprawling palace in the distance, built into the mountainside. Lights twinkled from the grounds, illuminating the meticulously manicured structures and landscape. It looked like a tumor. A great, malignant tumor that had attached itself to the base of the mountain and refused to let go. Refused to let everyone forget that it was here and it ruled them.

Kal ducked into the alcove of a nondescript adobe building and pulled a key from the folds of his cloak. He fitted the key to the lock, turned the handle on the door, and let himself inside. He replaced the bolt before moving farther into the darkened room. A lone candle flickered on a round table in the center, casting weak yellow light on the empty table and the few worn wooden chairs surrounding it. The rest of the room was cast in shadow.

A voice came from the darkness. Female. "The city is lovely tonight."

Kal strode into the room and settled himself into one of the chairs. "The city is shit tonight, Santhe, as it is every night."

The female's slender figure emerged from the gloom, bathed by the flickering light of the candle. Her mouse-brown hair was tied back from a plain, but not unpleasant face, currently fixed in a scowl the likes of which rivaled Kal's own. Her hands were braced on her bony hips. Uh-oh.

"That's not what you were supposed to say. You were *supposed* to say, 'Lovelier than the desert bloom under a waxing moon.' What is the point of having a code phrase for these meetings if you won't use it?"

Kal relaxed back in his chair and stretched his long legs out in front of him, crossing them at the ankle. "Because it makes you feel better to have them. I could smell you when I came in, Santhe. I knew you were here alone."

Santhe wrinkled her little nose at him. "You're impossible. How was your trip? Did you have any issues getting into the city?"

Kal shrugged. "No more than usual."

Santhe gave him a wary look. "Meaning?"

"The army is three guards shy, but it'll be some time before they realize."

"Kal! Soldiers? You can't keep killing people, you idiot! You're going to get us caught."

Kal shrugged again.

A frown marred her brow, creating an 'M' between her eyes. "I'm serious. We take risk enough without you picking off soldiers each time you visit. The army is going to start tightening up security, not relaxing it like we need. Do you have to make everything more difficult?"

"Stop pacing and sit down. Based on the activity of the soldiers I saw in the city, no one is worried about a few missing guards. When they find the three I disposed of, it'll look like they went on a drinking binge, took one too many hits of *kossroot*, and died high as a cloud. Their superiors won't think anything of it. They'll probably commend their methods and confiscate the leftover powder for later use."

Santhe sighed and dropped into a chair. She put her head in her hands.

Kal reached over and squeezed her shoulder. "Hey. It's fine. I was careful."

"Careful isn't in your vocabulary." She peeked at him. "Where did you even get *kossroot*? Only criminals have those kinds of connections."

His deep chuckle reverberated in the small room. "You give this vagabond too much credit. You know I'm a scoundrel at heart."

Santhe rolled her eyes and smiled. She couldn't keep the warmth out of her expression, though the 'M' on her forehead didn't disappear entirely. She was frowning too much lately. "I've known you for years, Kalevar Kaine. You might be a scoundrel, but there's no heart truer than yours."

His smile didn't come as easily as Santhe would have liked. "Like I said. Too much credit."

"You look good," she said. "Could use a haircut, though."

Kal ran his fingers through the dense knot of curls on top of his head that were longer than he normally kept them. The sides were growing but still short. His hair was an odd texture. It was soft, not coarse, but thicker than one would expect. As a child, it grew in long ringlets, and people would tell him how pretty his hair was, something that deeply offended his boyish pride. His father had cut it when he'd complained, much to his mother's dismay. She had thought he looked too grown up without his long curls. Now they were both gone, and he'd kept it short ever since.

"I'd planned to have Cinah fade me up when I got here. Where is he, by the way?"

Santhe chewed her lip, and her brown eyes darkened with worry. "He's late. He should have been here ahead of you."

Kal's brow furrowed. Cinah took more risk than either of them coming to these meetings. Santhe worked as a barmaid in one of the local taverns and a seamstress on the side. She could easily move about the city without rousing suspicion. Kal no longer lived in Asteros but was able to come and go as he pleased, so long as he didn't attract any unwanted attention. Cinah worked for the king. There were times he was unable to get away and could not get word out. Twice before, he and Santhe had been waiting for him for hours before finally having to call off the meeting. Neither of them held it against him. Kal's blood boiled at the thought of his friend serving that prick. Cinah didn't have a choice. He was King Domitan's favored attendant, and Cinah used that connection to benefit others despite what it cost him. The information he was able to gather couldn't be obtained from other sources. And he hated it. Kal fucking hated it.

"He can't continue doing this," Kal growled.

Santhe looked at him sadly. "He doesn't have a choice, Kal. And if he did, he'd choose to help." She looked toward the door. "It doesn't make it any easier to deal with. Not for us. Least of all for him."

"I swear on the gods, if that fucking piece of shit king—"

A key turning in the lock of the front door cut Kal's raging short. He and Santhe both froze. Moments later, a dark head poked around the door, and a lean male body followed it. The door shut, and the lock was thrown. No one spoke.

"The city is lovely tonight," Cinah whispered.

Santhe got up from her seat, went to Cinah, and threw her arms around him. The tall, dark-skinned man looked down at her surprised and returned her hug. "You were supposed to say 'Lovelier than—'"

"Oh, shut up," Santhe said. She peered up at him, concern evident in her expression. "We didn't know if you would make it."

Cinah smiled, and Kal hated that it looked forced. Likely for Santhe's benefit. "I was delayed," he said. "I'm sorry. I came as soon as I could."

Santhe took his hand and guided him to the table. Kal stood and clasped the male in a quick embrace. He put a broad hand on Cinah's shoulder. "Alright, Cin?"

Cinah nodded. "Still above ground. It's good to see you, Kal."

Santhe moved into a shadowy recess and returned with a pitcher of ale, one of tea, and three mugs. She also brought a loaf of bread with butter, honey, and an orange-colored jam that smelled tart and sweet.

"Were you going to starve me until he got here?" Kal asked her. "What if he never showed?"

Santhe pegged him with a stern glare. "He's here now. So, you can quit complaining. Eat, drink, and tell us why we're here."

Cinah chuckled deeply and reached for the tea. "What did you do, Kal?"

"I did nothing."

Santhe huffed. "Nothing, my ass. He killed three city guards!"

Kal crossed his arms. "Honestly, Santhe. Snitching?"

Cinah's dark brow furrowed. "Kal. We talked about this."

Kal poured himself a healthy serving of ale and took a long swallow. "It was unavoidable."

Cinah raised a brow. "Unavoidable. Like the two tradesmen you killed the last time you were here?"

"That was a misunderstanding."

"And the time before that?" Santhe quipped.

"I was defending myself. And you, if memory serves me," he said, pointing his mug in her direction. "A little gratitude might be nice for a change."

"Kal."

"Cin, relax. I cleaned up after myself."

Cinah sighed. "Even if you covered your tracks, and we know you always do, the news of three soldiers' deaths will make its way back to Domitan. You know how obsessive he is over the stability of his army. This will...vex him."

Santhe reached forward and grasped Cinah's forearm, the concern back on her face.

Of course. Fuck. Of course, any threat to the king's precious army would inevitably cause a backlash of which Cinah would take the brunt. Kal cursed his own tactlessness. He hadn't considered how the ramifications of his mini killing spree would potentially affect his friend. It had been two years. Two years of being at that dick king's beck and call after the last attendant died of some mysterious illness. Cinah never complained, and when Kal came into Asteros, he always helped, whether it was smuggling goods, information, or people. That first year, he'd tried countless times to convince Cinah to let him sneak him out of the city. Santhe had sided with him for once, lending her own reasoning to Kal's arguments. His friend had always refused, saying he still had his part to play. Kal eventually stopped asking, but he never stopped hoping.

He rubbed a hand over his jaw, scratching the stubble. "Fuck, Cin. I didn't think."

Cinah waved him off and poured a mug of tea for Santhe, who situated herself next to him. "What's done is done."

"Cin…"

"Kal, it will be handled. And though I know you secretly wish to wallow in regret on my behalf, we haven't the time. Tell us why you called this meeting."

Kal took a breath, burying guilt he'd probably punish himself with later. "You both remember Rask?"

His companions nodded. Santhe said, "Blond locks, blue eyes? How could we forget your friend from Meress? He nearly got the three of us killed six years ago when you brought him to Asteros, and he tried to cheat at stones."

Kal dipped his chin. "That's the one."

Cinah took a sip of tea. "He's not from Meress, though. Didn't he say his family lived here in Asteros?"

"Yes. His mother and sister."

Santhe said, "What about him?"

Kal looked at each of them and said, "Rask's younger sister, Railah, was recruited as a Fate."

Santhe swore.

"When?" Cinah asked.

"A week ago, maybe? Rask received a letter from his mother several days ago. It found us outside Berdeen."

Santhe looked at him. "Let me guess. Rask wants you to get her out."

Kal nodded. "Santhe, have you heard anything? Talk regarding the Fates?"

She shook her head, then stopped, pondering. "Wait. A few days ago, there was talk in one of the lodges of a Fate being retired."

Cinah frowned. "Killed?"

"No. They talked like she got away. Got out. Maybe they recruited Railah as her replacement before letting her go?"

Cinah said gravely, "They don't just let the Fates go."

Kal asked, "But nothing of a new Fate being recruited?"

Santhe shook her head.

Kal swore. "I have to get Railah out of the city. Cin, can you get to her?"

Santhe spoke up. "Wait a moment. This isn't just another civilian that no one will notice is gone. Kal, if Railah is a Fate, she's going to be watched. Someone will know if she goes missing."

"What would you have me do? Rask is expecting me to meet him in two weeks with his sister. He's already planning to send word to his mother to leave Asteros."

Santhe soured. "Doesn't he understand the danger here? Of course, he sends you. Rask couldn't be expected to risk his own neck, I suppose?"

"Santhe."

She stood and started pacing again. "No. Tell Rask to come retrieve his sister himself. We have risked too much for the sake of others and none for ourselves. And we are *always* the ones paying the prices. We aren't talking about grain or weapons or intel. This is a *Fated Mother*. I won't tolerate either of you risking your lives for Rask's selfishness." She stopped and looked at both of them, emotion filling her eyes. Kal knew the source of that emotion, the desperation in her gaze. Santhe lost a brother to this rebellion. Collateral damage of risks that shouldn't have been taken. Kal and Cinah were the only family she had left, yet what could they do but continue to try? The Faithful Cursed and their oppressive beliefs, the crown and its chokehold on the people of Ilistaar, had to be stopped. More than just Santhe's brother needed avenging.

"Santhe," Kal said again.

She looked at him, biting her lip to keep it from trembling. "It's too dangerous."

Kal turned to Cinah, who gently placed a hand over Santhe's. "What is the potential fallout?"

Cinah sat back and blew out a breath. "Best case scenario? If Railah goes missing, the queen will have guards searching the city for any sign of her. Maybe Domitan's hunters. When she's not found, it's possible she'll let it drop. See it as a sign it wasn't meant to be. The queen may be distracted enough by how close we are to the Prima's presentation." He paused. "Worst case? She'll turn this city upside down to find her in order to silence her. Anyone suspected of aiding in her escape will be in danger."

The grimness of Santhe's expression intensified.

Cinah continued. "Domitan never had much involvement with the Fates. That is the queen's enterprise. Army elites guard the females in a place called the Stronghold, and the location within Asteros is secret. If Railah has already been taken there, it won't be difficult to get to her; it'll be impossible."

Kal muttered a curse.

"There could be one option, though," Cinah mused. "It is possible that Railah hasn't yet been retrieved. If this is the case, it will be much easier to reach her."

"Where would they be keeping her if she hasn't yet gone to the Stronghold?"

Cinah looked at Santhe. She took a long draw of her tea despite the steam still wafting from the lip of the mug. "She would be in the Starlight Lodge off Kinsmet Road," she said. "The queen has a private suite there, kept for guests of importance and anyone that requires a discreet stay. The normal staff runs the lodge, but the queen's personal attendants are the only ones allowed in and out of that suite. Short of taking Railah onto the palace grounds, that's the one place she'd be secured in the city before going to the Stronghold."

Kal frowned, thinking. "Why wait? Why not just take her straight to the Stronghold after recruiting her?"

Cinah answered. "The queen has turned the Fates into a sort of spiritualistic class. They are seen as servants to the Goddess, meant to serve a greater purpose. From what I can gather, the induction has become somewhat involved. A cleansing period is required before the females are allowed to enter the Stronghold with the others. I don't know much more than that."

"Fuck," Kal said, disgusted. "Okay, well, the first thing we must do is determine where she is. Santhe, is there any way you can safely find out if Railah's in the queen's suite at the Starlight Lodge?"

She hesitated, clearly unhappy, and Cinah squeezed her hand. She gazed at him for a long moment before she nodded. "I pick up shifts there a few times per month. I have a friend who runs the front house on weekends. She can get me in on short notice without any fuss. If the suite is occupied, I'll know."

"Good. Cin, if we can verify Railah's presence at the Lodge, can you get a message to her?"

Cinah considered. "If she's there, it's possible, yes."

Kal nodded. He drained his mug of ale and wiped his chin. He set the mug down on the table with a thud. "Well, my friends, if you can accomplish this much, I will handle the rest."

"You're sure, Kal?"

He looked at Santhe. "I told Rask I'd get her out safe. Even if she wasn't my friend's sister, if I have the opportunity to save a female from that kind of fate, what kind of man would I be to waste it?"

Santhe gave one last effort. "The kind that lived a long, happy life?"

"There are no guarantees, San."

She grimaced. "Ugh, I know." Then firmer. "I know. Okay. I'm on board. I'll get what information I can about Railah's whereabouts. Give me two days. Kal, meet me back here at the same time. Cinah, I'll leave word at The Crowned Doe for you."

"Railah may not have two days," Kal argued.

Cinah interjected before Santhe could retort back. "Two days, Kal," he said in a voice that brooked no argument. "We do this the right way, the safest way, or not at all. Agreed?"

He couldn't disagree with the man's logic. It was this city. This place. It was making him antsy. The sooner he got Railah, the sooner he could get the hell out of here. "Agreed."

Cinah nodded and moved to clear the drinks from the table.

Kal pulled out a straight blade and a comb when Cinah returned and twirled them skillfully between his fingers. "Any chance you've got time for a cut before we call it a night?"

Cinah sighed but smiled, holding his hand out for the blade and comb.

Santhe grabbed the last piece of bread, dunked it in a vat of honey, and stuffed it into her mouth. "Be thankful all he cuts is your hair," she mumbled. Kal couldn't help but laugh.

Chapter 9

Tunnels

FELÍNE FOLLOWED IMOGEN DOWN THE spiraling stone staircase. She only knew where the female was based on the sound of light steps ahead and the rustle of a gown with gentle movement. She couldn't see a thing in front of her, and she hoped, with Imogen's superior eyesight, the female had an idea of where she was leading them so that neither unexpectedly plummeted to their deaths.

"You're sure you know where you're going?" she asked.

"Yes."

"You've been this way before?" She was surprised. Imogen had been an elder all of three days. She'd clearly been busy.

"No."

Oh.

"That's not reassuring."

Imogen stopped suddenly ahead of her, and Felíne stumbled straight into the elder's back, nearly falling flat on her own. Imogen reached out surely and braced Felíne's arms, keeping her upright. The stairwell had ended, and they were once again on level ground.

"This way," Imogen said, her soft voice seeming loud in the dark. She took Felíne's hand, guiding her forward to the left. Felíne felt an overwhelming urge to keep looking over her shoulder, certain they would be found out. She half expected her mother to come charging through the shadows or for one of the wraiths to manifest out of the darkness.

Felíne had the sense of being weighed in on all sides. When she reached out, she realized that they were, in fact, squeezing through a narrow passage.

She had a moment of tightness in her chest, and she sucked in a wheezy breath.

"Easy," Imogen whispered. "Not far now."

She was right, thank the Goddess. Within a few seconds, the passage widened, Felíne's panic receded, and a glorious, dazzling light sparkled ahead. It was little more than the wavering flicker of a single candle set into a sconce in the recess of the wall, but as far as Felíne was concerned, it might as well have been the holy light of all the heavens leading them to immortality.

Imogen moved to a rather worn-looking wooden door with a brass ring for a handle that Felíne hadn't initially noticed. The passageway they'd come from extended forward, continuing into darkness. The walls here were stone and dirt, the tunnel clearly old and unused. Felíne bypassed the passageway and followed Imogen through the door into a small room no bigger than a closet. It had a single stool in one corner with legs that looked mostly chewed through by some nocturnal creature. Imogen dropped the canvas bag on the floor, told her to sit, and went to retrieve the candle from across the hall. Felíne was doubtful the stool would bear the weight of an empty boot, let alone her whole body, and she perched delicately. Her seat gave an alarming creak but otherwise held.

Imogen returned with the candle, which she handed to Felíne, and produced a bronze oil lamp from the canvas bag. Once lit, they had considerably more visibility, and Imogen set the lamp on a small shelf that protruded from the wall. She'd never considered herself to have a fear of the dark, but this excursion already had her realizing how much she valued the airy, illuminated halls of the palace with their abundance of natural sunlight. That, and she distinctly preferred life above ground.

"This might be a stab in the dark," Felíne said. Oh, the witticism! "But I'm going to venture a guess that you aren't planning to conduct my first lesson in an ancient broom closet in a moth-eaten crypt under the palace."

Imogen had gone back to rummaging through the canvas bag and glanced up briefly, giving Felíne a look that said *Why, Prima, that's exactly what I'd planned to do.* Felíne sighed.

"Of course not," Imogen said at last, after gathering a collection of supplies, including what looked like kohl, lip stain, a small handheld mirror, rouge, and a tin palette of other flesh-colored paints. "But you need to look the part before we reach our destination."

Felíne eyed the cosmetics. "Which is where, exactly?"

Imogen began sharpening the stick of kohl. "What do you know about servicing a male?"

The question caught Felíne off guard, and she momentarily blanked. "I…The basics, I suppose. I know male and female anatomy. I know the mechanism of action that results in procreation. I know…how…*things*, uh, fit together." Gods, she was awful.

Imogen stared at her. "How did you learn this?"

Felíne felt incredibly foolish. This was preposterous. She was a grown woman. Why did she suddenly feel like a child caught doing something inappropriate? "Books."

"Books?"

Her cheeks warmed. "Well, the elders taught me basic anatomy. Mender Alcuin gave me physiology texts to read. They explained the reproductive process and fundamental physiological functions, including the differences in fertility based on form. There were…pictures."

"Pictures."

Felíne blinked. Her face was on fire. Why did she have to repeat everything she said and make it sound infinitely more absurd? "Yes. Diagrams. Of…of body parts." Gods above, what was wrong with her? She'd taken care of patients. She knew what bodies looked like beneath clothing. But somehow, when her imagination assigned a sexual role to the male and female forms, those bodies transformed into something erotic and forbidden. They stopped being a simple collection of parts and became an entirely unfamiliar entity. One that made her hyperaware and altogether uncomfortable in her own skin.

Imogen stopped sharpening the kohl and sat back on her heels. "Oh dear."

Enough meaning was sunk into those two words to make Felíne's uneasiness spike.

"Tonight, you are going to see more than pictures, Felíne," Imogen said. "But we are going to take things slow. I'm taking you to a pleasure house."

Her eyes flew wide.

"I assume your mortification is an indication that you've never been touched."

She sputtered. "Of course not!"

"Okay. Take a breath. You will remain that way. No one will touch you. However, you will see more than you likely anticipated. The best way for me to teach you what will be expected of you during your servicing is to show you. Ideally, the art of pleasure is something best eased into, but I don't have the luxury of taking the time necessary to ensure your comfort. For that, I apologize."

Felíne swallowed and nodded numbly.

"Also, tonight is simply an introduction. First forms only. Your particular servicing will be distinctly different, considering the intent is to produce a child." The light in Imogen's chocolate eyes guttered and Felíne wondered at the reason, but the female mastered whatever passed over her before she could ask and said, "But one life-altering step at a time."

Imogen took the stick of kohl then and began smudging it around Felíne's eyes. They sat in silence as Imogen worked, and Felíne struggled to control the vivid wanderings of her imagination. After the kohl, Imogen applied rouge to her cheeks and painted a berry-colored stain on her lips. The quiet slowly shifted away from being oppressive and instead acquired a cathartic quality as Imogen patiently decorated Felíne's features with graceful precision. The sudden tension she'd felt started to dissipate until she was once again mostly relaxed, left with only a small kernel of apprehension that was far easier to manage than the earlier smothering blanket of anxiety.

"There," Imogen said moments later. She held the little mirror up so that Felíne could inspect her handiwork. She looked and let out a little gasp. It was a stranger. Queen Serebine preached chastity and favored purity, so Felíne did nothing to alter her natural features. "You will go to the Primordial Male pure as the Goddess made you," her mother had said. The female that looked back at her now was someone different entirely. She was still chaste. Still pure. But she *looked* like a temptress. Imogen had somehow accentuated all of her best features. Her almond honey-green eyes appeared larger and more enticing, winged out with the dark liner. Her lips looked fuller, glossy, and red like she imagined they might after a night spent kissing a lover. Her high, round cheekbones popped with subtle color, and the hollows of her jawline were masterfully shaded, giving the shape of her face sharper, alluring angles.

"Who is she?" Felíne breathed.

Imogen smiled, clearly pleased with her handiwork. "Someone who will not draw the wrong sort of attention where we are going."

Imogen then had Felíne hold the mirror for her as she painted her own face. When Imogen looked equally like a siren, she carefully packed her supplies and pulled two suspicious-looking garments from the canvas bag. One she handed to Felíne.

"Last part of the costume."

Felíne quickly undressed, and Imogen helped her don the under-gown, a lovely gossamer length the shade of sheer midnight. It draped over her shoulders, hugged her bosom, and fell loosely and femininely to her feet. The fabric was surprisingly comfortable and made Felíne feel entirely naked. Gooseflesh peppered her skin.

Imogen began to clothe herself in a similar, floor-length shift, which was cocoa-colored. When she was finished, she closed the canvas bag.

"Where's the rest?" Felíne asked.

Imogen tucked the bag to the side of the room and looked up at her questioningly. "The rest of what?"

Felíne blinked, and Imogen stood. "The gowns."

"There is no 'rest.' These are the gowns."

She couldn't be serious. Felíne blurted, "But I can see your breasts." Before she could stop herself, she pointed at Imogen's chest as if to remind the female she did, in fact, have two unmistakable breasts visible through the fabric of her garment. She then suddenly seemed to remember that she herself had a pair. Felíne looked down at her own heavier set and the beautiful blue-black fabric that did nothing to hide them from view. Felíne immediately crossed her arms over her chest and looked imploringly at Imogen.

"This is the traditional garb of Madame's," Imogen said. "If you wear anything more modest, you're going to draw attention, and that is not something either of us wants. You must remain anonymous."

"I'm practically naked!"

"Trust me, you're more clothed than others will be."

"But—"

"Felíne," Imogen said. "Trust me."

But that little seed of panic had exploded into an invasive weed that was hellbent on choking the air from her lungs and the logic from her brain.

"I can't do this."

Imogen bent, pulled a thick cloak from the bag, and draped it around Felíne's shoulders. Felíne immediately fisted the material closed and hugged it to her chest.

"Do you want to go back?"

"What?"

Imogen regarded her seriously. "We can go back. I can give a false report to the queen. If you truly cannot do this, I will take you back and have you escorted to your chambers. You can wash your face, put on your nightclothes, and crawl into the comfort of your bed. Tomorrow morning, you can meet me in one of the classrooms with which you're familiar, and I can stand in front of you and lecture you on sexual positions and show you diagrams of how males and females can touch each other for pleasure, then how they join to make children." Imogen's voice took on a hardened edge, one that Felíne felt had nothing to do with her. "I'll show you a picture of a birth. Describe the stages of pregnancy and the feelings you may or may not experience when your own time comes to carry a child. Walk you through how to push that child into the world. We can be done by noon and have lunch in one of the garden rooms. Nice and safe."

A comfort zone was an interesting place in which to exist. She'd spent years inside it, seeking any way she could imagine to get out. To experience life. To see and feel and do new things. To test her limits, stretch her curiosities. Yet the moment she was thrust outside the boundaries of familiarity, her first instinct was to run back inside. Was that what she wanted? To live a life cushioned and complacent? Imogen was painting a picture of her childhood. Of lecture halls and explanations, and the occasional controlled demonstration. She'd been presented with shadows of real-life experiences, relying on her imagination to fill in the gaps where reality had fallen painfully short. Yet she would be expected to perform in a very real way. With no actual practice. Zero actual understanding.

Imogen was right. You could read recipes from dawn until dusk, but how did you learn your own culinary competency unless you watched the chef in the kitchen? Unless you wielded the knife? Physically stirred the pot?

She'd rather had enough of her emotionality and indecision. Where was the youngster who jumped into the moat just to see how long she could hold her breath? That girl wasn't afraid of drowning.

Felíne slowly unclenched her fists and slipped the cloak from her shoulders like releasing the weight of expectation. She inhaled deeply, blew out a determined, cleansing breath, and squared herself. She held the cloak out to Imogen, who looked at her with no small measure of pride. Imogen took the robe and dropped it on top of the bag.

"Very good, Prima," she said, then led her out of the little room and into the hall.

The walk through the underground tunnel was uneventful. There was no movement other than their own, no noises other than the ones they created, such as the soft padding of feet on the dirt floor and the rustle of clothing. They didn't speak, and Felíne was glad for it. She felt if she began discussing the path her life was suddenly taking, she'd find some way to second guess her decisions. She already told herself she wasn't going back. Only moving forward.

The pathway only branched off twice that she noticed, and then she stopped paying attention, distracted by her thoughts.

She thought of her mother, and what the queen would inevitably have to say about her new nighttime excursions underground. She imagined the expression on the queen's face if she saw the garment Felíne currently wore. The thought made her want to laugh and vomit at the same time. She wondered at her mother's own introduction to sexuality. As the queen, was it something that had been taught to her? Had she been instructed on how to please the king before being faced with the task? Somehow Felíne had difficulty picturing the queen, always so put together, always so self-assured, as a diffident young female entering her first servicing. Imagining her mother with the king was even more difficult. She'd never seen them exchange any genuine affection. True intimacy taking place between them behind closed doors seemed an impossibility. Clearly, Felíne's existence stated otherwise.

She thought of Mender Alcuin. She was dying to ask him if he knew about this tunnel beneath the palace. It was old and seemed forgotten, something very different from the subterranean channels the mender frequented to maintain access to his infirmaries in the city, which seemed more modern and well-kept. She wondered at the patient he had wanted her to visit. Wondered if the female had worsened or was yet on the road to recovery. She hoped Mender Alcuin had reached a breakthrough in her care and had developed a definitive treatment plan that would prove successful. If anyone could figure out how to better the female's prognosis, it was Alcuin. She made a mental note to check in for an update regarding the female in the next day or so.

Ahead of her, Imogen shifted her gait slightly to accommodate the gradual decline in the pathway. The journey back on a constant uphill gradient would not be enjoyable.

Felíne's thoughts wandered to her meal with Imogen in the terrace hall earlier that day. How Gen had confided to her that she'd been a Fate. How Felíne had thoughtlessly demanded to be told *everything* in her excitement to gain information that had eluded her for years. Mender Alcuin had said Fates had been hurt. Had died. She didn't want Imogen to think her calloused to any plight she might have faced. Gen was going out of her way to help Felíne, taking risks to teach her in a way she felt would be most effective. Whether her intentions were wholly altruistic or not, Felíne was grateful for the consideration. She wanted Imogen to know it.

"Gen?" Felíne said, and the female glanced sidelong at her as they walked side by side. "I haven't exactly proven myself to be a model student this evening."

Imogen's eyes were soft as they regarded her. "It is a lot to take in. Change is difficult."

"It is, but that's no excuse. You've been kind to me. Understanding and patient. I have been…afraid. Hesitant."

Imogen didn't say anything for a few paces. "You carry a great responsibility, Felíne. Given the circumstances, I think a little fear and hesitation would be natural."

82

Feliné nodded. Then said, "I have also been inconsiderate. A poor friend."

Imogen quirked a brow. "Oh?"

Feliné gazed ahead. "You confided a piece of your past with me and I demanded you lay yourself bare. I believe my words were 'I want to know everything.' I had no right to ask that of you. I'm sorry for my insensitivity."

The tunnel turned abruptly to the right, maintaining one path, and they followed. The dirt floor gave way to rough stone and Feliné had to concentrate, so she didn't catch her foot on an elevated paver lip. Imogen seemed to glide over the uneven ground, completely unaware of how effortless her movements appeared.

"You are forgiven," Imogen said. "I did not hold it against you, but I appreciate the concern for my feelings. I don't mind sharing. Some things, at least. If you have questions, you have my permission to ask them. I would only ask that any answers you obtain you keep to yourself."

Feliné considered. She *did* have questions, but she didn't want to offend Imogen by prying for sensitive information. Then again, she had the feeling that if Gen didn't want to answer a question, she wouldn't.

"How did you become a Fate?"

"The pleasure house we are visiting tonight, Madame's, is not unknown to me. My mother worked there as a prostitute after my father died when I was fifteen. It was just the two of us, and my mother didn't possess many skills. She hadn't received any formal schooling and my father's construction business died when he did, along with all of the profits. She was teaching herself to become a dressmaker, and she ended up mending several gowns for Madame. When she saw the ladies, how beautiful they looked, the lavish gowns they wore, she wanted that for us again. Dressmaking was barely providing food and shelter. Madame offered her employment, a room at the inn, and three square meals per day for both of us. She even proposed to pay my mother extra for inspecting and mending the ladies' gowns. My mother felt she couldn't refuse. We lived at Madame's for five years. My mother is a beautiful female. She did well for herself and Madame was fair."

It sounded unimaginably different from Feliné's upbringing. "What happened?"

"One of her clients was too rough with her. I found her in her room the morning after with bruises and a bloodied lip. I told her I was going to tell Madame, but she begged me not to. She said the male had paid double and it would cause trouble for her with Madame. She didn't want to complain."

Oh, Gen. "Did you tell?"

Imogen shook her head, but her expression said she wished she had. "It happened three more times. The last time, she'd been choked until she passed out. Her eyes were bloodshot, and he'd broken the skin on her neck. Those were just the marks that I could see. I should have said something, but my mother was genuinely afraid when I told her I would. I think the male threatened her."

"Gods, Gen. I'm so sorry."

"I had to get her out of there. But I was twenty years old, had lived in a pleasure house with sparse responsibilities for five years, and spent selfish little time planning an exit strategy. I needed money. Enough to pay for our own place, safely away from Madame's, in case that male came looking for her. Enough to allow my mother the freedom to make her dresses at leisure without worrying where our next meal would come from or what we'd have to do to get it."

"The Fated Mothers. You volunteered?" What little Felíne knew about the Fates included that they were compensated exceptionally well. Significantly more than a common prostitute. It would have been the only thing Imogen could have offered herself up for to guarantee that sort of income on such short notice.

"Yes."

"And your mother? Were you able to get her out of Madame's? To a safe place?"

"I was."

Felíne smiled. "I'm glad. The next time you see her, tell her I'll buy her gowns."

An odd look briefly passed over Imogen's features, and Felíne noticed it too late to discern whether it was pain, confusion, or regret.

"Thank you," Imogen said somewhat distractedly. "She is finally getting the care she deserves."

"And what about you, Gen?" Feline asked. "You helped to take care of your mother. Does anyone help take care of you?" She hoped Imogen had someone special to appreciate and attend to her the way that she'd appreciated and sacrificed to care for her mother.

"I was young once and trusting," Imogen said. The female was once again focused, and the hardened edge to her voice sent a chill down Feline's spine. "Then I became a Fate, and now I am an elder. I take care of myself."

"Of course. I only meant—"

Imogen cut her off, but her voice softened a touch. "I know what you meant. There is little opportunity for romance when your body is not your own. But we will talk more about this later. We're here."

Feline didn't even have a chance to think on Imogen's words because the tunnel ended abruptly at a stone staircase and within moments they were up and through the slanted door overhead, emerging into the night and the heart of Asteros.

Chapter 10

Madame's

THE FIRST THING THAT FELÍNE noticed was the warm, dry night air as Imogen helped her step up over the last stone stair and onto a withering patch of grass. The temperature felt the same as it would on an evening in the palace, and she felt silly for subconsciously assuming it would feel different. Of course, the temperature was the same; they were still in the same city, the same desert. It was only that *she* felt different. As though she'd just stepped into another world.

The second thing that she noticed was the smell. And that *was* different from the palace. She wrinkled her nose at the sour, putrid stench that was unmistakably body excrement, though which kind she couldn't tell. Likely a combination of several. Imogen noted her expression and said, "You'll get used to the smell. The cleanliness in this part of the city is not held to the standards you're accustomed to. Nearer Madame's, it's not as foul, and inside, you won't even notice."

Felíne had no intention of growing accustomed to the odor. Any time she'd been in the city proper, it had been at one of Mender Alcuin's clinics. Inside those buildings, it smelled sterile and clean on account of the mender's strict policy on sanitation. She'd never gone outside. This was awful. It turned her stomach.

She took a moment to look around. They were in a small yard, guarded on three sides by a high wooden fence that was mostly intact. A condemned adobe building occupied the fourth side. The wall she could see was crumbling, and sizeable holes peppered its side. The window had long since broken, the remaining shards of glass were weathered and dull, and the single door was hanging by a rusted hinge. A scraping sound made her turn, and she watched as Imogen covered the door in the ground that they'd come through. There was an overgrowth of shrubbery and tangled weeds that bordered the entrance to the passage, and once shut, it was nearly invisible unless you specifically looked for it.

"This is somewhat arbitrary, but why did you go through the trouble of petitioning the queen for Veely's arrival to the palace when you could have simply snuck her in through this tunnel?" Felíne asked.

Imogen dusted her hands. "Because, while I like Veely, I do not trust a hair on her curled head. I don't want her to know where this passage leads in the city and risk the temptation of her using it without my knowledge. Or worse, sharing its entrance with someone else."

"Couldn't she just follow us through the boudoir?"

Imogen walked to a particularly large gap in the wooden fence. "She won't. She knows the room is guarded, and she knows what is at stake if she jeopardizes this assignment. I made sure she was escorted in through the front entrance for another reason. The crown now knows her face. If we were caught, there would be repercussions, to be sure, but you are the Prima, and I am an elder. Veely would be considered nothing more than a common whore. There is nowhere she could hide if suspected of treachery."

Felíne shuddered slightly at the thought of being caught, and she couldn't help glancing around to be sure there were no sets of watching eyes on them.

"Besides," Imogen said. "I know Veely. She loves money despite her attempt to decline my payment. She's also quite lazy and not overly perceptive. Right now, she is very much appreciating a free meal, a full purse, and a chance to lounge in comfort for an evening."

Felíne smirked. "You obviously hold your associates in high esteem."

Imogen huffed a laugh. "I hold people to their standards, not mine. If you hold others to the standards you set for yourself, you will be forever disappointed. Better to spend your efforts understanding them so that you know where you stand."

Felíne couldn't argue with that logic.

Imogen slipped through the gap in the fence and motioned Felíne to follow. They were in a dark alleyway. She could hear the echo of raucous voices around the corner at the far end and was thankful when Imogen moved in the opposite direction. The alleyway branched into another and then turned into another. The foul smell began to fade slightly, and the posteriors of buildings appeared better kept.

"Should I be concerned about who knows of this passage into the palace? What if someone with ill intent wanders upon it?"

Imogen stopped at an intersection between the alleyways and checked to confirm both ways were clear before moving across into the shadows on the other side. "That tunnel is a closely guarded secret. It has been used by select members of the palace staff, none of which are a threat to you. As for someone stumbling upon its whereabouts, the particular lot where it's hidden is foul by design."

"What, someone comes and sprays the surrounding area with emesis and fecal matter and urine?"

Imogen laughed. "You can say 'vomit, shit, and piss,' you know. I won't tell."

Felíne grumbled. "Vomit. Shit. Piss."

Imogen laughed again. "Much better. There's hope for you yet. And to answer your question, yes. Several someones do just that. There is little risk of anyone lingering long enough to discover the door. Even the lowest of us city-dwellers prefer to sleep somewhere that doesn't smell like excrement."

"And how did *you* find out about the tunnel?" Felíne asked.

Imogen shrugged. "When you spend enough time watching people, you start to learn who to ask for information. I asked the right person."

They continued in silence, avoiding the sounds of the city, using the shadowed alleyways as cloaks. Thankfully, they didn't encounter any wandering citizens. She was still mortified by the thought of anyone seeing her dressed so immodestly. As they went, Felíne watched her feet more than her surroundings, trusting Imogen to lead the way. She had to sidestep questionable pools of liquid on more than one occasion. Already she wanted to bathe.

After several blocks, they reached the backside of a tall brick building with a single iron door set into the façade. Two females were lounging against the back wall, smoking and talking quietly. One was dressed nearly identically to Felíne and Imogen, except her gown was pale blue. The other would have been dressed similarly, but the entire top of her garment was missing. She was bare from the waist up, her small breasts heaving with each inhale of her hand-rolled smoker. Felíne was then embarrassed less for herself, and more for the bare-chested female who appeared to take no issue whatsoever with her state of half dress.

"Relax. Try not to stare and let me talk," Imogen said in a low voice as they approached. Felíne immediately averted her eyes.

"Gods above, Gen, is that you?" The first female said. Her red-orange hair was piled on top of her head with several thick tendrils escaping their containment to fall near her face and neck. She looked dainty, like a doll, with wide blue eyes set into a round face with rosy cheeks.

"Hello, Riki. It's been a long time."

Riki moved forward and briefly squeezed Imogen before returning to her spot by the door.

The second female with straight ink-black hair shorn just below her chin, put out her smoker on the brick wall and flicked the butt of it into the alley. "I'll say. How long, Gen? Eight years?"

"Ten."

Riki whistled. The second female said, "That's another life."

Imogen laughed, and the sound was bitter. "You have no idea."

"How's your mum, Gen?" Riki asked, her quiet voice lilting unfamiliarly. "Madame told some of us ladies that she'd been ill. I tried looking you up years ago, but it was like you dropped right off the edge of the world."

Imogen smiled easily, and Felíne couldn't help thinking the expression was more instinctual than genuine. "She's on the mend. She'll appreciate you asking after her."

The female with the dark hair studied Imogen with sharp, hooded brown eyes that were tilted up at the corners. The kohl smudged around the lids gave her a slightly feline appearance. "What brings you to the back door after dark, Gen? Ten years later, at that," she asked. "And who's your companion?"

Imogen motioned to Felíne. "Riki, Suja, this is Wren. She's a new girl. I brought her to learn from the best."

Suja turned her cat eyes onto Felíne and looked her up and down. The scrutiny made her skin crawl. "She's a pretty one, Gen. You should let her come play with me and Riki. We can teach her how things are done."

"Another time, perhaps," Imogen said, and Felíne thought, *not likely.* "Madame is expecting us."

Imogen moved toward the iron door and the couple of wide steps that led up to it. Felíne followed closely behind.

Suja shrugged, and Felíne caught the movement from her periphery. "Suit yourself. I only offered because you said you wanted the best. Only half rates upstairs tonight."

Imogen gave Suja a cool stare. The female seemed unfazed.

"Bye bye, bunny," she crooned, waggling her fingers at Felíne. "I'm sure we'll be seeing you." She smiled unkindly, revealing a chipped tooth.

"You're terrible, you know that, Suja?" Riki scolded. Felíne heard Suja laugh and then hack in a coughing fit before the door shut behind them and cut off the sound.

Stepping into Madame's was like passing through a rift in time. The exterior of the building was brick, customary of desert dwellings, but inside, it was transformed. Whereas most structures in this region favored large open windows to allow plentiful lighting, tiled floors, and plastered walls, Madame's was dark with no windows that Felíne could readily identify.

As they moved farther into the building, down a short hallway, they soon emerged into a modest foyer. There were intimate lamps set to a low burn on small side tables, mounted into wall sconces, and resting on shelves that jutted out from the walls in no discernible pattern. There were lounges and chaises in every corner, against every wall, most of which appeared well-used. Carpets of all different colors and patterns covered every inch of the floor. The walls were dark polished wood, and a matching wooden staircase spiraled up to a second floor to Felíne's left. Above, a glittering crystal chandelier floated in space, sending fragments of dim amber light reflecting off every surface.

Several scantily clad females emerged from a door beyond the staircase to their left and moved languidly up the steps. They gave the newcomers a brief once-over before continuing on their way. Imogen surveyed them, but there was no sense of recognition in her features.

Imogen led her in the opposite direction through a set of double doors with frosted glass etched with twisting vines and frilly flowers. They entered a small sitting room, similarly furnished, except with a lovely heavy wooden bar that took up an entire side of the room. Gods, a drink sounded like just what her shot nerves needed right about now. She doubted the cart was stocked with *maruchi* powder.

"Keep your guard up around Suja," Imogen said. "She's worked at Madame's since before my mother and I lived here. She's old and bitter and mean."

"That delicate flower? I would have never guessed."

Imogen's lips tilted up. "Riki is alright. She's been here a while, too, but she hasn't let the life ruin her. She works to care for her younger sister, and I think that helps keep her grounded. That being said, don't trust anyone you meet. Varying levels of altruism exist, but at the end of the night, each female working here will prioritize her own interests above all else."

The frosted glass doors opened then, and a grand female swept into the little room. She was tall, nearly six feet, and well-built. She had a wealth of shiny black hair styled in an intricate updo, and her makeup was impeccably applied. Gold dust glittered on her eyelids and high, sharp cheekbones. Her gown was lavish. Dark purple material hugged her generous bosom, black lace peeking up underneath, and fell in voluminous pleats and folds to the floor. More black lace filigree decorated the skirt and hem, as well as the capped sleeves, which ended in a delicate frill at her wrists.

Felíne couldn't imagine how the female breathed in all that fabric, especially during summer when the temperature remained suffocatingly warm even at night. But the female wore the gown like she belonged in it, not a bead of sweat dotting her wide brow.

Imogen dipped her head. "Madame."

Felíne bent into a brief curtsy, years of etiquette overriding her actions despite feeling entirely exposed. Madame's dark eyes lit with amusement.

"Imogen, you are as lovely as the day you left us," Madame said and placed a pale hand on Imogen's smooth brown cheek. "It has been quite a long time, my dear. How is Miriam?"

Imogen met Madame's dark gaze with her own. "She is being cared for," Imogen said softly.

"Mmm. I am happy to hear it. I must admit, I was surprised to receive your letter," Madame said and moved to the bar to pour a shallow drink. "You have brought me quite a rare jewel." She turned toward Felíne and the female's scrutiny made her suddenly wish she had a more concealing disguise. Which was silly; no one knew the Prima's face. Her identity was safe. Yet Madame's eyes seemed to bore straight through her flimsy gown, past her flesh, and into her hammering heart.

Felíne looked at Imogen, unsure if she should respond.

"This is Wren."

"Wren." Madame wrapped the word around her tongue like she was tasting it. "A name I am not familiar with, and I do pride myself on my memory. I know many of the families with young girls that live in this city, and I remember many names. An entrepreneur must always keep a watchful eye for new talent. There is a familiarity in your face, though."

"I appreciate you allowing this, Madame," Imogen said, noticing Madame's unwavering attention.

Madame continued to watch Felíne. "Consider it a debt paid, dear," she said, waving her hand absently. "I never thought I would agree to train my competition, but I was indebted to your mother and, by extension, you. Though I cannot promise that I won't attempt to employ this gem of a lass and keep her for myself."

Imogen smiled apologetically. "Unfortunately, she won't be staying in the city. I am training her for private employment."

"So, you said." Madame moved closer to Felíne, her eyes having never left her face. "There is something about you, my dear. I just can't quite put my finger on it." She swirled the clear liquid in her glass, and she was near enough that Felíne caught the astringent scent of liquor before Madame tossed the contents back and swallowed.

"You have a sense for potential, as ever, Madame," Imogen said. "Do you have a room available for us?"

Madame finally tore her eyes from Felíne, and the feeling of relief that flooded her was immediate. "I do. You'll be in the fourth suite, upstairs, with Sashara. Shall I escort you?"

Imogen's eyes widened in surprise, and Madame watched her carefully. Gen quickly dipped her head, possibly to allow herself a moment to recover from whatever it was that had unsettled her. "That won't be necessary. I remember the way, assuming the room assignments are unchanged?"

"Unchanged for nigh twenty-six years, dear." Madame moved forward toward the door and as she passed, she reached a hand out and caught Felíne by the wrist before she could finesse avoidance. Felíne had the urge to snatch her hand away but refrained, afraid of the older female's response to an offense. She could recognize a woman in power within her territory. This was Madame's domain, and it was very evident that inside these walls, she ruled.

Madame raised Felíne's wrist and rubbed a soft thumb over the skin of her palm and up to the pads of her fingers. She lifted her hand and inhaled once before releasing her grasp. Felíne allowed her arm to fall to the side, resisting the instinct to cradle the limb protectively. "Oh, to be young and unmarred by the wickedness of this world," she said. "It was lovely to meet you, dear. I do hope we see each other again soon."

She turned to Imogen. "Take care of this one, darling. And try not to wait another ten years before stopping in on an old friend. Give Miriam my best."

Then she was gone.

Felíne felt very tired all of a sudden. "You lived with her? For *five years?*"

Imogen glanced at the bar as though debating whether or not to pour both of them a drink. "Yes."

"Is she always so…intense?"

"Yes."

She wanted to sit. It was hard to believe their night was just beginning. "What did she mean when she said she was training her competition?"

"Madame runs the most profitable pleasure house in the city. Any females allowed to train under her roof are inevitably employed by her. She has never permitted an outsider to learn and then leave."

"Yet she's allowing me because she owed you a debt?"

"Yes," Imogen said. "My mother and I saved her life and her livelihood. That, and I assured her that you were going to be bound by a private employer far from Asteros, so you wouldn't be a direct competitor."

Felíne opened her mouth, and Imogen said, "Save your questions, Wren. We should not keep Sashara waiting."

"I need to make a list," Felíne muttered. "So I remember what to ask later."

"Do that," Imogen said. "I have no doubt you will only add to it as the night progresses."

Felíne didn't have a chance to ask her what she meant before she hurried to follow Imogen out the frosted glass doors and up the winding staircase.

Imogen led Felíne up the stairs and down a long hall that resembled the first level of the building. Everything was dim and sensual. The walls were papered with a broad floral pattern, deep burgundy, and muted shades of green. They passed many closed doors, each numbered with a small painted wooden plaque hanging on the outside.

As they passed, one such door opened, and a man emerged. Felíne startled, but Imogen didn't give him a second glance as he left the room open and moved away from them down the hall. Felíne resisted the urge to turn her head and look after him. The peek she'd gotten only told her he had brown hair and an unlined face before he'd ducked his head and left. She had seen grown men her age before. Patients and staff in Mender Alcuin's clinics. But somehow, here, in this setting, everything was infinitely more interesting. More forbidden. Instead of turning back toward the retreating male, she directed her gaze into the open room he'd vacated. She caught a glimpse of rumpled bedsheets and a naked female lighting a smoker. The fragrance followed them out into the hall, and Felíne rushed to keep pace with Imogen, who had moved on ahead.

They stopped not much farther up the corridor in front of a wooden door with a painted number four on the front.

Imogen knocked.

They waited.

Enough time passed that Felíne was about to suggest that maybe the room's occupant—or occupants—hadn't heard the soft rap of knuckles when the door swung inward.

A woman in a heavy robe stood before them. Her long, lustrous golden hair fell to her waist in a cascade of waves. Large, kohl-lined, ocean-blue eyes looked over Felíne briefly before turning to Imogen. They widened in recognition.

"Gen!" she exclaimed, a smile transforming her pleasant face into one of radiant beauty.

Imogen smiled, truly smiled, and the sight was so shocking that Felíne was momentarily stunned. The new expression transformed Imogen's face as well. Gone was the reserved, untrusting female, and in her place stood someone full of happiness and youth with a life of limitless possibilities in front of her.

The golden female peeked her head out, scanning the open hallway, and grasped Imogen's hand.

"Come, come in!" She beckoned. "We have a few minutes before the next one arrives."

The female ushered them into her room.

It wasn't large, at least by Felíne's frame of reference, but it was cozy. Still dark like the rest of the house, but the curtains covering the lone window were buttery gold, a chair in the corner was upholstered in a light sage green, and there were feminine touches throughout that helped to soften the space: jewelry in a stand on the dresser, a framed painting of a vibrant landscape, and a turquoise shawl hanging on the edge of a privacy dressing screen.

Once the door shut behind them with a soft click, the female threw the deadbolt, and then she threw her arms around Imogen's neck, squealing a distinctly feminine sound of pure joy.

"Gods above, I can't believe you're back!"

Imogen hugged her fiercely before stepping away. "It's been far too long. A lifetime too long." She turned to Felíne. "Wren, this is Sashara. Shar, this is Wren."

Felíne dipped into a curtsy and said, "It is a pleasure to meet you, Sashara."

Sashara's deep blue eyes sparkled with delight. "Oh, please call me Shar. And goodness, you don't have to bow. Not to me. Come sit."

Felíne immediately liked her.

She led Felíne to the sage chair. "Where are you from, Wren? Certainly not Asteros, bowing to a whore. Unless you're the princess of the palace, and you don't know any better." She chuckled, and Felíne nearly choked.

Imogen sat on a cushioned bench at the foot of the bed. "She is from another world. And that story, we don't have time for. When did you start working for Madame, Shar?" Her voice held a note of something Felíne couldn't quite place. Disapproval? Disappointment? Regret?

Sashara sighed and leaned on the dresser. "Two years ago. And don't give me that tone. I know what you're thinking."

"I'm thinking you were the last person I would expect to let Madame sink her claws into."

Sashara's eyes dropped. "Mom died, Gen."

Imogen's lovely dark eyes widened with compassion, her brows drawn up. "Oh, Shar. I didn't know. I'm so sorry."

Felíne offered her condolences.

Sashara smiled sadly and hugged herself. "Thank you. Both of you. It was sudden. She didn't suffer, thank the Goddess, but it was unexpected. I didn't give up on my goals, Gen. I had planned to leave for the theatre in Pantamore that week. But after my mother…I don't know. I just couldn't go. It felt like leaving her behind. I couldn't do it."

Imogen nodded, understanding suffusing her features. "And now?"

Sashara shrugged. "Now, it doesn't matter. My life is what it is."

"But you've got so much talent, Shar. The theatre was your dream. It's all you ever talked about growing up."

A small jeweled clock chimed at the top of the hour. Ten o'clock. Gods, was that all? Felíne thought it felt like the night had lasted ages. Sashara pushed off the dresser. "I still get to act, Gen. Just for a different audience."

Imogen's expression was unreadable. "I don't mean offense. You know that. I just hoped for better for you. You deserve better."

Sashara placed a hand on Imogen's arm. "We both deserved better," she said softly. "But you know just as well as I that life rarely listens to our plans, and deserving has little to do with it. We do the best we can with what we've got." She spread her arms. "This is what I've got. I'm doing my best. Besides," she added with a wrinkle in one sunny brow, "isn't it poor taste to be chastising me when you've brought a new lady to learn the same trade?"

Imogen seemed to gather herself. "You're right. Forgive me, Wren." Then to Shar. "Madame spoke with you?"

Sashara glanced at Felíne and dipped her chin. "She did. I've got a full audience tonight, it seems. Dimon will be thrilled. He enjoys giving a show. The more, the merrier."

Imogen said, "He will abide by my rule?"

"Yes, of course. Madame will speak to him herself when he arrives."

Felíne tilted her head. "What rule?"

Imogen stood. "No touching. You are here to watch, to learn, but not participate. Shar's client is not to put his hands, or anything else, on you."

Anything else? Thank the gods for that.

"It will be fine," Shar said, seeming to sense Felíne's obvious nervousness. "Dimon is a frequent customer. He won't do anything that might put him on Madame's blacklist. He enjoys coming too much." She smirked at the double entendre. "Is this your first time?"

Felíne nodded.

Shar's eyes were soft with understanding. The female had no idea. "You're here with Gen. She's the best person I know, and my closest friend," said Shar, looking over at Imogen. "Any life can be hard, and this one tends to really test your limits. But once the initial shock is over, you'll learn that a person can become accustomed to just about anything if given enough time."

Felíne thought her body was doing a rather fine job becoming accustomed to the amount of stress and adrenaline she'd been experiencing this evening, and she hadn't given it nearly the amount of time it probably needed.

"Wren, you will be here," Imogen said, indicating a spot along the wall near the door where a low-lying lounge sat topped with a few tasseled velvet pillows. "You don't have to do anything. Just relax and watch."

The watching she didn't think she'd have an issue with. It was the relaxing part that Felíne thought would be next to impossible. But she could sit. Sit and stare. "And you?"

"I'll be in the room. Another spectator. If you have questions, which I'm sure you will, save them for after."

CLOAKING FATE

Sashara opened the top drawer of the tall, bleached dresser and pulled out three masks. One, decorated with aquatic blue feathers and glittering amber rhinestones, she handed to Imogen. A second one, which had pale green crystals and a beautiful border of beige lace woven with delicate strands of black and gold threads, she gave to Felíne. The third, red with silver filigree and a single gray plume, she kept for herself. "For dramatic effect," she said and winked.

Imogen helped Felíne tie the mask behind her head, careful not to knot her hair in the bow. Felíne returned the favor. Imogen was striking in the amber mask. The bright blue color against her dark hair and brown skin was eye-catching. Only her eyes, full mouth, and chin were visible.

"Ready?" Sashara asked, donning her own mask. The red and silver matched the pattern on her floor-length robe. Imogen nodded and Sashara left the room.

Felíne moved to the lounge and sat among the pillows. She had the urge to hug one to cover her chest. That wasn't entirely true. What she *really* wanted was to bury herself under a mound of pillows and disappear altogether. She refrained from either.

"Shar is covered head to foot," Felíne whispered to Imogen, who had positioned herself on the opposite side of the room near the window. "I feel on full display."

"Trust me," Imogen said. "Shar will be commanding the attention in the room tonight. Her client isn't here for either of us. Just remember. Questions after."

"I *can* keep my thoughts to myself, you know."

Imogen quirked a brow, and Felíne rolled her eyes.

Then the door opened.

Sashara swept into the room, a man in tow, and the door shut behind them.

Felíne straightened, and her heart hammered as the male surveyed the room and the shurii in it, another dose of adrenaline flooding her bloodstream. He was not in costume. He was tall and broad with brownish-blond hair and light brown eyes set under thick brows. He had a nose that would have been perfectly straight had it not been broken at some point and probably left to heal without being properly set. His jaw was strong and square, and short stubble shadowed his jawline and throat. His eyes connected with Felíne, and she attempted desperately to get a grip on her racing heart, erratic emotions, and scattered thoughts. It was like trying to catch minnows wearing an oven mitt.

He smiled, his white teeth slightly crooked, and Felíne swallowed. "Sasha, what did I do to deserve such a treat? Not one, but *three* beautiful women to spend the evening with?"

Sashara came up behind him, still wearing her heavy robe, and ran a hand possessively over his shoulder toward his chest as she wound her body around to his front. She practically draped herself over him, rubbing parts of herself along his in a way that made Felíne flush, and she was eternally grateful for the mask that hid the top half of her face. Shar's blue eyes gazed alluringly up at the man, who dragged his own away from Felíne and focused on the oceanic ones beckoning his attention. This was what Imogen had meant. Gone was the charming, genuine woman who had welcomed them into her suite. In her place was a temptress, a siren, and she was calling to the male that had walked so willingly into her den. He had no plans to deny her.

"Yes, three beauties," Sashara sang. Even her voice was no longer her own. It was throaty and rich. "One for your pleasure and two to judge your performance." She'd reached the male's other side and reached up on her tiptoes to speak into his ear. "Don't you want to impress them, Dimon? Don't you want them to see what you do to me?"

She reached her hand around again, but this time she trailed it along his torso and down to the front of his pants. Felíne's gaze followed Shar's hand and snagged on the bulge that it rested on.

"A show, hmm? You want to give your friends a show, Sasha?"

She hummed low in her throat as she rubbed her hand back and forth.

He chuckled. "I think your friends would like that," he said. "This one likes to watch."

Felíne's eyes popped back up and found the male studying her watch Shar's hand. Shar laughed throatily. "They both like to watch, Dimon. That's why they're here. You put on such a good show."

Sashara moved her hands to the leather belt of Dimon's trousers, but he held her wrists, stopping her from unbuckling them. "Me first," he said.

Sashara made to step back, and he released her. Dimon turned, facing Shar, all focus now on the female that peered at him behind her red and silver mask. He approached her and reached for the tie that kept her robe secured at her waist. Slowly, he pulled the sash free and let it fall to the floor. The robe was still closed, only a peek of black fabric showing behind the two sides. Shar didn't move, only watched the male as he reached for the lapels of her robe. He slid his fingers under the edges of the fabric, near her collarbone on either side, and opened the two halves. The weighty material slipped from her shoulders and fell to the floor.

Felíne gasped.

Dimon didn't look her way, his focus entirely on Sashara's body, but he said, "Yes, beauty. Isn't she something?"

She was. Under the discarded robe, Sashara's body was a gift tied up in ribbons and bows. She was wearing thin strips of black satin that ran up over her shoulders and crossed under her arms and between her full breasts. The material continued to weave over her slender waist and her full hips, passing between her legs and under each swell of her buttocks. The strands were held in place by scraps of sheer black lace. The ensemble was tied in the back with black ribbons that curved down her spine, leaving a trail of shiny black material like a satin tail. Her legs were bare, as were her arms and sides. The garment left absolutely nothing to the imagination, nor was it meant to. She was on display, her luscious body an invitation wrapped in an erotic package.

Felíne completely forgot about her own exposure.

Dimon circled her, a predator taking in every angle of his prey as though deciding where to begin his feast.

Shar stood proud and tall and let him visually devour her. He reached her front and lifted a hand to gently touch the edge of her mask. "I like this," he said. "I think we'll keep this."

He moved his hand then, trailing a finger under her ear, down her neck, and along the curve of her shoulder to the place where one of the thin satin strips of fabric rested. Felíne saw a fine tremor run along Shar's flesh, and the female's lips parted on an inhale. Dimon slipped a finger under the strap and tugged on it. "This, though. As pretty as it is, this has to go."

"Whatever you like," Shar said, her voice breathy.

"Mmm," he growled approvingly.

Dimon moved behind Shar again, and she looked over her shoulder, arching her back slightly. With practiced fingers, he undid each bow along her spine, slowly unraveling the flimsy garment. When it was all but hanging on her, he gave it another tug, and the satin fell away, leaving Sashara standing in naked glory. Dimon reached from behind her and pulled a curtain of her golden waves back over her shoulder. The strands of hair glided over her breasts, and her nipples puckered. Shar's head tilted back, and her lids shuttered at the sensation. Dimon watched her with rapt attention, Felíne and Imogen all but forgotten where they watched from opposite sides of the room. Felíne was glad she was stationed to sit. She didn't trust any of her body parts to behave at the moment and she doubted her legs would agree to support her weight.

"Look at you," he said, glancing into the mirror on the opposite wall. He ran both hands down her arms and back up again. Dimon placed his mouth on the side of her neck where he'd previously pulled her hair away. He kissed her hungrily as he rubbed against her backside, and Shar leaned her head to the side to give him more access.

"Your turn?" she said after a moment.

Dimon stepped back and Sashara turned to face him. He alternated between watching her in front of him as she began to unbuckle his trousers and watching her in the mirror, the curve of her rear on display. Shar didn't waste time. In a few moments, the belt was off, his pants unbuttoned. Shar slipped her hands under the hem of his white linen shirt and pulled it up and over his head.

Dimon's hair was tousled with the movement, and his eyes gleamed with a carnal light. Shar dropped onto her haunches in front of him, her hands resting on his hips, and Dimon's brown eyes darted back to the mirror.

Shar tugged on the waistline of his pants, and Felíne was transfixed as they fell to the ground, his cock bouncing free.

Then Shar stood and put her hands on him. Dimon groaned, and his hips jutted forward as she stroked his length. He put his hands on her hips as she moved, then slid them to her ass, one hand on each full cheek.

The two shurii in the center of the room might as well have been alone. They were entirely focused on one another. Sashara was running one hand firmly up and down Dimon's cock, the other cupped under his balls. Dimon squeezed her ass, then dipped his mouth to cover one puckered breast. Breaths quickened. Moans escaped throats. Eyelids became heavily hooded.

Felíne flushed from head to toe. Suddenly the room seemed hot, the air heady and thick. She didn't exactly know what she'd expected. But this? This made her realize just how unprepared she really was. How sheltered she'd been. Suddenly, she felt as if she were underwater, sinking to the bottom of the moat. In way over her head.

She was completely entranced as she watched Shar and Dimon touch each other. An odd feeling began to unfurl low in her belly. It was warm and pulsing, and she felt breathless.

One of Dimon's hands left Shar's ass and slipped between her legs. Shar let out a throaty moan, her head falling all the way back, and Dimon groaned around her breast.

Then everything changed.

Dimon lifted his head, Shar's wet nipple popping free of his mouth. He withdrew his hand and turned them, backing her up until she hit the bed. She scooted onto the edge, legs dangling off the side. Dimon gripped her left leg and propped it up so her foot rested on the mattress, fully exposing her sensitive flesh. He moved closer to her, still standing, glutes flexing, and held her firmly by the waist. Then he reached between them, positioned himself, and thrust into her. Shar cried out and fell back onto her forearms, the force of Dimon's hips shoving her back as he simultaneously held her in place. Pinning her with his hands, pushing her with his cock.

He pulled back, the head of his shaft glistening with Shar's wet heat, and then slammed himself home once again.

Shar's breasts bounced with each thrust, and Dimon reached forward with one hand to fondle them. She moaned, and he grunted and picked up his pace. Several minutes passed, and Shar reached forward to grip Dimon's ass. He seemed to lose control then, bucking wildly. Shar sank her nails in to keep herself steady, and the act was Dimon's undoing. He clenched, ramming himself forward, sinking between Sashara's legs to the hilt, his whole body spasming.

Then he stilled, dropping forward to brace himself on the bed, his chest heaving. Shar released him and ran her hands down his chest. Dimon straightened after a few moments and slipped free of her. He walked to the wash basin next to the mirror and dipped a clean cloth in the water. Sashara followed him and wet a second cloth. Dimon cleaned himself and then went to retrieve his clothes. Sashara, after cleaning herself off, went to the simple boudoir and collected a light, silky robe, which she slipped on and fastened. She removed her mask and set it on the dresser, clearly indicating the show was over, and her performance concluded.

Shar walked to the door and opened it once Dimon had donned and righted his clothing. Felíne stood, amazed that her legs were obeying her brain's commands, and situated herself slightly behind Sashara. Imogen joined her.

Dimon approached, tucking his shirt into the waist of his trousers.

"Always a pleasure, Sasha," he said, his gaze sweeping the length of her body, a knowledge of her intimate form evident in his expression.

"Dimon," she said.

He started to move past her but stopped, looking at Felíne, who watched as a bead of lingering sweat escaped his hairline and trickled slowly down the side of his face. His eyes found hers but didn't linger, traveling down her body, snagging on her breasts, barely hidden behind the thin midnight fabric. The desire to move away from his roving returned. It didn't feel right that he should be looking at her with hunger after he'd just feasted so thoroughly on Sashara. The warm feeling in her belly from before evaporated.

Dimon raised his hand toward her, his eyes having returned to her face, a curious look on his own.

Imogen moved ever so slightly, but before she could intervene, Shar slipped her hand into the crook of Dimon's elbow and drew him away from Felíne.

"Forgetting the rules already?" she chided. "You don't want Madame to ban you from the premises, do you, Dimon? I'd be so sad if you weren't allowed to visit again."

Dimon looked down at her, seeming to remember himself. He smiled smugly. "Jealous, Sasha? You never minded sharing before." He looked at Felíne again briefly, then at Imogen. "Well, ladies? How would you rate the performance?"

Neither of them spoke.

Shar crooned, "Oh, Dimon, you've left them speechless. Let's leave them to think on it. Maybe next time, my dear friends will have an answer for you."

"Maybe next time they'll join."

They moved out of the room and down the hall, their voices fading.

Imogen shut the door behind them and deflated a little, seeming to relax now that the male and Sashara had left. Felíne blew out the breath she hadn't realized she was holding. That was…an experience. One she was having a hard time finding words to describe.

"You okay?"

Felíne nodded, feeling a bit shaky. Imogen watched her with a mixture of concern and uncertainty. "I…yes. Do you think we can sit somewhere? Somewhere, not here?"

Imogen dipped her chin. "Yes. I know a place."

A moment later, Shar returned to the room, a velvet pouch clinking as it swung from her fingers.

"Drinks?" she asked cheerfully. "Appétit is still open late, Gen. My treat."

"Lead the way, *Sasha*," Imogen teased.

Shar made an ugly face. "Ugh, stop. I *hate* it when they call me 'Sasha.' Let's go before Madame finds another straggler to send in."

Chapter 11

Preparations

KAL LEFT SANTHE AND CINAH at the meeting house and returned to prowling the streets.

Two days. That's what he'd agreed to give Santhe. Time enough for her to secure a last-minute position at Starlight Lodge and verify Railah's whereabouts. Two days to verify. Another day at least to get word to Cinah and have him, in turn, get a message to Railah. Likely another day after that to allow her time to comply with his instructions and get her out.

Gods.

It was too many days. What the hell was he supposed to do in this godforsaken place for four days? And that's if it only took four.

Rask expected him in Meress in two weeks, Railah in tow. If everything went as planned, and gods knew it never fucking did, that cut his travel time down to ten days. Meress was roughly a week's ride from Asteros via the main road traveling at a moderate pace. Domitan had the main roads patrolled past Berdeen and Pantamore, the fucker. That meant taking the easy way was out of the question. He'd have to skirt the patrols to avoid unwanted attention, especially once Railah's absence was noted. He was pushing it for time. If he made it to Meress in two weeks, he'd shit a rainbow for how happy he'd be. Hell, he'd throw in a pot of gold if Rask stayed put that long and actually waited the two weeks for him to arrive without going off and doing something stupid.

He hadn't told Santhe, but Rask had wanted to be the one who got his sister out. Had insisted. Kal had convinced him otherwise, which had been no easy task, and he'd done it for the safety and benefit of everyone involved.

CLOAKING FATE

Rask was a decent fighter with balls the size of powder kegs, but he was hotheaded and brash. Thinking things through before acting wasn't on his list of strengths. Between the two of them, Rask tended to find his way into trouble, while Kal tended to find the way out. Most of the time, Kal didn't mind. Rask kept things interesting, and Kal rarely found himself in situations he couldn't handle. This one, though, getting a Fate out of Asteros with minimal casualties, was a situation that Rask would fuck up *and* down if left to his own devices. Kal had told him as much, and, big surprise, the message hadn't been well received.

At first, Kal tried to talk him out of the whole thing, which went over about as well as anyone might expect: fucking horribly. Finally, after much debate, a hearty brawl, a dangerous amount of liquor, and choice words, Rask relented to Kal's argument that he should be the one to get Railah out and he should do it alone. He had the resources that Rask lacked. As well as the skill and forethought, though he'd left that detail out lest it send his friend into another tantrum. Rask's emotional involvement would put Railah at increased risk. That was something he couldn't deny. Kal, on the other hand, had a head cool as an iceblock, excelled at emotional detachment, and wouldn't allow his feelings to compromise his plan of action. He also possessed an uncanny ability to talk his way into or out of almost anything. If that failed, he had no issues killing people and was quite good at it. He was, as he'd assured his friend, *the* man for the job.

Now, he just had to prove it.

Four fucking days.

This was a shit show already, and it hadn't even gotten started. The more he thought about it, the more he had serious doubts about his decision to involve himself. He could have been in his bed in Meress, sleeping like a corpse. Or better yet, in someone else's bed, not sleeping at all.

Instead, he was stomping around Asteros, sidestepping puddles of piss in this godforsaken heat, trying to formulate a plan to save his friend's sister from the monsters in this city and the grim future they'd planned for her while at the same time preventing his other friends from having to suffer the consequences of any potential fuck up of said plan.

Yeah. He should have stayed home.

Kal turned down a familiar street and approached the smallest, and probably shabbiest, stable in Asteros. The paint on the outside was mostly chipped, and where it wasn't chipped, it was faded. This particular stable sat at the far end of a quiet street in an industrial part of town. Traffic was infrequent here during the evenings, and he was grateful for the reprieve. Here, the night was silent. Kal only heard the soft hooting of a nearby owl and the shifting of horses' hooves on straw.

He strode to the front door and gripped the rusted handle. It swung open with a creak, as if protesting the movement. Kal knew the stablemaster was still awake, even at this hour. As he entered the dim barn, the smell of fresh hay, grain, and horse manure flooded his senses. It was comfortingly familiar.

He passed by a stall, and a handsome red roan head shoved out at him, offering a curious nicker.

Another not-so-handsome red head shoved out of the doorway to the tack room a bit further down and offered a curious, "Who the hell is it, and what do ya want?"

Kal raised his hands and lowered the hood of his cloak. A set of watery brown eyes squinted at him through the low light.

"Gods, Kalevar, I coulda hacked ya to pieces. It's an ungodly time o' night. Don't ya know how to come during normal business hours?" The head with thick, wiry red hair, a ruddy face spattered with freckles, and an equally wiry beard was attached to a stout frame covered in more hair than Kal had ever seen on a shurii in first form. The stablemaster emerged fully from the tack room carrying a leather cinch over one shoulder and a hatchet in the opposite hand.

"Normal business hours are for normal clientele, Brune. I knew you'd be up."

Brune, the stablemaster, harumphed. "I've had enough of yer nefarious dealings, Kalevar Kaine. I'm not interested."

Kal smiled, and Brune scowled, clearly not trusting the expression on Kal's face. He clapped the male on a beefy shoulder as he approached. "That's a big word, Brune. I'm impressed. Have you been reading while I've been away?"

Brune's scowl darkened.

Kal bent his head so it was level with the older man's. "It's also a lie, and we both know it. My nefarious dealings pay you far too well for you to lose interest."

Brune grunted and hung the cinch on a rack that held several others of similar make. The hatchet he hung in a leather holster at his hip. "I don't want any trouble, Kal. Every time you come into town, there's trouble."

"Merely an unfortunate coincidence."

"Ha! Clucking coincidence. Coincidence, my left boot."

Kal placed a hand over his heart. "Brune. You wound me."

The first time he met Brune, Kal was eighteen. Gods, nearly twelve years ago. He'd been in a hurry to get out of town after he drugged several soldiers as payback for mistreating the pretty barmaid at the tavern where he'd been staying. Apparently, the captain of the guard didn't appreciate having his ale spiked with a hallucinogen that would have him stripping in public and sticking his cock in lamentable places for the next three hours.

Regrettably, the drugs had no effect whatsoever on the man's memory, and Kal was unfortunate enough to cross paths with him the following day.

When Kal found himself in a crowded street facing the murderous military captain and several lieutenants with witnesses abound, he did something he rarely did and hadn't done since: he ran.

Right into Brune's stable.

Kal had dumped a full purse of gold into Brune's meaty palms, likely six months' worth of earnings for the stablemaster, and asked for the fastest horse he had.

The older man had denied him the horse but, sensing something was up, instructed him to hide out in the hayloft. Kal just wanted the horse, but climbed up the ladder and ducked behind a stack of bailed straw just as the captain and his soldiers burst into the barn.

Kal would later find out that Brune harbored an intense dislike of the military in Asteros after King Domitan's endorsement of a competing stable had nearly put Brune out of business. The stablemaster had gone ballistic at the soldiers' intrusion and began verbally assaulting them with phrases like "clucking army," "pig-sucking goat cluckers," and "get the cluck out of my stable!"

The new captain fumbled, apparently not expecting to face such vehement treatment from a common business owner.

Kal had been perched above, ready to intervene, but the soldiers were so disturbed by the red-faced tirade they must have decided their pursuit wasn't worth the effort. After a few cursory glances, they'd left.

Kal had descended from the hayloft, looked at Brune, and said, "What the fuck was all that?"

Brune had grabbed Kal by the front of his shirt and informed him that he didn't tolerate cursing in his barn and that if he was going to use such filthy language, he could get the cluck out, too.

Kal had come here with his business ever since. And he kept his swearing to himself.

"Ah, you ain't wounded. Go on. Stable's closed. I'm locking up." The stablemaster moved past him, trying to shoo him toward the door.

Kal glanced at him but didn't move. "You really want me to take my business elsewhere?"

"Course not. Come back tomorrow."

"I'm here now."

Brune turned, exasperated. "Cluck, Kalevar! It's late! Why can't ya come back in the morning like a normal person, hm? You coming at this hour will make people think yer up to no good."

"That's exactly why I've come at this hour. No witnesses? No opinions. Unless, of course, you go gossiping about your nocturnal visitors with the city folk? Then they'll certainly have something to think of my presence. Just imagine the rumors."

Brune sputtered, his red face turning redder. "Not clucking likely!"

Kal smirked. "I thought so. Now that we've established there will be no trouble, can we get to the reason I'm here?"

Kal's business with Brune didn't take more than twenty minutes once the old shurii put his cantankerousness aside and focused on his fortune in having a willing customer. He purchased two horses from the stablemaster at a reasonable price: The red roan he'd initially seen when he'd entered the stables that evening and a stout bay gelding with a wide white blaze. They were strong, sturdy creatures. The bay wouldn't be winning any races, but he'd be reliable through difficult terrain and had an even temperament suitable for a novice rider. He had no idea how much experience Railah had, and he figured it was better to underestimate her riding abilities and hope for an advantageous surprise. The roan stallion was huge, had stamina for days, and a wicked intelligence lighting his eyes that had Kal itching to open him up.

Brune would keep the horses for him for the next few days, ensuring they were well-fed and primed for travel. Kal also purchased extra packs and supplies, some of which he'd procured in town earlier in the day, that would be fitted to the saddles ahead of time. Brune was no fool. He knew Kal was up to something, but he'd never guess what, and Kal felt the stablemaster didn't want to know anyway. He'd have the horses ready for a quick departure; that was all he needed to concern himself with.

Brune's stable, imaginatively named Brune's Stable, was conveniently located on the city's eastern border, furthest from the heart of the military's occupancy. There were patrols at every entrance and exit of Asteros, but at the east road, any guards Kal would have to deal with would be farther from reinforcements, allowing them precious time to get out of the city and off the main pathway.

Now that his transportation was secure, he needed to figure out the best place to secure Railah and how exactly to go about it. He knew little about the female, mostly because once he and Rask had agreed on Kal retrieving her, there hadn't been much time to review the particulars. In any case, Rask hadn't seen his sister since she was young, and the twenty-five-year-old version of her was likely very different from Rask's brief descriptions of the awkward pre-teen. He'd leave the identifying her to Cinah, who was obsessive enough over details that he'd not make the mistake of delivering a message to the wrong female. Kal wouldn't be able to pick her out of a crowd, having no idea what she looked like, but Cin would make sure Railah was where she needed to be when Kal needed her to be there. From what his friends had gleaned, only one new female was being inducted to the Fates; there'd be no mistaking her.

Kal traversed the streets of Asteros with practiced ease. As much as he despised this city, he knew it like his own reflection. There were new buildings each time he returned, unfamiliar businesses that now stood on old familiar street corners, but the city's core hadn't changed since he'd left it at sixteen. It was still a desert metropolis that once had the potential to be an oasis, a place of refuge, peace, and prosperity. That is what it should have been. Instead, it became a cesspool of corruption and depravity. Ruined by greed, the goodness bled out of it.

He'd once loved this city. His innocent boy's eyes had been wide with hope and wonder, imagining his future in Asteros.

Who could have known it would hold his greatest torment, deepest pain, and the seed for his vengeful heart? Kal had not been a boy for a long time now. Like this city, he'd also been ruined by greed, but what had been bled out of him was innocence. Now, his hope was tainted with bitterness, and the wonder he'd felt when he was young had long since been replaced with the cold, harsh bite of reality.

He supposed he should be grateful. At least he'd gotten out of Asteros alive. That was more than he could say for his mother and father. If it hadn't been for Kal's path colliding with Santhe's and Cinah's all those years ago, he might have shared his parent's fate. None would have predicted that a boy on the run from the crown would find safety and friendship while hiding in the alleyway between a bar and a merchant's shop. They'd found him dirty, bloodied, and broken, and somehow helped to heal his wounds. Those that could be seen, anyway. His father would have called it fate. His mother would have said he was damned lucky.

Kal glanced up at the night sky, looking for the twinkle of stars, something he did when thoughts of his parents weighed on him. He didn't have a pair of graves to visit. No stones to place flowers on. No spot where he could sit and reflect and speak to them. Their bodies had turned to dust, rotted in some back alley, or been eaten by some desert predator. At this point, it didn't matter. They were gone. And he had nothing left of them. The only living person who tied Kal to the family he lost was as distant to him now as the far side of an endless sea. His uncle was as good as dead.

His friends? They were the family he claimed.

CLOAKING FATE

Not one twinkle shown in the heavens. Clouds rolled in from the south, smothering the heat and obscuring any fragments of light from the stars. Even the moon was choked behind the gray veil. His parents weren't watching tonight.

Once again, Kalevar found himself on his own. Alone in Asteros.

This time, though, he wasn't a boy. He wasn't helpless and afraid.

He had a job to do.

As Kalevar approached the intersection of Kinsmet and Crown, he stopped to listen to the subsiding bustle of nightlife. Madame's must've been busy with working girls still seen lingering outside, smoking and sharing last-hour drinks. Across the street, the Starlight Lodge rose several stories on the corner, its windows drawn shut and shuttered, its patrons likely sleeping soundly.

He wondered if Railah was that close. For a moment, he had the crazy desire to break into the lodge, find her, and drag her back to Brune's, where the horses waited to carry them off. He could be done with this insane responsibility and away from this wretched place that held so much anguish. To hell with plans. With involving Santhe and Cinah. To hell with putting them at risk.

He looked across from the Starlight Lodge to the southern edge of Crown Road. The grand gate to an elaborate botanical garden stood proudly, still open to the public even at this hour. A couple exited the lush entryway hand in hand, the path they'd walked obscured by the dense greenery of imported vegetation. The garden was probably as old as the city itself. It was thick, shaded by tall, closely growing trees with broad canopies that overlapped over the disappearing walkway beyond the gate.

Kal strolled over to the entrance to the garden. Dim lamps lit the path, casting weak light over the winding stones. A short distance ahead, nearly unnoticeable from the entrance, stood an old-looking stone bridge extending across a shallow stream. Beyond the bridge, the pathway turned and disappeared. The gardens were silent. Birds had nested down for the night, and other than the chirping and buzzing of a few insects, nothing moved, sang, or spoke.

Kal glanced back at the lodge.

Perhaps his original plans weren't such a bad thing after all. Logic won out over Kal's impatience. With his mind turning, he moved deeper into the garden, allowing himself to be swallowed by its dense green shadows.

Above, past the canopy of foliage, nearly beyond where Kal could see, the cloud cover broke for a few seconds, briefly bathing the street in moonlight and the flickering of a few faraway stars.

Chapter 12

Conversations

FELÍNE FOLLOWED IMOGEN AND SHAR out of Madame's into the warm Asteros air. There weren't many other shurii out and about this late into the evening, and those who were seemed to be finishing their nocturnal activities and retiring to whatever places they called home.

Madame's was situated in what seemed to be a nicer part of the city, especially if compared to the place where she and Imogen had emerged from its underbelly. Their journey to the pleasure house hadn't offered Felíne much in the way of scenery, considering they'd stuck mainly to the back alleys and rears of buildings to avoid detection. Now, however, they were on the main road, and Felíne took in every sight, sound, and smell, not wanting to miss a thing.

Shar had lent her and Imogen cloaks, for which Felíne was immensely grateful. She felt more herself now that her body was no longer on display, concealed by the weighty black material, and her mind could focus once again on everything around her. Her face was hidden behind a deep hood, and her eyes were wide open.

Shar had assured her that Appétit was no more than a city block from Madame's and wouldn't take long to reach on foot. Felíne didn't care if it was halfway across the city. The aftershocks of Sashara's performance upstairs subsided, and she was enjoying her first outing. Never mind that it was nearly midnight, nearly everyone was asleep or on their way to it, and she was only glimpsing one street. It was all new, and she could imagine how it would look midmorning before the heat drove everyone inside. People would be milling about, shopping, talking, conducting business, and catching up on the latest gossip. The empty road before her would be buzzing with activity.

Felíne stepped onto the next curb and glanced up at the grand façade of a multistory building with large double doors set back under an impressive marquee. An arched signboard declared the property The Starlight Lodge in intricate looping script. Tiny flickering lights had been set behind the sign, illuminating the title for anyone passing by to notice.

Felíne was tempted to go inside, curious to discover what the interior looked like, considering the face was so lovely. However, Shar and Imogen moved quickly away from the building, and she hurried to catch up.

She continued scanning the night as she followed her companions. Across the street, a vast gated entrance stood open. Two shurii, huddled close together like lovers, exited through the gate and ambled down the road. *Desert Bloom Botanical Gardens*, read the sign in bold letters.

A light breeze swept through, and Felíne swore she could make out the scent of star jasmine wafting from the gardens. The aroma was intoxicating, and she strained her eyes, trying to see beyond the gateway into the shadowy entrance. *That* was a place she'd like to visit. She loved gardens, and while the royal villa was home to a number of them likely grander than any others in the city, something about the depths of this one called to her. It was mysterious. Secretive. Peaceful. And this late at night, it was probably deserted, occupied only by the silent plants, humming insects, and the quiet creatures that nested in their sanctuary of flora.

Perhaps it was because she was viewing it on a cloudy night, with all quiet around her, but the dark shadowy expanse of greenery seemed like a place where she could escape reality for a time, walking among the company of gentle blooming things. Somewhere she didn't have to be who she was. The Prima. The Goddess's favorite. The people's savior. Somewhere no one expected the world of her, where her life belonged only to herself. Where her purpose was hers to decide. Felíne gazed into the yawning blackness, losing herself in the smell of jasmine and the blissful impossibility of her thoughts.

"Wren?"

Imogen's voice cut through her musing, and Felíne realized she'd stopped and was staring at the garden, having taken a step into the street toward the gate. A flicker of movement caught Felíne's attention just before she turned to answer the elder.

A man—there was no way that huge frame belonged to a woman—entered the botanical gardens and melded effortlessly into the shadows. She'd only just caught the sweep of his cloak, the breadth of his shoulders, and his impressive height before he disappeared from view. It seemed she wasn't the only one the garden was calling to. She envied the stranger's ability to answer.

Another breeze blew her way, stronger this time. Felíne raised her hands to reposition her hood, ensuring her face remained covered. Despite the warmth of the air, a chill raced down her spine. Moonlight broke through the clouds momentarily, bathing the street in its silver glow.

Imogen reached her. "Is everything alright?"

Felíne turned, stepping away from the street with Gen toward where Shar waited. "Yes, fine, sorry," she said, shaking herself. "I was distracted by the gardens."

Gen glanced over her shoulder at the gated entrance. A soft smile touched her lips. "Understandable. It is the largest public garden in Asteros. It was expanded not long ago and is a favorite spot of couples, young and old."

"There is something…strange about it."

Imogen hummed in agreement. "They call it the Lover's Verdure."

Felíne looked back again, unable to resist another glance. She wondered if the male she glimpsed entering just a moment ago was meeting his lover among the trees. She pictured a graceful female with cascading golden hair waiting for her beau. Imagined the way her face would light with anticipation upon seeing him emerge from the shadows, eyes and attention for her alone.

An unfamiliar pang clenched her heart, and she furrowed her brow, confused by the sensation.

Imogen studied her. "You're sure you're okay?"

Felíne offered a wan smile. "Gen? You're fussing over me like a mother hen."

Imogen looped an arm through hers and pulled her close. "That's because you're like my little chickadee. Freshly out of the nest with a whole new world to explore. Dangers around every corner. In every garden even."

Felíne laughed despite her mood having turned somewhat melancholy. They reached Shar, and the three of them continued to the café. Felíne made a heroic effort not to glance back at the garden's entrance and forced her imagination to relinquish its envisions of a shadowy stranger and his golden companion in the Lover's Verdure.

Appétit was a quaint little café with an unassuming exterior and an interior crowded with stools, chairs, floor cushions, and sofas surrounding little rough-hewn tables. The tables were overflowing with aquatic plants, roots tangled in shallow glass bowls filled with water and colorful stones, leaves and stems draping haphazardly off the edges, some to the floor. There was so much greenery that Felíne felt the furniture was more to accommodate the vines than the people who planned to use them.

The ladies chose one of the larger round tables in the far corner, which bordered a deep brown sofa backed up to a wall and a pair of bright yellow cushioned chairs. Felíne chose a chair while Imogen sank onto the couch. Shar went to collect their drinks from the bar. They were the only patrons.

She returned a few moments later, three full glass jars balanced expertly in her arms.

Felíne inspected the contents and sniffed. She noticed Imogen watching her, and they shared a smile. Felíne gave the female a self-conscious shrug.

"All right, Wren," Sashara declared, taking a healthy swig of her drink, which turned out to be some version of black tea with a modest serving of liquor. "What'd you think?"

"Hm?" Felíne took a tentative sip and immediately coughed at the burn of alcohol.

"Dimon's performance. Gen said that was your first time seeing a coupling. What did you think?"

Felíne's face heated. Her entire life, she had been taught that the joining between a male and female was an intensely private affair. She knew prostitution existed, but she never in her wildest dreams imagined sex being put on display for others to observe, for educational purposes or otherwise. Outside

Madame's, she'd pushed the whole matter and her feelings about it to the back of her mind, trying instead to focus on the newness of being outside the royal villa. Now that she was being put on the spot, having to examine her thoughts made her intensely uncomfortable.

That creeping anxiety threatened to reappear, and she clamped down on it. Still, thoughts sprouted unbidden to her mind like weeds invading a flowerbed.

Was that what her servicing was going to be like? A business arrangement between the Primordial Male and herself? Was that what she ultimately was? A glorified client? Her body and vulnerabilities displayed for others to critique and dissect? Another bothersome thought occurred to her. Sashara appeared to enjoy Dimon's attentions, but was that all simply an act? Shar may have been destined for the theatre, but Felíne was notoriously incapable of disguising her emotions. Sure, she could play the attentive student, feign interest in her lessons, but conjuring believable emotion or authentic desire for another shurii was something else entirely. What if Shar's reciprocal enjoyment was purely theatrical? Felíne wasn't sure she was capable of that level of deception.

"That bad, huh?" Shar said, and Felíne realized she hadn't answered.

"What did *you* think about it?" she asked, suddenly needing to know.

Shar looked surprised. "Me?"

Felíne nodded, hoping her inquiry wouldn't be taken offensively. "What does it make you feel?"

Sashara sat back, contemplating. "I think what you're really asking is, what does money make me feel? The funny thing about coin is that any ordinary task becomes a job when you add compensation. And with enough of it, even ugly jobs will find willing employees."

Next to her, Imogen had gone quiet, seemingly preoccupied with her own train of thought. Felíne waited.

"It's my occupation," Shar said finally. "At least for now. Is sex enjoyable? Sure, it can be when it's with someone you choose. The rest is…well, it's sex. Sometimes I hate it. Other times, it's not awful. Every one of them has different tastes. Some like it rough and fast, some like to be watched, some like a little pain, others need it slow and gentle. Touching or no touching. Bondage. Submission. Roleplay. I give them what they want, and every once in a while, their desires mesh a little with mine. It's a job. Sometimes, the work is easy. Sometimes, not so easy. But it's my job to pleasure *them*. Not theirs to pleasure me."

Just like it was Felíne's job to pleasure the Primordial Male. A male she'd never met. She didn't know his likes and dislikes. Didn't know his habits or preferences or tendencies. The enormity of her situation suddenly came crashing down around her ears. She was born to please a complete stranger. To bear his children. Even the best teacher in the world would never be able to guarantee she was adequately prepared for that task, not only because a fruitful coupling between a female in first form and a male in second had never before been accomplished, but because none of them knew the male that was going to be on the receiving end of her servicing. And if they did, Felíne was certainly never told. Her mother and the elders assured her that the Primordial Male was being prepared just as surely as she was, but she knew nothing beyond that. She'd never been allowed to meet him. Never seen his face. Felíne didn't even know where he was.

What if he couldn't stand the sight of her? What if he didn't like the heaviness of her breasts, the sound of her voice, the shape of her mouth, the width of her hips?

And what of her mind? Her heart. Her spirit. Would he even care about those?

She was expected to give her body, but how did she do that without it being tied to the pieces that truly made her who she was? Shar may have been able to offer herself with detachment for a client's coin, but this wasn't a job for Felíne. It was her *destiny*. And that destiny was written into her soul.

Felíne's silence stretched, and Shar glanced at Imogen questioningly. After another uncomfortable moment, Shar changed the subject, asking Imogen about things that had happened since she left Madame's. Gen answered, but Felíne wasn't listening.

She thought she had a handle on her life. She knew who she was and what she was tasked with. She had become adept at carrying the responsibility resting on her shoulders. Felíne knew how to deal with stress. She had ways to talk herself out of a panic and calm racing thoughts before they spiraled out of control. Recalibrate. Recenter.

CLOAKING FATE

Yet in that moment, after witnessing Shar and Dimon's intimate display, after having her own body displayed, hungry eyes groping her figure in jealousy, criticism, and hunger, a wave crested inside her and crashed, and she was underwater. She was drowning in a bottomless ocean of expectation.

Her lungs were full of air, and she was drowning.

Felíne was a child all over again, overwhelmed by the prospect of her fate. And yet, while her childhood self had not even considered a way out, her adult sense of self-preservation demanded she find a way to escape this course of her life—even if escaping was more impossible than completing the task itself.

That was the funny thing about desires. They were seldom governed by logic.

Vaguely, Felíne noticed Sashara stand, collect two empty glasses and Felíne's full one, and take them to the bar. Imogen followed her, and after a brief exchange that Felíne didn't hear, the two females embraced, and Shar left the café.

Imogen returned and sat next to her. She made to rub her eyes, then seemed to remember they were lined with kohl and settled her hands in her lap.

"Felíne?" she said softly. "Would you like to talk about what's going on inside that head of yours?"

She wanted to cry, and she was furious with herself for it.

"Tonight was a lot," Imogen said. "I'm sorry."

Felíne shook her head. "It's not your fault. You're just doing your job. So I can do mine." She tried unsuccessfully to keep the bitterness out of her tone.

Imogen sighed. "You're not just a job to me. I want you to know that. I want you to succeed in this. Not just because the fate of the shurii race depends on it but because I care."

The hot sting of tears gathered behind her eyes, and Felíne fought them with everything she had. "I can't do this," she said hoarsely. "What Shar did back there? How elegant she was? It was effortless. Sensual. I can't do that. I can't *be* that."

Imogen studied her, determination hardening her dark eyes as though she could infuse that same resolve into Felíne. "I think you know well who

120

you are but don't know what you can do. You haven't tried," she said. "Besides, you don't have to do what Shar did. I only wanted you to have an example of what a servicing entailed in the most basic sense, and this was the best way for me to achieve that. I don't know what your other teachers have told you, but you aren't required to pleasure the Primordial Male. Only withstand a successful coupling with him."

"In second form!" she said, exasperated, then lowered her voice. "I *have* no second form, Gen. Do you understand? I am completely outmatched in every way. It's not possible. I can't do it."

"It is possible," Imogen said, steel in her voice. "And you *can.*"

"How could you possibly know that?" Felíne said, her anxiety heating to frustration and bubbling over.

"Because. I did it."

"Oh, right. Because you—" Felíne blanched like boiled greens plunged into an ice bath. "Wait, you, what? You did what?"

Imogen leaned forward, voice lowered, and repeated. "I. Did. It."

Felíne stared, earlier retorts evaporating.

Imogen had successfully been paired with a male in second form while in first form herself?

The Fates. Oh, dear Goddess, it actually worked?

Imogen glanced around the café briefly and then stood. "If you want answers, I will give them to you. But this is not a conversation that can be had here. We need to go."

Felíne followed Imogen out of Appétit and through the back streets of Asteros toward the run-down lot and the hidden tunnel. The city was completely deserted now, and Felíne could only guess how late it was. She knew they were getting close when the telltale stench grew unbearable. Once safely back in the tunnel, the trapdoor was closed above them, and the lamp Imogen had left was lit to provide an amber glow by which to travel. Imogen considered her.

"The last thing I want to do is overwhelm you, especially with everything you've seen and learned tonight. But I must start from the beginning if you wish to understand."

Felíne squared herself and nodded. "I want to understand."

CLOAKING FATE

Imogen dipped her chin and took a breath. "When the Fates were initially created, females were selected on a volunteer basis. We were offered exorbitant amounts of money, more than any of us could make in a lifetime otherwise. We were expected to serve a term of ten years, or until we successfully carried a child to term, whichever came first. The purpose of the Fated Mothers was to determine how best to mate a first form female with a second form male to produce offspring."

Feline nodded. This she knew. The Fates were created by the crown and approved by the elders for her benefit. They wanted the Prima to have a safe way to service the Primordial Male and bear a child, thus fulfilling the Goddess's requirement and breaking her curse. It would do the people no good if the Prima were to die in the act of her servicing. She wasn't expected to enjoy it, only to survive.

"I joined when I was twenty," Imogen continued. "Ten years didn't seem like such a long time back then, and I needed the money. Badly."

"I imagine ten years seemed a lot longer after you joined?"

Imogen looked over at her, and Feline almost started at the tortured expression on her friend's face. "It was an eternity. The term limits are a joke. No female made it ten years. Not one. Many didn't make it past the first coupling."

Feline's eyes widened in shock, her hand going to her mouth. She'd thought the program was ultimately successful. Her mother had told her not to worry because their efforts proved promising, and the details would be shared with her when the time came. This...this was not what she'd expected. "But...why?"

Imogen looked ahead, the ridge of her brow tensed. "Have you seen a male in second form?"

"Yes, but only once," she said. "One of the elders for a lesson."

Imogen hesitated. "This...no elder will have ever spoken what I would tell you. If they knew, they would cut me from their ranks. And the crown? I would be...removed. Permanently."

Feline swallowed, watching Imogen's drawn features in the dim glow of the lamp. She understood the risk her new friend was taking.

"You can trust me," Feline said. "I promise."

Imogen inhaled deeply, giving a purposeful nod before continuing.

"The Godking's design was not flawed, contrary to what the Faithful Cursed believe. Our second forms serve a purpose. Males are faster, stronger, and less susceptible to fear. They make excellent warriors capable of incredible endurance and feats of heroism without hesitation. They are the perfect protectors."

Felíne remembered the elders and their second forms during the demonstration that she'd had. She remembered her awe, how fluid their bodies moved, how natural they seemed despite their beliefs that the second form was inferior to the first. They had both seemed so composed, if not a little predatory. She'd been exceptionally jealous at her lack of a second form. "They are impressive. But why so dangerous to the Fates?"

Imogen lifted the hem of her gown to step over a jutting piece of stone. "Males in second form are notoriously difficult to control, and in some cases even more difficult to reason with. Their humanity is not lost when they shift, but everything that makes a shurii who he is becomes…intensified in second form. When they make up their minds about something, deterring them from their course of action is nearly impossible. There are varying levels of this depending on the male, but it serves as a general rule. The second is a form dominated by instincts. Do you remember me telling you about my scenting ability drastically improving in second form?"

"Yes," Felíne said. "The poisons. You said you'd be able to detect it across the room." Something else of which she was intensely envious.

Imogen nodded. "Part of that ability is physiological. My actual sense of smell is vastly improved in second form. This is true for all shurii," she said, and Felíne felt a sting of jealousy, but she quashed it quickly. "However, there is another sense that is not so easily quantifiable. More a general, inexplicable sense of awareness that exists. If your drink were poisoned, I would almost *feel* that there was something wrong before the smell of poison reached me."

Felíne pondered. "A built-in defense mechanism. Like your gut told your nose to look for the poison?"

"Yes," Imogen said. "Exactly. Most all shurii have this ability as well. It's something we are born with, god-given some say. Some shurii ignore it and lose their sensitivity to it; others practice it routinely and can develop an extremely heightened ability to perceive things before they could physically know them."

CLOAKING FATE

Perhaps this was what Felíne experienced when she felt her 'premonitions.' Maybe her form wasn't so handicapped after all.

"This sort of innate sense is particularly strong in second form males, to the degree that they sometimes cannot control their reaction to it. Specifically during mating. When they scent a female in her fertile cycle, they experience a craze. You've heard of bloodlust on the battlefield? Males becoming drunk on death? This is the same, only they become drunk on the prospect of procreation. Males in first form experience lust, but in second form, they become obsessed with claiming their female. They're virtually unable to resist their design. A female in second form can withstand the intensity of those instincts. It's what our second forms were made for. Everything goes into overdrive. Smell, sight, sensation. Our bodies are more durable, the perfect match for our male counterparts. If they push, we can push back. When they are demanding, we can hold our ground. We are the cliff face upon which they crash. In first form, a female has a distinct vulnerability, something you know better than anyone."

Yes. Felíne had her own sense of hyperawareness, particularly regarding her vulnerabilities.

"The first Fates enrolled in the program were brought before second form males when they were in cycle with little forewarning," Imogen said, her voice biting with disgust. "It was like the elders had all this knowledge of what would happen, but they threw them together anyway just to witness it firsthand. The females were understandably terrified. They would shift on instinct, their bodies understanding they needed the change to survive the males' attentions. But that defeated the purpose of the experiment, and the elders couldn't have all of their efforts wasted. They threatened the females, withheld food and water, and subjected them to emotional and psychological abuse to try and *properly motivate* them to refrain from shifting. Nothing worked. Their bodies were designed to change, and so, despite the females' sincerest efforts, they changed. It was self-preservation. They couldn't consciously prevent it."

Those poor females. Felíne's stomach churned, filling with acid. How could this treatment have been permitted?

"That's when they brought in Vulgren." Imogen spat the name as though it were a foul-tasting word. "He figured out a way to physically

124

prevent the shift. When we entered our cycle, we were drugged to keep us from shifting to second form. Imagine Dimon's intensity earlier with Shar. They were both in first form. Now multiply that by a thousand, factor in a distinct lack of control, and wrap it all up in a lethal package equipped with jaws that can crush steel and claws made to rend flesh."

Feline was appalled. Her imagination needed little motivation to produce horrific imagery. The females were no better than lambs led to slaughter. They had no way to defend themselves. She wondered if these were the practices with which Mender Alcuin refused to involve himself. She would bet all the coin in the royal vault on it.

"Many of the females that joined when I did died within the year. After Vulgren took over the program, they did away with volunteers. Rumors started circulating about the dangers of the position. What Shar said earlier about money? It's mostly true; people will do just about anything for enough coin. Except when your life is the price of compensation. Then coin doesn't hold the appeal it did before. When volunteers became harder to come by, they started enlisting females by force to keep the program going. Young, healthy females were randomly selected from families in the poorer sections of the city. They would leave to join the Fates and never return."

Feline was going to be sick. How was this possible? How was it allowed? Her parents, determined as they were, would never have knowingly permitted this kind of atrocity. They must have been deceived by this…this Vulgren.

"Who is Vulgren?"

The hate that flashed in Imogen's eyes was frightening. "A mender. Or at least he was. Some said he was stripped of his title, and I wouldn't doubt it. He's a man with a single-minded determination to elevate his esteem in the eyes of the crown. And he will do whatever is necessary to accomplish that, regardless of who gets hurt in the process. The elders relinquished their involvement. Vulgren is the current unchecked master of the Fates."

Vulgren. It was a name Feline felt certain she would never forget.

"And now?" Feline asked. "He is gone, right?"

Mender Alcuin had said he thought the mender in charge of the Fates had been asked to leave the city.

Imogen hardened. "I was still a Fate as of four days ago, and if Vulgren had any intention of leaving the city, we have all yet to hear it. He considers the Fates to be his life's work."

Felíne could not believe what she was hearing. Her parents would have this exiled mender's head on a spit if they knew what he was doing to shurii in the name of the crown. "This cannot be allowed! When we get back, I'll go straight to the queen. Vulgren will answer for his crimes."

Imogen stopped her suddenly, gripping her arm. "You can't. I swore a vow of secrecy and signed it in blood. It's in my contract. Vulgren reports directly to the queen. If you go to your mother, they will know I told you. It is a crime punishable by death, even now that my contract has been fulfilled. You cannot say a word."

"But they must learn what is happening! This must be stopped!"

Imogen faced Felíne, her tone serious, her eyes tired. "They know, Felíne. Maybe not everything, maybe not all the details, but they know. They *gave* him the power he holds."

Vulgren reports directly to the queen.

What? No. *No.*

Imogen must have seen the disbelief in her eyes because she said gently, "It's true. Vulgren is the queen's creature. At least he started that way. I don't know exactly how much information he feeds her, but he keeps her updated regularly. The Fates are your mother's enterprise. She brought Vulgren in when she felt the elders were failing. I doubt much happens in the Stronghold of which she is unaware."

Mender Alcuin's words entered her mind then. He had known. About the deaths. The females that had suffered. He'd warned her to address Imogen with caution to avoid causing her additional trauma. And he'd plainly stated that things were being done that violated his vow as a mender. It was why he'd refused to become involved despite the queen's requests. But did he know they were *still* going on?

"And the king?"

Imogen cut her head to the side. "I'm not sure. I know that his men provide security for the Fates and for the males that service them, but beyond that, I have no idea how much he knows."

He knew. Felíne was almost certain of it. King Domitan and Queen Serebine were not what anyone would consider close in terms of affection, but she knew how obsessed the king was with his military enterprises. If his soldiers provided security for the Fates, the king undoubtedly knew exactly who he was protecting.

How involved were her parents in this scheme? How much did they knowingly turn a blind eye to? Considering the answers made her physically ill. Those females and the males who serviced them were taken from their families, forced into servitude, and abused physically, emotionally, and psychologically. Her arms went around her middle, trying to settle her soured stomach, holding herself together. Imogen had warned her, hadn't wanted to overwhelm her. Two opposite poles in Felíne's world were suddenly reversed, and she struggled to orient herself. And yet she'd asked Imogen to explain. She'd wanted to understand. She was sick from what she was learning, and she wasn't even the one who'd gone through it. Imogen endured all of this and somehow, miraculously, fulfilled her contract. She barely knew Felíne. Imogen didn't seem like the type of person who trusted easily, especially considering what she'd been through, and yet she placed an extraordinary amount of trust in her.

"Why tell me all of this?" Felíne asked. "Why would you take that risk? You've known me only a day."

"Because," Imogen said firmly. "If you fail, then none of it matters. Everything the Fates have done, male and female alike, all we've gone through and sacrificed will have been for nothing. You cannot fail."

The pressure of that last statement was astronomical.

"How? How did you survive as long as you did?"

Imogen swallowed and looked away. "I was lucky."

Lucky? Felíne spared her companion a glance. Somehow, she felt luck had little to do with it.

"The male they paired me with had…experience. Vulgren told me he was from a promising line. That male…he hated it. He hated it with every ounce of his being. He…took great care with me."

Felíne noticed the way Imogen's face softened as she spoke. There was a tenderness there that she'd not displayed before. "This male, he cared for you?"

Imogen nodded, eyes going distant. There was pain there. Buried deeply, expertly concealed, but there nonetheless, and the rawness of it squeezed Felíne's heart.

"You cared for him too."

Imogen focused on her.

"What happened?" she asked gently.

The tenderness disappeared as quickly as it arrived, pain replaced with icy determination and bitterness. "We did it. It worked, and I became pregnant. He is still there, likely tasked with servicing another female, and another after that, and still another after that because that is all we were to them. That was our only value. Just a statistic. A successful experiment. While I'm here, now uniquely qualified to instruct you. Promoted to elder. One life sentence traded for another."

Felíne was horrified. "Life sentence?"

"It started as a ten-year term, like the rest. Ka—" she caught herself and corrected. "The male I was assigned to couldn't bring himself to touch me. I can only guess he'd had particularly awful experiences with other females before me. He was filled with self-loathing, and I was terrified. We weren't monitored as closely then. So, we rebelled. When we were paired initially during my fertile cycle, we sat in that room, staying as far from one another as possible. He would enter in second form, then quickly shift to first so he wouldn't be so affected by my scent. At first, we didn't speak; we simply kept each other silent company, both of us consumed by our private thoughts. Then, eventually, we began to talk. We were separated during my off cycle and wouldn't see each other. Four times a year for two weeks at a time, we would be paired, left alone together in a designated room with a single bed and connecting bathroom."

A shurii female became physically mature around age sixteen. Cycles were typically irregular until eighteen to twenty years old when they settled into the normal fertility schedule every three months. The fertile cycle lasted anywhere from one to two weeks. Felíne's cycles lasted about a week and a half and arrived every three months nearly to the day. The elders and her mother had closely monitored her body's rhythms since she'd entered maturity at seventeen. Her presentation to the Primordial Male was scheduled after her twenty-fifth birthday during a projected fertile period, which just so happened to coincide with the Autumn Reaping, the Goddess's holiday.

"At first, we simply used each other as a source of information. We'd share our observations of the Stronghold, where the Fates are kept, and happenings in the city since the females were allowed to leave with an armed escort during their off cycle for short periods. After the third cycle, we became each other's only source of peace. Something changed. We warmed to each other and opened up. I was the first person he'd spoken to in years who didn't see him as a thing to be used. And he became the only person I could share my fears and hopes with."

The two of them rounded a corner in the tunnel, Imogen holding the light ahead to illuminate the way.

"After three and a half years, I grew worried that someone would suspect us. At that point, I had survived longer than any other female. I was unmarked and not pregnant. I overheard one of the handlers whispering, and it made me paranoid. The next fertility cycle I had, I told him we had to try for a child. We'd been together in first forms by then, and our friendship had become something more. But he was extremely hesitant. I think he was horrified at the thought of harming me. It took me nearly a week of convincing, but ultimately, my argument won out over his hesitation. If we didn't do *something*, we would either be reassigned or found out and probably terminated."

"And it worked."

"Yes. It worked. It was difficult, and I did not leave that room unscathed, but we did it. I found out three weeks later that we succeeded. I was pregnant."

Felíne didn't know whether to feel joy for Imogen's success or terrible heartbreak at its circumstances.

"I was sequestered after that. Vulgren all but put me in a glass box. I had the best meals, the most attentive handlers, all these luxuries that had been denied to me the past nearly four years to ensure that the baby growing in my womb, *our* baby, was healthy and successfully delivered."

Imogen's voice was flat. It didn't hold the note of happiness one would anticipate from a mother reflecting on a joyful pregnancy. Felíne wanted to hug her friend, but she looked fragile enough to break, and she didn't want Imogen to lose the courage she'd pulled together to tell her story.

"What about the father? Your male?"

"They kept us separated. I don't even know if he was ever told."

She reached out to squeeze Gen's hand. "I am so sorry. That must have been impossibly difficult for you. You didn't deserve it. Neither of you did."

Imogen didn't squeeze back, but she looked at Felíne. "You're right. We didn't deserve it, but perhaps it was better he didn't know."

Felíne frowned. "What do you mean?"

"The baby was stillborn. A girl carried to term and born without a heartbeat. They took her before I had a chance to hold her."

Felíne squeezed Imogen's hand again, words failing her. Her eyes filled with tears. She thought maybe Gen's eyes had no tears left. Felíne opened her mouth to say something, anything, to offer condolences, to yell her frustration for her friend's tragedy, to weep, but Imogen spoke before any sound came out.

"You asked about my life sentence," she said as though determined to push past a pain that threatened to overwhelm her. "After my pregnancy, my contract was fulfilled. Vulgren didn't want to let me leave, but he couldn't ignore documents that were legally binding and signed by the crown. My ten year-sentence ended at five. When I got out, I found my mother had fallen ill. I threw all of my energy into taking care of her. I was with her every day for four years, going from mender to mender, using every penny that I'd earned as a Fate to try and heal her, and nothing worked. If she died, I don't think I could have lived with myself."

Of course. Imogen had already lost the man she'd loved and a child she hadn't even had a chance to know. Her mother was all she had left. The whole purpose of her volunteering as a Fate in the first place was to take care of her mother.

"I had nowhere to go, and my remaining fortune was dwindling to nothing." Imogen took a deep, shaky breath. "So, I made a bargain with Vulgren. I would return to the Fates if he would get me an audience with the queen so I could petition her for my mother's care. Better care than could be found anywhere else in Ilistaar."

Something clicked into place. "Mender Alcuin."

Imogen dipped her chin, a few strands of woven hair falling over her shoulder. "My life of servitude for Alcuin's care. He has no idea his new patient is the mother of a Fate. His unparalleled expertise paid for in blood."

"Gods, Gen," Felíne breathed.

Imogen smiled weakly. "Vulgren was overjoyed to have his favorite test subject back. He helped convince the queen that my life contract was invaluable and worth whatever boon I requested."

Felíne's features twisted. "I don't understand why you're smiling."

"Vulgren didn't account for one thing. The queen has the power to overrule any contract at any point in time. Her word is law. Vulgren got greedy. He didn't initially tell Queen Serebine I was the former Fate who'd successfully carried a child to term. She learned of it within a day of my return to be prepped for service. I made sure of it. As expected, she deemed my expertise highly valuable to the Prima."

Felíne's eyes widened. "You were more valuable to her than to Vulgren. My mother voided your contract."

They had reached the side room that held their hidden bag of belongings. Felíne hadn't even noticed the journey she'd been so engrossed in Imogen's tale.

"She did. But she did more than I expected. I was taken from Vulgren before he could even properly celebrate my return. He can't touch me now that I am an elder. And he wouldn't dare endanger his standing with the queen. She has the power to take everything away from him."

Imogen was brilliant. She'd ensured her mother received the best possible care available in all of Ilistaar while simultaneously orchestrating her escape from a life of servitude. It was masterfully done.

"You are incredible. Truly," she said.

Imogen didn't smile, just looked at her with dogged determination. She appeared as though she'd just expended every bit of energy she possessed, pouring every reserve into their conversation. Felíne couldn't imagine what it must have taken out of her to bare her soul the way she had, and Felíne felt privileged to have been the recipient of such a gift.

"Your secrets are safe, Gen. I need you to know that. And if there is anything I can do, anything at all, you need only ask."

"Thank you," she sighed. "For now, I think I've asked enough of you. We both deserve a hot bath and a warm bed. Tomorrow, perhaps, we can continue our quest to save the world."

Chapter 13

Tests and Messages

TWO NIGHTS AFTER KALEVAR WANDERED the expanse of the Desert Bloom Botanical Gardens, he found himself in a modest local tavern where Santhe ran the bar on Tuesday and Wednesday evenings.

It was a Sunday night, and Santhe wasn't working. In her place, a plump woman with greasy black hair pulled into a haphazard knot at the base of her neck worked the usual crowd. She bustled to and fro with drinks and bowls of the night's stew. Kal watched her deposit a third serving in front of two males sitting in a booth against the wall across from where he sat at the bar. The soup sloshed over the sides, coating the barmaid's fingers, which she promptly wiped on her already soiled apron. He wondered if she noticed that she hadn't cleaned her hands by the action, only succeeded in further smearing herself with grease from the stew. The female, who introduced herself to her patrons as Lou, moved on to another table and left greasy fingerprints on the mug of ale she delivered.

No, she didn't notice. He had been there three hours, and she'd been at this for the better part of the evening, leaving a trail of lard everywhere she went.

Kal looked away.

Lou approached him for the sixth time in the past two hours and leaned a meaty forearm on the bar. He ignored her.

She extended a hand for his mug, and he deftly moved it out of her reach.

"No refill?" she pouted. "Cuttin' yourself off early? That's a damn shame, sweets."

Kal gave her a tight-lipped smile and tried not to notice the constellation of blackheads that dotted her bulbous nose. He should have gone to the Dovetail instead. Screw subtlety. Kal would have rather taken the chance of drawing unwanted attention at the upscale pub than be the subject of Lou's overattentiveness for another unbearable hour. Of all the nights he could have been here, it had to be Sunday. Hell, he'd have preferred Trixie over Lou. At least she made an effort to bathe before work, and her breath didn't smell like last week's tripe.

"You asked me only five minutes ago if I wanted a refill, Lou," he replied patiently. "The answer hasn't changed."

She tried to peer into his mug, but he angled it away, so she peered at his face instead. He was disappointed he couldn't angle that away from her quite as effectively.

"Now, what kinda bar maiden would I be if I didn't take care of my customers?"

Bar *maiden?* Kal wondered vaguely if Lou had always been this unpalatable or if she'd been ruined by some tragic event in her past. Somehow, he couldn't picture her as anything but what she currently was. Maiden indeed.

Lou leaned dangerously close. "So, what about that drink, sweets? Hmm?"

"Ever the vigilant alewife, Lou," he said. "However, I find myself unable to drink as fast as you can pour."

She leaned a fraction closer, and Kal made a sincere effort not to forcibly remove her from his personal space. He really *was* trying to avoid trouble, despite Santhe's opinion of him. She wouldn't dare doubt his control if she could see him now. She'd applaud it. Lou's scent assaulted his nostrils.

"What's your name, sweets?"

"Crow."

She smiled, showing him yellowed teeth bracketed by swollen red gums, and squinted her eyes. "That's not your real name."

"Hm?" He'd turned away from her again. Somehow, ignoring her only endeared her to him more.

"Are you playing hard to get, sweets? I can take a hint." She winked at him. "I'm off at ten."

"Oh good," he said. Where the fuck was Santhe's messenger?

Someone across the room whistled.

"I have other clients, Mr. Crow. I can't have you monetizing all my time now. You gotta share til I'm done later."

Did she mean *monopolizing?* Kal didn't correct her. Gods, she was as bright as she was beautiful. He sure as fuck wouldn't be *monetizing* anything where Lou was concerned.

It wasn't the looks. He didn't place a high value on a person based on their appearance. Kal had met his fair share of wretched souls wrapped in beautiful skin, but it had been a long fucking two days, his patience was thinning by the minute, and Lou went out of her way to personally test it despite his every effort to evade. He'd had just about enough.

She sauntered away from him, trailing a finger along the bar top behind her in what she undoubtedly thought was a tantalizing gesture.

Kal waited until she was thoroughly engrossed in the demands of another pub dweller before reaching behind the bar and filling his mug. He drank deeply, draining the slightly bitter, citrusy ale.

A pale, delicate hand reached around him. His own shot out and gripped the wrist it was attached to. What was it with females going after his mug tonight? Couldn't a man enjoy a beer in peace?

Kal turned and looked up into the bemused expression of a shurii female who couldn't have appeared less like the bothersome barmaid.

Her hair was fire-red, long, silky, and pinned back from a heart-shaped face. She had blue eyes lined with kohl to give them an elongated, cat-eye shape. Her lips were thin but pleasantly shaped and currently tipped in an appreciative smile as she surveyed him. She had an ample bosom, the creamy crests of which were threatening to spill over the lacy top of her gown, and her waist was narrow enough to fit neatly encircled in both of his hands.

She dipped her blue eyes to the slender wrist, still firmly in his grip. "Might I have my hand back?"

Her voice was high-pitched in a musically feminine way.

"That depends on what you plan to do with it," he replied. "I'd like to keep my drink in my possession."

"It's empty. I thought I might refill it for you."

Kal released her. He reached around the bar and let the foamy amber liquid pour into his mug. He swiped a second glass from a washed stack and filled that one as well before closing off the tap.

"It turns out I'm capable of procuring my own drink."

The female eyed the second glass. "Quite capable, I see."

Kal took a sip from his mug. "Are you thirsty?"

She watched him, eyes the color of indigo iris petals fixed on his mouth as he licked the foam off his upper lip. Her slender throat bobbed as she swallowed. "Yes," she said. "Very."

She sidled closer to him, placing a hand on his forearm. He looked at her hand, then at her face. She leaned forward, her mouth close to his ear, and whispered, "Something tells me that a man like you would more than satisfy my thirst. I think I'd like a taste."

He leaned back. "Is that so?"

"Mhm."

The woman reached for the second glass, but Kal lifted it and sipped from it before her fingers could close around the handle. Those violet eyes lit with amusement. "That was mine."

He smiled, showing teeth, and then leaned to her ear. She arched her neck, presenting it to him.

"Oh no, sweetheart. They're both mine," he said seductively. "But if you tell me who sent you to distract me, I might just give you a sip and let you walk out of this tavern with that pretty head still attached to your shoulders."

Her smile faltered slightly as his words registered. She recovered quickly, but he'd already caught it. His eyes bored into hers, and he saw the flash of uncertainty in them. Noted the change in her scent when her confidence and arousal became tainted with fear. He could practically hear the adrenaline flooding her bloodstream as her instincts warned she was in the presence of a predator. Her instincts were correct. It was just a matter of time before her conscious brain got the message.

She glanced over his shoulder.

Kal turned and saw Lou making a beeline for them. She'd noticed his attractive companion and had a look of pure determination set into her features.

He stood abruptly, slapped a few coins onto the bar, gripped the red-head gently but firmly by the upper arm, and pulled her close. "What do you say we take this conversation somewhere more private?"

Before she could respond, Kal ushered her quickly around the few tables separating them from the exit and slipped out the door. Lou would have to find another unwilling participant for her after-hours enterprise. He had some new, unexpected business that needed to be handled quickly and quietly.

Once outside, Kal repositioned himself with one arm around the female's shoulders and tucked her into his side, his other hand still gripping her upper arm. He dwarfed her. Anyone passing by would assume he was a protective man gathering his lover close after a few drinks at the local pub. He dipped his head to murmur into her ear. "If you scream, yell, or make any other undesirable noise to draw attention to yourself, things will become rather unpleasant for you."

He nodded politely to a couple passing them in the opposite direction.

The female stumbled, her feet slipping out from under her, tangling in the length of her gown. She didn't move to catch herself, though Kal had no doubt she was perfectly capable.

The well-dressed man passing reached out a hand to help. Kal pivoted out of reach, easily supporting the woman's weight to prevent her from hitting the cobblestones.

"That's it. No more wine, dear," he said, chiding her lightly. "Let's get you home." He smiled apologetically to the gray-haired man, who gave him a sympathetic look before glancing at his partner as if to acknowledge he understood Kal's predicament.

Kal steered them toward the alley that ran between the two buildings. It was dark and unoccupied. The female became dead weight, clearly unwilling. That was fine. He'd carry her if needed.

"You don't have a strong sense of self-preservation, do you?"

"You're hurting me," she hissed.

"Not even close," he said. "But keep dragging your feet, and I can arrange it."

She miraculously found her footing.

"Better."

"You're a fucking brute bastard."

His eyebrows crept up. "Darling, your mouth is even dirtier than I imagined."

She seethed next to him. "Fuck you."

Kal spun her suddenly, and her eyes widened in surprise. He pinned her against the brick wall with his body, one broad hand lightly bracing her throat. He could crush her without so much as a twitch. It was terribly unfair.

He gave her a dazzling smile. "Listen, sweetheart. It's been a trying few days. I consider myself a patient man, but my patience is wearing dangerously thin. I don't want to hurt you, but I also won't lose a wink of sleep if it becomes necessary." He squeezed briefly in emphasis, and she squeaked. "So, please, do us both a favor and drop the fucking act. Okay?"

The female nodded rapidly, tears gathering at the corner of her eyes. A nice effort but a wasted one. She wanted empathy from him? She'd have an easier time wringing water from a stone.

"Good girl," he said. "Who are you?"

She blinked up at him. Her lip trembled. He heard her heart rate accelerate.

Kal sensed the blade before he saw it. The female's arm came up in a wide side arc, and she attempted to plunge her knife into his neck.

Sloppy.

She'd wasted precious time trying to stab him from above, even though he towered over her by at least a foot. She would have had a better chance of landing a blow thrusting up from below. The kidney, the gut, hell, even the groin would have been a better attempt. It still wouldn't have worked, but he could have given her some credit.

This was just pitiful.

Kal easily caught her by the wrist and knocked her arm back against the wall above her head, hard enough to dislodge the blade from her hand but not hard enough to break her fragile bones. He stepped on the knife, securing it under his boot.

Who the hell was this amateur?

Kal wracked his brain for anyone he might have unintentionally scorned but came up empty. He might not have a clean conscience, but he'd been sitting on his hands for the past two days. He'd been good. Just like he prom- ised. And it had been fucking hell.

Regardless, he wasn't about to miss Santhe's messenger because of some redhead with a death wish. His entire being here in Asteros hinged on ob- taining the information Santhe was scheduled to provide.

"That was cute," he said, and the female's eyes flared in anger. "But you have no idea what you're doing. No technique. No training. I said before I did not want to harm you, and I meant it. But if you don't start talking, I will be forced to consider you an actual threat. I'll give you one guess what I do with threats. Here's a hint. It rhymes with 'marry them.'"

She growled. She actually *growled* at him.

He was tempted to growl back but instead took a measured breath. "Lis- ten. I am running late, and you are running out of time." Authority suffused his voice. "Last chance. Who. Are. You?"

No answer.

She needed motivation? So be it. Kal leaned his weight into her to what he knew was an uncomfortable degree. His grip on her throat tightened, and her free hand dug into his forearm, her nails biting into his flesh like little bee stings.

She was afraid, her indigo eyes wide, her nostrils flaring, but she wasn't as afraid as she should have been. A considerable amount of defiance blazed in her expression as though calling him on a bluff.

That was how she wanted to play? Fine.

He locked his gaze on hers, black eyes to blue, his face mere inches from her own, and let a little bit of the monster inside him rise to the surface. He didn't have to change forms for her to get the picture. She might not know who, but he saw the moment she realized precisely what she was dealing with. Just a glimpse of what lurked beneath the skin.

Kal didn't enjoy killing as a general rule. He made an effort to avoid causing unnecessary loss of life. However, when it was unavoidable, he did what he had to without question or regret. He was a reasonable man. Not evil. Not someone who relished exercising power over those weaker than him.

But the part that lived under his skin? The beast of his second form? *That* version of himself was merciless. He had no limits. No morally inveigled scruples. Threats were eliminated without discrimination.

The female saw a shallow impression of it, and the blood drained from her face. Terror shone in her wide eyes.

"Your test," she managed. "I'm your test."

Whatever he'd expected her to say, it wasn't that. "What do you mean, test?"

She took a forced breath, as if her lungs were starving for air but afraid of drawing it in without his permission. "Santhe sent me. I'm the messenger."

Kal's lips peeled back in a snarl. What the fuck was going on? He closed the gap between them again. "What do you mean you're my test?"

She winced. "Santhe told me to try and seduce you. She wanted to make sure your head was in the right place. Focused. She wanted to make sure you couldn't be easily distracted."

Kal watched her closely for a moment. She wasn't lying. He stepped back from her and swore. What the fuck, Santhe? What was she playing at? Did she think he'd just be whoring around while he waited for an answer? Didn't she know him at all? He turned to the female and pinned her with a furious glare. "Are you fucking insane? I could have killed you."

She swallowed and watched him warily. Her prior defiance was gone, withered by the knowledge, limited though it might be, of what lay beneath the surface of his skin.

"That was another part of the test," she said. "Santhe said if you can't control your urge to kill everyone that annoys you, then you have no business dragging her into this mission. She would consider you to be a liability."

Kal stared at her in disbelief. A liability? *Him?* If he killed everyone who annoyed him, his body count would be too high to number. Oh, they would be having words, Santhe and he. And *her*, whoever she was. She was hardly an innocent bystander. "I would have been justified killing you. You tried to stab me!"

"She knew I wouldn't succeed."

Kal ran a hand over his face. "You're insane," he said again. "Do you have any idea what could have happened to you? What I could have done?"

Her expression narrowed. "I do now."

"Why? Why would you agree to this?"

The female shrugged. "I owed Santhe a favor. She said there was a risk, but she didn't think you'd actually hurt me. She said it might be a good night for me if rumors are to be believed." Her gaze dipped to an indecent level. As if he had difficulty understanding her meaning. She had fucking balls, this one.

He stared at her. A favor. Fuck. He hoped it was one hell of a debt that was now repaid. And rumors? That was years ago. Another life. Santhe should have known better. "Are you hurt?"

She rubbed her wrist. "Just a bruise. It will heal."

He nodded, satisfied. Santhe should be rejoicing at his level of restraint. "What is your name?"

She turned blue eyes to him. "Reese."

"And your message?"

She hesitated.

Kal stooped and retrieved her knife. He held it out to her hilt first, and she took it.

Reese pulled a sealed piece of parchment from the bodice of her gown and handed it to him.

He inspected the seal briefly and ripped it open. Santhe's telltale scrawl marked the inside of the paper.

The location has been confirmed. Your instructions have been received and will be delivered by tomorrow morning. The north window shall be left open tomorrow night at your place, two hours after sundown. DO NOT be late, or your window will close.

A pious female garbs herself in the colors of the Goddess.

Kal got the message loud and clear. Tomorrow night, then. Everything was going as planned, just as he hoped it would. A familiar cold calm settled over him. His wait was nearly over.

Chapter 14

A Cloak of Midnight

FELÍNE FLUNG HERSELF ONTO HER bed, scattering the pillows, and stared at the chandelier that hung overhead. She watched mindlessly as the too-bright light of the setting sun filtering through the window lit the dangling crystal strands and refracted, scattering a kaleidoscope of colors across the room.

Her thoughts had been a whirlwind for the past three days. Trying to organize them felt like standing in the middle of a typhoon and attempting to pluck blowing debris from the air as it spun chaotically around her.

Tonight marked the third night since Imogen had taken her to Madame's. It felt like an age. They'd returned well after midnight, and Felíne had been convinced they'd been found out. When they emerged from the false door in the boudoir into the sitting room, they had found Veely snoring lightly in a chair, cushions padding her every side, and a thick woven blanket tucked under her chin. Imogen scowled and woke her up with a rough shake. Veely had glanced panicked at the clock and assured her in hushed whispers that she'd only fallen asleep ten minutes prior.

Imogen threw her a hard stare before she righted the blonde female's gown, thrust her cloak and the bag containing the sheer garments Felíne hoped to never see again into her arms, and ushered her to the door. The guards still dutifully waited outside.

Felíne had been exhausted after the night's events, and she could only imagine how Imogen must have felt having to relive the details of her painful past. Few things sapped the energy and strength from a person the way strong emotion did. Gen's short fuse was understandable, considering.

They wasted no time in the drawing room after Veely departed. Facing the wraiths and being escorted back to her room was another nerve-wracking experience. Try as she might to calm her racing heart, she was convinced they could hear its erratic beating through the halls. Not only that, but they'd surely notice the uncharacteristic kohl painting her face. They likely had, but no doubt dismissed it as a result of her 'lesson.' She'd been too tired and nervous to be embarrassed.

Felíne had collapsed when she reached her bed. She hadn't bothered with changing her clothes or turning down her coverlet. She even forewent washing her face and cleaning her teeth. The next morning, she'd been promptly woken a half hour past sunrise with black kohl smeared across her cheeks and a tangled mess of hair that likely pointed to questionable nighttime activities. If the queen's attendants only knew. And, thank the Goddess, they did not. At least her mother would have sufficient information as to her disheveled state. It should keep her satisfied that Imogen had been thorough in her instruction.

Since that night, Felíne had spent nearly every waking moment with Imogen. They hadn't spoken again about Imogen's past or the treatment of the Fates and all that she'd revealed during that walk through the tunnels. Felíne hoped that Imogen didn't regret opening up to her. Tonight, she had the evening free of lessons, but she planned to ask Imogen the next time she saw her.

Felíne had meant to broach the subject at some point in the past two days, but there had hardly been time. Her days had been filled with continued instruction.

The other elders had all but relinquished their roles in her daily life, having been instructed by the queen that Elder Imogen's one-on-one time with the Prima took precedence with her presentation less than two months away. She'd learned as much as the other elders could teach her, her mother reasoned. Felíne knew the histories. She knew the details of the curse, as much as could be known. She was poised, polished, and educated. At this point, she needed to remain focused, undistracted, and concentrated only on things relevant to her presentation and servicing.

Imogen seemed to be taking that task with no lack of seriousness. She wasn't distant, so to speak, but seemed thoroughly controlled during their interactions, as though placing her efforts on ensuring Felíne's understanding of various concepts instead of expanding their friendship.

The day after their meeting at Madame's, they spent an untold amount of time in one of the lecture halls discussing every mortifying detail of shurii male anatomy, the differences between first form and second form genitalia, and how a female handled specific parts to elicit pleasurable sensation. Shar's coupling with Dimon was referenced several times. Then Imogen explained how to position her body to meet her future partner's desires. *Then,* how to manipulate her body to ensure her own pleasure. Thank the Goddess Imogen hadn't insisted on another demonstration. The discussion alone left Felíne's face so red she was confident it would take days to return it to normal color.

Yesterday, they'd taken another unsanctioned trip outside of the palace walls. This time, they visited the private home of a female that Imogen knew through an acquaintance. An older female shurii had answered the door for them and ushered them quickly inside.

As soon as the door opened, Felíne heard low moaning from somewhere in the modest home. The elderly woman escorted them down a short hallway with bare walls into a small bedroom with one shuttered window and a cramped tub opposite the bed. A heavily pregnant female paced in the space between the two pieces of furniture.

She'd glanced up at the newcomers and then questioningly at the older woman who said, "They are here to help, Jess."

The female, Jess, only gave a curt nod before leaning against the edge of the tub and grunting as another round of contractions gripped her. Beside Felíne, Imogen was a pillar of stone.

Felíne had seen pregnant females before at Mender Alcuin's clinics, but never for a delivery. That was traditionally handled by a specialized branch of menders called birthers. Mender Alcuin had undoubtedly been present for new births in the past, but his interests regarding pregnancy and fertility had focused more on research and data collection than the care involved in safely delivering the babes.

After all, Mender Alcuin had identified the physical manifestation of the Goddess's curse, which had been activated upon Felíne's birth. He found that every shurii child born after Felíne bore the same small starburst-shaped birthmark on their lower abdomen. The mark had been foretold in the *godscripts*, but it was Alcuin who had correctly interpreted it. The people called them *lastmarks*, and every child with a *lastmark*, male and female alike, was sterile.

Felíne Lochlan Faelstrom, the Prima of Ilistaar, was the last fertile shurii born; no others born after her would bear children regardless of gender or form.

Not unless she successfully serviced the Primordial Male and bore him a child. Only then would the curse be broken and the people restored, their infertility reversed. Otherwise, the shurii would suffer a slow decline. They would live normal lives, perishing by blade, sickness, accident, or advanced age. Eventually, the population would dwindle, Felíne's generation producing the last generation. When they finally died, the shurii would be no more.

Felíne had watched the pregnant female before her sweat and pant as she labored. She appeared to be only a year or two older than her. The older woman, a birther named Greer, had Felíne fetch another bucket of boiling water and clean cloths. Felíne set about helping. It was different than closing wounds or setting broken bones in the clinic, but Jess was still a patient, and Felíne fell into the familiar role of assistant, helping Greer with her assessments and ministrations. She bathed Jess's forehead with cool water, walked with her through the house, and opened the door to let her feel the rare cool breeze that graced the balmy night. When Jess's contractions became too frequent and too intense for her to continue walking, Felíne let her squeeze her fingers and murmured words of encouragement with each wave.

Greer came to undress her, gently stripping the heavier clothing from Jess's trembling form. She stood before them with only a strip of fabric covering her swollen breasts. It was a completely different kind of exposure than Felíne had witnessed at the pleasure house. Jess couldn't have been less concerned with maintaining modesty. Every bit of focus she possessed was occupied with withstanding each contraction. Greer steered her toward the tub, which had just been refilled with warm water, and helped her into the bath. She sank in as low as she could go. It seemed to help soothe the female's agony, if only a bit.

Absently, Felíne noticed that Imogen had excused herself from the room sometime earlier. Her heart squeezed for the young elder, but she didn't seek her out. If she'd lost a baby during delivery, the last person she'd want to spend time with was a woman imminently expecting her own.

Felíne had no idea how much moving about laboring women did. She felt helpless as Jess squirmed, repositioned, stood, sat, and lay down. Into the tub. Out of the tub. In the bed. Onto her hands and knees. Squatting at the side of the tub, arms over the edge. Leaning against the wall, against Greer, against Felíne. Jess's dark blonde hair became soaked with sweat, and her brown eyes squeezed shut in concentration as she doubled over, her huge belly tightening painfully for seconds at a time, longer and longer.

At one point, Felíne turned away to retrieve another fresh cloth from a stack on the single side table, and a wail of agony sounded behind her, followed by a ripping sound and a roar of pain. Felíne spun around, and Jess crouched on the now too-small bed in second form, her light brown pelt damp with perspiration, jaw clenched against the pain, claws gripping the sheets. Her fur-covered belly heaved.

Felíne froze, eyes wide. Greer calmly retrieved the cloth from Felíne's hands and went to stand by a panting Jess. She murmured to the female, dabbing her furred head and prominent brow, and then began to massage behind Jess's small triangular ears, which were pinned back with tension. The female relaxed again a fraction, trembled violently, and then shifted back to first form. The strip of fabric that had covered her breasts lay shredded next to her, forgotten.

Greer looked over to where Felíne stood. "It won't be long now," she said quietly.

Felíne glanced up at her, concerned. "Is it safe for her to shift like that? For the babe?"

The birther nodded.

"It's completely normal. The shift is an instinctual reaction to the pain. When a female reaches this point in labor, the body changes to try and make accommodations. The babe will suffer no harm, and in fact, the change to second form, even briefly, helps the mother by releasing a flood of endorphins that lessen the pain and relax the pelvis. They won't take it away entirely, of course, but it is enough to offer a small reprieve for that last leg." Greer smiled fondly down at Jess, the expression transforming her rough, slightly wrinkled face into one of motherly affection. "You're doing so well, dear. You're almost there."

Felíne had watched the scene before her and dipped into private thoughts. They weren't exactly comforting. Should she succeed in becoming a mother, there would be no reprieve for her own labors. As there had been none for Imogen.

Greer hadn't exaggerated. The babe came shortly following Jess's brief shift to second form. The female bared down with grim determination and produced a wet, wailing newborn baby boy. The infant was swaddled in a clean cloth and thrust onto his mother's bare chest, where he wiggled, kicked his little feet, pumped his tiny fists, and exercised strong lungs. But not before Felíne noticed the telltale mark on the lower left side of his round little abdomen. The *lastmark* was two shades darker than the baby's creamy pale skin. Another shurii infant was born whose ability to one day welcome his own children to the world depended entirely upon Felíne's ability to survive her servicing.

The thought deeply bothered her.

Jess was spent. She lay there limp and exhausted while Greer fussed over cleaning her, changing the sheets, and wrapping both mother and baby in fresh, clean blankets.

Felíne excused herself once Jess was soundly sleeping, her infant cuddled close and nursing eagerly. She had found Imogen standing outside, keeping a silent vigil. She'd looked heavy, Felíne remembered thinking. Weighed down, the same way Felíne often felt when contemplating future events. But Imogen was likely burdened by events already unfolded.

Felíne's disposition had turned inward, and she remained quiet the rest of that evening, consumed with thoughts of the *lastmark* and the aftermath of seeing it mar the otherwise flawless skin of that sweet infant.

She retired to her bed chamber later that evening, emotionally and physically exhausted.

The more Imogen exposed her to, the more thoughts of her presentation plagued her. They weren't happy thoughts. They were frightened, anxious, worrisome thoughts, and she had difficulty letting them go.

Tonight was no different.

CLOAKING FATE

She knew Imogen intended to encourage her. To show her that what she needed to do *could* be done. Imogen said the more she knew, the better equipped she would be to deal with what lay ahead. The logical part of her mind understood this. It assessed the situation and prepared her for action. The emotional part of her mind, which tended to unfairly outweigh its counterpart, told her all was hopeless, and she needed to run away as far and fast as she could.

Felíne took a deep breath, drawing air into the very bottom of her lungs, filling her chest to capacity, then holding a moment before slowly blowing out through pursed lips.

Again.

In through her nose slowly, out through her mouth. Just like Mender Alcuin had coached her when she'd been on the verge of panic.

She hadn't seen him since that first day meeting Imogen. It was unlike her to go so long without a visit, and she'd sent word explaining the reasons for her absence. He replied, saying he understood, but she still felt guilty. Guilty and a little morose. She missed working alongside him. Learning from him and watching his practice. He had a calming, steady presence that she tried to emulate when she tended to patients, and she missed the peace of performing simple tasks.

She missed being faced with a problem and being able to fix it. Lately, it seemed she was only reminded continually of a problem she had yet to solve, and the lack of resolution was draining.

Felíne wondered how Imogen's mother was doing and whether or not Mender Alcuin had solved the riddle of her affliction. She hoped so. If anyone was capable, it was him.

Imogen had given her this evening off to go over the expected procession of events when her presentation arrived. Felíne had been looking forward to having the evening to herself, to have a moment of quiet that recently had become such a rare occurrence, but now that she was secluded in her rooms, she was restless. She could not escape her mind and felt trapped by her thoughts. Felíne needed something to do. She needed motion, something to occupy her focus that had nothing to do with the impossible weight of expectation resting on her chest.

Having decided, Felíne straightened and went to her dressing chamber.

She donned a fitted pair of black riding breeches and a light long-sleeved cream-colored tunic that fell to mid-thigh and laced up the deep vee in front.

As a girl, she was taught the basics of horsemanship but hadn't been permitted to ride. It wasn't a skill deemed necessary for the Prima and was much too dangerous. The elders and the crown wouldn't permit any unnecessary risks concerning the Goddess's chosen. Felíne would likely never sit in an actual saddle, but she liked how the breeches hugged her legs, butter-smooth against her skin beneath the sometimes-scratchy fabric of her undergown.

Over the breeches and tunic, she wore a simple yet fashionable sleeveless pale blue gown with beige stitching that matched her tunic's loose, exposed sleeves. It was one of her favorites. The gown laced up in front and back, hugging her waist and flaring over the widest part of her hips before falling in a loose curtain to the floor.

She'd change once she reached Mender Alcuin's lab before taking the tunnels to his clinic. He'd undoubtedly have something to occupy her evening.

The wraith guarding her door didn't so much as blink when she informed him they would be visiting the mender. He followed her silently as they made the familiar trip through the hallways to the small building. The night was clear, and the stars twinkled prettily overhead. It was a full moon, the glowing orb shielded behind a particularly thick cloud, making the world seem a little darker than normal.

Felíne entered the front waiting area expecting darkness. Instead, a soft lamp glowed at the reception desk ahead. Behind it, a pretty middle-aged woman looked up from the papers she was writing on. She set the ink pen down and smiled.

"Hello, Prima," she said. "What may I do for you?"

Felíne dipped her head. "Apologies for the interruption, Tahnia. I had hoped to speak with Mender Alcuin."

Tahnia offered a pleasant smile, but her eyes shone with sympathy. All of the mender's staff knew about the Prima's 'therapy visits.' It was the only way Felíne and Mender Alcuin could maintain the ruse of her assisting him with his work and patient care. However, Mender Alcuin typically did not keep a receptionist at this building unless he was away. Felíne's heart sank, already knowing what the female would say.

"I'm very sorry, Prima. The mender is away on an urgent errand. He is expected back late this evening. Do you wish to leave him a message? Or shall I call an elder for you?"

Felíne forced her lips into a smile. "No, thank you, Tahnia. The matter is not urgent. I will speak with him when he returns."

Tahnia dipped her chin. "I shall inform him you asked for him."

Felíne thanked the female and left the building. There was nothing she could do with Mender Alcuin gone. His lab was locked tighter than the royal treasury any time he left. In any case, she wouldn't have tried to visit his clinics in the city without him. She had promised not to and it simply wasn't in her to break his trust.

With her planned distraction unavailable, Felíne headed back to the palace. She didn't want to go back to her chambers. If she had to sit alone in her room, surrounded by silence, with only her thoughts to keep her company, she'd go insane.

A detour, then.

When they reached her familiar corridor, she turned right down an adjacent hallway instead of continuing toward her bedroom doors. Her guard smoothly adjusted and positioned himself next to her instead of behind.

"I don't suppose you'd like to continue to my rooms and wait for me there?" She glanced up at the wraith.

His eyes didn't even flick in her direction.

She sighed.

The trip to the elders' quarters was short. They had an adjacent building connected to the main villa by a breezeway. Imogen's room was separated from the main elder complex by a hallway, two rooms designated for conferences or educational purposes, and the common room, which was used for meditation or prayer. Hers was in the last suite, on the edge of the building. Felíne had been here with her once before when Imogen had needed to retrieve a few books from her personal collection for a lesson, which was the only reason she knew its specific location. Imogen had commented that she preferred the disjointed rooms despite the suite's smaller size because they offered more privacy, something of which she'd had precious little for much of her life.

When Felíne finally reached Imogen's door, she hesitated. If she knocked and Imogen didn't answer, her guard would expect to escort her back to her rooms. Though it wasn't terribly late, it was well after sundown. There were few other places she could go within the palace grounds that would be expected of her at this hour. Even a trip to the gardens or the reflection pool would be questioned. If it hadn't already, word would undoubtedly reach the queen of her unsuccessful visit to Mender Alcuin's. Tahnia was employed by the mender, but she would report to her mother without a second thought if questioned. Serebine's eyes were everywhere. If an attendant saw her walking toward the clinic after hours, the queen would follow up.

No, she couldn't risk appearing as though she was wandering after a failed *therapy* visit. That would raise a red flag. Her mother was highly sensitive to any perceived changes in Felíne's behavior. If she found Felíne to be aimlessly perusing the grounds, she would immediately be suspicious of Felíne's resolve, mental state, and emotional disposition.

Felíne loved her mother, but after all she'd learned concerning the Fates, she didn't think she could withstand an interrogation without doing some questioning of her own. She promised Imogen to guard the information she'd shared. Better to avoid drawing the queen's notice and let Imogen continue to report positive progress. She also bore some of the responsibility of ensuring that Imogen's reports were believed. Giving her mother a reason to question her now would undermine what favorable information Imogen was surely relaying.

That meant this was her last stop of the evening. She'd be forced back to her rooms if she was turned away. Felíne felt the anxiety ripple deep within her. She couldn't afford to have a fit.

She needed the distraction. Time to utilize a secret weapon. She'd have to accept the consequences of Imogen's potential wrath.

Felíne turned to her guard. "Elder Imogen and I will be engaged for some time. You don't need to wait. She can see me back to my rooms."

CLOAKING FATE

The wraith looked at her for a long, silent moment. Then he turned around and took up position to the left of the door with all the formality of a funeral attendant.

Well, she hadn't exactly expected him to listen. At least he wasn't watching her and wouldn't enter the rooms.

Felíne reached into an inner pocket of her gown that she'd engineered to hide trinkets. She withdrew the universal key and fitted it to the lock in Imogen's door. She felt the mechanisms in the key shift and click into place.

The key was a gift from Mender Alcuin. He didn't gift her things frequently, but when he did, they were extraordinarily valuable. This key, for example, would mold to any shurii-made lock and allow her access. It was unbelievably useful, and she guarded it fiercely. Her necklace had been another gift. The heavy, weathered gold coin was a comfortable weight around her neck, her name engraved into the back. She was sure it was probably some priceless rarity dug up from an ancient shurii civilization. Even if it had been a common mark, she would have treated it as a prized possession. She never took it off.

Felíne let herself into Imogen's room.

"Gen?" she called softly after shutting and locking the door behind her. The lights were out, and it took a moment before her eyes adjusted to the darkness. There was no answer.

Suddenly, she felt like an intruder. She was wrong to be here in Imogen's personal space uninvited. An overwhelming piece of her felt guilty, but she couldn't bring herself to leave. Between guilt and anxiety, tonight, she chose guilt.

Felíne moved deeper into the room and lit a lamp on a small side table beside Imogen's bed.

The room was impeccably clean, as it was the one time she'd been here with its tenant. The modest, narrow bed was situated directly ahead and arranged neatly with a few pillows. The sheets and single blanket were smoothly folded and tucked precisely at the corners. Her side tables were sparse save for the lamp on one and a single book on the other. A bookshelf sat against the wall to the left of the bed, occupied by various tomes and well-organized rolls of parchment. Next to the bookshelf, an arched doorway led to what appeared to be a dressing room. To her right, a simple wooden dresser was situated against the wall. A glass vase with freshly cut starflowers rested on top. A washroom with a single shuttered window was through another doorway next to the dresser. Directly to the right of the entrance sat a table for two nestled into the corner to make the most of the room's limited space.

Felíne parked herself at the table and resolved to wait for Imogen's return, pondering where the elder might have gone. Unlike Felíne, Gen wasn't restricted to the palace grounds.

It was quiet here, and she was still alone, but the space was not her own, and somehow, the solitude didn't feel oppressive like it would in her chambers.

As she waited, Felíne let the tight grip on her thoughts loosen, and they unfurled, her mind flitting from one mental image to the next. She had always needed time to process things. New information, feelings, concepts, ideas. No one would have ever been able to consider her witty or quick of tongue. She was intelligent and had an excellent memory, but retrieving the information once it was filed away took time. If she ever got into an argument, she would be the person who identified her brilliant rebuttal after the time for delivery had passed.

This was likely why she felt so off-kilter the past few days. Her routine had been violently interrupted, and she'd been forced to face a tsunami of new information without adequate time to come to terms with it. Every day was a new challenge, a new task, a new piece she was expected to fit into the puzzle of her life, and before she knew it, she was overwhelmed with pieces and left with no idea where to put them. There was a bigger picture here, but she couldn't see it yet.

Her role as the Prima was one thing. Her responsibility toward the Primordial Male and the shurii people was something she could carry, as heavy as that alone proved to be. *How* she was going to fulfill that obligation was something she was still trying to figure out.

The Fates were something else entirely. She felt accountable for the atrocities that had been committed against those shurii. For those still being committed in her name for her supposed benefit. She was horrified and felt compelled to do something, and yet, at the same time, she was powerless to stop it. But something had to be done. Vulgren's operations had to be gridlocked. She'd discuss that with Gen when she saw her tonight. If anyone had insight on how to dismantle that enterprise, it was one who had experienced it firsthand.

For it wasn't just the Fates that had suffered. Felíne had initially questioned the males' roles in this whole experiment. Shouldn't they also be held accountable for the damage they'd inflicted upon the females subjected to them? When she'd voiced these thoughts to Imogen, the elder had given her a look of such overwhelming sorrow that Felíne was taken aback. The males, Gen had said, were just as abused. Many went mad with grief after learning the outcomes of the Fates they'd serviced, and suicide became common.

"Shurii males are natural protectors," Gen had explained. "It's in their blood to defend females and young. That drive is one more thing heightened in second form."

Felíne had been skeptical. "Born to protect, and yet they're the cause of the harm?"

Imogen had sighed. "It is the nature of our creation. We were perfect before the Goddess's curse. Balanced. Males have overwhelming mating instincts in second form, which isn't typically an issue because a female's second form can match that intensity. The curse changed everything. It crippled you, and I don't say that disrespectfully. The Goddess put you at a distinct disadvantage while simultaneously shouldering you with the responsibility to fix it. It's not fair, nor is it your fault. The males cannot be blamed for their biology. Their otherwise perfect design has been perverted and used to harm females despite their intentions for the opposite."

The knowledge added yet another weight to Felíne's chest.

Minutes dragged on, and Felíne's restlessness slowly returned. She could not find a clock in the room, and she had no idea how much time had passed. Still, Imogen did not arrive. Belatedly, she questioned what her wraith would think when Imogen *did* show up, considering she'd insinuated that they had spent this time in her room together. Did the wraiths even have opinions? She decided it didn't matter. She was already here. Better to plan on asking forgiveness since she'd decided against asking permission.

Felíne worried her gold coin necklace and zipped it back and forth along the chain around her neck. She stood and paced the room. The curtain that partitioned off the dressing room had been left open, and Felíne peeked inside as she made her twelfth pass.

Imogen had only a few common gowns hanging from a rack inside the closet. Two pairs of simple shoes were lined underneath. Her three extra garments were elder vestments, neatly hung alongside the rest. It was practically bare. Most of the space was unused. She thought of her wardrobe and the countless hung gowns and shoes stacked on racks lining a dressing room larger than Imogen's entire suite. Undergarments practically burst from drawers and shelves. Gross overabundance; that's what it truly was, she realized. Imogen's lack of clutter was surprisingly refreshing.

Felíne turned to pace back to the washroom on the opposite side when her gaze snagged on a robe hanging at the far end of the closet.

Without thinking, she entered the dressing room and stood before the robe. Her fingers reached out and touched the supple, buttery fabric. The robe had a deep hood and hung so low it would drag on the ground when worn. It looked heavy and luxurious. The color was black but hued like a raven's wing. The dark length was interrupted by tiny spots of silver reflective stitching that made the cloak appear as though woven from a galaxy of stars. A cloak of midnight. It was beautiful. Expertly made. Where in the world had Imogen gotten it? And why was it hidden in the back of her closet as though forgotten?

Felíne couldn't help herself. She lifted the robe from the hook and shouldered the fabric. She'd been right. It was heavy. She made her way to the washroom and looked at herself in the mirror hanging above the basin. The front of the robe was visible now, and she stared at the vibrant yellow and crimson of the flaming sun emblazoned into the material. The sun of the Goddess appeared like a beacon, burning through the darkness of the cloak of night. Felíne drew up the hood. Her features disappeared completely, swallowed by shadow. She could see out as clearly as if she wore nothing, but her own mother would not recognize her while wearing this garment. She felt invisible. Like shedding the exterior of her skin and donning another's. The fantasy tempted her.

Oh, to have the liberty to walk without an escort, where no one knew her face and her intentions were hers alone. No wraith to serve as a perpetual guardian. Her identity safeguarded, and no one forcing her to reveal it. Privacy. Freedom.

Tempting indeed.

CLOAKING FATE

If she had one night to herself, left entirely to her own devices, where would she go? What would she do? She would have been able to answer if she'd asked that question of her ten-year-old self. Even fifteen.

But now? At twenty-four?

She was an adult woman. Any shurii female her age should know the answer to such questions.

An image of a tall, broad stranger disappearing into the green shadows of a botanical garden entered her mind. The moment in her memory was one of quiet, crystal clarity.

She didn't know. What she would do, where she would go. She didn't know this adult, duty-bound version of herself, and it bothered her. She *should* know.

She looked into the darkness of the midnight cloak, her face obscured by its depth.

Felíne glanced at the window, opened the shutters, and viewed the night beyond. She thought of the tunnel behind the boudoir.

She thought of the garden in the city. The Lover's Verdure.

She had no intention of looking for a lover, but perhaps she could find herself instead.

Chapter 15

Hunter

KAL WAS READY.

He clung to the shadows of the botanical garden, letting them envelop him like a second skin.

While he waited, he replayed Santhe's message from memory. He'd burned the original soon after receiving it.

The location has been confirmed. Your instructions have been received and will be delivered by tomorrow morning. The north window shall be left open tomorrow night at your place, two hours after sundown. DO NOT be late, or your window will close.

A pious female garbs herself in the colors of the Goddess.

Santhe had taken precautions to conceal the meaning of her missive, just as they'd discussed was necessary in case the messenger was intercepted.

The location was the botanical gardens in Asteros that Kal had scouted days prior. It was large, offered an abundance of cover, and, for the most part, was deserted after dark. If any shurii lingered, it would be easy to avoid them. There were also multiple exits, which he favored. It would be difficult for anyone to corner him in the expanse of greenery.

Cinah would have delivered his instructions to Railah. They contained specific directions for the female to meet at the garden bridge, however she would not believe herself to be meeting Kal. He kept himself, Cinah, and

Santhe entirely out of it. Instead, Railah would think she was meeting an attendant of the king to offer his blessing before her official induction to the Fates or some such nonsense. Kal had left the specifics to Cinah, who knew better than he what information would be believed. The message wouldn't be questioned by Railah's guards or any of the queen's attendants. Not when it bore the seal of King Domitan. Cinah had taken considerable risk, and he didn't even want to consider what his friend had to do to obtain the seal. It couldn't be helped. He could think of no other way to draw Railah out of the lodge, and he'd been expressly told that going in to get her was out of the question.

There was no north window, and he had no place of his own in the city. The window itself referred to the time frame he'd need to be ready to intercept Railah. Two hours after sundown actually equated to four hours after sundown. If the message was confiscated, or if Railah decided to share it with someone and their deception was discovered, the garden would be crawling with city guards at the time indicated in Railah's note, and Kal would be poised to disappear.

He'd been staking out the location since the sun vanished over the murky horizon, and there hadn't been a peep of activity. All good signs. At three hours past sundown, he'd entered the garden where he'd been waiting since. If there was any suspicion regarding their plan, he would have known already. But all was quiet.

Now, he just had to watch for a female wearing the cloak of the Fates, a garment only members of that group were permitted to wear. Cinah had obtained information regarding its make, and good thing. Otherwise, he'd have no idea if he was grabbing the right female, considering Kal hadn't a clue what Railah looked like. Cin said it would be impossible to miss. A cloak like a clear star-filled night with the Goddess's sun emblazoned on the front. Easy enough. Even a fool would recognize it, and Kal was no fool.

Kal had tried to determine the best way to approach Railah when she entered the garden. She'd likely be under guard, and disposing of her escort would be his first order of business. Between the three of them, Santhe had reasoned that it was probably best that Kal not identify himself or his intentions. Not until they were well out of the city and out of immediate danger. If Santhe had it her way, he wouldn't reveal his identity to her at all. Railah could be carted all the way to Meress and dumped into her brother's arms without having any clue who had facilitated it. If anything went wrong in her apprehension, it was best the female didn't know who was involved. Kal agreed with Santhe's logic, and Cinah conceded it was the safest option. The poor girl would be scared half to death, but better that than her revealing their identities to the crown. Santhe would be executed without care or thought, Cinah would likely suffer a fate worse than death, and Kal would take his own life before surrendering himself to that insufferable prick and his bitch queen.

That wasn't an option.

With explanation and a quiet retreat out of the question, Kal had no choice but to take her by force. He'd manage.

Kal hunkered down, deeper into the foliage. He checked his weapons for the seventh time, almost methodically. Knife. Sword. Bow. Quiver stocked. Second knife. Third knife.

He liked his knives.

Kal's muscles tensed with anticipation. He checked the pocket watch he'd obtained earlier that day, his keen eyes seeing the time even in the absolute darkness. He chose this one specifically because it produced no noise. Not even the softest tick as the weighted mechanism sent the hands around its face. The predator inside him stretched its powerful jaws, gnashed its teeth, and flexed, wanting to be let out. He was hunting, and the instincts of his second form recognized the thrill of waiting for prey.

He wrestled the beast down.

Not much longer now, he thought, unsure who he was reassuring: himself or the monster within. He pocketed the watch. Not much longer at all.

Chapter 16

A Complication

SANTHE WORKED THE CROWD OF the Dovetail Tavern with less skill than she was otherwise accustomed to. It was unusually busy for a Monday evening, and she wondered what divine being above was cursing her with wretched luck. Normally, she could handle twice the number of patrons with practiced ease. She could remember orders of fifteen tables, keep up with local gossip, and slather on the perfect amounts of charm that would earn her a few extra marks in tip money for her service. Not tonight, apparently. This was the third order she'd forgotten and the fifth drink she'd delivered to the wrong table. Fifth!

Mr. Gib's broad, weathered face pinched in distaste. "Santhe, I ordered the lager. Not the hops brew. You know I hate this bitter shit. Where's your head tonight, girl?"

Make that *sixth*.

She withered inside and offered sincere apologies. Another drink out of her pocket. At this rate, she'd be paying her customers to drink the tavern's ale. She needed to snap out of it. Unfortunately, that was easier said than done.

She had been a bundle of nerves all day. Reese had found her early this morning and assured her that Kalevar had received her message. She shot up a silent prayer for the woman returning alive and unmarked. Cinah had already delivered the instructions to Railah, and now all they had to do was wait.

Everything was in order. Everything so far was going to plan.

So why in the name of the Godking was she so damned nervous? Dread curdled in her belly like soured milk. She hated this. All of it. All the risk, all the danger. The sneaking about, secret meetings, and having to constantly pay attention to everyone at all times. A glance could contain a deeper meaning. A misspoken word could spell disaster. Threats lived and breathed around every bend, and they navigated them blindly, like dodging submerged rocks in the rapids.

Kal lived for this sort of thing. He loved toeing the line between safety and danger. He lived on it and thrived in that constant state of adrenaline.

Not her. She just wanted a quiet life with simple work. She hated this treasonous bullshit.

She just hated the crown more.

Santhe apologized again to Mr. Gib and delivered the lager, free of charge, as promised. She was heading to check on the next table when she looked up and spotted a man who had just entered the tavern.

Alarm shot through her like shards of ice, and she froze.

Thank the Godking she wasn't carrying a tray of drinks or a platter of food. They would have crashed to the floor and caused a terrible scene.

Cinah.

What was he doing here?

Santhe forced herself to look away and took measured steps back to the bar. She grabbed a rag and began wiping the counter to disguise the shaking in her hands.

Cinah entered smoothly, dressed in plain clothes. He was handsome but didn't stand out in a crowd like Kal did. Where Kal's features were striking and commanded attention, Cinah's were broader and appealing in such a way that encouraged one to look, appreciate, and then pass over. He possessed a kind of quiet, natural poise. You could have a pleasant conversation with him for half an hour and then forget him fifteen minutes after saying goodbye.

Santhe watched him from lowered lashes as she scrubbed the bar. He moved between patrons, his face a pleasantly neutral mask, and settled himself at a single table bordering a raucous group of shurii that worked in the smithy on Tresor St.

She dumped the rag into a bucket of soapy water and wiped her hands on her apron. She wove her way to his table, forcing her breathing to steady and praying her heart would slow.

He was here for her. Something had happened. Cinah knew her work schedule by heart and wouldn't have risked coming unless he urgently needed to speak with her.

He wore civilian clothes: a shabby pair of brown trousers, basic boots, and a faded linen shirt rolled up at the sleeves, revealing the dark skin of his lean-muscled forearms. He had dirt caked under his nails and smudged haphazardly on his clothes. There was even a bit of wheatgrass in his hair's tight, coarse curls. He looked just like a farmer who came directly from working the fields in need of a hot meal and a cold ale.

Cinah hated feeling unclean. He was obsessively meticulous about his appearance. This was serious business.

"Welcome to The Dovetail, sir. What can I get for you?" Santhe kept her voice low and even.

Cinah looked into her eyes, pretending to see her for the first time. He smiled, and it would have fooled any casual observer, but she knew better. Whatever news he brought was not good.

Oh, gods. Kal. Something happened to Kal.

"I will have whatever soup the cook is serving with hard bread, please."

Santhe dipped her chin, her mind working furiously. "Potato with bacon fat. Right away."

Cinah lowered his eyes to inspect his hands. She was about to turn when he spoke so quietly she barely caught his words. She hadn't even seen his lips move.

"A complication," he said.

The table beside his roared with laughter, drowning out any other murmuring. Santhe walked away from the table to collect the soup before her lingering appeared unusual. She made a point to stop by three other tables on her way to the kitchen.

A complication? He had to mean with Kal and Railah. What the hell happened? As if navigating these past days hadn't been harrowing enough. Now, something was amiss, she had no idea what it was, and the one person who'd come to warn her couldn't even speak plainly for fear of being over-heard by the wrong set of ears.

Damn it all to hell.

She forced herself to take a measured breath. Cinah was here, and she would find out what he came to say. She just had to be patient. There was too much at stake for her not to be.

The next few hours were torture.

Cinah had managed to inquire about a room, to which she responded that they had one available. She retrieved a single key with a number written on one side and slid it face down on the table toward him. He'd nodded and paid her in advance for the meal and board for one night. She pocketed the coins, fully intending to return them to him later. Then, she was forced to go about work as usual.

If she thought her nerves were frayed before, they were shredded to ribbons now. Every single monotonous movement, conversation, and task was unbearable. She felt brittle, like weak glass that was prepared to shatter at any given moment.

Cinah finished his soup and retired to his room before she could make it over to retrieve his empty bowl. He hadn't touched the ale, and she hadn't expected him to. He only pretended to sip it while he ate. She had a break in an hour. She'd sneak up to his room then and figure out what the hell was happening.

Santhe's break came sooner than anticipated. She was walking with a tray full of drinks, and one of the drunker patrons stood suddenly with an exorbitant amount of enthusiasm mid-conversation. He crashed right into her. She hadn't been paying attention and lost her hold on the tray, sending the mugs and their collective liquids splattering down her front. The male had landed on his ass at her feet. His companions hollered with laughter as he sputtered a slurred apology and tried to wipe her soaked hair, dress, and apron with his equally wet hands.

One of the other barmaids saw the commotion and rushed over with a stack of rags to help clear the mess. Santhe excused herself to go clean up. The washroom was right next to the back stairwell that led to the guest rooms on the second floor. She took the stairs two at a time, neverminding the dripping trail she left as she went. She'd wipe it up later. No one else would be up this way for a while yet.

When she reached the right room, she knocked as quietly as she could. Cinah opened the door immediately and let her inside.

"Thank the gods. I've been waiting for an age." He bolted the door and then turned. Cinah looked at her, likely seeing what resembled a drowned rat, and frowned. "What happened? Are you alright?"

She waved him off. Forget her sopping. "Just a spill. It doesn't matter. What's wrong? What's happened to Kal?"

Cinah's brow furrowed further, and his full lips formed a hard line. "It's not Kal. It's Railah."

Santhe hated the feeling of relief that flooded her limbs. Kal was okay. But wait. "What about Railah?"

"My message was delivered too late."

Santhe scowled. "What do you mean, too late?"

"Railah was taken from her rooms at sunrise for an audience with the queen. Her final rite was earlier than we anticipated. They've taken her to the Stronghold."

Santhe just stared at him. Somehow, his words weren't penetrating. She had too much adrenaline in her system. It was blocking her mental pathways.

"What?" she said numbly.

Cinah gripped her by the upper arms, his hands warm against her wet, chilled sleeves. "I said she's gone," he said. "She did not receive my message. We were too late."

Santhe's brain finally caught up. Gods. "What time is it?"

Cinah checked a watch. "Fifteen minutes to midnight."

Nearly four hours past sundown. He was waiting for her. They had to warn Kal. Their plan was over. Doomed. She knew it would never work, yet Kal insisted. Now, he was sitting out there in the dark, in the middle of the city, waiting for a woman who would not be coming. They had to tell him. They had to tell him now.

She was suddenly panicked. "Cinah, why are you here? You should have gone straight to Kal!"

He looked at her like she sprouted a third eye. "Santhe, I only sealed the message. I didn't write it; you did. I have no idea what it said or where they planned to meet."

That's right. They had agreed Cinah would not know the letter's contents for fear of discovery and what horrors he might face if implicated. She'd insisted. Cinah had only relented. He'd not been in favor of the plan, arguing that it put her in considerably more danger, but she wouldn't budge, and he begrudgingly yielded. She would write the letter, and Cinah would "contribute monarchial rhetoric so that its authenticity would not be questioned."

And now they were too late.

"How do you know? Where is the letter?"

"Destroyed," he said. "I instructed my page to burn it if it was undeliverable."

"But that would have been this morning. Why are you so late?"

Cinah's features twisted in chagrin. "I failed to instruct him to immediately notify me if the aforementioned circumstance arose. He is quite reliable but not very bright. It was my error. I misjudged his capacity for critical thinking."

Santhe stared at him, wide-eyed. What did they do?

"I came as soon as I found out."

Oh gods, what did they do?

Cinah shook her. As if in a daze, she looked down at her arm. He never shook her. "Santhe. Where is he?"

Santhe looked up at the face she adored. She saw the concern in his warm brown eyes, in the lines of his broad forehead, and bracketing his generous mouth.

"Desert Bloom," she said. Her voice sounded strange to her ears. A shiver wracked her soaked frame, and Cinah rubbed her arms with his warm hands. When did it get so cold in here? "He's meeting her at the bridge in the Desert Bloom Botanical Gardens."

Cinah nodded, purpose steeling his gaze. "Go downstairs and clean yourself up. Finish your shift. Go home and wait for me. Bolt your door."

Of course. She always bolted her door.

Cinah pressed a kiss to her forehead and moved toward the exit.

CLOAKING FATE

Outside, a call went up through the city streets. Cinah froze with his fingers on the handle and looked back. His eyes guttered with fear, and Santhe's heart dropped to her toes. They heard it even through the closed window.

The alarm sounded, and they heard the city guard shouting. Santhe and Cinah shared a knowing look. Somewhere in the night, within the gates of Asteros, a fugitive was being hunted.

Chapter 17

Encounter

FELÍNE'S ESCAPE TO THE HIDDEN tunnel behind the boudoir was surprisingly easy. In fact, it was so easy that she kept glancing behind herself, convinced that someone was following her, watching her every traitorous move, just waiting for her to reach her destination so they could jump out and proclaim her obvious guilt.

But, no. No one followed her. She ran into no guards, no attendants of the queen, no elders, no queen herself—praise the divine—no one at all.

The most difficult part of the whole affair was maneuvering her woman's body through the ridiculously narrow window in Imogen's washroom while taking care not to snag the heavy material of the cloak on the sill. She'd climbed through plenty of windows as a child without much trouble or thought, but the feat was significantly more challenging while in possession of breasts and hips.

Felíne had folded the front of Gen's cloak in on itself, gathering the crimson and gold fabric of the sun inward so that only the star-studded midnight portion remained visible. It would do her no good to escape Gen's suite only to be spotted dashing through the grounds with starfire emblazoned on her front.

Ha! As if she were that naïve.

Felíne felt an almost giddy sense of exhilaration course through her, something she hadn't experienced since childhood. Sneaking out with Imogen was one thing. Her excursions with her elder friend caused her anxiety, likely because the agenda was never her own. Their secret outings together were ultimately business. The two of them were duty-bound by their roles. If she weren't the Prima and Imogen not the elder assigned to instruct her, their adventures together wouldn't even exist. And while she appreciated the new things she'd experienced under Imogen's tutelage, it was difficult to enjoy herself while constantly being reminded of her burden. Perhaps one day, their friendship would not bear the onus of responsibility.

Even her work with Mender Alcuin didn't bring her this kind of elation. She loved their time together. He'd become more than a mentor, a grandfather. But even Mender Alcuin guided her. He gave her considerably more autonomy than her mother or the elders. He didn't treat her like a fragile piece of art in danger of ruination at the slightest disturbance. But he was still a vigilant guardian. Ever present, ever watchful.

Now, this? This agenda was hers and hers alone, and no one was there to guard or guide her. She was doing something for herself strictly because she wanted to. Not because she was obligated or compelled. Not because she'd been told it was necessary or required. No. The excitement and anticipation she felt was on account of the one thing she could never fully acquire: freedom.

It didn't matter that it was only for a few hours. It was freedom all the same, and, by the gods, she planned to savor it.

The trip through the tunnel went without incident. It was virtually impossible to see where she was going, considering she didn't have a light for the lamp like Imogen had their first night through. Thankfully, there were no branching corridors that would have made it easy to get lost. The dark spooked her a bit, and she stumbled more than a few times. She was unable to see her feet, but determination pressed her onward. Felíne didn't let herself even consider the potential consequences she'd face if her absence were discovered. If she did, the part of her personality that had been cultivated to meet the expectations of others would talk her out of what she'd decided to do and turn her right around to turn herself in. Guilt would take root and prevent her from taking one step further. So, she resolved not to think about it and instead continued in the dark.

Freedom. Freedom. Freedom became her mantra.

Felíne finally reached the end of the winding underground pathway and emerged onto the dilapidated property. The stench was more wretched than she remembered. She pulled her hood even further over her face and squeezed through the loose board in the fence. Now, if she could just remember which way to go...

In the end, she'd only gotten turned around twice before making it back to her intended path. She stayed in the alleys, avoided noise and people, and soon came upon the telltale brick back of Madame's. Instead of going up to the building, she turned early, slipping through the space between the pleasure house's neighbors until she reached the front of the street.

It was busier than she would have liked. She hung in the shadows, watching with rapt attention as shurii milled about. Some stumbled out of taverns, and others called out to draw attention and the promise of a warm bed for an hour. Still, others stood engaged in what was left of their nighttime conversations and companionship.

A group of soldiers walked by, and Felíne flattened herself against the building, praying she was invisible from the street. They passed without even glancing in her direction.

Across the street, she saw the entrance to the garden. For all the lingering commotion on this side of the road, the Desert Bloom looked invitingly vacant. Now, she just needed to get there without being seen.

Felíne backtracked, winding her way through the alleys and side avenues until she found a quiet, narrowing of the street far enough away from the businesses that the nocturnal shurii wandering the city would not notice her.

In moments, she passed under the arched gateway and disappeared from view among the dense greenery, positively tickled with her stealth. Her giddy affect quickly dissipated, replaced by awe.

The garden was magical.

The full moon glowing overhead reached its peak in the sky, bathing the world in its silver luminance. From inside the garden, the moonlight filtering through the canopy of leaves looked like radiant filaments of fluorescence piercing the darkness, like a multitude of fantasy skylights in a verdant ceiling.

Felíne dropped her hands and floated down the path in a trance. Peace settled over her. The quiet rustling of little desert-dwelling creatures, the affectionate twittering of birds nestled down for the evening, and the rolling flow of water in the gentle stream that cut through the plant beds surrounded her, cloaking her in tranquility. This was exactly what she needed.

CLOAKING FATE

Here, she wasn't the Prima. She wasn't the Goddess's chosen. She wasn't the savior of the people. She had no titles or responsibilities. She was not important, not needed, and there was no expectation hanging over her perfectly styled head.

She was simply Felíne.

The stress of the past few days, of her very existence, faded slowly away.

She wandered deeper into the garden until the entrance disappeared from view. Felíne had the distinct feeling that she was here for a reason. It was meant for her to shed her reservations and self-restraint tonight. She was supposed to come. The combination of the midnight hour and the delicate beauty of the vegetation that surrounded her held some unknown sense of purpose. She wasn't sure exactly what it was or what it meant, but it was tangible. As though she'd been called. She could no more refuse that summons than she could refuse to drink water or draw air.

Up ahead, Felíne saw the bend in the path that led to a graceful wooden bridge with iron filigree woven into the railing. Jasmine vines clung to the rail posts, coating the entire thing in emerald drapery with tiny white star-shaped flowers. The green living things in this place had claimed the tattered wood and twisted iron and transformed it into something beyond itself. It looked ethereal. Timeless. The moon broke through the canopy overhead, setting the bridge aglow and making the rolling waters below look like liquid silver bordered by beryl moss. The fragrance beckoned her.

Felíne stepped onto the bridge.

Once she reached its center, she paused and lowered her hood to better appreciate the view. A tiny sand squirrel scampered up one side of the rail and crept toward where she leaned against the edge before rocking back on its little haunches. Its bushy tail fluffed up behind it, and its overlarge eyes stared at her as if to determine whether she was a friend or foe.

She cooed to the little creature, and her low voice sounded overloud in the silence, almost like the disturbance was unwelcome. The garden was so quiet. The sand squirrel straightened, whiskers twitching violently. Then, it whipped around and scampered off into the protection of flora.

Well, alright then.

Felíne straightened, stepped back from the rail, and froze.

An otherworldly prickling sense of awareness skittered down her spine like spider feet.

There was something behind her. Something large. And it held the fine, honed edge of a blade against the hammering pulse of her throat.

Felíne's brain shorted out in panic. Her heart raced, and her lungs pumped like a bellows to draw life-saving oxygen into her body, prepping her muscles for action. Her eyes were wide open, and suddenly, she saw everything in the garden in striking clarity. Even the deeper shadows were visible to her. Her senses went into overdrive. She saw every color in vibrant detail, every stir of the leaves in the breeze. She could smell each individual scent of the blooming flowers and feel the cold line of steel that graced her skin under her jaw. Could taste metal on her tongue, the bitter bite of adrenaline. All of it assaulted her. She started to sweat. The potent stress response piloted her system. What had Mender Alcuin called it? To fight or to flee.

Her muscles tensed.

"Easy, now. No sudden moves." A deep, masculine voice sounded from somewhere above and behind her.

Her instinct was to yell. She should yell.

"No yelling."

Felíne didn't curse often. She was taught a dirty mouth did not belong on a pretty face. Intelligence married eloquence; ignorance bred profanity…But, fuck.

Fuck, fuck, fuckfuckfuckfuck*fuck*.

"Just back up with me, nice and easy. Slow."

She had no choice. The stranger had her around the middle with one iron forearm, and his blade rested at her throat almost like an afterthought. She took a step back with him.

"That's it. Good, girl."

His voice was low, and he spoke the way one would if trying to coax a frightened creature from its burrow with promises of safety. It would have been soothing, hypnotizing even, if she weren't trapped in a pit of fear.

Stupid. She was so *stupid!*

What in the name of the Goddess did she do now? For all the adventure in her soul, nothing within her prepared her for a moment like this. She was alone, far from her guards, the shelter of the palace, and anyone who would answer her call for help. She was entirely vulnerable. At the mercy of this strange male. She didn't even have the benefit of a second form to give herself a fighting chance. This was exactly the type of situation her parents had guarded her against. The reason why she'd been sequestered within the palace walls. Hidden away from the world.

This man could slit her throat and dump her body in the silver stream, and no one would be the wiser. The king and queen would turn the city upside down to find her, but first, they had to discover she was missing. It could be hours. Her guard would stand outside Imogen's door all night if the elder never showed. They'd all been explicitly instructed by the queen not to interrupt her and Gen during their meetings.

Ironic how she'd started her evening praying to the Goddess that her absence wouldn't be noticed. Now, she was praying for the opposite.

The male backed her off the bridge and onto the opposite path, which she'd previously noticed disappeared into the dark depths of the garden. No wonder she hadn't seen or sensed him. The foliage was so thick on the path's edge that it could have hidden a peacock in full feather.

They continued to move slowly, carefully along. The stranger gave no indication he intended to release her.

"I will say I'm surprised by your lack of a guard," he said casually, his voice a rich, rolling timbre. "I had expected more of a challenge. You couldn't have made it easier if you gift-wrapped yourself for me."

Gods, he was taking her!

Felíne's heart stuttered. He knew who she was, and he was taking her! Why? To what end? Was he a member of the Cozened? One of the followers of the Godking, hellbent on undermining the work of the Faithful Cursed? Was his plan to remove her from the equation altogether?

Or worse…

What if he made to molest her? Oh gods, the Goddess would never forgive her. The king and queen would disown her. If she became despoiled, it would mean the end of the people. The Primordial Male would never have her. She would be cast aside, forgotten, her entire life's purpose dismantled by the perverse intentions of a felonious thug.

She felt sick.

The man gripped her tighter against the hard plane of his body as he guided her another step backward, and his scent invaded her nostrils.

Felíne wanted to sob. She stumbled. Her feet felt strangely numb. She was trapped between the solid, muscled wall of the male's body and her own ineptitude. Her wide-eyed gaze swung left and right, hoping to find something, anything that she could use to defend herself and secure her release. There was nothing but green. She was being swallowed by plants, strangled by the lush flora that moments before had offered her such comfort. Now, it was choking her.

There was no one here. If she screamed, no one would hear her. She struggled to draw air into her lungs, but her throat was closing up in panic.

"Please," she rasped. "Please, no."

"Shh. None of that, now. Trust me, you're going to thank me later."

This was it. He was going to rape her.

Felíne struggled, her hysterical brain forcing movement into her wooden limbs with the sole intent of securing her survival. She stomped a numb foot down onto his own as hard as she could.

He grunted and shifted his grip. The blade left her throat. "That wasn't very nice," he growled.

His words were like a catalyst, and they broke something inside her. Felíne had never before fought for her life. She'd never stood faced with her end and clawed like a savage to escape it. She did so now. Felíne kicked and punched and squirmed and bit and scratched. She struggled with every shred of every fiber of her being. She became a hellcat. A spawn from some dark depth in the forgotten places of the world. A demon with razor claws and a frothing mouth with a forest of teeth. If she had possessed a second form, it would have ripped this villain to ribbons.

But she did not have a second form. She didn't have claws, only neatly clipped, manicured nails. No jaws filled with fangs, no superior strength, no everlasting stamina.

Her captor, on the other hand, seemed to have strength and stamina abound, and he used it to withstand her onslaught. Soon, Felíne had exhausted every last reserve of energy she possessed. She felt dizzy and weak, and her breath came in wheezing gasps.

"A valiant effort," the male commended. "Truly. But not enough."

Felíne dropped. Her feet no longer felt attached to her body. She was spent, and she couldn't breathe. The stranger supported her full weight without the slightest strain, lifting her into the cradle of his arms. Darkness crept in on the corners of her vision. Her focus clouded.

"Puh...pl..." Her lips were moving, but the air had gone. She was like a fish on the shore, mouth gaping, trying. She was trying so hard.

Two deep obsidian pools stared down at her. Or was that the darkness that finally claimed her?

"Please?" His rich, silky baritone caressed her ears. "Only because you asked so nicely."

Then Felíne knew no more.

Chapter 18

Farewell

KAL LOOKED DOWN AT THE limp female in his arms. She was utterly spent. While he wasn't thrilled about the prospect of carrying Railah back to Brune's, he supposed it was more efficient than dragging her along unwillingly. At least she hadn't shifted. And she'd been early. He'd get to get the fuck out of here ahead of schedule.

Kal took a moment to study her as he moved silently through the garden. She really was a lovely creature. Fair complexion, a wealth of thick, dark hair that fell down her back in waves, a delicate natural arch to full matching brows, large almond-shaped eyes, a straight feminine nose, and lovely pink lips with a perfect cupid's bow all set into an oval face.

He'd seen her standing there on the bridge with moonlight spilling onto her face, gilding her in silver, and he couldn't help but take a moment to appreciate the sight. That appreciation lasted about until she'd tried to claw his eyes out. She looked nothing like her brother, but she certainly had his temper.

Rask was also fair, but the blond hair and blue eyes didn't match his kin. He hadn't noticed at first, with her form concealed beneath the heavy layers of the cloak she wore, but now, holding her, Kal realized she had the kind of curves that most males would fantasize about. She was heavier than she looked. Another difference. Rask was tall and lean. He'd be wiry if he didn't train with almost fanatical intensity to try and maximize his muscle content.

Perhaps they had different sires.

Kal approached one of the rear exits of the garden and paused in the shelter of shadow, surveying the street. It was past midnight, and this part of the city was not busy like the business district on the opposite side. A couple of pubs stood between here and Brune's stable, where his horses waited. He'd considered going an alternate route, but it would take him extra time through a residential area patrolled by alert soldiers lacking the lure of nearby taverns. If he took the shorter route near the pubs, at least any guards would have a higher chance of wandering inside for a final drink before the establishments closed and they were forced back to their stations.

Staying in the garden until everything shut down wasn't an option. He needed to get out now before anyone realized Railah was missing. Besides, the sooner he put the sights and smells of this rotten city behind him, the better off he'd be. His mood suffered a steady decline the moment he set foot inside the Asteros gates and didn't begin to lift again until he left.

Kal readjusted his grip on the woman's sleeping form and ducked out from the cover of green. He kept to the shadows, slinking along the sides of buildings and alleyways, pausing in alcoves to allow nighttime stragglers to pass before continuing with his unconscious load.

They approached the first pub. *The Staghorn* was written in faded white ink on the sign outside the entrance. One solitary window in the front of the establishment offered a view of the thinning crowd. As he'd hoped, Kal spied two males in the signature crimson cloaks worn by militia inside near the bar, engrossed by one of the barmaids.

He smirked. This was too easy. Santhe was all tied up with worry and for what? He'd give her no small amount of grief for it later.

Railah twitched slightly, and Kal glanced down at her. She lay still. He paused in the shadow of a high wooden fence separating two buildings and watched her. If she woke now, he'd have to adjust his strategy to account for potential resistance. She didn't move again. Her chest rose and fell with even breaths, and her heart beat a relaxed rhythm. He spared another glance for the soldiers through the window. They were still engaged. He continued on-ward.

The next mile went without incident. Railah remained soundly sleeping, and Kal encountered no one of consequence. He'd had to sidestep one drunken shurii who had wandered down the street, but the man couldn't even hold his head straight, let alone raise it to look at Kal with any amount of suspicion.

The first phase of the evening was nearly complete. He had to pass by one more pub, and then he'd have no more busy streets to navigate on the way to Brune's stable. There would be little chance of him encountering anyone in the industrial district at this hour. At Brune's, he'd gather his belongings, find some way to get Railah onto a horse, and escape the city by the eastern road. Beyond the gates of Asteros, the desert wilderness would claim them, and by then, it would be too late. They'd be long gone. He would finally be able to take a full breath.

Kal approached the final straightaway and noted the distant change in surroundings. Markets and business structures gave way to large, empty, fenced-in properties, storehouses, feed lots, and livestock yards. The industrial district.

At the corner just ahead, the road came to a tee. To the right, the street would curve and head back toward the main district: Madame's, The Starlight Lodge, The Dovetail, where Santhe would be working the bar, the entrance to the gardens, and other various whorehouses, bars, shops, and cafes. To the left was the heart of the industrial district, Brune's, and freedom from this wretched city. On the lefthand corner stood the final tavern he had to pass.

Even before Kal approached, he could tell there were more occupants than he cared for. The noise behind the closed door made him wish he could avoid the place entirely. He saw no soldiers and could only hope they were inside, equally distracted from the goings on outdoors as their colleagues at The Staghorn.

Kal kept an even pace, moving past the tavern. He would have absolutely no cover for about thirty seconds before turning the corner and vanishing down the darker eastern road.

A few things happened simultaneously.

Two soldiers burst through the tavern door with a loud bang, laughing at some private quip. Railah tensed and opened her eyes. Kal looked down into startled gold-green orbs, and a female-sized fist flew right toward his face.

Kal was so startled by the flash of pain in his nose that he nearly dropped her.

She fucking punched him! For a fraction of a second, he stared at her, incredulous.

The guards noticed the odd commotion in the exposed street and moved toward them curiously. They each moved a hand to identical swords. Kal tried to turn away from them, blocking Railah with his body to prevent them from seeing her, but he hadn't accounted for *her* seeing *them*.

She screamed. "Help! Guards! Help me!"

Was she out of her fucking mind? Kal put her down, threw his cloak over her own to disguise the sunburst on its front, and smothered her next scream with a hand over her mouth. "Shut up, you stupid girl!" he hissed. "You'll get us killed."

She tried to yell behind his hand and it came out a muffled cry. He had half a mind to strangle her and be done with it.

"You! Stop there!" One of the guards yelled.

Fucking divine. He waved his free hand behind him in a casual gesture. "Nothing amiss, sirs. Just making our way home."

Please fucking go back inside. He shoved Railah forward. She locked her knees and dug in her heels, pushing against him.

"Hey! I said stop. Release the lady."

Kal closed his eyes, cursing his rotten luck. His imagination procured an image of Santhe's face wearing her signature "told you so" expression. Railah struggled to free herself from his grip, and his cloak slipped off her shoulders. Of all the ungrateful, ill-tempered, self-sabotaging females he could have been tasked with retrieving...

He glanced over his shoulder, looking toward the guard, and knew he would be fighting his way out of this one. They were well past effective negotiations, thanks to his mouthy companion. The guard on the right saw Railah's cloak, and recognition flared in his eyes.

"A Fate!" he hollered. "There's a Fate trying to escape!"

Both guards drew their swords. Two more soldiers exited the tavern to investigate the commotion outside. Somewhere down the street, a call went up. "He's got a Fate! That man's helping a Fate escape! Guards! Call the guards!"

Normally, four against one were odds he'd accept without issue. However, Railah began struggling in earnest, inconveniently cured of her prior exhaustion. He had to run for it. If he stopped to fight, he might be able to make quick work of the soldiers, but he couldn't both fight them and keep hold of Railah.

He let go of her mouth so he could grab her around the middle with both hands, intending to hoist her over his shoulder. Kal regretted it a moment later.

"Let go of me! Guards! Help! Help me! I've been abducted!"

He shook her once, hard, and her jaw clicked. "Shut up, or I'll kill you myself," he snarled. No female was worth being captured by the crown, sister of a friend or not. "Got it?"

She gaped at him.

He didn't waste another moment. Kal turned and swiped the bow off his back with one fluid movement while concertedly grasping a barbed arrow from his quiver. It was the practiced work of a moment to notch the fletching, aim, and fire. A second more to release another. The first arrow took the closest guard in the neck. The male had barely begun to fall before Kal's next shot found his companion through the eye. Never take off your helmet while on duty. Domitan's general needed to maintain better discipline among his ranks.

The two soldiers that had most recently exited the pub stood shocked, taking a moment too long to process the bloody scene before them.

Amateurs. The most violence they'd ever seen was likely a tavern brawl. They had certainly never been in a real battle. Never seen their allies and fellow soldiers cut down around them.

Unfortunately for Kal, their hesitation didn't last long. One soldier ducked back behind the safety of the pub's solid door, and the second took cover behind a metal water trough. Kal could have killed them. Would have killed them, but the call had gone up, and reinforcements were undoubtedly inbound. He couldn't waste precious time angling for a better shot while Railah made it clear she had no intention of complying with his escape.

Kal took advantage of the guards' temporary retreat. With a growl of frustration, he grabbed Railah from where she stood, stunned, watching the spray of blood that matched the soldiers' crimson cloaks. Kal tossed her unceremoniously over his shoulder and took off down the street without a backward glance.

CLOAKING FATE

What felt like a blur later, Kalevar boomed through Brune's stable doors and dumped Railah onto a bale of hay. It was a wonder he hadn't torn the barn door off its track he was so angry. The horses whinnied at being startled awake, rolled their eyes, and danced nervously in their stalls.

He rounded on her. "You idiot female. Are you *trying* to get us killed?"

She scrambled to her feet, putting distance between them. "Not us," she retorted. "Just you."

She *was* an idiot. Fantastic. Kal knew her beauty could only be skin deep. She was just as obtuse as her damn brother. He had rescued a simpleton with a bad attitude. Didn't she know the soldiers in the street would have killed her as quickly as him? She was no use to the crown on the run. Not when she could have revealed all of their twisted secrets. The royals prized the Fates as long as they did what they were told. If they stepped out of line? Those females were as expendable as a lame horse, easily put down and replaced. All she had to do was keep her damned mouth shut, let him talk their way through the soldiers' initial curiosity, and they'd be free to escape unscathed.

Now, instead, they had two guards likely close on their tail, two more dead in the street, and an alarm gone up through the city about a missing Fate. Reinforcements would be moments behind. The whole fucking army would be mobilized to prevent their passing through the city gates.

They had to leave. They had to leave immediately.

Kal hurried to the closest stall, the one housing the massive roan.

A disgruntled Brune appeared, holding a lamp above his head, the light casting his disheveled figure in an amber glow. They'd woken him, and he looked none too pleased.

"What in the clucking blazes is going on out here?"

Railah gathered herself and ran to the stablemaster. "Please, sir!" she implored. "This man has taken me captive. He means to molest me! Help me, please! I beg you!"

Molest her?

Brune blinked at her in surprise and then squinted in Kal's direction, where he was saddling Sig. "Kal? What's the meaning o' this?"

Kal tossed him a hard look and then shot one toward Railah that promised violence. She stepped behind Brune, using his body as a shield of sorts. "There isn't time," he said, biting off each word. "I need the bay. We need to leave."

He'd made a quick retreat from the tavern after putting the soldiers down. If they were lucky, they wouldn't be immediately found. If they were *really* lucky, they'd be on their way out of Asteros before the soldiers even made it to Brune's stable to inquire about fugitives in the area. The last thing he wanted was to bring the royal army to the male's doorstep.

Brune grumbled and swiped a meaty hand over his ruddy face. "Clucking slop buckets," he groaned. "I told ye I didn't want any trouble, Kal. Do ye have any clue what time it is?"

Kal gave him another stare, and whatever was in his eyes made Brune take off toward the far end of the stable to gather the gelding, grumbling to himself. Railah looked after him, mouth agape, limbs trembling.

"You killed them," she accused. "You killed the soldiers in the street."

Kal didn't answer as he cinched the saddle and checked the fastening on the bags. Sig, the roan, tossed his handsome red head. His eyes rolled wildly. Kal patted the thick column of his neck.

"Oh gods, you're in on this together. You planned it," she continued as though to herself. Brune hurried back from the depths of the stable, the bay gelding in tow. They were running out of time.

Kal moved to the second horse and threw a saddle onto its back. In a few moments, the creature was ready. He gathered both reins at the withers with one hand, then held his other out for Railah.

She didn't move.

"Up," he commanded.

She shook her head and stepped back.

Kal gritted his teeth. "Now. Please." The courtesy nearly killed him.

"I don't know how to ride."

"You will learn tonight."

She shook her head again. Blasted female.

"I will tie you onto this horse if I must."

"I'm not going anywhere with you," she insisted.

Brune looked between them, evidently trying and failing to deduce how they had become affiliated.

Kal had enough. He strode toward her. She darted faster than he'd have given her credit for, but not in his direction. She lunged at an unsuspecting, sleep-deprived Brune and, a moment later, brandished his hatchet at the two of them.

"Hey!" exclaimed the stablemaster.

Railah swiped the hatchet once in front of her. "I said I'm not going."

An angry fist thundered on the front barn door. They all three looked toward the sound. The horses shied from the clamor, and Kal gripped them tightly to keep them from bolting.

"Open up! In the name of King Domitan!"

Brune shot Kal a look of fierce accusation. "Soldiers, Kal? Ye brought clucking *soldiers* to my stable?"

"Here! I'm in here!" Railah yelled.

Kal was going to kill her. He was going to kill her and dump her miserable corpse right in her brother's lap.

A moment later, the glass pane of a high front window shattered. The roan kicked out, and Kal dodged, narrowly avoiding a dangerous hoof.

"Here!" Railah shrieked again, holding the hatchet aloft.

The soldier in the broken window aimed. Railah's elated expression turned to horror in the split second it took her to realize the arrow he wielded was pointed at her.

Kal dropped the reins and lunged forward. A horse reared. He gripped Railah's cloak and jerked her to the side. A crossbow snapped. The bolt intended for Railah whistled past her and took the gelding behind the shoulder. The horse screamed in pain and terror.

Railah turned, gasped, and watched as the poor creature went down, its lung flooding with blood.

Brune yelled.

Kal jerked a knife free from its sheath at his waist and hurtled it through the air. The soldier disappeared from the window. He grabbed Railah, her knuckles gone white where they still gripped the hatchet, and all but threw her onto the roan's saddle. He turned back, reaching for Brune, intending to load him onto Sig as a second passenger. The two of them could find a safe place to wait while he took care of the soldiers outside.

The stablemaster looked over his shoulder, opened his mouth, and gurgled. Bloody foam coated his lips and slid into his beard. A bolt protruded from his chest.

No. *No. Godsdamn it, no!*

Kal reached the stout older male right as his knees gave out. He lay Brune back on the cobblestones. Kal gripped the bolt's shaft, and the male's eyes flared wide. He grunted and shook his head once violently.

"I'll pull it free." Even as he said it, Kal knew it was pointless. Brune took a direct hit from a double crossbow. He knew the kind of barbed tip that graced the shafts of the projectile weapons Domitan favored for his militia. The head was buried somewhere deep in Brune's chest. By the bright, bloody spittle that leaked from his mouth, it was somewhere vital.

"Fuck!" Kal hammered a fist into the stone floor.

Behind him, Railah clutched Sig's saddle as the beast snorted and tossed his head. He smelled blood. The bay gelding finally stopped screaming and lay still.

"Go," Brune choked. "Burn it. Those fu...cking cunts can't...have my...b...barn."

The stablemaster clutched the edge of Kal's leather jerkin and struggled to focus on Kal's face, trying to communicate his resolve. It was a plea—a final request to prevent the crown from seizing his property. Brune had no more clucks to give. This was the male's one last authentic fuck you to Domitan.

Kal would see it done. The male deserved whatever Kal could give him.

The front door shuddered under renewed pounding.

"Go!" Brune gurgled. He used the last bit of his strength to shove Kal away from him. The light of awareness faded from his eyes, a wet rattle left his lungs, and the stablemaster lay still.

Kal pushed to his feet. His fisted hands itched to become claws. A snarl lodged in his throat. He could kill them. He could tear them all to pieces in a blink.

Instead, he made himself move to the nearest stall. He forced the claws back beneath the surface of his skin and unlatched the door. The dun horse inside showed him the whites of its eyes. It knew a predator when it saw one.

Kal darted from stall to stall, making quick work of the doors, setting the frightened beasts free. The horses flooded the center aisle of the barn, crowding each other.

He ran back to where Railah sat elevated in the herd, her eyes as terrified as the beasts' surrounding her. Sig lay his ears flat and bit into the rump of a black gelding that bumped him. Kal reached up and grabbed the front of Railah's starlight cloak.

That damning cloak.

"No!" she yelled, but he wasn't after her. He broke the clasp on the front, and the midnight fabric fell from her shoulders. He spread it over Brune's body, rested a palm on the male's chest next to the bolt, and murmured farewell. Then he retrieved the lamp Brune had carried from his room, shattered the casing, and tossed it into the hay.

The front door thundered. The soldiers were nearly through.

The straw ignited. Hungry flames lapped at the dry wood of the barn posts, the hay fueling its destructive rage. The animals shrieked in terror as smoke began to fill the space.

Kal strode to Sig and swung himself up into the saddle behind Railah. The beast moved purposely through the herd toward the rear exit. The other horses sensed the shift and mirrored Sig's direction.

Kal rode up to the rear door, threw the latch, and shoved it aside. Four guards were waiting, and they rushed the opening, but the fear of the captive horses was a tangible, driving force. They broke, galloping out of the smoke-filled barn, ravenous flames growing to an all-consuming inferno behind them. Kal imagined they must look like a cavalry burst free from the depths of the underworld, his burning red stallion leading the charge. The soldiers dashed to the side to avoid being trampled. One wasn't quick enough and fell under Sig's flashing hooves. He heard the male's pelvis crack.

More bolts flew in their direction. Kal forced Sig to the center of the herd, intentionally using the other livestock to prevent them from making an easy target. The horse to their left was hit in the flank, and it went wild, kicking, rearing, and throwing iron-clad feet. Kal let Sig run with the herd past the remaining soldiers who guarded the rear exit. They galloped, and then the herd turned as if to loop back toward the other soldiers streaming around the sides of the barn from the front. Kal counted nine. Not the entire army, then. Not yet.

Kal urged their mount forward, toward the dirt road and the dark. Horses were herd animals. To leave the safety of the group was to die. Sig didn't even break stride. He broke from the rest and plunged down the path at his rider's command, away from the shouting of King Domitan's guards, away from the stable that was now wholly wreathed in flame. Forward, they rode into darkness, swallowed by the black of night, leaving safety burning behind them.

Chapter 19

Escape

FELÍNE LOOKED TOWARD THE HORIZON, the black silhouette of mountains nearly invisible in the distance against the still-dark sky. A thunderhead spit flashes of lightning that briefly illuminated the desert landscape, far enough away that she couldn't feel the storm's effects but close enough that she knew it was coming. There was no wind, no rain, but she could smell the moisture in the air, and they were riding directly into it. The first monsoon of the season would soon be upon them, and if her judgment of the sky were any indication, they would be wise to seek some form of shelter. The region's monsoons were notoriously brief but fierce, and when they hit, they hit hard, drenching the parched landscape in rain that could turn into dangerous floods and mudslides within minutes.

The sky overhead was clouded, the stars and moon obscured from view. She couldn't say the hour was late anymore. They'd likely ridden into the morning but were still hours from welcoming the sun.

The way she currently felt, it might never rise again. That thundercloud was here for her. Ominous and foreboding. A punishment for her curiosity, her betrayal of the Goddess and birthright. It made her positively morose.

The knuckles of Felíne's right hand were white where she still clutched the hatchet's handle, stubbornly refusing to release it. The solid wooden shaft was currently her only comfort, and she was loath to give it up. She gripped the saddle of the monstrous red horse beneath her with her left and shifted her weight ever so slightly. The tiny movement was more habit than anything. Her butt had gone numb an hour ago, and any attempts to restore feeling were futile. Besides, anything more than a subtle shift in her position brought her painful awareness of the man seated behind her. A hard wall composed of chest and torso was to her back, strong, muscled arms rested on either side of her, large hands gripping the reins, and powerful thighs braced her own smaller ones. She could feel them flex and tense, and the roan beast would change gait, shift position, or alter their course. Some odd form of communication that she was excluded from.

Felíne was not a slight female; she'd never been petite. But the man whose body currently caged her made her feel dwarfed. She'd never felt so small. So helpless. She shuddered at the thought of encountering him in his second form, considering how imposing he was in his first.

Felíne didn't turn to glance behind her, but she knew what she would find if she did: The lights of Asteros winking out one by one, the wall surrounding the city growing smaller and smaller before it was finally swallowed by the span of terrain behind them. Their increasing distance erasing the city from the landscape altogether. No more sun-drenched palace, no more mandatory lessons, no more secret trips to work in the clinics, no more forbidden visits to an enchanting botanical garden by the light of the moon. It was all falling farther and farther behind her with every step.

Felíne had no idea how she'd get back to it.

She'd gone to those gardens seeking a moment of freedom. Instead, she had traded one form of captivity for another. The difference was, she knew her previous prison. She was precious there, protected. Here, she was exposed. Outside the city gates, far from the palace walls, she was completely at the mercy of her captor. She hadn't a clue what his intentions were, and he'd given no indication that he planned to discuss them.

He simply sat behind her, silent as death, guiding their mount into the approaching storm. A thundercloud in his own right. He'd been this way since their escape from the city.

How exactly that escape had been achieved, Felíne wasn't sure. If she was honest with herself, she hadn't wanted to know. Still didn't. They'd galloped away from the burning wreck of the stable and down a dark, deserted road. Structures flashed by them. They had made several turns, came to abrupt stops, and then launched into flight once more. She had been so preoccupied with holding herself in the saddle without dropping her stolen weapon that she couldn't even begin to keep track of where they were. But who was she kidding? She wouldn't have known even if she'd followed the same path on a leisurely stroll in the middle of broad daylight.

Before she knew it, they'd come to a halt between towering rows of great wooden casks stacked fifteen feet high. There were hundreds of them. Some sort of storage yard on the edge of the city. Beyond the shadowed aisles, she could make out a wooden gate in what appeared to be a perimeter wall. It was large enough to fit two sizeable wagons passing through side by side but not grand by any means, almost nondescript. Four guards stood at attention on the ground in front, weapons sheathed but ready, their gazes darting around, watching for any sign of movement or threat.

Her male captor had slid from the saddle behind her and pulled the horse back farther into the shelter of the barrel rows until the gate and its guards were no longer visible. The male gripped her leg with a broad hand, and she jumped in surprise, making the horse shy away. He held her fast. His voice was quiet but its menace was unmistakable.

"You will wait here until I return. Do not scream. Do not run."

Felíne had given him her best impassive stare. He really thought she'd just sit here and wait for him? When her father's guards were only a stone's throw away? Fool.

The male seemed to sense the direction of her thoughts, and he narrowed his gaze. "Don't even think about it."

Perhaps she didn't do impassive very well. Felíne tried scowling instead.

"Those guards will not save you from me." He leaned closer. "And if you disobey me again, nothing will. I have your scent. There is nowhere you can hide that I cannot find you."

She hadn't been able to formulate a response. Half of her wanted to scream at him in fury, the other half wanted to scream in fear, and so she just stared at him mutely, not trusting herself to make any noise at all.

His eyes were like two burning coals inside the hood of his cloak as they bored into her own. "You saw what I did to the guards in the street?"

Her mind helpfully thrust the image of a soldier holding his neck, bright arterial spray squirting between his useless fingers, painting the stones crimson.

She swallowed involuntarily and nodded.

"Good. Remember it."

188

In other words, let that be your motivation to stay put.

Fine.

She saw how accurate he was with a crossbow. Had seen how quickly he'd thrown that knife at the guard in the barn window. The man hadn't even taken time to aim. He'd just swung his arm overhead in a terrifying arc of speed, and a moment later, the soldier in the window had fallen back, never to get up again.

Felíne wanted nothing more than to escape this nightmare, but she wasn't deluded. If she tried to run, she would be running blind. She knew no one, no one knew her, and she was clueless as to her whereabouts. Felíne was completely lost inside her city. A stranger in her hometown. She was born here and had lived here her entire life, yet she was an outsider. The thought made her feel some strange combination of disgust, regret, and anger. No, she couldn't run. If she did, he would most certainly find her, and the very last thing she wanted was to be the object of this male's single-minded attention.

At least if she stayed put, she might have a chance at escaping in the future. She had a weapon, and if she bided her time, she would eventually get an opportunity to use it. More importantly, her decision to stay and wait put only herself in danger. If she tried to escape and seek the help of someone else, this male would inevitably kill whomever she allied with. There were enough lost lives on her conscience. He clearly didn't suffer any reservations snuffing them out, but she wouldn't give him an excuse to take any more on her behalf.

Felíne looked away from him and stared ahead, mustering up as much resigned defiance as she could. She could feel him watching her a moment longer, his eyes burning a hole into the side of her face, then he slunk off into the shadows and left her alone.

Felíne let out a breath. She sat on the horse and tried to be still. Her mount's ears twitched, turning this way and that as he listened for the slightest sounds.

She considered inching forward again, not to gain attention, but to see what, if anything, was happening. Then she remembered the dying soldiers and figured it was best to play the obedient prisoner—for now. Maybe it would throw her captor off guard enough to allow her a chance to take advantage of him.

So, she sat and listened and waited.

It wasn't long before her mind began to wander. She let it, needing some form of distraction from the silence of the night and the fear that had begun worming its way through her.

If she wanted to get herself out of this mess, she needed a plan, and she would need to execute it herself. Felíne decided she couldn't rely on someone else to rescue her. She had already tried, and her earlier attempts this evening had proved disastrous. Her cry for help had only resulted in the deaths of three guards and one stablemaster, who may or may not have been entirely innocent.

Don't forget your own near death.

Of course. The soldier in the window.

How could she? The look in his eyes would likely haunt her dreams for the rest of her life.

She'd been so thrilled they had come for her. So relieved that her nightmarish capture would be a thing of the past. The soldiers would valiantly defeat her enemies and then escort her back to the castle, where her family would fuss over her safe return. This whole affair would be an unbelievable story that she could tell.

And then she had seen the guard's face. The cold determination, the anger. No one had ever looked at her that way. He had looked like a man on the verge of glory, a trigger pull away from putting down a loathsome criminal. He'd aimed that huge crossbow, and it hadn't been at her captor. Hadn't even been at the stablemaster. The soldier had pointed his deadly weapon directly at her. Right at the center of her chest. Time had frozen in that moment and suddenly, all of her status, importance, and prestige evaporated as if it had never been. She was no longer the Prima. In that moment, she was a no-name female wearing a pretty cloak, and she was going to die. She'd been sure of it. The soldier she thought might be her savior would become her slayer instead.

Then, without warning, her body had been jerked to the side, and the bolts meant for her had instead taken a poor horse and an unfortunate bystander.

190

The man. He'd saved her. But why?

Perhaps a ransom. If she had a hefty price tag attached to her head, she'd be no good to him dead. Whatever price was asked, the crown would pay it. Of that, she was certain. Maybe he was a member of the Cozened, and her capture was intended to further some form of treasonous political agenda. Maybe he was simply selfish, saw something he liked, and decided he wanted her for himself.

Yet, he'd saved her and sacrificed another. Knowingly or not, that second bolt had killed someone he knew. The stablemaster had been a friend of his—an acquaintance at the very least.

Guilt twinged inside her. There was nothing she could have done, even if she hadn't been frozen in shock. The twin of the bolt that took the stablemaster in the chest had put down a twelve-hundred-pound animal. He hadn't stood a chance.

That death had pained him, her captor.

Kal. The bearded horse keeper had called him Kal.

Well, perhaps that was one thing in her favor. She had a name, at least. Or part of one. If she was smart, kept her emotions under control, and used her brain, she could survive this. She could get away.

As though her thoughts had summoned him, Kal had emerged from the shadows like an apparition.

He didn't say two words to her, but his eyes appraised her with the fleetest moment of speculation, and then he was swinging up behind her in the saddle and urging his devoted steed forward out of the gloom. He expected her to try and make a run for it. Maybe she should have.

Felíne looked around. The place was deserted. Sconces were lit with torches on either side of the gateway, which stood open, and there wasn't a guard in sight. There was no blood, the ground was undisturbed, and there were no signs of a struggle. None that her unpracticed eyes could determine, anyway. It was as if the soldiers had never existed. The road was clear, the night was calm, and the mouth of the gate yawned ahead, beckoning them through.

Anxiety bit at her. Something was wrong with this.

"What did you do with them?" She'd whispered.

Kal ignored her.

Did she really want to know?

No. She didn't.

She did not ask again, and he did not offer any explanation. He kicked his heels into the horse's flanks, and they shot through the gate, out of the city, and into the desert.

And in the desert, they remained, with the Asteros border now far behind them and not a single soldier in pursuit.

They turned off the main road leading out of the city some time ago and were winding their way through the terrain toward a rocky mountain range. Felíne wondered if Kal knew where he was going because everything around her looked the same, and they weren't following any discernible path.

It was dark here. So dark, Felíne thought they could walk straight off the edge of a cliff and not even realize until they were falling to their deaths. Everything existed in shadows. She could make out shadows of native plant life, shadows of the mountains on the horizon, shadows of the clouds that drifted in front of the moon, smothering the glow. Every once in a while, lightning would spark, and the gray thundercloud in the distance flashed in stark relief, appearing to billow upward like smoke pouring from the well of a giant cauldron buried somewhere beyond the skyline. The storm was closer.

Their initial pace had been grueling. Felíne had been terrified for a long while that she would be thrown from the saddle, and she'd nearly tossed the hatchet so she could use both hands to hold on. She was glad she hadn't. Eventually, they slowed into a loping canter that lasted for miles. Finally, they settled into a brisk walk, the roan weaving between the dense thorny shrubs and cacti that peppered the landscape. His sides heaved, and she could see the sweat darkening the red and white hairs on his neck.

If they didn't stop soon, the horse might collapse from exhaustion, and she could kiss escaping goodbye. Forget trying to run away. If she didn't get out of this saddle, she'd never walk properly again.

A deafening crack thundered overhead. Felíne jumped, her back pressing briefly against her silent companion's wall of leather-clad muscle. He clicked his tongue and pressed his calves into the roan's flank, urging the overworked animal to increase their speed. The horse valiantly picked up the pace.

Felíne could barely make out a rocky outcropping ahead of them. The jagged outline of huge boulders was visible if she squinted hard enough. Another flash of lightning lit up the landscape, and she briefly saw the mountainside. That was close. Thunder and lightning were directly overhead, but there was no rain. Maybe they'd get lucky and avoid the typical deluge that accompanied such storms.

As soon as the thought entered her mind, they loped straight into a wall of water. The rain of the Saraat Desert monsoons didn't sprinkle. It didn't even pour. It crashed to the earth in great sheets, flooding the hard, packed surface. The ground was so dry throughout the summer months that when rain finally did fall, there wasn't enough residual moisture in the soil to absorb the torrent quickly enough. All that water accumulated so swiftly that new temporary rivers with muddy rapids could form within minutes, following a path of least resistance, sweeping away anything in its vicinity. They were drenched in a matter of moments.

The monsoon rains brought relief from the heat, but the water remained comfortably warm. She remembered running out into the courtyards as a child, playing in the rain until an elder, her mother, or an attendant forced her inside. She wasn't comfortable now. She was soaked and suffered a chill that had nothing to do with the temperature. If they didn't get to higher ground soon, escaping her kidnapper would be the least of her concerns.

The horse picked his way through the muddy trail. His front legs lifted, and he threw his muscled chest into the effort of raising each hoof. They were climbing. The ground was becoming less packed earth and more rocky hardscape.

A swell of dirty water swept toward them up to their mount's ankles. It wasn't deep, but it crashed into them with unexpected force. The horse slipped, one knee going down, and Felíne's world pitched forward. She barely managed to keep herself seated. They slid backward.

The horse righted himself with a grunt of effort and began trudging up the precarious slope. That's it. She reached forward and patted the thick neck in encouragement. Felíne sat back and met open air. The body that had been seated behind her was gone.

Her captor. Oh gods, had he been thrown?

CLOAKING FATE

Felíne twisted in the saddle, searching the ground. It was still pitch black, but the lightning flashes lit the sky every few seconds, and with each burst of light, she strained to see. All around her were rock and mud and plants either facing their last monsoon or enduring their hundredth. The initial flood had slowed, and only an inch or so covered the ground, flowing downhill. She wrenched the other way. Craned herself completely around and braced one hand on the rear ridge of the saddle to try and see behind them.

She couldn't see him. Felíne kept imagining a prone body, face buried in mud, but the image didn't manifest in reality. What if he was gone? She had a moment of irrational indignation. How dare he go through all that trouble to capture her, keep her alive, sneak her out of the city, and then die on her in the middle of the desert. How was she supposed to get home? She didn't even know where she was or how to return to the main road. Would she even recognize the main road if she saw it? How would she eat? She'd die a slow, miserable death out here of starvation or heatstroke or rattlesnake bite.

Then again, this could be her chance. Surely, their horse had enough sense to get them back to civilization. Even if she didn't know the way, maybe if she turned them around, her mount would take her back the way they came. Asteros had to be the closest city. They couldn't have traveled *that* far in a few hours. By then, someone would undoubtedly be looking for her. A spark of hope flickered to life inside her, and she guarded it, refusing to let it extinguish.

They were suddenly lurched forward, and Felíne twisted back to face the front.

He hadn't drowned or been swept away. Kal had dismounted and was pulling their horse up the mountainside, guiding the exhausted creature on foot. The man was woven with threads of pure determination. Goddess, damn him.

She wasn't sure whether she should feel relief or regret, but she released a shaky breath.

Mercifully, the rain slowed. It was still falling but had gentled to a steady shower. Kal led their mount to the right and between a crevice in the rock that she never would have noticed if she hadn't been passing through it. The path briefly narrowed to an uncomfortable degree and then widened again.

One more turn and the rain stopped pouring. Felíne looked up to find the sky was gone. They were under a great outcropping of rock, a makeshift cave carved into the side of the mountain.

If Felíne thought it was dark out in the open, she was fully blind here. How Kal saw anything at all, she had no idea.

He led them a bit deeper into the cavern before they stopped. She sat there atop the horse, not sure what to do. Felíne heard shuffling behind her and turned. He was removing the saddle bags.

After a few more moments of Kal moving about the cave and her remaining in the saddle, his voice filled the space. It came from somewhere ahead and to her left.

"We will stay here for the night."

Felíne didn't move. She'd be sleeping here. In a cave. In the same space as this…man. A dangerous, murderous, terrifying man. But a *man*. It was unthinkable.

"Are you going to dismount, or do you plan on sitting there until morning?"

The voice was much closer now. Too close. She startled a little, and the roan snorted. Would she sit here all night? Yes. Yes, she would. With her hatchet. And he could sleep by himself in the far corner. Felíne cleared her throat. "I'm fine right here, thank you very much."

Was she being childish? Yes. Yes, she was.

"You may be fine, but my horse has earned a reprieve from the burden of his saddle."

Oh.

"And your ass."

Oh. Felíne scowled. Ass.

A hand reached forward and firmly found the one of hers that wasn't holding a weapon. She thought sincerely about snatching it away from him, but concern for the creature she sat atop outweighed her stubbornness. She allowed Kal to guide her down from the back of the horse until she was standing on her own two feet. It was only because she was soaking wet, exhausted, frightened, and disoriented from the darkness. At least, that's what she told herself.

She stepped tentatively away from the horse and clutched the hatchet with both hands. A moment later, there was a spark, and a small torch flared to life, bathing the cavern in a flickering red glow. Kal held the torch out to her, his face still masked by the hood of his cloak, which dripped residual rainwater onto the dirt floor. Gods, he was huge. And menacing.

"Take this and go sit by the bags." He gestured to the side.

Felíne took the torch from him and backed away to where he mentioned.

"I'll need more than a single burning stick if I am going to get dry and stay warm," she remarked.

"Your comforts are not my priority," Kal said as he continued unsaddling the horse. "His are."

Felíne's mouth opened in indignation. The nerve!

When he was finished, and the saddle was set aside, Kal spread the saddle blanket onto the ground. He rummaged in one of the bags and procured a stiff, bristled brush, which he held out to her.

Felíne just looked at it. First, he insulted her, and now he wanted her assistance? He was mentally inept if he thought she'd relinquish her hatchet in favor of a grooming tool. Not only that, but the torch was her only means of sight.

"Look, you can either wait for me to finish rubbing him down before I make a proper fire, or you can help."

Felíne gripped the weapon tighter. He tracked the movement of her fingers. "If I meant to take it from you, I'd have done so when you first stole it."

Kal still held the brush.

Felíne thought a moment longer, and a shiver worked its way down her frame. She was tired and sore, but she did need a proper fire. She took the brush.

Fifteen minutes later, the exhausted equine, named Sig, was dozing on his feet on one side of the cave, thoroughly brushed, watered, and fed, and a modest fire was burning on the other side, surrounded by a crude circle of stones. Kal had dry kindling in one of his bags, which had been treated with a thick salve that burned for hours. He'd left the cave to collect additional firewood while she rubbed Sig's short coat. When he returned, he stacked the cut wood in a neat pile against the wall to dry.

Kal undid his bedroll and laid it on one side of the fire. The saddle blanket was on the other. He removed his cloak and wrung the fabric out to remove the excess water near the entrance to the rocky overhang. It was still raining.

When he returned to the fire, Felíne had to make a conscious effort not to stare.

His face was fully visible, and she had time to properly study his appearance for the first time since he'd abducted her. What she found completely caught her off guard. She'd expected brutish, blunted features comprised of an ugliness that mirrored her image of his actions. She hadn't expected...*this*.

Kal's skin was light mocha, a shade darker than tan, as if he'd been caramelized by hours spent in the sun. He had shortish dark brown hair that hinted at soft, unruly curls if it were left to grow, longer on top and down the back and gradually fading into a closely cropped length near his ears. An interesting pattern of lines and symbols she didn't recognize was cut precisely into his hairline on the left side. His eyes were two obsidian pools, so dark they were nearly black, intelligent and profound, set under a heavy brow. He had a straight, masculine nose that widened at the nostrils and a generous mouth with a fuller bottom lip. His jaw was an angled set of lines that met at a strong chin. Short dark hair covered his jawline and framed his chin in a slight goatee, too short to grab but dense enough to add a bit of rugged appeal. He had the kind of face that would kick a female's ovaries into production on instinct. Kal wasn't just masculine; he was *made* of masculinity. There was nothing soft about him. He was all harsh lines and broad planes and strong structure.

Women likely fantasized about that face.

Felíne wasn't excluded. But her fantasy involved his face and the very sharp blade of her hatchet. Shame.

Kal began unfastening the front of his leather jerkin. In a moment, he shrugged out of it and laid it out by the fire. Felíne watched, transfixed, as he tugged on the hem of his tunic and pulled it over his head in one fluid movement. His bare torso twisted, abdominal muscles flexing as he set the shirt next to his vest. She could see the individual muscles cut into his ribs and the distinct outline of his pectorals, dusted in short dark curls that trailed down in a wide line that narrowed at his navel and traveled farther down to his...

"What are you doing?" she asked in alarm.

Kal's hands paused at the hem of his pants, where he was loosening the tie. He looked up at her, half-naked, a severe expression on his face.

"You may prefer to sleep in wet clothes, but I do not."

Another shiver wracked her. She wasn't sure if it was a chill from the drop in temperature or if it had an entirely different cause.

"Keep your pants on at least," she said.

He gave a yank, eyes not leaving her face, and peeled his trousers off his muscular thighs. Those, too, joined his other clothes by the fire where his boots were already drying. Felíne averted her eyes and felt her face flush absurdly. She would not look at him. It was positively indecent.

A rustling sound reached her, and she peeked over at him. She caught a glimpse of short, fitted briefs molded to a glorious backside before Kal pulled the saddle blanket over himself and turned his back to her.

She shivered again. Definitely the temperature.

Felíne sat by the fire, fully intending to sit awake all night if she had to. Kal's weapons had been set aside, but they were within arms reach of where he lay. She was willing to bet all her sopping clothes that if there was the slightest disturbance, he would be armed within a fraction of a second, pants or no.

Her determination didn't last long. A soul-deep exhaustion settled over her. She was tired, hungry, scared, wet, and uncomfortable. She squelched when she moved. How in the world was she supposed to execute a sneak attack when she sounded like that? The bedroll Kal had left for her sat at her feet. It was no down coverlet, but it looked warm, and it was dry. She glanced over at him. His back was to her, and his side rose and fell in an even rhythm.

Sleeping.

Fine then. Recover her strength tonight, plot murder, and escape tomorrow. She'd dry her clothes, but only so she didn't freeze to death. She couldn't very well run for freedom if she came down with pneumonia. It wasn't like she had a spare wardrobe, and as loath as she was to undress, she was even more loath to sit there soaked, shivering, and sleep-deprived. She'd keep her hatchet close in case he got any crude ideas.

Felíne quickly stripped down to her undergarments, laid her tunic, leggings, stockings, and gown out neatly by the fire, and burrowed into the bedroll. All her fear couldn't keep her weariness away. In that moment, the thin bedding on the hard ground was more comfortable than the most luxurious mattress. Within a few minutes, she drifted into a fitful sleep, the hatchet clutched to her chest and a burning black gaze haunting her dreams.

Chapter 20

The King

DOMITAN FAELSTROM, HIGH KING OF Asteros, The Shield of the Realm, and Head of the Crown, stood over the smoldering corpse at his feet and surveyed it with cool regard. He toed the edge of what was once a limb with the tip of his boot. The charred body part crumbled to ash, revealing the cracked brownish-gray bone beneath.

The barn on the eastern edge of Asteros was ruined, as was everything within it. Fallen beams reinforced with steel and the remains of half-scorched stalls littered the space. The blackened body of a horse smoked not far away, legs drawn up close to the body as if in mid-gallop. A crow perched on its shoulder and picked at its seared flesh. The acrid smell of burned wood and flesh hung in the air like a toxic miasma, refusing to dissipate. The roof was half caved in. The walls stood by sheer crude stubbornness, the adobe foundation refusing to yield entirely, while the lumber had been mostly incinerated.

Brune's establishment had never been a grand place. The dogged stablemaster had tried his best to establish his business as a fierce competitor to the king's royal stables and failed quite miserably. The only thing he'd ever succeeded in was proving himself a mild annoyance to the king by trying to sabotage his business pursuits. 'Trying' being the operative word. Even at that, he hadn't been adept enough to warrant the king's true attention. If the still-smoking remains before him were any indication, it appeared the sorry male had one last failure to add to a pathetically long list.

Something glinted, catching his eye. Domitan crouched and reached forward.

"My king! Here, let me."

A young soldier approached, eagerly offering his services. Domitan waved him off. He had no issue soiling his hands with the blood of his enemy, even when it had turned to ash.

Domitan plucked a barbed bolthead from the pile, careful not to snag his fingers on the wicked edges. He blew on it, revealing the once-polished iron underneath and his engraved insignia—a royal bolt. So, Brune had met his end before the conflagration consumed his carcass. Perhaps not an accidental fire, then.

Domitan rose and exited the ruin.

The blaze that had claimed the stable—no, the barn, for it could hardly be considered a true stable—had taken hours to extinguish. Domitan had been notified immediately, but he hadn't been the first to the scene and was just now surveying it himself.

The body of a common soldier lay out front and off to the side, hidden by shadow. He hadn't seen it upon his initial arrival. It had been burned but not entirely destroyed by the flames. A short, wicked dagger protruded from one eye socket.

Domitan's general of twenty-five years, head of his city command, peered down at the dead soldier. He glanced up at his king's approach.

"Well?"

General Markain Corstow bowed his head briefly before glancing back at the body. "The dagger is lodged to the hilt. Straight through the eye socket."

He saw that clearly enough, but Domitan let him continue. His general was a meticulous man and was more effective if allowed his particular chronologically inclined method of delivering information.

"I knew this soldier. Boress Hull."

Of course, Corstow knew the soldier. He knew all of them.

"He was competent in hand-to-hand. An excellent bowman. Not flashy. Reliable. Efficient." Corstow crouched. "Look here." He indicated the hilt. "The blade entered angling upward. Not likely a stab wound, and I feel confident in saying I don't believe this soldier fell on his own dagger."

Domitan narrowed his eyes. "You're saying the dagger was thrown?" Impossible. He knew every shurii in Asteros capable of a throw like that. He could count them on one hand, and they were all in his employ.

Corstow stood and turned to the window where a few jagged pieces of glass remained lodged in the frame. He nodded. "I believe so, my king. Boress sustained some manner of injury from what appears to have been a considerable fall. The angle of his legs is wrong. The dagger killed him, but he fell from some height. There is a ladder just there, to the side. I think someone inside the barn struck him."

Corstow bent back to the body and pulled the dagger free from the soldier's skull with a wet squelch. He wiped the gore and blood from it. His expression turned hard. "Goddess mercy," he said. "Look at this, Sire."

Domitan peered closer and inspected the dagger. The make of the weapon was fine, the hilt simple but soundly crafted. The slender blade gleamed. But the tip was wrong. Where the pointed apex should have been, only a blunt edge remained as though someone had taken another blade and cleaved the top several inches off. He looked at his general. "You come from a family of master smiths, Corstow. What is the likelihood of a blade breaking from a throw such as this?"

"By chance? Through the eye? I have never seen it, Sire. See this top edge? It's clean, perfectly horizontal. There are no jagged ridges or fissures. The blade was fashioned by no amateur. There are no imperfections that I can visually discern. I can consult my father to be certain, but my guess is whoever designed this dagger intended for the tip to fragment upon impact."

Domitan took a measured breath to control his rising anger. "If you are correct, then whoever threw it knew he would not miss. A dagger such as this would not be wielded by one prone to inaccuracy."

Corstow agreed. "Yes, Sire. One misthrow and the dagger's tip would shatter, leaving the weapon useless. But hit your mark? If the blade itself doesn't kill, the fragmented tip will break off inside the body, ensuring death."

"Take the blade to your father. I want his opinion on this before sunrise tomorrow."

Corstow pulled a cloth from beneath his armor and wrapped the weapon. "Yes, my king."

Domitan looked down at the dead soldier, one blue eye glazed and sightless, the other a ragged, wet red hole in his skull. "I want the assassin found. They cannot be permitted to leave the city. Lock down the gates. No one leaves. No exceptions."

Corstow inclined his head, then glanced from the cooling corpse at their feet to the smoking corpse of the barn. "Is it possible our assassin was killed in the blaze?"

If only they could be so lucky. But no, the Goddess was a temperamental bitch. She would make them work for the solution to their problems. Domitan handed the barbed bolthead to Corstow. "Brune's body lies in the barn. He was not capable of such a throw." And no other bodies were found inside.

Corstow considered the discarded crossbow several feet from its former owner. "Forgive me, Sire. You're sure it is him?"

Domitian's gaze was like ice, and Corstow had the sense to lower his own in apology. If he hadn't been a loyal servant and an excellent general for the past two decades, Domitan would have cleaved his head from his shoulders and added another corpse to the patchy front lawn for the insult.

"I am sure," Domitan said, though he didn't need to. His message was clear enough. And he was more than sure. He was certain. The remnant of that ridiculous belt was fastened around what had once been Brune's considerable midsection. He would have recognized that decorative buckle anywhere, charred or not. He'd only been surprised he had not also found a hatchet buried in the debris.

Another soldier approached them from the eastern side of the barn. The male bowed, and Domitan signaled for him to speak.

"Sire. General. There is another dead soldier behind the barn. Trampled, Sire."

Domitan turned furious attention to his general. "Where are the soldiers who witnessed what happened here?"

The newcomer grew visibly concerned, but Corstow did not cower. He held the king's gaze calmly, collected despite the pressure. And this was why he was general. "They are being held at Pub Black, nearby. Awaiting instruction."

CLOAKING FATE

"I want them questioned at once. We have rumors of a missing Fate, and whoever threw that dagger is loose in my city. Find out what happened here, Corstow, by whatever means necessary. I want this fucking mess cleaned up."

He didn't mean the smoldering ruin. That godforsaken barn could sit in ash and filth for the next millennia for all he cared. He'd look upon it and smile, knowing Brune lay burned and bloodless inside. But not if they didn't find the owner of that dagger. Domitan didn't like surprises. His control was absolute in his domain, which was wherever he chose to be. The stranger would pay once he got his hands on him. Dearly.

Corstow bowed at the waist. "Yes, my king. It will be done."

Domitan ordered his horse brought to him. As he mounted, he glanced at the sky. A storm was brewing. He could feel it. Could smell it. It was on the black horizon and boiling in his blood.

He kicked his mount viciously, and the creature launched into movement. Domitan was headed home.

Not to the palace and the bed of his dear wife, the queen. He would speak with Serebine soon enough, and it would not be a pleasant conversation. But before that, he needed to visit the Stronghold to learn the identity of the Fate that supposedly escaped and ascertain how such a blunder could have occurred in his city. If the rumors proved true, Serebine would be furious once she learned, if she didn't know already. Domitan intended to have answers before he met with her. The queen's asperity was one headache he didn't need added to the ones already plaguing him.

More blood would be shed before this night was over, and a wicked thrill filled him. There was something undeniably pleasurable about enacting justice where it was due. Some people sought love and companionship. Filled the desires of their souls with pretty things or flowery compliments. King Domitan's soul was filled with power and pleasure and law. He was made to rule, and he did so with an iron will. His subjects both feared and respected him, and any that dared disobey his commands would assume the full weight of his wrath—something he graciously bestowed upon those who deserved it.

Oh yes, vengeance was coming. Soon.

But first things first. Domitan needed to blow off some serious steam before he visited the Stronghold. His blood was pounding in his ears, and he was wound tighter than a drawn bowstring, liable to explode into his second form with the slightest provocation. He kicked his horse again and rode through the streets like a dark avenger toward his private suite, where his personal attendant would be expectantly waiting.

Domitan pulled his charger to a thunderous halt in the courtyard outside his private estate. It was not as large as the royal villa, but it was no less luxurious. His residence was one of a handful of homes that made up an exclusive gated community within the city, guarded day and night by hand-selected personnel. The king's was, of course, the grandest property in the development. He had personally funded the community, and its residents were there by the king's invitation. General Corstow owned a home nearby, as did Domitan's private mender, as well as other various shurii of influence and status, wealthy merchants, and the king's councilmen.

Domitan dismounted and left his stallion with the stable hand that ran out to greet him. Day or night, morning or afternoon, hours before sunrise or minutes after dark, his staff was prepared to attend him. They were always ready, always waiting. He could snap his fingers and have a feast prepared. With a wave of his hand, he would be clothed in the finest silks and the most radiant jewels. He needed but give a look, and he would have a handful of servants falling over themselves to do his bidding. They would move the mountains themselves if he commanded it. That kind of power was his and his alone, and he reveled in it.

The king strode up the front steps of his estate and passed through the grand double doors that swung open for him as though by magic. Inside the foyer, a servant took his ebony damask cloak. It was still too warm for ermine. Another retrieved his sword and riding gloves.

"Refreshments, Sire?" A servant held a silver tray bearing a decanter of clear liquid, a small lidded ceramic jar that likely contained a sleeping additive, and a single heavy crystal glass. The hour was late, but sleep was not on his current agenda. He'd opt for the liquor.

"In the study."

The shurii male bowed. "Right away, Sire," he said and departed.

Domitan entered the study to find everything as he'd left it at dawn that day. Two oversized crimson velvet chairs sat before a massive ivory stone fireplace. The creamy tiles were spotless, not a speck of ash staining the surface. Above it was a portrait of Domitan in full battle regalia, brandishing his bloodied sword atop his ebony stallion—a depiction after he put down the first rebellion. An enormous desk occupied the left side of the room in front of a plush leather seat fit for a king. A heavy, irregular wooden table filled the right side of the room. On it, a map of Asteros was stretched and weighted. A bookshelf was built into the wall behind the table filled with bound books and scrolls of new developments and plans for military expansion. A thick tome rested on one shelf containing the names and addresses of every member of his army and their families' whereabouts. Corstow had an identical copy that he kept locked in his safe. He had another smaller ledger containing information for all the shurii in his employ: servants, stewards, stable hands, chefs, messengers, and pages. He found disloyalty remained a rarity among his staff when he had access to their loved ones.

Domitan strode to the desk, where the servant had deposited the silver tray. He poured the *mezahl* and took a healthy swallow, letting the liquid carve a fiery path into his chest. He had an hour at most, and then he needed to get to the Stronghold and handle this mess.

Domitan stood staring at the desk, sipping his drink in silence. The clock on his mantle ticked. Thirty seconds passed. He frowned. A full minute. He was here for one thing and one thing only. And that thing was not readily available. A second minute ticked by. Domitan's eyes remained fixed to a point on his desk, and he lifted the glass to his lips, draining the contents. His countenance blackened. The two servants stationed against the wall shifted, eyes downcast. How dare—

The door to the king's study swung open, and the object of his thoughts walked in and knelt on the floor before him, head bowed in supplication.

"I humbly ask your forgiveness for my tardiness, my king."

Domitan looked down upon the dark head and surveyed the exposed neck.

"You know how I feel about waiting."

"Yes, my king," the male said, his voice cultured and even despite appearing slightly out of breath. "It will not happen again."

"Oh yes," Domitan said. "Of that, I have no doubt." He moved toward the mantle and glanced at the clock. Fifty-two minutes remained before he needed to leave.

"How may I serve you, my king?"

Domitan ignored the question. He would get to that. "Where were you, Cinah?"

Cinah remained kneeled. There was no hesitation in his reply. "In the city, Sire. Meeting with a merchant."

Domitan looked back with narrowed eyes and commanded him to rise. Cinah obeyed immediately and stood before him. The king took in the tall, lean-muscled body, perfect posture, and the wide, handsome planes of his face set into a pleasantly neutral expression. His brown eyes were intelligent and obeisant. Ah, yes, this was Cinah's humble servant mask. He had many that he donned for different occasions, some that Domitan preferred over others. All of them unique, all of them for him. He'd make him wear another before his hour was up. Forty-nine minutes.

"Shopping? At this hour?"

Cinah's lip twitched, and Domitan's gaze snagged on it. "This particular merchant has a very select clientele, my king. His wares are not the kind that can be obtained in the common street. It would attract…unwanted attention."

Domitan held out his glass, and a servant peeled himself from the wall to refill it. "Cinah, am I to understand that you had a nefarious business dealing with an illegal merchant in the middle of the night in my city? Without my knowledge or consent?"

Cinah bowed at the waist, one flawlessly manicured hand extended. His voice came out soft and low. "For your pleasure. my king."

Now, he *was* curious.

Domitan placed the glass on a side table and took the drawstring pouch from Cinah's hand. He tipped its contents into his palm and stared at the seven tiny, perfectly spherical, green beads. His eyes snapped to Cinah, who was looking at him with his patiently expectant mask. The king's lip curled in predatory glee.

Cinah had brought him *euphorium*—the most potent, purest form of it. One bead under the tongue would induce a pleasure-filled hyper-sensory trip that would last hours. It was illegal, banned from public use. Domitan himself had ordered several manufacturing operations of *euphorium* dismantled at the queen's request. Her elders deemed the substance offensive to the Goddess. Those found with it were imprisoned.

Cinah took a considerable risk in obtaining this. Domitan would have to punish him for that alone, but later. He only had forty minutes.

He carefully tipped the beads back into the pouch. *For your pleasure.* "Yes, it will be."

Cinah permitted himself a small smile and dipped his head.

"But not tonight," the king said, pondering his favored attendant. "I have urgent business that requires my direct involvement, and I am short on time."

"At your leisure then, my king."

"There is an urgent matter that has recently come to my attention, and I would have it addressed before I depart."

Cinah was back to pleasant neutrality.

Domitan strolled to the desk and returned his crystal glass to the silver tray. "You see," he said. "There is a thief at my estate. A treason has been committed under my roof. An item appears to have been stolen from my study."

Cinah watched him. The two servants against the wall stiffened.

Domitan placed a finger on his desk, just to the right of his inkwell, next to a half-used stick of hard wax. He looked at Cinah, his gaze like stone.

"Someone has taken the king's seal."

The room fell silent. The servants shifted on their feet. One visibly trembled. Cinah didn't remove his gaze from his king. His face was the picture of calm, but Domitan saw a muscle twitch in his right temple.

Slowly, deliberately, Cinah reached into the inner fold of his jacket pocket and withdrew the seal.

Fury punched Domitan. His favored attendant? His fucking bedmate? The betrayal flogged him.

"You had better fucking explain yourself." He barely managed to get the words out, he was so focused on preventing his second form from ripping out in rage.

Cinah swallowed, his breathing even, nostrils slightly flared. The muscle in his temple twitched again, and he clenched his jaw. "Forgive me, Sire. I only sought to borrow it."

"I should burn you alive for this," Domitan snarled.

Why? The thought came unbidden to his mind. He shouldn't have cared. It shouldn't have mattered. But it did, and that made him even more angry. He was too fucking soft with this male. Afforded him too much freedom. Now, he was paying the price.

Cinah reached into another pocket and produced a thick, unused stick of black wax flecked with gold. He held the solid golden seal and the wax out to Domitan, palm up. The explanation left his full lips as though Cinah knew one was needed. "An experiment. For your pleasure, my king."

Experiment?

Cinah slowly drew up the sleeve of his outstretched arm, the muscles under the dark skin of his forearm flexing. A round glob of dried wax the size of Domitan's seal was burned into Cinah's flesh, one edge having pooled outward. He could just make out the insignia: a *D* inside a five-pointed crown imprinted into the mark. It was fresh, the skin at its edge puckered and swollen.

Cinah had dripped hot wax onto his flesh and sealed it with Domitan's mark.

If he was cool-headed and thinking clearly, he might have questioned why Cinah had taken the seal covertly instead of approaching Domitan with a specific request to utilize it. He might have asked why Cinah had risked carrying the seal on his person when he left to go into the city instead of simply using it and returning it to Domitan's desk. Should have wondered what kind of treasons Cinah might have committed with the king's seal.

But he wasn't cool, he was fevered with need. His thoughts weren't clear, they were fixated on the sight of his initial in wax on Cinah's skin. Fury left him, replaced with raw, aching lust. His favored attendant was experimenting with pain and presenting him with the means of its infliction. Domitan had a vision of Cinah naked under him while he dripped a hot trail of wax onto his chest. He saw his abdominal muscles stiffen. Saw his face snap into that submissive mask.

For your pleasure.

Domitan reached out and took the seal and the wax from Cinah's hand.

He glanced at the clock. Twenty-four minutes. Time was short. But it was enough.

Chapter 21

Railah

FELÍNE WOKE BEFORE THE SUN crested the horizon. Weak light crept into the shadowed alcove where they'd spent a few hours resting. She immediately looked across the dead remnants of last night's fire to where Kal had slept. He was not there. The saddle blanket he'd used as bedding was gone, as was the horse.

He left her there? Rode on without her?

No, the saddlebags were still there, and the thief wouldn't so readily abandon the prize he'd worked so hard to acquire. Regardless, she was alone, and something in the moment of solitude caused the weight of her circumstances to crash down upon her.

A sob broke from her. Felíne choked on it, tried to reign it in and bury it, but she had no more adrenaline to steel her resolve. All of her fear, worry, anxiety, and uncertainty manifested in ugly, uncontrollable, spasming silent cries. She clutched her arms around her middle and doubled over. Her chest tightened, her stomach hurt, and her muscles clenched.

She let this happen. She had no one to blame but herself. Her cursed curiosity, that unshakable need for escape and adventure. If only she had accepted her responsibilities with a grateful heart. She had played the cultured student, the model daughter, the perfect Prima. But that's all it had been, hadn't it? Just a part that she'd been trained to play. Something inside her was broken, and if she was honest with herself, some small, vital part of her had been seeking a way out since she was a child. Age, maturity, and practice had smothered it, locked it away in a vault deep within her spirit, but the key had remained, and she'd unlocked it time and again to peek inside and remind herself that her life as the Prima was not what she truly wanted.

That was her ugly truth.

And she thought herself incapable of acting the way Sashara did to please her clients. Ha! Her whole life, she'd been acting to please her parents. Please the elders. Please the Goddess. Why did everything she wanted for herself exist outside the parameters deemed acceptable?

Felíne wiped her sleeve across her face in a very unladylike manner. It didn't matter what she wanted. Some people didn't get to choose their lot in life, and all people had to face unforeseen circumstances at some point. Things happened to people all the time that were outside their control. A resilient person chose their response to the situation. The weak allowed the situation to choose for them.

She didn't feel so resilient right now. She felt cowardly, feeble, and dumb. Evident enough by the smear of snot and tears on her sleeve.

The feelings are real, but are they true?

Mender Alcuin's words surfaced in her memory. Sure, she felt like a coward, but was she cowardly? She felt foolish, but did she prove herself a fool? The emotions were undoubtedly *real* in the sense that they existed. However, just because she experienced a feeling did not guarantee it was *true*.

Felíne scrubbed the final tears from her face. No. She wasn't a coward. She might have been scared, but she would not allow that fear to drive her. She made a mistake in venturing into the city without any means of defending herself, but she was not a fool. She was intelligent and capable and learned valuable lessons from her oversights.

Felíne picked up the hatchet lying on the ground beside her and slid it under her belt. It would have to do until she could obtain or fashion a better holster.

She got up, folded and rolled up the bedroll, set it next to the saddlebags, and ventured outside into the growing dawn light.

The mouth of the cavern was hidden by huge boulders and a sheer wall of rock that formed a narrow passage. To the left of the entrance, the gravelly path extended a short way before dropping off into midair. She peeked down over the edge. The fall was far enough that it would seriously maim anyone unfortunate enough to topple over if it didn't kill them outright. She looked up. The walls on either side of the passage were smooth, not a ledge wide enough to grab onto, and the opposite surface was far enough away to prevent her from shimmying up by bracing her body against both sides.

She looked toward the right and down the path. One way in and one way out. Very well.

Felíne followed the pathway until she emerged from the rocky façade. The valley spread out before her. Last night's monsoon had cleared, and the barren landscape from yesterday had transformed. As if coaxed by the flood of life-giving water, new greenery sprouted up from the earth in every direction, painting the drab land in color. The previous day's dried-up shrubs sported tiny new verdant leaves. Birds flitted about, chittering to one another. Bees and other insects buzzed as they floated from plant to plant, visiting each infant bud. The desert had come alive.

Felíne turned and shielded her eyes as the sun crested the horizon. The sky looked on fire. Vibrant pink, peach, and yellow blended with lavender and the brightest azure. A puffy smattering of clouds overlaid the scene, bathed in the colorful glow. The sky looked enormous, spreading endlessly in every direction. She'd never seen anything so lovely. In the palace, she caught glimpses of the sun rising over Asteros, but the walls and the city beyond them prevented an unobstructed view. She'd never gazed upon something with such infinite grandeur.

For a moment, she forgot about her current predicament and basked in the warmth of the emerging sun. A thought struck her, catching her off guard. This was the first morning in her existence that she greeted the day completely free of a mandatory schedule. Last night, the notion had terrified her and left her with a sense of loss and longing. But this morning, with the land so lush before her and the heavens so intensely hued overhead, that little spark deep inside of her flared a little brighter.

A soft thumping noise sounded to her left, and Felíne turned, brandishing her hatchet. The huge roan horse crested the rocky hill, Kal sitting upon him with his hood up, face shielded, and sword hanging at his side. A brace of rabbits was tied by the feet and slung over the horn of his saddle, their bodies bagged. Felíne glanced down and saw thick padded boots covering Sig's hooves, secured at the pastern, muffling his steps and preventing any shoeprint from marking his passage. Clever thief.

CLOAKING FATE

Kal stopped in front of her. She stared at him. He sat tall and proud, his broad shoulders held back as he looked down on her. He was the very picture of menacing masculinity, sitting astride his mighty horse with the cute little booties. He raised one gloved hand and pointed toward the pass and the hidden cavern.

And just like that, her moment of tranquility disintegrated.

Barbarian. He couldn't even use his words and ask politely?

Felíne continued to stare into the pit of his hood as she made a point of visibly sheathing her hatchet in her belt. She lifted her chin, turned, and marched back down the path in the rock. He wanted to play brute? Fine. She would listen only because she had little alternative, but she certainly wouldn't give him the satisfaction of cowering before his command. She wasn't a coward. She wasn't a fool. And she would not allow herself to believe otherwise, prisoner or not. She woke up, cried, gave herself a pep talk, dressed, and watched her first sunrise. Her captor should be wary. It's amazing what a good cry could do for a female.

Inside the cavern, Kal lit a single torch to light the space. He removed the brace of rabbits and set them on a flat stone. He then unsaddled Sig and retrieved the brush. Felíne approached him and held out her hand. Kal looked at her.

"I'll do it," she said. Sitting idly held no appeal, and she didn't have the first clue how to skin a rabbit. She doubted he would allow her the freedom to wander, and he didn't look in a mood to entertain the suggestion.

He wordlessly handed her the brush.

Kal separated his catch, took out a wicked-looking curved knife, and efficiently cleaned the carcasses. He separated the flesh and fur, removed the organs, and cut the meat from the bones, which he then sliced into fine strips. He took the hides and muscle outside and lay them in the sun to cure.

Felíne finished brushing Sig and returned to sit by the cold firepit, watching her nemesis with wary regard. Kal moved with an easy sort of grace. His movements were deliberate and sure, each action chosen and confident. He seemed to know exactly who he was and what needed to be done. No indecision. No hesitation. He was a man of action, that much was apparent. Even in the simplest of tasks, he had a sense of direction and awareness. She wondered what went on in that mind of his as he went about his day. What

214

were his days even like? Was all this routine for him? Just another run-of-the-mill kidnapping? Just another sojourn to his hideaway in the desert?

Come to think of it, what exactly did he have planned now that the sun had bathed the world in light? Surely, he hadn't smuggled her out of Asteros to hide in a dusty cavern a few hours' ride from the capital? They were in the middle of nowhere. Eventually, someone would come looking for her. He had to know it.

"Is this it?" she asked. "You can't mean to keep me here."

Kal ignored her.

"You know they will come for me."

No answer.

She tried again. "What is your plan for me?"

Silence, just the methodical swipe of a cloth across his blade.

"Kal."

He looked at her then, hood pulled back from the harsh planes of his face, black eyes boring into her. Something feminine and primal inside her stirred.

She cleared her throat, and he looked away, spreading out the saddle blanket. Kal set his sword, crossbow, and quiver beside the blanket, then lay down and closed his eyes. He seemed perfectly contented to ignore her. Perhaps that was better than a few alternatives her unhelpful imagination scrounged up.

Minutes went by. Felíne counted them.

Then she counted some more until she lost track. Outside, she could picture the sun rising steadily in the sky, turning the beautiful, dewy morning into an unforgiving afternoon. Did they realize she was missing? Did anyone yet know that she'd been taken? Surely, someone must have alerted the king. Her mother. Imogen.

Imogen.

Gods, what a mess she'd made of things. She sincerely hoped she hadn't caused trouble for her friend. How ungrateful and spoiled Imogen must think her. The thought twisted a guilty knife into Felíne's stomach.

Kal lay there, breathing steadily, completely unperturbed by her dilemma.

CLOAKING FATE

The silence was oppressive. Frustrating. All she heard was the shifting of Sig's feet on the stone and his occasional snorting, Kal's soft breathing, and her treacherous thoughts.

It swallowed her.

Kal, on the other hand, seemed completely contented to let her wallow in self-loathing. He refused her freedom, why would he give her the luxury of simple conversation? Why would he allow her the courtesy of an explanation? No, he was determined to let her brood in silence.

He may have preserved her life, but he had also doomed it. And if she didn't find a remedy for this predicament soon, countless other lives would be doomed as well. She could not allow that to happen.

Felíne shifted uncomfortably. Kal remained still. Only the rhythmic rise and fall of his chest indicated he still lived.

Minutes ticked by. She lost count of how many.

More silence.

Sig flicked his tail, the sound of coarse hair brushing his flank abrasive in the quiet. Her breathing seemed too loud. All the movement of the night before made the stillness of today disconcerting. Uncomfortable.

A lizard scurried past the opening of the hollow on tiny, clawed feet, and Felíne nearly jumped out of her skin. Her skittishness suddenly infuriated her. She looked again at Kal, seeking somewhere to vent her anger.

His eyes remained closed. His annoyingly attractive face was placid. Resolved to ignore her and the emotion boiling under the surface of her skin.

She couldn't take it. If he decided to kill her for asking questions, then so be it. She'd die anyway if she sat one more moment in silence.

"Why?" she said, voice low and laced with ire. "Why did you take me?"

No response.

"Do you have any idea what you've done?"

Not even a twitch of an eyelash.

"What are your intentions? I know you can hear me."

The venom in her blood blossomed into full-blown malevolence. Felíne stood and ripped the hatchet from where it hung at her side. Her arm was steady and strong as she raised it over Kal's body. He wanted to ignore her? Fine. She'd made it too easy for him to do so.

No longer.

216

She'd never intentionally harmed another shurii, never thought herself capable. But she'd also never been ignored. Not once in her life. It made her feel insignificant and low. Even her wraiths acknowledged her presence despite declining to interact with her directly. This male had opened a chasm of fear and chaos in her orderly life, and then he had the audacity to *ignore* her?

Her arm ratcheted back just a fraction, and she froze. Kal's eyes snapped open, the only thing about him that moved, and he stared up at her with a ferocity she had not been on the receiving end of. It scorched her. The ire that was so fervently stoked by this male's disregard was now fizzled by his attention.

Felíne was still, arm cocked back. That gaze of his penetrated sure as the bolt of a crossbow intended for her heart. A killing blow. Her resolve trembled. Slowly, she lowered the hatchet. She was still angry but no longer to the point of violence.

Kal continued to watch her. He swung himself into a seated position and leaned forward, muscled forearms resting on his knees. At the same moment, Felíne leaned back, away from him. She wasn't fooled. His body language was attentive yet relaxed, but somehow, she knew he could be on his feet and primed for killing in a fraction of a second.

Felíne sat, her axe lowered to the ground next to her.

They stared at each other. One predator, the other unwilling prey.

The silent confrontation strained.

She zipped the gold coin along the chain around her neck and made a heroic effort of insouciance. She felt anything but. "Nothing to say?" she said, pleasantly surprised at her unwavering tone. "No explanation?"

He studied her, lips closed but not pressed thin. Brow heavy, eyes assessing. A small line at the side of his mouth spoke of his displeasure, and she was once again indignant. Felíne wondered if he could read the waves of her emotions as they swelled and crested in her expressions. She knew he could. He gave little away, but her face was made of glass. She couldn't be more transparent if she wrote her feelings in ink on her forehead.

Felíne didn't bother controlling her temper. There was little point.

"You threaten my life, drag me out of my city, frighten me half to death, maroon me in a raging monsoon in the middle of nowhere, and then sit there like everything is right with the world? All going to plan, hm? One which you couldn't possibly be inclined to disclose."

His eyes narrowed.

She narrowed hers back even though she felt like a mouse caught in the sights of a raptor.

"The least you could do is answer me. You owe me that much."

A muscle twitched on the side of his face, and his jaw clenched once, twice. He was angry. Monumentally angry. Her father was terrifying when in a temper. He would yell and throw his weight, making himself more ferocious by his uproar. She'd seen larger men balk in the face of the king's anger.

Kal's silent rage was worse.

She had never been the subject of her father's wrath, but whenever she witnessed it, the safest response was a steadfast one. If one balked or fought back, the outcome was always worse. So, she steeled herself and waited.

Another moment passed before Kal unclenched his jaw. "All is not right with the world," he said with deceptive calm. "A good man is dead because of your stupidity, your need for attention. I owe you nothing. I saved your wretched life, and you've done nothing but make me question if it was even worth the risk. The sacrifice. The least *you* could do is show some gratitude."

She stared at him incredulous. Of all the responses she imagined, this was not one of them. *Gratitude?* For kidnapping her and subjecting her to the worst night of her life? Was he completely delusional?

"You call kidnapping me in the middle of the night 'saving my life?'" This was some terrible joke. "My call for help was a cry for *attention?*" She'd never been more insulted.

He shot her a murderous glare. "Of course, that would be the part you heard. Never mind my mentioning the death of a good man." If contempt had a face, it was his. "Typical selfish female," he muttered.

Selfish? Feline was outraged. "How dare you! You don't get to pin that man's death on me. Maybe if you hadn't kidnap—"

"You keep using that word," Kal cut in, low voice rumbling with disdain. "*Kidnapped.* Here I thought I was after a grown woman. But maybe you're right. Based on your behavior thus far, it seems I ended up with a child instead."

Felíne was on fire. The hatchet's handle once again found itself gripped in her shaking fist. Kal didn't even give it the decency of his concern. She pointed the curved blade at him. "You monster." His eyes darkened. "You had no right to steal me away. I didn't ask for this."

"You know, one would think you had hoped to avoid the path your life was taking. From the stories I've heard, I am willing to bet another would have gladly traded places with you if offered the chance to escape." He leaned forward, close to the blade. "I didn't kidnap you. I liberated you."

He may as well have slapped her. How…Was her heart's secret yearning for freedom common knowledge? Did someone know and contrive a means for her removal? Gods. This wasn't what she intended! Was all of this her fault? A result of her carelessness?

Panic seized her.

"Liberated?" she sputtered. The word meant to instill hope suddenly filled her with dread. "I have a responsibility! That *path* my life was taking is my duty! My calling. My only purpose. And you have undoubtedly jeopardized it!"

Kal laughed. It was not a kind or joyful sound. "This must be a joke."

Felíne stared at him in outrage. He thought she was joking? The fate of tens upon hundreds of thousands of shurii was no laughing matter. Was he that sadistic? That calloused to the fate of the race? A race of which he was a member? Of which his fallen friend had been a member? She was too stunned to speak.

"Not joking? Unhinged, then, surely. I would have been warned of a dullard."

Felíne could do nothing but stare at him. Fear and panic welling. How would she make him understand? This heartless, soulless creature who laughed at the idea of a whole people ending. Who thought the Prima an idiot. He called her insane.

Kal saw something in her eyes after another moment. "Fucking divine, you're being serious."

"Of course, I am serious!"

The ridge of his brow lowered, his gaze darkening. He had not expected her sincerity. "Those insufferable royals and their fucking agendas," he said, disgusted. "I didn't know it was this bad. They've completely brainwashed you."

Brainwashed? Her entire life, all of her lessons, all of her struggles and studies? Her overcoming crippling anxiety. Her deep-set insecurities, vulnerabilities, fears of failure. All of the elders dedicated to her education, to her preparation. The sacrifices of males and females in her name for her benefit so that the Prima could save their people. Her *friend's* sacrifice so that children would have a future. An image of Imogen cradling a dead infant filled her mind.

"How dare you," she seethed, voice shaking with quiet rage. "You know nothing of the crown. You know nothing of my life or what I have been through. The sacrifice and loss that has been sustained. You have no idea what you have done by taking me."

Kal's dark brow furrowed, and piercing black eyes peered at her from beneath them. "I could argue you on that first bit. But you're right. I don't know what you've been through. I can't even begin to imagine."

It wasn't said with compassion; she wasn't sure he was capable. He was only stating a fact. Still, Felíne hadn't expected him to agree with her at all. She'd expected him to dig his heels in and fight her on every detail.

She was still shaking with anger, but she forced her emotion behind a wall of logic and control. It felt like trying to contain a tsunami with a sand castle.

Kal had proven himself to be a killer, but was he cruel? Not that she could honestly discern. He'd had plenty of opportunity to harm her but hadn't seized it. He may have taken her, but he'd also saved her from taking a bolt to the chest. Kal was an ass, to be sure, but that didn't necessarily make him a monster.

Could her predicament be simpler than she thought? If she explained her situation to him, would he listen? The thought of pleading with him made her want to combust, but she would do it if it meant her safe return.

Felíne opened her mouth to do just that.

"You want to know my intentions? They are not mine. They are your brother's."

Her mouth clicked shut. Brother?

"I was supposed to wait to tell you until we were farther from the city, but it will be easier if you know since you seem determined to fight me on everything, and I would hate for another innocent to fall on account of your ignorance. Rask sent me. He is a friend."

She stared at him, suddenly unsure what to say. She didn't know anyone named Rask. She didn't have a brother.

"My name is Kalevar. Your brother asked me to help get you out of Asteros."

Felíne frowned. "I don't understand," she said tentatively.

Kal sighed and sat back against Sig's saddle as though trying to appear less threatening, more reposed. His positioning didn't matter; there was no diminishing his frame. "Your mother sent word to Rask when you were conscripted to join the Fates. She was afraid for you. Rask and I devised a plan to get you out of the city. He is waiting in Meress. That's where I intend to take you."

Her eyes widened in surprise. The Fates?

The wheels in Felíne's head were spinning, but they weren't producing any useful information. She was terribly confused. Why would he think the Prima would be intended for the Fates? Her mother would never...Oh, my Goddess. Did she have a brother? Did her mother have a son that Felíne didn't know about? Or her father? He spent so much time away from the palace...

"Railah?"

Impossible. It was not possible. Felíne flipped through memories furiously, trying to identify some clue. Some fragment to help her make sense of what was going on. It was like trying to find a single sentence in a thousand paged tome. There was no way. She would have known. She would have—

"Railah."

Kal's deep voice penetrated. Her gaze snapped to his, the name he spoke forcing her off her path of thought. She almost looked behind her, but she was captured by his attention.

Railah?

She said the name in her head. Slowly. Again. A piece snapped into place. She felt bloodless. Lightheaded.

"My...my mother sent for...my brother?"

Kal must have mistaken her horrified shock for relieved surprise.

"Yes," he said slow, quiet, as though speaking to a frightened horse. "Your mother wrote to Rask. She knew of your conscription. She did not want that life for you. Your brother did not want that life for you."

"And you…"

"I am a friend. Your brother's friend."

Did he…did he think she was someone else? The sister of his friend? Her eyes went wide. Dear gods…he thought he had saved her. His friend's sister was selected to become a Fate, and he'd staged a kidnapping to rescue her. But he got the wrong woman. Felíne gripped the coin around her neck so hard it bit into her palm. How did this happen? How could this have happened?

"You're free now," Kal said in what was supposed to be a reassuring voice. "No Stronghold. No forced servitude. No more cloak of stars. You're free."

Felíne gasped. A shaking hand raised to cover her mouth. Dear Goddess above. The cloak. Imogen's cloak. She was a fool. A damnable *fool*.

And now she was here. The Prima of Asteros mistaken for a rescued Fate.

And if she was here, what happened to—

"Railah?"

Tears pricked her eyes. *Railah. The real Fate.* She looked into Kal's face and saw a flicker of concern in his granite features. Oh gods, he truly didn't know. He thought she was her. Kal thought she was his friend's sister, Railah. He thought he'd saved her from a terrible future as a Fated Mother. Her lip quivered.

Kal regarded her a moment before he rose slowly to his feet. He didn't take his eyes off her as he stood. "I am sorry I frightened you. We thought it best for you to remain unaware, in case something went wrong. There is a strong opposition to the crown in Meress. You will be safe there. You have my word."

The Cozened. He was taking her to the Cozened. So, he was her enemy, after all. This was wrong. How? How had this all gone so terribly wrong?

He's sorry he frightened you.

No, she thought. He was apologizing to his friend's sister, not her. He had saved Railah from a life of servitude. Saved her from loss, sacrifice, and likely death. Kal had saved *Railah* from a bolt to the chest. If he'd known she was the Prima, the daughter of the crown, would he have let her take that fatal shot to the heart?

Felíne thought she knew the answer.

That knowledge broke her control, and a lonely tear slipped free. She could not tell him. He was allied with her enemies. If she revealed herself now, there was no telling the kind of danger she would be in. Kal had been angry with Railah over the death of his friend. What would he do if he knew the stablemaster died for the wrong female? And the female he meant to save was now suffering the fate he had intended to prevent.

No. Revealing her identity was out of the question. Her only chance was to maintain this unintentional ruse until she had a means of escape. Eventually, someone would come for her. She was sure of it. The only question was whether it would be too late when they found her.

"We are a week from Meress," Kal said. "But there is too little cover in this part of the desert to ride safely by daylight. Get some rest. We'll leave at sundown."

Felíne put her head into her hands.

"This is a lot, I am sure."

It was her turn to be silent. He had no idea, and she had no words.

"I'll give you some time."

Kal ducked out of the shelter and disappeared, leaving Felíne alone by the dead fire, her hopeful flame flickering weakly inside her with growing despair.

Chapter 22

Gone

DOMITAN STRODE PURPOSEFULLY THROUGH THE open halls of the royal villa. Weak morning light peeked into the darkness that blanketed the city, dissipating last night's storm.

He hadn't slept. He hadn't eaten. He'd received no good news from Corstow about the blade. The soldiers present at Brune's had not been able to identify the killer. Couldn't even provide a godsdamned generalized description, which meant the talented bastard was either running amok in his city, causing Goddess only knew what kind of trouble, or had escaped. His trip to the Stronghold had been less than enlightening. The missing Fate's identity remained a mystery. Apparently, the only thing his soldiers paid attention to was hair color. He could throw a handful of coins into the city square at midday, and nearly all of them would hit a female with tresses some varied shade of brown.

Domitan had more questions and fewer answers than he'd had four hours ago. Godsdamned incompetence. All around. It was a plague that surrounded him.

At least he'd fucked. His quick session with Cinah had taken a slivered edge off his temper, albeit briefly, but the effects had long since worn off. His mood darkened with every booted step that took him farther into the palace.

Domitan had been on his way to meet his wife when one of her attendants intercepted him. The queen summoned him urgently. Serebine rarely summoned him and never urgently. The King and Queen of Asteros presented a united front to the people, but they existed within two separate spheres. Duty and obligation were the threads that bound them, and though they were woven tightly, they shared little else. For Serebine to reach out meant something was far outside her control. She would be in a hell of a mood, he thought blackly. That made two of them.

It took him a matter of minutes to reach the villa.

The king rounded a corner and came face to face with two black guards posted outside a set of closed ornate doors. They bowed at his presence, and he moved past them into the council room.

Queen Serebine stood before a floor-length window, staring out the heavy drawn curtains into the weak morning light. She clutched a shimmering lace kerchief to her chest in a white-knuckled fist. Her formal attire was absent. Instead, she wore a wide-sleeved magenta nightrobe embroidered with nightblooms that fell to the plush, carpeted floor. Her hair was unbound. Not a jeweled ring or bracelet in sight. The king could count on one hand the number of times he'd witnessed her in such a disjointed state.

The grand oval table that dominated the room was laden with various refreshments and hors d'oeuvres, which sat untouched. The fire crackling merrily in a marbled gray hearth did nothing to warm the space. None of the elders were present. The queen's usual menagerie of attendants was nowhere to be seen. The only guards were those stationed outside the doors to the chamber. They were alone.

Serebine heard Domitan's entrance and turned to look at him. Red-rimmed eyes stared at him from an uncharacteristically blotchy face. It seemed he was not the only one who had foregone sleep.

"Husband," Serebine said by way of greeting.

Domitan had grown accustomed to the way his wife addressed him. Her voice was always heavy with duty, sometimes resignation, mostly respect, occasionally ire, and never love. That morning, a new emotion suffused the single word she spoke into the silence: desperation.

He glanced about the room, half expecting some hidden threat to reveal itself. None did.

Domitan stepped forward and looked his wife over more closely, though he did not touch her. "Are you hurt? What's happened?" He shared no true depth of feeling for this female, nor did she him, but this was his wife and the Queen of Asteros. Any threat to her was a threat to him, to their rule, and Domitan did not tolerate threats. He dealt with them swiftly and with liberal violence.

"She's gone."

Domitan's considerable brow lowered. "Who?"

A hysterical note entered the queen's voice. "She's gone, Domitan! Someone has taken her!"

The queen couldn't have received word about the Fate. If this level of hysteria was regarding a missing servant girl, Domitan had serious questions about his wife's involvement with this pet project. It was unlike her. A servant was a tool. If broken or lost, they were easily replaced. Goddess knew Serebine had supplanted enough of her own. The king focused on her. No, something was not right here. He asked again.

"Who is gone?"

The queen hugged herself. She stared at him, but her eyes were unfocused. "Goddess, forgive us. Oh, my Goddess, please forgive us."

Domitan resisted the urge to reach out and shake her. "Serebine," he commanded. "Serebine! Look at me. Who is gone?"

Something in her snapped. Changed. The queen lifted her bloodshot gaze to his. The King of Asteros cowered to no one, but a lesser male would have wilted. "The Prima," she said, voice like an omen. "Our daughter is gone."

Domitan could not disguise his shock.

Queen Serebine raised her hand where the kerchief was fisted between slender fingers. It wasn't a lace kerchief, Domitan realized. It was a fine layer of chainmail reserved exclusively for royalty and, by extension, the royal guard. *Silverskin,* the smiths called it. Or as close to the actual thing as they could get. Its original creator was long dead, his methods of fashioning the material dead with him despite the king's prior efforts to extract that information.

Domitan's wife held the piece of *silverskin* in shaking hands and slowly, with incredible effort, began to tear it apart. It was a replica, Domitan realized. Likely torn from one of the guards. True *silverskin* was virtually indestructible. Still, the strength required to shred their best imitation with one's bare hands was significant. The queen's perfectly manicured nails elongated into claws as her self-control slipped, fury peeking through a normally cultured façade.

"Find them, Domitan," she demanded, her words punctuated by the tiny bursts of each link as they reluctantly gave way. "Find whoever took her so I can tear them apart."

It took forty minutes and an uncharacteristic amount of reassurance from Domitan to reel Serebine back from the edge of the proverbial cliff she perched upon. The bottom of said cliff was an abyss of irrational emotions and decisions based upon them that tended to fare poorly for all involved. He knew from experience. If he let her fall into that well, she would lose all effective functionality and make his life a living hell. The effort it cost him to reinforce the queen with logic and reasoning was as much for his advantage as it was for her sanity. He needed her alert and clear-headed.

Females and their emotional tides. If only royalty were bred exempt from such weaknesses.

The Prima was missing.

He pointed out that this was a grand distinction from *gone*, a term upon which Serebine had originally fixated. 'Gone' could refer to any manner of absence, including 'dead,' which, as he explained *again*, they had no proof of. 'Missing' simply meant the Prima was not where they expected her to be.

Domitan projected calm authority, but inside, he was fuming. The Prima's disappearance was a disaster. One which infuriated him. If anything happened to the Goddess's chosen, the crown would face not only a besmirched reputation, but a doomed race. Serebine would be forever known as the queen who lost the key to the shurii's salvation, and Domitan would share in that notoriety. He would be seen as the king who lost control of his kingdom. The thought alone made him see red.

"Call your staff," he said. "We need to figure out which of them betrayed us."

Serebine's previous state of stunned panic had been wholly replaced with vehemence. She pierced him with glacial green eyes.

"If there was one, there could be any number," he continued. "The villa has been compromised."

"*My* staff?" The queen seethed. "None of my staff would have committed such an atrocity. The guards belong to you, husband. Which of *your* staff betrayed us?"

King Domitan drew himself upright. Of course, she would pick a fight over petty possession instead of focusing on the issue at hand. Never mind that the queen had personally approved each of the royal guards employed. They'd taken vows before *her* priests in *her* temple.

"It doesn't matter," she said. "We must find her. We must find her *now*. That is the only priority. Everything depends on it."

Domitan had already locked down the city, hoping to locate Brune's mystery killer and prevent his escape. His soldiers were scouring the streets, looking for him. The matter of the missing Prima was a touch more delicate. They couldn't publicly declare her disappearance for fear of creating widespread panic and civil unrest. He'd dispatched General Corstow to hunt for her and instructed him to hand-pick a select number of his inner circle that could be trusted with discretion. If the Prima was within Asteros, she would be found. The city was large, but no place was populated enough to remain outside Corstow's reach. If they had any fortune, he'd have the assassin and the Prima in hand by nightfall.

Domitan declined to tell Serebine about the killer. If she knew there was a dangerous, highly skilled criminal at large in Asteros while her daughter was missing, there would be no end to her hysterics. He had neither the patience nor the time to withstand another of her emotional tirades.

However, he'd had no choice but to disclose rumors of the missing Fate. Domitan had personally questioned his guards at the Stronghold and received no helpful information. As far as they knew, nothing unusual or suspicious had transpired under their watch. They knew who came in and out of the fortified bunker, but they did not have intimate knowledge of how many Fates were in service at any given time. The guards were not permitted certain access by the king's decree as an extension of his dear wife, so they warranted no punishment for their ignorance.

Only one shurii had access to detailed information pertaining to the Fates and was near obsessive about maintaining it. But he was the queen's creature. If Domitan had interrogated him, news would undoubtedly reach the queen with unnatural swiftness, and he would have another headache to face for withholding such sensitive information.

For that reason, Domitan relayed what he knew, which was irritatingly little.

As expected, Serebine was none too pleased, but the majority of her focus was elsewhere. A missing Fate seemed a mere inconvenience compared to the bigger issue they faced. The queen sent an attendant to summon Mender Vulgren, almost as an afterthought. Her mind was on the Prima.

"Tell me again," Domitan commanded.

The queen's emerald eyes flashed with mild irritation, but she complied. "One of my attendants passed the Prima's chambers and noticed the absence of her guard. I was notified immediately and checked on her myself. She was not there. My attendant alerted the remaining guard staff at my direction. The Prima's guard was found posted outside Elder Imogen's quarters. The room was searched and found to be empty."

"He was guarding an empty room?"

If it weren't an expression fit below her station, the queen would have certainly rolled her eyes. "It was not empty when he arrived," she said with exceeding patience. "The guard conveyed he had escorted the Prima there earlier in the evening. The room has only one entrance, but there is a rear window."

Domitan paused his pacing. Anger bubbled up anew. "An unguarded window."

They shared a look. The queen shared his feelings about the level of incompetence. It was unacceptable. Judging by the discarded remains of the replica *silverskin* that Serebine had no doubt torn from the body of the offending guard, she'd had a chance to vent her displeasure. If there was anything left of the guard to question, he would be surprised.

"And the elder? Is she missing as well?"

"She is not," the queen said tightly. "I was informed Elder Imogen spent the evening away from the villa. One of my attendants has been sent to retrieve her. She should be here shortly."

"And the Prima was not aware of her elder's absence?"

"Obviously not," Serebine clipped. She was pushing it.

King Domitan narrowed his eyes. "How well do you trust this elder?"

Serebine regarded him. "Elder Imogen has shown herself to be a loyal servant of the Goddess and the crown. Her dedication to the Prima's education has been enthusiastic. They have unrestricted access to one another, and the reports I've received have been encouraging. I am hopeful Elder Imogen will be able to provide some insight."

A non-answer.

Domitan considered. Why would the Prima remain inside the elder's rooms upon discovering they were empty? He hadn't yet had Corstow's men do a thorough sweep of the rooms, but based on the preliminary report he'd received from the royal guard, there were no signs of an obvious struggle found, which made an abduction seem questionable. What if the young female was coaxed out of the room by someone she knew? What if she left of her own accord? He was dipping a toe into treacherous waters, but a king was obligated to consider every angle. "And the Prima? Is she to be trusted?" She had been a willful child, after all.

Serebine's voice gained a dangerous edge. "Be careful what you insinuate, King of Asteros. Even your throne does not sit higher than that of the Goddess."

Domitan released a controlled breath, choosing to ignore the threatening tone. The alternative, then. Any guard posted outside the door would have undoubtedly heard a disturbance and moved to intervene. Unless, of course, that guard was an accomplice to the crime. But why remain at the post to be implicated? It didn't make sense. They needed more information.

An attendant moved silently into the room and bowed before the queen before leaning to whisper in her ear.

"Send him in," Serebine said. The attendant bowed again and left. A moment later, Mender Vulgren entered the room.

The wiry, middle-aged shurii male did not just bow; he prostrated himself before the queen. Long, thin gray hair was combed neatly back and bound in a leather tie. His milky pale forehead appeared overlarge due to a severely receding hairline, which gave the appearance of age beyond years. The naked skin there shined as though waxed. Mender Vulgren straightened and looked to Domitan with blue eyes so pale they were nearly colorless. He dipped modestly in the king's direction before angling once again toward Serebine.

Domitan's lip curled in disgust. The male's loyalties could not be more apparent.

"Your Majesties," the mender said in a high, breathy voice. "How may I be of service?"

"There is a matter that requires clarification," Domitan growled.

Mender Vulgren twisted to return reluctant attention to the king. Domitan disliked the male. He visually criticized his wide, unsettling eyes, hooked nose, thin lips, and careful posture. Something about him gave the impression that he was a man prone to guarding secrets. The bad sort.

"Of course, Majesty."

Domitan briefly recounted the information Corstow had relayed after interrogating the soldiers involved in the previous night's events without providing unnecessary detail. "The female was not recognizable, but she wore the Fate's garment. If there is, in fact, a Fate missing, we must identify her."

A troubled wrinkle appeared in Vulgren's expansive forehead. He appealed to the queen. "I inventoried the Fated Mothers yesterday, forty-seven minutes before the midday toll, and again when they retired to their chambers. All were accounted for."

Serebine glanced back from the spot she'd resumed by the window, looking regal despite her disheveled state. "What of the newest female? Her cleansing was to be completed yesterday."

Vulgren bowed again ridiculously low, obviously overjoyed at the queen's address. "The cleansing of your new female was concluded without incident, my queen. She arrived at the Stronghold last evening and was settled into her quarters ahead of schedule. I was present for her escort. Her orientation is set to begin in a few hours. I think you will be most pleased with her. In fact, I was in the process of—"

"Check them again, Mender," Domitan interrupted. His tolerance had been exhausted. "I expect a response within the hour."

If Mender Vulgren was put out by the king's dismissal, he did not show it. "Yes, Your Majesty. Of course. I will return with a complete headcount."

Domitan snapped his fingers, and a guard entered the room. "No need," he said. "Your escort will wait for a report."

The guard gave Domitan a proper bow and moved to accompany the mender toward the exit.

Mender Vulgren gave one last look at the queen as though hoping for her to intercede on his behalf. When she did not, he left, the guard covering his retreat.

Domitan approached the table and poured himself a shot of fiery liquor. It had been a long day, and the sun was barely hours into the sky. Something told him it was only going to get longer. He got a moment's reprieve before another attendant called upon the queen.

Serebine came to life. Elder Imogen had returned.

Chapter 23

Return

IMOGEN FELT REFRESHED IN A way she hadn't in what seemed like years despite receiving only a few hours of sleep. She had spent the night at her mother's bedside in one of Mender Alcuin's private specialty clinics, which blessedly seemed less like a medical clinic and more like a comfortable inn. Light House, he called it. Her neck and back retained a dull ache from the chair she had dozed off in, but they were minor complaints. She'd do it all over again without a second thought to feel her mother reach her frail arm out to touch Imogen's face and witness the faint smile that graced her lips.

The mender checked in on her mother shortly after Imogen arrived. Imogen had been watching her chest rise and fall in a reassuring, steady rhythm when the mender entered the room. Miriam was already exhausted from the few moments of effort it took to maintain a conscious presence and greet her daughter. She'd fallen asleep several minutes prior.

Imogen had watched as Mender Alcuin began a brief assessment but quickly excused herself to 'attend to her own needs.' She'd walked a short way down the hall and waited quietly, focusing on taking deep, slow breaths until he was finished. When she returned to the room, there wasn't a medical apparatus in sight, to her immense relief. The mender stepped out to confer with one of his associates who had been attending his patients before returning to speak with her.

The update he'd provided had not been a guarantee by any means, but he was hopeful, and that had raised her spirits considerably. Mender Alcuin's optimism was catching. Imogen found herself daring to place a small bit of faith in the old shurii male's ability to reverse her mother's condition, something she hadn't reserved for any mender before him.

Mender Alcuin was leaving, Imogen learned, traveling to seek the advice of a friend and colleague who he hoped could assist him in pursuing a curative therapy. All other available options had been exhausted. His destination was far enough away to be considered a journey, and though she did her best to disguise her doubts about the old male's traveling capabilities, she felt he could sense them.

"I am sure your concern for my wellbeing exists in direct relation to the wellbeing of your mother, my dear, and while I consider it to be altogether unnecessary, I thank you for it nonetheless," he had said with a small smile that made the skin around his eyes crinkle deeply. "I can only assure you that this trip is necessary. It is, frankly put, her best chance. She will remain in excellent, capable hands while I am away, and I will make all haste."

Imogen had no choice but to trust him. The alternative was unthinkable.

So, with that little kernel of hope tucked away in her heart, she had left the role of distressed daughter at her mother's bedside, resumed that of the competent educator, and returned to the royal villa.

She felt light, thinking the little clinic was aptly named. The sky overhead was clearing, waking, and she drew in a lungful of city air. Somehow, it tasted a little less foul.

Imogen turned the corner and nearly ran into a cloaked female moving briskly in the opposite direction. She barely had a chance to steady herself when the female formally addressed her.

"Elder Imogen. Your presence is requested. Quickly, please."

One of Queen Serebine's attendants. A summons from the queen was not something that frequently warranted cause for concern, but Imogen dreaded it all the same. Especially considering her less-than-traditional approach to Felíne's instruction and their routine covert maneuvering. Moments like these made her worry less for herself and more for her mother, who she reminded herself remained well within the queen's power to use as leverage or punishment against her if desired. Imogen buried that worry deep under a thick layer of dutiful obedience as she followed the attendant through the city. The only way to pass under the queen's scrutiny unscathed was to meet her expectations.

It took little more than twenty minutes to reach the palace. They made their way past the front guard, over the drawbridge, and toward the portcullis in the perimeter gate.

It was early. Her lessons with Felíne would begin at full light. She'd need to take something to boost her energy so she didn't seem unfocused. Time was growing ever shorter before Felíne's presentation, and Imogen needed some way to fortify the young female's confidence. If only she had access to the Primordial Male. If she knew more about him, she could gauge that introduction and better prepare Felíne. Unfortunately, the male was kept under lock and key in some undisclosed location. He was rumored to be guarded closely, likely completing his version of preparation. Imogen didn't even know where to begin looking for him, and asking after his whereabouts was out of the question. Any female inquiring after the sacred male would meet a swift end. It had happened before, and she had no desire to claim that fate for herself. She'd just have to make do.

Imogen followed the attendant through the gate. Creeping ivy clung to the stone walls and hung from the arched entrance like the green tentacles of some vined monster reaching toward the passersby. It grew at an alarming rate and encompassed much of the wall despite the gardeners' best efforts to keep its appendages at bay. Imogen thought the plant took personal offense at being amputated. They passed underneath, avoiding ensnarement.

Once inside the villa, unease squirmed through Imogen, which had nothing to do with the creeping ivy. Guards swarmed inside the walls. She looked around. The king's soldiers, heavily armed, stood at attention at every visible entrance. The villa should have been quiet at this hour, with only the soft bustle of palace staff beginning their daily duties. By contrast, the grounds were crawling with unnatural activity.

Something was amiss. Queen Serebine was explicit in her instructions regarding outsiders, especially males. Only her chosen royal guard was permitted within the villa's walls—no exceptions.

This was unheard of. Impermissible. Had something happened to the queen?

Imogen kept pace easily with the attendant as they made their way through the courtyard and into the main hall. Her mind churned through possible explanations, none of which provided any reassurance.

They turned a corner ahead, and Imogen saw another guard striding toward them, a second man following closely.

The male looked up, and his eerie, colorless eyes found hers. Instantly, razor shards of ice ripped down her spine. Her steps faltered. In that moment, she was no longer walking down a tiled hallway in the palace accompanied by a queen's servant. She wasn't an elder. She had not spent the evening watching her mother rest peacefully in a warm bed. Instead, she was transported to a sterile, windowless room with an exam table and cold, whitewashed stone walls deep underground. Cabinets lined the walls containing vials of tinctures, needles, knives, cruel polished metal contraptions, and potions that could be seen through the glass doors. Countless oil lamps lit the room, casting unnatural shadows of medical instruments as they were picked up by a meticulous, long-fingered hand and used on her.

Imogen was strapped to that table. There were leather restraints pinning her arms to her sides. A thick leather strap was buckled across her chest, preventing her from rising off the table. Her thin gray robe was parted slightly in the front, leaving her bare from the waist down. Her legs were up, locked in wooden stirrups and spread, displaying her sensitive anatomy. A shiny, pale forehead raised from between her knees, and equally pale eyes peered at her. Gooseflesh pimpled her skin.

"Well done, my dearest," he beamed. He moved his hand, and there was a cramping sensation low in her belly as he removed one of his instruments. The touch of his fingers on her tender flesh made her want to vomit. Her legs shook, and she couldn't stop them. "Well done indeed. A viable specimen has been achieved."

A female who did not belong there entered the room. She spoke, and her voice sounded far away, though she stood beside the table.

"Elder?"

The male with pale eyes smiled wide and wiped a cloth lovingly along the blood-tinged edge of his instrument.

"Elder Imogen. Elder, is something the matter?"

Imogen startled back into the present, finding the queen's attendant standing over her. Her palms were clammy, sweat beaded her hairline, and she shivered with cold despite her gown, elder's vestments, and hooded cloak. Her breath came too fast.

Imogen craned to look past the female before her and scanned the hall-way. He was gone. There was no one in either direction. But she'd seen him. She'd been sure of it. Vulgren was here, and he recognized her.

"Elder?" the female said again.

Imogen looked at her, feeling half-crazed. "A man passed by here. A mender. The one with the guard."

The female's eyes darted past Imogen down the hallway where they'd just come, then returned to Imogen's face. "Come, I'll help you stand. We should not delay. Your presence is expected."

Imogen realized she was crouched on the floor, back against the wall, and she stood on weak legs. She took a moment to brace herself and slow her breathing, then smoothed her clothing. Gods, it had seemed so real. She could smell the astringent in the room and feel those awful hands. She suppressed a shudder.

"Lady," she said because she did not know the female's name. "What of the mender?"

"Come."

Imogen gripped the female's forearm, refusing to budge. "The mender."

"He is gone, Elder," she said.

"What happened?"

The lady must have guessed from the look on Imogen's face that Imogen would not take one step until answered. If so, she guessed correctly.

"You fell against the wall. I thought perhaps you had misstepped, but when I turned, you looked frightened. The mender came forward to help you, and you started screaming. Another attendant heard, and we tried to calm you, but you would not stop until he moved away. You would not let him near you."

Imogen swallowed the knot in her throat.

"He spoke with the attendant who came to help and then left with the guard. You passed out for a few minutes. Are you well, Elder?"

No, she was not well. Not in the slightest.

"Where is the other attendant?"

"Gone ahead, Elder. Likely to advise Her Majesty, The Queen."

Imogen closed her eyes and took a deep breath. She didn't need this. Her past was behind her. Not by much, but behind her all the same. All the pain and fear and trauma and loss. She'd buried it. Dealt with it and laid it to rest in an iron coffin. She didn't need it rising up to drag her under again. Certainly not where anyone could witness. But someone *had* witnessed. Several someones. Even if the attendants and guard could not make sense of her reaction, Vulgren knew. He knew her hysteria was for him. She was sure of it. Now, the queen would know as well. The ramifications of such knowledge were unclear, and Imogen was not in the current headspace to explore them.

She took a step forward, and the queen's attendant matched her.

"What is your name?"

The attendant glanced uncertainly over at her. "Gilda."

"Thank you for staying with me, Gilda. I am sorry if I frightened you."

She was not a particularly beautiful woman, Imogen noted, but she had lovely, large cornflower-blue eyes rimmed with honey-blonde lashes. Eyes that were currently filled with skepticism as they surveyed her.

"The queen tasked me with your retrieval, Elder. It is expected that I remain with you until you are delivered. And please, 'attendant' or 'lady' are permissible."

Imogen looked ahead. Of course, she chided herself. Unquestioning loyalty was a trait Queen Serebine undoubtedly prized in her attendants. They did not use formal names because individuality was not valued in their line of work. They operated as one obedient body and carried out the queen's bidding unquestioningly. Gilda had likely provided her name only because Imogen's title superseded her own. There were no friends to be found in this retinue, she realized. The thought made her look forward to Felíne's company.

Elder Imogen shook herself, trying to dislodge the remnants of terror that clung to her. She steeled her spine as best she could and strode forward, head high.

"Then let us continue, lady. We mustn't cause Her Majesty any further delay."

Imogen wasn't sure what she'd been expecting when she entered the council room, but it wasn't this.

The first person she noticed was Queen Serebine, who stood before a grand window with light spilling onto her face, which remained lovely even unpainted. Her hair was uncharacteristically unbound, her robe intimate. The woman turned to look at her. Only the Queen of Asteros could clothe herself in informality and still exude such regal poise.

King Domitan stood near the table, armored, armed, and hulking. Imogen had never seen the man up close. Doing so now gave her a new understanding of the fear that his name inspired in the streets. She knew the king did not frequent the royal villa, choosing instead to invest his time with the men he commanded. Felíne had even said he did not sleep here, opting to maintain a private estate where he could remain close to the heart of his army. She imagined the females in residence might prefer that arrangement, considering the way he currently radiated dark menace.

Gilda moved ahead of her into the room, bowed before the king and queen, murmured her introduction, and stood along the far wall beside another attendant. Judging by the brief look the two shared, Imogen ventured a guess it was the same attendant who heard her screams and witnessed her earlier episode in the hall.

Imogen dipped gracefully before her sovereigns.

For a heavy moment, nothing happened. A deafening silence pressed in from all sides, and Imogen raised her head. All eyes focused on her. Something was not right.

"We understand you spent the evening outside the palace walls, Elder. Can you confirm your whereabouts?"

Imogen glanced at the queen but ultimately turned her attention to King Domitan, who had addressed her. His words sounded like an accusation.

"Yes, Your Majesty. I was visiting my mother. She is receiving care at Mender Alcuin's clinic, Light House."

"And can anyone corroborate your story?"

She blinked, taken aback. He thought she was lying?

"Yes, of course. Mender Alcuin can confirm my time spent there."

King Domitan looked to the queen.

"Alcuin is not here," Serebine said. "He left the city before sunrise. Some medicinal inquest."

King Domitan stared. "That is not possible. The city was locked down last night by my command. No one was permitted to enter or exit unless by royal consent, and I have given no permissions."

Asteros was locked down? But why?

"I have," his wife said.

King Domitan paused. His voice was deceptively soft. "What do you mean you have?"

A fine tremor flickered across the queen's delicate brow. She looked like a cat that had just encountered another predator in her jungle. One with bigger teeth and sharper claws. Her nostrils flared slightly. "Alcuin carries a gold missive embossed with my seal. It provides him with independent authority in his therapeutic pursuits. Your guards would not have impeded his departure."

The king appeared to be maintaining a very tentative hold on his composure. Imogen saw the thick vessels in his neck throb with his increasing pulse. Something about his expression told her the king was neither aware of nor had approved his wife's decision to bestow the mender with such an autonomous endowment. She had a feeling the matter would be discussed at length later and was grateful she would not be present for that conversation.

"And you did not think to notify me before this moment?"

Imogen stood perfectly still, wishing she were transparent instead of fully corporeal. Clearly, the conversation was happening now. The attendants against the far wall might as well have been carved from stone.

The queen's chin raised a hair. "It was not pertinent."

Domitan's fist came down on the table with a shuddering boom. The females flinched involuntarily. His lip curled over too-big teeth. "I think it is pretty fucking pertinent."

Serebine recovered quickly. Her eyes flashed at the expletive. "Mind your language, husband. I am your *queen*. Of course, it is pertinent *now*." She smoothed a hand over the front of her robe, reeling calm back into her posture. "Had I been forewarned of current situations, I would not have allowed Mender Alcuin to retain such freedoms. Alas, that was not the case, and here we are."

"So, send someone to go fucking get him."

Serebine's lips pursed. "I can't. I do not know where he went."

King Domitan visibly seethed but decided to temper his behavior with no small amount of strain. Imogen wished she were nearly anywhere other than in this room, caught between these two colossal shurii powers. The king looked liable to explode at any moment, and Serebine's projected calm did little to convince Imogen that anything other than a geyser of scalding water bubbled just under her surface.

Queen Serebine made a monumental effort to ignore her husband's ire. As a result, her attention regrettably returned to Imogen.

"Now, then. Who else can provide witness to your time at Mender Alcuin's clinic?"

Imogen readily gave the assistant's name that the mender had assigned to care for Miriam in his absence. "Forgive me, Majesties, but have I done something wrong? Elder Frest led me to believe my title permitted me to leave the royal villa as needed, provided my responsibilities to the Prima remained uncompromised."

"Indeed, Elder. And have they?"

"Your Majesty?"

"Have you prioritized your responsibilities to the Prima?"

Imogen's eyes widened imploringly. "Yes, my queen. Yes, of course."

The queen faced her. "And you display that prioritization by leaving the Prima? By leaving her to sit by your mother's side?"

Imogen didn't know what to say. Queen Serebine was transmuting the king's displeasure with her into her own displeasure with Imogen. It would help if she knew exactly what she'd done to cause offense. "Majesty, I—"

"Do you deny it?" The queen was closer now, and Imogen saw the shadows under her round green eyes. She fought the urge to step back.

She couldn't very well argue with the queen, whether the female was justified in her inquisition or not. This was dangerous ground, and she needed to tread carefully. "Forgive me."

King Domitan, who appeared to have errant angry emotions in check once more, stepped in. "What time did you leave the villa yesterday?"

Imogen told him.

"And is it your habit to leave your chambers unlocked?"

She frowned. "No, Your Majesty. The door to my rooms is always locked." Whether in or out of them, she never left her personal space unsecured, especially now that she had the freedom to maintain that privacy. Imogen reached into the pocket of her robe and produced the key to her room as though it symbolized her sincerity.

"Not always, it seems," Queen Serebine said.

She was missing some crucial piece of this conversation.

"Majesties, has something happened that I should be aware of?"

The queen looked about to speak when King Domitan intervened, his tolerance of his mate having reached its limit. "Sit down, dear wife," he said. "I fear the stress of recent events has taxed you."

Queen Serebine did not look taxed. She looked ready for war, flowered robe notwithstanding. The king, however, left her little choice but to obey him. She sat.

"The Prima is missing," he said without further preamble. Imogen gaped. "She was last seen in your chambers. Her guard claimed she was attending you there for a late lesson. We do not know how she secured access, considering your absence and your claim of bolting your door prior to your departure. We do not know how she was removed or when. We only know that she is missing. You are the elder who has spent the most time with her these past days. If there is anywhere you can think she would have gone—"

"Who would have *taken* her," the queen insisted.

"—then it must be shared immediately. Every moment we delay is a moment we cannot afford."

By the time King Domitan left, Imogen had also taken a seat, exhaustion having won out over her resolve to maintain a brave face. She complied without reservation in the king's and queen's questioning. Even the king's general had come to make detailed inquiries of her.

A thorough search of her rooms had been performed. Nothing was out of place with the exception of her Fates ceremonial garment, which she'd considered burning on multiple occasions since having left the Stronghold.

Instead, she had exiled it to the rear of her closet, the reminder of a painful memory she hadn't been fully ready to abandon. Its absence was disconcerting, but she did not know what to make of it. Felíne didn't know the cloak's significance. She wouldn't have taken it. Imogen reported it missing to the king, who appeared positively malevolent as a result and left it at that.

Her mind was fogged with fatigue, clouded with worry for her friend, and compromised from having pulled every minute detail of the past seventy-two hours from it, all while excluding any condemning information that would have revealed her and Felíne's forbidden educational pursuits.

Imogen couldn't help feeling she was somehow responsible for Felíne's disappearance. She only hoped the young female hadn't gone far and would soon be found safe and whole with the king's most skilled hunters searching for her. She wracked her brain, trying to think of anyone they'd encountered who would wish to harm her. Any stranger they had met or look they had received that had lingered too long. She had been careful. More than careful. No one knew Felíne's true identity. She hadn't even trusted that information to Shar, and Veely's real identity had been a ruse to prevent unwanted snooping.

Still, Madame's would be a good place to start looking, and the crown would not know to search there for information. Nor, she admitted, would they likely gain much if they did. The people recognized the crown as power and feared its henchmen, but they didn't trust them, and many would not freely offer known details. She could make inquiries on her own in the gutters of the city. But first, she needed to excuse herself.

Imogen rubbed her eyes and pushed herself to her feet. The queen was the only other person in the room, and she hadn't said anything for some time now.

"Your Majesty, if it pleases you, I should check my rooms again. Perhaps there is something that has been overlooked."

"Your rooms have been searched since before you returned to the villa," she said without turning. "If there were some clue yet to be found, it would have been."

Imogen couldn't continue to sit and do nothing. "Then I could assist hunting in the city. I am capable of discretion. Even one extra person looking for the Prima might result in her safe return."

The queen raised a brow. "You have experience as a hunter?"

"No, majesty. However—"

"And exactly what manner of discretion do you believe will be maintained if an elder, of all people, is witnessed making inquiries after a particular missing female in Asteros?"

"But I—"

"Your presence in the city will not help. It will hinder."

Imogen bit back her irritation. "How, then, might I be of service, Your Majesty?"

Queen Serebine was quiet for some time while she regarded her. "I commissioned you for one particular thing," she said, almost to herself. "That one thing you accomplished when all others failed in hopes that you would be able to utilize your experience to assure the Prima's success. To transfer your proficiency to her."

And gods knew she had been trying her hardest. She just needed more time.

The queen tilted her head to the side, her gaze penetrating, the wheels in her clever mind spinning. Uncertainty prickled tiny feet along Imogen's arms.

"Now the Prima is missing. And you are an elder without her only pupil."

The sensation reached her shoulders and danced toward her neck, raising the minute hairs there on end.

"I am aware you met Mender Vulgren on your way in."

That name sent an involuntary shiver through her limbs.

"My attendant informed me the encounter was less than pleasant. A shame. He was so terribly fond of you. Proud like a father of his most cherished offspring."

Horse shit. Vulgren prized her like a farmer would prize his fattest sow. Bred to bursting before being lovingly led to slaughter.

"He quite regretted relinquishing you to my care, poor man. You do know how important you were to him?"

Imogen needed her anger, needed it to clear the haze of fear clouding her thoughts, but it was slipping through her fingers like silk ribbon, and try as she might, she couldn't sustain her grip.

"And how important you are to your queen?"

"Yes, majesty." Her voice sounded feeble. She had no fight; it was left floundering in the wake of her growing unease.

"I must admit," the queen mused, "I do wonder if your skillset could still be used to serve the Prima despite her absence."

Imogen worked her throat on a swallow. Her mouth was so very dry. It wasn't a rhetorical question. The queen wanted an answer from her. "How, Your Majesty?"

Queen Serebine approached her and tucked a thick coil of hair behind Imogen's ear. She looked upon her with fond features, but her eyes seemed to glow with a wicked light.

"You would like to help the Prima, wouldn't you, Elder? You swore to serve in her interests."

"Yes."

The queen smiled, showing teeth.

"Then you will help those who travail in her name. You are the best at what you do, Elder. No other has accomplished what you have accomplished. We cannot allow such talents to be wasted. Not even for a moment."

Unease blossomed into the worst sense of dread, and it dashed unforgivingly down her spine, where it burrowed deep and took root in her belly.

"You will return to the Stronghold, Elder Imogen. You will return to the Fates until my daughter is found."

Chapter 24

Cindamar

RAINY DAYS IN THE DESERT possessed their own dreary sort of beauty. The thickly overcast sky was varying shades of charcoal, fog, and lighter powder gray. The vegetation in its sage, sand, and drab yellow clothing seemed to quiver in anticipation of that next drop of life-sustaining water that fell from the heavy blanket of clouds overhead. Mountains rose in the distance like graphite megaliths standing guard over the valley as they peeked through the low-hanging mist on the horizon.

Beautiful though it may have been, traveling through the Saraat Desert terrain was miserable. On days like this back home in Asteros, Felíne would take her lessons inside next to a roaring fire, sipping black pearl tea with honey. During her lunch hour, she would bundle and step out into the garden where the undeniable happiness of the colorful, sated flora would lend vibrance to her soul.

There was little vibrance now. Just a cold, soggy spirit and slipping resolve.

Felíne unclenched her frozen fingers where they'd locked onto Sig's pommel and rubbed them together, desperate for a bit of blood flow.

Felíne used to love rainy days. The dreary weather was easy to enjoy when you weren't far from a warm shelter and a hot bath. That enjoyment vanished when you had no choice but to withstand the persistent, penetrating damp with no place to retreat to and no warmth within reach. Now, she would give her left kidney just to be dry again. She only hoped the late summer sun would make an appearance at some point and burn off this miserable morning drizzle. Though, if her luck had anything to do with that outcome, she wouldn't hold her breath.

The one lamentable indulgence that existed was the constant source of steady warmth radiating from her riding partner. Kalevar was a veritable furnace, and his body heat seeped into her back, muting the chill. She was slightly bitter about the significant difference it made.

They'd been riding for three days. Three days with no sign of rescue. Not even a whisper of pursuit. No cavalry to come thundering over the horizon, kicking up dust and mud in their desperation to reach their Prima and avenge her capture. Felíne found hope was a slippery thing to hold onto. The farther they rode, the more tentative her grasp.

Three days of cold, dreary, plodding flight.

In that time, her fervent stubbornness had faded into grudging acquiescence when it came to accepting those spare things her captor offered. His warmth was one of them.

That second night since leaving Asteros, the two of them had ridden furiously for hours, demanding every bit of stamina poor Sig had to offer. The rain had relented around midnight, thank the Goddess, and the ground was reasonably dry by the time they stopped a few hours before sunrise. Kal had deemed it safe enough to continue during the day on account of the distance they'd managed to cover and the distinct lack of identifiable pursuit—to her considerable dismay—and had announced they would rest for a while before continuing.

Those few hours were spent hunkered down in a shallow recess in the ground. The temperature dropped significantly in the early morning hours before the sun rose, and it was a matter of moments before Felíne was physically shaking with cold. She had doggedly refused to sleep close to Kal, and he'd dispassionately replied that if she wished to freeze to death, it would be discourteous of him to dissuade her from her intended fate. He also refused to relinquish his blanket to her, not that she'd asked for it, and informed her that he had no desire to share in her demise. She had given him a glare of pure, undiluted feminine defiance, breath puffing out in a frosted cloud, and promptly curled away from him.

She lasted forty minutes. When she lost complete feeling in her distal extremities and began trembling so violently that her teeth clacked together, she drew the line, choked down her pride, and scooted into his backside, nearly whimpering at how good his body heat felt. Kal had reached behind him and unceremoniously slung half the blanket over her quivering form without saying a word. She spent the next moments while her tremors subsided justifying to herself that she couldn't very well run away from him if she lost her toes to hypothermia.

Kal's food was another commodity she took full advantage of.

Felíne quickly realized she was a poor outdoorswoman. Her knowledge of medicinal plants was substantial, but knowing which weed would help staunch a bleeding wound or what herb could settle an upset stomach served little benefit when it came to keeping herself alive in the wilderness. It certainly did not keep her constantly growling stomach full.

Kal suffered no such predicaments. He was half wild animal himself. The man was perfectly at home in the middle of the desert with no civilization in sight. Nothing phased him. Not the elements or the unforgiving terrain or the scarcity of wild game. He was a problem-solver to his core, and he faced each challenge they encountered with single-minded, undeterred obstinance. The man's tenacity was an indubitable force of nature.

No shelter? Fret not. Kal will miraculously construct a tent from only the tatters of his cloak and the skeleton of a towering desert cactus to break the wind whilst you rest your head.

No food? Never fear. He will fade into the darkness and utilize his irresistible powers of persuasion to lure the edible wilderness creatures from their burrows and return shortly later encumbered with their consumable corpses.

No bath? Pah! Real shurii men have no need of *baths!* They revel in their tameless aromatic pungency. When Felíne had asked for one, he'd made a sarcastic noise of disbelief, then offered her a roll in a cluster of nearby *stinkweed* if her delicate feminine sensitivities were so offended by her odor. She hadn't asked again.

The infuriating yet undeniable fact remained that while Kal was the sole reason she was stuck out here, countless miles beyond the boundaries of her comfort zone, she was also unmistakably dependent upon him. She knew it, and he knew it, and he was impossibly irritating in his resourcefulness. Felíne made it her mission to find a weakness in him. There had to be *something* at which he was inept. Some skill with which he was unequipped. He did little to provide what he determined to be unnecessary luxuries, but when it came to survival and necessity, he was a selfless provider.

Felíne stuffed her stiff fingers back into the pocket of hare skin pelt tied to the saddle and resumed her grip. Kal had given the pelt to her after their first day in the cave, and she was reasonably sure she'd have lost at least a few fingers by now without it. Her innate propriety's sense of obligatory gratitude was a loathsome thing.

She felt him stir slightly behind her. "I can have it fashioned into a proper pair of gloves when we reach town," he said.

Felíne perked up, cantankerousness temporarily forgotten. "Town?"

Kal grunted his assent.

Her eyes hungrily searched the horizon. "With proper buildings and actual beds to sleep in?"

His breath was warm, his voice a low rumble near her ear. "Pillows even. Dry clothes. Maybe a hot stew and crusty bread."

She shivered, cold momentarily displaced by something else.

"A bath?" she asked expectantly.

"Yes, Railah," he said, mildly amused. "Perhaps we can find you a bath."

Even the extreme irritation and ruinous guilt she typically experienced at being addressed by the other female's name barely diminished her audible sigh of pleasure at the thought of a hot bath laden with sweet smelling oils and herbal soaps. She would be warm again. Dry. Fed a meal of more than meat and ruffage. There would be other shurii. Surely, Felíne could find someone to help her escape from Kal and return to Asteros.

A town. There was possibility in a town. Hope even.

"How far are we?"

Kal shifted slightly in his seat. "We'll be there by sundown. Possibly sooner."

Felíne smiled. Finally, in three days, something to look forward to.

By late afternoon, maybe an hour and a half before the sun would disappear behind the far edge of the landscape, Felíne became convinced she was hallucinating. They were finally nearing the foothills of the once-distant mountain range that marked the transition to the High Country, but it still stood some way off, the rocky outcropping appearing to shift farther and farther away from them the harder they tried to reach it. It wasn't the permutating landscape that caused her to doubt her visual acuity but what she saw preceding the ridge.

Felíne saw an oasis. Towering palms spread their fans toward the finally thinning cloud cover where fleeting slivers of blue sky teased her, dancing between the overwhelming expanse of gray. A pool shimmered tantalizingly, silver and azure against all the surrounding nude earth, with clusters of squat proliferative ferns dotting its banks. She spied a sizable camp, where little joyous specks of people scuttled about erecting tents, gathering water from the pool, and herding livestock.

She was definitely hallucinating.

But the oasis did not vanish. The closer they got, the more Felíne debated whether the mirage did, in fact, exist. If not, she'd finally lost all rational sensibilities, the stress of the past few days having exacted the entirety of their toll.

"Please don't mistake this for any amount of trust in your capacity for sound judgment because I assure you, I have none," she began, "but do you see anything...odd ahead?"

"Define odd."

"A sprawling tropical paradise in the middle of nowhere."

"Tropical paradise is a bit of a stretch," Kal replied. "But Cindamar does tend to sprawl, I suppose."

Felíne rubbed her eyes. Still there. "Cindamar?"

"The Disappearing City."

She wrinkled her brow. "I thought you were taking me to Meress?"

"I am," Kal confirmed. "This is a temporary detour."

She wasn't going to complain. After plodding through the desert for miles, she was very much looking forward to a reprieve. She was just surprised to find civilization in the middle of a relative wasteland. "There's a city? *Here?*"

Felíne figured their destination had to be close if Kal thought they'd make it before sundown. Still, she assumed they would be traveling up into the shelter of the mountainous crags before reaching any settlement. When Kal initially mentioned a town, her imagination had conjured a charming village tucked up in the elevation, rustic cabins surrounded by cozy pines with aromatic smoke rolling lazily from stone chimneys. She had not imagined…this.

She felt Kal's broad shoulders shrug behind her. "Less of a city. More of a trade post. The founders suffered mild delusions of grandeur, but the name stuck."

Felíne considered herself to be moderately studied in geography, and while she preferred to sneak fiction from the crown library rather than cartographies of Ilistaar, she was relatively certain she'd never seen any such city labeled on any map. She couldn't recall specifics, but the name Cindamar was unfamiliar. She'd never even heard stories of such a place, and she explained as much to Kal.

"You wouldn't have," he said. "The wealth of Cindamar is a closely guarded secret. Few people know it exists, and fewer still have been granted access. It cannot be found on any map. Especially not one in Asteros."

"Why?" She asked.

"It is a free city."

"And that prevents its name being recorded?"

Kal gave a humorless laugh. "You think the crown would tolerate the existence of a thing it could not control?"

"Of course not," she admitted a bit defensively. "But if they do not recognize the authority of Asteros, then whose?"

"Cindamar is law unto itself."

She frowned. "How do you mean?"

"I mean they choose to exist outside the influence of the monarchy."

"Impossible," she said.

"Hardly," he replied. "Most of the shurii here would die to maintain their independence."

It was difficult for Felíne to wrap her mind around the foreign concept. She spent her whole life bundled in a cocoon of monarchical structure. Why be the hand that removes itself from the body? Asteros was the beating heart of the land, its influence reaching all the way to the Sun Sea in the west and the elder city of Doceo far in the north. Any part excised would be cut off from all sustenance, sure to eventually wither and die. For a city, that meant the loss of access to resources, trade, culture, and protection. Not to mention the Goddess's favor. It would be a life of dangerous isolation and eventual doom.

"Don't they suffer for it?"

Kal was quiet a moment, and Felíne wondered if he had heard her. She nearly turned to look back at him when he spoke. "Better to bleed in the dark than die in the light," he said, voice low and distant.

"What?"

"It is better to suffer a little and remain hidden than to die for discovery. You can't kill what doesn't exist."

Felíne could only think of one group of people that would prefer to live a life in exile than repent and reform.

"The Cozened," she said.

"No," Kal said, surprising her. "These traders operate by their own code. The feuding of such opposing factions is not permitted. Bad for business."

Felíne frowned. People did not exist outside either association. You either worshipped the Goddess and recognized the crown as sovereign as a member of the Faithful Cursed, or you were a blasphemer, a heretic who followed the Godking and his mutinous teachings as a Cozened.

"Then who do they worship?"

"Not who. What. You'll find no temples here. Coin is their god, and profit, their prayer."

She startled. "That is treason."

"Oh yes," Kal said with a dark chuckle, though she failed to find the humor in it. "And you would be wise to keep any opinions on the matter to yourself. When I say feuds are not permitted, I mean it."

She scoffed at the rebuke. "Oh? And what will they do? Jail me for disagreeing with their impiety?"

Kal sat back heavily, and Sig stopped. "No. Cindamar has no jails."

She bristled at his tone but didn't answer, and he continued. "You need to understand something. There are no soldiers policing the streets here. There is no king to dole out punishments for crimes committed. The only law is that there is no law. You are not important enough to run your mouth here without consequence. So, disagree all you like, but piss off the wrong person, and it'll make time in a jail cell sound like an afternoon picnic."

The implications of his meaning sunk in like a stone descending to the bottom of a sandpit. Kal squeezed his legs into Sig's ribs, and they started forward again, slower. After several paces, he sighed. "You are entitled to your own beliefs," he said, his tone still stern but less severe. "The traders here are like people anywhere else. They flock to affluence. The more coin you carry, the better your friends will seem. But money makes for fickle alliances. These shurii are easily insulted, and the last thing they will tolerate is a threat to their way of life or business, impending or perceived. Asteros and her crown are both. Mention loyalty to either, and it will be difficult for even me to protect you."

And there it was again. Another reminder of her dependence on him. First, it was on his resourcefulness. Ironically, now it was on his protection. Felíne's earlier plans of finding an ally in the town to aid in her escape were evaporating like raindrops on a hot stone. She doubted she'd find assistance in such a lawless place. Once again, helplessness pressed on her. It chafed.

"Railah? Do you understand?"

"Quite," she snapped, projecting anger rather than her underlying despair. "I shouldn't be surprised you, of all people, know how to find this place. It's obviously full of traitorous miscreants like yourself."

She was being childish, immature. Her foul attitude and the blatant display of it were hardly doing anything to convince Kal that she had the self-control necessary to hold her tongue despite a hot head. She couldn't help it.

No. No, she could. Right at the moment, she just didn't want to. What she wanted was to dig at him. Chip away at his impenetrable armor so he would feel even a fraction of how she felt, pockmarked with holes, eroded by stress, guilt, and fear. And that blasted name.

Railah.

Felíne knew she needed Kal to relax in her presence. To watch her a little less, lower his guard a little more. But every time he addressed her by that other female's name, she felt like a dune adder being jabbed with a barbed rod, and she rattled back without thinking. She took a measured breath through her nose and attempted to bury her irritation.

"I understand," she tried again. Her pride was thick and viscous going down, but Kal took a page from his own book. Whatever opinions he held regarding her tantrum he kept to himself. She was silently grateful. They rode on for some time without speaking, and Felíne watched as Cindamar became clearer.

She had no idea how the city maintained its secrecy. There was no perimeter wall, no border through which to pass that she could identify. The town just sprouted up as though manifesting from the hard desert soil.

They were still some distance away, but details became more visible. Horses stood on the banks of the pool, led by caretakers, parched throats working on great swallows of the clear water. A fuzzy, woolen flock of sheep was herded into a square pen by two leggy males, a third gangly adolescent holding the wooden gate wide for them to pass. Dogs barked. Several mules, heavily laden with cargo, stood tied to posts with half-lidded eyes as their owners unloaded their packs into nearby wagons and carts.

The city itself stretched farther than she could see from their current location. There seemed to be no formal roads. No paved streets with directional signs. Just winding, packed dirt paths that seemed to form at random, carved out by an army of frequent foot traffic.

And tents. Everywhere tents. There wasn't a single tiled roof in sight. Not one building of any discernible permanence. Just a camouflaged sea of canvas that stretched in every direction, their inhabitants erecting the temporary structures according to their individual whims, seeming to plant themselves wherever space allowed. The place was bustling with activity in the crepuscular light.

"I thought you said there would be proper buildings." Her heart sank as she scanned in vain for any sign of a multi-storied inn.

"I said there would be pillows. You assumed there would be buildings."

Sig snorted and danced to the side.

Felíne's excitement at sleeping on a feathered mattress in her own private suite faded along with her prospects of enjoying a long, hot soak in a large tub. "What kind of town has tents instead of homes?" And wagons and carts instead of stores? She leaned forward, straining for a better look. Even the plants were mobile. Those towering palms were potted into massive clay urns on wheels, hauled by teams of thick-yoked oxen, and parked at varying points of interest. What in the name of the Goddess?

A male voice sounded. "One that can vanish into the hills at the first sign of trouble."

She started, and Sig stopped abruptly. Kal's muscled forearm came securely around her midsection to keep her from jumping out of the saddle.

The voice was not Kal's.

She turned. What Felíne saw was so unexpected that she was stunned into stillness.

It belonged to a monstrous male hulking near Sig's left flank. Felíne stared in wide-eyed shock. The male was in second form. *Second form!* Standing close, in the intense early-evening glow, his bulk silhouetted against the rugged terrain, he looked like a warrior of the Godking's own ranks.

Critical eyes the color of freshly tilled soil scrutinized them without shame. His pelt was a deep, earthy brown. A custom helm covered the male's broad forehead back to the base of his skull with a cutout on either side to accommodate full movement of his erect ears. Side guards extended forward to shield each cheek while leaving his toothy muzzle free. A deep scar marred his left upper lip. The rest of his considerable frame was similarly armored, the design of his gear expertly crafted to protect vital organs while still allowing unrestricted range of motion. A heavy blade was sheathed along his back, the only weapon visible. Not that she imagined him needing to use it. He was a weapon himself. His claws were nearly three inches long, tipping the digits of broad hands that looked like they could easily crush anything they couldn't shred. His feet were bare, insulated by thick bottom pads with shorter claws that provided traction in the dirt. A segmented, flexible armor shielded his soft belly and extended lower to protect…Felíne's eyes snapped up. The male saw her looking and smiled, a terrifying display of pointed white teeth.

She felt her face flush uncomfortably. His tail swished once, eyes still on her face, and Kal's arm tightened a fraction.

Dear Goddess above. Every bit of the conversation she'd had with Imogen in the tunnels beneath Asteros regarding the shurii male second form and its distinct lack of self-control came flooding back. Tension surrounded her like a copious cloud, thick enough to cut with a dull blade. She sent up a silent prayer of thanks that she was not currently on her cycle.

"Speaking of trouble," the male said, unbothered by Felíne's considerable nerves. "What do we have here? Seems the Saraat spit out a couple regular roughnecks."

"Garren," Kal said, nodding, his voice holding an edge she'd not heard before.

"Grisham didn't tell me you were coming," the male said, finally glancing up at Kal.

"I imagine there are many things your brother declines to share with you."

Garren's eyes narrowed, and his ears flicked in annoyance. He stalked closer, coming to stand near Sig's shoulder. The horse twitched and raised his head, whites of his eyes flashing, but otherwise didn't shy. Their mount was braver than she, Felíne admitted dourly. She wanted to find a rock to hide under.

"Been a while, Kalevar. Grish is going to love this. You know how much he enjoys unexpected drop-ins."

The way the male, Garren, said it gave Felíne the impression that whoever this Grish was, he enjoyed 'unexpected drop-ins' about as much as he enjoyed a venomous snake dropped into his sheets while sleeping.

"Grisham and I have an understanding," Kal said calmly.

"Right. And how about me and you, Kal? Do we have an understanding?"

Kal was quiet for a moment, and Felíne wished he wasn't sitting behind her so she could gauge his expression. "My agreement is with the Trade Master, Garren, not the Trade Master's brother. There's a reason Grisham is the head of the family."

The male's lip curled, canines flashing in warning. Felíne was half convinced Kal had pushed him to violence, but after a moment, his expression turned to what could only be described as a sneer. Whatever issue Garren had, he appeared to be shelving it for later, choosing instead to refocus on Felíne, to her considerable chagrin.

"Grish know you brought a pet?" The male's voice was gravelly, words slightly distorted by the teeth. Felíne didn't like the way he was looking at her. It made her feel like a rabbit ensnared by the intent gaze of an apex predator. She swallowed.

"You know the code on outsiders."

"I am permitted a guest," Kal said, tone clipped. She had the sense he was already tiring of the conversation.

"Even *your* guests must be inspected, Kal." Garren looked much too enthusiastic about volunteering his help in that regard.

Whatever that inspection involved, Felíne wanted no part in it. Kal wanted her to keep her opinions to herself? Well, she would be having an opinion on that.

"I know the code, Garren. This will not be an issue."

"He'll want to meet her. Give his approval. Discuss your other…agreement."

"Of course."

Garren smiled again. Sig pawed at the ground.

"What's your name, pet?" Garren asked Felíne. He lifted his muzzle slightly, nostrils flaring, and she got the distinct impression he was tasting her scent.

Self-consciousness moved in like an unwelcome guest, irritation shouldering in closely behind. She had zero personal experience interacting with males in second form, but she had been thoroughly educated in etiquette, and uninvited sniffing was on par with gross impertinence. Felíne was tired, soggy, and probably smelled like a flourishing microbiome. Not only was this newcomer disrespecting her, but he was goading Kal, which would undoubtedly make him even more insufferable and further complicate her predicament. Somehow, miraculously, her irritation outweighed her terror.

She didn't need complicated. She needed dry clothes, a hot meal, and a warm bed.

Felíne looked down at the male with a patient smile that she reserved for Mender Alcuin's more confused patients. She patted Sig's neck affectionately. "His name is Sig. Though I think 'pet' an erroneous title. Meritorious steed would be more accurate."

Garren's furred brow pinched.

"Now then," she continued before he recovered. "It was so thoughtful of Trade Master Grisham to send his seneschal ahead to receive us, but we are quite looking forward to some much-needed respite. I must admit I have overindulged my time in the saddle. Doubtless, my companion shares my sentiments. Perhaps you would be so good as to ensure accommodations are prepared? We will be along forthwith."

The male did not move. Felíne stared for a breath, feigning obliviousness, allowing the air to grow pregnant with awkward tension before twisting in the saddle to blink innocently up at Kal. "Does he require a tip?"

Kal rewarded her with the ghost of a smile. He reached into the folds of his cloak and produced a heavy, worn silver coin with the image of two balanced scales engraved on one side. "This should cover it," he said against the shell of her ear. She trilled a little, unexpectedly.

Kal flipped the coin to Garren, who snatched it out of the air, and pressed his legs into Sig's sides. "What the lady said," he tossed back as their mount danced in a tight circle. "You can tell Grisham I'll find him once I'm settled."

A delayed sense of mortification bled into her haughty self-satisfaction as they sped toward Cindamar. She dared a peek behind them but Garren was nowhere in sight.

"Dear Goddess. Kal, you actually tipped him! Like he was a butler!"

The first genuine laugh she'd ever heard from him rumbled in Kal's throat, surprising her. She liked the way it sounded: deep and earthy and *real*.

"I believe seneschal was your term."

Felíne shook herself. "You're laughing? Did you see the size of him? He's going to kill us!"

"I warned you about offending the traders."

"I didn't think you'd actually pay him!"

Kal chuckled again. "Hard to resist. It's about time he got a taste of his own tonic. You don't have to worry about Garren, Railah. He isn't that big. Though I'm sure he'd love to hear you think so."

She slouched a bit, sulking. How would she know? In her estimation, he was monstrous. She'd never even seen her father in second form. She had no frame of reference. Absently, Felíne wondered what Kal's looked like—what color his fur was, how tall he stood. He was probably the picture of masculine perfection. He was so irritatingly faultless in first form, why wouldn't his second form be equally transcendent? She bet his long limbs would be corded with muscle, ending in ferocious claws. She imagined a strong, proud male, sheathed in maybe dark gray or deep mahogany, with bottomless black eyes that stared out of a regal face…

Some part of her mind realized she had leaned comfortably back against Kal's broad chest. Felíne sat forward and snapped out of it, scolding her boldly wandering imagination. She needed to get a grip. Fatigue, hunger, and fear were scrambling her senses.

Kal eased Sig to a walk as they neared the edge of Cindamar. Felíne saw now how organic the city truly was. The outskirts of town seemed to consist primarily of personal tents. Shurii milled about feeding animals, organizing wares, and cooking meals over modest campfires. Families bickered and told stories. Groups of children darted between horses, people, and tents, squealing and yelling at one another. Most people she saw were in first form, but some, to her astonishment, were in second.

"Kal," she said softly, without turning. It was impossible for her to drag her eyes away from the shurii in second form. There were so *many*.

"Hmm?"

"How…" How did she word it? She'd been taught her entire life that the second form was lesser than the first, weaker. A base part of self that was ruled by temptation and impure impulses. All shurii, males especially, were taught from a young age to resist it at all costs. Self-control was the primary foundation of basic education. Shifting, unless absolutely necessary, was an affront to the Goddess and would result in punishment after death. All Asterosians knew this. Her conversation with Imogen in the tunnels confirmed it. She now knew it went beyond a sense of spiritual obligation. Males were dangerous. They could not be controlled; couldn't be wholly trusted. The act of procreation was one of the rare exceptions when a second form was permitted.

And yet here, in the middle of the Saraat Desert, shurii walked about in whatever form they pleased, with no discernible fear of consequence. Garren was a shock. This…all these shurii, it was unimaginable.

She tried again. "How…do they control themselves?"

Kal followed her gaze to where two tawny-colored males lifted cumbersome crates into neat stacks on the back of a wagon. "I don't follow."

Felíne glanced up. "The people. The *males*. In second form. How is there no...violence?"

He was quiet for a moment before responding. When he did, his voice was laced with disdain. "You mean, how are the males you see not raping every female they scent? Picking fights to the death? Succumbing to their inherently foul impulses?"

Felíne blinked. "Well...yes."

Kal scoffed. "Because. That's a load of horseshit."

She twisted in the saddle, shocked by his anger. "I beg your pardon?"

Kal's scowl was unsettling. "Is that really what they taught you? I know the crown sits on a fucking nest of lies, but I didn't think most people bought into it. Is that what your family told you happens with the shift?"

A nest of lies? Felíne almost allowed herself to fall down that rabbit hole. She wanted, no, *needed* to know what Kal meant by that. But he was looking at her. He wanted a response.

"I..." Felíne paused, remembering that it wasn't *her* family he was referencing. She had no idea what Railah's family would have taught her, but she knew the female's brother was a friend of Kal's, which meant he likely wasn't Faithful. Meaning his family might not be either.

But Imogen was a Fate, and she'd had first-hand experience with the horrors the second form could inflict. She's seen those females after...Felíne shook herself. Railah would have been trained similarly if she was destined for the Fates, if not by her family, then by whoever prepared her for service.

"Yes," she said. "That's what I was taught."

Kal didn't speak for some time, and the air grew pregnant with his displeasure. Finally, he shook his head. "Well, you were taught wrong. You're all being taught wrong."

Felíne waited for him to elaborate, but he remained silent. She wasn't sure what he meant and wanted to ask, but it seemed neither the time nor place for detailed discussion. Kal's earlier moment of playfulness was once again replaced with dour stoicism. He didn't currently appear in the sharing mood.

Instead of questioning him further, Felíne tucked her curiosity away for later examination and contented herself with watching the people around her in quiet fascination. A ponderously pregnant female with fur a color somewhere between fawn and clotted cream emerged from behind a canvas flap. She carried a heavy iron pot cradled against one hip and a babbling babe against the other, the telltale *lastmark* visible on his naked round belly. The baby was putting forth his best effort to squirm away from his mother's careful grip and remove his nappy.

Felíne's heart squeezed seeing the baby's *lastmark,* but she was awed despite herself. The way these shurii displayed their second forms was a wonder. The more she watched, the more she realized no one was exploding into displays of aggression, and the more she allowed herself to observe. Could Kal be right? Had her teachings been wrong?

No.

The Goddess set unmistakable parameters and spoke to her mother's priests through the *godscripts.* Imogen was a testament to the truth of the second form. And yet, Felíne couldn't help but wonder how the mother of their race felt about this irreverent exhibition. She wasn't sure how *she* felt about it. What she was sure of was that these people, too, were ones Felíne was destined to save.

They stopped briefly at the oasis pool to allow Sig a moment to drink his fill before leading him deeper into the camp. There was a main road, Felíne realized, though it was unmarked and unpaved. The perimeter residential tents expanded out around a roughly ten-acre area of land where people kept their places of business. Carts and wagons were organized in a rough circle, most closing their windows, locking up their goods, or hauling off their caravans for the evening. However, some were still open to serve the day's final straggling customers.

Kal brought them to a stop outside one such vendor, its keeper currently haggling with a patron over the material quality of a thick indigo robe. All manner of scarves, gloves, and hats were neatly stacked and hung in the rear of the wagon on staggered wooden display shelves. The vendor had a considerable selection of wearables from what had to be a dozen different species of animal. Felíne saw a pair of boots that looked to be sewn from the hide of some colossal scaled creature. A hand-painted sign beneath them read,

CLOAKING FATE

Authentic Water-dragon Leather: Dry feet guaranteed or your money returned! A moderate-sized tent with heavy bronze curtains for an entrance stood slightly behind the wagon. Presumably containing additional wares.

Felíne felt Kal dismount from behind. The day's last rays of radiant sunlight bathed his masculine features, accentuating the hollows of his cheeks and the sternness of his brow, making his skin glow as he stood looking up at her with that depthless gaze. With the light hitting him from this angle, she could see flecks of gold illuminated in his dark eyes like forbidden gilded treasures flickering enticingly at the bottom of a dangerous black sea.

What would it be like to venture into those depths? His anger was still there, churning like a tempest, but it was fading, receding like the tide. The waters were still treacherous but no longer raging.

Felíne felt a slight pressure on her right calf. The one closest to Kal. She glanced down. He was touching her. His hand was on her leg.

"I promised you dry clothes, Railah."

Railah? He wasn't touching Railah's leg. It was hers. His hand was on *her* leg. Her skin heated beneath her clothing. Odd? Absently, she reminded herself that she couldn't let him know. She couldn't let him know she was *her* and not the her he thought she was.

He was still looking up, eyes on her face.

"Yes," she said. "You did." Did her voice sound funny?

His lips curved ever so slightly. Was he amused? What was he thinking? She was looking at his lips. Why were they so interesting? Her own parted slightly.

"Can you move your leg?"

She blinked, brain puzzling out the meaning of his words with a slight delay. "What?"

"My coin is in the bag under your leg. Unless you'd like to cover the bill?"

Felíne looked down to where he indicated. Her faculties returned in a mortifying rush. Her leg gripped the saddle so tightly that Kal would have had to forcibly pry her knee away to reach the slim leather bag fastened underneath. The bag containing his money. To buy them clothes. Her cheeks flamed.

Kal was no longer smiling. Had he ever been? Or had her addled female brain imagined that, too? Ugh. She needed to get a grip—a good, firm one.

Hurriedly, she swung her leg farther back than probably necessary in her haste to move away from his touch.

Kal smoothly retrieved his coin pouch and slid it into a pocket.

"Wait here," he instructed, not looking at her. With a fond pat on Sig's neck, Kal turned and ducked into the tent, leaving Feline outside to watch the sun paint the western sky in shades of flame to match her obvious embarrassment.

Chapter 25

Kitty

THE EMBARRASSMENT DIDN'T LAST LONG. The more minutes that passed, the more her prior humiliation morphed into indignation.

Wait here.

Leave it to the notoriously unaffected thief to intentionally provoke a terrifying second form male, dash away into the town he'd previously emphasized was full of shurii possessing highly questionable moral standards, and then leave her *by herself* so he could go shopping. Never mind the part where he made her feel all sorts of irrational, unnecessary, confusing…things, and then sauntered off altogether unperturbed.

Unbelievable.

The city, if she could even call it a city, was in the process of a collective wind down. Two more shops closed while she waited, the neighboring owners chatting for a few minutes before bidding one another a friendly farewell.

Even though Cindamar seemed to consist of a haphazard arrangement of random residential canvas structures toward its perimeter, the trade center was seemingly well organized. It was divided into two rough concentric circles, the traders' shops positioned along the edges, facing the wide space created between them. The outer circle's inner boundary and the inner circle's outer boundary were bordered with wide-planked segmented boardwalks that fit together to form walkways between establishments.

The outer circle was lined with wagons, carts, and tents offering an expansive array of goods for sale. She saw several for clothing, one for luxury fabrics, and another for custom jewelry. On the opposite side, a broad space that could easily fit five trade wagons boasted what appeared to be a makeshift smithy. The smith was bent over a forge, seemingly unfinished with his day's work. Next to the smithy was a weapons vendor, and beyond that, an armory.

The inner circle of the trade center also sported mobile shops, which faced outward and consisted primarily of food vendors. A butcher, a bakery, and an herb merchant were visible.

A generous pathway cut between two carts leading to the center of the innermost circle. Through it, Felíne could see a large open area of odd-looking green grass. On its edge sat a charming garden that appeared to be constructed from a conglomeration of potted plants, flowers, shrubs, and small trees. A worn wooden bench bordered the garden's fringe, along with several tables in the grassy area where she imagined people would sit and dine.

Felíne could envision the trade center in broad daylight. The place would be bustling with activity, packed with people: families shopping, lovers seeking gifts for their partners, children pleading for treats and toys. Felíne had never been shopping; any luxuries were readily provided for her. What would it be like to walk through a crowded market and enter a store of her choosing to browse at will?

Just near the entrance to the circle center was a cart, its oak shutters still thrown wide over a counter where a vendor was cleaning up the remainder of his goods. A grand butter-yellow sail extended off the front façade of the cart to provide shade. Two thick wooden posts anchored it to the ground. Felíne watched the man behind the counter collect several containers and carry them to a deep can on the ground near the edge of his cart where he dumped their contents. Felíne caught a whiff of something delicious. Her stomach gave an appreciative grumble.

Felíne glanced at the tent where Kal was still occupied. What was taking him so long, she couldn't imagine, but she was hungry and curious, and her butt ached from hours in the saddle. She looked back at the food vendor. It wasn't far, just on the other edge of the circle near the garden. Making up her mind, she slid off Sig's back, looped his reigns loosely over a nearby hitch, and wandered toward the cart. She made a considerable effort to refrain from rubbing her backside and inner thighs, which were chafed and sore.

A prepubescent boy wearing an overlarge cap resting on wide ears stood not far off. A skinny, wiry-haired dog sat near the boy's feet, thumping its happy tail into the boy's ankle. The boy looked up at her as she passed, and she offered him a friendly smile before coming to stand under the cart's yellow sail.

The vendor grabbed another container and a handful of brightly colored fruit, preparing to toss them into the can. He hadn't seen Felíne approach.

"Excuse me, sir?" The man jumped a little and looked at her. "Forgive me. I couldn't help but notice you're throwing that food away."

The vendor recovered and looked her over. He appeared middle-aged with thin hair, warm brown eyes, and deep smile lines set into a full round face. "Course, miss," he said in a rough, unfamiliar accent. "Day's done. I've sold all I will by this time." He scraped more food into the can. "Won't go to waste, though. The butcher up the way has hogs need feeding. I get a regular fat slab of bacon for these leftovers."

"Isn't it early to be closing for the day?"

The vendor pulled a wooden sign from the edge of his cart that folded out to stand on three legs. It read *Hamme's Breakfast Best* in cheerful, sunny print. "Occasionally do a midday menu, but if you want a fine dinner place, Rovena's at the north end has the best beef shank and vegetable medley in town. Makes a mean honey corn biscuit, too."

"That does sound good," Felíne admitted, her stomach giving a rumble of agreement. She glanced at the remaining contents of his container. "But *that* smells delicious."

The man, supposedly Hamme, swelled with pride at the compliment. "This is just scraps, miss. Couldn't in clear conscience feed you hog food. But you come back tomorrow for first meal, and I'll have a proper feast for you."

He held out a fruit, and she smiled apologetically. "I'm afraid I have nothing to trade."

"On the cart," he insisted, and she gratefully took the fruit. He nodded in her direction. "You consider that coin round your neck, and I'll give you a peek at my whole recipe catalog."

Felíne gripped her necklace, zipping the coin once before tucking it beneath her dress. "I'm afraid the only value this old thing has is sentimental."

"Sure?" Hamme lowered his voice dramatically and waggled bushy eyebrows. "They're *secret* recipes. Five generations. Ol' Mel around the corner's been trying to get my leavened hot iron batter right for four years now. Four!" He leaned forward conspiratorially, one meaty hand near his mouth. "Course, he'd never know I tweak it a skosh whenever he gets close."

Felíne laughed a little. "Tempting, but I'm afraid I must decline. I haven't yet tested your culinary skills myself, after all," she teased.

"Oh ho!" Hamme leaned back and chuckled, his considerable midsection bouncing. "Right, you are, miss. Right, you are!" He pointed a finger. "Well, I expect to see you first thing tomorrow, and you'll have your proof. Then we'll haggle!"

She smiled. "I will do my best. For now, thank you for the fruit."

Felíne stepped back, and something brushed by her leg. She glanced down to see the wiry dog from earlier had crept up and sniffed toward Hamme's can of discarded food. She looked around but did not see the boy.

"Shoo, mutt," Hamme said, waving a towel in the dog's direction. "Git!"

The dog was not dissuaded. Hamme shooed it again and was met with a commotion of incessant barking.

Felíne figured now was a good time to return to Sig. She backed away from Hamme, who was preoccupied with this new distraction, and turned to retrace her steps toward the outer circle where the red roan patiently waited when a startling crack and a crash sounded behind her. She had a moment to glance up before the thick canvas shade came down on top of her, the dog, and Hamme with his discarded food.

The weight of the sail was heavier than anticipated, and it smothered her to the ground. Felíne extended her arms to try and push it away and scrambled to the side. Something crashed into her, knocking her head painfully. "Ow!" She struggled, someone struggling along with her. The boy from earlier disentangled himself and scurried furiously toward where the dog and Hamme were still scuffling.

"Oi! Cook! Get off my dog!"

Felíne found the edge of the canvas and was about to shove out from under it when she suddenly became weightless. Someone lifted her easily into the air and set her firmly on her feet.

"Are you hurt?" Kal loomed over her, broad hands gently bracing her arms, looking her up and down.

She reached up to touch her temple and winced slightly. The poor kid had smashed right into her in the confusion. Kal noticed, and his expression hardened dangerously.

"It's nothing," she said. "I just bumped my head when the shade fell."

He looked at Hamme and the boy, who had both managed to extract themselves and were arguing over the ruined shade while the dog yapped excitedly between them.

"Wait here," Kal instructed, pinning her with a glower. "And I mean it. Wait. Here."

"You're going to pay for that, you little worm!" Hamme's face was red, his earlier kindness replaced with ire as he surveyed the damage.

"Piss off, cook! It wasn't my fault!"

Hamme extended a grabbing hand, but the boy was quick and jumped effortlessly out of reach.

"Wait!" Hamme yelled.

The boy made to dash around Kal and beat a hasty retreat, dog hot on his heels and a smug grin on his face, but he didn't have the chance. Kal moved with unexpected speed and accuracy and snatched the boy straight off the ground, holding him aloft as easily as if he'd plucked a ripe grape from the vine.

"Hey! Ow!"

The dog began barking with renewed vigor. Kal ignored the mutt and held out his unoccupied hand. "Give it back."

"Let me down!"

"I will not ask again," he said with deceptive calm.

The boy was pure childish defiance.

"Kal," Feline called. "Let him go. He's just a kid."

"Yeah," the boy said. "Listen to the broad, bully. I'm just a kid. Lemme go."

Kal showed no intention of complying.

The boy's skin started to darken, russet fur sprouting from follicles along his arms and neck, snubbed fingernails elongating. He was going to shift!

Bark!

Kal shook him once, hard, and the boy's second form reverted.

"Ow, ow, dammit."

Bark, bark, bark!

Kal turned a murderous glare on the bothersome animal, a deep rumble sounding low in his chest. The mutt immediately ceased barking and let out a whine of submissive canine terror, tail tucked tightly between its legs, urine dribbling into the dirt. Satisfied but no less menacing, Kal returned his attention to the boy dangling in his grip.

The fight promptly went out of the youth. "Okay, okay. Damn. Just don't hurt my dog. Here." The boy fished in the pocket of his worn trousers and withdrew a length of chain threaded with a familiar gold coin.

Felíne's eyes went wide, hand fruitlessly searching her bare throat. She hadn't even realized it was missing. The little scoundrel! She watched as the boy dropped her necklace into Kal's outstretched hand. He inspected it briefly, then set the boy on his feet, one hand firmly gripping the base of his neck. He walked the boy to Felíne and dropped the necklace into her hand. Her name, written in a worn, delicate script, showed on the flat surface. She lifted the precious coin over her head and tucked it away once more.

"What do you say?"

The boy glared up at Kal from under his ruddy eyebrows and muttered a reluctant apology.

"Good enough. Now get lost," he said, releasing him. "And be thankful your only punishment is a wounded pride. If I catch you again, it'll be trade code."

The boy ran off a short way before skidding to a halt and looking back. His dog was still cowering at Kal's feet, belly down in the dirt, licking his lips, eyes reproachful. The boy called for the wiry canine, but it didn't move.

"Hey, bully, can I have my dog? I gave your stupid coin back."

Kal regarded the pitiful pup, then cut his glance firmly to the side as Felíne looked on with mild amusement. The mutt scampered off after his companion, and the two of them disappeared into the growing dark.

Kal faced her. Oh, wow.

"I told you to wait."

Clearly, he was unaccustomed to disobedience. "I didn't go far."

"I can see that," he growled. "But evidently, trouble finds you regardless of distance. I left you alone for five minutes, and you managed to get yourself injured, robbed, and involved in the destruction of someone's property."

"His name is Hamme," she supplied unhelpfully. "And it was more than five minutes."

"That is *not* relevant."

Okay then. "It wasn't my fault."

"Oh? Please. Explain."

Ugh. He was insufferable! "How was I supposed to know the kid was a thief!"

"A blind man could have seen that kid mark you from a mile away."

So, he'd known? Had Kal been watching her the entire time? Somehow, that thought only irritated her more.

"If you're so clever, why didn't you step in sooner? Stop the whole fiasco?"

"I turned my back for two seconds! Fuck, Railah, were you raised in a temple? The streets of Asteros are crawling with lifters and pickpockets. I thought you'd know better."

Felíne's temper snapped. "Stop calling me that!"

Kal did not back down. "Calling you what?"

"Railah! Railah, Railah, *Railah*. That is not who I am!" She realized her mistake the moment the words left her furious tongue, but it was too late; she couldn't retract them.

Kal was angry, but he wasn't stupid. His brow dropped over those heated black eyes, and she felt momentarily like he could see straight through her skin into her mendacious heart. Felíne swallowed, still furious but no longer impulsive. She had to fix this. Her very life might depend on it. "That is not who I am *anymore*. I...I don't want to be her."

Those twin obsidian orbs bored into her, no gold to be seen. The sea was dark, treacherous waters hiding a monster in the dangerous depths. In that moment, Felíne realized she did not want Kal as an enemy. She would rather face a hundred Garrens in second form fury than be the sole focus of this one male's undiluted wrath. Felíne met Kal's gaze with her own, praying whatever he saw was the sincerity she was attempting to portray and not the deception she was obligated to disguise. Gods, she hated lying. At least that last part was spoken honestly.

After a tense moment, Kal softened, if only a fraction. His eyes were still hard, still heated, but his posture relaxed, no longer primed for violence. "I don't know anything about what being chosen as a Fate took from you." He looked away from her then, voice low, eyes focused somewhere over her head in the distance, on the past. "But I do understand the need to let go of who you were to become someone else. Someone new. Sometimes, the only way to leave pain behind you is to leave behind the person who experienced it."

His words were meant to reassure his friend's sister. The one chosen as a Fate. The one he thought he'd rescued. They weren't intended for *her*. But Felíne felt a little less calloused toward the man who stole her away from her home. From *her* fate. If only it were as simple for her to let go of her responsibilities and step into a new life. For her, that was not and never would be an option. However, Kal's words made Felíne exceedingly curious about his past. What could have happened to this male that caused him to walk away from the life he lived to become who he was today? Who had he been? What kind of pain did he carry? Because somehow, she didn't think he'd left it entirely behind. It was still there, locked behind an impenetrable wall of iron will and cemented with spilled blood and bad decisions.

"You'll not hear that name from me again." His words were a vow. Felíne found herself believing them. "But it doesn't excuse the fact that you deliberately disobeyed me."

She sighed. He was like a raptor locked onto a hare. Once engaged, he wouldn't alter course until he'd sunk his talons into the object of his focus.

The boy had called Kal a bully, but that didn't fit. Bullies preyed on those weaker than them to perpetuate their self-aggrandization. Flexing their power was an attempt to fill a deep well of insecurity. Kal was undoubtedly powerful, but he didn't need to showcase it to boost his confidence. Self-actualization already rolled off him in waves. Controlling the kind of power he possessed had to take an enormous amount of restraint. Bullies did not have restraint.

If she thought about it, the kind of anger she saw Kal display earlier toward the boy was the first she'd witnessed, and he had been in undeniably more stressful situations during their short time together. He'd been on the brink of violence, clear danger in his eyes. What could have possibly made that unwavering control slip?

Felíne thought back to the moment she recalled a change in his demeanor. When she had touched the tender spot on her head.

Was he…had he been worried about her?

No, she reminded herself. If he was worried, it was about his friend's sister. Despite knowing any concern for her was not really *for her,* the thought warmed her a little. Instead of inciting the desire to exploit this potential weakness, the idea of Kal caring about her well-being made her surprisingly agreeable. She found herself wanting to avoid causing him unnecessary stress.

"I'm sorry," she said.

Kal was momentarily caught off guard, her response clearly unexpected. What he had been expecting was a fight. His eyes narrowed in suspicion.

"You're stubborn."

She nodded. That much, at least, she could not argue. "I know."

"And your lack of awareness is impressive."

They reached Sig, saddle newly laden with additional packs of what had to be Kal's recent purchases. "That didn't sound like a compliment."

"It wasn't."

She blew out a breath.

"And you're too trusting. I thought I explained enough about how potentially danger—"

"*Kal.* You're right, okay? I didn't listen." He was standing close, gaze still burning with what she assumed was lingering anger stoked by his underlying worry. She had the feeling he didn't particularly appreciate the latter emotion. Her heart made the irrational decision to increase its tempo, irrespective of her current exhaustion. "I apologized. It was sincere. Please don't lecture me."

Some of the ire dissipated. Something possessed her to reach out and lightly place a hand on his forearm. He wasn't expecting the gesture.

"I'm alright, Kal."

That wildfire in his eyes was doused by an autumn rain, still hot, still smoldering, but no longer capable of catastrophic destruction. "I should have intervened when I first saw the kid. I assumed you'd had experience dealing with petty thieves."

She lifted her brows, amused. "Like you?"

The corner of his mouth twitched. "There is nothing petty about me."

Felíne rolled her eyes.

Kal grew serious once again. "Despite the impression you likely have of me, I don't make a habit of stealing. You aren't a captive, and I don't want you to feel like one."

Her heart squeezed. Foolish, she argued with herself. If he knew who she really was, that's exactly what she'd be.

"You're sure you aren't hurt?"

"Yes," she assured. "Barely a bump."

He nodded, the monster seemingly satisfied. Kal helped her into the saddle and then led Sig back to Hamme's cart. The vendor was finishing righting the remaining mess caused by the ruined canvas shade. Kal offered to help repair the damage the following day, paid in advance for breakfast to be delivered in the morning, and finally mounted behind her, turning them down a less obscure path away from the mostly emptied trade center.

"Where are we going?" Felíne asked after they'd walked some distance. She stifled a yawn.

"To the inn," he said. "I promised you a bath, Kitty."

She craned her head to look back up at him, surprised. "Kitty?"

"I have to call you something," he said. "If not your name."

"Why Kitty?"

He raised a brow. "You're wearing a necklace with the word *feline* engraved into it."

Felíne choked a laugh. "Feline. *Fee-line.*" Not *feh-leen.*

"Yes, feline," he parroted. "As in demanding, temperamentally unpredictable little beasts. Just as likely to sink their claws into you as to crave your affection." He shrugged. "Kitty seemed to fit."

Felíne laughed in earnest, suddenly unable to contain the hilarity that bubbled up inside of her at the sheer ridiculousness of it. She laughed until tears leaked out the corners of her eyes. Kal's visage said he no longer believed her prior head trauma to be as benign as she'd assured and was noticeably convinced she had indeed suffered significant cognitive damage. He said nothing while she giggled uncontrollably and remained silent as her mirth finally subsided. Dear Goddess, she needed food, to bathe, and to sleep.

"Sorry." She took a deep breath, once again under control. "I'm fine, I promise."

"Like I said. Temperamentally unpredictable." His words earned another snort of amusement.

"Well, as far as me craving your attention, I wouldn't hold your breath," she said, then curved her fingers playfully. "But the claws…"

Kal huffed behind her, and she smiled.

"Thank you," she said after a few moments of listening to Sig's soft plodding as he walked the dirt path. The sound was lulling. Her eyes were heavy, her head heavier, and after several more paces, she gave up holding her rigid posture and rested back against Kal's chest.

He seemed to accept her weight, relaxing into the closeness. His warmth enveloped her.

"You're welcome," he said.

Felíne's eyes finally fluttered closed, soothed by Kal's secure presence, the swaying of the saddle, and the rhythmic thud of horse's hooves.

Chapter 26

The Inn

THE INN WHERE FELÍNE AND Kal were headed turned out to be less of a traditional inn—not that she expected anything even remotely traditional at this point—and more of a collection of rentable tents. The tents were spaced far enough apart to allow some moderate level of privacy between tenants but close enough to be identifiably part of the same collective establishment. The place didn't have a name. It was simply The Inn.

One main larger structure functioned as the innkeeper's residence, business office, and dining hall. Most of the apartments for rent were single rooms. However, the three closest to the innkeeper's tent were grand in comparison, and each was partitioned into separate sections that functioned as 'extended suites.' Kal had purchased one such suite for the evening. Or rather, he'd helped slip Felíne off Sig's back, pressed three coins into her palm, and instructed *her* to purchase the suite. She grumbled a bit but did as she was told.

The innkeeper was an ancient shurii woman named Leanara, fondly known among locals as Lele. She had so many wrinkles in her face, Felíne couldn't count them, and an impressive amount of stark white hair that was pinned halfway on top of her head. The rest trailed down her slightly hunched back like a wisping waterfall. Despite her withered appearance, Lele had clear, shocking blue eyes that shone with old, ornery intelligence. If her body was a dull blade, the woman's mind was a razor.

Felíne gave Lele the coins Kal had handed her and politely asked for a suite. Kal came in behind her, and Lele regarded him momentarily, eyes twinkling with mischief and crinkling deeply at the edges. She placed a piece of paper in front of Felíne.

"Just a standard rental agreement, dear. Sign here." Lele pointed a gnarled finger.

Felíne looked back to Kal, but he made no move to sign.

She didn't have the energy to puzzle out the situation. Felíne signed *Kitty* on the indicated line, unable to think of a suitable pseudo surname quickly enough, and handed the paper back to the innkeeper.

After handling their business, Lele assured them that dinner was still available in the dining compartment at their convenience—a robust lamb stew with root vegetables. Per Kal's request, one of her employees would ensure the suite was outfitted with a wash basin and hot water for a bath.

Felíne was so exhausted she was willing to skip dinner, but the bath was a physical requirement at this point. Even without all the aromatic oils and herbal scrubs—Lele had provided Kal with a rough chunk of soap smelling strongly of citrus and something woodsy—the thought of soaking her aching body in steaming water was enough to make her suppress a whimper of anticipatory relief.

Kal stopped Sig in front of their suite and unlocked the door with the key Lele provided. It took Felíne's sluggish brain a moment to realize there was an actual lock. On an actual door. Upon closer inspection, she saw that stiff wood planks had been sewn into the canvas walls at intersections, creating a barrier that was significantly more secure than simple cloth construction. The tent itself sat on a slightly elevated platform and was anchored in place by thick woven cords and heavy stakes. It wasn't adobe or stone, but it was stable enough to provide the occupants with a decent forewarning if an intruder attempted forced entry.

The inside of the suite was sparse by Felíne's standards but appreciatively functional. There was no unnecessary decoration. No heavy furniture. Only basic, maneuverable pieces that could be easily packed and hauled off if required. The suite had three separate sections. Two had beds, thick padded mattresses on simple wooden pallets piled with furs and pillows, as Kal had promised. The third room, situated between the bedrooms, functioned as the washroom with a standing basin in one corner near a rack holding neatly folded towels. In the center was the loveliest monstrosity of a copper tub that

Felíne had ever beheld. It was scuffed, worn, and dented in multiple spots, but it was clean and deep enough to comfortably fit a shurii in second form.

The tinkling of a chime sounded somewhere inside the suite. Felíne wandered back toward the main entrance and looked up to see a small swinging bell dangling from the ceiling. She looked questioningly at Kal.

"It's a doorbell," he said as though casually explaining a great mystery of the universe.

Kal opened the door to their suite, folding it back and securing it, to reveal two shurii males in second form, each carrying an overlarge drum, the contents of which were throwing off copious amounts of steam.

The first male, large with a thick russet coat, dipped his head in greeting. He wore a simple linen shirt and trousers tailored to accommodate his bulk and tail. On his shirt front was an emblem: the outline of an upside-down triangle sewn in crimson thread surrounding two balanced gray scales. Felíne recognized the scales. The image was the same as the one on the coin Kal had flipped to Garren.

"Innkeeper Lele sent us to fill the bath. May we?"

Instead of allowing the males over the threshold, Kal blocked the door. The movement seemed a little silly, considering the male standing outside towered over him and likely outweighed him by double. Kal, however, wasn't cowed.

"He can," Kal said, nodding toward the smaller, tawny male standing behind the first. "*You* can inform your employer that I'll meet him shortly."

The second male dipped his head and hurried past Kal with his heavy load, making for the bath.

The russet male's amiable act dropped like a heavy stone in a still pond. "You would be well advised not to delay." He peeked over Kal's shoulder, gaze landing on Felíne. "If only to avoid any unnecessary consequences."

Kal leaned a fraction closer. If he'd had hackles in first form, they would have shot into the air. "My companion is a paying guest of The Inn. She is protected by trade code." Kal glanced down to where the male's clawed foot toed the threshold. "You are trespassing, Bodemere."

The male's eyes widened, and he regarded Kal with new wariness, ears twitching. He hadn't expected Kal to know him by name.

"If you don't want a delay, I suggest you get moving," Kal said. "I said I'd meet him once I was settled, and I will. He can expect me within the hour."

The russet male lowered his drum and stepped back from the entrance, clearly unhappy but bound by invisible shackles of what Felíne assumed were duty or obeisance.

"Oh, and Bodemere?"

The male stopped his retreat and looked over his shoulder to where Kal stood.

"Don't ever fucking threaten me again."

She was in heaven. Floating in the watery halls of the Goddess herself. Felíne stretched a bare foot up out of the bath water. She extended an arm. It was clean. Then, she promptly resubmerged everything from the neck down. She'd been in the bath for over an hour, and her hands were wrinkled like a crone's. She was scrubbed raw, skin pink and smooth from the rough soap, not a speck of dirt in sight. And while she smelled more masculine than she would have preferred, at least she didn't smell like sweat and grime and Sig.

Felíne released a contented sigh and finally rose out of the tub, tepid water sluicing between her breasts and down her body. It had long since ceased steaming.

The second male who'd arrived with Bodemere, a young male named Shel who happened to *actually* be an employee of the innkeeper, had offered to return in an hour with fresh water to refill the bath. Kal had declined, and Shel departed. Kal had an errand to run, he'd told her, and would be back when he was finished. She guessed he was going to meet with the Trade Master. Felíne had been instructed to remain in the suite while he was away, which had now been nearly an hour and a half. Kal had given her a hard look before he left, likely in an attempt to impress upon her some deep obligation to obey, but if he was worried about her wandering off, it was a wasted concern. Shel had brought her a heaping bowl of stew with warm crusty bread just before

Kal's departure, so she hadn't needed to skip dinner after all. She had no desire to do anything except eat, bathe, and sleep.

The first two items on her agenda for the evening were done. Now, she only needed to sleep. Tomorrow would be a new day to plan an escape.

Felíne toweled off, wrung out her hair, and combed through the tangles with her fingers. When Kal returned, she'd have to ask if Lele could provide a comb.

She slipped on the thick gray robe Kal had left for her and wandered back into her suite to inspect the items he'd purchased. Felíne found a new pair of boots made of soft leather with thick, durable soles. She pulled out a pair of dark chocolate-colored breeches lined on the inside with a heavier material that would keep her warm in colder weather and a second pair in a lighter color that were unlined but with slight padding to protect her legs in the saddle. Two long-sleeved cotton tunics were there, both of which would fall to about mid-thigh and laced up the front. One was a lovely deep wine color with simple dove-colored stitching, the other a muted hunter green with tawny laces and a buff inner sheath. Kal's attention to detail was acute. He had chosen pieces similar in style to what she'd already been wearing, and while the material of the new garments wasn't nearly as fine as what Felíne owned, they were clean, new, and looked comfortable.

Felíne pulled out two identical pairs of socks, a set of simple undergarments that made her blush furiously at the thought of Kal purchasing them on her behalf, and a final third garment that caused her to forget her embarrassment in lieu of confusion. She held up the bronze-hued piece of clothing for inspection. There was no way this was intended for her. It was feminine in style, but it was at least three times too large for her and oddly cut. The shoulders were too wide, the waist too narrow, and the way it flared just so...

Oh!

Realization dawned on her. Kal had purchased a garment for her second form. He bought an outfit for her just in case she decided to shift. She thought back to his words.

You aren't a captive, and I don't want you to feel like one.

He was trying to be thoughtful. Felíne pictured the female she'd seen when they'd entered Cindamar. The one with the toddler on her hip and the creamy fur. A sting of jealousy pierced the gratitude she felt at Kal's consideration. She stuffed the garment back into the bag. It was one she'd never wear.

Felíne laid out the wine-colored tunic and darker breeches, not yet ready to give up the snuggly comfort of her robe. At home, she wore a sleeping gown to bed but there were no night clothes in the bag Kal provided.

She was just about to pull back the comforter on her mattress when she heard movement in the main compartment. Someone entered the tent.

Felíne swiped her hatchet from where it rested by the bed and crept back to the shared tub room. She peeked around the heavy canvas flap that separated the two compartments and relaxed. Kal was back.

He was gathering his belongings, stuffing things back into his pack, and glanced up at her entrance. Kal stopped, hand suspended mid-reach, and looked at her. Felíne could tell he was unhappy about whatever had transpired during his errand, but for a brief moment, there was something entirely different than irritation in his gaze. And that thing, whatever it was, gave her pause.

She suddenly became acutely aware of every inch of naked flesh under her robe. The way Kal was looking at her gave Felíne the impression he shared in that awareness. Gooseflesh pimpled down her arms and legs. Her nipples tightened. She was covered from shoulders to shins by dense woolen fabric, but she may as well have been completely nude for how exposed she felt. They were both silent and still, ensnared by a web of shared focus, neither so much as twitching to break the tension. Water dripped quietly from a thick strand of Felíne's wet hair and hit the rug under her bare feet.

She should move. Say something. Stop whatever it was that Kal was thinking as he looked at her like that. It was wrong, she knew. Expressly forbidden. He was looking at her the way she imagined a man looked at a woman he wanted but shouldn't. A look she was currently returning. And she needed to stop it.

But Felíne didn't move. She barely breathed. Kal was so dangerously beautiful, it was sinful. His hard, powerful body was sheathed in sun-kissed golden-brown skin and leather armor. Long legs and the tight curve of his muscular ass were clad in fitted black trousers. His hooded eyes were dark, brow heavy, his masculine features strong and defined. A muscle feathered in his temple. She wanted to reach out and run the pad of her thumb across his fuller bottom lip. Feel the soft skin there and then the contrast of the short black hair of his goatee and the scratchy stubble along his jaw.

As if she spoke her thoughts aloud, Kal's gaze darkened, heated. Blessed Mother, it was wrong, but Felíne *wanted* him to keep looking at her like that. The heat from his eyes pooled low in her belly and settled there. The sensation was strange and unfamiliar. It turned her joints to liquid, making her feel pliable and fluid. Her gooseflesh melted, skin suddenly molten. Kal's nostrils flared, scenting, and Felíne thought this was distinctly different from Garren's earlier intrusive sniffing. The attention of this man made her feel feminine, powerful, alluring. She wanted him to smell the heat coming off her skin. Wanted him to t—

The doorbell chimed above them and broke the spell, the sound dousing them as effectively as a bucket of icy water.

Kal peeled his attention from her, growled, and stalked to the door. Felíne swallowed a lungful of air.

Lele stood outside leaning on an ivory cane flanked by two males. Shel and another. "I am sure that foul temper is a result of the Trade Master's instructions and not my visit," she said with a raised brow.

Kal grunted and left the door open, but Lele did not enter.

She peeked inside, intelligent blue eyes taking in Felíne's undoubtedly flushed face and robed figure. "I trust I am not interrupting?" A hint of a smile tugged at the corners of her thin lips, adding yet another wrinkle to the old woman's face. Her snowy hair floated around her like a corona.

Kal did not answer, and Felíne did not know what to say. The memory of Kal's fiery gaze muddled her thoughts. What in the Goddess's name had they put in the bathwater?

Lele hummed. "Your new accommodations have been prepared. Shel and Dem here will help transfer your belongings."

Felíne turned questioningly to Kal. "What new accommodations?"

The fire was gone. He was back to being surly. "Trade Master Grisham has taken it upon himself to provide alternative lodging for us for tonight."

"Why? What's wrong with this suite?"

Lele smiled wider, showcasing a set of surprisingly intact teeth. "The Trade Master has paid for a fully furnished luxury apartment."

"Gather your things," Kal said to her. "It's not far."

Felíne didn't budge. "Why?" She repeated. "We've already paid for this suite."

"Oh, you will be fully refunded, dear."

"It would be considered impolite for us to decline," Kal said tightly.

"So?" Screw being polite. She was exhausted. Kal was on edge. They needed rest. "Is it not also impolite to inconvenience your guests by insisting on relocating them after they've already retired for the evening?"

Lele laughed, delighting in Felíne's uncustomary irreverence.

Kal glowered. "The Trade Master and I have had business dealings in the past. He knows me, but he does not know you. As Garren mentioned, I have never visited Cindamar accompanied by…"

"A lady friend?" Lele supplied helpfully.

Kal ignored her. "Your presence is unexpected, and Grisham does not appreciate being surprised. He has agreed to postpone your inspection until tomorrow, provided we accept his hospitality."

Felíne frowned and folded her arms across her chest. "So, in other words, he doesn't trust me, and he wants to control where we stay until he has a chance to decide for himself whether or not I'm a threat."

Kal dipped his chin in agreement. He was pissed. Grisham might not like surprises, but Kal did not appreciate being manipulated. Unfortunately, his pride painted him into a corner. He'd agreed to keep from dragging Felíne before the Trade Master tonight, which was apparently the only alternative and one with which she did not abide.

This had to do with trade code. Felíne was somehow protected as a paying customer of The Inn. By providing their lodging, Trade Master Grisham side-stepped that protection, reestablishing his control until he could meet Felíne and see for himself if she was cause for concern. He might know Kal, but he didn't trust him entirely. Either that or this was a play for dominance on Grisham's home turf.

Fine. If Kal had agreed, even grudgingly, she had little choice but to go along with it. In the grand scheme of things, she didn't care which bed she slept in as long as it possessed those two details: bed and sleep. Felíne returned to her room to quickly change and collect her things.

Fifteen minutes later, Felíne stood in the doorway of another tent owned by Lele, the innkeeper, and stared at a single, exceptionally large bed piled high with lush furs, extravagant throws, and a miniature mountain of down pillows. It was the only piece of furniture in the one-room apartment. That is if you didn't count the single deeply padded chair or the monstrous oval tub in the right corner, obviously large enough to comfortably fit two adult shurii, which was nearly overflowing with steaming hot water and a cascade of aromatic blush rose petals.

She looked back at the bed and squinted. A distinctly identifiable herb was scattered across the top throw. *Wombwillow.* The herb of fertility.

Felíne turned to Kal, who had an unreadable expression on his serious face.

"No."

Absolutely not. Her earlier lapse of judgment had been fully rectified, and sleeping in the same bed as Kalevar was strictly out of the question. Especially one that had been contaminated with a blessing for fruitful coupling.

Kal's glower returned, and he stalked into the room, dumping their packs onto the rug by the foot of the bed.

He unbuckled his belt and shoulder sheath and tossed both onto the bed. Hidden weapons were carefully revealed and set aside. Next, he removed his leather jerkin and cuirass. Felíne could see the imprints of sweat and dirt where the armor had stained his white linen shirt a dingy brown. Kal undid his boots and tugged them off his feet, discarding them unceremoniously to the side. She watched as he stood and reached for the tie at his pants.

Alarm bells in her head blared in warning. "What are you doing?"

He looked up, unbothered by her alarm. "What does it look like I'm doing?"

"Taking off your clothes!"

"Ah, so she does have some sense of awareness after all." Kal tugged the dirty shirt over his head, revealing an obscenely cut torso. He may as well have been carved from marble, chiseled by the masters with exceptional skill and painstaking detail. On closer inspection, Felíne was startled to find Kal's body was marred with a multitude of scars that stood out like a network of pale runes scattered across his flesh. One particularly wicked mark disfigured the otherwise smooth skin of his chest near his heart. He'd seen his fair share of fighting, whether by choice or circumstance, she did not know.

His pectorals were dusted lightly with dark hair that trailed a line down the ridges of his abdominal muscles toward his navel and lower, where the tie of his pants was partly undone.

She turned promptly away from him and wound up facing the bath and the petals. The sight did nothing to reroute the immodest direction of her thoughts. Or her burning curiosity. There was shuffling to her left where Kal stood near the bed. Another piece of clothing was being removed. Her heartbeat kicked up its tempo. "You can't just get naked. I'm standing right here! It's inappropriate."

"Oh?" Felíne jumped. He was much closer than he'd been a moment ago. "Like you were earlier?"

"I wasn't naked. I was in a robe!"

Kal chuckled, and it was absurd how sensual the sound was. "Barely," he said. "That robe was indecent."

Her face heated, and Felíne wished she could force the blood that was currently painting her cheeks into her brain instead so maybe she'd get a handle on her obvious lack of common sense. "You left it for me! Besides, I had expected some privacy. How was I supposed to know you were going to barge in unannounced? You're lucky I had finished bathing."

Kal moved past her to the tub and into her line of sight. Blessedly, he still wore pants, though his socks had been removed. He dipped a broad hand into the heated water and swiped the petals floating on the surface onto the floor. "You're right, I *am* lucky. Considering the way you were looking at me, if I had returned to find you still naked in the tub, my virtue would have undoubtedly been compromised."

His virtue? She huffed. "Oh, you think so, do you?"

Kal's fingertips beaded with water. He watched several drops fall, creating ripples on the surface. "I know so. You were dripping wet." Drip, *drip.* "And not from the bath."

"You dare!"

His lips quirked. "Oh, Kitty, I haven't dared anything yet."

284

Felíne forcibly shut her gaping mouth. She was in trouble. She needed distance from this man. Physical distance. There was no way she could sleep in the same room as him. At this rate, she needed a different continent. "I demand my own tent."

Kal wiped his hand on his pant leg. "You can't have your own tent. I already tried that, and Grisham outmaneuvered me." He grimaced and ran a hand over his head, tousling the infant curls. "Since you're no longer a paying customer of The Inn, I am your only protection. Tomorrow, when you meet the Trade Master, he'll either deem you safe and extend a formal invitation to Cindamar by offering you a token or…he won't. Either way, it'll be easier for me to keep an eye on you here for tonight."

She should be concerned with what would happen if Trade Master Grisham decided to deny her welcome, but Felíne couldn't get past the half-clothed image of Kal or the idea of sleeping in the same room with him. Somehow, it felt infinitely more scandalous than sharing a shallow hole in the ground to preserve body heat.

"I'm not sleeping with you."

"I don't recall asking you to," he said, and her mouth clicked shut. Kal sighed. "Look, Kitty. You had a chance to bathe, to relax. I'm tired and filthy and would appreciate the same courtesy. Take the bed. I will sleep on the floor."

With that, Kal undid the final tie of his trousers, and they dropped to his feet. Felíne hastily turned away from him, wrestling her unanticipated feminine wiles into submission, and retreated to the bed. She heard the soft displacement of water as he stepped into the tub and lowered himself into the liquid warmth. A moment later, he sighed, the sound so unexpectedly contented, an echo of her earlier relief as the hot water soaked away the stress and strain of the past three days.

Felíne busied herself collecting the softer furs off the bed and adding several fluffy pillows to create a makeshift pallet on the floor, eyes kept firmly away from the bath. She listened to the swish of the water as Kal scrubbed the dust and muck from his body. It was then, while her impossible imagination conjured images of his warrior's body floating in a sea of fragrant rose petals, that the canvas wall behind the tub shredded with a terrible rip, and the room exploded into chaos.

Chapter 27

Addict

DOMITAN GRIPPED THE MAN BEFORE him by the throat. He struggled, but the king's grip was an iron vice. He applied pressure, cutting off the wheezing flow of air through the windpipe. The man's eyes were wide with shock and something that sent a pleasurable thrill running down Domitan's spine, suffusing his limbs with increased strength, honing his awareness to a keen edge.

Fear.

The man in his grasp was naked. Wet.

Domitan's armor was saturated from the splashing.

"You still don't remember? Not even a single detail?"

The man wheezed, desperate to draw air into his starved lungs.

"No? Pity."

At the king's nod, a deluge of freezing water plunged onto the man's face. Domitan eased the force on his throat, but the additional restraints kept him in place. He sputtered, lungs begging for air only to fill with water.

A few more seconds.

A few more.

Domitan held up a hand, and the flow stopped. The man choked. Gasped. Shivered uncontrollably. Then he began to weep. Pitiful creature.

"P…pl…please, Majesty. I don't know an…any…thing. I s…sw… swear to you."

He nearly bit off the end of his tongue with his chattering. Partly from the cold, partly from the withdrawal.

They'd been at this for the better part of the morning. The man was nearing expiration. Domitan had tortured enough filth to be able to identify the breaking point's approach. Sometimes, he pushed them to the edge, tipped them over, and watched them fall. Other times, he pulled back just enough to allow them that precious pretense of hope, that yearning for on-coming relief that kept them just inside the brink of madness and allowed enough recovery for Domitan to start again.

He could have done this for days. But addicts had their limits. For all the drugs that it took to get them high, their tolerance for torture was disappointingly low.

"It's all right. Shh. I believe you."

"You d...do?" The man began crying in earnest now.

"Of course."

A brief, undiluted glimmer of relief shone in the man's red, watery eyes before they widened in confused surprise. A bloody bubble popped as his mouth opened on an exhale. Domitan raised his blade for the man to see and watched as bright crimson droplets fell from the edge to mingle with the man's tears. He wondered if the addict even realized the blood was his own before his eyes glazed over, pupils dilating for the last time.

The stench of piss filled Domitan's nostrils as the dead man lost the contents of his bladder. He stepped back from the corpse, tossing the knife he'd used to cut its throat onto a table of others. He washed his hands at the door to the stone chamber and left the gaoler to clean up the mess.

General Corstow was waiting for him at the top of the stairs.

"Anything?"

Domitan growled. "Nothing. Not a fucking thing."

Corstow had the decency to mirror his king's disappointment. "Perhaps I can find an accomplice. A witness even. Dealers are careful, but addicts are sloppy. They make frequent mistakes."

Domitan toweled off his forearms. His wet clothes clung uncomfortably. He needed to change.

"Perhaps you should have been looking already."

Corstow dipped his head and offered an apology.

Domitan waved him off. "This was a waste. That miserable shit didn't know anything. He had a limp prick where his spine should have been. If he had anything of substance to share, he would have sung."

Corstow's expression turned grave. "Whoever paid him with that dagger received enough *kossroot* to keep an entire den of druggies high for a month. At least we got that much. The buyer is our culprit. He has to be."

Yes. He was. The blade Corstow had found in the addict's possession was a twin to the one that had killed the soldier outside of Brune's. Corstow had thrown it into a pig and examined the fragmented tip. It matched. Whoever their killer was had purchased a shit heap of *kossroot* from the lowlife dealer. Now Domitan had one less worthless addict in his city, but still no answers. They needed *something*.

"Go back to the addict's territory. Find me a fucking clue, Corstow. I need a godsdamned name."

The general bowed stiffly. "Yes, Majesty."

He made to depart but stopped. "My king, if I may?"

Domitan gestured him on with forced patience.

"The Queen requests an update."

The king turned, radiating menace. "And do you answer to the queen, Corstow?"

Corstow bowed deeply. "No, my king. I am sworn to you and you alone. I only wished to inform, Majesty."

"Get out."

Domitan did not have to say it twice.

Serebine.

His wife was driving him to the very last shreds of sanity. Her incessant inquiring was approaching the realm of obsession. She didn't sleep. Didn't eat. For a female who typically shared his disdain for habitual pedantic motions, the queen could now be found pacing her chambers in the middle of the night or tapping her foot in anxious staccatos. Her attendants were beside themselves, lost without their mistress's confident direction. She did not entertain company save for Vulgren and his reports of the Fates, and even during those briefings, Serebine was only half attentive.

She had approached him the prior evening after another day with no word as to the Prima's whereabouts and asked him to stay the night in the villa. Domitan had barely concealed his shock. She'd not asked because of any feminine desires for affection or even because she craved his companionship, but because she wanted him close in case news of her daughter reached the king's ears ahead of her own.

Domitan had promptly declined and ordered her to the temple. He couldn't allow her to continue wandering the halls of the villa like a raving banshee. Sooner or later, word would spread beyond the palace walls, and once her erratic behavior reached the ears of the people, impossible speculations and malignant theories would be on the lips of every shurii in Asteros. The king's containment of the situation would be at an end.

He would do whatever he could to prevent that from happening, including sequestering his wife.

She'd fought him. Argued against going, but Domitan did not take no for an answer. Not from anyone. He had her escorted to the Temple of the Rising Dawn early that morning, and that's where he expected she would remain until such time that he deemed necessary to retrieve her. As devout as his wife claimed to be, she could spend this time exercising it. Prayers to the Goddess for the Prima's safe return were all the woman could currently offer. And maybe apologies for her own gross incompetence. If the girl had remained under his protection, they wouldn't be in this fucking mess.

No, Serebine would remain in the temple. In prayer. She had little power to help their situation in any other way.

Domitan had thought she would finally be someone else's problem and allow him the presence of mind to concentrate, and yet she still found some way to bypass the watchful eye of her priests and nag him for information. Pestiferous female.

Domitan left the shadowed alcoves of the Asteros dungeons and pushed into the light. Guards snapped to attention, spines straightening as though impaled with rods of steel by his presence.

He entered the guardhouse and stripped the soiled fabric from his body before donning fresh garments and clean armor.

No missives had come.

Two days ago, he and Corstow had concluded that they needed to broaden their search for the Prima. While clues as to her captor's identity and whereabouts might have existed within the walls of Asteros, the Prima herself had undoubtedly been taken beyond them.

The eastern gate had been compromised the night of her disappearance. Four soldiers had been found strewn in a stinking heap of unconscious flesh in one of the nearby buildings covered in vomit. Two dead. The military mender's assessment pointed to another overdose.

Shooting *kossroot* had been a problem among the soldiers in years past. One the king had demonstrated little tolerance for. He'd personally made examples of several guilty individuals, their punishments witnessed by the mass of his militia in a public fashion, and the issue had been overwhelmingly resolved. Instances of use still presented themselves in isolated occurrences, but it was rare. Now, he wondered if the recent drug use had more nefarious origins.

Domitan possessed a reserved belief in divine intervention, but he also didn't lend much credence to coincidence. His instincts told him those soldiers at the eastern gate had been lured into abandoning their post and left blitzed on *kossroot*. *Kossroot* purchased in bulk by the Prima's captor from the addict, who by now was being incinerated in his dungeon kiln. That wasn't happenstance.

He couldn't continue wasting his time scouring the city. Corstow had agreed, not that the king required it. His hunters' talents would be better spent outside the walls of Asteros. That's where the real answers would be found. So that's where he sent them. His three sharpest hunters were on whatever trail could be found. Domitan wouldn't receive word until they had something valuable to relay. They didn't waste time with ineffectual correspondence.

If the Prima's captor was out there, hunkered down somewhere in the Saraat, they would find him. And if it was a ransom he expected for the Prima's return, the king's hunters would willingly pay it.

In blood.

His instructions had been to deliver the thief alive—he wanted his own uninterrupted quality time with the male—though he'd be a tyrant king indeed if he denied Tavene, his prime huntress, a little bloodletting in the process.

The prey had taken flight, and the predators had been set loose.

All Domitan had to do now was the thing he despised most.

Wait.

Chapter 28

Might, Mind, and Blade

TAVENE SAT CROSS-LEGGED NEAR the sputtering flames of the mediocre campfire that Drexan had haphazardly thrown together to stave off the late-night chill. It was unnecessary; their uniforms provided enough insulation to adequately regulate their core temperatures, but idleness was Drexan's most formidable foe. They'd been waiting for over two hours now, and the male's patience tended to wane around sixty minutes, fully tapping at ninety. Tavene learned long ago what became of his particular brand of boredom, and they didn't need complications like that now. Not when they were so close, and all focus was required. She needed Drexan fully hinged and swinging both ways.

Hence the fire. Sometimes, all a man needed was a little responsibility to satisfy that inherent desire to feel useful.

Every few minutes, he prodded the kindling, causing a flurry of miniature sparks, as though it were an imperative task requiring his undistracted attention. The prodding was also unnecessary. The fire, pitiful though it was, wouldn't immediately die if he looked away for ten seconds. Or an hour. But she wasn't about to tell him that. Not when this little distraction provided her a reprieve from his otherwise constant badgering.

Tavene slid the whetstone along her sword's edge at a precise thirty-degree angle in practiced strokes. She was careful to leave just enough of the edge blunted to ensure its efficacy and maintain its strength. Too sharp and the blade would become brittle, increasing the likelihood of chipping upon impact, and she couldn't have that. An unreliable tool was an unacceptable one.

CLOAKING FATE

She passed the stone once more. Her movements were methodical, ritualistic.

Femoran should have been back any minute with his report on their target and additional intel on an identifiable extraction point. The man's mind was a labyrinth of details and information, and reconnaissance was his specialty. You could walk him blindfolded into a room full of people, remove the blindfold for a full second before replacing it, and he would be able to recall each person's distinguishing features and attire, identify all exits visible from his current position, and provide an assessment of any potential threats. He possessed the personality of a dull river rock, but what he lacked in animation he made up for in intelligence, which was infinitely more useful.

"Flaming shit balls!" Drexan cursed and rubbed his muscled forearm where a particularly belligerent spark had landed.

This one, on the other hand, had animation to spare.

The third point of their little coterie triangle couldn't be further opposite Femoran's lackluster predictability. Drexan was a mammoth of a male and possessed a personality as large and loud as his physique. If Femoran was a flat grassy plain, Drexan was a rugged mountain range with low valleys and soaring precipitous peaks. His first form was huge by typical standards. He stood well over seven feet tall, nearly two feet over lean Femoran, and three times as wide. His humanoid first form was fearsome indeed, but it was his second form that made him invaluable. He had the raw strength of ten males. And while Tavene preferred stealth to pure power, all that brute force and bottled rage came in handy when things went sideways.

And things often went sideways.

Drexan sent another cascade of orange sparks into the settling darkness. "Been too long," he complained.

Tavene did not look up from her bladework. "Patience."

His prodding gained an aggressive edge, and the sparks responded in kind. "And what do you think we've been doing, hm? We've *been* patient. I say it's been too long."

"He will return. And he will expect us to be here when he does."

"Well, *we* expected *him* ages ago."

Tavene did not answer.

292

Drexan glowered at her. "All he set to do was look. *Look.* Not engage. Not pursue. Just look around and plug information into that lockbox brain of his so he can puke it up for us later. How long does that take, hm?"

She extended her arm. *Swiiiiipe.* "As long as it takes."

"Blow this, Tav," he growled. "Fem's comp'd."

Tavene bit back a sigh. She set down her task and looked at the huge man. He was bald except for a thick, dingy blond braid that grew from the base of his skull and hung limply over his ridiculously muscled shoulder. He was hunched doggedly over his little fire, and despite the menacing tattoos painting the sides of his head and face, he looked like a great child on the verge of an even greater tantrum. Tavene knew of Drexan's tantrums, and unfortunately, they tended to result in damage, the likes of which was no childish matter.

"Drexan, he will return. Femoran is not compromised." He should have known as well as she. Femoran's level of caution bordered on obsessive. A feature with which they were well acquainted.

"How do you know?"

The great child was looking to dear mother for reassurance. No one would dare call her motherly, but they trusted her judgment and sought her approval all the same. Tavene provided these two killers a consistent, calm stability they didn't even realize they craved. She was the thread that bound them together. Awkward Femoran and his inability to express all that stoppered psychological excess. Simple, volcanic Drexan and his persistent impulsivity.

Femoran was a bottomless sea, Drexan the hurricane rolling across its surface.

And she was the moon. Anchoring. Guiding.

She leaned forward. "How many missions have we completed, Drexan?"

He was still surly, but he accepted the distraction. "At least fifty."

Forty-seven specifically, but close enough for her purposes. "And how many have we failed?"

His answer came quicker. "None," he said, unable to damper his pride.

"And when has Femoran ever allowed himself to become compromised?"

"Never."

Tavene returned to her blade. "That is how I know, Drexan. We are the Hunters of Asteros. The elite. The king's reserve. An extension of his will. You are his might. Femoran, his mind." *Swipe.* "And I am his blade."

The big man's eyes followed her movements as though hypnotized.

"Our king calls us when others fail, Drexan, because we do not."

He nodded, serious, fully satisfied by her reasoning.

Tavene's pep talk would settle him for about twelve minutes before he returned to his fatalistic train of thought. Might as well hack off the next tantrum before it even took root.

"He will return," she said again. "And he will be hungry."

Drexan puffed his already bulging pectorals and poked his fire again for good measure before pushing to his feet. Resolve colored his expression.

"Then he bloody well better take his time, hm? You can't rush the fixing of a proper meal."

Femoran crept silently from the darkness forty-two minutes later, just as Drexan was putting what he called 'the final touches' on his stew. He was an above-average cook, which was an unexpected talent that offered their trio a particular luxury while away doing the king's bidding. He carried a compartmented pouch with various dried herbs that he replenished on the road and would use to spice and flavor the meals he prepared. Tonight, they dined on white-peppered dune adder stewed with hard bread and *thistleroot*. Tavene had no idea how Drexan had managed to concoct a broth from naught but the water from their skins and emaciated plant material, but he had.

"Ah, right on time," Drexan said with a self-satisfied smile as he spooned a steaming heap of fleshy stew into a bowl and handed it to Femoran.

The lanky male blinked owl eyes at the bowl in his hands and looked at Tavene in question.

"The reconnaissance was moderately successful," he said in his typical monotone when she remained silent. "I project our odds of success to be eighty-six percent."

Drexan wiped his bear paws on a towel, re-draped it over his shoulder, and glared at Femoran.

The male continued, unperturbed, stew forgotten. "Higher, provided we remove the—"

Tavene held up a hand and accepted a bowl from Drexan.

Femoran waited, suddenly lost amidst the social innuendo and nonverbal cues. Tavene blew lightly on her stew and tasted a sip. The serpent meat was tender, the broth rich and earthy.

"Compliments to the chef are in order, Drexan," she said. The big male preened. "Manners, Femoran. Try your food."

Femoran brought the dish to his lips and gulped a steaming mouthful, chewing and swallowing efficiently, inconsiderate of the scalding temperature.

Tavene dipped a petrified corner of bread into her broth. "What is your assessment of the meal?"

"Calorically, it is less than one-third of our daily requirements—less than a fifth in Drexan's case—however, we have trained for such dietary restrictions and will not suffer detriment provided a balanced ration be consumed within the week. It is lacking in fat content but provides enough carbohydrate from the tuberous root and sufficient protein from the..." He took another gulp and worked his jaw on a chunk. "Adder meat, to provide immediate sustainability."

Drexan's head threatened to explode.

Tavene pinched the bridge of her nose. She should have known better. Three days with only two hours of sleep was finally catching up to her.

"Femoran, please thank Drexan for the meal and tell him that you like the way it tastes."

Femoran turned to face the volcano. "Honorable Drexan, thank you for preparing this meal. It is delicious."

The volcano flashed a wide grin, satisfied, and settled in with his own portion. Eruption averted.

CLOAKING FATE

Necessary pleasantries exchanged, Tavene and Drexan listened as Femoran relayed the details of his surveillance.

"The town is widely unprotected," Tavene mused. "Little more than an overgrown campsite."

Femoran nodded. "It possesses no discernible defensive structures. I saw no wall, no towers, no moat. I was unable to visualize any manner of fortifiable construction. The surrounding terrain provides no natural deterrent to siege. The bordering mountain range is not close enough to successfully shield the settlement from attack. I saw no soldiers or other organized militia."

Drexan laughed and wiped broth from his lips with the back of a bear paw. "So, our target is squatting in an unguarded campsite with nothing but a bunch of sky-bellied civilians keeping watch? Ha! Have you heard of an easier assignment, Tav? Hm?"

Tavene frowned. In theory, sure. But nothing about tracking this thief had been easy so far. Drexan's short-term memory loss must have relieved him of their extended sojourn through the Saraat in the wrong direction just two days past. Even with the monsoon, she had enough experience to effectively hunt even the most elusive prey. And yet whatever the Prima's captor had done to cover his tracks had wasted nearly an entire day of pursuit. No, this was no ordinary thief. He was skilled. Dangerous. Tavene found it hard to believe he would have chosen an indefensible location with such a rich prize in his custody. He took time to obscure his retreat, which indicated he expected to be followed. Instinct told her rushing in blindly would be a mistake. When her instincts whispered, she always listened.

Femoran continued. "There is a narrow possibility the town itself is equipped with traps to deter unwanted visitors or the unnatural bodies of water may conceal some manner of weaponry, though I believe both to be improbable."

"Foolsplay! Tav, let's go now. We'll be back in Asteros before the week's end. Fem, you'll be back to your pigeons, and I'll be nestled between the ample bosoms of my sweet maidens."

Any female that braved the bed of the mercurial monstrosity was no maiden and couldn't hope to be described as sweet. Even seasoned whores kept their distance despite what he was willing to pay. It was a known fact that the life expectancy of Drexan's bedmates was discounted, and crippled prostitutes didn't earn. He gave the adage 'one night knocker' a haunting sense of finality.

Femoran's straight shag of chin-length coffee-ground hair shifted as he tilted his head. "They are not pigeons. They are a rare breeding pair of Amorous Fleetwing doves."

Drexan waved him off. "Pigeons, man." He then held his palms up in front of himself as though fondling a pair of enormous tits.

Tavene addressed Femoran before he had a chance to further argue the species of his avian pets. "What of the guards?"

"Stationed in the desert surrounding the camp. At least four at one time, each patrolling a perimeter quadrant. I would venture an assumption that these guards rotate shifts. It is likely not a standard six hours due to what I would perceive as a limited number of available bodies. Twenty-four would fatigue. I believe twelve or eighteen hours before the next rotation. I require a day of additional observation to be certain."

"Denied," Tavene said. "We haven't the time. Describe the guards."

"Second form exclusively," Femoran said. Drexan popped his knuckles with a malicious grin. "Two were armed with blades. One with a bow. One purportedly unarmed. All appeared in good health, moved with ease and without visible malady. They did not linger in any one place. All remained alert for the duration of my assessment. Above-average precaution was required on my part to remain undetected."

"Trained."

"Yes. I do not anticipate a level of combat skill or weapons proficiency tantamount to our own. However, it would significantly increase our statistical advantage to avoid engaging all four simultaneously, considering current unknown variables."

"And that's just the perimeter guard. We have no way to verify their internal number without getting past the initial four."

Drexan had abandoned groping the imaginary breasts to ladle himself a fourth helping of stew. "Blow the four," he said. "We crush the guards. Sneak into the camp. Grab and go before anyone's the wiser."

Tavene raised a raven brow. There was no sneaking anywhere with Drexan. Based on Femoran's intel, the male was as big as many of the housing structures in the camp. He'd be recognized as an outsider immediately. Any efforts to employ stealth would become futile if they brought the big male in.

He did have a point, however. The guards were a problem. Twelve hours—provided that was the length of the guard shifts, another thing they didn't have the time to properly verify—was a big enough window to allow them ample time to enter the camp, locate their target, and be on their way out before a formal alarm was sounded. That is, if they were able to force their own window early in the guard shift.

"Femoran, is there any way to sneak into the camp without alerting the perimeter guard?"

"Avoiding casualty entirely? On your own, your chances of initial success would be roughly forty percent. That rate decreases substantially if I were to accompany you and becomes zero with Drexan's inclusion."

She shook her head. No good. Even if she were to get in undetected and managed to secure their target on her own, there was no way she'd be able to sleuth her way out again. There was a reason she had a team. The triangle was most effective when they combined their unique skill sets.

"One guard per quadrant," she mused. "The camp is large enough that we can afford to put down one quadrant without the other's awareness. Correct, Femoran?"

"Yes, at least initially," he said. "I did not observe interaction between guards. Their quadrants did not appear to overlap. I am fifty-seven percent confident in this assessment. Our favorability decreases the longer we remain inside."

More than half to start. She'd take it.

"And if they do notice, then we crush them all," Drexan said around a mouthful of snake and *thistleroot*. He looked very much like this was the outcome he preferred.

"This infiltration requires a high level of maneuverability, reticence, and stealth," she said. "Extreme covertness."

Drexan grunted his agreement and took another bite.

Femoran watched her silently.

"You have a knack for the extreme," Tavene said carefully. "But there is nothing covert about you, Drexan."

298

The giant paused his chewing and narrowed his eyes in her direction. "We cannot hide you."

"Tav…"

She set her jaw. "If you enter that camp, any element of surprise that we possessed would be forfeit. Even in full dark, you would be recognizable. Drexan, you know this. You present a liability."

He slammed his bowl down, cracking the wooden dish right through the middle. She'd have to purchase *another* set. Bits of milky flesh flew into the air. Broth splashed onto the sleeve of her uniform.

"I'll be dead before I let you two skinny shits leave me here while you go have all the fun!"

Tavene's irritation reared its ugly head. She dabbed calmly at her sleeve, but her eyes flashed. "You will be dead if you compromise this mission with your petulance, Drexan. Do not make me arrange it."

He stood. All seven and a half plus murderous feet of him. He was no less intimidating with chunks of stew dripping from the towel tucked daintily into his collar front to catch the dribble. But intimidation or not, Tavene maintained her position as point for a reason, and she would not tolerate insubordination.

Drexan shifted his weight, eyes dipping to where her sword lay balanced across her lap. She really did not want to put him down.

"I can hide him," Femoran said.

Drexan and Tavene both turned to the smaller male with identical looks of skepticism.

Femoran waited.

"What do you mean?" Tavene asked, still eyeing the big male.

"I can hide him in the camp," he clarified.

Drexan's skepticism slowly transformed into pure, joyous delight as the slighter man's words registered. He took a step toward Femoran.

"Please do not embrace me," Femoran said, with a note of uncustomary alarm.

Drexan paused his advance and Tavene loosened her grasp on her sword's hilt.

"Explain," she said.

Femoran looked to Tavene. "I possess an extreme aversion to being touch—"

"No," she said, jaw flexing. "Explain how you plan to hide Drexan."

"There is a section of the camp designated for wares storage on the western border. It is not heavily populated and is guarded only by a single large canine. Drexan's size can be fully concealed between the stacked crates."

Kill the dog. Hide the bear. If they could get him into the camp and keep him hidden, they may need him to help punch a hole for their escape if they encountered a shitstorm.

"Very well." She fixed Drexan with a stare and pointed her spoon in his direction. "But you *will* remain hidden until we call for you, no exceptions. If you jeopardize this mission, I will have your balls and keep them for our king. He will want to reattach them so he can remove them again himself. Are we clear?"

Drexan grinned, and it did nothing to reassure Tavene of his understanding. He rubbed his hands together with enthusiasm.

"Let's go bag us a princess and kill us a thief."

"Not exclusively the thief. The single perimeter guard and dog as well. Additionally, I expect the potential for multiple casualties beyond our initial estimation. Your inclusion in this mission exponentially increases that potential," Femoran offered helpfully.

Drexan roared with laughter.

Tavene did sigh then. "It's settled. Tomorrow at sundown, we commence night zero. Drexan, you're first watch. Don't wander. And don't shift. Your second form's stench could be scented from five miles. Femoran, get some sleep."

She certainly planned to do the same.

Chapter 29

Surprise

FELÍNE LOOKED UP AT THE sound of shredding canvas to see just that. A wicked serrated blade carved a jagged tear in the fabric between two of the heavier inlaid wooden panels of the tent's back wall.

Her eyes went wide. Kal was already moving, his powerful body sluicing sheets of water as he rose in the tub. His black gaze found hers for a fraction of a second.

That fraction was too long.

A huge iron-pelted blur shoved through the man-sized rip in the wall and collided with Kal before he could fully turn. A thick, furred forearm closed around Kal's throat from behind, further hefting his body up. Felíne watched, horrified, as the same blade that carved through the tent wall rose into Kal's line of sight.

Kal stopped struggling.

"Well, well," the male said, chuckling darkly. His voice was smooth and pleasant, a stark contraposition to the deadly blade that hovered too close to Kal's face. "I would say I've caught you with your pants down, mate, but it looks to me as if they're clean off."

The newcomer's accent was one Felíne couldn't place. His second form was tall and layered with lean muscle. His coat was dark gray, like aged iron, and shaggier than those of the sleek shurii she'd seen in Cindamar. His body was sheathed in the same style of flexible armor that Garren had worn. He wore a svelte pack draped over one shoulder, close to his body. The blade he held was the only weapon she could see.

Kal growled menacingly low in his throat. He looked positively murderous.

"Now, now, none of that," Ironhide chided. "It's a first for me too, mate, but no need to be prickly about it."

Felíne hesitated, unsure of what to do. She could run. She *should* run. But Kal...

Felíne glanced down to where her hatchet rested against the edge of the mattress on the ground. If she could just reach...

"Easy there, love. I wouldn't do that if I were you."

She froze. Two sets of eyes were trained on her. One, thundercloud gray. The other, black like a starless night sky.

"That's it. Now just step to the left side, love. To the wall. Nice and slow."

Felíne found Kal's gaze, no less piercing for the water dripping from his sodden curls. There was no fear there, only anger. And beneath that anger was a well of calm. She was terrified, but the confident certainty she saw in those dark orbs filled her with a sense of purpose. Bolstered her resolve. She couldn't deem Kal a true ally, especially considering her dishonesty, but she knew something without question: Kal would go to great lengths to protect her. Perhaps even to his detriment. If Kal was out of the picture, she was on her own. Any escape that had proven difficult with Kal keeping watch would become impossible with Ironhide's attention on her.

She needed to distract him.

Felíne stepped slowly to her right.

Those gray eyes tracked her movement with chagrin. The shorter hair above and below his right lid was slightly distorted, the direction of growth disrupted oddly. "Wrong left, love."

Her knees trembled slightly but not solely from fear. There was so much adrenaline flooding her system that she had a hard time controlling the fine shaking in her limbs. It worked to her benefit, however. Ironhide noticed the tremble and considered her the way he would a frightened female, not an adversary.

She looked up as though confused. "Where..."

Ironhide sighed. He pointed the serrated blade to the opposite wall. "Just over th—"

Kal exploded into movement. He rocketed an elbow back into Ironhide's abdomen, somehow knowing exactly where to find the softer joint in his armor. The bigger male grunted in pain, his grip slipping as he instinctively bent to protect the injury. Kal spun to face his attacker, displacing more water from the copper tub.

The male recovered quickly and jerked his knife forward. Felíne cried a warning, but Kal's hands shot out, bringing the male's arm forward and trapping it close to his body. In a second expert maneuver, Kal forced Ironhide's clawed hand to spasm open, and the serrated blade fell from his grasp into the murky water at Kal's feet.

"Damn you," he growled, displaying an impressive set of sharp white teeth. He snapped them less than an inch from Kal's face.

Felíne felt trapped in a bubble. Time felt thick and viscous, like she was watching events happen underwater. There was no way Kal would overpower the second form male. He was incredibly skilled, more so than she imagined could be expected for a common thief, but unless he shifted himself, he was completely outmatched. Not only was he already exhausted, but he was unarmed, and she couldn't forget *naked*.

No, she certainly hadn't forgotten that.

Ironhide brought a thick fist around in a nasty hook. Kal blocked the first blow, then the second, but the third punch caught him on the right side. Something crunched, and Felíne's stomach dropped.

Kal feigned back, the muscled line of his calves bumping the inside edge of the tub. For a moment, he looked as though he'd lost his balance and would topple backward over the side. Ironhide sensed an opportunity and advanced for another attack. Kal's head swung forward with unexpected momentum and connected with the taller male's snout. Ironhide roared. Blood poured from his nose.

Kal did not waste the moment and leapt forward out of the tub. The males collided again, grappling. Kal was significantly outweighed. If he didn't shift, and soon, Felíne doubted he would be able to maintain his advantage for long. What in Goddess' name was he waiting for?

Whatever it was, she wouldn't stand here and watch him slowly get torn to pieces. She bent and swiped the hatchet from the floor, then quickly shouldered one of the packs. A pang of guilt gave her a moment's pause as she made up her mind.

There was a crash, and the tub overturned, sending water flying everywhere.

An inhuman snarl ripped from Kal as he struggled to maintain his hold on Ironhide's larger form. His biceps bulged, veins standing out in his neck, jaw set in determined ferocity.

Felíne gave him one last glance and dashed to the front door, leaving him to his fate.

Felíne didn't bother securing the door. Sounds of the struggle inside the tent could be heard behind her, but she didn't pause, even as the oily feeling of shame slid over her. She had to get away, and there was no way to determine how much time she had. Kal was a skilled fighter. Her presence wouldn't give him any advantage, and she might never get another chance to get away. He'd be fine.

Of course, he'd be fine.

Another crash and a muffled curse sounded. A painful cry. She couldn't tell who it belonged to. Why did that bother her?

She shook herself. It didn't matter. She needed to focus. Sig would be bedded down for the night at The Inn's makeshift stable. She needed a mount if she stood any chance at getting out of Cindamar and back to Asteros. There was no way she'd make it on foot.

Felíne flew off the tent's platform, rounded a corner to head in the stable's direction, and hadn't even made it out of the row of suites when she stopped dead in her tracks. A lithe form, several inches shorter than her own, emerged from the shadowed alcove between two of The Inn's tents to block her path.

"Leaving so soon?" The voice was soft, feminine, and held a note that promised violence.

Felíne stepped back.

The figure crept closer. "Stay a while."

Felíne whirled and ran in the other direction. There was a whisper of sound behind her like the rustling of leaves. Something grabbed her by the ankle and jerked her leg sharply backward. She went sprawling forward, hitting the ground with a painful thud. Felíne barely managed to keep hold of her hatchet and miraculously avoided hacking herself to pieces when she fell.

She glanced back to find a thin braided coil wrapped around her ankle. The other end was held aloft by the oddest female she'd ever seen.

"That wasn't a suggestion," the woman said. She was petite and clothed in close fitting leather armor that shielded her chest and torso and extended down in a pleated skirt to protect the top half of her thighs. She wore dark breeches and tall boots that covered her small calves. A cream-colored linen shirt was worn under the armor, and dark leather vambraces that were lovingly decorated with odd lines of symbols sheathed her forearms. Her clothing, however, wasn't what made Felíne stare.

The female had a wide, flat nose, slightly upturned loamy eyes, and a full mouth. Her skin was a warm Morena, healthy and innately glowing as though the sun that set each night went to rest within her, its beams of warmth pushing out through the surface of her complexion. She had hair like midnight, sheared short on the sides, with more length on top that transitioned to a vibrant tangerine color at the ends. It was styled upright in a dramatic wave that flowed with her movements like the dancing flame of a candle.

A thunderous clattering sounded, and Felíne glanced toward the noise, back the way she'd come. The odd female didn't even flinch, eyes trained on Felíne at her feet. An eerie silence followed in the wake of that final racket.

A sense of urgency came over her.

"Let me go," Felíne said. "Please."

The woman's eyes narrowed scornfully, her nose wrinkling. "Go? When we haven't even been properly acquainted? Now that would just be rude."

The female bent and hefted Felíne to her feet with surprising strength and coiled her whip. Felíne clutched the handle of her hatchet, but the woman paid it no mind. "Besides," she said. "The evening festivities have only just begun."

She gripped Felíne by the arm and steered her forward.

The already narrow window for Felíne's escape was rapidly closing before her eyes. Despair hung in the air about her like a heavy cloud. The female was small. Smaller than Felíne. Perhaps even without a second form, she could overpower her. She *was* armed, after all. She hadn't lugged the former stablemaster's hatchet around with her the past several days merely for show.

Felíne dug her heels in.

The woman turned, graceful like a dancer, and a thin dagger twirled playfully between her delicate fingers. Felíne hadn't even seen her reach for it, nor could she see where it had been hidden. The dagger pointed in her direction, nothing playful about its owner's expression.

"Shall we get acquainted now, then? Or would you prefer to follow along like a good little princess?"

Felíne stiffened. Did she know?

Her weapon was three times the size of the small blade the female wielded, but Felíne was out-skilled. She gritted her teeth, eyeing the pointed tip of the dagger with irritation. She'd had just about enough of being frightened and threatened. However, she saw no choice but to reluctantly follow the strange woman back to the suite.

"Good girl," the female said, dagger once again hidden in some nameless place on her person.

It did not take them long to approach the platform supporting the tent Felíne had fled moments before. All was quiet within. The door no longer stood ajar. If she didn't know any better, Felíne might think she'd fabricated the entire conflict.

The female extended a slender arm. "After you, princess."

Felíne steeled herself. The adrenaline that had threatened to drown her earlier was rapidly receding like an ebbing tide, leaving her stranded on an island of weariness. She was less afraid to open the door and face the iron-pelted male than witness what might be left of his attack. She'd seen lifeless bodies before, working with Mender Alcuin. Death did not bother her. It was *who* might be dead—seeing the lifeless form of someone familiar.

A nagging at the back of her mind said it was more than familiarity that had her so horrified at the prospect of confronting Kal's demise.

"Oh, blessed stars above, we haven't got all night."

The female pushed Felíne forward, unlatched the door, and shoved her through.

Felíne stumbled into the confines of the single room and stared in stunned silence. What she saw was entirely the opposite of what she'd expected.

A small round table had been brought into the tent, along with a single wooden chair and an overturned empty crate. Water still stood in puddles on the floor and dripped slowly from the near wall, but the tub had been righted and shoved against the opening that had been ripped in the canvas behind it.

A stack of towels was tossed onto the mattress along with clean rags, and a small bucket filled with chunks of ice rested on the floor nearby.

A trim, broad-shouldered man sat slouched on the overturned crate, holding a block of ice wrapped in a waterproof skin to his face. He was dressed in a simple loose cotton shirt that hung open at the collar, showing off the beginning of defined pectorals, and plain brown trousers. His feet were bare. He raised his shaggy head of iron-silver hair at the sound of the two females entering. Storm gray eyes landed on Felíne then found the odd female that moved past her into the room.

Next to the male, lounging moodily in the single chair, was Kal.

He looked to be nursing a battered set of ribs, and there was a gash across his brow that hadn't been there before, but he was alive and breathing.

Something swelled in Felíne, and it took her a moment to realize it was relief.

The petite woman plopped onto the single bed and relaxed back into the pillows, hands folded behind her head, ankles crossed daintily.

"Well, fellas, what's the final tally?"

Ironhide removed the ice to reveal a ghastly purpling that was already spreading from the center of his face to create a ring under his left eye. A swollen ridge marred the bridge of his otherwise straight nose. He winced. "I claim first blow and first blood. But the wily bastard—" He looked at Felíne apologetically. "Pardon my tongue, love—outmaneuvered me and took the finish."

The female let out a short laugh. "*Again?*"

Kal sat forward with barely a grimace, but Felíne could tell he favored his side. "You don't get to claim first blood. That's mine."

Ironhide shot him a side eye. "You headbutted me. A broken nose doesn't count."

"The fuck it doesn't. Your swollen sniffer was spurting blood like a geyser. It counts."

The gray man was affronted. "Even if you get first blood, I got the drop on you. I claim surprise points."

Kal huffed. "There are no surprise points."

Ironhide looked to the female pleadingly. "Oph."

She shook her head, the orange hair atop it waving. "No surprise points."

Ironhide slumped back with a defeated sigh and winced at some unnamed injury.

A smug expression bled through Kal's ire. "Rules, *mate.*"

His mocking earned him a foul glare. Ironhide retorted, "I should get something for the ambush. I bloody had you, mate."

Kal glowered. "You fucking attacked me in the *bath.* With a blade. In second form. I beat you bare-handed *and* bare-assed. In first. You lost. Swallow it."

"Disgraceful," Ironhide grumbled.

The female straightened and took out a small, worn leather book. She leafed to a page and marked something down. "Better luck next time, Adder. You get one mark for first blow, but first blood and final go to our reigning champ. That's two to one in Kal's favor for this match. He's up twelve to one overall."

Felíne's legs finally forfeited their match of keeping her upright. She sank onto the edge of the mattress, confusion and exhaustion finally exacting their toll.

Kal's self-satisfaction faded as he looked at her. She had a hard time reading his expression. He was clothed again, at least. Thank the Goddess.

"Adjust the ledger, Ophelia," he said, then nodded in Felíne's direction. "I think the win tonight goes to Kitty."

Ironhide grimaced at Kal, but his gray eyes warmed, and he quirked a smile in her direction. "Good call, mate. That was a right beautiful distraction, love. You saved your boy from a sorry whooping. I'm ashamed I fell for it."

Her boy? She looked between the two men. She was baffled. Tired. Not a little irritated. "I...It was a *game?*"

Ironhide had the decency to look halfway sheepish, halfway apologetic. "More than a game, though. It's become somewhat of a ritual between us when crossing paths."

The female, Ophelia, rolled her eyes. "Oh yes, very serious stuff. They make a damned mess of anything in their vicinity. It's costing us a blessed fortune." She pegged both battered males with a hard stare. "I keep the ledgers, but do you think they listen? Pah. Men."

Felíne looked incredulously at Kal. "So, you weren't in any danger?"

He shook his head.

"Adder did lose a toe once," Ophelia supplied. "Was that the seventh bout?"

Ironhide—Adder—made a pained face. "Let's not revisit that one, Oph. It still pains me." Then to Felíne, "I'm sorry if I scared you, love. I rarely get a chance to ambush this wretch. Didn't realize you'd be in the room with him."

Kal's eyes were serious and bored into her with something like concern. The intensity in them only irked her. "Are you alright?"

"No," she said firmly. "No, I am not alright. I've been dragged across the desert, trudged through the mud and rain and cold, been stolen from, scared half to death, threatened, and manipulated. I'm tired and pissed off and…and freaked out."

"That's fair," he said. "But you're unharmed."

"That isn't the point!"

Ophelia popped up off the mattress and took the ice from Adder's hand. "Come on, *mate*. Let's go see the innkeeper. Lele will want payment for the damage you did. Then, a mender will patch you up for the damage *he* did." She bent when she passed Kal and murmured something to him that Felíne couldn't hear. Then she said, "We'll give the two of you some privacy."

Felíne scowled. "We don't need privacy!"

Adder made eyes at Kal and avoided Felíne's as he limped to the door. The two of them exited, leaving her alone with the primary source of her ire.

His posture relaxed, revealing the first sign of fatigue. She rounded on him.

"What did she say?"

Kal smirked a little. "She told me to select my bedmates more carefully. Apparently, it's unwise to choose a lover who would leave you in a fight for your life to save her own."

Felíne's hands found her hips. "But you weren't in a fight for your life."

A twinkle of amusement lit Kal's dark eyes. "True. But you didn't know that."

The way he was looking at her made her fidget. Why...? *Gods*.

"And we are not lovers!"

The amusement deepened. "But *she* doesn't know that."

Goddess, save her. He was confoundedly insufferable.

Kal raised his hand to touch his forehead. His fingers came away bloody. The gash that had clotted was oozing again, dripping into his brow. Felíne grabbed a clean cloth from the pile on the mattress with a huff and pressed it to the wound. He didn't shy away from her touch.

Felíne avoided his gaze, focusing instead on the folded piece of cloth in her hand. "Will they be back?"

"I expect so."

"Ironhide won't try to attack you again?"

Kal frowned, and Felíne repositioned the cloth. "Who? Oh, Adder?" He snorted a laugh. "He'll love that. No, he won't try anything. He lost. There won't be another bout until we haven't seen each other for at least a full month. He was lucky I was...distracted. Next time, he won't find it so easy."

"So, they're friends of yours."

Kal dipped his chin.

"Good." Felíne lifted the edge of the cloth. The laceration was still seeping and would likely require sutures. "When they return, you can clarify the nature of our relationship so there isn't any confusion. I'd hate to have your friends thinking you chose a cowardly bedmate."

Her tone was only a little bitter.

Kal reached up and lowered her hand, peering up at her face. "Why did you run?"

Felíne hesitated. She'd been scared, sure. But she'd also been trying to get away. She looked down and realized she was standing over Kal, positioned between his knees, tending to an injury she had no obligation to tend. She was standing too close. Anyone walking in on them now *would* assume they were lovers. It certainly seemed like something lovers did. Felíne was horrified to admit that it felt good being close to him. Somewhere between three days ago and now, their proximity went from feeling wrong to feeling…okay? Safe, even. Comfortable. And that *was* wrong. That was why she'd run. She'd been trying to get away from him. Away from *this*.

But she couldn't very well admit any of that to Kal. She couldn't tell him why it was imperative for her to return to Asteros. Couldn't tell him what was at stake if she didn't.

"I went to find help," she said somewhat lamely. "Ophelia? Found me instead."

Felíne couldn't tell by Kal's expression if he believed her or not. Another pang of guilt twinged deep within her, and she promptly shoved it off a cliff. He nodded after a moment.

"You'll need stitches," she said, changing the subject. She eyed the spot above his brow to avoid his penetrating stare. She was suddenly finding it difficult to lie to him. Which was ridiculous. She didn't owe him anything.

Kal shrugged, then paused, his features pinching slightly in discomfort.

Felíne knelt and lifted the hem of his shirt, noting the bruising coloring his right side. "He likely cracked your ribs," she said with some consternation. "I doubt there's anything to be done for those other than a *sweetwater* salve to lessen the pain."

"I'll manage," Kal said, shoving to his feet.

"But your head."

"Thank you, Kitty," he said. He was standing and once again well inside her personal space. "I'll see that Lele's mender takes care of it."

Felíne shifted on her feet. "Oh. Okay. Good." She didn't mention that *she* could take care of it if given the proper supplies. Nor did she admit that she *wanted* to. Only to practice her skills, of course.

Kal moved toward the door. She felt the increased space between them acutely.

"You're going now?"

He looked back. Of course, he was. She'd just told him he needed to be sutured. Why did her brain turn to mush whenever she was left alone with him? Ugh.

CLOAKING FATE

"Ophe's outside," Kal said, having utilized some sense of their surroundings that Felíne did not possess. "You'll be safe with her watching the tent while I get this—" he gestured to his forehead, "—situated. There will be no more surprises tonight; you have my word. Try and get some rest."

Kal left, and Felíne finally collapsed on the bed. She stared at the ceiling, thinking of the fiery young female standing guard somewhere in the night, her polite yet violent silver-eyed companion, Imogen and Mender Alcuin, home, and what in Goddess's name would become of her future. Before her lids grew too heavy to keep open and her thoughts became fuzzy with impending sleep, Felíne thought of the male with the jet, bottomless gaze that had stolen her from fate and was beginning to unknowingly steal his way into every corner of her mind.

Chapter 30

Cheers

KAL LEFT AN EXHAUSTED KITTY in the tent behind him—the hole Adder had slashed into the rear wall having been mostly reinforced—to hopefully achieve some measure of rest under Ophe's watchful eye. She'd be safe there. Ophelia's attention to detail bordered on manic, a trait that was mostly incredibly useful and occasionally incredibly irritating. If Kitty tried anything, Ophe would handle it. Shit, if *anyone* tried anything, Ophe would handle it.

Kal was exhausted himself. His feet felt like leaden bricks as he trudged through The Inn's grounds. His eyelids had weights attached to them, as if his lashes had suddenly become a burden he could no longer continue to lift. All he wanted was a quiet place with an uninterrupted span of five hours so he could crash and recharge without worrying about some unnamed catastrophe taking place.

Unfortunately, it was a prospect that seemed less and less likely the longer he spent with Kitty in his care. Kal was unaccustomed to being responsible for another person the way he currently found himself. Any jobs he did were completed solo or accompanied by shurii capable of taking care of themselves. In fact, he typically made a point to avoid claiming responsibility for others. He was adept at giving directions, but he was also accustomed to people following them. This female, her stubbornness, and her apparent lack of experience maintaining self-sufficiency tested his resolve.

It hadn't been long since they left Asteros, but in the short time he'd spent with her, Kal could already discern Kitty was a magnet for trouble. Not entirely surprising, considering who her brother was. However, aside from that similarity, she and Rask couldn't be less alike. It was worth mentioning that Rask tended to cause trouble for himself, whereas his younger sister appeared to unintentionally attract it. While stubbornness was a thing they had in common, Rask's stubbornness was born from a sense of irrational male pride and an unwillingness to display vulnerability. Kitty's stubbornness was like an unleashing, reminding Kal of a breaking dam. It was as though she'd been bottling an abundance of thoughts, opinions, and ideas for so long that when they emerged, they did so in an uncontrollable cascade.

Another curious dissimilarity was Kitty's unmistakable poise. She carried herself with a level of grace and entitlement that seemed to be bred into her very marrow. He recalled the way she'd spoken to Garren. Half the words she'd used were rarely spoken in casual conversation. That depth of self-assuredness wasn't often taught. It was carefully cultivated over years. Something normally afforded to the wealthier upper echelons of society. Kal would know.

Rask didn't strike him as someone who possessed affluent origins. The man walked around with a chip on his shoulder the size of a colossus, like the gods had cheated him, spawning the insatiable need to prove to himself he was worth more than the pittance of his birthright. The man frequently mentioned his family as all he had. A thing that had prompted Kal's reluctant agreement to retrieve his sister from the clutches of the Asteros crown.

Kitty's sense of privilege stumped him. But perhaps she was the favored child in Rask's family. Doted upon and coddled. That would certainly explain her lack of life experience. The woman acted like she'd never cooked a meal for herself or slept without a feathered mattress and down coverlet.

And yet, underneath all of that obstinance and expectation and bluster, there was a genuine sense of curiosity, compassion, and thirst for life.

Kitty fought him at every opportunity, yet she cared about what happened to him. He suffered no illusions that she'd fled upon Adder's earlier arrival out of fear for herself, but there was something else at war within her in the moments before she left. She was a terrible liar, and Kal was an excellent judge of character. A combination that worked decidedly in his favor. You could learn a lot about a person without exchanging words if you knew what to pay attention to, and Kal did. He'd had lots of practice. It was in the eyes. And he'd seen hers when Adder had had him by the throat. She'd been worried. Deeply concerned. Not for herself but for *him*. Enough to cause her hesitation.

The image of her frightened gaze resurfaced as though emblazoned in his memory. *It was in the eyes.* Kitty's were the strangest he'd ever seen. The most peculiar shade of green gold, like warm honey poured over lichen. To say he was captivated might be a stretch, but he would be lying to himself if he said he wasn't drawn to her for some unfathomable reason. Kal stopped lying to himself a very long time ago.

Kitty was a beautiful woman, but beauty was a fickle thing. Many women were beautiful to him. The appeal she possessed was something that existed beyond her appearance.

She was a desert flower, lovely and fragrant. She'd been planted in the most hostile of environments and was determined not simply to grow but to *thrive.*

She possessed an unmistakable eagerness despite the unnamed weight she carried. For there was something about Kitty that she was unwilling to share. Something that she took pains to conceal. Kal thought back to their conversation earlier that evening on the way to The Inn. She'd been so vehemently abhorred by his use of her name. *Railah.* Something tied to that moniker caused her a pain significant enough that she wanted to shed it like a too-tight skin. Was it trauma? Abuse? Some manner of suffering that transpired after being named a Fate? Before?

Kal turned a corner. The image his mind produced of someone intentionally harming her made him angry. Violently angry.

He knew all too well what it meant to suffer at the hands of others. To watch that suffering claim those he loved. To possess all the will in the worlds and still be powerless to stop it. He might still use the name he'd been given at birth, but he knew what it felt like to want to discard an identity that was tied to an irreparable past. To leave things behind that were once integral parts of his being. People, a life, a purpose.

It was not his place to pry, and he would not ask her—gods knew he didn't want anyone rummaging through *his* past—but Kal couldn't deny he was curious. He found some odd and unexpected sense of kinship with the young female, and perhaps, in time, she might reveal whatever scars she concealed of her own accord.

CLOAKING FATE

Despite his growing interest, Kal would not discount the fact that Rask obviously cared very deeply for his sister, and his priority was to deliver her safely. Kal might be a scoundrel, but he respected his friends, and there were certain lines he would not cross.

Yet Kal couldn't shake the nagging feeling that while he would do his damned best to maintain his boundaries, those very lines he'd drawn had been etched in shifting sand instead of immovable stone.

He thought of Kitty standing before him in nothing but her skin and that godforsaken woolen robe. He'd gawked like a fucking prepubescent pup. She was sweet and supple, skin scrubbed pink and fragrant, hair unbound and dripping and…and he needed to get a fucking grip. It was bad enough he hadn't been able to help goading her. It had been too long since he'd shared a female's bed. Withdrawals. That's what his damned problem was.

Kal made it to the main tent where Lele housed the dining area, her private front office, personal residence, and mender's ward. He entered to find Adder at one of the long tables hunched over a bowl of hot food, the only occupant aside from the cook, who was cleaning up for the evening. Kal sat down across from his friend and rubbed his temples as if that would erase the image of Rask's sister from his traitor's memory. He winced as the already-forgotten cut above his eye was stretched with the movement.

Adder looked up with a glorious bruise decorating his left eye and a swollen nose, courtesy of Kal's earlier headbutt. His smile was unreserved and genuine.

"You look like balls, mate," he said.

Kal huffed a laugh. "You'd know, I suppose."

Adder chuckled and ran a hand through his dark silver mane. Ironhide, Kitty had called him. It fit.

"Yeah, well, it wasn't my best plan, I'll admit. But it was damned effective."

"And yet you still lost," Kal said, saluting him.

Adder leaned forward with a grin. "Matter of perspective there, mate. You may have won the bout, but I gained something quite valuable."

"Oh? And what's that?" Kal nodded to Adder's face. "A disfigured mug?"

Adder chuckled again. Humor had always come easy to the male. He had an uncanny ability to always find the positive in every situation, no matter how dark or difficult. It was a trait that Kal had admired since they were young and one he'd tried many times to duplicate himself with limited success.

"Ah, I'm not so worried about that," he said good-naturedly. "Mender said he can't do much about the shape, and we won't know how off it is until the swelling subsides, but I told him as long as it works the same, I don't much care what it looks like."

"I'm shocked," Kal said. He wasn't, though.

"Gods, Kal. Didn't anyone tell you *this*—" he pointed to his nose, "—isn't the bulge that females care about? No wonder you're so damned lonely. You've got a fine-looking snout, mate, but I'll tell you right now, it's not doing you any favors."

"Alright, alright," Kal said, waving off his friend's teasing. "If it wasn't a busted bridge, what'd you gain that was so valuable?"

Adder grinned wickedly. "Knowledge."

"Of?"

He held up a finger. "I'll tell ya," he said. "But first, I brought something for you, and I figure it's a fine enough time to *crack* it in celebration."

"What are we celebrating?"

"Two things. Your hard-fought, ball-dangling, *barely clenched*, victory—"

"Ass jokes. Hilarious," Kal said, voice dry as a roasted bone. He'd never fucking live it down.

"—And my newfound discovery."

Adder reached beneath the table and pulled a large, sleek glass bottle out of his bag. He flagged down the cook and requested two squat glasses, which were promptly delivered. Adder popped the corked top off the bottle and poured a measure of fragrant bronze liquid into each glass. He slid one toward Kal, who sniffed it with pleasure.

"Gods," Kal said, eyes closed. "Do you know how long it's been since I had a good bourbon?"

Adder swirled the liquor in his glass. "This isn't good, mate. It's fucking phenomenal. My best cask. Aged four years in a charred white oak barrel with a high-country pinesap casing. No one knows this recipe. It can't be replicated. And you're the first one to share it with me, you lucky sonofabitch. Oph is gonna castrate me. Cheers."

Kal raised his glass to clink the one across from him and sipped. The spirit swirled in the back of his throat, coating his palate with an intoxicating mixture of vanilla, caramel, oak, spice, and honeyed burn. The liquid bite worked its way into his chest and lit a fire there, restoring some of his vitality. He might have moaned.

Kitty's eyes once again entered his mind as the liquid heat settled behind his rib cage.

Adder's eyes widened suggestively and he dipped his head to peek under the table.

Kal quirked an eyebrow.

"You made noises. Thought maybe you were hiding a nymph."

"Idiot."

Adder smirked. "I take it you approve."

Kal leaned back in his chair. He had to hand it to him. The man knew how to distill a fine bourby.

"It's fantastic, and you already know it," Kal said. "You get no additional ego stroking. Now out with it. What's this big discovery?"

Adder sat back, mirroring Kal's relaxed posture. The scars above and below his right eye—the result of a serpent's strike and the source of his moniker—dimpled as he grinned. "I discovered your weakness."

"A good—sorry, *fucking phenomenal*—whiskey? That was never a secret, my friend. I'm a sucker for that liquid gold."

"No," Adder said with a shake of his head. "Your vulnerability."

Kal frowned. Adder was toying with him. "Most people would consider themselves vulnerable whilst bathing."

"Blessed stars, mate, you're dense. The woman!"

Kal's frown deepened. "Who, Kitty?"

His friend took another swig of glorious molten honey. His lips pursed in brief annoyance. "Gah," he said. "Can't fucking appreciate the taste with this damned nose clogged." He tilted the glass again anyway and nodded. "Yes, Kitty. She's the fault in your armor, mate. The only reason I got even close to having your ass was on account of you being distracted by her presence. And the only reason you had *my ass* after she ran was because you were in a frenzy to go after her."

Kal narrowed his eyes. "I was not in a frenzy. And I didn't go after her."

"Only because we both heard Oph walking her back before you could make it out the door."

Kal grunted, displeased with the turn this conversation had taken.

"Disagree with me all you like, mate. I've known you a long time. Seen you with a number of different females. I'm keen on that shit."

Kal chose to occupy his mouth with his bourbon rather than allow it to form a retort.

Adder laughed, presumably at Kal's denial, then leaned forward, gray eyes glowing. "Who is she then?"

Kal told him, the burn of the alcohol melting his stress, pouring liquid into his limbs and a pleasant heaviness into his head.

"Well, I'll be damned," Adder said, his glass empty. "Though I don't know if I believe it. She looks too good to occupy a branch on Rask's family tree."

Kal murmured his assent and emptied his own glass. Adder refilled them with a heavier pour.

"So, you'll be heading to Meress, when, tomorrow?"

"Sooner would be better," Kal said. "But we'll see how tomorrow goes." He just needed to settle this business with Grisham, get Garren off his fucking back, and be on his way. But gods, it was good to see Adder and Oph again. The circle of people he trusted was continually growing smaller, and he appreciated these moments spent with those he had left. With the way things tended to go, Kal never knew how many remained to him. They were part of the reason he'd made the detour to Cindamar.

Adder was Kal's oldest friend. The two of them met as boys when Adder's family sent him to stay as a ward under Kal's parents. Adder had found Ophelia in the city near Kal's home two years later, the little street urchin having stolen Adder's coin purse. The three of them had been inseparable. Until Asteros. When everything went to complete shit.

Adder was privy to Kal's business dealings with Grisham and was stationed in Cindamar to keep an eye on the Trade Master and his brother in Kal's interest. Grisham was unaware of Adder's relationship with Kal, a secret maintained easily enough considering Adder's position as head of Grisham's personal guard. The appointment had boiled Garren's blood, to Kal's immense satisfaction.

Kal hadn't been surprised by Adder's elevation in Grisham's esteem. His friend had always possessed an inexplicable talent for garnering people's affections and trust. As a result, Adder became privy to all kinds of interesting information that Grisham tended to guard from all but his closest confidants. He learned of trade deals, personal feuds, and future plans for development. In the year since Kal last saw him, Adder had gone from outsider to trusted inner counsel and maintained a good portion of Grisham's business dealings with surrounding cities. This included smuggled information and goods in and out of Asteros as well as continued assistance and resources to Meress, the latter activities of which Grisham would remain unaware until Kal had sufficient leverage to sway the Trade Master's impartiality. It was a delicate balance, exacting his plans.

The two friends talked late into the evening. They drank and laughed, draining Adder's bottle to the last remaining glasses.

Kal was pleasantly buzzed a few hours later when he realized he never had the cut above his eye sewn by the mender. Kitty's irritated face floated before him, and he couldn't tell if the warmth he felt was a result of her concern or his consumption. Probably a little of both, he decided. Either way, the bleeding had stopped on its own.

After another half hour, Kal shoved himself up from the table. He was bound to manage at least three solid hours of deep sleep between his frank depletion of energy and the bourbon currently swimming through his bloodstream. However, if he didn't leave now, he'd end up passed out at this table and at Adder's mercy. When he woke up in the morning, he'd then be at Ophelia's mercy for leaving her in charge of watching Kitty all night. The latter prospect seemed significantly more terrifying. Ophelia would not appreciate being forgotten.

"Last pour?" Adder emptied the remainder of his coveted cask into the glasses.

Kal shook his head, pouring his half-full portion into Adder's. "You had better save that for Oph. It's good enough she might only take one of your balls."

320

Adder pointed a finger in his direction and squinted at him with one bleary eye. "That's why you're my best mate, mate. Good looking out."

Kal clapped his friend on the shoulder, promising to send Ophelia his way, and headed back toward his tent and the alluring young female that he couldn't seem to get out of his brain.

Chapter 31

The Trade Master

"KITTY."

"Mmm."

"Kitty, wake up."

Felíne murmured again. At least, she thought that was her sleep-laden voice. She was having a pleasant dream featuring a stern, hardened warrior, warm sun on an open field of green, and a decadent breeze that smelled of amber honey and rich spice. She nestled deeper into her pillow, reluctant to let go of the fantasy. The warrior had turned away from her, but she was catching up. She just wanted to see his face. Was that smell on the air coming from him? Goddess save her, he smelled divine.

Wait! She tried to call out. There was something he needed to tell her. Something she wanted to tell him.

A firm yet gentle pressure found her upper arm. It gave her a slight jostle.

"Kitty, I know you're awake."

Felíne rolled over and squinted against the light. She found herself looking up into Kal's amused dark eyes.

"And how exactly do you know that?" she rasped.

He raised a brow. A brow that was no longer caked with blood but was also absent recommended sutures. The fool. It would undoubtedly scar.

"You mean aside from the fact that you're scowling at me, your mouth is moving, and words are coming out?"

Her scowl deepened. He smirked, displaying a set of dimples that made him even more ridiculously handsome.

"Your breathing changed," he explained patiently, as though normal people always paid attention to such details. "Get up. There's breakfast in the main tent, and then we have to meet Grisham."

Grisham. The Trade Master. She groaned and rolled back into her pillow, pulling the blanket over her head.

"Suit yourself. Just remember, I'm not the one with a first impression to make," he chided. "I already have my token. If we are late, it'll be taken out of your hide, not mine."

Felíne seriously doubted Kal would let anyone take anything out of her hide, master of trade or otherwise, considering all the trouble he'd gone to retrieve said hide. Still, she ceased her grumbling and shoved herself up from the comfortable warmth of her pillowy nest. She turned to make a choice retort to Kal, only to find he'd already left the tent.

Damn him and his stealthy, silent…well…everything.

Felíne got up and made the bed, enjoying the simplicity of performing a task she'd not been permitted at home.

After the pillows had been appropriately fluffed and the comforter smoothed, Felíne changed her clothes. Finally, she splashed water on her face, tamed her hair into a presentable half-braid, and rinsed her mouth.

Before she left the tent, she noticed the spot on the floor where Kal slept was already tidied. The blanket he'd used had been folded neatly and set at the foot of the bed. What time had he woken? He couldn't have gotten more than a few hours' rest.

Felíne tried to remember him returning last night and sifted through half-fogged memories. She'd been so tired once she finally fell asleep, she thought she might never wake. But she had woken. *He'd* woken her.

Kal had come in last night quiet as ever, but something had disturbed her sleep, though she couldn't remember what. What she could recall was turning over to find Kal kneeling by the side of the bed, looking at her with an uncharacteristically soft expression on his face.

"Are you alright, Kitty?" he'd asked her.

She'd almost given a spiteful retort, but the quiet sincerity in that molten voice of his gave her pause. Instead, she merely nodded.

He'd been so tired, lids heavy with exhaustion, but relaxed in a way she'd not yet witnessed. Content. Dark curls hung limply on his forehead as if they, too, had finally succumbed to weariness. She wondered how they'd look if allowed to grow, and she imagined loose velvet ringlets that would soften the harshness of his expressions. The masculine lines of his face were shadowed, all that male intensity muted by fatigue and yet still entirely focused on her.

He had looked good, she remembered thinking. Heartbreakingly good. She'd had the oddest impulse to gather him close and watch over him as he fell asleep. She'd listen to the steady lullaby of his breathing and let his redolence cocoon her until she drifted into her own contented slumber.

Felíne took a deep breath. The scent on the breeze from her dream had been his. He'd been leaning right on the edge of her bed, breath warm near her face. Kal had smelled of honey and oak and a darker, earthier spice that was entirely his. It intoxicated and overwhelmed her senses.

Felíne flushed, remembering the way she'd felt. The way he'd made her feel. *Continued* to make her feel.

What in the world was happening to her? Was she so willingly tempted?

She took a few moments to compose herself and then went in search of the one person she should be taking pains to avoid. She didn't make it very far, however. Ophelia waited for her just outside the door.

"You get enough beauty sleep, princess?"

Felíne smoothed the front of her shirt, feigning indifference. It was the third time Ophelia had called her princess, but Felíne was no longer concerned the female knew who she really was. She refused to be riled. "I did manage sufficient sleep, thank you."

Ophelia pushed off from where she was leaning against one of the corner posts of the tent. "I'm so glad."

She didn't sound like she was glad at all. In fact, the little she-devil seemed downright hostile. This was one of Kal's friends? She seemed more prone to violence than even her male companion, Adder. And *he'd* been the one to actually attack.

"Did you see where Kal went?"

Ophelia looked up at her and somehow managed to make Felíne feel like she was being looked down upon. "I'm just going to say it," Ophelia said, ignoring her question. "I know you're Rask's sister, and I know Kal got you out of some sort of mess back in Asteros."

Felíne nodded tentatively, wondering where this was going.

"I also know you left him last night to save your own hide. Like a coward."

Oh.

"Deny it if you like."

Felíne denied nothing. How could she? *Actually, Ophelia, I ran to escape the clutches of my unwelcome, yet irresistible, kidnapper because it just so happens that said kidnapper kidnapped the wrong dame. Oh, and my aforementioned escape is imperative because the fate of the entire shurii species rests upon my shoulders. It's me, the Prima of Ilistaar.*

Right.

Ophelia continued. "We don't leave the people we care about. I don't know the particulars of your relationship, but I've seen the way you look at him, and even an eyeless old goat could see the way he looks back. If your intentions regarding Kalevar are anything less than genuine, I will devise and enact a punishment so horrific that even the whisper of my name will cause your very ancestors to shudder with fear."

Goodness.

Felíne had never been in a physical altercation, but she was relatively certain if Ophelia had given her this speech last night, she might have tried to punch the little female right in the trachea, propriety be damned. However, last night, Felíne had been very tired and very stressed. This morning, after having received an acceptable amount of sleep in an actual bed with real pillows, she felt capable of tackling just about anything with her usual measure of refinement, which unfortunately dictated punching tracheas was beneath her.

"That was oddly specific," she said, gaze drifting betrayingly to the female's slender, exposed throat. "And while I commend your creativity, I am admittedly curious what this punishment would entail. You seem to have planned it all so meticulously. It'd be a shame not to share."

Ophelia's hooded eyes narrowed to slits.

Perhaps goading her wasn't the best option. Plan B, then. Felíne smiled in what she hoped was a pleasant, unthreatening manner. "Forgive me. That was rude. Let me try again. I have not known Kal for long, nor do I claim to know him well, but it is clear that he has friends willing to do just about anything to defend him from any manner of threat, real or imagined. In that, he is exceptionally fortunate."

Ophelia folded her slender arms across her chest and studied her for another beat before speaking. "Well, I didn't believe you were Rask's sister when Adder told me, but you're definitely not a hooker either. Not with that well-rinsed mouth."

Felíne blinked.

"I am sorry we met under strained circumstances," Felíne said after a moment and realized she meant it. Hostile or not, the woman cared about Kal's wellbeing, and that was something Felíne couldn't begrudge her. As someone who'd been prohibited from friendship of any kind, she placed an exceeding value on that particular manner of relationship. "I can promise you; I have no disingenuous intentions where Kalevar is concerned."

What her intentions *were*, she had yet to decide. The more time she spent with him, the more difficult it was to lie, the guiltier she grew, and the less convicted she felt in her plan to escape him. She needed to. That hadn't changed. But the way she planned to go about it, with trickery and deceit, felt…wrong, somehow.

And then there was Kal himself.

Even an eyeless old goat could see the way he looks back.

Being around him had planted a seed of bitterness in her heart that shouldn't be there. A seed that, if allowed to sprout, would create within her a root of discontentment for her very purpose and the male to whom she was destined. Whether or not that little seed was a result of Kal specifically or simply because he was the first male to which she found herself attracted, she did not know. If she was being honest, Felíne was afraid to find out.

Ophelia was watching her but thankfully remained unaware of her inner conflict. Felíne extended a hand. "Shall we try again? You may call me Kitty. I am pleased to meet you."

After a pregnant pause, Ophelia seemed to make up her mind about something and accepted Felíne's offer of peace. "Ophelia. Or Ophe or Oph. Just don't call me Lia."

"Only if you stop calling me princess."

Ophe snorted. "Come," she said. "I'll walk you to the dining hall."

The two females walked quietly, each with their silent thoughts. When Felíne's turned unsurprisingly back to Kal after a few moments, she decided a distraction was her best defense.

"Forgive me for saying so," she said. "But you do not look like an Ophelia."

"Why is that?"

"Well," Felíne said. "It just seems like a name that would belong to someone…elderly."

Ophe gave her a side eye. "How do you know I don't have a brood of grandchildren? Perhaps I'm simply well-aged."

No shurii aged *that* well. The female couldn't be more than a decade older than Felíne, and even that was being generous.

The woman gave a little shrug, her leather armor creaking slightly with the movement. "My mother thought it would be fashionable. That all the names of past generations would come back into style."

"Did they?"

Ophe looked at her. "How many thirty-something-year-olds have you met named Gertrude, Dorothy, or Eunice?"

"None," Felíne admitted. Though, the question itself was biased. Felíne could count the number of females in their thirties she'd met on one hand.

"Well, there you have it."

"I did meet a Gladys." The elder had not been one of her favorites, but she'd been unbelievably skilled with a needle and thread. Felíne had been enthralled by the painstaking amount of detail the woman wove into her tapestries, a talent Felíne couldn't duplicate with ten thousand hours of practice.

"How old was she?" Ophelia asked.

"Oh, nearly a hundred and forty."

Ophe snorted again.

Felíne allowed herself a quiet smile. A beat passed, and she said, "I believe your mother was onto something. Ophelia was a lovely choice. And even if others do not think so, her daughter became terrifying enough to ensure they never admitted it." She dropped her voice to a conspiratorial hush. "Blessed forbid their ancestors be cursed to shudder with fear at the whisper of your name."

Ophe didn't respond, but after a moment, the corner of her lip tilted up just slightly. They walked the rest of the way in comfortable silence.

In the dining hall, Hamme did not disappoint. Breakfast had been delivered, as promised, and it was a feast indeed. Felíne gorged herself on thick, crispy slices of pork, mounds of fluffy eggs with rich cream and melty cheese, crusty bread that was still warm from the oven topped generously with butter, and freshly squeezed citrus juice. There were fruit muffins and delicate, flaky pastries that she wanted to try but couldn't bring herself to stuff into her already overfull stomach.

Kal watched her consumption with an odd fascination. Felíne subconsciously worried that she was being impolite—she wouldn't dare indulge herself so ravenously under the watchful eye of the elders or, Goddess forbid, her mother!—but she was too hungry to care. Felíne wondered absently how in the world Kal could afford such a banquet, then decided she probably didn't want to know. When they were finished, Felíne offered Hamme abundant praise for the meal, for which he appeared thoroughly flattered. Kal had already assisted him in repairing the damage to his cart and even suggested improvements to its structuring. The vendor considered himself in their debt.

After, Ophelia departed, having her own business to attend to in the city. Adder was nowhere to be found.

Kal had one of The Inn's employees saddle Sig, but Felíne opted to walk instead, preferring to stretch her legs after the large meal. Kal kept a comfortable pace with her as they made their way to the trade center, Sig following along like an overgrown puppy.

Cindamar's city center hadn't yet reached its busy peak, but carts were pulling into their designated lots, and vendors were opening their mobile businesses to display their wares. A few early risers ambled along the boardwalk or sat in the center drinking from steaming mugs. The place would be bustling with activity in a few hours' time.

They passed the merchant where Kal had purchased their clothing the evening prior, then the jewelry cart, then the baker on the opposite side of the street. Up ahead, Felíne could make out a grand tent, larger than any others, with rich, heavy canvas walls and thick, sturdy support beams that bowed in embellished arches, seeming to defy gravity. This establishment was situated at the northernmost section of the center, occupying the space of at least ten regular businesses. It seemed to preside over the other structures in the trade center, a lord among vassals. When Kal halted Sig in front of one of the decorative panels, Felíne knew this was the Trade Master's dwelling.

Felíne stared up at the entrance. Two heavy curtains—though curtains seemed an unsuitable term given the grandeur of the panels—were drawn closed and guarded by an armored shurii male in second form. Each panel was embroidered with opposite halves of a gargantuan scale. The left side was weighted with treasures of gold and colorful jewels, diadems, and decorated goblets. Stitched with painstaking detail into the right side were the decayed skeletons of shurii corpses. The scales were balanced.

Felíne's meal turned to lead in her stomach.

Kal seemed to sense her unease. "I have known Grisham for years," he said. "He is ruthless and cunning, but he is not known for cruelty. He is a businessman above all else, and Cindamar is his enterprise. You don't pose any threat to his operations or his city. Once he establishes that, you will receive your token and be free to visit Cindamar whenever you wish."

Felíne had difficulty dragging her eyes away from the shurii graveyard piled atop the righthand scale. "And how exactly will he determine that I don't present a threat?"

"An interrogation."

She swallowed.

"Relax, Kitty. You might be from Asteros but it's not like you're a member of the royal family."

Her eyes shot to his. "Because that would mean what?"

The words slipped out, but Kal didn't seem to think the question odd. "Death, certainly," he said. "The biggest threat to Grisham's entire way of life is the Crown of Asteros." His voice dropped. "Don't forget you were also recently at the mercy of their cruelty. Use that as common ground. Just be honest. There is nothing to worry about."

Just be honest. Right. What's the worst that could happen? Oh, just certain death. Nothing to worry about.

CLOAKING FATE

Kal spoke quietly to the guard after tying Sig's reigns to one of the hitching posts in the front of the tent. The guard cranked a massive wheel on the far side of the entrance that drew back one of the heavy curtains. He disappeared inside. Kal waited quietly while Felíne began to sweat. It wasn't long before the male returned to escort them inside.

The interior of the Trade Master's dwelling was undeniably befitting a master of trade. They entered a large, open foyer that was decorated floor-to-ceiling with opulence. Priceless pieces of abstract art covered the walls, statues carved by masters of marble and bronze stood in life-sized poses, and a table constructed entirely of crystal with a glass top as thick as Felíne's wrist held artifacts that looked older than the oldest elders. The ground was covered with plush rugs dyed in a kaleidoscope of colors. Overhead, a dazzling chandelier hung suspended from a thick beam, refracting light that entered the room through retracted panels in the ceiling.

The Trade Master must have been confident indeed if such valuable pieces were left on display in his entryway. Felíne wondered if it was a test for any who visited. Or a testament to the Trade Master's reputation as though to proclaim that no one would dare thieve from him.

Kal and Felíne were led into an adjacent room, plainly furnished with a wide cushioned stool and a long, narrow tapestry depicting a swath of barren land with a single tree in full foliage. Instead of fruit, the tree's branches were laden with jewels the size of grapefruits. Several shurii bodies lay tangled among its roots.

"I'm noticing a theme," Felíne whispered, indicating the tapestry.

Kal dipped his mouth to her ear. "Very astute of you." Felíne suppressed a shiver. "Grisham has dedicated his life to his pursuits and collected many things of value. He's gained much but lost much as well. The irony amuses him."

They did not have to wait long before another shurii retrieved them. This one was a woman in first form. She was not beautiful but alluring. Tall and willowy, she glided into the room draped in gossamer lavender fabrics from chin to floor. Her light hair was coiled neatly on her head, and her perfume was at the same time sharp and sweet, the aroma immediately filling the space. Felíne thought it a bit overdone.

"The Trade Master will see you," she said in a voice like a song.

They entered a room even grander than the foyer but somehow more intimate. No open panels allowed light into this space. Instead, it was lit by torches encased in glass columns along the walls, each stained a different shade so that the otherwise dark room became a prism of multicolored shadows. There were no treasures here. Just an expansive wall-to-wall carpet the shade of new winter grass. Felíne immediately recalled the grass in the center of the trade circle and realized it wasn't grass at all but a replica of this rug. *Nothing of permanence,* she thought. *Not even the earth.*

In the middle of the room, seated in a simple wicker chair, was a middle-aged shurii man. He had a stern face. Wide-set, intelligent blue eyes bordered with the beginnings of age lines surveyed them as they entered. His black beard was neatly trimmed and streaked with gray. Matching hair was pulled back from his face and secured in a leather tie. He wore an unadorned but fine gray robe fastened over a black shirt and pants. On the middle finger of each hand, he wore a ring: the left was a heavy gold signet, the right a skull. They were the only pieces of jewelry.

Trade Master Grisham.

Behind him were two shurii males in second form, one standing to each side. Felíne recognized both. To his right was Garren, the male who had stopped them outside the city—the Trade Master's younger brother. Garren's eyes found Felíne, and he sneered. To Grisham's left, standing tall and solemn, seeming every bit as formidable as he'd originally appeared upon entering their suite the night before, was Adder. All trace of familiarity was gone, his previously friendly disposition buried beneath a stony iron hide. Icy gray eyes surveyed them with cold detachment.

Felíne glanced over at Kal. He showed no sign of recognition. Odd. She decided it prudent to act accordingly.

"Kalevar Kaine," Grisham said, smiling. He spread his arms wide but remained seated. "I am pleased to hear of your return to our humble city. You have no doubt come to make good on your promises."

Promises? What promises?

"Trade Master." Kal dipped his chin in respect. "I haven't forgotten. I had planned to discuss the particulars."

"Good. That is good to hear," Grisham replied, nodding. He settled back into his chair. "Yet you did not seek me out upon entering the city. I admit I was curious to learn of your…uncustomary request for a delayed audience." He looked over his shoulder at his younger brother's imposing visage. "Even more so surprised by Garren's report of your interesting companion."

Kal placed a hand on Felíne's lower back. "My companion is the younger sister of a personal friend. She is traveling to meet her brother under my protection."

At the word protection, Garren's sneer seemed to intensify, and Grisham's eyes lit with interest. Adder's face remained impassive. "Indeed," the Trade Master said. "And yet I do not believe we have met, she and I. Kalevar, I am admittedly surprised that you have kept such a rare jewel to yourself for an entire evening without so much as an introduction."

In other words, *you brought an uninvited stranger into my city and spent a whole twelve hours or more with her before seeking my approval.* Felíne may not have possessed a wealth of worldly experiences, but she was no idiot. Grisham might be playing polite, but he was not happy about Kal's clear dismissal of traditional etiquette. He struck her as a male who was unaccustomed to his expectations being impugned.

Yet Kal did not offer an introduction. Instead, he looked down at her and waited. Felíne stood there for an awkward moment, unsure of what to do with all attention focused on her. It took a moment for her to realize that Kal was not introducing her out of respect. Not for the Trade Master, but for her. *How do you wish to be announced?* his eyes seemed to question.

Felíne stepped forward and dipped into a flawless curtsy, ignoring the fact that she wore a tunic and breeches instead of a lavish gown. "My name is Kitty, Trade Master. Please forgive the discourteous delay. I was terribly fatigued from our travels, and Mr. Kaine only sought to allow my recovery before arranging for my presentation."

Grisham folded his hands in his lap, the gold signet and the skull coming together. "Mr. Kaine is ever the gentleman, I see," he said, eyes twinkling with interest. "I can see why he would wish to keep you all to himself."

Felíne stood, straightening her spine. Grisham noted the posture.

"Where are you from, Kitty?"

Felíne hesitated. *Just be honest,* Kal had said. Weren't the most effective lies buried in truth?

"I am from Asteros."

Garren looked pointedly at his brother, but Grisham was entirely focused on Felíne. He leaned forward with fascination. "Is that so?" he mused. "It has been a long time since we had a visitor from the capital city. Based on proximity alone, you would think our populace would consist of many Asterosians, but the crown has a suffocating grip. It is not often that it relaxes enough to allow liberations. I would imagine one's departure avoiding notice from such a watchful eye as the crown possesses would prove...difficult."

Felíne glanced at Kal. He was the picture of calm, but there was a tension within him that she all but felt rippling in the air. Did the Trade Master think her a spy?

"I was fortunate," she said carefully. "Thanks to Kal."

"A tale I am eager to hear," Grisham said. His expression was calculating. "However, trade code rules here and must be followed. All outsiders are treated accordingly, without exception. And you are an outsider, dear Kitty, regardless of Kalevar's assurances of your trustworthiness."

Adder moved forward and produced a polished cane made from black wood inlaid with carmine filigree. Grisham took it and laboriously pushed himself to his feet. Felíne hadn't noticed before, but one of the Trade Master's legs was twisted and deformed, previously concealed behind his robe while seated. The movement seemed to cause him a great deal of pain, though he masked it well.

Her curiosity as to his condition was soon forgotten, however, for the Trade Master gripped the cane with both hands and spoke. The skull on his finger seemed to stare at her with its empty sockets. "Welcome to Cindamar, Kitty of Asteros. You have entered the disappearing city. Here, strangers may enter, but only friends may leave. Come. Step before the scales, and let us weigh your worth."

Chapter 32

The Scales

WHEN THE TRADE MASTER SAID her worth would be weighed, Felíne figured he meant it in a metaphorical sense. She did not expect to have her character weighed *literally*.

Felíne found herself in another chamber within the Trade Master's tent, standing before a set of very tangible silver scales. Where his receiving room was filled with muted color, this room for judgment was black as pitch. The walls were black, seams between the floor, ceiling, and each panel sealed completely to prevent even a sliver of light from entering. The carpeted floor was also black, giving Felíne the sense that she was standing upon a bottomless chasm. It was disconcerting and disorienting.

The only source of light in the room was ahead, a lone thick candle illuminating a single chair that sat before what appeared to be a table carved from a solid block of stygian wood. Normal trees grew in such a way that when cut, a particular grain could be seen inside, the variations in color adding to the character of the final piece. Stygian trees were not normal. Their bark was uniform in color from exterior to core, producing a solid black piece of lumber no matter which way it was cleaved. How Grisham had managed to get his hands on that table, she had no idea. It was incredibly rare and must have cost a fortune.

Upon the midnight desk in front of her sat the scales. They were currently balanced, each weighing plate empty. A platter of smooth polished stones rested on either side, identical except for hue. The stones on the left were opaque milky white, those on the right, obsidian.

The female who escorted her and Kal earlier also led Felíne into this room and then promptly departed. Kal had seemed taut as a drawn crossbow, and Felíne could feel his eyes on her until she disappeared from view, but he'd made no move to prevent her from being led away. Felíne told herself it was because he knew she wasn't in any danger, but now, standing alone in the dark, she wasn't so sure. If Grisham's scales found her lacking, would Kal be able to deliver her from whatever punishment awaited? Would he even attempt to?

Felíne glanced around, heart picking up speed. Her hatchet had been stripped of her before they'd been granted access to Grisham's receiving chamber. She was entirely unarmed and unprepared to meet her end in a dark room and a strange city.

"Contemplating your fate?"

Felíne jumped at the voice behind her. Her heartbeat stuttered. It was not a voice she wanted to hear.

Garren chuckled and stepped into view, the candlelight from the desk casting ominous shadows over his second form. The first time she had seen him had been from Sig's saddle, and she'd had Kal guarding her back. Facing the male now, on her own, was a different experience entirely. He was huge, towering over her, covered in muscle, sleek brown hair, and leather armor. He could crush her skull with the squeeze of a clawed fist. And without a second form of her own, Felíne was more vulnerable than any of them could know.

"Are you ready for your weighing?" When Felíne didn't answer, he said, "Have a seat, pet. Let's see what the scales have in store for you."

Garren stalked to the stygian desk and palmed an obsidian stone. It was dwarfed in his hand. Felíne waited for the judge to enter. Surely the Trade Master had someone appointed to conduct these questionings if he did not preside over them himself. Garren watched her expectantly. A moment of uncomfortable silence passed. No one else entered.

A sense of dread descended upon Felíne.

"*You* are going to judge me?" But how? Garren didn't know her. All he knew was that she was traveling with Kal. She didn't know what kind of history the two had, but the animosity between them was palpable. How could Garren possibly judge her fairly? She was already guilty by association.

"Weigh, not judge," he said. "A weighing is a critical piece of trade code. All newcomers must submit to the scales."

"Why you, though?"

Garren returned the obsidian stone to its brethren. "Only a member of the Trade Master's inner circle can perform a weighing in his absence. It is an honor reserved for a chosen few."

"But he's not absent," Feline argued. She'd rather face Grisham's serious intelligence than his younger brother's hungry arrogance. "I just saw him."

Garren stiffened, displeased with her rebuttal. "He is busy. I am not. Now sit so we can get on with it."

Feline did no such thing. She wasn't simply going to subject herself to a tendentious assessment. She turned to look for an exit but found nothing but darkness in every direction.

"He's not going to save you," Garren said, his voice a condemning growl. Somehow, she knew he was referring to Kal. "He can't. No one interrupts a weighing. If you plan to beg for salvation, pet, you might as well beg me."

Garren had a better chance of convincing her to sprout wings and fly. She'd stick a hot poker in both eyes before she got on her knees for him. Feline reached out in front of her as she stumbled away from the scales and Garren, hoping to find a wall of the room and a way out.

Before her hands met any resistance, something clamped down on her forearm. Feline yelped. Garren dragged her back toward the desk and deposited her unceremoniously in the chair. She hadn't even heard him move.

The Trade Master's brother bent down, his muzzle and predator's teeth inches from her face. His scarred lip was curled in a snarl. Feline drew in a sharp breath.

"Go ahead and yell. Call for help. Scream for *him*. Waste your breath, pet. No one is coming for you. Countless others cried for help. No one came for them either."

This had to be some kind of nightmare.

"Here's how this works," he said, straightening. "I'm going to ask you a series of questions. If you're honest, you get an honor stone. Lie to me, and I place a death stone on the scale. If your honor outweighs your deceit by the time we're finished, you will be granted a token. But if deception is your trade…well."

"Let me guess." Felíne crossed her arms across her chest, partly in defiance and partly in a weak attempt to put space between them. "You're the executioner, too?"

Garren smiled, displaying teeth. Somehow, Felíne thought he enjoyed that second role a little too well.

"How will you know if I'm lying or telling the truth?" There were ways of guaranteeing an honest response, but she wasn't about to tell him if he didn't already know.

"Call it a predator's instinct." Garren moved behind the stygian desk, the silver scales and sets of stones looking delicate in the foreground of his bulk.

Felíne eyed the plates. "How do I know the stones are of equal weight? Black could weigh twice that of white."

Garren's chest rumbled, and he pegged her with a frosty glare. He placed an obsidian stone onto one side of the scale. It dipped in response. A second stone, this one white, went into the opposite pan. The scale balanced. Garren added another set of stones. Again, the scales leveled.

"Satisfied?" He emptied the pans, returning each stone to its respective platter.

Not by half, she thought. "And how many questions must I answer?"

He leaned forward, bracing his considerable weight on the edge of the desk, and sneered. "As many as I decide to ask."

Felíne shot to her feet. "That is hardly fair!"

In a blink, Garren again stood before her, his patience expended. "If you like, pet, we can skip the theatrics and get straight to passing judgment, as you put it. Guilty or…not guilty? I'll give you one guess which direction I'm currently leaning."

Felíne almost cursed the Goddess for denying her a second form. She wanted nothing more in that moment than to shift and give Garren a taste of his own tonic. Instead, she ground her teeth. "The word you were looking for is *innocent*. And stop. Calling. Me. *Pet*."

Garren smiled again, hackles raised, eyes hungry. His tail swished. "Or what? Is that other little form of yours going to come out and play?"

Just then, a door opened behind her. Garren snarled, and Felíne whirled, hoping to see Kal.

Adder stalked into the room, and her expectation deflated. He wasn't who she'd anticipated, but she had to admit, he struck an imposing figure. He was taller than Garren, though not as wide. And while he didn't exude pure power, Adder was no less intimidating. He looked lithe, calculating, and deadly.

"What the fuck are you doing here?"

Felíne thought if Garren puffed up any harder, his fur would decide to stop straining and detach from his body entirely.

Adder stopped near Felíne's chair. He looked at the empty seat, at her, at Garren, and finally at the still-empty scales on the desk behind them. His icy gray eyes turned frigid. "Trade Master Grisham is requesting your presence, Garren. I am here to relieve you."

Garren seethed. "You do not have the authority to interrupt a weighing."

"It doesn't appear to me that any weighing has taken place. What have you been doing in this restricted chamber, Garren, if not your brother's appointed task?"

"We are not finished!"

Adder's voice was quiet, calm, and dangerous. "Oh, you're finished. Trade Master's orders. I will commence the weighing."

Garren drew himself to his full height and growled a challenge.

Adder was unmoved. "Unless, of course, you'd rather I relay your disregard for your brother's demands?"

A tense moment ensued. Felíne braced herself for violence as the two males locked gazes. Finally, miraculously, Garren gave a snort of derision, shot Felíne a final glare, and stalked out.

Felíne watched the space in the far wall where he'd exited, the panel identifying the doorway invisible now that it was closed once again.

She heard Adder blow out a breath. "He's a right brute, that one," he said. "Gods damned piece of work. Pardon my tongue."

Felíne turned and was shocked at the transformation. Adder was still in second form, but the iciness was gone from his eyes, now a warm gray as they regarded her. His posture relaxed, shaggy pelt softened, and his expression was friendly, if a little concerned.

"I don't believe we met under the best circumstances, love. What with my trash timing last night. Devereux Santaire," he said, placing a clawed hand over his heart and dipping his head like an absolute gentleman. "And I am told you are Rask Harless's younger sister. Kitty, is it?"

"I…yes," Felíne said. "I thought your name was Adder?"

"A nickname, which you're welcome to use," he said, smiling, then gestured to the scars near his right eye where the silvery hair was missing. "Sweet Ophelia took to calling me Adder after one of the wretched serpents nearly took my eye. Two weeks of fever and almost a month blind. Can't blasted well stand snakes." He shuddered, fur standing on end briefly before settling. "Oph and Kal found it endlessly amusing, of course."

"Goodness," Felíne said. "I'm so sorry."

Adder waved off her concern. "Nothing to be sorry for, though I appreciate the sentiment. It was a long time ago, and the eye works fine now. But enough about me," he said, growing serious. "He didn't hurt you, did he, love?"

Felíne looked down at herself stupidly. Like she needed to check to be sure? Gods. She was wound too tight. "Who, Garren? No," she said. "He's a bully, but he didn't hurt me."

Adder breathed a sigh of relief. "Thank the gods. We won't have to kill him."

"We?"

Adder quirked a smile. "Well, Kal mostly. I'd be obligated to help, mind. Never let your best mate pick a fight without backup. As much as I'd enjoy it, handling Garren would complicate a few things."

Adder moved to a spot behind the desk, reached up, and grasped something Felíne hadn't known was there. A moment later, a panel retracted back in the ceiling, letting daylight stream into the darkened room. It was smaller than she'd realized and certainly less ominous with the morning sun shining through the skylight. Adder propped a leg up on the desk and gestured to the chair. Felíne sat.

"Why would Kal want to kill Garren?" she asked. "Doesn't he have business dealings with his older brother?"

Adder's brow furrowed slightly, and his ear twitched. "He does. And I don't think he wants to kill anyone. But he would be honor-bound to retaliate if Garren had harmed you."

"Because I'm his friend's sister?"

"Because you are under his protection. Aside from the fact that there are few things Kal loathes more than a male who would intentionally damage a woman or child, Kal has given his word to see you safely delivered to your brother. That is something he takes seriously."

Of course, she thought. Kal did have a sense of honor. And displaced as she might believe it to be, he would keep his word if he gave it. However, Kal's motives were purely anchored in his moral obligation to keep his promises, not because he was concerned about what happened to her specifically. Any interest he held in her welfare was generalized, not individualized. Women. Not *woman*. It was a desirable trait in a male. So, why was that realization disappointing?

"I suppose you're here to judge me now?" She looked up at Adder, trying to alter the irrationally dismal shift in her mood. "To weigh my character?"

Adder rolled his eyes. He reached over, grabbed a handful of white honor stones, and dropped them onto the scale, which descended at an alarming angle. Felíne's eyes widened at the irreverence.

"Too much?" He plucked three obsidian stones and added them to the other side. The scale barely lifted the honor plate. "For good measure," he said, winking. "Everyone's got at least a little dark in them. Wouldn't want anyone thinking you were god-chosen."

Felíne was thankful she had the fortuitous presence of mind to keep her jaw from dropping to the floor in alarm.

"Wait, that's it?" she sputtered after recovering from the momentary shock. "I thought this was a sacred ritual. Garren said it was a required part of trade code for all newcomers."

"Oh, it is, love," he said amiably. "I've seen three executions in the time I've worked with Grisham. Untrustworthy foreigners. Nasty business earning those death stones."

She should have kept her mouth shut, just nodded her head in bemused agreement, but she wanted to understand. "Then why not complete my weighing? Why would I be exempt? Could you not get in trouble?"

Adder shifted his weight where he perched on the edge of the desk and regarded her. "Well, to be honest, I am counting on you to keep this interaction to yourself, love. If Grisham or any loyal to him were to discover I shammed your weighing, they'd no doubt assume the worst. The consequences would be...dire for all involved."

They'd assume all of them—Adder, Ophelia, Kal, and herself—to be spies. A direct threat to Grisham's trade empire. Everything he'd built in Cindamar. They would be killed without a second thought.

"Why take that risk? You don't even know me."

Adder quirked a brow and leaned forward, resting an elbow on his knee in a very humanoid gesture. "If I didn't know better, I'd think you would rather I left Garren here to question you on his terms."

"No," Felíne said immediately and meant it. "I am grateful. I just don't understand why you'd risk your life and the lives of your friends for a complete stranger."

Adder smiled, soft eyes glinting with something she couldn't decipher. "Kal."

Kal?

"Kal vouches for you, love. To him, you are worth the risk, and his judgment has long been good enough for me."

Adder must have noticed her surprise because he added, "Give yourself a little credit. He is the one who sent me in here for you, after all."

Felíne swallowed, her chest swelling with gratitude.

"And you're not worried about Grisham or his brother?"

"What takes place during a weighing is between the scale keeper and the appraised. Grisham might be Trade Master, but seeing as he's temporarily passed the task of scale keeper to me—thanks to a bit of brilliant manipulation by Kal—I don't much think he needs involving, do you?"

Relief swept through her. She smiled for the first time since breakfast. "Thank you, Adder. Devereux. Truly."

He gave her a shallow bow. "A pleasure, lady. Besides, if worse comes to worst and our position with Grisham is compromised, Kal and I have an infallible insurance plan."

"Which is?"

Adder gave a dazzling display of teeth, and Felíne was suddenly reminded that she was still in the presence of a dangerous predator. "Ophelia," he said with reverence. "She'd murder the lot of them to avenge us, the dear little psycho."

Chapter 33

Token

"I'D SAY WE'VE HAD ENOUGH time to conduct a proper weighing. Any longer and Kal will have a fit from the suspense. Shall we?"

Feline seriously doubted Kal cared that much about what happened to her to allow himself to become preoccupied, but she was more than ready to leave the confines of the dark room. Even with the skylight, the room held an ominous air simply because she knew a number of shurii before her had met potentially untimely ends at the plates of those scales. She got eagerly to her feet.

Adder led her to the only exit and stopped abruptly before opening the door. "I almost forgot," he said, turning. "We need to make it official, yeah?"

He dug briefly into a pocket of his armor and produced a silver coin, which he extended to her between two clawed fingers. She proffered her hand, and the coin fell into her open palm. It was identical to the one Kal had flipped to Garren outside the town. A token of Cindamar. It marked her a friend of the Trade Master, a guest welcome to come and go as she pleased. Even though her method of obtaining the invitation was about as far from honorable as one could get, she still felt some measure of...*something*, knowing she had a piece of freedom within this settlement. Even if it was only in the eyes of its leader.

"You'll need to present the token to Grisham. It will serve as an indication of your honor and trustworthiness. No one will be able to dispute it unless you do something to specifically call it into question," he warned. "Grisham will return the token when you leave. When he does, keep it safe. If you lose it, you'll not be given another. Any time you visit Cindamar, present the token to one of the guards when you're stopped outside the city and say this: *Super omnia libra.*"

Balance above all. A fitting password for the Trade Master's city. She would have no issue keeping it hidden even after returning to Asteros. She'd had years to master safekeeping precious items she wasn't supposed to have.

A thought occurred to her as she pondered the coin. "Kal didn't say those words to Garren when we were stopped outside Cindamar."

Adder gave a half-hearted chuckle before opening the door. "Can't say I'm surprised. Kal rarely does what's expected of him and even less what he's told. The ass. Doesn't blasted well know what's good for him."

Felíne thought maybe that was part of the reason Kal and Garren had such issues with one another. Garren seemed like the type who enjoyed using his station to exercise control over others, and Kal certainly seemed like a man who did not suffer being controlled. By anyone.

She followed Adder out of the room with the scales and through another hallway before returning to the Trade Master's receiving chamber.

Kal was there, standing stiffly to the side, grooves of agitation carved between his brows. Her stomach gave a silly little tumble when she saw him. As soon as she entered, his gaze immediately locked onto hers. His eyes roved over her, searching for what, she wasn't sure, but it made her intimately aware of his attention. The tumble in her stomach morphed into a flock of doves taking flight.

Felíne forced herself to look away from him and address Grisham. For Kal's weren't the only eyes on her. The Trade Master watched her with a neutral sort of expectation from his seat. Garren waited slightly behind his elder brother, his own expression predatory.

Felíne pointedly ignored Garren. She produced the token Adder had given her and bowed slightly at the waist. She held the token out for Grisham and said, "Super omnia libra," as instructed.

The Trade Master's eyebrows rose in surprise. "Perfect dictation," he mused. "As though the old tongue was your mother language and not the new. How interesting."

Felíne mentally kicked herself. She had no idea if the average citizen of Asteros was instructed in language as extensively as she had been. She should have marred the accent.

Grisham studied her with sapphire eyes that seemed to know more than she'd like. He didn't ask for an explanation, however, and so she did not give one. She only remained standing silently with the token outstretched.

After another beat of silence, the Trade Master accepted her coin, inspected it, and gave her a small smile. Felíne released her breath with forced steadiness to conceal her relief. Grisham ignored the skeptical glower that Garren sent in Adder's direction. "Welcome, Kitty Harless," Grisham announced, arms spread wide. "Friend and ally. The scales of Cindamar have found you worthy. May yours be balanced all the days of your life."

Felíne wasn't sure how to respond. Adder hadn't advised her beyond the initial greeting.

"Thank you, Trade Master."

She was a fraud. Adder knew it; Kal knew it. She could only hope Grisham didn't suspect it. She felt a slight pang of guilt, but it was dwarfed by an overwhelming appreciation for having not been executed after an unfair weighing, which she would have undoubtedly received had Garren remained in charge. That was something to be happy about. Felíne stood, glanced at Adder, who gave her a private wink, and then looked at Kal. Her face broke into a wide smile that she felt all the way to her toes.

Kal stared at her, transfixed, for what felt like several long seconds. Then he blinked and shook himself as though suddenly remembering where he was and whose company he kept. He stepped forward, close to her side. Felíne felt his warmth without touching him, and the closeness was a comfort.

"I believe our business has been settled with mutual satisfaction, Trade Master. By your leave, I would like to show Kitty the city."

Grisham shifted in his seat, pushed himself upright, and suppressed a grimace of pain. He smiled, though Felíne's practiced eye saw how forced it was. He was hiding the depth of his discomfort, and she wondered if anyone had offered a remedy. "Yes, of course. Go. Visit the shops. Dip in the pools. Spend some coin. Enjoy yourselves."

Kal inclined his head and placed a hand on Felíne's lower back to guide her out of the chamber. Just as they reached the exit, the Trade Master called out to Kal.

"Meryl knows that you are here, Kalevar. She will be expecting your presence tonight."

Kal hesitated, his face an unreadable mask.

Felíne tensed. Who was Meryl? Also, why was she suddenly so irritated by the list of possible explanations that immediately presented themselves to her imagination? Was she a friend? A family member? A former lover? A *current* lover? Heat crept up her neck. Felíne had the completely unreasonable thought that whoever Meryl was, she didn't like her. In fact, she didn't like any female who held expectations of Kal's presence after dark.

And that was simply ridiculous. Dear Goddess. What was wrong with her?

Kal smoothly dipped his chin again, his hand not leaving Felíne's back. "Please let her know I won't disappoint her."

Felíne's breath caught. Suddenly, she felt wrong with his hand on her. She stepped toward the exit, but Kal moved fluidly with her.

Grisham gave a nod of acquiescence, and they left the chamber.

As soon as Kal and Felíne emerged from the Trade Master's tent, she faced him. Probably against her better judgment.

Adder chose that moment to slip through the closing canvas panels to join them outside.

Definitely against her better judgment.

But the words were already on their way out.

"Who is Meryl?"

Kal raised both brows, clearly not expecting the hostility in her voice. *She* hadn't expected the hostility in her voice. Adder's eyes widened, and he glanced between them.

Kal recovered and assumed an air of nonchalance.

"Why so interested?"

She scowled, wishing she could take the words back. Why *was* she so interested? She shouldn't be interested at all. But it was too late, and now she had to face her infuriatingly inappropriate curiosity. Felíne crossed her arms. "Do you frequently answer a question with a question?"

Adder hid a smile.

Kal tilted his head, studying her. "Do *you* frequently show gratitude with displays of aggression?"

Her eyes narrowed. "You think *this* is aggression?"

"Who's answering a question with a question now?"

Felíne made a very un-lady-like noise of aggravation. Adder doubled his efforts to conceal his grin. Kal looked down at her, amusement softening the handsome planes of his face. Ugh. Why couldn't he have a face like a toad?

He didn't want to answer? Fine. She didn't want to know. It didn't matter, anyway. Wasn't any of her business.

He wanted gratitude? Also fine.

"Thank you, Devereux," she said with a sweet smile, pivoting toward Adder, who was momentarily caught off guard by the use of his given name. Kal glanced at his friend with curiosity. "I am so appreciative of your timely intervention. You...saved me. I won't forget that." The look of indifference she shot in Kal's direction couldn't have been more dishonest. In fact, she felt anything but. She lied through her teeth anyway. "And I retract my initial question. I don't care who Meryl is. I hope you have a lovely time with her this evening."

Felíne turned on her heel with unmatched grace, head raised with all the poise expected from the Prima of Asteros, and marched off toward Sig.

"That one's all you, mate," Adder murmured after a moment, clapping a hand on Kal's shoulder. She didn't hear his response.

Sig was startled awake by her sudden approach. He tossed his head, sensing her agitation. She immediately felt bad for bothering the animal with her emotional baggage.

"Sorry, boy," she said softly, trying to calm him. Trying to calm herself. "I don't know what's gotten into me."

Why should she be bothered by the thought of Kal spending time with another female? She had zero claim on him, nor he on her. The notion of such a thing was preposterous. He didn't even know her. Not really.

Felíne squeezed her eyes shut.

She shouldn't feel guilt for her lies. She was only doing what was necessary to survive. Besides, how did one betray a mere acquaintance? And yet, if Kal ever learned of her deception, that's precisely what he would feel: betrayed. The thought shouldn't bother her, but it did. Deeply.

Now, she felt doubly guilty for treating him poorly because of her senseless jealousy.

CLOAKING FATE

Felíne stood rubbing Sig's velvet nose, her irritation slowly ebbing with each warm breath blown into her chest by the horse's great lungs.

The trade center of Cindamar had come alive in the time they'd spent in the Trade Master's tent. Shurii from what seemed like every corner of the world roved the street, first and second forms alike. Some wandered from shop to shop, cart to wagon, merchant to vendor. Others strode with purpose to familiar displays. All manner of goods were being traded and exchanged and carted about. The sheer amount of diversity in the little city was staggering. Even the brief glimpse she'd gotten of Asteros during her secret outings with Gen gave Felíne the impression that the variety available in her home city didn't compare to this.

She watched in quiet fascination.

The people here were so different, yet so comfortable. There was no military presence, no threat of arrest if a blasphemous word was uttered or an unacceptable behavior displayed. Second forms were worn proudly here without apprehension or shame. In Asteros, the second form was seen as lesser. It was the cursed form. The one given by the traitorous Godking that was a grudging necessity, good only for the purposes of procreation. Here, that wasn't the case at all. The shurii here were free. So long as they abided by the trade code, no one took issue with whichever form they chose.

Felíne wondered if the Goddess looked down on this with condemnation. Her mother would certainly insist as much. Yet if what Kal said was true, the shurii's second form wasn't one to be feared. Maybe it didn't lack control in the ways she'd been told. The notion only raised more questions she didn't have answers to. Yet.

She thought of Imogen back home. What the female had been through. What others were still going through. Railah likely included. Felíne held a well of compassion inside her, but her determination to get to the bottom of why those females were allowed to be abused was like a hot blade dipped into that water; it sizzled. As soon as she got home, there would be answers. Her mother might have been the queen, her father might have ruled, but the future of the race was hers. That had to count for something. What good was all that responsibility if it didn't afford her certain privileges? Certain powers.

By the time Kal's quiet presence approached her, Felíne had lost all desire to argue. The fight she'd picked over something so trivial now seemed immature.

She peeked up at him, her hands ceasing their gentle stroking of Sig's nose. Kal watched her with that calm, ever-present awareness that he seemed to always possess. He didn't speak, and Felíne sensed he was waiting for her to initiate so that he could appropriately gauge his response. Sig shoved his nose into her chest, and she resumed her petting. His large equine eyes grew lidded.

"I apologize for my earlier...aggression," she said, clearing her throat. "It was childish of me, and you didn't deserve it."

She half expected him to goad her, but he stayed silent. Watchful.

"Thank you for sending Adder. I was...he came just in time." Felíne looked down at her forearm. The place where Garren had grabbed her. He hadn't harmed her, but she'd been rattled just the same.

Kal noticed her attention, and a darkness crept into his eyes that had nothing to do with their color. When she saw it, a chill skittered down her spine.

"If he put his hands on you..." Kal's deep voice was quiet and laced with menace. "There is nothing that will save him. Not his station. Not his brother. Nothing."

Felíne's gaze was captured by his. Kal's words were a vow, and she remembered what Adder had said about him. This is what he meant and what he'd been hoping to avoid. When Kal gave his word, he kept it. If she told him that Garren had grabbed her, Kal wouldn't just kill him. He'd dismantle him. But he'd also destroy any ties held here in the process. He would make himself an enemy to Grisham, crippling whatever business dealings they had. Felíne had no idea what those entailed, but the obvious wealth and prosperity of the city gave her the sense that their agreement was significant. And Kal would forsake all of it for her?

No. He would forsake all of that to keep his word. And he'd promised to keep her safe.

Felíne reached out and touched his hand. Kal's eyes hadn't left her face, not for a moment. "I told Adder he didn't hurt me."

That, at least, wasn't a lie.

Kal wasn't satisfied. He bent closer to her, seeming to cage her with his body. "Kitty. You're sure?"

It was less a question than a demand for an answer. She almost told him in her sudden desire to obey. But she hesitated. Not because she had any concern for Garren. He'd been a brute and a bully. No, she hesitated because she didn't want Kal to jeopardize whatever he'd established here. Not on her account. Not when she was perfectly fine.

"I'm sure," she said more firmly. "I promise. I'm fine."

Kal searched her face, dark eyes roving, and Felíne hoped that whatever enhanced senses he possessed didn't include mind-reading or truth-seeking. She held his gaze, and after a moment, the intensity receded. He nodded.

Felíne let out a steadying breath.

"Meryl is Grisham and Garren's younger sister. She and I became friends years ago when I first found Cindamar. My relationship with Meryl is the primary source of Garren's animosity toward me."

Felíne's eyes snapped to Kal's. She swallowed the swell of emotion and the sting of disappointment. So, she'd assumed correctly.

"I...see," she said. Suddenly, Felíne felt like an intruder. Kal had probably stopped in Cindamar to spend time with his lover and instead, he'd been stuck watching over her the whole time. She briefly, *vividly* recalled standing before him in nothing but a robe. Feeling as though he'd been caressing her with his eyes. She'd watched him *bathe*. Like a total creep.

Gods, she was such an idiot.

And he was still standing too close.

"She must be anxious to see you."

"I'm sure."

Felíne studied a leather buckle on Kal's vest, unable to hold his gaze. She recalled Grisham's words from earlier. *Meryl knows that you are here.* The way he said it and the way Kal responded made it seem like Kal hadn't expected that information.

"You didn't tell her you were here, did you?"

"I did not."

Felíne huffed a humorless laugh. "Bad move. She's going to be furious with you."

Kal's head tilted, his curls shifting, and Felíne had to mentally chastise herself for wanting to reach up and touch them.

Stop it.

She needed to get away from him. Felíne leaned back and bumped into Sig's shoulder. The roan transferred his weight away from her to allow her extra space. Kal moved with her. An hour ago, she would have welcomed the closeness. Now, she felt trapped by it. Knowing that it was another woman whose space he should be invading—*would* be invading later—changed things dramatically. She absolutely would not intrude upon another female's relationship.

"Why would she be furious?"

Felíne's brow furrowed. "Are you serious?"

Kal watched her, his expression sincere. "I want to know what you mean."

Irritation spiked. "If you were *my* lover and neglected to tell me you were in town, I'd be furious. Doubly so if I had to find out that information from someone else. *Triply* so if I found out it was because you were preoccupied babysitting another woman."

Kal blinked at her, completely caught off guard. Then he laughed. He *laughed.* It changed his entire countenance. It made him even more attractive. Impossibly, irresistibly so.

And that made her even more irritated. "I am so curious as to what you find hilarious about this."

"Is that what you think I've been doing?" he said, eyes sparkling with mirth, gold treasures glittering briefly in their depths. "Babysitting you?"

She didn't provide an answer. He didn't deserve one.

Kal's lip lifted, and a stupid, adorable dimple appeared in his cheek. "You're not a baby. I haven't been babysitting you."

"Does *she* know that?"

Kal gifted her with another laugh. "I supposed we're both going to find out. You're coming with me to see her tonight."

Felíne's eyes went wide. That was *not* what she'd been expecting. She might actually have gaped. Why would Kal invite her along to visit his lover? She recalled a particular lesson with Gen, in the days following their visit to Madame's, that had detailed a coupling with not two, but *three* shurii. That one, thank the Goddess, had not involved an actual demonstration. It was hard enough for her to come to terms with the idea of becoming intimate with one partner, let alone multiple. The visual aids alone had caused her to blush from hem to hairline. Was *that* what Kal had in mind?

She was most definitely gaping.

Why was it so suddenly stifling? Felíne fidgeted with the neckline of her tunic.

Kal was once again studying her with entirely too much focus. Felíne threw up a silent prayer that her thoughts weren't being publicly broadcast via her facial expressions.

"I would really like to know what you're thinking right now," he said, dipping his head to eye level. His voice was low and rich. Inviting. She leaned away and got nowhere.

"Actually, I think it's best if I don't say." Because it was nowhere near appropriate.

"Kitty."

She shook her head and clamped her lips together, looking at anything other than his probing gaze. If he thought for a moment that she would even entertain the possibility of—

"Kitty, look at me."

Her traitorous eyes lifted to his without her consent.

"Meryl isn't my lover."

"I don't care, I—wait, she's not?" Why did her voice sound weird?

Kal wasn't smiling now, but his eyes were soft, and there was something else there. The way he was looking at her made heat bloom in her face. "No. She never has been."

"Oh." It was such a lame response for such a significant revelation. "Then why…?"

"She's getting married," Kal said. "We've been invited to the celebration."

"Oh. That's why she was expecting you?"

Kal nodded. The dimple was back. It was less stupid now. "Exactly what had you been thinking?"

It wasn't stifling any longer. Now, it was just hot. "Exactly nothing."

"I think you're lying."

352

He regarded her like he had just caught her with her hand in a coin purse that wasn't hers. Smug. The scoundrel. She refused to give him the satisfaction of discovering that 'liar' was her new middle name.

"Hang on, you said 'we.' Are you sure you want me to attend?"

Kal straightened, puzzled by the shift in conversation. "Of course," he said. "Why wouldn't I?"

Felíne shrugged. "I don't know. It's your friend, not mine. Are strangers typically invited to such events?"

"Kitty. Do you think I'd leave you alone in an unfamiliar city while I went off to a party?" He seemed genuinely offended.

"I…" Well, yes. If she was being honest, that's exactly what she expected him to do. With the addition of a guard to keep her from doing anything rash. Isn't that what her entire upbringing had consisted of? Felíne was used to being excluded. She'd never attended a wedding. Never been invited to a celebration of any kind. Temple rituals hardly counted as 'celebrations' even if that's what her mother's priests insisted they were. The fact that Kal was even considering her feelings by including her was unexpectedly touching.

Felíne worried her bottom lip. Kal missed nothing as his eyes tracked the movement. "I don't want to intrude."

"You won't."

"But it's your friend," she pressed. "The invitation was for you."

He shrugged. "Where I go, you go. And vice versa. I made it clear to Grisham we're a package deal."

Felíne blinked, surprised. "You did?"

Kal nodded.

"We are?" Why did her stomach do a summersault?

"Yes." He was completely serious. "Though, if you really do not wish to go, I won't force you. Meryl will just have to deal with her disappointment."

"It's not that. It's just…" She was running out of excuses. How did Felíne explain that she wanted to be sure it wasn't too good to be true? It seemed such a small thing, the invitation to a party. Kal desiring her company. And yet, to her, it was everything. "I have nothing to wear."

Surely a wedding required attire more formal than a pair of breeches and a tunic? She vaguely remembered her parents attending a wedding when she was younger, and her mother had had a gown made specifically for the occasion. Her father had been dressed in full regalia.

"You don't have to change a thing, Kitty," Kal assured. He took her hand and gently pulled her from where she was pressed against Sig's shoulder. With a hand on her upper arm, Kal turned her to face away from him, out at the bustling trade center. He dipped close to her ear and gooseflesh ran down her arms, all the little hairs standing on end. "But if you insist, I don't think you'll have trouble finding something special. In case you've forgotten, you now wield a Trade Master's token. We are in the famed trade center of Cindamar, after all."

Chapter 34

Move

"YOU MEAN...ARE WE GOING shopping?"

"Would you like to?"

Felíne looked out at the people wandering along the boardwalk and through the street. A sense of pure, undiluted excitement slowly spread its way through her chest. Would she ever. Felíne had never been shopping. She remembered being hopeful she would get to browse the vendors' goods when they'd first arrived in Cindamar, but she hadn't given it much thought beyond her initial longing. Any exposure she had to the business district of Asteros was in the dead of night when shops were locked up, people were mostly home asleep in their beds, and she was required to sneak about to avoid attracting unwanted attention. And even then, her focus hadn't been on perusing merchandise; it had been consumed with her lessons as the Prima.

Here, though, she wasn't the Prima of Asteros. She wasn't even Felíne Lochlan Faelstrom, Daughter of the Crown. Those titles might not be gone for good, but they could be shelved for a time. Her destiny wasn't coming to claim her today. Would it be so bad if she allowed herself to be as others saw her here? Could she just be Kitty and go shopping with her brother's friend?

She became aware of Kal's quiet attention. The bright midday sun warmed his brown skin and bathed the longer hair on the top of his head with golden light. It was a rich coffee color, not black like she'd first assumed, and naturally highlighted with several strands bleached by his time outdoors. The sides were still shorn close to his skull, though they'd begun to grow out a bit, which softened the harsh designs shaved into them. The planes of his face were all masculine angles and lines, with a strong jaw and an expressive brow. His goatee was slightly fuller, and ebony stubble shadowed the edges of his jawline.

He looked good in the intense daylight rays. Like a midnight prince worshipped by the sun.

One that was still waiting for her response.

"Oh, yes!"

Kal extended an arm, and Felíne stepped into the street. She hadn't gone more than a few steps before stopping abruptly.

"Kal, I haven't got any money." Well, she did, but her trove of coin was buried in a vault in the heart of the royal villa of Asteros. She couldn't exactly make a withdrawal. It's not like she ever really had access to it anyway. She never had any need.

"I know," he said simply. "It's not a problem."

Felíne frowned. "It is a problem. I don't expect you to continue paying for me." She was already wearing clothes he'd purchased for her.

Kal looked down at her, his expression matter-of-fact. "It isn't a problem unless you make it one. It's not like I gave you time to pack a bag before we fled the city. Paying for you until we reach your brother is the least I can do."

He was being generous. Felíne knew he *had* packed a bag for her. It had been attached to the other mount that had perished in the barn just before everything went up in flames. Including Brune. Those losses weren't strictly her fault, nor did she believe Kal blamed her for them, but he was still replenishing items lost in what he believed to be an attempt to rescue her. And she could not deny her involvement in those events, even if they'd seemed well outside her control at the time.

"Rask owes me anyway. If it makes you feel better, whatever you buy can be tacked on to his debt as interest."

Felíne was being stubborn, but this was important to her. She shook her head. "Rask is not responsible for me. My debts are my own."

"Kitty." Kal rubbed his cheek. "You can either allow me to pay for whatever you like and let yourself enjoy it, or we can skip the shopping altogether, and you can attend the wedding tonight in the traveling clothes you're currently wearing. Either option works for me, but you need to decide."

Felíne hesitated. She wanted to attend the celebration. And she really didn't want to be underdressed. "Is this a formal event? Will the females be wearing their finer garments?"

Kal shrugged. "Nothing more extravagant than what you would see at a typical Asterosian wedding."

That didn't help her at all. But Rask's sister, Railah, had likely attended at least a few marriage celebrations. Kal would assume his response had satisfactorily answered her question.

"Fine," she said, making up her mind. "But I won't accept charity. You'll need to find some way for me to pay you back."

Kal raised a skeptical brow. "Are you sure you trust me with that kind of bargain? Unnamed favors are a dangerous sort."

Felíne narrowed her eyes. "Something *appropriate*. And mutually agreed upon."

He smirked. "Deal. Where to first?"

Felíne once again faced the town center. The commotion was exciting, but she'd be lying if she wasn't a teensy bit intimidated. Navigating crowds existed within the realm of uncharted territory. In fact, pretty much everything except daydreaming in solitude, furthering her education, and assisting Mender Alcuin was uncharted territory. She wanted to explore, but it made sense to start with what she needed. "Clothes, I suppose? Perhaps the shop you bought these from?" She indicated her outfit.

The space between Kal's eyes furrowed. "If you want something nicer than what you're wearing now, you won't find it there. You'll want a dressmaker's shop."

Of course. Again, that would be something any typical female raised in the city would be expected to know. She deflected to conceal her ignorance.

"Didn't you tell Grisham you planned to show me the city? Lead the way to the dressmaker."

Kal started down the boardwalk. "There are several, I believe. I haven't ever sought one out myself, but all the clothing vendors are this way."

Felíne felt pressed in on every side, and she was grateful Kal was with her. Shurii seemed to flow around him without even realizing it. Clusters of people moved to get out of his way as though their collective subconsciouses recognized an apex predator approaching and some survival mechanism within them activated to avoid his attention. All Felíne had to do was stay close behind him, and the crowds parted for her by default.

Kal stopped before a tent with an interesting entrance. Instead of the canvas curtains pulling laterally to allow passage between them, the blush-colored panels were pulled toward the center of the entryway and cinched with a thick swath of pearlescent fabric that gathered in a lovely pleat and cascaded to the floor. Two shorter, delicate tasseled pieces rested on either side of the collected panels near the top of the entryway. A custom line of embroidery was stitched into the curtains so that when closed as they were, a deep vee was visible in the folds.

Felíne's lips parted in awe as the image was discerned. The gathered center panels looked like an exquisite ball gown with a plunging neckline and lace-capped sleeves. There was no sign out front, but the owner didn't need one. There was no mistaking this was a dressmaker's establishment. And a fine one at that.

Felíne glided toward the entrance and turned before crossing the threshold. A thick section of her hair slipped over her shoulder. "Aren't you coming?"

Kal eyed the fancy doorway. "Is this something that requires my presence?"

Was the mighty Kalevar Kaine reluctant to enter a woman's clothing store? The notion was too good to let go unpunished.

"Why Kalevar," she purred. "Are you *embarrassed* to be seen entering a ladies' dress shop?"

One moment, he was standing back near the edge of the boardwalk. The next, he was directly in front of her, occupying her space, breathing her air, and claiming her proximity. There was a slightly sinful gleam in his dark eyes, a flash of gold. "Oh, Kitty," he purred right back in that rich, throaty voice of his. "I don't get embarrassed."

She swallowed. "Ever?"

He turned his head slowly. "Not ever. Not by anything. If you want me in that dress shop with you, you only need to ask."

What she should have asked was for him to wait outside.

"Will you accompany me into the dress shop?"

Kal's lips quirked. He extended an elbow, and Felíne slipped her hand through to rest on his biceps. She was touching a man. Voluntarily. And not just any man. *Him.* And he'd invited it. She'd touched him before, but this felt different. This seemingly simple gesture felt like she was crossing an invisible line of demarcation. She was taking a step forward, toward what, she wasn't sure, but it was away from where she'd come. That much she was certain of.

"What kind of person doesn't ever get embarrassed?"

He glanced down at her, tucked close to his side. "The kind that doesn't care about the opinions of others. Embarrassment implies concern for another's judgment. I stopped caring what others think of me a long time ago."

And what sparked that transformation? she wondered, not for the first time.

Kal led her over the threshold into a simple tent filled with natural sunlight. A small round table sat against one wall topped with a vase of pale pink roses, and several tufted chairs lined another. Gowns of all cuts and styles were displayed throughout the space. Felíne was stunned by the amount of care and detail that went into the designs—the intricate patterns and the painstaking amount of specificity that had been hand-stitched into the bodices. She wandered over and fingered a skirt. Even the quality of fabric was comparable to those of her gowns back home. The owner here possessed no average skill.

A petite, raven-haired female pushed through a curtain that concealed a side room, holding several bolts of velvet in different colors and a mouth full of pins. Her dark hair was streaked with gray and collected up onto the top of her head with long wooden hairpins. Several strands had fallen loose around her face, which was unlined. Her blue eyes went wide when she saw them, and the straight pins fell out of her mouth.

"You cannot be in here!" The woman looked directly at Kal. She set her bolts of fabric on a nearby cushioned armchair and hastily made to shoo him out of her shop. Kal didn't so much as budge an inch. He regarded the woman the way a cat would a cockroach: not quite edible, but capable of being squished just the same.

"I am here with the lady," Kal said, indicating Felíne. "She would like to find something suitable for a wedding."

The woman squinted up at him, her delicate brow pinched. "Obviously," she retorted. "But you still cannot be in here. No males. Don't you know it's bad luck to bring your bride in to choose a gown? You can't see her! Not until the ceremony!"

Kal glanced down at Felíne. She watched as his initial moment of bewilderment transformed into understanding.

"Out. Out!"

The little woman made to physically turn Kal. He grinned.

Oh no.

He leaned forward predatorily, and the dressmaker looked up in alarm, conceding a small step. "The ceremony is tonight," he said. "And I'll be seeing everything. Luck be damned."

Felíne poked her head around Kal's intimidating bulk to address the smaller female, who was liable to suffer an apoplexy. "He and I aren't getting married," she clarified. "We are attending a friend's wedding, and I have nothing to wear. I hope you can help me find something appropriate despite the short notice?"

The dressmaker looked back and forth between them as Felíne's words registered. Finally, she pegged Kal with a dubious glare. "Must he stay?"

Felíne nodded, patting Kal's forearm. "If it's not too much trouble? He will be on his best behavior."

The dressmaker pointed to another set of curtains at the rear of the tent. "Wait there," she ordered, gathering her fabric and spilled pins. "I will be with you in a moment."

She disappeared into another room to attend to what Felíne could only assume was another client. Kal walked with Felíne toward the smaller dressing room. She elbowed him in the ribs. "Adder said you hated males who treated women poorly," she whispered accusingly. "You scared the poor lady half to death."

"I would never put my hands on a female in anger," he replied, not bothering to keep his voice down. Kal held the dressing room curtain aside for Felíne to pass through, then ducked in after her.

"Unless she was trying to kill me." He was standing so close in the tight space that Felíne could practically feel the vibrations of his voice reverberating in her bones. Kal closed the curtain, shutting them in together.

Felíne faced him. "Well, you intimidated her."

"It was harmless." He tilted his head. "A little intimidation was probably good for her. She was being presumptuous."

"You were rude."

Behind Felíne stood a small round platform in front of a full-length mirror. Near the entrance was a single chair. Kal opted to stand while they waited.

"Me?" Kal's brows flew skyward. "The old sprite tried to physically force me out of her shop. What do you call that?"

"Confused," Felíne snapped. "You deliberately misled her."

"She assumed. Should I have allowed her to push me out?" He crossed his arms, biceps bulging beneath his sleeves. "I might remind you that I was prepared to wait outside. *You* insisted I come."

That's right. And why had she done that, exactly?

The curtain blew open, and the dressmaker whisked in. "You," she pointed at Felíne. "Stand here." She indicated the platform. Then, she turned haughtily to Kal. "Will you be watching her change as well?"

Felíne's face flamed. Really, now. Maybe she'd been a little hard on Kal.

But Kal only smirked, a dimple flashing. "Don't ask me," he said, voice like velvet. "Ask the lady."

Felíne glanced around for a rock to crawl under. When none were found, she muttered, "You can leave." The dressmaker grumbled something under her breath that sounded very much like "scoundrel."

Kal ignored the remark. Instead, he grabbed the chair, lifting it easily with one hand. "I'll be right on the other side of that curtain," he said to Felíne. He shot a warning glare at the little dressmaker. "I don't trust her. If she attacks you, yell."

Before the woman could make any retort, Kal disappeared behind the curtain, leaving Felíne at her mercy.

The dressmaker turned to her, hands clasped, clearly determined to ignore the recent exchange. "Now then," she pronounced, all business. "You said you are attending a wedding."

"Yes."

"Whose?"

Did that matter? How many weddings could there be in the little city on the same night? "The Trade Master's sister. Meryl." She didn't know her surname or even who she was marrying.

The dressmaker's eyes cut briefly back to the curtain behind which Kal was waiting. "Ah ha! Well, you came to the right place. I designed Meryl's gown. I am Policarpa."

"Kitty," Felíne introduced herself. "My…companion is Kal. Thank you for your help. I know this is quite last minute."

Policarpa waved her off. "No matter. It is good you came to me. The other dressmakers do not have even half the selection I can offer you. Turn."

Felíne did as she was told and rotated on the platform. Policarpa took out a length of tape and began measuring. "You want lace? Full skirt? Something to accentuate the high waist and generous breasts, I think. Good hips, too. Yes."

Felíne looked at the dressmaker in the mirror. "I don't want to stand out."

Policarpa returned her gaze. "Clever girl. You wear one of my gowns, and you won't have a choice. Shurii will notice."

"I am serious," Felíne insisted. "The evening is not for me."

Policarpa studied her and nodded her approval after a moment. "Meryl's gown is special. Imported fabrics. Very expensive. There is no other like it. Don't worry, the night will be hers." She rolled up the tape and tucked it away. "Wait here."

Felíne waited as the dressmaker left to select items for her to try on.

She was gone only a few minutes and returned positively laden with fabrics.

After a bit of tying, tugging, cinching, and a brief squeeze, Felíne stood on the platform in an absolute dream. The gown was trumpet style in a champagne-colored satin. An asymmetrical neckline hugged her breasts with an elegant bow capping one shoulder. An extra layer of fabric trailed from the neckline, which elevated the dress from simple to chic. The body hugged the lines of Felíne's waist and wider hips before flaring slightly and extending to the floor. It was lovely.

Policarpa stood back and appraised Felíne with a smile. "Beautiful," she said.

Felíne ran her hands down the length, smoothing the sides. "It is."

The dressmaker tsked. "The gown, yes. But a dress is just a dress until a lady steps into it and makes it something more. You want to blend in, but you would stand out clothed in a flour sack. You are accustomed to finery. I can tell. You wear this simple gown like a queen."

Felíne swallowed. "Is it too much?"

Policarpa scoffed. "What is too much? It is perfect."

She needed to show Kal. He was making the purchase; it was only fair she got his approval. And maybe she wanted it—just a little.

Felíne stepped off the platform and exited the dressing room. Kal stood with his back to her, hands folded behind his back, inspecting one of the feathered dresses hanging nearby.

Felíne cleared her throat, anticipation swirling in her stomach as he turned. Kal froze. He was backlit by the sunlight streaming through the entrance. His eyes were shadowed, and she couldn't make out his expression, but she *felt* his gaze. Every place his attention touched, her skin heated beneath the satin. From her neckline all the way down the length of her body. Back up again. Slowly.

After a moment, he stepped closer. She saw his eyes then, and something new stirred in those dark pools. Something powerful. Something that turned the heat she felt into a fire of pulsating energy. It…it was hunger. *Desire.*

"Well?" Policarpa looked positively smug. "You trust me now?"

Kal forcibly dragged his gaze away from Felíne and eyed the little female. She was grateful. Another moment of the way he'd been looking at her, and she was liable to combust.

"No."

A single word from him and the moment fractured.

What? Felíne stared. Shocked.

"What do you mean, *no?*" Policarpa voiced what she'd been feeling, looking equally incredulous. Possibly more so.

"I mean, no. This dress won't work."

Felíne's face fell.

Policarpa was outraged. She practically vibrated with anger. "You animal!" she hissed. "This female is magnificent."

CLOAKING FATE

Kal was unbothered by the little woman's ire. "She is," he said with quiet confidence, and Felíne's gaze snapped to his. "However, the dress will not work."

"*Why.*"

Kal faced the dressmaker. "Because," he said. "She cannot move."

"Nonsense," Policarpa snapped. She threw a finger in Felíne's direction. "Walk to the front."

Felíne hesitated, feeling caught between their conflict.

"Go ahead, queen. Show him you can move."

Sighing, Felíne walked easily to the entrance of the shop, spun smoothly, and made her way back.

"You see," Policarpa stated triumphantly. "She is elegance made flesh. She does not walk, she glides—"

Kal shot unexpectedly toward Felíne, startling both women. Felíne saw the flash of a dagger thrust in her direction and panicked. She lunged away from the danger on pure instinct, but the skirt of the gown restricted her legs. She stumbled, balance compromised, and fell backward. Policarpa cried out.

Kal's forward momentum shifted, and he caught her effortlessly, his arm cradling her with surprising gentleness. He sheathed his dagger, taking care not to damage the gown as he helped her steady herself.

"What in the world is wrong with you!" Felíne cried. "You could have ruined the dress. Are you out of your mind?"

Kal ignored Felíne's fuming and looked instead at the outraged Policarpa, who had turned a furious shade of red. "She cannot move," he repeated calmly, still holding Felíne by the waist. "She cannot run or sit a saddle or react to a threat."

Felíne was livid that he'd used her as a demonstration, but she paled. Did he know something that he wasn't telling her? "Are you expecting an attack?"

His eyes found hers. They were hard. "No. But that doesn't mean I won't be ready for one. I'm not taking any chances with you." To the dressmaker, he said, "Please, find something else."

Policarpa threw up her hands with an exasperated cry and, muttering to herself, went deeper into the shop.

Chapter 35

A Matter of Repayment

IN THE END, FELÍNE WAS not disappointed. While she'd loved the satin champagne gown, Policarpa solidified her claim as the best dressmaker in Cindamar—and undoubtedly beyond—by providing an exquisite and entirely unique garment as an alternative. It was three garments, actually.

First, Felíne stepped into a cream-colored pantsuit with wide cottony shoulder straps, loose through the bodice, and flowing wide-cut legs that gave the illusion of a floor-length skirt. Next, a pastel rose corset went about her waist, securing her breasts with modified boning that allowed Felíne plenty of room to move and breathe. Policarpa cinched up the back with thick satin ribbon. A beautiful lace design decorated the front of the corset with a row of delicate pearl buttons extending down her abdomen. The outfit was completed by a sleek, high-collared vest accentuated with extended shoulders and secured with matching pearl clasps. The vest was closed from her chin to the swell of her breasts before flaring out in a flowing train that matched her pants, leaving the design of the corset on display.

She'd never worn anything like it. It was, at the same time, bold and graceful. Fearless and feminine. It felt like the type of thing a warrior queen might wear to a formal event to remind her subjects that while she was beautiful and benevolent, she could also cut the hearts from her competition.

Kal was positively thrilled. Evidenced only by a taciturn nod of approval.

He *wasn't* so thrilled about the cost of the outfit. Or at least, he couldn't have been. When Policarpa told him the price, Felíne's jaw nearly hit the floor. Not that she had much frame of reference, but it seemed outrageously expensive. She immediately declined, saying they'd find something else, but Kal only reached into an inner pocket, counted out the required amount, and told the dressmaker that the garment could be delivered to their current room within the next two hours.

"It is too much," she said as soon as they left Policarpa's shop and stepped back into the bustling center.

Kal held out an arm, stopping her from colliding with a passerby. "Do you like it?"

"Of course," she replied. "But—"

"Then it's not too much."

Felíne opened her mouth to argue, but he led them once again down the boardwalk. Kal looked sidelong at her. "Is there anything else you'd like to see? Any other merchants you want to visit?"

"Not after spending what you just did on an outfit," she mumbled. At this rate, she'd have to pawn her organs to pay him back.

The corner of Kal's lip tipped up. "Don't be ridiculous, Kitty. It's only money."

She frowned. *Only money?* "It's your livelihood."

He tilted his head thoughtfully. "I can always make more. Besides, it's made to be traded. And you looked...well, it was money well spent."

She looked what? What had he been about to say?

"Also, you owe me now." His lip curled higher, one dimple winking. "And I'm very much looking forward to deciding upon an appropriate method of recompense."

Something about the way he said it made Felíne think he wasn't considering anything appropriate at all. Or maybe that was just where *her* thoughts were venturing. And that was a problem.

"Exactly," she said. "I don't want to be indebted to you any more than absolutely necessary."

When Kal offered no reply, Felíne peeked up at him. His playful demeanor had changed. She was surprised to see what she thought was a flash of disappointment cross his features before it was masked with careful neutrality. Or had that been irritation? Confusion? Now, she wasn't sure if she'd seen anything at all.

"Why don't we establish this method of repayment that seems to be such a burden to your pride?" Kal finally said, eyes still up and scanning the street ahead. "That way, you can enjoy your time today without being plagued by guilt for accepting my generosity, small thing that it is."

"That's not—" Felíne had half the words out before her mouth clicked shut. He hadn't said it maliciously. There wasn't even a hint of sarcasm in his tone. He'd stated it as though commenting on something as mundane as the weather or traffic.

Was she being prideful?

Kal said his generosity was a small thing, but it certainly didn't feel that way. The truth was, she *did* feel guilty. She had no idea why her conscience chose to take issue with this, but she didn't like the thought of accepting any form of generosity from Kalevar knowing she only planned to escape him, repaid or not.

Kal still wasn't looking at her. Was he offended by her refusal?

"You're upset with me," she said, somewhat stunned by the revelation.

"No," he answered. "Why would you assume that?"

She blinked up at him. "Shall I repeat what you said?"

Felíne pulled up short as a small child raced between them. The girl's mother was close behind, offering a quick apology before snatching her laughing daughter into a secure embrace. "I will, you know. Don't worry about it wounding my pride or plaguing me with guilt."

Kal ducked into a small space between two vendors and pulled her in with him. They were suddenly standing quite close. She could feel the heat coming off his body. Oh, *now* he was looking at her. There was heat in his gaze as well. Or maybe it was just a trick of the shadows. Felíne squirmed in the tight space, and Kal tensed. "Do you have any idea how frustrated you make me?"

"Aha. So, you *are* upset with me."

He frowned. "I said frustrated, not upset. There's a difference."

Felíne shrugged, doing her best to pretend that Kal wasn't occupying her space, breathing her air, and making her insides squirm...in a good way. *No. A bad way*, she chided whatever reckless streak was running wild within her. "Barely," she countered. "I think 'upset' would be more accurate, given the furrowed state of your brow."

Feline watched a muscle twitch in Kal's jaw. Was it always this *hot?* They were standing in the shade. Surely, that should offer some relief.

"No? Perhaps you're looking for a different word," she offered, somewhat breathless.

The twitchy jaw unhinged. "Fine," he said, leaning even closer. "Do you have any idea how *aggravating* you can be?"

"An inkling," she said. "But what have I done this time?"

He blew out a breath and leaned back slightly, returning some of her breathing room. "You want to go shopping."

It wasn't posed as a question, but she felt the need to confirm it anyway. "Yes."

Kal nodded. "Yet you have no money with you."

Go on and rub her nose in it. Was he trying to aggravate *her?* "Yes," she said again tightly.

"I offer to pay for your things. Something any halfway decent man would do—and I haven't even made it halfway to decent. You decline. Yet you still want to explore the trade center. Still want to go shopping."

"Your point?"

Kal ran a hand down his face. "I'm offering you a solution, but you refuse to accept it. *That* is frustrating. What do you want, Kitty?"

Feline froze. What did she want? No one ever asked her that. And now that someone was, unexpected as they might be, she couldn't even give a definitive answer. Feline had never even stopped to truly consider her wants, because normally no one else did, either. But she knew what she *didn't want* and that was a debt she didn't require to a man she couldn't repay. One that she liked. One that was probably a lot closer to decent than he gave himself credit for.

But to put that into words?

"I don't know," she said finally, lamely.

Feline avoided his gaze like the complete coward that she was, but she could feel it on her face, and her cheeks burned in response. Pretending to be someone she wasn't was much more difficult than she could have anticipated. It was hard enough being herself in a new environment. Being someone else in an environment that might or might not be new to said someone else was nearly impossible.

Kal seemed to sense her discomfort and, blessedly, gave her a break. He gently placed a hand under her elbow and guided her out of the small space between tents, folding them seamlessly back into the throng of people.

Kal led her into the inner circle of the town center, which was situated in an open carpeted area where several shurii children ran and laughed while their parents chatted amongst themselves. There were wooden benches throughout the space where several families sat eating their midday meals. The makeshift garden of potted plants was off to the right at the far end of the inner circle. An open two-seated bench sat near a large, spiked plant with orange and white blooms the size of Felíne's head. This was where Kal stopped, indicating they sit.

"Are you hungry?"

She wasn't. She'd eaten enough at breakfast to last her until evening. Felíne cleared her throat, which was dry, thankful for the neutral change in conversation. "Just thirsty, actually."

Kal nodded and left her sitting alone while he disappeared into the crowd bustling along the inner boardwalk. Was the town center this busy all day? Was the level of activity even something expected for this time of year? She always imagined people would wish to stay inside on hot late-summer days, but the shurii here didn't even seem fazed by the heat or the blazing sun overhead.

She dabbed the back of her neck, where her hair was growing damp with sweat. She'd have to ask Kal about the pools when he got back.

Heat aside, it was nice inside the center, especially closer to the little garden. Bees and other plant-loving insects buzzed about, the air was filled with a fragrant mix of flora and freshly baked bread from a vendor farther down, and the sound of children laughing was background music. It was quieter here, almost like the innermost heart of the city was insulated from the commotion outside. For once, Felíne was contented to sit and wait instead of wander. She might have a stubborn streak the width of the Yawning Canyons, but she was also capable of learning from prior experiences. There was no need to cause Kal any additional stress, which would undoubtedly happen if he returned and found her missing. Again.

CLOAKING FATE

It wasn't as though she'd have much success trying to run off in broad daylight anyway. Given Kal's attention to detail and his tendency toward overbearing, it was highly unlikely he'd gone far.

As if her thoughts summoned him, Kal emerged from the crowd like a specter. He carried two large mugs, one of which he handed to her.

"Thank you. What is it?" Felíne sniffed the contents. It smelled sweet and tart.

"Cindamar regulars call it nectar. A local favorite. It's a mix of water, sugar, some form of citrus, and agave pulp. All the food vendors carry it, each adding their own variation to the recipe to try and outdo one another. They even have an annual festival with contests to judge the best brew."

Felíne took a tentative sip and then a greedy one. It was delicious. "That sounds like fun."

Kal sat next to her and leaned back, his long legs stretched out in front of him. "Oh, it's a good time. The vendors take it way too seriously. There's always at least one brawl over who the real champion is. Grisham jacks up security around that time every year. But there's also dancing and games for the younglings and every kind of delicious food you could imagine. This whole corner of the desert becomes ripe with the smell."

Felíne smiled. Partly at thoughts of what the festival would be like and partly because of how unusually talkative Kal was being. She didn't know him to be one to overshare, which was exactly what he was doing. She didn't dare bring it up. It was nice listening to him. Relaxing. She sighed, surprisingly contented. Kal's gaze found her face.

"You have a token now. You'd be welcome to see it. And if he doesn't get his invitation revoked before then, Rask would be happy to join. He loves any excuse for a party. But you know that."

Felíne's smile faltered, and she forced it in place, though it no longer felt like it belonged there.

They sat in silence for a few minutes, listening to the center hum around them. Felíne drank her nectar and tried to turn her mind to happy thoughts instead of dwelling on the inevitable future and its terrifying uncertainty.

"What is it you did in Asteros?" Kal finally asked, his deep voice low and quiet as if he were speaking to a frightened doe. "Before the Fates."

Felíne stared at the mug in her hands. What did she do? Well, she...No. What did *Railah* do? What kind of answer would be acceptable? Believable. She didn't know the first thing about Rask's sister or what the female's life was like before being summoned to the Fated Mothers. She didn't know her interests or talents or routines. Goddess help her, she didn't know what *any* normal female's life was like. She'd only met a handful of them, and they would hardly pass for normal. She didn't think Sashara's chosen profession could be considered typical. Nor would it be favorable for her to describe her leisurely activities as the ones she'd witnessed that night at Madame's. Her face flamed at the memory. And it wasn't like she could tell the truth. *I spent every waking hour preparing myself to successfully service the Primordial Male to save our species.* Somehow, that was even worse.

Think, Felíne. Think.

Kal watched her, waiting patiently for an answer. He could probably hear the racket her heart was making as it bashed about inside her rib cage. A hardness entered his eyes, and Felíne wasn't sure if it was directed at her or at some other thought that entered his mind, but it made her nervous all the same. She needed to answer before he grew suspicious.

"Um, could you elaborate?"

She mentally kicked herself in the shins. She was stalling.

There was an undeniable edge to him, but his words were surprisingly gentle. "Did you work? Do you have any hobbies? Skills?"

Felíne raised her gaze to his. She didn't understand what she found there. He looked at her with a warring expression, a mix of anger and concern that confused her.

She cleared her throat, an idea forming. She had to sell something that he'd believe and the best option she had was a truth because Goddess knew she was a terrible liar.

"I was training to be a mender. I didn't have many hobbies. Any free time I had was spent at the clinic."

Kal's brows raised slightly. It wasn't an answer he'd been expecting. Felíne swallowed, racking her brain for a follow-up explanation. Something to save herself from inevitable scrutiny. He probably already knew what Rask's sister did for work. What she did for fun. He was going to call her on her lie. Color bloomed more intensely in her cheeks.

"Sorry," he said, mistaking her panic for embarrassment. "I don't mean to be surprised. It's just that I've known Rask for some time. I hadn't expected anyone who shared his blood to be…well, capable in a capacity such as…" He ran a hand through his hair, agitating the growing curls. "You know what? Never mind. Now I'm just being rude."

Felíne gave a shaky laugh of relief and took another gulp of nectar. Her mug was nearly empty.

"Did you enjoy it?"

Felíne rubbed a sweating palm on her pant leg. "Assisting the mender?"

Kal nodded.

Felíne's chest tightened suddenly. "Yes," she whispered. She did. She wished she could escape to Mender Alcuin's lab, bolt the door behind her, and unload all of the past week. He was a safe haven. A source of wisdom and kindness, and she missed his quiet brilliance and uninhibited honesty with a fervor that threatened to overwhelm her.

"How long before you finished your training?"

Well, there was a question she'd never been asked. Technically speaking, she wasn't being officially trained to assume her own patients. Her future lay along another path entirely. One from which she wasn't permitted to detour. "I…I'm not sure," she said, sticking with another safe version of the truth. "I suppose I was never meant to finish." That was a terribly depressing thought now that she voiced it.

The hardness in Kal intensified. She could see the tension bracketing his mouth, forcing his shoulders into a rigid slope, and flexing the tendons in his forearms. *What now?*

"Did I say something to upset you?"

Kal turned away from her, facing some unnamed point in the distance. For a moment, he didn't answer, and she wasn't sure if he would. Then, "I know what it's like to have the future you wanted stolen from you. I'm not angry with you. Only angry on your behalf."

"What future did *you* want?" she blurted.

Two black pools of unfathomable depth turned in her direction and sucked her in. "One that didn't involve my family being slaughtered."

Felíne gasped.

His voice didn't waver. Not a muscle twitched. There wasn't even the hint of emotion in his expression, though his brow was a set of hard dark lines, and the eyes underneath were still locked on her. Eyes that were far too bottomless. They held too much of a void, one that reached to the core of who he was.

She hadn't expected Kal's answer and was transfixed by his attention, his admission. A wave of compassion crashed inside Felíne's chest, ripping a ragged hole in her heart. Surging into that new space was an unexpected yearning to heal his hurt. She fought the overwhelming urge to wrap her arms around him.

Kal had experienced an inexplicable pain in his past. Whatever had happened to his family had carved a chasm into his soul and rebuilt the man he was around it. Some unnamed horror had claimed his loved ones and left him a shell without them.

Felíne didn't know what that entailed. Who exactly he'd lost. Had he children? A wife? How had they died? He said they'd been slaughtered, and what she saw in him now made it terribly clear it hadn't been an accident. But who would do such a thing? And why?

It would be callous for her to ask. Whatever fragile trust they'd grown in the past few days would be obliterated if she attempted to pry. No amount of curiosity was worth that. Besides, Felíne got the sense that he'd already revealed more than intended. 'I'm sorry' would sound shallow, and even though her heart was reaching for him, she doubted he would appreciate her sorrow.

People who carried true pain didn't crave sympathy; they craved understanding.

She didn't understand, but she could still offer a kindness. Felíne reached out and took his hand, squeezing slightly, careful to keep her expression neutral.

Kal allowed it, and they sat like that for some time without speaking. They watched a family of four finish their meal, pack up their things, and amble away, fat and happy. The sun crested in the sky and crept slowly forward. The trade center did not slow.

"If you find it acceptable, you can repay me by working as a mender."

Felíne cocked her head. "You don't look like you need a mender. Besides, I gave you my professional opinion last night, and you ignored it." She nodded to the cut above his eye.

"You're not wrong," he said with a shallow grin. "But I don't mean for me. You chose a reliable profession. There is always need for capable menders. You can charge handsomely for your services." He cocked a brow. "If you're any good, that is."

Felíne raised her chin a hair. "My skills are adequate."

More than adequate, but there was no need to be boastful about it.

"You're sure? If you start killing people by mistake, they won't offer compensation."

Ha.

He shrugged. "Then again, they'd be dead, so I doubt they'd care if we helped ourselves."

Felíne's jaw slackened in shock. "Kal!"

He showed her both dimples. "What do you say, Kitty? Do we have an agreement?"

"I have never killed anyone," she said sternly. "Nor do I plan to."

The dimples stayed put. It was a little disturbing how much she liked them. "You're a better person than I," he said.

She pointed her empty mug in his direction. "No pilfering from dead bodies."

Kal took the mug from her and replaced it with his own, much fuller one. "What if they're already dead?"

Felíne pegged him with a formidable scowl, retort poised on her tongue.

He scooted to the opposite edge of the bench in mock alarm. "You're sure you've never killed anyone?"

"Kalevar…"

"Okay," he said with a rough laugh. "No body-robbing. On my honor."

"Do you *have* any honor?"

He winked. "Debatable."

The corner of her lips twitched. Felíne extended her hand. "Alright. We have an agreement."

Kal gripped it with a warm, rough palm. "Great." He reached down to his waist and tossed her a leather purse full of coins. Felíne barely managed to catch it without spilling her drink. She palmed the surprising weight, clutching it against her chest.

"I have one stop that I need to make, but otherwise, the next three hours are yours, Kitty."

She allowed herself a small smile. "I can visit any shop I like?"

Kalevar slid smoothly back to her, dipped his head, and looked into her eyes with absolute sincerity. The dark pools once again warmed from within. "Anywhere you like. Wherever you go, I will follow."

Chapter 36

Daybreak

FELÍNE STOOD BEFORE A FLOOR-LENGTH mirror in the tent she and Kal had been designated at The Inn. She fingered the delicate pearl buttons that ran down the front of her corset. She'd done her hair with hot irons that Lele had provided, and it now sat curled, coiled, and pinned to near perfection with a few tendrils tactfully chosen to frame her face. Felíne knew how to style her hair. Her face, however, was another challenge that she'd done and redone several times over. If it weren't for Imogen showing her how to embellish her features, she'd have been entirely clueless about how to use the tools the thoughtful innkeeper had left. Finally, she was mostly satisfied with the result.

A fine line of kohl accentuated her eyes. The mix of fat, antimony powder, and soot was brushed onto her eyelashes, making her already large almond-shaped eyes look even more pronounced and feminine. The mossy green color in them shone. A pinkish gloss painted her lips, creating a fuller appearance, and some sort of powder in the same color was patted subtly into the apples of her cheeks.

She stood back and critiqued her appearance in a way only women did.

Felíne supposed it would have to suffice. She was far less grand than her mother, but hopefully, she looked suitable to attend the wedding. A little thrill lit her nerves. Another first. She wondered if the excitement of participating in things she was never meant to experience would wear off. Felíne doubted it. As guilty as she should feel for enjoying these forbidden adventures, she couldn't deny that she *did* enjoy them and even...craved them. The knowledge that they wouldn't last forever…couldn't last, made them all the more exhilarating.

She glanced at the clock. Kal would be there to escort her in a few minutes.

Felíne went to the side table and picked up the small velvet pouch that contained a custom assortment of mixed herbs in a little glass vial as well as a salve, which she'd made an hour before. Policarpa had the forethought of a prophet and had sewn deep pockets into the pants of Felíne's outfit. She slipped the medicinal pouch into one of them, along with a handwritten note for later.

Felíne's first stop after her conversation with Kal earlier that afternoon had been the apothecary. If she was going to be working as a mender, she needed materials, equipment, and supplies. She could have spent all day in that little herb shop. It was stocked floor to ceiling with some of the rarest plants, poultices, and potions. *Saltleaf* from the western coast. *Miner's bloom* from the far Caves of Solace. Even *sanctitium*, which was rumored to grow exclusively in the elders' private gardens of Doceo. She'd been awed at the variety, and for a brief moment, all thought of feeling remorse over her debt to Kal fled as she considered buying a little bit of everything. The ailments she could treat with these! Even Mender Alcuin wouldn't have been able to leave empty-handed, and his personal pharmacy was the most extensive she knew of.

Eventually, though, her senses returned, and she purchased what would provide the most practical applications while remaining easy to transport. When she finally made her escape back to Asteros, she wanted to be able to take whatever she hadn't already used with her.

After the apothecary, Kal stopped by the weapons vendor to speak privately with the owner. Felíne had remained outside, watching the blacksmith next door and his apprentice alternatively heat and quench a piece of metal. Kal's appointment lasted a few minutes, and they were off again.

Felíne walked by every single vendor in the town center, though she purchased nothing else. Just being able to peek into carts, peruse open tents, touch trinkets, and inspect little treasures for sale according to her whims was an unbelievable treat. Kal accompanied her to each shop, keeping silent guard as she flitted from merchant to merchant, only speaking to answer any questions she posed. His earlier talkative spell had abated, but his quiet watchfulness didn't bother her. She'd been so preoccupied she forgot all about the heat and completely neglected to ask about the pools.

The little bell that hung from the center of the tent's ceiling tinkled musically, startling Felíne out of her reverie.

"Come in," she called.

A moment later, Kal pulled back the tent entrance and stepped inside. Felíne stared. It wasn't polite, but she couldn't help it.

He looked like a forbidden dark lord that just stepped out of a tantalizing fiction. His short, dark curls were as unruly as the man they belonged to. It appeared that a somewhat unsuccessful attempt had been made to tame them with some pomade, which only succeeded in defining each coil's opposition to tranquility. The sides had been freshly shorn and faded to precision; new designs were shaved into one temple that followed the crest of his ear. He wore a fitted long-sleeved shirt so dark brown it was almost black. It matched perfectly with his oil-colored leather armored vest, which was secured at each side and hugged his muscled chest and trim torso. An oddly familiar crest stamped the vest—a shield emblazoned with the head of a roaring lion that possessed a strange serpentine body. Behind was a crashing wave, and underneath, a sword crossed with an axe. She could have sworn she'd seen it somewhere before but couldn't place the occurrence or identify what it represented. Felíne's eyes traveled downward of their own accord. Kal's long, toned legs were clad in black trousers, and he wore dark boots that sheathed each calf.

The only weapon Felíne could see was a dagger strapped to his waist. It had a lovely pearlescent hilt that shone milky white with delicate veins of turquoise running through. It was beautiful. She thought it a shame for something so graceful to be destined for violence.

"The dressmaker chose well."

The dark lord spoke, his voice rich and deep. Every cell in Felíne's body that identified her as female came alive with the sound.

So, all of them.

Felíne mentally slapped the nonsense from her femininity.

"Policarpa is a talent above talents," Felíne replied, hands clasped before her. "I am honored to wear one of her designs."

"She should bear the honor. You wear it well."

Felíne flushed a little at the compliment and murmured her thanks.

Kal stood there watching her, not saying anything. She deliberately did not meet his gaze. Felíne had begun to lose trust in her sensibilities when she looked into those deep, hooded eyes. She desperately needed her wits about her.

After another moment of silence, Felíne cleared her throat. "Are we waiting for something?"

Her words seemed to break some kind of abstraction. Kal straightened a little, as though remembering why he was standing there and what they planned to do. What was he so preoccupied with?

"No," he said, glancing at the clock. "We can go."

Felíne gave herself one final glance in the mirror before walking to the exit. "Is there anything that I need to bring?"

"Actually, yes," he said. "Your weapon."

Her weapon…the hatchet? Did she need that? They were attending a wedding.

Kal's words from earlier that day in the dress shop resurfaced. He was prepared for anything. At all times. Felíne's enthusiasm deflated a little. Policarpa's outfit was near perfect. She would look ridiculous with a thick leather belt strapped about her waist and the weathered old axe looped through it.

She sighed. Eyesore, though it might be, she scolded herself for wanting to leave it behind for the sake of appearances. Kal was right. She needed to be prepared.

Felíne moved past Kal toward the bed and stopped. She turned to him as something dawned on her. "It's not here," she said, regret surfacing. "The guards took our weapons before we met with Grisham. I didn't even think to ask for it back."

Kal stepped toward her.

Felíne frowned. "What's that?"

Kal produced a rough, oblong package wrapped in simple brown paper and tied with a piece of twine. He handed it to her. "A gift. One that you should be able to use."

He got her a gift? Felíne sat on the edge of the bed, not quite knowing what to think or say. She undid the twine and carefully unwrapped the package.

Felíne stilled. For a few heartbeats, she could only stare at the work of art that lay in her lap.

It was a hatchet. The exact same size and shape as the one she'd taken from Brune, but stunning. The freshly honed bit gleamed silver. The cheek of the blade had been etched with the profile of a lioness framed by a rising sun in the background. The handle was smooth blonde wood so light in color it was almost like bone, its lower portion wrapped in a buffed cream leather. It fit her grip like it was made for her hand. Felíne ran her fingertips over a delicate engraving on the side. She peered closer, trying to make out the symbols.

"Every good weapon has a name," Kal said softly. "It says *Daybreak*. I wanted something that represented a new beginning. I thought it would be fitting."

Felíne's throat swelled with unexpected emotion.

Under the hatchet rested a holster fashioned from the same cream-colored leather with a guard for the blade and clasps that were at the same time decorative and functional. It would match her outfit flawlessly.

Felíne had to restrain herself from jumping up to embrace Kal. Instead, she raised eyes brimming with tears of gratitude to his twin dark wells. "Thank you," she said thickly. "Thank you so much."

Kal remained unsmiling, but his eyes warmed, and his brow softened. "You're welcome."

She inspected the etching again, appreciating the detail crafted on such short notice. The sunrise made sense considering what he'd named the weapon, but... "Why the lioness?"

Kal shrugged. "For Kitty. I asked for a feline. I guess that was the best he could come up with, considering the time restraint. I think it works, though."

Felíne smiled and ran her hands again over the craftmanship of her new weapon. "What will you do with Brune's old blade?" Perhaps he could lay it to rest with his old friend one day.

"That is Brune's blade."

Felíne's eyes shot to his.

"I had Adder take it to the weapons master and relay my instructions after we left Grisham's. He engraved the original head and refitted it to a new handle. It isn't perfect, but it should work well for you."

A fresh tear welled and spilled over, and Felíne smiled, uncaring of the emotional display. "It's perfect," she said. "Will you help me put it on?"

Felíne stood, and Kal stepped closer to her. She could smell him, the spice of bourbon, honeyed amber, and masculinity. He reached around and fastened the holster so the hatchet hung like a reassuring weight at her hip. Felíne was intensely aware of Kal's broad hands lingering at her waist.

Goddess help her, he was looking down at her again, and she was letting him. The heat in his hooded midnight eyes suffused her with warmth. It crept through her blood, making her limbs feel heavy and languid, and settled in her belly. The longer he looked at her, the heavier it grew until Felíne felt a pulsing sauna pooling low in her abdomen. Lower. That liquid heat sunk right between her legs. Her lips parted at the sensation, and she inhaled. The rise in her chest brought the front of her corset in contact with Kal's chest armor. Her nipples hardened, suddenly sensitive, and more heat pooled.

A gold spark glinted in Kal's eyes, the monster at the bottom of the dark sea stirring. His nostrils flared, scenting. Whatever he sensed hardened his gaze and intensified his own scent. Felíne became intoxicated with it.

A wildly inappropriate thought flashed into her mind. But instead of immediately dismissing it, Felíne allowed herself to entertain it. Whatever sensible part of her conscience that normally exercised control had been en-tirely submerged. The echoes of common sense floundered at the bottom of the hot spring that Kal churned low in her abdomen. It was wanton. Forbidden. But right at that moment, Felíne didn't care.

She…she wanted him to touch her.

She imagined it. Standing there, so close to him. Feeling the fever of masculinity that he threw off in waves. Felíne was swallowed by the darkness of his gaze, and she let herself go under.

She imagined him palming her breast, taking the weight of it. Imagined that broad, calloused hand travel lower than where it currently hovered by her waist. Imagined the press of it between her thighs. As she sank further into those twin dark pools, she could almost feel him sinking into that damp cove right along with her.

Dipping into *her* pool.

Another pulsing sensation swept her, and Felíne's knees felt weak.

Kal made a very masculine sound. His hands hadn't moved from where they originally rested near her hips after buckling the hatchet around her waist. Felíne's imagination was creating a very dangerous scenario, and based on the way he was looking at her, Kal knew precisely what kind of picture was being painted.

In vivid detail.

A gong sounded somewhere outside the tent. Somewhere in the city.

"What was that?" Felíne asked, still distracted, her voice coming out a little breathless. She made a heroic effort to regain some modicum of self-control, which wasn't much. She was hot and bothered, but she drew the line at panting—a line she currently toed.

Kal didn't break eye contact, looking very much like he wanted all self-control—his and hers both—to go straight to damnation. "The event carillon," he said, voice like smoldering coals. "It marks the start of the wedding."

Oh gods, the wedding. You know, the thing you spent all this time preparing for, which you're ready to completely undo over a gift and a heated look like some hussy in heat?

Her conscience was back, head forcibly thrust above the surface of her newfound pool of imaginative pleasure.

It was *a very thoughtful gift,* the wanton part of her argued.

Felíne's conscience looked positively murderous, treading water in her lake of lust, and shot a hefty dose of common sense her way, which had been entirely forgotten in her bout of temporary insanity.

She cleared her throat and stepped back from Kal, breaking eye contact and placing appropriate distance between them. "We should go. We'll be late."

Kal looked like he would gladly miss the wedding altogether in favor of a completely different type of event if Felíne asked it of him, but her sensibilities returned, and finally, it seemed, so did Kal's.

"We have time yet," he said with surprising steadiness, moving toward the door. "They won't be looking for us during the ceremony. Are you ready?"

No. "Yes."

Kal extended a hand, and Felíne took it. It was warm and rough. Just the way her imagination remembered it.

Together, they stepped out into the gathering dark.

Chapter 37

The Wedding

THE CEREMONY WAS LOVELY.

Felíne had never attended a wedding, so she hadn't known what to expect. She and Kal slipped inconspicuously into the crowd of attendees near the rear and still caught the second half of the joining.

The event took place at sunset on the bank of Cindamar's largest pool, which was a surprising shade of aqua. Felíne had anticipated a murky, mud-filled body of water, not the filtered clarity of the oasis. An elevated platform had been erected by the water's edge where Meryl and her betrothed stood, joined at the wrists by thick swaths of red silk ribbon underneath an arch of white jasmine. The mountain range behind them dripped gold in the last light of day. More white petals had been cast into the pool and floated tranquilly atop the still water.

Tiny lamps were scattered throughout the area, attached to feeble posts of varying heights. They looked like a host of fairies that had drifted down from the High Country to float among the people and gift the venue with their soft illumination. An expansive tent stood open a short distance from the ceremonial platform that was large enough to house a hundred shurii comfortably. If she raised on her tiptoes, Felíne could see an army of staff laying out a veritable feast on long wooden tables inside. Even further to the right, a massive unlit firepit circled by a ring of heavy white stones was being stacked with thick cuts of timber by two shurii males in second form.

Felíne forced herself to ignore the final preparations for the post-cere-mony celebration and turned her attention back to the bride and her mate.

Meryl was a stunning creature with soft, honey-blonde hair that fell in gentle waves just past her shoulders. She had a pretty round face, rosy cheeks, turquoise eyes, and a small mouth with full lips. The gown Policarpa had designed for her hugged her small breasts, slim waist, and generous hips with a caress of ivory lace that fell gracefully to the floor. A deeply plunging neckline was the showstopper of the piece and some kind of shimmery semi-translucent material occupied every area of the dress that would have otherwise left Meryl's skin on display. It was daring without being garish. Felíne thought only a select number of females could pull off that style of gown and still manage to make it look tasteful. Meryl was one of them.

A balding man wearing priest robes carefully looped the ribbon that joined Meryl's hand to her betrothed's. He looked at each of them with kind eyes that crinkled at the edges and explained the ribbon's significance. The red indicated the blood to be shared in joining their lives together as one. The remnants of cut white ribbon that once signified their individual lives lay at the couple's feet. That life was no more. For a joining such as this was permanent. A vow taken before witnesses to pledge loyalty, protection, and devotion to one another forever. For once their hands were joined, once their blood was shared, once their bodies bound, only death could cleave them apart.

A hush settled over the crowd as the priest spoke. Meryl looked up into the awed eyes of her husband as the final tie was made.

Felíne glanced up at Kal but couldn't read his expression. Was he thinking about Meryl? Was he thinking of his own family? Someone he lost? Maybe this brought back memories for him. Had he stood on a platform like that before friends and family, pledging his life to a woman he loved? Had he hoped for forever, too, only to have it end before it even had a chance to start?

That was a sad thought.

She turned back to the couple. She didn't know either of them, but it was obvious that they were unbelievably happy. The pure, undiluted joy that bathed Meryl's face as she was tied to her husband radiated like the twinkling beams of light trailing from a shooting star. Her man saw and was captivated. He only had eyes for his bride.

CLOAKING FATE

Felíne couldn't help but feel happy for them. The excitement they must feel. *What would that be like?* she wondered.

Her thoughts trailed to her own joining. The male she would be bound to for life. Her divinely chosen mate. The soft smile that lit her features while watching the wedding faltered. Something that once filled her with a sense of purpose and even…pride felt less and less like a meaningful path and more like a walk to a gallows. Like unwelcome finality. She'd always been nervous. Always felt apprehension at the unknown. But she'd carried a sense of resolute understanding that her destiny was something bigger than herself. It still was. But now, standing under the waterfall of happy expectation that Meryl and her husband were pouring out, Felíne realized that was an experience she would never have. She would never get to choose a mate for herself, allow herself to be chosen by a male. Never stand under an arch of jasmine with hands tied, looking up into the eyes of the man she knew without a shadow of a doubt that she wanted to spend the rest of her life with.

Meryl turned to glance at the crowd with a radiant smile. Her husband's eyes didn't stray from her face.

No male would ever look at her like that. With attention only for her. With devotion.

With love.

The understanding settled into the bottom of her heart like one of the black death stones from the Trade Master's scales.

The priest said some final words and raised the couple's hands, presenting them as husband and wife, mates forevermore, to the waiting crowd. Felíne swallowed her selfish despondence and forced a smile. Cheers went up, and handfuls of tiny white flowers were thrown into the air. Meryl laughed, threw one arm up around her new husband's neck, and kissed him full on the mouth. More applause erupted.

Felíne saw Grisham sitting in his chair toward the front of the crowd, just at the foot of the dais. He smiled as he clapped quietly for his younger sister. Garren was there, too, Felíne realized. She'd never seen him in first form, but she recognized the judging brown eyes and umber hair combed hastily back from his broad forehead. His face was clean-shaven, and he would have looked dapper in his buff-colored shirt, mahogany jacket, and light trousers if not for his somber demeanor. She wondered if the man possessed any emotions other than disdain, arrogance, and anger.

Meryl slipped off the platform, dragging her new spouse with her, and greeted her brothers warmly. The crowd began to disperse, individuals, families, and couples approaching the newlyweds to offer their congratulations and well wishes. Felíne looked around but didn't see Ophelia or Adder anywhere. However, she noticed several of what could only be Grisham's personal guards posted throughout the venue, keeping an eye on the scene.

She and Kal hung back toward the periphery and waited for the well-wishers to move on toward the feast. None of the food would be touched until Meryl and her husband were seated at the head of the table and took the first bites of their meal.

Finally, with only a few stragglers left standing near the platform, Kal and Felíne approached the couple. Grisham looked past his sister, who was laughing and telling a story with an abundance of enthusiasm, and nodded in greeting. The moment her brother's attention shifted away from her, Meryl knew. She turned, saw Kal, and squealed. She flung herself at him and wrapped him in a hug hindered only by the one wrist still tied to her husband, who was jerked forward in his wife's excitement.

"Sorry, sorry!" Meryl laughed, untangling herself from the ribbon. "Kal! I'm so glad you came!"

Kal smiled down on her without reservation. "Congratulations, Mer."

She scowled then, perfect brows turning down over her bright eyes. Meryl swatted at him. "You cur. I sent you an invitation, and you never responded. I had to find out last minute that you were even here. Not even a hello."

Kal tucked his hands into his pockets and gave a noncommittal shrug. "Sorry, Mer. I haven't been in one place long enough to receive a letter, let alone send a response. It's pure coincidence that we arrived in time to help celebrate you both."

Meryl gave him an exasperated look and turned back toward her groom. "Why does this not surprise me? He's about as static as a desert wind, this one."

Kal overlooked the quip and nodded toward her new husband. "Does the poor sod know what he's in for?"

"The poor sod's name is Boden Ceen," Meryl said, linking her arm through her husband's. "And yes, he knows *exactly* what he's gotten himself into. Willingly, I might add."

Boden extended a hand to Kal who accepted it easily. "Please, call me Bo. Happy to meet you, Kal." He glanced fondly down at the fiery female attached to his arm. "I'd accept your congratulations, too, but I wonder now if I should ask for luck instead."

"Smart man," Kal said. "Though I don't know if luck will help you."

Meryl waved off their teasing. "Okay, I can see the two of you need to be separated already." Bo chuckled, and Meryl's aqua eyes found Felíne.

Felíne extended her hand toward the smaller female. "My name is Kitty," she said. "Congrat—"

Meryl put her arms around Felíne and squeezed. "—ulations."

When she pulled back, Meryl took Felíne's hands in her own. "I cannot tell you how happy I am that Kalever finally found a girl."

Felíne blinked.

"Not that he hasn't *been* with girls. I'm sure he knows what he's doing in that regard, but he's never actually brought one *here*." She leaned in conspiratorially to whisper. Felíne was quite positive everyone standing in their small group heard each word. "I honestly started to wonder if he might prefer men." Meryl cut wide eyes to Kal, who watched her with mild bemusement. "Which would have been fine! I mean, it would have been *someone*." She looked back at Felíne. "But I'm so glad it's you. He's been broody and serious and kind of an overall wretch for years, and I was convinced last time he left Cindamar that he would just wander out into the desert and die of loneliness."

"Meryl…" Bo started.

"But he didn't!" She said cheerily. "And Kitty, you have my utmost gratitude." She leaned in and kissed Felíne on the cheek. Felíne looked up at Kal for direction, but he only shrugged as though to say *this is what we all deal with*.

Meryl was a whirlwind. Delightful. Lovely. But a whirlwind all the same.

Felíne suddenly felt foolish for her earlier jealousy. Meryl seemed to be the kind of woman who doted undivided attention upon anyone she encountered. She was so genuine with her interest and intensity that it was impossible not to be charmed by her. If Kal *had* had a relationship with her, Felíne could hardly blame him.

Again, not that it was her business.

Boden slid a hand under his wife's elbow, recapturing her attention. "Let's make our way to the feast, Mer," he said. "Your guests will be waiting to eat."

"*Our* guests will be just fine waiting until we're ready," she said, turning back to Kal. "I want to know what you've been up to since I last saw you. How you met this lovely lady. When we'll be getting an invite to *your* wedding." She pivoted again toward Felíne and leaned in without waiting for a response. "On second thought, never mind him," she said knowingly and slipped a delicate hand through Felíne's arm, angling her away from the men. "I'll never get any ripe details out of that one. I want to know *everything*. Tell me your secrets. How'd you fell the great oak that is Kal?"

Bo sighed somewhere behind them. Kal stepped easily up to Felíne's other side as they made their way toward the large tent. He leaned in and said, "Do not feel obligated to answer any of her questions. Meryl's a glutton for information, and she can be rather demanding. Don't let her bully you for answers."

Meryl stopped their forward progress and shot an accusatory glare around Felíne in Kal's direction. "I am not a bully."

His voice dropped an octave. "Though you can't really blame her, considering who her older brother is."

Before Meryl could further voice her growing indignation, Garren's bulk approached them from behind. "If you're all about finished running your yaps, there's a tent full of people waiting to eat. Listen to your husband and get seated, Mer, so we can get on with it." He stalked past, glaring at Kal as he went.

Boden and Grisham joined them a moment later, the latter relying heavily on a thick cane. "Kitty, please excuse my brother's loutish manner, something to which the rest of us are unfortunately accustomed," Grisham said. "His impatience gets the better of him when hungry."

Felíne glanced up at Kal teasingly before replying to Grisham. "Oh, not at all. Compared to this one, he's a veritable ray of sunshine."

Meryl chimed with musical laughter and clapped her hands. "I love her, Kal. Please keep her."

"He is not wrong, Meryl," Grisham counseled. "It is inconsiderate to keep your guests waiting much longer. And let us not suffer any delusions. They are your guests. Besides, I am sure we are all hungry."

Meryl sobered and collected her eldest brother's arm. "Yes, Grisham. Of course," she said and walked with him toward the throng of people waiting. "Don't go anywhere, Kitty," she called over a shoulder. "I still want all the details."

Kal dipped his head once again as they fell behind their departing group. "If Garren's a ray of sunshine, what does that make me exactly?"

Felíne braced herself as a little thrill worked its way down her spine. She got a rise out of teasing him, though she knew she probably shouldn't. She looked up into his black gaze, a glint of gold flashing in the growing dark. "A solar eclipse," she said before thinking through her response. Something shifted behind Kal's eyes as they locked onto hers. Something powerful and predatory and entirely too focused on her. Before she got sucked into his vortex, Felíne tore her ogling away and took a forced step toward the feasting tent. Then another. Trying desperately to ignore the attention of the man she could feel shadowing her every move and attempting to prevent herself from enjoying it.

Thankfully, the feasting tent offered enough distraction to pull Kal's attention elsewhere, and Felíne was spared from having to suffer Meryl's promised inquisition. She and her husband, Bo, were seated apart from the remaining guests at a private table. After tucking into their meal, food was served to the crowd, and the tables were laden with savory delights. Kal had chosen a seat near the edge of the gathering, closer to the exit, and Felíne knew it wasn't unintentional. If they needed to make a hasty retreat, they were positioned to do so. The man did nothing without purpose.

Halfway through their meal, a band started to play, upbeat music filling the venue and drowning out the drone of a hundred conversations. Felíne watched the people laugh, talk, eat, and mingle. It was fascinating. Closer to Meryl's table, she spotted Grisham sitting with an older woman she recognized as Lele, the innkeeper. Garren sat with his back to a wall, arms crossed, surveying the crowd. Apparently, Kal wasn't the only one primed for action at all times. Other than those few, Felíne didn't recognize another face.

"Were Adder and Ophelia not invited?"

Kal took a sip of spiced cider and set down his glass. "Adder is on perimeter guard tonight," he said. "Ophelia may or may not make an appearance depending on her whims. She tends to do as she pleases, though I don't believe she received a formal invitation. Oph isn't the social sort."

That wasn't exactly surprising. "Earlier in Grisham's tent, you and Adder didn't greet one another. Does the Trade Master not know of your friendship?"

"Grisham knows that we know one another, but no. He doesn't know the depth of it." Kal regarded her. "An ambiguity we'd like to maintain. And I don't believe he knows Ophelia beyond just another female he'd once granted a token."

Felíne nodded. She had no desire to betray the information. "I assume the three of you have been friends longer than you've known the Trade Master."

Kal accepted a refill of his cider and waited until the server moved away before replying. "I have known both of them since I was a boy. I only found Cindamar five or so years ago."

So, she was right. Whatever past Kal had walked away from, these two friends of his had likely either witnessed that transformation or were privy to it. Felíne wanted to know more about the dark male sitting next to her, sipping cider. However, this was not the place for weighty revelations, nor was she necessarily the female to which he would impart them. Instead, Felíne went for something lighter. "And that would make you...how old?"

Kal sat back and crossed his arms, quirking a small smile and taking the bait. "Guess."

Felíne made a show of assessing him. "Let's see. No gray yet. Not even in the beard." One of Kal's broad hands ran over his stubble. Felíne closed her own around her drink to keep from involuntarily reaching toward him, smothering the desire to run her hand along his jawline. "Dark circles under the eyes," she continued. "Though that could be related to stress rather than age—"

"Definitely stress."

"—Or even lack of sleep." Her gaze traveled down the column of his neck to his shoulder and the curve of his biceps that was visible under his shirt sleeve. "Good muscle tone. Firm skin. Abundant stamina."

Kal's brow quirked at that one, and his eyes hyper-focused once again. She ignored him, her expression turning impassive. "Which I only know because of the past three wretched days of travel together."

"Ah."

"I guess no older than forty," she said, disregarding that single loaded word. "Hot or cold?"

He leaned toward her. "Lukewarm."

"Forty-two?"

"Cold."

"Thirty-two."

He smiled, dimple reappearing. Curse that dimple. "Much warmer."

"Thirty?"

Kal took another sip of his drink, somehow making the simple motion look seductive. He nodded, still watching her.

Thirty years old. Just over five years her senior. Younger than she'd thought. He seemed much older than thirty.

"My turn," Kal said.

Felíne's eyes widened. *Crap.* "You want to know how old I am?"

He shook his head. "I already know that."

She puzzled a moment before understanding. Of course. "Rask." And just like that, they'd stepped into dangerous territory. Kal undoubtedly knew things about his friend's only sibling, but what exactly those things were, Felíne had no idea. It was nearly impossible for her to anticipate which questions were safe and which would give her away.

Kal made a noise of agreement. "Twenty-five. You're a baby, yet. Though, I would have guessed older had I not known. You carry yourself more maturely than I expected."

Felíne paled slightly, momentarily distracted. Gods. Railah was only twenty-five years of age and called into service as a Fated Mother? Barely older than Felíne herself. It seemed so terribly young. Wrong. And all in the name of her own potential peril? It was unfair, and…No, she couldn't go there right now. Felíne pulled herself back from that path of thought. "Alright," she said, collecting her wits. "If not my ripe old age, what would you like to know?"

Kal watched her, clearly trying to identify what unknown aspect of her he found most interesting. Felíne tried very hard not to fidget. Just then, a young woman approached the table and offered them dessert. Kal looked over the paper menu she provided before passing it to Felíne. Her stomach was too knotted to entertain the idea of sweets. She also politely declined, and the waitress bowed before moving on to another table.

At the head table, Meryl's telltale laugh sounded and cut through the noises of the crowd, drawing attention. Felíne turned and saw a smiling Boden attempt to wipe pieces of some frothy, ivory-colored dessert from his chin while Meryl, still laughing, leaned in to kiss the sweet cream off his face. Her husband picked up his utensil, laden with confection, and extended it to his golden bride. Meryl squealed, leaning out of the way to avoid being similarly smeared with sugar.

Felíne's lips quirked in a smile that slipped as soon as she leaned back and glimpsed Kal's expression. He watched Meryl and her husband, but his features didn't reflect happiness. They were almost…pained.

"You're sure seeing her married to someone else doesn't bother you?"

Kal's attention cut to her, his expression smoothing. "Why would that bother me?"

Felíne's smile was a little sad. "Because you were just looking at her like you wished it was you sitting next to her at that table."

"No," he said earnestly. "I am happy for her. Meryl may have wanted more from me at one point, but that was never something I was going to be able to provide. She is with someone who can truly make her happy. She deserves that."

Ah, so there was potential for a relationship between them. Yet, Kal walked away from it? "So that's why Garren hates you."

Kal nodded. "Garren is very protective of Meryl. He doesn't exactly show it, but she is the weak point in his armor. She loves him dearly. Garren and I were actually friendly when I first began visiting Cindamar." Felíne's eyebrows rose in surprise, and Kal laughed. "I know. Shocking."

"So, what happened? Tell me you didn't break his sister's heart."

Kal shrugged. "I don't know if I'd state it so dramatically, but something along those lines. Meryl and I were friends. She frequently tagged along when Garren and I made business runs for Grisham. We spent quite a bit of time together. After a while, she made her intentions toward me clear. I was the only one surprised by her confession. I think Garren assumed I would be pulled into the family, become everything his little sister wanted in a mate, and work alongside him to help the Trade Master further Cindamar's enterprises."

"But you didn't."

Kal's onyx eyes fixed on hers. "No. That was never something I could have committed to." He sighed. "It became clear that I needed to distance myself. My proximity and the time I'd been spending were giving others expectations of me that I never intended. I began pulling back from my involvement, spending more and more time away from the city. Garren tracked me down at one point and demanded an explanation. I told him I wasn't interested in a relationship with his sister, something I thought I'd made clear to her early on. Meryl had unknowingly followed him and heard the entire conversation."

Oh dear.

"Things were said. Feelings got hurt." Kal's shoulders lifted in another shrug. "Meryl made things difficult for her brothers for some time after that. She is…intense."

"I hadn't noticed," Felíne said, and Kal smirked knowingly.

"She eventually forgave me and moved on from her interest. Her brother, however, did not. Garren holds a grudge. To him, I will always be the man who slighted his little sister."

Felíne pondered. "More than that," she said. Garren might love his younger sister, but he was also intensely devoted to Grisham. "To him, you'll always be the man who didn't want to be his brother. He took it personally."

Kal's brows rose in surprise. "I think you're right."

"Yet, despite all that, you still work with Grisham?"

Kal nodded, clearly intrigued by her deduction. "A tie Garren attempted multiple times to sever. Grisham, however, is not so emotional a creature as his siblings. I was far too valuable a business connection for him to let go over a simple misunderstanding."

"Too good a thief?"

Kal laughed. "I told you I don't make a habit of stealing. People or otherwise. You happened to be an exception."

Felíne tilted her head, thinking. "Then what is it you do for the Trade Master that is so valuable?"

Kal's smile was predatory, and he leaned in, his voice dropping. "Nice try."

Okay, so that topic was off limits. For now, at least. That was fine. Kal was in a sharing mood, and she'd take advantage of whatever information he was willing to provide. "If not for lingering feelings," she said. "Then why the pained expression earlier when you watched Meryl and Bo?"

Kal straightened, gaze shuttering slightly, and Felíne wondered if that, too, might be a conversational path he was unwilling to travel with her. Then he spoke, surprising her. "They reminded me of my parents," he said. "My father always begged my mother for a specific dessert. A sort of raisin cream stuffed pastry. She made it infrequently because it was so time consuming. I was thinking of the last time we had it. My mother acted like she was going to feed him a spoonful and instead smeared it all over his face." Kal's smile was soft and nostalgic. "He chased her around the kitchen with thick, sweet cream dripping off his nose."

Another piece of the puzzle that was Kalevar Kaine fit into place. "You lost them." In that moment, she knew it with certainty. He had loved them fiercely, and they were gone.

Kal's expression iced over so suddenly Felíne thought maybe she'd imagined any previous tenderness. "No," he clarified. "They were taken from me."

Felíne didn't shy from his hostility. She wanted to know more. Wanted to understand who would have done such a thing. And why. Surprisingly, she felt anger bubble up inside her on Kal's behalf. How dare anyone orphan the boy he once was. How dare they steal his family from him. Take that future from the man he would become. Felíne opened her mouth to ask when a shurii male dressed impressively well stood on a platform and addressed the crowd.

"Boden and Meryl hope everyone has had adequate time to sate their appetites. We will now move outside into the plaza for the gift-giving, which shall be followed by dancing and libations."

Kal stood, ending the possibility for her to voice her curiosities. The time for sharing was over. He extended a hand to her, which she took. "Come on," he said, seemingly relieved for the interruption. "I need a drink."

Chapter 38

Gifts and Blessings

FELÍNE LET KAL LEAD HER out of the feast tent into the outdoor venue with the other wedding attendees. It was full dark, but the night was alive with flickering lanterns and scattered bonfires that cast their amber glow on the scene. The stars twinkled happily above, not a cloud marring their shine. The band had moved to a corner space that had been cleared for the dancing, and a great many additional small tables had been erected around it for people to sit, watch, and refresh themselves. A number of drink carts scattered the periphery of the gathering and were already being frequented by guests asking for ale, wine, and liquor, all of which seemed to be provided free of charge. Grisham had spared no expense for his little sister's celebratory evening.

Meryl and her husband were once again seated apart from their guests. The same shurii who had announced the start of the outdoor activities addressed the crowd and informed them that the gift-giving would commence forthwith.

Felíne waited next to Kal as one of the drink cart staff poured a generous portion of bourbon into a shallow glass. Kal turned and asked if she wanted anything from the cart. She opted for a sweet wine. With drinks in hand, Kal led them to a table of his choosing. This one was slightly closer to Meryl and Boden's table but far from the center of the group.

A line of shurii bearing an assortment of items had formed before the bride and groom, which conveniently passed Grisham's chosen seat. Felíne noticed nearly everyone waiting to present their gifts to the happy couple cast what they hoped to be inconspicuous glances in the Trade Master's direction. If it was obvious to her at this distance, Grisham must have noticed, too.

She snorted, drawing Kal's curious attention. She nodded in the direction of the line. "All these people are waiting to give their gifts to Meryl and Bo. But they're not really for them at all, are they? What these shurii really want is Grisham's approval."

Kal seemed once again pleasantly surprised by her assessment. "They're not nearly as clever as they think they are," he agreed. "Grisham is the most powerful person in this city. Whoever holds his favor attains a certain status in the trade ring. They all want to outdo one another with the lavishness of their gifts in the hopes that the Trade Master will take notice and find one of them a desirable business associate."

"They aren't Meryl's guests, after all," she mused. "They might be here to celebrate the bride, but what they seek is Grisham's attention."

"Many, yes," Kal replied. "Though Meryl certainly doesn't mind."

It was true, she saw. Meryl preened as each gift was presented. She accepted each treasure with genuine gratitude, passing them tenderly to her husband for appreciation and then setting each aside into a growing pile of ridiculous riches.

When one shurii hauled up a golden miniature in Meryl's likeness, Felíne laughed out loud, unable to stop herself. She was immediately grateful they were seated far enough away to avoid being heard. She found the flamboyance hilarious. "Do you suppose they'll set that one up in their bed chamber?" she asked Kal, unable to keep from giggling.

He chuckled and leaned closer to her ear. "No, Bo will keep it in his private bath for the nights when he's done something to earn Meryl's displeasure."

She looked at him, confused, and then blushed full crimson when he made to explain the joke, which made Kal laugh even harder.

They watched as a few more gifts were delivered, and Felíne sipped her sweet wine, which tasted like sugar and tart berry. Kal drank his bourbon sparingly, seeming reluctant to finish the liquid. Felíne's glass, on the other hand, was nearly gone. She felt warm and bubbly.

"Is it no good?" she asked him.

Kal arched a brow and offered his drink for her to taste. She sniffed it and wrinkled her nose. Somehow, the scent of the bourbon directly from the glass was much harsher than it smelled when combined with Kal's scent after he drank it. He watched her intently as she lifted the squat glass to her lips and sipped. The liquor was peppery on her tongue and burned a line of fire down to her chest as she swallowed. She coughed and made a face, which made Kal laugh again and pat her back.

"Forget I asked," she wheezed. "It's awful."

"It's not from one of Adder's casks," he said. "But it's not the worst I've had."

"It's all yours," she said, handing the glass back to him. "I'll stick to the wine. Besides, it smells better on your breath."

"Oh?" Kal rested his elbows on the table and smirked at her. "Kitty, have you been smelling my breath?"

She took another sip of wine, only to find her glass was empty. "No."

"What does my breath smell like?"

Felíne couldn't look at him. *Like warm honey and amber spice and Kal.* "Like a dragon's lair."

Kal's laugh was deep and throaty. "Dragons aren't real."

She shrugged. "If they were, they'd smell like your breath. Hot and foul."

He smiled widely, showing straight white teeth, both dimples on display. Her own breath left her lungs. She needed more wine. Immediately.

"I think you like my breath, Kitty. I think you like the way I smell."

"I think you've had too much whiskey. It's scrambled your wits."

Kal leaned closer. Too close. "On the contrary. I have all of my wits thoroughly unscrambled and not nearly enough whiskey."

Felíne felt somewhat emboldened, though she wasn't sure why. Possibly the wine. She leaned in until she was inches from Kal and could feel the gentle warmth of his breath, which smelled *nothing* like a dragon's lair. Definitely the wine. "In that case," she said, "perhaps you should finish your drink and get us both a refill."

Kal's eyes didn't leave hers as he tossed back the contents of his glass, draining the remainder in one smooth swallow. He collected both empty cups and stood to fulfill her request. As soon as he left the table, Felíne took a deep breath, already missing the scent of his, and wondered if tonight spelled more trouble for her than she could have imagined.

Felíne watched the continued presentation of gifts while waiting for Kal to return with their drinks. She'd convinced herself by the time he'd returned that the wine was poisoned and was directly responsible for her lapse in mental acuity and self-control.

"Kal," she asked when he returned and placed the bubbling rose-colored liquid in front of her. "Did you know we were expected to bring a gift?" Saying *we* out loud made it sound like they were together. Kal had told Grisham that they were a package deal, and everyone else seemed to assume they were a couple, but Felíne needed to make sure her brain understood and remembered the reality of their situation. Of *her* situation.

"It's not an expectation," he replied. "We'd be here until morning if every guest felt obligated to present something. Over half the people waiting are there to get Grisham's attention, remember?"

That's right. But still, they spent a good portion of the day in the trade center. She could have found *something* for the newlyweds.

"If it makes you feel better, I do have a gift for her."

Oh? Felíne watched as Kal gently pulled the decorative dagger from his waist. Of course. She should have known that he wouldn't choose to wear something so formal, even to a formal event. Felíne was learning more and more that Kal was a man of functionality, not flash. The dagger was far too ostentatious for his taste. Kal removed the dagger from its sheath, and Felíne was surprised to find that the blade was a dark silver color woven through with intricate black veins, a stark contrast to the ivory and turquoise handle. She was no weapons expert, but it looked extremely unique. She'd never seen a blade like that. Kal resheathed the weapon, and something about the care with which he handled it made her feel like it was exceptionally special.

If that was for Meryl, what had Kal brought for her husband? She asked.

"You remember when Grisham said that the guests were Meryl's?"

Felíne nodded. She'd said as much earlier. Even Bo said that the guests were his wife's. It was Meryl who corrected him by saying, 'Our guests.'

"When gifts are presented at a wedding celebration, people don't typically gift both the bride and groom unless they happen to know both equally. You gift the person that extended the invite."

Felíne eyed the still-staggering line of people waiting to give gifts. "You mean to tell me all of those people were invited personally by Meryl?"

Kal smirked. "Or by her eldest brother on her behalf."

Felíne thought she might prefer a smaller gathering of close friends and family instead of an overwhelming cascade of strangers. She imagined all of her father's men, the entirety of the Asterosian army, attending her presentation to the Primordial Male. It was enough to send her into palpitations.

"And Meryl asked that of him?"

"No," Kal said. "But the Trade Master is cunning. Boden has no family. He brings no wealth to their union, only a fair reputation from his late father. By extending these invitations, Grisham has single-handedly ensured that his sister will need for nothing entering into her marriage. And he's done it without insulting her new husband by offering his own riches to support her."

Clever indeed. Felíne watched another shurii male hoist a priceless hand-woven rug before the couple. Meryl reached out to inspect the quality and beamed at the extravagance. Grisham sat just to Meryl's left side, far enough from the dais to not claim the spotlight, yet close enough to have a first-hand view of each item presented. It was a resounding victory for him from a business standpoint. Grisham kept his sister's reputation—and, by extension, her husband's reputation—intact while simultaneously making them fabulously wealthy and having a front-row seat to all the affluent merchants in the land.

"I should have brought something to give," she mused.

"No," Kal said, drawing her gaze. "You aren't their guest; you're mine."

Oh. All the bubbles from her earlier consumed wine decided to float to the surface of her stomach. *You're mine.* She cleared her throat. "You may as well go present your gift," she said. *Yes. Please go. Stand far away.* She once again needed time to collect her scattered senses.

"I planned to go later, after the line dispersed."

"I think now is fine," she insisted. "The line isn't that long anymore." She looked at the line. It was forever long.

Kal studied her, and Felíne sincerely hoped he didn't sense her discomposure. Whatever he *did* sense made him unusually agreeable. "You'll be alright while I wait?" He said the last word like it tasted foul on his tongue.

"Absolutely," she said, relieved. "I'll stay right here."

Kal hesitated a moment before he stood and wove his way through the throng of people, not disappearing from view entirely but settling far enough away that Felíne once again had breathing room. She sank back into her seat a little and watched the nearest lantern reflect its gentle light on the surface of her wine.

"Come on, Felíne," she muttered under her breath. "Get it together."

She needed to stop becoming so flustered by everything that was Kal and start focusing on how in the world she was going to get herself out of the mess she was in. Seeking help from anyone in Cindamar was out of the question. Kal had spent an untold amount of time in the city, working directly with Grisham's family. If Kal himself didn't maintain connections with a vast number of people here, which she strongly suspected he did, then Grisham did without question. No, she'd find no allies here. Not in this lawless city where the Crown of Asteros was seen as a threat instead of a haven.

Unfortunately, she was starting to gain an understanding of why people felt that way, and it turned everything she knew right on its head. The capital wasn't perfect. The way things were run needed serious reevaluation. Whether or not her parents were privy to the extent of the abuse her people suffered was yet to be seen. She hoped they weren't. Either way, her people needed a light. Those Fated Mothers needed an advocate. She could be that for them. She would be.

Felíne reached forward to collect her drink when something collided with her from behind. She barely managed to save the majority of the wine from splashing everywhere.

"Oh, my goodness!" said a distressed feminine voice behind her. "I'm so sorry. Are you alright?"

Felíne turned to see a young woman with wide midnight-blue eyes and raven hair woven into a lovely intricate braid that covered the entire left side of her head. The shiny strands extended through their pattern, over her ear, and flowed down to drape across her shoulder. The stranger was dressed in an unremarkable navy blue gown with billowing sleeves capped securely at each wrist, a slack bodice that hid her figure, and a full skirt that fell to the floor. Her expression was so concerned that Felíne smiled reassuringly on impulse.

"I'm fine," she assured.

"Please," the female said. "I'm so terribly clumsy sometimes. Let me get you another drink."

Felíne waved her off. "No, honestly, there's no need. I spilled very little."

The female eyed the table and stopped a passing staff member to ask for a cloth. One was presented to her immediately, and she reached over to clear the few splashes of wine on the table. "A little is still some," she argued, holding the soiled cloth. "And it was my fault. The least I could do is make it right."

Felíne smiled in thanks, but the female didn't leave. In fact, she looked somewhat out of place, standing awkwardly looking into the crowd.

The band played in the far corner. An upbeat song floated on the air, and a handful of shurii couples moved into the space cleared for dancing.

"Are you looking for someone?" Felíne asked, noticing the female's searching gaze. She was moderately pretty, with large eyes, a long pointed nose, and sharp features. The woman worried her full bottom lip.

"Sorry," she apologized again. "I seem to have lost my friend. She left to collect drinks some time ago and must have gotten distracted. I tend to get a little anxious in crowds by myself."

"Would you like to sit?" Felíne offered a chair. "My…companion is waiting to present a gift to the bride. Once he's finished, I'm sure he can help find your friend. I would offer, but I'm afraid I wouldn't be much assistance. I don't know anyone here."

The female looked positively relieved. She sat with a whoosh of her skirts. "Thank goodness," she breathed. "I don't know anyone either. Thank you."

"Not at all," Felíne said. "My name is Kitty."

The stranger tilted her head in a way that reminded Felíne of some kind of bird. "So nice to meet you, Kitty," she said. "I am Eveant Moor. Please call me Evie."

"The pleasure is mine," Felíne said. "Are you here for Meryl or Boden?"

"Neither, actually," Evie said somewhat shyly. "My friend, Tula, is a distant cousin of the groom's, but I was coerced into attending when her most recent relationship ended unexpectedly. I suspect she became distracted looking for companionship when she left to collect drinks."

"Oh, dear." Felíne smiled apologetically, and Evie huffed a quiet laugh.

"I know. Not unexpected, I'm afraid," she said. "It would not be the first time she's forgotten me in her romantic pursuits. I can only hope she doesn't travel all the way back to the capital without me."

Felíne started and lowered her voice. "You are from Asteros?"

Evie nodded amiably. "Have you been?"

"I…" She hesitated, unsure how much to share. Then, she mentally pinched herself. Could she be so fortunate? Hadn't she been trying unsuccessfully to figure out how to get home for the past several days now? And without her even having to lift a finger, a stranger happened upon her who could potentially provide her with exactly that. The Goddess was gifting her an opportunity. She would be an absolute fool not to accept it. She glanced toward the line where she could just make out Kal standing proud and strong among the other gift-givers.

Look away. Focus on your future.

Felíne returned her attention to her new, entirely incognizant blessing. "Yes," she said, forcing the conviction. "In fact, I am expected back."

Evie's eyes twinkled. "That's grand," she said, placing a hand atop Felíne's. "Tula and I plan to return first thing in the morning. You and your…companion would be welcome to travel with us."

Felíne fought the desire to look back over her shoulder.

To Kal.

You're mine.

But she wasn't, was she?

"Just me," she said firmly. "It would just be me joining you."

Chapter 39

Whiskey Dance

EVIE ACCEPTED FELÍNE'S RESPONSE WITH evident enthusiasm. "That's fantastic," she exclaimed. "Now, just to find Tula and let her know the change in plans. Do you need to make arrangements?"

Felíne glanced back. Kal had moved closer to the podium, where Meryl seemed to possess endless patience and zeal for her seemingly infinite line of guests. He glanced in her direction, and she guiltily turned away from him to face Evie. "I know this is an odd request," she began. "But do you mind keeping this travel arrangement between us?"

Evie's brow furrowed. "Is everything alright?"

"Yes, yes," Felíne assured her. "I just…" She searched her witless brain for an acceptable excuse. "I'd rather slip away from my companion quietly than make a show of it. He knows a great number of people in Cindamar. If it became common knowledge that I planned to leave with you, it would undoubtedly get back to him, and he'd feel…" Confused. Angered. *Betrayed.* "Slighted."

"Oh," Evie breathed, midnight eyes turning knowing. "Of course. I won't breathe a word."

Felíne sighed, simultaneously relieved and appalled at telling yet another lie. Deceiving another innocent person. She hated this. Hated lying. Hated sneaking about. Hated the oily feeling of guilt and shame that accompanied both. At the rate she was going, no one would be able to trust another word she spoke ever again.

"Tula has to be around somewhere," Evie said, craning to see through the crowds. "And don't worry. Despite her typically poor choice in bedmates, she is a vault. She won't betray your plans." She turned in the other direction, still looking. "My bet is the lonely drink cart across the way. Why don't you join me? Just there."

Evie indicated a shadowed section on the periphery of the venue. A lone firepit cast flickering light on a single drink cart where only a few stragglers had wandered over, unwilling to wait at the busier, closer carts. Those that did loiter near the farther flame seemed to be entirely engrossed in their partners. It seemed a perfect place for two shurii to find uninterrupted time alone, away from the main body of the crowd. Evie rose as Felíne deliberated.

"Which plans are we not betraying?" asked an unexpected third voice.

Felíne jumped. Evie's eyes flashed. Ophelia materialized seemingly out of thin air and settled herself at the table. She looked dressed for battle rather than a wedding, wearing her customary leather armor and boots. The female was also likely fully armed despite the lack of visible weaponry.

"Gods, Ophelia," Felíne said, clutching her chest. "You scared me halfway to death."

Ophelia quirked a brow. "Only halfway?"

Felíne stopped herself from voicing a choice retort. She turned back to Evie, who stood stiffly near her recently occupied chair. The female scrutinized Ophelia with what looked like cold suspicion. Or maybe irritation? "Evie, this is Ophelia. Please excuse her abrupt arrival."

Evie seemed to shake herself, countenance slipping into one of awkward surprise.

"Sorry," she said with a shaky laugh. "I get a little out of sorts when I'm spooked. Nice to meet you, Ophelia."

Ophelia ignored her. "Which plans?" she repeated, addressing Felíne. The female's tone was mildly curious, but her expression demanded an answer.

How much had Kal's friend overheard? Felíne's stomach flipped. Oh gods, what if she'd heard the whole conversation? She fumbled for a response. Ophelia's eyes narrowed, assessing.

"Plans to get another refill," Evie filled in helpfully. "And to convince that dashing creature she arrived with to take her around the dance floor."

Felíne gaped at her new acquaintance. Ophelia eyed her dubiously.

"Sorry," Evie apologized to Felíne. "Should I not have said anything? I assumed she was a friend."

"I…no, it's fine," Felíne sputtered.

"Speaking of dashing creatures," Evie said, glancing behind Felíne. "I think I'll leave you to look for my friend on my own. Enjoy your evening," she said to Ophelia. Then, to Felíne, "Let's get a drink later, Kitty?" Evie turned on her heel, narrowly avoiding colliding with another passerby, and departed to search for her missing counterpart.

A moment later, Kal arrived, looking not a little disgruntled. "That was a mistake," he declared. "I'm never bringing another gift to a wedding. To hell with tradition." Felíne saw the dagger was no longer in his possession, having been successfully passed on to its new owner. Now, all he held was a long-empty glass of what was once whiskey and his paper-thin patience. "Oph," he said after a moment as though just acknowledging her presence. "You came. You hate crowds."

"I almost didn't," she said, still eyeing Felíne. Gods, could the female find another target for her ceaseless scrutiny? "But I'm glad I did. It's been enlightening."

Kal looked between the two of them, curiosity replacing his earlier irritation. "Did I miss something?"

"No," Felíne said at the same time Ophelia said, "Yes."

Kal's brows rose.

Ophelia glanced up at her friend. "Apparently, you're a dashing creature, and Kitty here wants you to sweep her onto the dance floor."

Kal's attention swung in Felíne's direction, where she sat wholly saturated in a fresh wave of mortification. She couldn't even deny it because Evie had ingeniously saved her duplicitous hide with her quick thinking.

Felíne couldn't look at him. Couldn't face the object of her torment. Instead, she gripped her wineglass with more fervor than was strictly necessary and gulped down its meager contents. She shoved the drained glass in Ophelia's traitorous direction, still refusing to look at Kal.

"I'll take another, please," she said, and Ophelia laughed.

Beyond their table, more guests had moved onto the dance floor. The music was quick and cheery, and shurii men and women slid and flowed to the rhythm. Smiles and laughter surrounded the scene like an enticing cloud of positivity.

Felíne watched in misery.

Drinks poured.

Except into her glass. Apparently, Ophelia wasn't taking requests.

"Kitty."

Why? Why did his voice do that to her? Felíne's eyes lifted to Kal of their own accord. The firelight from one of the nearby pits cast warm light onto his hard features, projecting magnetizing shadows on his frame. He was tall, broad, and severe. She was powerless and pitiful when faced with his allure.

"Would you like to dance?"

What? Had she heard correctly?

He couldn't be sincere. And yet, there he was. Looking at her. With expectation.

The words she tried to form were 'No, thank you.' What came out of her mouth instead was, "*You* know how to *dance?*"

Ophe pushed up from the table with a smirk. "Who's being rude now?"

Kal reached over and deposited both empty glasses into Ophelia's hands. She gawped at him. "Refills are in order, Oph. Do the honors, will you?"

She laughed and pointedly dropped both glasses onto the table between them. "Piss in your cups, Kalevar Kaine. You must have lost your damn mind." The hostile little female promptly departed, leaving Felíne and Kal alone with their drinkware.

He looked after her briefly. "I take it that's a no."

Felíne momentarily forgot all about the dancing. "She is going to hate you forever," she said, still somewhat stunned by his irreverence. "Why would you do that?"

Kal flashed a dimple. "You'd be surprised what Ophelia's had to put up with between Adder and me. Don't worry too much about her. She's sour now, but she doesn't play fair, and she loves having an excuse to contemplate revenge."

Felíne thought that to be a positively terrifying concept.

"Besides," he said, "she was giving you a hard time."

She blinked. Kal was defending her against his childhood friend? Against a strange threat, sure, but his friend?

"And to answer your earlier question, yes, I can dance. Would you like to?"

Feline looked around. More and more shurii couples had made their way to the open area near the band. The music slowed into a melodic hum. Meryl and her husband, Bo, still accepted the last remaining gifts. She saw an attendant slip close to Bo and exchange a mug of what had to be some form of spirit for the empty one he held. His smile looked a bit more forced, his posture less composed than when she'd looked only thirty minutes prior. They were ready to be done so they could join their guests in celebration. Grisham had seen as much as he must have cared to. He had taken up a spot near the edge of the dancing, Garren standing stiffly next to him.

Kal extended a hand to her, waiting patiently for a reply. It would be the last night she might ever have to dance with a handsome man at a party where no one knew her name. Tomorrow, possibly sooner, if everything went as planned, Feline would be on her way home to Asteros, and all of this would be behind her.

She reached up and placed her hand in his.

No areas of the dance floor were entirely unoccupied, but Kal led her to a quieter section. Feline could see Grisham and Garren from where they were. Garren's assessing gaze found them immediately, tracking their progress. Kal knew it and pointedly ignored the other male. His attention remained focused on Feline.

"Have you been to many dances?" he asked as they found their space.

None, actually. She had instruction, she knew the steps, but she'd never been permitted any authentic practice at an actual ball. However, she wasn't sure how believable that would be, so she settled for a simple "No."

"We have that in common, then," he confessed. "It's been a very long time."

Feline eyed him. "Is that safe?"

His lips tipped up in amusement. "Moderately."

One of Kal's broad hands slipped around Feline's waist. His other gathered her hand close to his chest. Her breath hitched as he pulled her flush to his body. She could smell his intoxicating honey-spiced scent and feel the hardened contours of his chest, abdomen, and thighs. Kal lowered his face to whisper against the shell of her ear. "Relax, Kitty. You're stiff as a board."

He was right. She stood solid as a marble statue. *It's only a dance*, she told herself. But with how close he was, how good he smelled, and the way he was holding her…it felt like much more than just a dance. It felt like another step in the wrong direction. Another step away from where she was supposed to be headed and toward a place expressly forbidden to her. A place she was finding she actually might want to explore.

Curse her internal warring, her indecisiveness.

"I think maybe I should have pressed Ophelia for that wine."

Felíne gave a nervous laugh. "I don't know if one more glass would have made any difference."

Kal pulled back to look down at her. "Whiskey?"

She made a face, wrinkling her nose, and he laughed, the sound reverberating in his chest. "I'll have to get you to try a decent bourbon," he said. "The stuff at this party is mediocre at best."

"I don't think you can convince me."

His eyebrows rose over obsidian eyes that glinted with the challenge. His mouth settled closer to her ear once more, and Felíne's world tilted slightly. "Mmm," he hummed. "But a really good bourbon isn't harsh. It's warm…" She felt the heat rolling off of his body and seeping into her own.

"Silky…" The hand he held at her waist shifted, gliding toward the small of her back where a smooth section of her pantsuit disappeared under the edge of her corset.

"Complex…" Kal spun her then, and her feet followed in a flawless maneuver. Felíne hadn't even realized when they'd begun dancing. Her body no longer seemed to operate according to her brain's instructions. It simply moved when Kal moved, went where he asked, followed where he led. And goodness, he led well. She hadn't expected that level of skill from a common thief. Yet he wasn't a thief, isn't that what he'd told her? And Felíne was coming to learn that there was nothing common about Kalevar Kaine.

He spun her away only to bring her back closer than before. The rest of the party melted into inconsequence. They no longer glided over a space of packed earth but the belly of a cloud. Felíne danced among stars. Two black voids in the cosmos held her captive. Riveted.

"Rich, spicy, floral…"

The dance was ending, the song approaching its outro. Kal sent her into a final lazy twirl, then reeled her back in to settle against his chest. He wasn't even breathing hard; all his movements were so practiced.

"Sweet?" she asked, a little breathless. She wet her lips with her tongue, and Kal's gaze snagged on the movement.

He stared at her mouth. "Oh, definitely sweet."

Kal was magnetizing. He drew her in effortlessly, and somewhere in the back of Felíne's mind, she knew they were embracing. His strong arms held her, and she melted in his grasp. "I think I give up," she whispered. "You convinced me."

The music faded out. Kal's mouth was so close she could practically taste him. He would be everything he'd described. Silky. Warm. Rich. Complex.

Oh, my dear Goddess. He was going to kiss her!

Kal's head began to lower, and all of Felíne's insides knotted with raw, forbidden anticipation.

Then he stopped. Tensed.

No!

Kal's arm tightened around her waist, and he moved, tucking her close to his side. All of his attention focused with intensity somewhere over her head.

Felíne craned around to look, wondering what could possibly be so interesting to have distracted him from—

Adder strode through the crowd. Not toward the two of them but toward the place where Grisham sat at the edge of the dancers. Before he passed, he cut a set of serious silver eyes directly to Kal. Whatever it was he meant to convey, Felíne wasn't sure, but Kal seemed to understand.

She stiffened. Something had happened. Something was wrong. Kal said Adder was on perimeter guard tonight and wouldn't be attending the celebration. *He shouldn't be here.*

As he passed them across the floor, she saw him clearly, and her breath caught. The music began to play again, the band speeding up their beat. People moved around them jovially, completely oblivious to the scene unfolding just on their periphery.

Garren saw Adder's approach and stepped up to Grisham's side in a protective stance. Grisham's expression turned grim, and he held out a hand, stopping Garren from causing a scene. Adder finally reached the pair and dipped his head to speak into the Trade Master's ear. The ferocity that transformed Grisham's features made Felíne understand the level of respect the man commanded. Even with his disability, he was not a male that you wanted as an enemy.

Grisham conveyed some set of orders, and Garren immediately left. The Trade Master leveled a hard gaze in Kal's direction.

At the same time, Adder straightened, tucking his hands behind his back.

But not before Felíne saw the blood that stained them.

Chapter 40

Report

KAL CAUGHT ADDER'S SCENT BEFORE he saw him.

Then he caught the scent of blood.

Thankfully, if any of the other guests noticed that unmistakable metallic tang on the air, the freely flowing drink combined with the mixing of phero-mones and the smoke from a dozen bonfires did a thorough job of conceal-ing it. The hundreds of shurii who had arrived to celebrate weren't looking for one singular reason to worry—they were looking for a hundred reasons not to.

Kal, on the other hand, was always primed for a dilemma. And fuck if it didn't just ruin his night.

One look from his friend confirmed it.

"Kal. There is blood on Adder's hands."

He glanced down at the female tucked protectively against his side. Kitty Harless was surprising him lately with her attention to detail. Her green-gold eyes were no longer filled with yearning. They were brimming with concern. She may not have known what was happening, but she was no foolish twenty-five-year-old. She knew something was awry.

Maybe he should be thankful for the distraction. Two minutes ago, he was fully intent on claiming those sweet lips of hers in front of everyone, and he hadn't given even the whisper of a damn if she was Rask's little sister or not.

He wanted her. All of her. And badly.

It was a complication he didn't need, the fact of which he was growing increasingly less inclined to consider.

"Come on," Kal said, shoving his yearning behind an iron wall of obligation.

"What's happened?"

Kal maneuvered them quickly to the edge of the dance floor. Right on cue, Ophelia emerged like an apparition. The woman missed nothing.

He stepped back from Kitty and instantly missed the way her soft figure fit against his. "Oph, don't let her out of your sight."

Kitty's concern cranked up a notch as she realized he was leaving her in Ophelia's care. "Kal," she said more insistently. "What is going on?"

He leveled a hard stare at Ophelia. "Not for an instant."

Kal didn't have to say it. She knew. She'd defend Rask's little sister with her life if he asked it of her, though he didn't expect it to come to that. Ophe nodded. "Figure it out," she said. "Don't do anything stupid."

He quirked a humorless smile. Famous last words.

Kal looked at Kitty. "I don't know," he said in answer to her question. "But I'm going to find out. I'll be back."

She wasn't satisfied with his answer. He could see the demand to join him in her expression, regardless of the potential danger involved, and a piece of him commended her for her courage even if she didn't realize that was what it was. But instead of inviting her along and keeping her close like he wanted, he turned his back on her. She'd be safer among the crowd under Ophelia's guard than walking into the lion's den for information. He left them to catch up with Adder and Grisham.

"Kal!"

He ignored Kitty's cry and followed the earlier scent of blood through the crowd. It wasn't Adder's, that much he knew. The thought gave him a small measure of reassurance. *This could turn out to be nothing*, he reasoned. But if Kal knew Adder, the look he'd pegged him with said otherwise. He picked up his pace.

Kal found Adder and Grisham beyond the celebration venue, already halfway to the trade center. Grisham was mounted, strapped into a custom saddle atop his favorite bay mare, and Adder had shifted back to second form. He was strapping his armor back into place as he prowled alongside the horse.

414

Kal fell into stride with them. Two other armored shurii materialized from the darkness and flanked their trio. Grisham had triggered the silent alarm. His guard was on high alert. Any reassuring thoughts that this might turn out to be no serious incident vanished with the realization. Whatever it was, it wasn't good.

"Who?" Kal kept his voice low in case unseen others were within ear-shot.

Adder's response was clipped. "Bodemere."

"Fuck."

The five of them arrived at Grisham's business tent, where they'd all been earlier that day. Two additional guards at the front stepped up immediately to help the Trade Master dismount. Garren pushed through the front panel and gave orders to the existing guards. "No one in. Question anyone coming out. Keep your fucking lids peeled. I don't care if it's your sweet old granny; no one gets close to this tent."

"Sir."

Everyone was in second form, save Grisham and himself. Also, not good. Grisham avoided shifting in all but the direst of circumstances on account of his condition; the transformation tended to go badly with the advanced deconditioned state of his legs. But the rest of them had gone full shurii. They wanted all senses fully functional, reactivity primed.

Kal followed Garren, Grisham, and Adder into the receiving chamber. The lights were low where they flickered in their glass lanterns save for the heart of the space where additional light had been gathered to illuminate the area.

What a fucking mess.

Bodemere, or rather, what was left of him, was laid out on a long table in the center of the room. Grisham's mender was surveying the wreckage that was the male's body with solemn, professional detachment.

The Trade Master rounded on Adder, his fine face lit with controlled fury. "Report."

Instead of answering, Adder turned his attention to another male. He was younger, fawn in color with a long muzzle, standing mostly in shadow. The male stepped forward into the light, trying and failing to avoid looking at Bodemere's ruin. Kal didn't recognize him. He must be a newer addition to Grisham's reserve.

Grisham sat in silence, eyeing the youngster. The male looked between the guards in attendance and then back at the table. He swallowed, clearly rattled.

"Speak!" Garren barked, stalking behind him. The male balked.

"Harris," Grisham said, voice calm but firm. The male, Harris, turned pleading eyes on the Trade Master. "*Report.*"

"Sir," he managed. "I was stationed in the west quadrant. Bodemere was north. Adder was holding position to the south—"

"We know the fucking rotation, you watery shit," Garren growled. "What. Fucking. *Happened?*"

"Right. S-sorry." A tremble jarred the young male's limbs.

Gods, this was painful to watch.

"We knew the party was going on, Bodemere and me." Harris glanced to the table again, and misery welled. "H-he was sour at having shift tonight. He said something about missing out on meeting up with a sweet piece. I...I convinced one of the staff to sneak us a bottle...we planned to share—"

"Name," Grisham demanded.

"Name..."

"The staff who delivered the bottle."

"Oh...uh, Lex, sir."

Grisham cut eyes to one of the guards who had joined them on their way to the trade center. The male left the room. Grisham nodded to Harris to continue.

Fine tremors wracked the male's frame. His fur dampened, and the tang of sweat mingled with the stench of blood, body fluid, and excrement that leaked from the table.

"Bodemere was supposed to meet me at the northwest intersection. We were going to share the bottle, then go back to patrol. But he wasn't there. I waited thirty minutes, then went to look for him. I...I didn't find him, so I stashed the bottle and went back through my quadrant perimeter, looped south, and found Santaire. He called in a shift replacement and went to look for Bodemere. He...he found him."

Kal glanced at Adder. He'd found Bodemere alright. In fucking pieces.

"He was buried, boss," Adder said. "Shredded. I found his head and torso in one location, lower half fifty meters farther into the desert. Whatever killed him caught him unawares and quite literally ripped him limb from limb."

Garren's arms were crossed over his broad armored chest, biceps bulging under his brown pelt. He was eyeing Harris like a jaybird eyed a fat wriggling worm. "Wonder if he was caught off guard because he was too preoccupied with scoring some tail. Or getting liquored up with his delinquent chum stationed in the west quad instead of doing his *fucking job*." Harris flinched.

Kal stepped forward. "At this point, it doesn't fucking matter why he was caught off guard. We need to know what the fuck caught him."

Garren turned his brimming hostility on Kal. "Yeah? What a genius concept. From the hairless wonder."

"*Enough*." Grisham's infinite patience was wearing thin. "We need information. Evidence."

"Well, I think it's pretty obvious it was no animal, mates."

"No," the Trade Master agreed with Adder. "It was no animal. This was shurii. And that presents a problem, gentlemen."

All eyes settled on Grisham.

"We have an imposter. There is at least one shurii inside Cindamar without a token, and they've killed one of our own. Finding them is priority number one."

Garren straightened to his full height, a growl rumbling through his deep chest like a challenge issued to his as-yet-unknown enemy. Kal knew that Garren could hold his own in a fight. He was battle-tested to some extent and made a formidable foe. The posturing, though, was unnecessary. A peacock puffing up his feathers, but no one here was impressed with the display. Or intimidated, for that matter. Except maybe the poor kid, Harris, who was intimidated by his own pitiful shadow at this point.

"Call your reserves, Grish," Garren petitioned. "Send us out. We'll turn the fucking city upside down. That fucking worm will be found within the hour."

Kal spoke from his position on the edge of the group where he leaned against a support beam, arms crossed. "There is a celebration yet underway,

Trade Master. Half the city is either drunk or well on their way, and right now they're all happily so. A search the likes of which Garren is suggesting will create a panic. Instead of one person in the city outside your control, you'll instantly have several hundred. This killer will capitalize on that chaos."

"How the fuck would you know?" Garren challenged.

"Because," Kal said, eyes flashing. "That's what I would do."

Garren curled his lip. "So, you'd have us leave a murdering madman loose in Cindamar to save the civilians a bit of fucking worry?"

Kal turned his head in Garren's direction. "We aren't dealing with a madman."

"Oh, and you know that for a fact, do you?"

Gods, he could use another bourbon. Or a smoke. Fuck.

Kal suppressed a growl. "For a fact? No. But I know people, Garren. And whoever ripped Bodemere in half wasn't crazy. They chose the most advantageous quadrant to enter the city, where the storage yards sit on the edge, sparingly guarded. Bodemere was no coward. He would have put up a fight. Which means whoever killed him came prepared to face some measure of resistance." He turned to Grisham. "You unleash bloodhounds into the city baying, and they'll play right into this killer's hands. People will get hurt. Send panthers instead. Hunt quietly."

Garren faced Kal. "Who do you think you are giving suggestions?" His eyes lit with fury. "Still in your fucking trousers like some soft-bellied cur. You aren't even ready to hunt!"

Kal ignored him, waiting for Grisham to make a decision. The Trade Master's face was drawn in lines of tension as he silently contemplated their situation. Sharp blue eyes surveyed the room.

Garren stalked forward and fisted his claws in Kal's shirt. "I'm talking to you, cur."

Kal's monster thundered at the other male's advance, but outwardly, he remained calm. "Maybe you've forgotten, Garren," he warned, voice deceptively low. Inside, he was roaring. "I'm always ready to hunt. And I don't need to shift to handle my shit. So, how about you quit throwing that extra weight around and try getting yours together."

Garren snarled, muzzle inches from Kal's face.

"In case you hadn't noticed, we're in a bit of a situation here, mates. Let's compare cocks another time, yeah?"

Kal didn't even glance at Adder. He exercised every bit of self-control to keep himself in first form and avoid adding Garren's dismembered pieces to the ones on the table behind them.

Garren seemed to sense his restraint and smirked. Kal loved when people mistook control for cowardice. It made the reckoning that much more satisfying.

Adder was right, though. This was not the time for a cockfight. "Meryl is out there," Kal said after another tense moment. Garren growled again, but Kal ignored him. "And her husband and a hundred other innocent people." *And Kitty.* "So, get your fucking paws off me, and let's find this bastard. You and I can have it out later," he promised. "If you can survive the hunt."

Garren eyed Kal for another span before lifting his scarred lips in an ugly sneer. He stepped back from Kal, menace still radiating off him but tempered for the time being. Gods, Kal wanted so badly just to beat his pompous ass. But Garren's pride wasn't his priority. Finding this killer was. He had a bad feeling whoever had entered Cindamar uninvited wasn't here to loot the Trade Master's treasures. He'd bet his only token they were here for Kitty. The crown's hunters were after their missing Fate. Which meant he didn't have time to sit around entertaining overinflated egos. He needed to get back.

"Kal's right," Grisham said finally, ignoring the outrage in his brother's eyes. "We handle this quietly and cleanly. I want a name. I want a motive. I want fucking answers." He pegged several males with a hard stare. "Trackers. Get moving."

Three of their company immediately left the room.

"Grish."

"Fenn? Take Harris and sweep the perimeter, starting in the western quadrant. I want those stockyards searched. Work back to the interior and meet with Rendall outside the venue." The two males left. Grisham looked at Adder. "Notify the guard outside the city to stay on high alert. No one leaves without my say. Then meet us back at the venue. We will need additional eyes on the crowd."

Adder nodded and departed without another word.

"Grisham—"

"Those are my fucking orders, Garren!"

The younger male grudgingly backed down, offering his elder brother a stiff nod.

Grisham stood and took several laboring steps toward Kal, sheer will propelling him. "We do this your way, for Meryl's sake," he said. "But if we don't find Bodemere's killer within the hour, I'll bring the force of a mountain down around us and damn whoever's unlucky enough to get in my way."

Chapter 41

Unfinished

FELÍNE WAS ANGRY. WORRIED, TOO. But mostly angry.

How dare Kal leave her behind with Ophelia! As though she were a helpless child who required supervision by a capable adult. *She* was an adult. And capable. She certainly didn't need Ophelia over-analyzing everything she did. Every shift of her seat, every glance, every huff of frustration. The serious female didn't say anything. Didn't try to make conversation or engage or get to know Felíne. Didn't show any actual interest at all. She offered no opinions. No explanations. She just watched. *Everything.*

But it wasn't just Ophelia's overattentive severity that had Felíne on edge. Adder had blood on his hands. Literal blood. The male had looked unharmed as far as she could reasonably tell, but that didn't mean much. Even if it wasn't his, the blood belonged to someone that might need her help. Yet here she was, sitting on her hands instead of putting her skills to use. So much for Kal utilizing her as a mender.

Meryl appeared behind them, interrupting Felíne's sulking. She crashed to a seat one chair over, draping an arm around Felíne's sullen shoulders. The bright-eyed bride was out of breath from dancing, face flushed a pretty shade of rose.

"Kitty!" she exclaimed. "Come and dance with us!"

Felíne pushed a tall glass of water toward Meryl. "I'm not sure I can keep up," she replied, attempting to bury her attitude. "I'm winded just watching you."

Meryl laughed and accepted the glass but didn't drink. "Nonsense," she said. "You haven't had a single dance!"

Felíne lifted a shoulder. "That's alright. I much prefer—"

"Pouting on the sideline?" Ophelia remarked. "She did have a dance. Just one."

Felíne glared at Ophelia. Oh, *now* she had something to say?

"With who?" Meryl pivoted toward Felíne, wide eyes practically ravenous for a bit of gossip.

"No one," Felíne said, trying and failing to divert the attention away from herself.

"Kal. Who else?"

Ophelia could clip her lips any time now, Felíne thought, irritated.

Meryl's aqua eyes sparkled knowingly, and she leaned closer, delighted. "And I missed it? What happened?"

"Nothing happened," Felíne insisted a bit defensively. "It was just a dance."

Just a dance. And almost something more. Not that she'd ever admit it aloud. She could barely admit it to herself.

Ophelia snorted, and Meryl honed in on the little female like a shark sensing the single drop of blood in a crystal sea.

"He was practically undressing you on the floor with his gaze. The fool has no self-control."

Felíne frowned but kept her retorts to herself. If she challenged Ophelia's claim, it would only increase her culpability. Besides, she disagreed. She thought Kal had an almost unreasonably excessive amount of self-control. And there had been moments—she was ashamed to admit—she wished he had less.

Meryl sighed, eyes searching for her husband and finding him across the floor at one of the drink carts talking with another of the guests. "Ah...love," she said, smitten. Then she looked back at Felíne, tilting her head. "Where is that man, anyway? Kal, I mean."

"Gone with your brothers and—" Ophelia cut stern eyes in Felíne's direction behind Meryl's back. She had to stop herself from scowling in return. Did the woman think her an idiot? She wasn't going to give away their association with Adder by mentioning his name. "—one of the guards."

Meryl rolled her eyes. "Of course, he would leave a perfectly good party and exceptional company—" she winked at Felíne. "To be lured by my brothers into some mysterious business situation. It's my wedding! Ugh. Men!"

"I'll drink to that," Ophe said, raising her drink.

But it wasn't some mysterious business situation. Whatever had happened was serious enough to have drawn Kal away from the celebration. Felíne suspected Ophelia knew something, but if she did, she wasn't sharing. With her, *or* Meryl, apparently.

Meryl, oblivious to Felíne's contemplation, grabbed the glass in front of her with a show a feminine camaraderie in response to Ophelia's toast and gulped the contents. She made a face. "Kitty. Girl," she said, eyeing the glass of water with obvious disappointment. "There's your problem! You need wine, not water."

She stood, not waiting for a response, and gathered her gown. "Wait here! We'll get you nice and fortified with a strong pour, and you'll be out-dancing all of us! Let Kal return to find you in the arms of some brawn, handsome stranger. See if he leaves you lonely then!"

Felíne had no intention of finding herself in the arms of any stranger, regardless of Kal's feelings on the matter, but she tipped her lips up in a smile for Meryl's benefit and watched as the bride wove her way through the crowd to meet Boden at the drink cart. Boden bent, arms winding affectionately around Meryl's trim waist to pull her close as he said something in her ear that made the lovely bride positively glow.

"Why didn't you tell her where Kal went?" Felíne was still watching Meryl, and Ophelia followed suit, not looking directly at her.

"Because I don't know," she said simply. "And because whatever it was, Adder wanted it kept quiet."

Felíne looked over then, questioningly. "Did you talk to him?"

Ophelia shook her head.

"Then how do you know?"

Ophelia turned slowly to face her. "He was in first form."

Was she supposed to know what that meant? What significance it held? Felíne wished Imogen were there with her. She'd know what to make of this situation. Gen's quiet confidence wouldn't be shaken by Ophe's acerbity.

Ophelia looked at her like she was a bit slow in the head. "Adder was on perimeter guard. He shifted back to first form before he came to deliver whatever news he had for Grisham. Some of the people here would have easily recognized his second form. He didn't want to draw attention."

Felíne nodded, a bit put out that she hadn't come to the conclusion herself. It made sense. Adder was a sight in his second form with his long silvery coat and icy eyes. People would certainly have noticed. Though whatever had happened hadn't allowed him time to clean up before delivering his message. "He had blood on his hands," Felíne said quietly.

"Not his."

So, she'd assumed correctly. "You know for certain?"

Ophelia had a strange expression on her face. One Felíne had seen on Mender Alcuin's when trying to puzzle out one of his patient's more complicated diagnoses. "Of course, I know for certain. I could scent that it wasn't his. Couldn't you?"

Felíne sat back. "How would I know if the blood was his?"

She'd asked the question without thinking. Ophelia narrowed her eyes, and little alarm bells went off in Felíne's head. "You smelled his blood last night when he and Kal were fighting in the tent. Kal busted Adder's nose. You should have scented that the blood wasn't his."

She should have. Except for the fact that Felíne had no enhanced senses to speak of and kept forgetting that everyone else assumed she did. Ophelia's growing distrust made her squirm.

Felíne needed distance. Before her entire façade began to unravel.

"I need to use the water room," she said, standing. "If you'll excuse me, please."

Ophelia got to her feet. "I'll show you."

"No need," Felíne insisted. "I know the way." She'd seen the closet-sized tents designated for toilet use when she and Kal had arrived earlier in the evening. They were situated on the edge of the venue. Close enough to be convenient yet far enough to provide some privacy and insulation from potentially unwelcome aromas.

Clearly, they were too far by Ophelia's standards—not that Felíne was asking permission—because Ophe stepped around her seat, planning to accompany her anyway.

Goddess bless it all. She would *not* be escorted to the toilet.

424

"Ophelia," she reasoned bluntly. "If Kal were here, he wouldn't be taking me to pee. I am going by myself."

"He told me not to let you out of my sight."

Felíne pointed. "You can see the tents from here."

The female was unmoved.

This was preposterous. "Listen, you can treat me like the adult that I am and watch me walk all by my grown self, or you can insist on treating me like a child, and I can really start acting like one. You tell me which you prefer."

Ophe visually measured the distance to the toilets, scowled, considered Felíne for longer than necessary, and finally sat back down with a light thump. "Fine," she said, crossing her arms with begrudging resignation. The orange hair on her head waved with the movement as if sharing her agitation. "Don't linger."

Oh, yes. Goddess forbid she *lingered* in the water room. Honestly. "Would you care to time me?" she asked innocently.

Ophelia continued to glower in silence, so Felíne took the opportunity to walk away while she still had the chance. She made her way between the fire pits and past one of the drink carts that had collected a line of guests waiting for refills until she reached the tented section. It didn't exactly offer the breath of fresh air that she needed, but it was a space she could claim as her own for the moment. It was also far enough from Ophelia to allow her a temporary reprieve from the woman's uncompromising analyses.

She couldn't fault Ophelia for her loyalty to Kal nor her determination to comply with his request to guard Felíne. However, being the target of that scrutiny tainted her appreciation for the female's commitment with annoyance.

Felíne scooted out of the way as a happily drunken patron stumbled to the door of one of the water tents. He smiled at her as he passed in what he probably hoped was a charming beam, but he had a bit of spittle stuck in his beard, and there was a dark stain on his shirtfront that was likely the remnants of an earlier meal. One he might be tasting again shortly. She gave a close-lipped smile in return and eased away from his unpredictable trajectory into a shadowed recess.

Beyond the alcove, Meryl's wedding celebration reached a crescendo. Loud, raucous laughter carried across the crowd as more and more people found their way to the dance floor, and the band upped its tempo. Shurii swung and swayed, entirely focused on personal enjoyment, freely flowing libations, and the allure of festivity. Sweets were passed out on trays between those who reclined around the fires or sat grouped at low tables.

Felíne thought about Kal as she watched and sifted through an impossible list of possibilities that could explain his whereabouts and the circumstances surrounding his absence. The longer he was gone, the more tense she became, caught between concern and feeling like she was running out of time to take advantage of his truancy.

The door to Felíne's right opened, and a familiar dark-haired female stepped out.

"Kitty!"

Evie beckoned Felíne forward. "Were you waiting for a toilet?"

Felíne glanced back across the crowded dancers where Ophelia was probably counting the length of time it took for her to pee. Thankfully, she was just out of sight past the first few tents. "Not exactly," she admitted. "Just needed some air."

Evie followed her gaze before her midnight blue eyes returned to Felíne's. They looked serious in the dark. Mysterious. "I see."

"Did you ever find Tula?"

"Hm?"

"Your friend that was missing. You wanted help looking for her."

"Oh," Evie said, focusing. "Yes, I did. In fact, we've decided to make an early departure. She's gone to ready the horses."

Felíne's heartbeat kicked up a notch. "You're leaving tonight? Now?"

Evie nodded, eyes darting occasionally in the direction from which Felíne had come. "I was coming to tell you. You still plan to travel with us, I hope?"

"I..." Of course, she did. This was it. This was her chance! A more fortuitous opportunity would not present itself again, Felíne was sure. She'd been schooled enough about the infrequency of the Goddess's blessings to know that they weren't to be squandered when granted.

So why was she faltering? The thought of Kal returning to the party to find her missing sent a pang of raw guilt through her. He would assume the worst. He'd think something happened to her. And he'd never find out that she'd left entirely on her own. For she would return to Asteros, be cocooned behind the walls of the royal villa, and once again be set upon the path to fulfill her destiny. A gift to the Primordial Male. A panacea for the curse that plagued the shurii people.

She would never see him again.

"We don't have time," Evie insisted. "Tula will be waiting. We should go now."

Felíne glanced back again, searching for a tall, broad frame, dark hair, and serious onyx eyes among the crowd. She didn't find them. Somehow, she knew she wouldn't.

"Okay," Felíne said, setting the irrational hesitation within her aflame.

Evie didn't give her a second glance. She took her hand and led them away from the water tents. She heard someone retching in one of them as they hurried past. Evie dragged her around a corner and past one of the lonely drink carts that bordered the venue. This far out it was mostly abandoned, the attendant working the cart lounging lazily against the counter. Behind her, Felíne could hear the party continuing, but the sounds faded the farther they went.

It wasn't long before the reality of her decision fully settled in her mind. She was going home! The realization, coupled with Evie's suddenly harried pace, stole her breath. She was having a difficult time keeping up. "Evie," she gasped. "Slow down."

The raven female didn't slow. She didn't even turn her head. She was entirely fixated on her course. "We cannot delay," she said as clearly as if they were taking a leisurely stroll.

"Why the...urgency? I...I can't keep up. Evie!"

A loud crack sounded ahead, and Felíne stumbled to a halt as Evie stopped in her tracks. For as clumsy as she claimed to be, the woman was remarkably agile when she wanted to be.

Felíne bent over, hands braced on her thighs to catch her breath. They couldn't have gone far, but it felt like miles. She really needed to start working on her endurance. Beside her, Evie was still. When Felíne finally lifted her head, she understood why.

CLOAKING FATE

Ophelia stood before them, fury etched into her usually flat features. "Kitty," she said with deceptive calm. "We've got to stop meeting in dark alleys like this. It sends the wrong message, don't you think?"

Shit. Felíne had the irrational thought that Imogen would be proud of how easily the expletive entered her mind.

Evie's initial innocence was replaced with cold detachment as her navy eyes assessed Ophelia. "Are you expecting a fight?" Evie nodded toward the whip that rested uncoiled in Ophelia's left hand. Her right wielded a dagger with a curved blade. Felíne's heart sank. That open window of escape was rapidly closing.

Ophelia ignored the question. "Where are you rushing off to ladies? There's a party underway."

Evie lifted her chin and slid a hand possessively into the crook of Felíne's arm. "Kitty and I desired a bit of privacy," she said, voice heavy with insinuation. "We were going to my room."

Felíne's eyes bugged, and she looked at Evie as if seeing her for the first time. Privacy? That's the best excuse she could come up with?

Ophelia's eyes narrowed, missing nothing. "I don't think so."

"You aren't her mother," Evie pushed. "She can choose her own company."

In the time it took Felíne to blink, Ophelia had moved. The terrifying little female had been several strides away, and now she stood directly in front of them, nose to nose with the taller Evie. "Based on how you've been dragging her, it doesn't look like she's chosen anything. She's returning with me."

Evie stared coldly down on Ophelia, miraculously unbothered by the obvious threat of violence should she present any opposition. She didn't know the kind of company the female kept. Felíne did. She also knew that Ophelia wouldn't be a member of Kal's cadre unless she could hold her own. Evie didn't stand a chance.

"Ophelia. Evie," Felíne pleaded, not trusting Ophelia's hairline trigger and not wanting Evie to get hurt. "Please. This is a misunderstanding."

Evie looked about to challenge Ophelia's demands when her attention snapped up, over Ophe's head. Something moved in the shadows. She glanced down, and Felíne was suddenly caught off guard at how predatory

Evie appeared. The woman seemed to war with some unnamed decision before making up her mind.

"Fine," she said, releasing Felíne's arm. "Another time."

That was it?

It was, Felíne realized. Evie decided to leave without her. The window of escape that Felíne desperately needed just slammed shut in her face, hand on the sill.

"Not likely," Ophelia commented.

Then Evie retreated. One moment, she was there, the next, she'd gone. Evaporated like the whisp of hope Felíne held for an uncomplicated departure.

Ophelia rounded on her immediately. "You said you were going to pee."

She had, hadn't she? What started as a moment's need for space had shifted rapidly to a decision to leave with the opportunity Evie had presented. Now she was gone, and the opportunity with her.

"Instead, you try to sneak off with some hen that wants to get in your pants? Not even an hour ago, you could barely keep your hands off Kal! Which is it?"

Felíne was becoming accustomed to the disappointment of her escape plans going awry, but the continued besmirching of her integrity was a difficult thing to swallow. "I lied about having to pee," she admitted, unable to hide her frustration. "And I have no intention of letting anyone inside my pants!"

"Then what the hell were you doing?"

"You were smothering me! You think it's miserable for you to play protector when you'd rather be doing…whatever it is that you do? Multiply that by a hundred. I am sick of being treated like a fragile doll liable to shatter with the tiniest friction. I'm not made of glass, Ophelia!"

Ophelia opened her mouth to reply, but Felíne wasn't finished. "We had *one* moment where I thought maybe we could at least be cordial, if not friendly, but you're right back to treating me like I'm the enemy. You don't trust me, but have you made any effort to try to understand me? To get to know me? No. No one here has. Do you know what it's like to be known only as the title assigned to you? To be surrounded by people who are *obligated* to share your company? Kalevar is the only person outside Asteros who has made any effort to make me feel like I'm not a complete outsider, and even he's bound by duty!"

She snapped her mouth shut. The words were out before she even had a chance to process the reality of what she was saying. The truth of them hurt. Imogen was a friend, but they only met because the young elder was forced to become the Prima's instructor. She wouldn't have chosen that role for herself if given the option. Even Mender Alcuin, who was Felíne's safe haven, had initially been assigned as her personal physician. The loneliness that her status carried was suddenly crushing, and she wondered if anyone alive could genuinely understand how isolating that was. Possibly only one other: her intended. And the Primordial Male was about as alien to her as the world outside the royal grounds.

Ophelia coiled her whip and fastened it at her hip. The look she finally settled on Felíne was hard but no longer accusatory. "I won't pretend to win any awards for social pageantry," she said matter-of-factly. "I know what I am. I also know that the world isn't going to cater to your feelings. The sooner you come to terms with that fact, the better the chance that you'll succeed in it."

That did little to assure her. "Right now, I feel like I'm just trying to survive long enough to get back on the right path. I just wish it wasn't so…desolate."

"I can apologize for making you feel unwanted," Ophelia said, not sounding very sorry at all. The woman was unyielding. "But I won't apologize for my suspicion. It keeps us alive."

That was about as close to a proper apology as Felíne suspected she would ever get. She didn't, however, get a chance to reply.

Two males in second form materialized out of the darkness behind Ophelia. They were in second form, armored, and thoroughly armed. These were no inebriated guests who had strayed too far from the celebration. They were guards. Their eyes were clear and sharp as they scanned the area, their nostrils flaring as they scented the two women.

Ophelia recognized one of the males and nodded her greeting. He seemed to be calculating. "Ophelia," he said in a gravelly baritone.

"Hunting for a good time, Shaw?"

The bronze-pelted male cut his head to the side. "Not tonight, Ophelia. I suggest turning in or returning to the party." He glanced at Felíne, giving her a once over. "And quickly."

"Trouble?"

"Orders. The streets are unsafe tonight."

Ophe's lips tipped up, but her eyes were humorless. "Sure, Shaw. We were just heading back."

The male nodded, and the two prowled off silently, scanning the street.

Felíne watched them disappear, phantoms in the dark. "What was that about?"

Ophelia looked after them, tension lines bracketing her generous mouth. "Those are Grisham's trackers. That male, Shaw? He's a dangerous fucker. Grisham only sends him out if it's serious. They're hunting."

"Hunting for what?"

The smaller female glanced over. "Not what. Whom. Let's go."

Felíne had no choice but to follow. Gods, she wished she knew what was going on. Kal pulled away from the celebration. The Trade Master's predators stalked the streets. And all the guests at Meryl and Boden's wedding party were none the wiser. As they returned to the celebration, it was obvious no one had any idea that something within Cindamar was amiss.

The table Felíne and Ophelia had previously occupied was taken by an engrossed couple. While Ophe searched for another empty seat, Felíne scanned for Meryl. She couldn't help feeling like something important was going to happen. What, she wasn't sure, but it would give her some comfort if Meryl was close in case of trouble.

The bride found her instead.

"There you are," she said happily. "Bo and I brought drinks, but you'd gone. I was worried you left."

"Sorry," Felíne said. "Did we miss anything?"

Meryl tucked a sheet of short blonde hair behind an ear, a fine sheen of perspiration glistening on her forehead. "No, but it's time for Bo's speech." She pointed excitedly. Felíne looked over to the platform where Meryl and her husband had stood to be joined under the jasmine arch near the edge of the pool. The water was black and still in the night. It looked like a dark mirror dotted with tiny white flowers. Boden stood on the platform, overlooking the crowd. His arms were raised, a drink in one hand. The musicians quieted their instruments, and a hush slowly fell over the attendees as they strained to see over one another.

Boden smiled broadly, eyeing those gathered, and he swayed just a bit, catching himself before he pitched too far forward.

"Is he alright?" Felíne asked.

Meryl giggled. "Oh yes," she whispered loudly. "He's terribly drunk. Oh, don't look at me like that. It's partly your fault. You and Ophelia left, and he had no choice but to finish your drinks, too."

"Friends! Family! Strangers, even!" Boden boomed. "Thank you all for coming to drink with us, dine with us, and celebrate this union!"

People cheered. Whistles split the air.

Boden waved from his podium, spilling his drink. Everyone laughed. The groom's blue eyes squinted in the lantern light as he searched the crowd. "Mer! Where are you, love? Look at me. I've lost her already!"

More laughter.

Beside her, Meryl's hand shot in the air, waving. "Here!" she yelled.

Bo found her and pointed. "There she is. Everyone! Look at how beautiful that woman is! My wife! My love. My…"

All heads turned to focus on Meryl. The female was no stranger to attention, and she didn't shy from the spotlight. But something kept Felíne from turning to look at the bride next to her like every other person in the venue. Instead, all her focus remained on the stage, where Boden swayed, a joyous smile spreading his handsome features.

So, she was the only one who saw when the shaft of an arrowhead split the skin of Bo's throat with a spray of blood. Whatever he'd been about to say would remain unfinished. The final words came out in a gurgle, and red stained his lips. A look of confusion twisted his expression before three more bolts pierced his chest in rapid succession. The drink Bo had been holding fell from his grasp and shattered at his feet a moment before he crumpled on the platform.

Felíne whirled. Meryl's aquamarine eyes flew wide.

And then the screaming started.

Chapter 42

Chaos and Loss

PANDEMONIUM.

The yellow lantern light that had just moments before suffused the venue in a warm, magical glow now cast the scene before them in gruesome flickerings of eerie horror.

Boden Ceen crumpled on the platform like a tower of cards collapsing inward. Felíne's eyes were transfixed on the body and the blood beginning to pool beneath it, but she sensed the moment Meryl's attention joined her own.

The cry that rent the air cleaved a jagged laceration through any remaining merriment among the party goers.

Felíne rushed forward. There might be a chance. He'd only just fallen. If the bolts, by some miracle, hadn't pierced anything essential, he might have a chance.

"Murderer!" someone screamed.

"He's dead! Someone killed the groom!"

The guests finally began to take notice. Finally. To Felíne, it felt like an age, though it couldn't have been more than a few seconds. That awareness spread through the crowd like plague mice, and suddenly, everyone seemed to be infected with it. Within moments, she was boxed in by a panicked crowd.

Felíne turned to grab Meryl's hand before the mob swallowed them, but a large man dressed in the armor of Grisham's guard was already there, shielding the horrified bride with his menacing bulk, shoving guests carelessly out of his way. Meryl would be fine. Not fine, she amended, but at least safe. Safer than the rest of them.

CLOAKING FATE

Felíne returned her attention to the platform. Unbelievably, none of the attendees tried to reach it. They were like a colony of drunken roaches put under a direct beam of sunlight, and she was disgusted by their selfishness. Someone pushed carelessly into her from the side, elbowing her painfully in the ribs. She shoved back. Another person trod heavily on her foot. It took longer than it should have, considering the short distance, but Felíne finally managed to reach the edge of the platform where Boden lay.

The few steps leading up had been dislodged and overturned, so she scrambled up on her hands and knees. Felíne was grateful, not for the first time that evening, of Kal's insistence that she have an appropriate outfit in case of an emergency. She couldn't imagine wearing the tight-fitting gown she'd initially favored in Policarpa's shop.

Boden was still. Her heart dropped like a boulder into a mountain lake, but she put her hands on him anyway, praying for some sign of life, some flicker of a pulse in the ruined throat beneath her fingertips.

There was none.

The arrow was larger up close, the head notched with a wicked barb that didn't just split the anterior skin of Bo's throat but shredded it. The shaft had broken when he fell, and the piece that protruded from just below the base of his skull wrenched his head to the side unnaturally. The shooter didn't have to fire the additional bolts into his chest. The first arrow killed him. The extras were for show.

A rage unlike Felíne had ever felt lit her blood on fire. He was young and happy and looking forward to a vibrant future with the woman he loved. The smile on Boden's face when his gaze had rested on Meryl was pure joy. Complete devotion. His bride had returned it.

And now he was dead. Felíne's hands fisted. He was murdered. That future stolen from him. Stolen from both of them. Furious tears blurred her vision.

"Kitty."

Felíne wiped angrily at her eyes and found Ophelia. "He's gone," she said, though the explanation was unnecessary. Ophelia could see clearly enough.

434

"We need to go." Ophe's tone was urgent, though her body was relaxed. The woman seemed to look at everything but Felíne. Scanning methodically, her brain digested information as her eyes relayed their surroundings.

Felíne pushed to her feet. "We can't just leave him."

"He is dead. We aren't, but we can be. You're a target on this platform."

The noise of chaos was deafening. People shouted, cried, and ran blindly into one another in search of friends or loved ones. Others drunk and fighting. Second forms exploded recklessly on instinct, shredding fine clothing like worthless rags. The band had abandoned their instruments, leaving expensive equipment to be trampled. A fire started somewhere to their left as a firepit was overturned, and smoldering coals sparked a tablecloth.

Felíne didn't know where Kal had gone, but if he were still within the city, he'd hear the roar of bedlam. He would be coming back. The thought shouldn't have given her the comfort that it did, but she couldn't deny the sense of security his presence provided, which had somehow manifested within her over the last twenty-four hours. If anyone knew what to do in this mess, it was Kal.

"Kitty, now. We need to get somewhere safe."

Ophelia had moved off the platform. Her hand reached up to where Felíne now stood on the edge.

Felíne searched the thinning crowd, wondering where they would go that could be considered safe. The oasis sat to their back. They'd have to get through the remaining tumult of the venue to access the rest of the city. Her gaze tracked a potential path, and that's when she saw him.

She wasn't sure how she knew it was a *him*, but she did.

The man was of average height and thin. Not frail, but slight in a hard, wired way. He moved with sure steps, face hidden by a deep hood. There was a heavy bow at his side, and as he moved closer to the now roaring fire, Felíne could see the fletching of thick-shafted arrows peeking over his left shoulder. Her breath caught as the male picked his way slowly toward them from across the venue.

Felíne tore her eyes from the stranger and looked back at poor Bo's body. She would bet her fate that she had just found the owner of the arrows protruding from his chest and neck.

CLOAKING FATE

A shriek distinguishable from the other commotion reached Felíne's ears, and her gaze flew back to the stranger just in time to see the man raise his left arm. He slashed downward and to the side. A small, horrified cry left Felíne's lips. The smaller female in front of him didn't have a prayer. Her head separated from her shoulders and rolled under a table. The woman's body pitched forward, knees hitting the dirt. The male kicked the headless torso with such violent disregard that Felíne's stomach lurched. She turned to the side and vomited.

Felíne wasn't the only one who'd seen the slaughter. Ophelia's chest rumbled with a menacing growl that sounded like it belonged to a wild mountain cat instead of the petite woman she was.

"You fucking monster," she spat. She unsheathed the curved dagger that Felíne had seen earlier and a longer, wicked-looking knife from a hidden sheath at her thigh. "I'm going to filet you."

Felíne wiped her mouth with a sleeve. She was too stunned to feel guilty for soiling it.

"Kitty. You see the palms to your right, along the shore?" Ophelia didn't look back. Her focus was fixed on her prey. Felíne saw the tall palm trees she'd referenced. They sat potted in heavy wooden planters among several other thicker hedges. The area lay beyond the border of the wedding venue, but it wasn't far.

"I see them."

"Go. Hide. If I don't find you there shortly, Kal will."

Felíne's wide eyes tracked the male. He was closer. Too close. She wanted to cry, but her fear choked her tears. "Come with me," she pleaded.

Ophelia turned to her then, and Felíne realized that the woman was no damsel. She was a cold, calculated assassin, and she'd found her next mark. "*Go. Now.*"

Her fear of Ophelia warred with her fear *for* Ophelia. If she stayed, she would only be a distraction. He was coming. She didn't have time to deliberate. That man killed Meryl's husband. He killed an innocent woman. Someone needed to put him down.

Felíne didn't need any further encouragement. She scrambled off the ledge of the platform and ran. When she looked back, Ophelia was stalking into the venue. Felíne threw up a silent prayer for her safety. She'd never prayed for death before, never envisioned herself wishing harm on anyone, but, in that moment, she did it with all of her heart. She wished death on the hooded killer, and she prayed for it to be delivered by Ophelia's blades.

Felíne darted off the path that passed the palms and scurried behind the hedges where Ophe had instructed. The palms themselves didn't offer much cover, but the dense hedges planted among them did. She hid relatively close to the edge of the larger pool, but no one would think to look in this corner. The plants likely provided a pretty landscape beside the pathway that wound along the waterfront, but it was pitch black at night, without any lantern light. The water shone like dark glass. Even from the other side, she wouldn't be seen.

The sounds of the venue quieted. Blessedly, she didn't hear any more screams over the crackling of the flames. The problem with remaining unseen was that she herself couldn't see. She wanted desperately to peek over to try and find Ophelia, but she kept her head down. All she could do was sit and pray and attempt to keep her overactive imagination from envisioning Ophe's broken body being unceremoniously discarded as the hooded nightmare resumed his meaningless slaughter.

It was difficult for Felíne to acknowledge the possibility of that kind of evil existing inside a person. What was the motive? Where was the purpose in such mindless violence? Meryl's expression upon realizing Boden's fate burned into her mind's eye. The woman's head rolling like a misshapen ball. She'd never be able to unsee that. And now Ophelia went out to face him alone.

Tremors wracked her body. Fear and adrenaline flooded her system. Felíne's heart raced. If anything happened to Ophe while she crouched here and hid...

Come on, Kal. Where are you?

A hand gripped Felíne's upper arm, and she yelped in alarm. She swung her opposite fist around on instinct, but it was easily caught midair before it collided with a slender jaw. A cloud broke overhead, and moonlight spilled into the cluster of hedges just enough for Felíne to make out a pair of harsh navy eyes and raven hair.

"Evie!"

"Quiet," the woman snapped. "Get up. We need to go."

Felíne was practically dragged to her feet. "I thought you left! I…"

Felíne paused. The gown Evie had been wearing the last time she saw her was replaced by boots, tight traveling breeches, a fitted long-sleeved tunic, and leather armor. Draped across her shoulders was a black cloak with a deep hood. One that looked like…

No. This was wrong. Something about this was—

"Now, Prima."

The title sent a ripple of shock through Felíne, cutting off her previous thought. "Who…who are you?"

"My name is Tavene, a hunter of Asteros. I am here at your father's behest, tasked with returning you home. But we cannot wait. Femoran's distraction will not last much longer."

A hunter! Sent by the king! She *knew* someone would be coming for her!

Yet, Felíne remained unmoving. Who was Femoran? What distraction? What…the understanding dawned so suddenly that it physically jarred her. She couldn't believe she hadn't connected the pieces earlier. Boden. The woman. *No…* "The hooded man," Felíne breathed, hating the truth of it. Hating herself for not realizing it sooner. "He's with you."

"Yes," Tavene said. "Femoran. One of my soldiers."

She felt sick all over again. Any momentary relief at being rescued evaporated with the realization. It was her fault. How had she not considered it before this moment? They were here for *her*. And innocent people—good people—lost their lives because she was here.

Tavene pulled Felíne behind her, stopping at the edge of the last hedge to check the clearing before continuing.

"Boden, the groom, was innocent. And the woman in the venue…your soldier butchered her."

"Good," said Tavene dispassionately.

Felíne gaped. "But…you knew?"

"Of course, I knew. He is acting on my orders. Trackers are combing the streets. I needed a distraction large enough to draw their attention and a threat dangerous enough to occupy the little bitch guarding you."

The contrast between this woman and the shy, apologetic female she'd met earlier couldn't be more pronounced. It had all been an act from the beginning. Evie had been a disguise with the sole intent of singling Felíne out and luring her away from her company. Even the meeting near the water tents hadn't been an accident. Eveant—Tavene—had been watching her the entire time. She'd only retreated after Ophelia met them in the street outside the venue and Grisham's trackers approached. Tavene must have realized that while she had a chance against Ophelia alone, she couldn't take all three of them. This female had been sent by her father to bring her home. She was the rescuer Felíne had been hoping for. And yet, Tavene felt like the enemy.

These people she'd spent the last day with weren't bad people. Ophe, Meryl, Adder. Kal. They were just people. *Her* people. Wasn't it her duty to save them all? Not just the Faithful, but the Cozened and those who didn't claim either faction as well? They didn't deserve to die just because their beliefs didn't align with those of the crown. Felíne wanted to go home, but this was wrong.

She pulled against Tavene's hold. "Call him off."

Tavene huffed a laugh. "Not going to happen."

"She doesn't deserve to die because you needed a distraction."

Disgust twisted Tavene's features. She leaned in. "They *all* deserve to die. They're all sinful, blaspheming curs. Better to send them to judgment now, before they can further stain shurii-kind with their treason. Thinking they can hide from the Crown of Asteros in their secret city." She laughed cruelly. "Well, they've been found. And when the king learns of this place, he'll send the greatest militia of the ages to wipe them from history."

This woman. Her soldier. *They* were the stain. How could her father employ people possessing such malevolence? Was that how he felt, too? Did her mother carry similar sentiments? *Look at what they did to the Fated Mothers,* she reminded herself. What they did to Imogen. Think of how those females had been treated. How they were *still* treated. For her own supposed benefit. And those females were Faithful Cursed, not traitors at all! Was it a stretch to consider her parents might tolerate or even favor the extermination of anyone outside their faith? She imagined the bustling town center of Cindamar full of people falling under the steel boots of the Asterosian army. Families cut down by their blades. Children stilled by their crossbows.

No. Felíne could not let that happen. She needed to get home, but Tavene and her soldier couldn't be permitted to reach Asteros ahead of her.

"I'm not going with you unless you call him off."

Tavene looked down on her like a bird of prey. "You don't get a choice in the matter, Prima. I take orders from King Domitan alone."

"You cannot do this!"

Felíne fought. She pulled and wrenched to try and free herself from Tavene's grip to no avail. The woman's grasp may as well have been an iron shackle about her wrist.

"If you do not cease your struggling, I will be forced to incapacitate you, Prima."

She wouldn't dare. Felíne voiced as much.

Tavene's cold response bit her. "Don't test me. Your title might offer a shield from my blade, but I will not hesitate to use other methods to ensure your compliance. The king demanded you be protected by any means necessary. Even from yourself."

Felíne felt trapped. Her fighting proved useless. The axe hanging at her waist might have been a jeweled talisman for all the difference it made in her talentless hands. She didn't even want to reach for it for fear that Tavene would take notice and disarm her completely. She wasn't strong or fast enough to overpower the female and get away. If she yelled or continued making any commotion, she'd likely be knocked unconscious and further restrained. Then she'd really be helpless.

Her only hope was Kal. He would come back. Ophelia said he'd be looking for her. However, the longer Felíne considered that chance, the slimmer it seemed. Tavene dragged her away from the venue, keeping to the shadowed sections between tents, avoiding notice. The direction they traveled seemed to lead away from the city and closer to the outskirts. Kal would be returning to the venue, not searching the quiet, dark periphery along the water's edge.

Felíne stumbled, scraping her knee, and Tavene's relentless hold hauled her forward. A bit further and Tavene pulled to a halt, shoving Felíne back against the edge of a wagon. Felíne didn't even bother checking to see the damage to her leg. She could already feel it swelling, and a smear of blood stained the front of her pant leg. Policarpa would never forgive her.

"Fenn. Anything?"

A familiar male voice lifted Felíne's head, grabbing all of her attention. It came from ahead, somewhere beyond the wagon and out of sight. Tavene got within inches of her face, her severe expression clear. Quiet. Or else.

"Nothing," a second male answered. "Harris is sweeping from the opposite direction. He should be here shortly. We checked the stockyards—"

Beside her, Tavene tensed.

"—but nothing. The mutt is missing again. Always fucking running off after a rabbit or gopher instead of doing his damn job. But nothing's been tampered with."

"Fuck. Alright," Garren said. "If you've checked the western perimeter working inward, there's not much else on this side. Get Harris and make your way back to the venue. They need fucking backup."

A slight breeze lifted the deflated coils around Felíne's face and chilled her dampened hairline. Tavene was so still Felíne wondered if she was even breathing. The males couldn't have been far from the other side of the wagon. If Garren was this far from the venue, maybe Kal or Adder had made their way to the periphery as well. Even if they hadn't, maybe Garren would help her. They may not be on the best of terms, but if he took a few steps in her direction, he would provide enough distraction for Tavene that maybe Felíne could get away.

"We smelled the smoke," Fenn said. "Your sister?"

"Safe," Garren said. "But her husband is dead."

Fenn cursed.

"I just came from the venue. Fucking mess. Dead groom. Two dead females. The bastard responsible ran off into the city. Shaw's on his tail, but they need help."

Felíne bit back a cry. She suddenly couldn't breathe her chest was so tight.

He said *two* females. *Ophe...*

"We're on it, boss."

"Check every tent," Garren said. "This fucker doesn't leave the city. I'm going north around the Jasmine Pool."

There was a grunt of assent and the males moved off in the opposite direction. *No!* Felíne's shoulders slumped. Ophelia was dead. Garren had gone. Kal was nowhere to be found. Tavene waited, listening intently.

Minutes dragged by. When she tugged on Felíne's wrist again, she jerked forward like a rag doll. A deep sadness wrapped around her heart like a vice. She hadn't considered Ophelia to be a friend, but the loss of her was an unexpected pain. It was a strange, sobering thing to face the death of someone you knew. Contemplating an unexpected casualty hurt, regardless of the depth of emotional tie. Loss was loss. And the truth was, no one wanted to lose.

"The horses aren't far," Tavene whispered. "Just around that—"

The females froze simultaneously. A huge, clawed hand gripped the back of Felíne's neck, its twin around Tavene's.

"I thought I smelled you, pet," Garren's gravelly voice grated from above as he palmed them from behind. "Sneaking in the dark with a little friend?" He lowered his head next to Felíne's own, lip curling over deadly white canines that gleamed in the dark, and inhaled deeply. Then he shifted position and similarly scented Tavene. His tail swished. "Smells like a couple of traitors," he growled, claws flexing. Felíne winced. "Start talking."

Chapter 43

Little Lamb

FELÍNE STOOD FROZEN. THE PRESENCE of Garren's deadly claws around her neck and his formidable teeth inches from her face made her seriously reconsider her desire for his intervention.

Next to her, Tavene was cool as a glacial tidepool. "We aren't traitors," she said, assuming the feminine lilt her voice had carried when coming from Evie's mouth.

"No?" Garren gave Felíne a little shake. "Then why do you reek of Boden Ceen's blood? Makes you look pretty damn guilty to me."

Felíne started. Gods. She'd touched him. Boden's blood *was* on her, but not for the reason Garren assumed.

"Garren," she tried. Her voice came out strained. She could feel his claws pressing in on the delicate flesh above her carotid. "I tried to help him. I'm trained as a mender."

"I call sheep shit on that one, pet."

"Garren, please."

Beside her, Tavene was quiet. He had both of them by the neck, but their arms were free. Garren's attention was trained on Felíne, so he didn't see Tavene reach for the blade at her side, hidden beneath her cloak. Felíne did. She caught the movement out of the corner of her eye.

"No!" Felíne yelled.

Tavene moved so quickly, her hand was a blur. Garren tried to evade at the last moment but was caught off guard. The short blade of Tavene's weapon buried to the hilt in his side. She didn't get the angle she'd been going for, but the blade came away bloody regardless.

"You fucking bitch," Garren snarled. He released his hold on both females. Felíne had to admit to some level of admiration. Instead of bending to cradle the wound or even pausing to inspect the damage, he moved into a fighting stance, fully primed for battle.

Garren tossed Felíne to the side and faced off with his larger threat. His armor protected his chest, soft belly, and head, but gaps in the leather joints left him vulnerable to a foe who knew how to exploit them.

Tavene did.

She threw off her cloak and drew a long, slender katana. Felíne watched in horror as the two opponents circled one another. Garren was intimidating in his second form as he stalked Tavene's willowy figure, but Tavene moved with poise and quiet confidence. She already believed she would emerge the victor.

Dark blood stained the brown fur of Garren's left side, but the injury didn't slow him considerably. Not an artery, then. Felíne breathed a sigh of relief. Garren pulled a heavy broadsword from his back. Tavene's sword looked delicate in comparison, but the size and weight difference would likely also mean a difference in speed. One that put Garren at a disadvantage.

Tension rippled in the air while the two predators assessed each other. Felíne backed away. Now would be an opportune time to retreat, but the scene unfolding captivated her. Rooted her.

Garren attacked first. He charged across the circle toward Tavene, lifting his huge sword above his head. He brought it down with staggering force. Despite his bulk, Garren was surprisingly quick.

But he wasn't quick enough.

Tavene easily evaded his swing. To Felíne, it looked almost like the female flowed around Garren's blade, avoiding being cleaved in two by mere inches. Her counterattack was nearly invisible. A quick one-handed flick of her arm and Garren staggered. Felíne couldn't even see where she'd connected, but Garren held his free hand over his abdomen. It came away bloody.

Felíne gasped. Tavene hadn't used any discernible force, yet her katana sliced clean through Garren's armor plating and into the delicate flesh beneath.

444

He growled, furious. "You crafty bitch. When I catch you, I'm going to cut you in two."

He wasn't wrong. If Garren connected just once, it would be over. Even Tavene, with her evident skill, was no match for his power, especially in her first form. Yet she gave no indication that she planned to shift.

"*If* you catch me, you mean. I'll have you watering the ground with blood long before you even get close." Tavene swished her sword, taunting.

Come on, Garren. Use your damned brain. Tavene wouldn't be defeated by brute strength. Felíne was no swordswoman, but even she could see the level of skill with which Tavene fought. The woman moved like a dancer. Her steps were deliberate, her body bending like a young sapling, springy and pliant. She was calm. Intentional. If Garren even had a chance, he needed to develop a strategy that capitalized on his strengths.

They clashed again. This time Garren managed to block a devastating blow that would have crippled him. Tavene charged again. And again, Garren barely managed to deflect.

Tavene laughed.

She circled to the left, raising her blood-stained sword to pass the edge beneath her nostrils. "Mmm. Smells like inadequacy."

Garren growled, baring his teeth. The wrinkled scar on his upper lip made him appear even more menacing.

Twice more, they collided. Both times, Tavene struck out with what would have been a fatal slash, and both times, Garren managed to move just enough out of the way that the wound was merely superficial. He now had a stab wound to his left flank and lacerations to his belly, chest, and inner thigh.

She's toying with him, Felíne thought. *Marking him.* Her sword was wet with his blood, and he had yet to land a single blow. The look on his face told Felíne he knew it. His initial cockiness had tempered, replaced with gritty resolve. Even with the advantages of his second form against Tavene's first, Garren needed to end this soon.

Garren considered his opponent. Though Felíne may not have believed him to possess an impressive intellect, he wasn't a complete fool. Garren drew air into massive lungs and let out a deafening roar. Felíne flinched at the ferocity.

Tavene's features twisted with loathing, and Felíne couldn't help but appreciate the tactic. Clever male. His roar would be heard from miles away.

Then he charged.

Tavene positioned herself. She was ready for his attack even before he initiated it. Garren barreled toward her, raising his sword. Tavene made a minute adjustment. Then Garren's blade left his hands, spinning wildly behind him. Felíne saw Tavene's surprise. Garren's now empty hands splayed, deadly claws swiping forward blindingly fast.

Felíne's heart leapt. He had her! She'd been prepared for a slower overhand power move with the heavier sword. Garren knew it and made a last-ditch effort to throw his challenger off guard. He was going to kill her with his bare hands!

The moment before he connected, something enormous collided with Garren's right temple, throwing the male off course. He crashed to the side like he'd gotten hit with an avalanche.

Felíne gasped, hand flying to her mouth.

Where Garren had been stood a second form male twice his size. Blond fur sheathed a broad skull and short muzzle. Arms the width of tree trunks bulged from a barrel torso. His massive hands could have crushed even Garren's skull the way she might squish a grape between her fingers. He stood on powerful hind legs, and his tail was as thick as Felíne's forearm. He was also completely naked, clothed only in his honeyed coat. The male's beady blue eyes peered at the smaller male's prone form with a crazed expression, a trail of saliva dangling from one corner of his maw.

Garren was still. From where Felíne huddled, she could see his helmet dented in at a concerning angle. The monstrous newcomer turned his attention to Tavene, her katana still held aloft and ready. She shot the great beast a dirty look.

"You took my kill, Drexan," she said. "That was rude."

The giant crouched, lowered his massive head, and squinted up at her with puppy dog eyes.

"Don't give me that sad shit," she scolded, pointing the tip of her blade in his direction. "You're lucky we're pressed for time."

Tavene produced a piece of linen and wiped the length of her sword. Once satisfied, she discarded the soiled cloth as though the worth of Garren's blood was nothing. The colossal male, Drexan, stalked over to Garren's body. Felíne had begun to creep toward the spot where he lay, hoping against all odds that he was somehow alive. She scrambled the rest of the way, placing herself between the monster and the motionless male. She owed Garren no allegiance. He'd been somewhat awful to her from the moment he met her. And yet, she felt some small measure of protection over his vulnerable form. It was wrong that Meryl's brother lay here unprotected at the mercy of the same villains that had just taken the female's husband. He was also Kal's former friend, and that meant something to her.

Drexan smiled, the moonlight glinting off his many glistening teeth. The effect was quite terrifying.

"Hello, little lamb."

Felíne's defiance wavered under the male's appraising eyes. Her gaze dipped below the giant's hips, and what she beheld horrified her more than his claws and teeth. The evidence of this monster's deranged delight plunged her terror to new, unexplored depths.

Drexan's clawed hand palmed furry balls the size of small boulders. "You're a pretty thing, aren't you? Like what you see?" He stepped closer, grinning wickedly. "They're not just for looking."

Oh gods. Impending vomit bubbled in Felíne's esophagus.

Tavene approached from the side. "Put that shit away, Drexan. She's not meant for you."

Drexan slathered her with another hungry look but relented, stepping away. Felíne had never in her life been so thankful for being promised to the Primordial Male as she was in that moment.

Drexan's ears twitched, cocking his head to one side. "Incoming, Tav. I wasn't the only one who heard his battle cry."

Tavene didn't bother to listen herself to confirm. She nodded toward Felíne. "Bring her."

Drexan scooped Felíne off the ground and tossed her over a shoulder, touching her more than was required. She fisted her hands and hammered them into his furred back. The giant didn't even twitch.

"Drexan, if you soil her in any manner, I will personally remove your favorite parts myself. We don't have time for this." They retreated. Felíne watched Garren's body disappear from view. The fallen male hadn't so much as twitched as far as she could tell. She hadn't even had the chance to assess the damage.

"Two other scouts moved off toward the venue, but they could still be nearby."

"Dead," Drexan reported happily. "Found them before I found you. Like taking a teat from a suckling cub. Too easy."

No. The male, Fenn, that Garren had been talking with earlier, and Harris. Two more dead tonight. Possibly three. She prayed Garren was still alive, but Felíne's optimism rapidly depleted with each new occurrence.

"You were supposed to stay hidden," Tavene scolded.

Drexan's breath huffed in indignation. "It's a good thing I didn't! I knew you'd need my help!"

"What I needed was to avoid a fucking bloodbath."

"I like bloodbaths."

"That's because you're a barbarian," Tavene said. "This was supposed to be a quiet mission. In and out. Minimal casualties. It's more difficult to extract a single sheep from a slaughterhouse with all the animals in a panic and the guard dogs on high alert."

Drexan's chest rumbled. *Did he just purr?* "But more fun," he rumbled. "Besides, I ate the guard dog."

As huge as the male was, he moved silently through the abandoned street. They only paused once or twice, Tavene ensuring the coast was clear before hurrying forward again. They had to be nearing the edge of Cindamar. The main body of the city lay behind them, along with all potential allies.

"Where's Femoran?"

"Engaged. He'll meet us at the camp."

"What if he needs help, Tav?"

Tavene showed impressive patience. "Drexan, I think tonight you've helped enough. We reconvene at the camp. That was the plan. We stick to the plan."

"But—"

"I need your escort, Drexan," she said in a tone that was coaxing more than commanding. "We have the target. We need to finish the mission."

Ahead, Felíne heard the shuffling of horses' hooves and a low nicker. After a few more paces, Drexan deposited her unceremoniously onto a patch of packed earth. Her knee ached where she'd previously skinned it. The two horses tethered among a rocky outcrop stamped their feet, visibly nervous around the massive blond predator. Tavene gathered the reins of the smaller horse and tied them to the saddle of her steed. She hauled Felíne to her feet.

"Mount up."

Felíne didn't move. Drexan growled at the disobedience, and the little mare reared slightly, both animals showing the whites of terrified eyes.

Tavene's angular features grew harsh in the dark. "Prima, if you do not get on that horse, I will be forced to compel you. There are hundreds of children in this piss poor excuse of a city. If you are silly enough to believe I would hesitate to put a child to my blade, then look at him and let me know if you think the same."

Felíne glanced up at Drexan's impossible bulk and made the mistake of looking into his wild eyes. The male was pure menace, edged with insanity. The thought of him anywhere near an innocent child filled her with dread. She stepped toward the skittish horse, trapped.

Tavene mounted in front of her.

"Hold on, little lamb." Drexan grinned and shoved her into the saddle. Tavene kicked her horse, and they shot off into the Saraat.

Chapter 44

Out of the Dark

"WHERE THE FUCK IS HE?"

An hour after their flight into the black heart of the desert, Felíne sat uncomfortably, hands bound behind her back with a length of rope, as she watched Drexan's hulking mass pace back and forth in the dark.

They were in a camp. The remains of a cold fire occupied the center of the cramped clearing. Except for a jagged cluster of rocks to one side and the scattered shrubbery dotting the periphery, they appeared to be predominantly exposed. It was impossible for her to visualize the surrounding desert in the dark.

Felíne had made a thoroughly unsuccessful attempt to steal away with one of the horses thirty minutes prior and ended up thrown from the saddle of the terrified creature when Drexan caught up to her. All it earned her was a bruised hip, a—thankfully—shallow abrasion to the left side of her temple, and a pair of skinned forearms, still currently peppered with debris. Oh, and a set of bound hands to prevent any further unwanted excursions.

She was getting really good at this.

Felíne shifted her weight off her right rump, which tingled unpleasantly. The slight movement caused a spike of pain to radiate up her left side. She ignored it. Drexan paused his pacing to glare in her direction, ears twitching in irritation, before continuing his single-file patrol. She ignored him, too— the troglodyte.

Across from her, Tavene sat motionless, a stern expression fixing her shadowed features. Felíne had a hard time believing she'd fallen for the act.

The cold, detached sense of duty fit the female better than Evie's awkward clumsiness.

Drexan made another rigid pass.

They had only stopped to rendezvous with the final member of their party, the hooded killer from the venue, Femoran. The horses stayed saddled. No fire had been risked. Drexan remained in second form—though, thank the Goddess, he'd donned some gear to cover his nakedness—to take advantage of the heightened senses and advanced warning in case of pursuit. He did this against Tavene's wishes. The female had all the reservations about utilizing the second form one would expect from an Asterosian who had grown up indoctrinated by the Faithful Cursed. It seemed that even her father's soldiers were reluctant to wear the Godking's skin. Drexan didn't seem to care so long as it provided them an edge. Tavene had eventually relented. It appeared she prioritized her mission over morality.

It had been over an hour now, and no sign of Femoran.

Felíne hoped he was a mutilated corpse somewhere back in Cindamar. The violent direction of her thoughts concerned her less than it should have. She was well on her way to fitting right in with the group of thieves and cutthroats.

No Femoran. But there had also been no sign of Kal and company, something that seriously disheartened her. My, how the tables had turned. She'd very recently been praying to the Goddess for deliverance from Kal. Now that her initial prayer had been answered, she asked for Kal to deliver her from her deliverers. The Goddess was probably up in her holy sanctuary laughing at the irony of Felíne's situation. If Goddesses known to curse an entire species in vengeance for the actions of one even did petty things like laugh. It seemed unlikely.

Overhead, the moon passed behind a cloud, once again cloaking their little camp in darkness. An owl hooted somewhere nearby. Tavene's tension ratcheted up another degree.

"*Tav.*"

Tavene stood. "We can't wait any longer. It's too great a risk."

The great blond beast paused his pacing and swung his head in his leader's direction. "Let's go get him."

Tavene didn't even hesitate. "No."

Drexan thundered toward her, his hackles on end. "So, we leave him for the worms?"

Tavene snarled, the sound inhuman. "Femoran is not the mission!" She thrust an angry finger at Felíne. "*She* is the mission. It doesn't matter if it takes all of us or one of us so long as we get her back on Asterosian soil. So, yes. We leave him for the fucking worms."

Drexan didn't like it.

Felíne didn't like it either. The longer they lingered, the better her chances of Kal picking up their trail. That is, if he was looking for one...

Tavene's patience was clearly at its limit, but she took a deep breath and when she spoke again, her rage had simmered. "We finish the mission, Drexan." He growled menacingly, but Tavene held up a finger. "Then, once our target is safe behind the palace walls, I will return with you, and we'll kill them all. We will find Femoran. The rest...we'll raze to the earth."

The giant eyed her dubiously.

"Help me finish this, and you can pillage to your wicked heart's content."

Drexan grinned, a slow, ugly show of teeth in gruesome delight. Felíne looked away in disgust. How easily the great troll was distracted.

Tavene took two steps toward Felíne. A subtle breeze lifted a strand of raven hair that had come loose from her plait, and she froze in place. Her head whipped to the side. Drexan's chest rumbled with a low growl, and he lifted his great snout to scent the air. Beady blue eyes cut to Tavene.

She didn't return the gaze. Her own was fixed ahead, entirely focused on a spot of blackness beyond their little gathering. Felíne craned to see what she saw, wrists pinching painfully behind her.

The steady sound of unhurried footfalls reached her ears. Her new captors were still as statues made of meat and bone. The three of them listened, watched, and waited. Then, out of the dark, Felíne witnessed a villain's nightmare materialize.

Kal separated from the darkness, his body emerging like a piece of midnight made flesh. He was clothed head to toe in armor black as the surrounding void of desert. The planes of his face were harsh, and a coal-colored substance had been smeared over the few parts visible beneath the helm he wore. Normally, Felíne had difficulty identifying the secret places Kal kept his weapons hidden on his person. Not so tonight. He'd come advertising his strength with a multitude of knives and daggers tucked securely along his frame. Two short swords crossed his back, their wrapped hilts peeking over broad shoulders. A compact bow accompanied the pair, and Felíne spotted a cache of thick bolts secured in a modified quiver at one hip. An oddly reflective silver cord wrapped around one armored forearm from wrist to elbow.

Kal strode forward, a Lord of Night, come for war.

As far as she could tell, he'd come alone.

His gaze tracked the gathering and landed on her. Felíne's breath caught. Kal's usually onyx eyes were laced with radiant shards of gold. Not the flickering specks she'd occasionally seen reflected in their depths, but luminous, gilded strands that pierced the shadows. These were inhuman eyes that belonged to a being from another time. Another world. And in that moment, as they assessed her, they flared with a primal fury that could be felt from where she sat strained across the space. Somehow, Felíne understood it wasn't just the Kal she'd begun to know looking at her. It was the part of himself that he kept hidden behind that handsomely cultured façade—his second form. The monster within peeked behind the curtain of Kal's iron will.

A shudder worked its way through her. Not from fear, she realized, but a mix of awe and nearly overwhelming relief. He came for her.

Kal tossed a heavy cloak onto the ground before Tavene and Drexan, returning his attention to his enemy. Felíne hadn't even noticed he'd been carrying it. Now that she did, she recognized the crumpled pile of fabric.

Tavene's brow came down in a furious slash, and Drexan's growl promised retribution. They recognized it, too.

"Good," Kal's voice rumbled. "Saves me an explanation. Let her go, and he'll be returned alive."

Drexan lowered his great blond head. "He lies. Femoran wouldn't allow himself to be captured by the likes of you, traitor!"

Kal reached into a pocket and tossed a small drawn leather pouch at Tavene's feet. She crouched, eyes not leaving the place where Kal stood, and retrieved it from the dirt. It took only a moment to open the tie and inspect the contents. The female's navy eyes burned though she said nothing. She held the pouch out for Drexan. His reaction was not so reserved as his companion's.

"You son of a festering whore!" he roared. He thrust a clawed hand forward. In it was a severed tattooed finger, blood congealed over the exposed bone at one end. "You're a lying cunt!"

"I said he'd be returned *alive*. I said nothing about remaining whole."

Drexan roared again.

Kal glared, wholly unintimidated. "Last chance. Give. Me. The woman."

Tavene had recovered from any initial shock, her expression severe. She spoke before Drexan could respond. "We don't barter with treasonous filth. That woman belongs to the Crown of Asteros, and she will be returned." At that, Kal's lips peeled back from gleaming teeth. Tavene ignored him. "As for you, thief…" She motioned to Drexan, who was liable to explode into violence at any moment. The monster stepped forward. "You'll be coming along as well. My king has special plans for you."

"The butcher king's plans will have to wait," Kal replied, voice low. "I'm a little busy this evening, so he'll get to keep his head a while longer."

Felíne's eyes flared.

"Bring him here, Drexan," Tavene spat. She drew her sword. "I'm going to cut that disrespectful tongue out of his mouth."

Drexan exploded forward like a beast unclipped from its master's leash. Felíne gasped. There was no way. Kal wouldn't even have time to evade, let alone draw a weapon. It wouldn't matter how many blades he had strapped to his frame if that powerhouse leveled him. One swing from the monstrous male had put Garren down, and he'd been in second form. Kal was significantly more vulnerable in first. Why, then, hadn't he shifted?

Felíne didn't get a chance to further contemplate. The giant blond male's arms spread wide as he barreled on, intending to crush Kal in a deadly embrace. Two powerful limbs swept forward and closed on nothingness. Drexan's momentum pitched him ahead, rage rippling to confusion.

Felíne had thought Tavene flowed like water, but Kal moved like wind. No shurii man could move like that. One moment, he stood in Drexan's path, the next, he was to the male's right flank. Kal hammered a sickening kick into the bigger male's ankle as he passed. Something crunched. Felíne's stomach knotted, and Drexan roared in pain and fury. The small crossbow Kal carried was leveled in the time it took Felíne to blink. He shot two surreptitious bolts into the giant's back.

Drexan turned, furious blue eyes hazed with bloodlust. He rushed Kal again, hardly phased by the arrows sticking out of his back or his injured foot. Kal blocked a blow heavy enough to crush a stone wall like a pebble tower. How his forearms didn't shatter, Felíne had no idea. Drexan reloaded his fist, but Kal spun at the last possible second, dropping his bow and uncoiling the length of silver that wound up one arm. He slipped the reflective cord around one of Drexan's wrists as he turned and cranked the noose, pulling the great male's blond arm back at a painful angle. Drexan made to swing his free arm around in the opposite direction to catch Kal off guard, using his sheer power to his advantage. The strategy likely worked for him in a hundred previous battles. Not this one.

Kal captured Drexan's other hand with the remaining length of silver in one effortless motion and cinched them together behind his back. Something in Drexan's shoulder popped, and the beast roared. Kal brought his foot down onto the male's injured ankle with merciless force. The bones in the weakened limb fractured with a nauseating crunch. Drexan toppled.

Felíne's hope soared, but Kal had no time to celebrate. Tavene gushed forward, sword slashing ahead at staggering speed. Kalevar's knees bent, torso dipping backward at an impossible angle as the deadly silver flashed inches overhead. Kal twisted to the side, somehow managing to retrieve and reload his bow, and fired another two shots in Tavene's direction with one hand while the other dropped to the ground to brace the weight of his movement. She dodged them easily, the bolts shooting off into the desert, missing the female by a hair's breadth.

Tavene smiled smugly.

Kal discarded the bow and slipped two thick knives out of their sheaths.

Tavene wasted no time. She rushed him again, bringing her sword around in a terrifying arc. Kal somehow anticipated its course and caught the impact on the cross-guards of his own weapons. Tavene's sword was pitched to the side, but it didn't deter her. Kal had no chance to counter. She adjusted, turning her body away from Kal, and stabbed backward, aiming for his mid-section.

He spun, avoiding being skewered, and used the trajectory to his advantage. Felíne soon recognized that Kal didn't waste precious energy on theatrics. His movements were deliberate, intentional, and efficient. There was no fancy dancing. No unnecessary flourishes. He flipped one blade as he turned and brought it down in a wicked thrust. Kal aimed for the hollow between Tavene's neck and shoulder. Had he connected, it would have meant instant death, but Tavene reeled just in time, the blade grazing harmlessly off her chest armor.

Two more blows were exchanged. Three. Four. The fighters were exceptionally trained. Their styles differed, but they were evenly matched in skill. Tavene was a dancer, light on her feet, fluid, her sword an extension of her arm. Kal was a hurricane. Exploding, spinning, hammering every ounce of effort out of his opponent with brutal, beautiful efficiency. They had to be exhausted, yet neither slowed.

They were, however, both thoroughly engaged, which meant neither was paying attention to her. Felíne wrenched her bound hands to the side, causing a terrible ache to fire in her left shoulder. With one palm firmly grasping the hilt of her hatchet, she fumbled awkwardly until it came loose from the lovely holder Kal had fashioned for her. Trying very hard not to cut off her fingers, she wedged the handle between her wrists and a nearby stone and began sawing through her binding.

Kal and Tavene clashed again. This time, Tavene's sword came away bloody. Kal didn't even bother inspecting the wound, and Felíne couldn't tell where he'd been injured. Judging by Tavene's expression, it wasn't serious enough to hinder him. Kal dropped the larger daggers and unsheathed two smaller knives instead. He sent them flying toward his enemy with an invisible flick of his wrists. Tavene dodged the first and sent the second spiraling into the desert with a slash of her blade.

Kal bent as though to retrieve his long knives, projectiles depleted.

The third blade appeared in his hand as if by magic; even Felíne hadn't seen him reach for it. Kal sent it hurtling toward Tavene. The female hadn't been expecting it and couldn't fully avoid it. It took her in the right shoulder.

Tavene yelled in frustration, transferred her grasp to her left, and unleashed a flurry of swipes. Kal darted forward to grab his knives off the ground. He dodged and parried, pressed back by the attack. One of his knives was wrenched from his grip, whirling into the dirt.

Felíne sawed faster. Her hand slipped, and she felt the sting of steel followed by the trickle of blood. A small noise of pained surprise escaped her. Kal's attention flicked in her direction for a fraction of a second.

A fraction was all Tavene needed. Her sword cut ferociously to the side, aiming to take Kal's head clean off his shoulders. He leaned in at the last moment, and the blade connected with the side of his helm instead.

Felíne cried out. Kal grunted. The helm careened to the side, rolling into the dirt. Thank the gods, his head was no longer in it.

Felíne watched as Kal went to one knee, his back to her, and shook his head to clear the ringing in his skull. His other long knife had been lost during the impact. A trickle of blood dripped from one ear. Tavene bled from a busted lip, and the hilt of Kal's dagger still protruded from her right shoulder. Felíne would have forgotten it was there if not for the arm hanging limply at the female's side.

Kal hadn't forgotten and he recognized an opportunity. He unsheathed the twin short swords housed along his back. Tavene tensed. Kal surged forward without preamble, his foe's death in his sights. The moonlight broke through the cloud cover and glinted off the slightly curved blades.

Felíne's binding broke with a quiet snap. She tore the remaining rope from her wrists.

Kal descended upon Tavene like a dark angel. The female made to block. Someone roared, and Felíne screamed, scrambling to her feet.

Kal's final blow didn't land. He was lifted off the earth from behind, arms pinned to his sides in a crippling blond grip. Drexan stood on his ruined ankle, his clawed foot twisted at a horrible angle, two thick bolts still protruding from his back. Bloodied wrists crossed over Kal's chest, one of them cut to the bone. Kal's silver cord was embedded in the flesh of the other, dangling where Drexan had finally snapped it.

"Now you die, cunt," Drexan growled. He squeezed his great biceps. Kal ground his teeth against the mounting pressure. Even his armor was no match for Drexan's brutality. Something cracked. Kal grimaced, fighting the inevitable. Drexan snarled and squeezed again. Kal's dark head reared back, and a groan of agony forced its way up his throat as his bones were ground together.

No! Felíne had never felt so small, so powerless. The moment held her suspended, doomed to watch Kal die in his attempt to save her. *No, she couldn't let this happen!*

Tavene strode forward with her ruined arm. "Stop."

Drexan didn't look like he wanted to obey, but he loosened his grip. Kal sagged, sweat-drenched curls falling forward as he clung to consciousness.

"As much as I'd love to watch Drexan grind your bones to dust, I want even more to see the delight in King Domitan's eyes when I throw you bound and gagged at his feet." Tavene smiled. Blood stained her teeth. "But first, I promised to cut that filthy tongue from your mouth."

Kal slowly lifted his head and glared pure defiance. Tavene sheathed her sword. She gripped the hilt of Kal's dagger with her left hand and, with an awful noise, wrenched the blade free of her right shoulder. Even the king's elite huntress was not immune to pain. She panted as the agony washed over her. Then she lifted the blade to Kal's face. "Say, ah."

"Argh!"

Kal's arms were pinned to his sides, but his feet were unrestrained. He kicked his right foot back into Drexan's shin with an obliging roar, activating some hidden mechanism. Felíne caught the flash of pointed steel flip out of the toe of Kal's boot before he raised his knee and kicked out viciously. Once, twice, three times, he connected, sinking the concealed blade into Tavene's abdomen.

The female staggered in shock. She dropped Kal's dagger, and her left arm cradled her belly. She slumped to the ground, seeping blood.

Drexan cried out like a wounded animal as he watched his leader fall. Kal wasn't out of danger yet. Drexan lifted him even higher, arching back as he tried to turn Kalevar's warrior body to pulp in his rage. Kal screamed.

Felíne fisted the handle of her hatchet and bolted forward. She raised the weapon above her head in a two-handed grip and brought it down with all her might. The head of the axe sunk into flesh with a thud. Drexan grunted. It was a sloppy hit. Her blade wedged into the muscle of Drexan's middle back but didn't sink deep enough to do any real damage. She was still holding the handle. Felíne wrenched back, trying to dislodge the weapon.

Drexan twisted his great snarling snout, finally distracted. Hate-filled eyes landed on Felíne. Forced to abandon her only means of self-defense, she released the handle and retreated several paces.

Drexan dropped Kal like a sack of grain as he rounded on her. He took a step forward, and his ruined foot crunched unpleasantly. It had to be excruciatingly painful, but the beast ignored it as he advanced. "Not a little lamb, after all," Drexan said, maw dripping bloody saliva. "Just a tiny buzzing bee."

Felíne backed up again, panic infusing her limbs. Drexan stalked her, taking his time. Not because he had to but because he wanted her frightened. He wanted her to feel hunted, helpless.

He succeeded magnificently.

"You seem to have lost your stinger, little bee." Drexan reached behind him and pulled her hatchet from his back with a stomach-turning lurch. It was dwarfed in his clawed hand.

He had her cornered. Felíne backed up to a tangle of desert thorn bushes too thick to navigate. Her pant leg snagged on a particularly nasty limb, and she tugged at it furiously, ripping the fabric and ensnaring it further. Drexan towered over her, eyes lit with maddened glee.

"Do you know what happens when a bee loses its stinger?"

Felíne stopped struggling and faced the giant, forcing calm into her racing heart. She swallowed, voice quiet but surprisingly steady. "It dies."

Drexan's maw split in an awful grin. He crouched low, ready to pounce. "But not before it signals the hive."

Kalevar reared up behind Drexan with silent ferocity and plunged twin short swords simultaneously into either side of the male's supraclavicular fossa. That delicate space on either side of the neck through which major blood vessels passed. Drexan didn't have a prayer. The mountain crumbled, arterial blood spurting from the wounds as Kal retracted his blades with a savage snarl.

She watched as the murderous rage faded out of the beast's blue eyes for the final time. The stillness of the night was sudden and complete.

Felíne sucked in a rush of air as though she'd forgotten to breathe the past ten minutes and was starving for it. Her chest hurt, and her courage crumpled. A strangled half sob escaped her on an exhale.

CLOAKING FATE

They were dead. The monsters who had come to drag her home. Those hunters who would have brought merciless slaughter to an entire settlement of people. They were dead. The people of Cindamar were safe, for now.

Felíne raised her bleary-eyed gaze to a pair of hardened onyx eyes shot through with brilliant gold. Kalevar. He came for her. He risked his life, broke his body…for her. To get her back.

Kal dropped his blades and stepped over Drexan's corpse. He didn't stop when he reached her. Kal's broad hands came up with possessiveness to cradle either side of her face. He was bleeding again. He'd been hurt. Before Felíne could even formulate the words of her concern, Kal's mouth came down over hers.

It wasn't gentle. It wasn't tentative. It was nothing like she imagined being kissed would feel. Yet something inside of her ignited.

Kal's hungry, possessive kiss consumed her. He tasted like woodsmoke and honeyed bourbon and something intoxicatingly masculine that lit Felíne's blood on fire. She didn't even know how, but she kissed him back, her body arching instinctively into his, her lips parting for his tongue. Kal's hand wove into her hair, which had come halfway undone during her capture and fell in a tangle to one side. His other hand gripped her waist. The stupid boning of her corset restricted her. Too much fabric. She wanted his hands everywhere. His mouth everywhere. Felíne was *alive*. She never felt anything in her life like she felt in that moment, and if he didn't touch her, she would die. She was sure of it.

A whimper escaped Felíne's lips into Kal's mouth, and she lifted a hand to touch the stubble of his cheek. He made a guttural noise of male need and deepened the kiss. His hands fisted in the fabric of her clothing, and he tugged her against his body.

Closer. She needed to get closer to him. Something was holding her, pulling her back from him. Somewhere in the shriveled rational part of her brain, she realized the silky material of her pant leg was still snared in the thornbush behind her.

Kal pulled back abruptly as if breaking free from a trance and rested his forehead against hers. Their breath mingled, both panting, not from exertion but something else entirely. The strong column of his throat worked on a swallow.

Minutes passed, then Kal touched his lips to her forehead, mindful of the abrasion at her temple. His hands came tentatively back to her face, and he assessed her, eyes still more golden than usual but not as intense as before. They were suffused with concern and brimming with what Felíne now knew with absolute certainty was desire. A desire that her own honey-green gaze undoubtedly mirrored.

"Are you alright?"

No, she thought. *You stopped kissing me.*

She nodded. "I think so."

Kal's eyes closed briefly, and he let out a breath of relief. When he opened them again, his lips curved into a slight smile, one dimple winking. "I think you saved my life."

Felíne laughed shakily, caught off guard by his teasing. "Not very well."

"Well enough," he said, glancing back at Drexan's motionless form.

Felíne shuddered. Kal pulled her clothing free of the thorns, then led her around the fallen beast and back toward the clearing.

"Are *you* alright? You're bleeding."

Kal made a noncommittal noise. "I'll live."

Felíne's attention snagged on Drexan's corpse. "He tried to crush you…"

Kal stopped. "Hey," he said, tilting her chin back to him. "I'm okay."

Felíne nodded but she wasn't convinced. "Will you at least let me assess your injuries this time?"

He paused, something unreadable in his expression. "Yes. Later."

The heat in her blood receded, and the events of the evening seeped back in to cool her head. "Thank you, Kal," she said. "For coming for me."

He regarded her, features softening. "Wherever you go, I will follow," he said, voice low. "Package deal, remember?"

Something in his words made Felíne's eyes well with tears. He'd said them before. Earlier in Cindamar, sitting in the center garden, sipping nectar. Then, he'd been referring to following her around the market, a teasing lilt to his tone. Kal wasn't teasing now. He said these words not out of duty-bound obligation but with a sense of protective regard. As though she mattered to him. Not because of what she was or to whom she belonged but because of *who* she was becoming to him. And…who he was becoming to her.

She reached out to squeeze his hand and took a steadying breath.

The sound of horse hooves thundered in the distance. After a moment, Kal left her to stalk around the clearing, collecting weapons that had been thrown or discarded during his battle. His movements were more reserved. He likely had a fractured humerus, and she wouldn't be surprised if several ribs were cracked. Tavene had also taken a gouge out of his left flank, but other than that, Kal thankfully hadn't sustained any life-threatening injuries. Drexan's body, on the other hand, lay in a terrible heap across the space, and Felíne made every effort to ignore it.

Three horses arrived, frothing and snorting—one riderless, the others carrying a pair of cloaked riders accompanied by two shurii in second form on foot. One male with a shaggy iron pelt, she recognized.

Devereux Santaire prowled forward, icy gray eyes surveying the scene. They landed on her. "Alright there, love?"

Felíne offered a tired smile. "I'll live. Thanks to Kal."

He nodded, some of the tension leaving his shoulders. "Glad to hear it."

"You're fucking late," Kal called from where he crouched over Drexan's body, inspecting his broken, blood-crusted silver cord. His brows pinched in disappointment as he fingered the shimmery length.

Adder scented the air. "Looks to me like you made out well enough without us, mate."

Us. Oh Gods.

"Adder…" Felíne's throat knotted, and thundercloud eyes turned back to hers in question. "I'm so sorry. Ophelia…I—"

Adder placed a clawed hand tenderly on her shoulder. "Don't even think it, love." He turned then, and Felíne watched the smaller of the two horsemen dismount. Ophelia lowered her hood, exposing fiery hair and wide-set loamy eyes. "What about me are you so sorry for?"

Felíne did cry then, the shock of seeing the tough little female alive suddenly too much to contain. She rushed forward and gripped the woman in a fierce hug.

Ophelia patted her back a bit hesitantly and addressed Kal over Felíne's shoulder. "You sure she's okay? I think she suffered a concussion."

Felíne pulled back. "I'm fine, you idiot. I thought you died at the venue."

"It wasn't Oph," Adder said. "That fucking coward—pardon my language—used one of the wedding staff as a shield when he realized Ophelia would best him. He killed her and took off into the city."

Felíne's heart squeezed for another nameless victim.

"We got him, though. He'll not harm another soul."

The two remaining shurii, one of them the burly, serious male called Shaw, spoke quietly with Kal before approaching Drexan's body. Kal made his way to where Felíne stood with Ophelia and Adder.

"On second thought, you look like you got your shit rocked, mate."

Kal leveled hard eyes on Adder. "We have an issue. The female huntress. Her body is missing."

Tavene.

Impossible. Felíne craned around to the spot where Tavene had fallen. A dark mark stained the ground, but the female was nowhere in sight. But how? Kal had practically disemboweled her with that concealed blade.

"What does she look like?" Ophelia asked.

Kal opened his mouth to reply, but it was Felíne who spoke. "It was Evie."

All three of them looked at her. Ophelia's eyes narrowed.

"She...she pretended to be a guest at the wedding. To try and get me alone."

Kal's now-black eyes churned with a fresh wave of rage.

"Where?" Ophelia demanded.

Kal pointed. "Both of the horses are gone. She's wounded, but don't underestimate her. She'll be flying toward Asteros as fast as that poor beast can carry her."

Ophelia nodded without a word and returned to her mount. She disappeared into the dark, leaving a cloud of dust behind her.

Kal looked at Felíne questioningly. He wanted to know what he'd missed after he left her with Ophelia at the venue. She shook her head. *Later,* she tried to say. *It doesn't matter now, anyway.* He seemed to understand and let it drop.

Adder eyed Drexan's corpse as it was hauled past them to be returned to the Trade Master of Cindamar. He whistled through pointed teeth. "Gods, that's a big fucker, Kal." When Shaw and the other male were a safe distance away, he added, "You know Grisham is going to demand answers. Three elite hunters from Asteros show up on his doorstep, murder his new brother-in-law, terrorize his citizens, and kill two women. Tonight devolved into fucking chaos. He will want to know why."

Felíne thought she was too tired to feel anything else, but she was wrong. That familiar nagging fear crept up her neck. Of course, Grisham would want answers. The problem was that all of those answers pointed directly at her.

Kal looked at her, seeming to sense her unease. Adder followed his gaze. "I'll handle it," he said.

Adder nodded. He turned and collected the reins of the additional mount and handed them to Kal. "What are you going to tell him?"

Kal still watched her. "The truth," he replied simply.

Felíne's heart grew heavy. If only the truth were a simple thing.

Chapter 45

Plans and Pleas

OPHELIA NEVER FOUND TAVENE. SHE searched for hours, even enlisting help from Shaw, and eventually returned empty-handed. By the time the morning sun broke the horizon, the swordswoman was either a meal for the desert beasts or well on her way back to Asteros and Felíne's father. Even the slim possibility of the latter meant the residents of Cindamar needed to flee.

Kalevar's conversation with Grisham was tense. Gradual livid realization bled into the Trade Master's features at Kal's tale. His cherished sister's future had been irrevocably changed, his only brother and battle champion lay injured, and his precious, profitable city faced future annihilation at the hands of the Asterosian army.

Luckily for her, Grisham directed the majority of his anger at Kal. All because he stole a Fated Mother from the capital city and snuck her in under the Trade Master's nose. They'd been reckless. Irresponsible. How could Kal not assume they'd be followed? How could he bring that kind of trouble to Cindamar? Kal overestimated his evasiveness. Pompous. Foolish. He'd have been better off wandering the desert and leaving their sun-bleached bones for the hunters to find rather than lead them straight here. Grisham berated Kal with color and enthusiasm. Kal withstood the assault like a solemn pillar of stone.

Felíne tried to imagine the look on Grisham's face if he knew it was the Prima of Asteros that had wandered into his city instead of a Fate. He'd likely suffer an apoplexy.

Then again, so would Kal.

CLOAKING FATE

While her savior shouldered the remainder of their collective verbal beating, Felíne busied herself by offering aid to those injured in the chaos.

The medical tent was less occupied than expected for the terrors she'd witnessed, and she was grateful. Cindamar boasted two full-time menders that flitted between patients who'd entered the previous evening with broken bones, abrasions, minor head injuries, one deep laceration to a thigh, and several superficial burns. Some who came seeking treatment suffered the after effects of emotional trauma rather than physical ailment.

Felíne soaked clean rags in boiling water, crushed fragrant herbs for poultices, delivered salves, and threaded sterilized gut-string through fine needles for suture. She held hands and offered condolences and murmured to a weeping woman. The familiar rhythm of work acted as an elixir to her anxieties. Felíne found herself soothed by the activity. It felt nice to be useful again.

An hour into her work, two guards forced a thoroughly disgruntled and most unwilling patient into the tent, causing considerable commotion.

Felíne looked up from the table and paused. She never imagined she'd be relieved to see the brute who entered.

A fully awake Garren spit a flurry of choice expletives at the two armored males who manhandled him.

"Trade Master's orders, Garren. You're still bleeding all over the damned place."

Garren tried to chin-check the burly male and was blocked. "To hell with the Trade Master's orders. I'm your godsdamned superior! Get your fucking paws off me."

They forced him onto an empty cot.

"Mender! This one's in need of patching," the other male called.

Mender Lew, a portly young shurii, hurried over with a few supplies and made an unsuccessful attempt at assessing Garren's injuries. Garren was in first form, and even she could see the blood staining his clothing from where she sat across the tent. The unwilling patient's companions stepped back to give the mender some space but stayed close enough to intervene if needed.

"I told you I'm fucking fine." He eyed the young mender with a gaze that could have chilled the boiling water Felíne had been tending.

"Remove your shirt, please." Mender Lew made the mistake of reaching for Garren's hem when his patient made no move to comply. Garren nearly knocked him back on his considerable rear. The mender stumbled into the guards, one of whom righted him. Mender Lew adjusted his glasses, huffing in indignation.

Felíne approached, carrying a tray of clean linen, a tin of thick salve, a few instruments, and her gut-string sutures.

Garren glared at her with open hostility from his perch on the cot's edge. His unkempt earthy brown hair hung loosely over his forehead. The scar marring his lip made his scowl even more intimidating. The last time she'd seen him, his claws had been around her neck, and he'd proclaimed her a traitor.

"May I?" she asked.

They all looked at her.

Garren's handsome features twisted into an ugly sneer. "No," he said. "You don't owe me a damned thing. I said I'm fine." At this, he looked at his companions. "I'm fucking leaving."

One male stepped up.

"Actually, I do," Felíne said, and Garren's attention flicked back to her. "I do owe you. You were wrong; I'm no traitor. But I am the reason those hunters were here. I can't give you back what you lost, but I can keep you from losing any more."

Garren leaned forward with an intensity that she was becoming increasingly accustomed to being on the receiving end of. "What the fuck do you know about loss?"

Felíne leveled with him. "You might be surprised," she said. "But I was talking about your blood, Garren. You aren't much use to your brother leaking like a punctured waterskin."

She nodded, and he glanced down at himself. Crimson stained his ivory linen shirt in a number of places. A tense silence ensued. After a moment, he turned his glower on his companions. "If the two of you don't quit hovering, I'm having you fucking demoted." Then to Felíne, "I don't have all godsdamned day, woman. If you're gonna do something useful, get on with it."

Garren yanked the soiled shirt over his head, revealing a broad chest covered in coffee-colored hair and a thick torso. More scars than Felíne could count at a glance peppered his tanned skin. One of the new lacerations Tavene had bestowed stretched with his movement and began seeping anew. The guards retreated, having established that Garren intended to behave at least moderately, and Mender Lew returned to more beholden patients.

Felíne got to work cleaning and suturing the visible wounds that had been added to his collection. Garren sat silent and unmoving while she sewed, soil eyes fixed somewhere over her head.

It was miraculous that Garren had only suffered a concussion after the hit he'd sustained. Drexan's blow should have caved his skull. The resilient design of the second form awed Felíne. No way something so intricately, expertly made could be an abomination. The menders here instructed their patients to shift after treatment and remain in second form for a prescribed amount of time based on their injuries. The Godking's form would ensure they healed at nearly double the rate they would in first. If Garren complied, his skin would be scarred over sooner than the stitches would dissolve.

Felíne could only imagine how much more effective their therapies would be if the people of Asteros harnessed the capabilities of the second form instead of demonizing it. Did those thoughts make her a pagan? What would the Goddess do if her chosen Prima admitted to sympathizing with those living outside the teachings of the Faithful Cursed? Find her unworthy? Doubtful.

Not for the first time, she found herself curious about what Kal would have to say on the matter. He'd told her she'd been taught wrong. That they all had. She made another mental note to ask him what exactly he'd meant.

Felíne tied off the last stitch and cut the gut-string. She smeared salve over the final visible wound to help seal her work and ward off infection. "Almost finished," she said. "There's just the one on your thigh."

Felíne turned away from Garren to retrieve another suture. When she looked back, she paused.

Garren leaned forward, forearms braced on his knees, a predatory glint in his eye. His expression was devoid of his usual malice and replaced with something she didn't wish to contemplate too closely.

"You're gonna have to do better than that if you want me dropping my pants for you, pet."

Felíne blinked. "That's not..."

Garren didn't wait for her to finish. He slipped the blood-stained shirt back over his head—causing her to cringe at the filthy fabric contaminating his freshly cleaned wounds—rose, and stalked out of the tent without another word. Garren's guards stepped forward, thanked her curtly, and followed him out.

Felíne sat back. She supposed she was finished, after all.

Kalevar sent word through Ophelia that he'd concluded with Grisham and would meet her back at their room at The Inn after he handled a few final tasks. Exhausted, but feeling more fulfilled than she had in days, Felíne relinquished the now-soiled apron she'd worn to cover Policarpa's grime-laden pantsuit and left the medical tent in search of someone she dreaded facing but knew she must.

The hazy late morning sun cast the city in a tangible gloom. Grisham had given the order to move. It amazed her how many of Cindamar's citizens compartmentalized the events of the previous evening, setting them aside like another box of belongings to unpack at a later time after they relocated somewhere safe and could afford the vulnerability it would take to deal with them. The few who had sought help in the menders' tent were but a small fraction of those affected by yesterday's events. The rest threw themselves into action. Not thinking, not processing, just doing.

Felíne wandered until she found herself in the venue that just hours ago had been packed with people celebrating. Now, it was the one place inside the city that seemed deserted. None of the mess had been cleaned. Tables were overturned, chairs lay broken, and a drink cart had spilled its contents, leaving scattered broken glass strewn in a burst on the floor. Several lonely shoes had been abandoned and forgotten. Plates of food were half-eaten, and a dessert tray still held a perfectly frosted small cake.

Leaden weights suddenly anchored Felíne's feet. Her saliva dried up. Her hand dropped to her side and found the reassuring weight of her hatchet. There had been blood crusted on the edge of the blade when it was retrieved from Drexan's body. Kal must have cleaned it for her before returning it, possibly trying to insulate her from the brutality. She would have worn it regardless. After last night, she would likely never take it off again.

She'd been mistaken, Felíne realized. The venue wasn't entirely deserted after all. A lone figure sat near the platform at the water's edge, where the jasmine flowers drooped dourly from their arch. Last night, they'd been radiant. Now, they looked in mourning.

Felíne found Meryl perched at a table splintered at some point in the chaos. A crack ran along one edge, and a deep gouge fissured into the once-polished wood. It leaned unsteadily to the side. The jubilant bride with glowing aqua eyes and sleek blonde hair that Felíne met yesterday vanished. In her place hunched the shell of a recently beautiful creature hollowed by sudden, unimaginable loss.

Meryl's dulled eyes stared lifelessly ahead at the still pool. Felíne eased down carefully next to her. Meryl didn't seem to notice or care. Next to them, lazy smoke wafted up from the smoldering remains of an overturned firepit.

They sat in silence, watching the glassy surface of water. Blood still stained the platform in front of them—Boden's blood.

"Meryl," Felíne whispered, heart breaking for the young widow. "I'm so sorry." And she was. The depth of which she hadn't fully understood until now. Guilt punched her. Those hunters. The death that resulted from them being here. Even the death that preceded their involvement. First, the soldiers in Asteros. Then Brune. Now Boden Ceen and the nameless women. Grisham's guards. They were added to the list of casualties Felíne meticulously carved into the flesh of her heart. She reached out and touched Meryl's elbow.

The bride just stared ahead. "Bo's mother died in childbirth when he was young. He would have had a sister." The words cracked, void of the emotion that must be churning beneath the placid surface of Meryl's damaged shell. "When his father died, Bo told me he couldn't marry me. He said he was cursed to lose the people he loved, and if I married him, I would die, too. He would be forced to live the rest of his life in misery because fate would take me from him."

Oh, Meryl...

She laughed a harsh, bitter sound. "I told him he was being ridiculous. That he was afraid for nothing. I told him I didn't believe in curses."

Felíne grasped her hand and squeezed. Meryl finally turned her tortured aqua gaze, and Felíne's heart splintered further. "I believe in them now," she whispered.

"It's my fault," Felíne choked.

Meryl returned to staring at the water. A slight ripple marred its surface where a fish or frog disturbed the shallows. "How?"

Felíne told her. She yearned to tell it all. The real version. The truth. Instead, she told her the same version Kal told Grisham. The story they all believed to be true. The one she knew was a lie.

"They were here for me," she finished. "Those hunters came and…killed because I was here. I put everyone here in danger."

Meryl watched her for a long moment, thinking. "It wasn't your fault, Kitty," she said finally. "You didn't even know Cindamar existed before Kal brought you here."

"I should have been more careful. We should have told your brother immediately upon entering the city. Kal covered our trail. He didn't think they would come this far, but…" Then, the truth did become too heavy to hold inside of her. "But I *knew*," Felíne whispered. Hot, angry tears spilled. "I knew they wouldn't let me go. My responsibility is too great. I am too important. I knew, and I said nothing."

Meryl's delicate brow quivered. "Yes," she said. "Maybe if you had said something, Bo and Mara and Stell would still be alive. And my brother's men: Bodemere and Fenn and Harris, too."

Felíne flinched.

"And maybe they would have died anyway," Meryl continued. "Now, it doesn't matter. The maybes don't count for a damn thing." Meryl's lip trembled and she fisted her hands. "Boden is dead. He's not coming back."

Meryl stood, suddenly restless.

"Your brother is mobilizing the city," Felíne said. "You all have to leave. You have to go somewhere safe. More hunters will come." She knew it with a certainty that saturated the very fiber of her being. Even if Tavene was dead, even if she never made it back to Asteros to report to Felíne's father, the king and queen would scour Ilistaar looking for her. They'd exhaust every possible resource, kill anyone who got in their way, make any sacrifice to get her back. Until Felíne could figure out how to return on her own, *everyone* was in danger.

CLOAKING FATE

Meryl stooped and dipped her fingers in ash from the ruined fire. She dragged the soot across her face, painting a jagged slash the color of death. She looked like Kal had when he'd come for her last night. It wasn't black for mourning; it was black for war.

"Asteros has stood unchecked for too long," she said. "Power and prosperity and greed sucking the lifeblood out of the land. They don't mean to save the shurii people. They've been slowly strangling them for years." A chill skittered down Felíne's spine. "They push their agendas, force their false religion, and persecute anyone who disagrees. Families torn apart. Communities burned to ash. Lives laid to waste. People who only hoped for a piece of quiet. A simple, happy life." Felíne knew she saw the future she'd hoped for, the one she'd counted on, slowly disintegrating. Meryl wiped the remaining soot on her priceless, once-white gown. Claws tipped her fingers instead of neatly manicured nails. The female's eyes glowed with blue fire in stark contrast to her blackened face. "Let the hunters come. This time, we'll be ready for them."

Felíne found Kal in their shared room at The Inn. He'd already packed her things. Filth coated her in an unwanted layer, and exhaustion permeated every sinuous fiber, but her current physical state didn't even phase her. A shift in perspective could be a real slap in the face.

"You have to take me back."

There were things she wanted to ask him. Things they needed to discuss. But none of that mattered compared to this. Felíne had to make him understand.

Kal looked up from tying his bag. His attention made her skin tingle.

"I just spoke with Meryl. She's going to urge Grisham to stand against Asteros."

Kal straightened. Why didn't he look as concerned as she felt?

"Grisham doesn't need urging," he said. "Asterosian hunters attacked his city and killed his citizens."

"Because of me."

472

Kal frowned. "If we're playing the blame game, technically, they were here because of me. It was my actions that sent them hunting in the first place. No one blames you, Kitty."

Why did everyone keep saying that? The only one blaming her was herself. But only because they didn't know what she knew. "They should," she muttered.

"Why?" Kal said with an intensity that surprised her. "Because you were practically enslaved? Devalued and dehumanized? Treated little better than a piece of livestock? A pretty broodmare to be abused, forced to produce, and then thrown away when her value finally fell below their impossible standards? And for what? So some spoiled brat of a princess elevated by some bullshit prophecy could sit in her tranquil palace garden and keep from getting her hands dirty?"

Shock ripped through Felíne. And…hurt. Was that how people viewed her? A pampered, privileged royal content to justify her people's sufferings to avoid sacrificing her own considerable comforts? Was that how *Kal* viewed her? *No*, she reminded herself, throat tightening. He didn't view her at all, did he? Felíne Lochlan Faelstrom, the Prima of Asteros, was little more than an obscure concept to him.

An obscure concept he didn't believe in. It cut her. Deeper than it should have.

"No, Kitty," he continued, oblivious to her inner torment. "No one blames you for escaping that hellscape. Least of all me."

Felíne shook her head, attempting to bury her wounds, to refocus. "I suppose it doesn't matter," she said. "What *does* matter is mitigating the risk that's been incurred as a result of my being here. You have to explain this to Grisham."

"Grisham knows the risk," Kal said. "What's done can't be undone. The man's got a mind for war."

Was no one hearing her? "There won't be a war, Kal. There won't even be a battle. It will be a massacre! My—" she swallowed. "The King's army will annihilate the people of Cindamar. They don't stand a chance against that kind of power."

"No faith, dear Kitty?"

He said it lightly, trying to lift her out of the pessimistic pit she'd fallen into. The effort was wasted. "Faith has nothing to do with it," she said adamantly. Hadn't he just made that abundantly clear? "This is a fact. Look at the damage three hunters did in a few hours. Think of what three hundred would do." And that was only a fraction of the number in her father's employ. Grisham might have his guard, but they were like a handful of stones tossed against the face of a mountain.

Kal watched her a moment, banter fading. "They will stand a chance." He spoke matter-of-factly, as if saying it made it so.

She narrowed her eyes, irritation spiking. "Funny. Meryl said the same thing when I tried to reason with her. What makes you so sure, exactly?"

"I've made some arrangements."

Of course he had. "Such as?"

Kal sighed and ran a hand through his still-damp hair, the short ends curling. His face was no longer war-painted, and his clothes were clean. Felíne noticed steam wafting from the tub, realizing fresh hot water had been poured recently, likely in anticipation of her arrival. The thought would have touched her under different circumstances. He continued. "My return to Cindamar was not unintentional. Grisham has been trying to broker a trade deal with me for some time now. A request I've been content to ignore until recently."

"One you previously promised to deliver on?"

Kal nodded.

Felíne crossed her arms. "What kind of deal?"

Kal moved to the edge of the mattress and sat as though standing suddenly required more effort than he was willing to give. He didn't answer, deciding how much to tell her. His hesitation stung, though Felíne had no real claim to his loyalty or confidence.

"I have…knowledge," he said at last.

One question only led to another. She took the bait. Again. "What kind of knowledge?"

"The kind that should have died with me when it died with my family. The kind worth killing to possess."

Her eyebrows crept up. "I can't imagine any knowledge worth dying for," she said sincerely. "Seems a bit counterintuitive." The dead couldn't use what they knew, after all. Not in this realm, anyway.

Kal gifted her a slight, sad smile. "If only the royals and warlords shared your sentiment. My mother and father did. It is why my family was so selective in sharing it."

Felíne frowned. "And this…knowledge you possess. You've shared it with the Trade Master?"

"In a manner of speaking."

Felíne pinched the bridge of her nose. A headache throbbed behind her right eye, and her frustration bloomed. "I have no patience for riddles, Kal. You either trust me or you don't. If you do, then please, for divine's sake, speak plainly. And if not, then just…leave me."

He sat back, intensity hyperfocusing on her in a way entirely unique to him. She stared back. He was heartbreaking, sitting there with his short, dark curls and midnight eyes. He aggravated her endlessly, and yet she still craved his closeness. The way he'd kissed her, yearned for her, surfaced readily in her mind as if her body would now keep that memory on instant recall so that she could torture herself on command. She had no right to it, had done nothing to deserve it, but she *wanted* him to trust her.

A long moment stretched as they sat silently studying one another. Then Kal spoke, decision made.

"My mother came from a long line of weapons masters. Her father was undeniably the most famous swordsman in an age. They called him the Bladesinger of Ilistaar. Not only could he wield virtually any bladed weapon with exceptional skill, but his family specialized in crafting uniquely superior blades. One in particular that would fragment upon entering the body of a viable target. In the hands of a novice, it was little better than a child's toy, breaking too easily to be considered a threat. But in a master's hands, these blades guaranteed the death of any enemy, no matter the strength or skill. All of this knowledge and ability was passed to my mother."

Felíne saw Kal in her memory as he'd been last night in the desert. The fierce, fearless way he fought. The confidence in his movements, his unshakable resolve. Kal was more than just well-trained. More than disciplined. He was a warrior born. The abilities he possessed had been imparted to him on a generational level.

"My father, on the other hand, was an artisan armorer and a brilliant scientist. He had a naturally insatiable curiosity about the world. Constantly exploring the way things worked and how they were connected." Kal's eyes grew distant as he spoke, hands resting in his lap. "During one of his pursuits, he discovered a way to meld a specific organic compound with traditional ore, which resulted in a nearly indestructible substance. He attempted to use this substance to enhance the armor he made, immediately realizing the potential application." Kal's lips tipped up with the ghost of familial pride. "It took him months, but he succeeded. His new armor was so durable, its wearer could take an unguarded hit from a heavy crossbow shot from six paces and sustain little more than a bruise. Yet, it was light and tensile enough to allow unrestricted movement. He called it *silverskin*."

Felíne's eyes widened in surprise. "The silver cord you'd used to bind Drexan's hands."

She'd read about the coveted substance. *Silverskin* armor was exceedingly rare. Some even said priceless. Only a finite number of pieces had ever been made, its mystery maker's method having never been documented. Countless had attempted to duplicate its composition, her father's scientists among them, with little success. Even Mender Alcuin, possibly the most intelligent man she knew, had spent some time trying to replicate it out of sheer curiosity. And that mystery armorer had been Kalevar's father.

Felíne was willing to bet every hot bath for the rest of her life that Kal carried the secret of that compound. He might be the last shurii alive who did. The revelation awed her.

Kal nodded and produced the length of *silverskin*, still stained with remnants of Drexan's blood. "It's not an original. Not one of my father's pieces, but it's close. My father's wouldn't have snapped." A shadow passed over his features. "Drexan would have fucking ripped his own hands off before breaking an original cord."

Felíne watched him. Pride lingered in his gaze, but a long-buried pain hovered under the surface.

"The Bladesinger's daughter and the infallible aegis," she mused, voice gentle. "Your parents must have been quite the power couple."

476

Kal's lips quirked. "Yes. They were. The Bladesinger's methods were famed. My mother's reputation preceded her. But very few knew my father was the original artisan of *silverskin*. That secret was closely kept."

To think. She'd been wrong. That *was* knowledge worth dying for. Her father would kill to get his hands on that information. She shuddered at the kind of power the king would possess if he obtained Kal's secret. The uncontested ruler of Asteros proved dangerous enough without it. A thought occurred to Felíne, and the blood drained from her face.

"Dear gods, Kal. Please don't tell me you sold that information to Grisham."

Kal huffed a humorless laugh. "I'll admit, I've made some questionable decisions in life, but I'm not *that* irresponsible."

Felíne sagged in relief.

"I just sold him enough weaponry and *silverskin* to outfit his entire personal guard while simultaneously solidifying myself as the single most important business connection Grisham has ever made."

Felíne barely stopped her jaw from gaping open. Did Kal have any idea what kind of wealth he dropped into the Trade Master's lap? It made the man's entire collection of riches pale in comparison. Not only would Grisham benefit personally by having secured a supply of deadly weapons and unmatched armor, but he could also potentially sell any piece for a considerable fortune. Of course, Kal knew this. He wasn't an idiot. But what had he been thinking? Did he trust Grisham that implicitly?

"What's in it for you?" she asked.

Kal raised a brow. "Unfathomable wealth?"

Nice try. Felíne shook her head. "Money is just a tool, utilized to achieve one's aims. Men who love money are slaves to their own greed." She leaned forward. "You're not a greedy man. So, what is it you're really after?"

Kalevar eyed her appreciatively. "I want Cindamar to take a side."

A side? She assumed Asteros was on one end, but who was on the other? Kal had verbally expressed his opposition to the crown, but he also hadn't claimed fealty to the Cozened either. Her father had made no secret of his enemies; they were many. So, with which of them did Kal sympathize? Regardless of his affiliations, Kal wanted Grisham's loyalty. Felíne stared. That meant...

"You knew," she said, disbelieving. "You knew the hunters would come for me. You led them straight here."

No. No, that couldn't be right. Would Kal allow an entire settlement of people to be endangered so recklessly? Would he intentionally lead Grisham into a dark corner so he could be the one to provide a lighted way out? To force the Trade Master's hand and ensure his compliance?

"I suspected you were important, but I had no way of knowing just how far the crown would go to get you back. Something I've been meaning to ask you, by the way." Felíne kept her face carefully neutral, but Kal kept going. "I didn't know the king would send his hunters, and I concealed our tracks well enough to fool all but the most skilled trackers, given the expedited nature of our departure. I underestimated Domitan. So, no. I didn't intentionally lead those killers to a defenseless city on the eve of my friend's wedding."

Felíne felt a modicum of relief.

"What I wanted was to present Grisham with the means to strengthen his position. To secure an alliance so that when the time came, he would be inclined to join my endeavors and lend his resources to my own. It's why Adder took steps to secure his position in Grisham's guard. He knew my plans. He's been hand-selecting recruits, training them, gaining their trust. I'd planned on all of this taking months, if not years, to accomplish." Kal's eyes softened. "Then your brother entangled me in his scheme to get you out of Asteros. Things…changed as a result."

Felíne's throat tightened.

"Those hunters finding us here was a terrible thing that happened to expedite my plans of stoking Grisham's slowly smoldering fire to blazing."

"And Asteros is the target."

"The Crown of Asteros is the target," Kal clarified. "Not its people."

Felíne didn't know how to feel. She cared for Kal. That much was undeniable at this point. She also cared about his people. Ophelia. Adder. Meryl. But she cared for her family, too. Despite their faults, despite the strained nature of their relationship and the way duty had diluted her tie to them, Domitan and Serebine were still her parents. She wanted them held accountable for their wrongs, knew change was imperative, but she didn't want them to die. War meant death. She'd had enough of that weighing her conscience.

Then there was the matter of who she was. Her purpose. It was perhaps the one thing that truly *did* matter in the grand scheme of it all, yet it remained the one thing Kal seemed to disregard. He might not believe in the prophecy, but she knew it was true. She'd seen the *lastmarks*. She'd read the *godscripts*. She *knew* who she was. What she was. Why else would she be the only shurii to have ever lived without a second form? It wasn't a genetic anomaly. No mere coincidence.

"Kalevar," she said again. "You have to take me back."

He pushed off the mattress and stood in front of her. She looked imploringly up at him, willing him to understand the reasons she couldn't explain. He lifted one hand to tuck a strand of hair behind her ear. Her appearance was in an utter state of disarray, and yet he looked upon her as if she were the most captivating thing he'd ever seen.

"No," he said gently.

Her heart sank. "Please."

"Why would you ever want to go back to that place?"

Why? If only she could tell him. If only she could explain. But what was the point? He'd expressed his opinions of the Prima of Asteros. She may as well be a mythical creature. Asking him to put his faith in the designs of the Goddess was pointless. Besides, what importance did a deity have to a nonbeliever?

"I am the only thing they want," she said hopelessly. "If you let me go, you won't need the weapons or the armor or the alliance. The hunters won't return. Cindamar and the people you care for will be safe."

The softness in his expression hardened. "The crown will always be a threat as long as Domitan wears it," he said. "He and his serpent queen must fall. Until then, no one is safe. Least of all the people I care for."

"Why? Why do you hate them so much?"

Felíne searched his gaze. What she found there arrested her.

"Domitan and Serebine murdered my parents. They destroyed my family." Kal's words were like blows to the soft parts of her soul. Felíne closed her eyes, fearing the worst and knowing what he said was true. She knew it as surely as she'd known Imogen had spoken true in the tunnels beneath the city.

"They intended to end my line and very nearly succeeded. I only survived because of my uncle, Karrick. He and I are all that remain, and even he is lost to me now. I cannot rest until that butcher and his bitch queen are brought to justice. Returning is pointless. Even if I took you back, Domitan would torture the rest of the world for spite."

Felíne wanted to hold him. She wanted to throw her arms around him and tell him how sorry she was. How unfair the world was. She also wanted to scream. To assure him she wasn't a monster. She wasn't her father's cruelty or her mother's schemes. She only wanted to do what was right. What she knew needed to be done for the good of *everyone*.

"Please," she said instead. The plea escaped her lips—a final, wasted plea.

"No, Kitty," he said, thumb brushing away the lonely tear that descended her cheek. "The Crown of Asteros has taken every person I have ever loved. Endangered everyone I care for." The gold in Kal's moonless eyes flared to life. "I will not let them take you, too."

Chapter 46

Truer Words

FELÍNE STOOD NEXT TO SIG, absentmindedly stroking the sturdy horse's thick red mane with one hand. The action was more to comfort herself than anything, though Sig could do with a little therapeutic touch. The animal pawed the ground restlessly. He knew they were leaving, anxious for their next adventure. At least one of them was. Their reliable steed stood saddled and laden with her and Kal's few belongings, in addition to a few things they had acquired during their time in the disappearing city of Cindamar. One precious pack, in particular, contained her brand-new collection of herbs, tinctures, elixirs, and a portable variety of other medicinal supplies.

The menders Lew and Oram, alongside whom she'd worked earlier that day, had arranged a special visit with the owner of the local apothecary before the shop owner stored and secured all his wares for transport. They'd gifted her with an assortment of goods she'd previously passed on purchasing, having deemed them too expensive to justify spending Kal's money. Their generosity and unexpected kindness had nearly moved her to tears. Somehow, she suspected the supplies would prove extraordinarily useful. She wasn't entirely sure if trouble always followed Kal or if it was simply because she had been added to his company. Either way, Felíne now expected some manner of catastrophe and felt better prepared to deal with any resulting physical damages should they occur.

Which they would. Because they did.

She'd known Kal all of a few days and he'd already needed mending twice. The second time because he had willingly put himself in harm's way on her behalf. He'd allowed her to attend to his wounds a few hours prior, once her crushing disappointment at him refusing to return her to Asteros had turned to resolved acceptance. She couldn't blame him entirely. Not after he'd bared his past to her, and she finally understood the origin of his hate for her family. No, she couldn't blame him at all. She would just have to find another way.

Felíne glanced over at the seemingly constant source of her thoughts.

The memory of Kal's warrior body partially bared for her inspection had felt like a sacred presentation. Those eyes and the way they'd watched her every move as she tended to obvious injuries and probed for those unseen had unnerved her. Her unhelpful imagination provided detailed images the entire time, torturing her with memories. She vividly remembered the sensation of his lips on hers and the feel of his hands in her hair and around the curve of her waist. She'd made the mistake of glancing up into the intensity of that dark gaze and knew instantly he was thinking about the same thing. She'd become so flustered that she reached for the wrong tin of salve and ended up with no feeling in the fingertips of her left hand.

She flexed them, remembering. The sensation barely returned.

Felíne knew the mending was for her peace of mind more than anything else. Kal insisted he wasn't seriously hurt, something she'd verified upon her assessment. When she told him his injuries would likely be completely healed within a week if he shifted to second form, he just shrugged, thanked her, and told her he'd be fine.

She learned quickly that men rarely did what they were told. And when they did, it was only to make the person doing the telling feel better. She supposed it was some convoluted form of compliment. If he didn't care about her feelings, he wouldn't bother.

Felíne shielded her eyes from the golden light of the sinking sun.

How very different it all looked compared to their arrival just two days prior. Cindamar lived up to its name. The efficiency with which the city's residents moved astounded and impressed her. Every able body pitched in to help. Even the children could be seen carrying trinkets and dragging small boxes to and fro at the direction of close-guarding adults. Within a few more hours, the teeming settlement would be entirely packaged and transported, disappearing up into the mountains of the High Country, leaving a dusty red scar where before dwelled a flourishing oasis. Even the pools would be drained—how that was accomplished, she couldn't fathom—to prevent unwanted squatters.

Watching the city deconstruct before her eyes filled Felíne with a mixture of awe and bittersweet regret. She'd experienced firsts here, in this unexpected corner of the world. She'd gone shopping, visited food vendors and indulged in sweet drinks, attended a wedding with a handsome man, and danced with him. Her lip trembled briefly. She'd also witnessed innocent lives senselessly stolen. Faced her own peril. Felt the surge of relief seeing Kal emerge from the darkness, knowing he had come for her. Experienced the thrill of being kissed for the first time.

Not knowing if she'd ever see Cindamar again seemed an unkindness. For despite his new transactional relationship with Grisham, Felíne and Kal would not be joining the caravan. They were headed to Meress where she would be proudly deposited into the anxiously awaiting arms of her dear brother, Rask. He was in for one hell of a surprise when he realized the sister he so feverishly anticipated remained stuck in the nightmare from which Kal had worked so painstakingly to rescue her. And in sweet Railah's place was the heir to the Crown of Asteros. The daughter of Kal's most abhorred enemy. Oh, to imagine the look on Kal's face if he ever realized he'd been in the company of Domitan and Serebine's daughter this entire time. The Prima. The spoiled brat of a princess for whom he held so much contempt. To see the understanding that he'd kissed her. Bled for her. Risked his life. Had even begun to care for her... All while she willingly deceived him. There wasn't an adequately colorful description of how he would feel. Disgusted was a gross understatement.

The thought made her ill.

"Ready?"

Felíne looked up at the source of the deep voice that intruded upon her melancholic musings. Kal wore simple riding attire: a cream-colored, long-sleeved shirt and light leather armor. He sported a woven, wide-brimmed hat to shield from the sun during daylight hours, a twin to the one he'd given her, which currently hung from a length of cord to rest between his shoulders. To any passerby, he would look like a seasoned traveler making his way to the next town.

She knew better. He was armed to the teeth.

CLOAKING FATE

Their little visit from the hunters of Asteros had given him a fresh perspective regarding personal safety. He hadn't let her out of his sight since she'd begged him to return her to the capital. She'd barely convinced him she was perfectly safe to bathe without his help or attention.

Felíne shrugged. Was he asking if she was ready to venture again into unknown territory containing untold dangers, accompanied by the slightly terrifying heir to a generation of weapons masters and armorers? One that her parents had attempted to wipe from existence for an as yet undiscovered reason? No, not really. But she'd spent a lot of time being afraid, angry, and pessimistic the past few days. Probably longer than that if she thought about it. Perhaps it was time to give sincere optimism a shot. Her problems weren't changing, but her perspective could.

"As ready as I will be, I suppose."

Kal's attention shifted over her head, and she turned to follow his gaze. A small party approached the little spot that had once been the outskirts of the city, where they'd been finalizing their preparations. Kal moved to stand in front of her, his posture slightly defensive.

When Meryl stepped forward, he relaxed and retreated a few paces to allow the females some space.

Meryl's transformation was jarring. Her flattering gown had been replaced with fitted leather armor that hugged her figure. Her golden hair was braided back from her face in neat rows, sharpening her soft features into harsh lines. Large blue eyes were painted in kohl, but even that did little to conceal their puffy red contours.

Shortly after Felíne had last seen her, the citizens held a short ceremony for their dead. The bodies hadn't been burned as was their tradition; they didn't want to attract unwanted attention from smoke that could be seen for miles. Instead, they were wrapped in fine cloth and would be taken up into the mountains where their loved ones could lay them properly to rest. Today must have been the worst sort of agony for her.

The jeweled dagger Kal had gifted her as a wedding present hung sheathed across her chest.

Felíne hugged Meryl tightly, wishing they were parting under different conditions. She should be congratulating a happy couple, not bidding farewell to a new widow.

484

"Take care of yourself, Kitty," she said.

Felíne nodded and squeezed her again. "You too."

She searched for words to express the complicated things in her heart, but everything sounded wrong, and she didn't want to cause this woman any more pain than she already had. Felíne felt so happy to have met her. So thankful for the way Meryl had welcomed her without question. And yet she hated that she'd ever come. Hated what these people had gone through. What they'd suffered.

Meryl seemed to intuit her struggle. "I know," she said. "Me too."

Felíne gave her a grateful nod, determined not to cry again.

Meryl looked over Felíne's shoulder to where Kal waited. "Take care of him, too."

Felíne nodded despite the enormity of the request. "I will."

A gentle smile lit the pretty young female's features for a moment. "He'll never admit it, but he's needed someone for a while now," she said. "I didn't think he would ever find a woman who fit him. Someone to lessen the darkness inside him. To lift his shadows." Aqua eyes met hers. "But he did."

Oh, gods bless it all. Now she *was* going to cry.

Meryl took Felíne's hands in her own. "What the two of you have is something special, Kitty. Neither of you realize it now because it is new and fragile, but you will. Don't let the chance to appreciate it pass you up. Promise me."

The words nearly choked her, but she managed. "I promise."

Meryl kissed Felíne on the cheek and embraced her like a sister. Then she moved on to Kal, reaching up to hug his neck and whispering something in goodbye that only he could hear.

The sound of wood rolling over the ground made Felíne turn again.

"You are an interesting woman, Kitty Harless," Grisham said from his wheeled chair. An older woman Felíne recognized from Meryl and Bo's wedding stood protectively near him. A caretaker, perhaps? A lover? "I only wonder what other hidden gems you've got buried behind those honeyed eyes. I regret that I shall have to wait to discover."

Felíne knelt before the Trade Master of Cindamar, and his eyes lit in surprise. Yet it was Felíne caught off guard. Grisham held out his hand. In it rested a token. The one she'd been gifted after facing his famed scales. Her key to the city.

She didn't take it. "I don't believe I deserve this, Trade Master," she admitted softly. "Perhaps your scales weighed wrong."

Grisham leaned forward and reached for her hand. He pressed the coin firmly into it. "Not my scales," he said. "Your mirror. You do not see yourself as clearly as you ought to."

Felíne tightened her grip on the token. "I am so sorry," she said. "For all of it. And yet…I do not want Cindamar to go to war."

"I believe you," Grisham said, settling back into his cushion. He grimaced and used one hand to rub a gnarled knee. The man looked decades older in that moment than he had since she'd met him. "Cindamar has been a neutral entity for a very long time. Not all change is bad, but sometimes the catalyst is painful. None can say exactly what the future holds. We can only prepare. One thing I do believe is that you will be a part of it. In what capacity, I'm not yet certain," he said thoughtfully. "Though I hope to be around long enough to find out."

Felíne fished in the pocket of her tunic for the small velvet pouch containing the vial, salve, and herbs she'd tucked away before Meryl's wedding, along with the note she'd written. She held them out to Grisham.

He looked at her questioningly and thumbed open the note.

"For your legs," she explained.

"The Trade Master of Cindamar has no need of a young woman's pity." The older woman standing just behind Grisham spoke up. She had sharp brown eyes surrounded by a web of soft wrinkles, and her thin mouth pressed into a hard line. She'd been lovely once, but difficult years had aged her poorly. Grisham swiveled to glance up at her, and in his eyes, Felíne saw a devotion he made no effort to conceal.

He looked back at Felíne. "What Leticia is too kind to say is that my legs are ruined. I have had all manner of menders attend me. Each year, it is worse. I thank you for your kind attempt, Kitty, but it is only that. An attempt. I have grown far too weary of failed treatments to try any more."

If only he'd met Mender Alcuin a few years ago.

"The mender I trained with in Asteros successfully treated a woman with your condition, though hers was not as progressed as yours appears to be. It is degenerative, as you said. My mender was not able to cure her, but he did manage to reverse her symptoms considerably and significantly slow their advance." Grisham listened to her intently, a small, cautious hope flickering to life in his expression. Felíne continued. "The note has all the instructions for the therapies he used as well as a few samples to get you started until your mender can make more. I cannot make any promises as to their efficacy, and I will not lie to you. Healing will be difficult and will require strict adherence to the regimen I provided. If you can do this, at the very least, you should be able to stand without much pain in a month or so. That is, if you are willing to try one last form of treatment."

Leticia's eyes widened in surprise. Grisham carefully folded the instructions as if that small piece of paper was the most precious item he'd ever held. He handed it to Leticia, a testament to his trust in the woman, and she tucked it, along with the velvet pouch, into the bodice of her gown.

Felíne stood, and Grisham dipped his head to her in respect. "We shall meet again, Kitty Harless. When we do, I shall know whether or not to thank you. Safe travels."

Leticia pushed the Trade Master's chair away, and Garren stepped into his place. Even in second form, he wore his customary stern expression. Perhaps she should feel grateful he took her advice and shifted to speed the healing of his injuries. Felíne wondered sincerely if the male had ever been happy. He could do with a dose of happiness. She imagined it would completely transform him.

Garren dipped his head to hers, bringing a mouth full of teeth dangerously close. She felt Kal notice from where he stood speaking with Grisham. Garren's voice was soft, casual. "If the potion you just gave my brother harms him in any way, physical or otherwise, I will personally make sure that whatever it costs him is taken out of your hide."

Felíne leaned away from the imposing male and arched a brow. They were back to threats now, were they? "And if it helps him?"

Garren's serious brown predator's eyes searched her green-gold ones. "Then I will pledge you my life and my protection for as long as they are mine to provide."

Whatever response she'd been expecting, it wasn't *that*. True to form, he stalked off before Felíne could formulate a response, leaving her wholly taken aback by the unexpected formality of his vow.

The small party bid their final farewells and retreated one by one until she and Kal stood alone.

"What was all that about pledging fealty and undying love?" Kal asked casually.

Felíne gave him a look, knowing full well he heard every word. "Why? Jealous?"

Kal's lips turned up in a slightly scary grin. "Of that pitiful sap?" He dropped his gaze until it leveled with hers. She saw gold. *Oh, wow.* "He can say whatever he wants, but if he tries anything, I guarantee you the only thing those flowery promises of his will be is empty."

Okay then.

"Has anyone ever told you that you can be seriously overbearing?"

He straightened. "It's been mentioned."

And she could see he had absolutely zero intention of changing it. "Could you at least reign it in a little?"

The monster looked amused. "I might be persuaded to try."

Felíne sighed. She patted Sig on the meaty part of his neck before hoisting herself into the saddle. Kal mounted behind her.

They planned to have a second horse for her to ride, but the insufferable beast beneath her had vehemently objected. It turned out that Sig also had a problem with jealousy. He attacked any poor creature brought within several strides of him. The last of which had nearly thrown Felíne in terror. After that fourth attempt, Kal gave up trying to force the disobedient wretch into submission and concluded they would have to ride double. He reasoned that anyone in pursuit would be looking for two sets of tracks, not one, so there was some advantage despite the slowed rate of travel. Felíne didn't argue. It would be easier for her to escape Kal on horseback if he was left without his own mount on which to follow.

"I'm surprised Adder and Ophelia didn't come to say goodbye."

Kal finished adjusting his left stirrup before answering. "Adder is still maintaining his guise as Grisham's guard. He was instructed to oversee the takedown of the Trade Master's tent."

She thought about all those treasures Grisham kept on display. Mounds of wealth. Poor Adder. Felíne didn't envy him that task and said as much.

Kal agreed. "He'll be busy a while."

"What about Ophelia?"

Kal pressed into Sig's sides with both heels, turning them away from the mobilizing settlement, and urged him forward. The horse tossed his head, all too eager to comply. "She's not much one for goodbyes."

A crestfallen sensation descended upon Felíne, which surprised her. She had met the two of them so recently, but it felt like she'd known them an age with all that had happened the past few days. They were Kal's friends, but they felt like hers, too. At the very least, she would have liked to say goodbye. Felíne experienced a momentary pang as thoughts of Imogen surfaced.

"You gave Grisham a true gift," Kal said after riding in silence for a few minutes. "If your tincture works, he will be indebted to you."

If? "No faith, dear Kal?"

He chuckled softly, recognizing his own words to her. "When, then."

"That's better."

Kal leaned down, his mouth close to the shell of her ear. She suppressed a shiver. "You know, a debt from the Trade Master of Cindamar is no small thing. You could ask for nearly any favor, and he'd be inclined to grant it."

While that might be so, she wanted nothing from Grisham. The boons that she would ask were not ones he could grant.

Then again...

"Next time we visit, I'll be sure to ask him for my own private suite suitably far from yours so I can avoid being inconvenienced by all the commotion you attract."

Kal laughed. It was a rich, wonderful sound. "Oh, Kitty, by the time we return to Cindamar, I have a feeling you'll be begging to share my room."

Ha! It was her turn to laugh. "Make that overbearing and *completely* delusional."

Felíne looked out over the red gold desert, waning light radiant in its final hours.

"It's still some way to Meress," Kal said, a smile in his voice. "A lot can happen in a few days."

CLOAKING FATE

Felíne thought back on ones recently passed. On all that had happened. Things that she'd learned. Ways in which she had changed.

"You know, Kal," she said. "I'm inclined to agree."

In fact, she didn't know if truer words had ever been spoken.

Epilogue

IMOGEN DESCENDED THE STONE STEPS in the Stronghold of Asteros with a suffocating sense of finality. Each footfall echoed off the underground tower's walls and ricocheted back to her, piercing another piece of her soul. She willingly lowered herself into the mouth of doom. By the time she reached the bottom, her spirit would be in tatters, chewed up and left at intervals along the way, marking her grim trajectory for any unfortunate soul who happened to follow and take notice.

The first time she came this way, she hadn't known what horrors awaited her. The second time, she knew, but she'd carried with her a sense of determination and conviction that she was doing what must be done. Her life hadn't mattered without her mother's, and that's what she would have been throwing away had she not come. The second time was to have been the last. She had promised herself, no *vowed*, that she would never again set foot on this stairwell. She would never again feel the chill that seeped through the stone in these dark depths that the lanterns did nothing to alleviate.

Yet here she was. No longer a Fate, yet just as unwilling. In possession of a newly elevated position and title, yet descending a third time.

The guard leading her turned into an adjacent tunnel before they reached the bottom. She stepped off the staircase onto a floor of stone pavers. The Stronghold wasn't entirely stone. The suites reserved for those Fated Mothers who had fulfilled the first portion of their contract by successfully becoming pregnant were relocated to lavish rooms with polished wood floors, floor-to-ceiling curtains, four poster beds boasting plush mattresses and down coverlets, private baths, and no shortage of additional small comforts. At least, that's what she assumed happened for any others. Imogen had no idea how many pregnancy suites the Stronghold maintained. To her knowledge, she was the only one who had ever carried a baby to term. She'd heard of many females who had succeeded in surviving copulation but died soon after.

Internal damages. That's what Vulgren told the queen. *They just weren't resilient enough.*

As if the women were to blame for hemorrhaging after the impossible attentions of the males forced to service them.

A soul-deep anger roiled inside her. She hated this place. The dungeons of Asteros were located somewhere else inside the city, but this was the true prison.

The guard pushed through a thick door that creaked as it swung inward.

"Yes, yes, Pollack here will take you to the examination room, dearest. Wait for me there. We will get you settled in no time."

The sound of that voice made Imogen grateful she'd foregone eating a meal before coming back here. She would have vomited all over the gray stone floor.

Mender Vulgren waited inside the modest room they entered. The chemical smell of sterilizer assaulted Imogen as she crossed the threshold. The vapors still hanging in the air sent a traumatic flash through her memory. Cold instruments. Colder hands. The nauseating pull low in her belly as Vulgren *assessed* her. The frigid intrusion of his thin probing fingers. Imogen forced herself to step forward. Mentally, she was already bolting back the way they came.

A slender, too-young female with unbound blonde hair the color of wheatgrass, blue-green eyes, and a spattering of freckles looked up at Imogen as she passed. She smiled shyly. The innocence in her expression pitched Imogen's stomach again. The girl had just arrived and didn't fully understand yet. That innocence was just one more thing that would be stripped from her before her time in the Stronghold was finished. Gods willing, the poor thing left with the rest intact.

The young woman followed her guard out of the room, and the door sealed, shutting Imogen in with the remaining guard and Mender Vulgren.

The mender beamed, his eerie blue eyes twinkling with an affection that made her ill. "My, how you've risen above the flock, dearest Imogen," Vulgren said. "My most prized Mother."

He called them *mothers*. They weren't. They were sows. Kept and bred until they became just scraps of meat, tossed out with the rest of the trash.

"Did you ever think that the daughter of a common whore could be so esteemed? You've done well for yourself, Elder. And now you've returned to The Stronghold. To me. To the Mothers."

Imogen lifted her chin. "Not for long," she said stiffly. "The Prima will be found. Her presentation is impending."

And once Felíne completed her servicing, the prophecy would be fulfilled. The Goddess's curse would be broken. The *lastmarks* would fade. Then, Asteros would no longer have need of the Fated Mothers. They would all be free.

Mender Vulgren slipped around the edge of the pale wooden desk to peer closely at her. "Ah, yes. But until then, you are here. With us. We must make special use of our time."

Imogen tensed, trying not to lean out of Vulgren's reach. Especially after her panicked episode in the royal villa. She didn't want to give him the satisfaction of seeing her unnerved by his proximity. "With you, but not one of you. As you said, I am an elder now."

And she would die before being forced to submit herself to further humiliation and abuse.

"Yes!" Mender Vulgren clapped his sallow hands. "And the Mothers require your tutelage, Elder! We've made some changes since you were last among us. I think you'll be pleased at the new order. Come. I will show you."

Mender Vulgren collected a thick robe from the back of his chair and shrugged it onto bony shoulders. He swept out of the room and beckoned her to follow. Imogen had no choice.

They returned to the main staircase and went down another four flights. If they kept going, they'd eventually reach what she'd come to think of as the cellar. The main floor of the Stronghold where all the Fates were housed in their individual rooms. All the way at the bottom, furthest from the light.

That level also held the servicing chambers. Spacious rooms containing several choice pieces of furniture. A chaise lounge. An overlarge bed. A pallet laden with plush pillows. She remembered the first time she'd entered that chamber. She'd thought the crisp white of the linens looked elegant. Now, she knew it better allowed Vulgren and his attendants to monitor how much blood had been lost during the servicing. White was also easier to bleach.

And then she'd discovered the leather bindings attached to each piece of furniture bolted to the floor. She'd never had them used on her, but she knew what they were for.

"We've been much more successful since you left us, Elder," Vulgren went on amiably. "Four more mothers survived their session with the male. Not a drop of blood was spilt! Imagine! You're still a legend, dearest. No viable pregnancies since yours. But I do think we're on to something."

Imogen trailed Vulgren at a barely tolerable distance, the bitter scent of his hair oil wafting unpleasantly into her face. They rounded a corner and passed through two more heavy doors. The corridor was unfamiliar to her. The third and final door they approached was inlaid with steel and bolted with the largest lock she'd ever seen. Vulgren produced a substantially ancient key from the folds of his robe, fit it into the lock, and gave it a crank. The door swung open with a horrible creak.

Imogen stepped under the threshold into a dank hallway. Something did not feel right about this. "You said male," she said, peering into the dark. "Not males."

Vulgren followed close behind her. She moved to the side to allow him to pass, not wanting to go further into the pitch. "Ah yes, Elder. Very good. Just one of the changes we've made permanent. I've said all along the issue was with the males, not my dearest Mothers. Savage brutes. Though it took some convincing to bring Queen Serebine around to my way of thinking."

Something moved in the shadows ahead. Something big.

Vulgren did not venture forward toward whatever it was. Instead, he opened another door adjacent. As soon as the new door was unlatched, light seeped between the cracks, and Imogen stepped into the room, eager to escape the dark and whatever lurked in its depths.

A table and two chairs stood in the center of the plain room, and two lanterns glowed wanly on the back wall. The front wall had been cut open and inlaid with a huge rectangular window. Impenetrable dark swallowed the place beyond the glass pane like the hallway they'd just stepped out of. At the table sat a single guard who stood to attention upon their arrival. Vulgren nodded to the guard, who promptly departed, leaving them alone once again.

"I don't understand," Imogen said. "What happened to the males?"

"Retired," he said in a way that made her think of a dog being put down. Something pierced her heart. "But not all of them, dearest. There is one left. The only one that matters."

Her stomach twisted unpleasantly, but she wanted to know more. As a Fate, she was never privy to the workings of Vulgren and his cronies. She was not permitted to interact with the other Fates and so did not know if they were subjected to the same treatment as her. If Imogen wanted to help any of them, she needed to understand how all of this worked. Vulgren seemed in a telling mood, and she was willing to take advantage of all the information she could get her hands on. "And this one male? He services *all* the females?"

Vulgren's eyes lit at his own perceived genius. "Of course! You see, after you succeeded so brilliantly while the others failed again and again—please don't take that offensively, dearest, I mean it with the utmost respect for your sisters—I knew there was something about your specific coupling that had to be harnessed if the Prima was to succeed. You were the first of your kind in more ways than one, you know."

Imogen once again caught movement in the dark, but this time, it was beyond the glass pane. "What do you mean? What other way?"

Vulgren stepped up beside her and followed her gaze. A soft smile lifted the wrinkles on his face. "You were paired with a special male, dearest. *The* special male."

Imogen glanced over at him, bowels knotting.

"I reasoned with the queen for weeks to be able to utilize him for our purposes. She was understandably reserved. You see, Queen Serebine was concerned our using him would foil the ultimate success of the Prima. She didn't want the Goddess to retaliate and go back on her promise. But I studied the *godscripts*. I spoke with the priests. I counseled with the elders. Nowhere did it say the *male* had to be pure of flesh." Vulgren's colorless eyes blinked at her. His expression turned to one of chagrin. "Meanwhile, my Mothers were dying at the claws of those brutish males—those sub-par specimens. I pleaded, and my queen finally relented. She released him to me to use. The perfect male was ours at last."

CLOAKING FATE

Vulgren reached out to touch Imogen's face with his slender white hands, and she had to close her eyes to concentrate on not flinching. Cold seeped into the place he touched her. Like it always did, as though the warmth of life abhorred him. "And you, dearest Imogen, were the first female we gave to him."

A light flickered to life somewhere beyond the window, and Imogen's eyes flew open. She saw a room through the glass with bars as thick as her arm from floor to ceiling—a giant cage.

The realization of what Vulgren was saying came crashing down upon her like the whole of the Stronghold and all its bleached walls and all its death-gray stone.

No.

Beyond the pane of glass, beyond the bars, the shape of a male took form.

The male. Her male.

He stood to his full height, dark charcoal fur glossy in the shadows, thick proud hackles raised in warning. His huge muzzle swung in their direction. She didn't know if he could see her, but something in his dark eyes said he knew she was near. He opened his mouth and bellowed.

Vulgren clapped his hands again. "Isn't he magnificent! But of course, you know that."

Imogen approached the glass and gingerly placed a hand on its surface. Yes. He was magnificent. Her gaze found the impossibly heavy shackles fixed to both of his ankles. The skin around them was hairless and raw. Scarred. An overwhelming sadness descended upon her. He was a prisoner here, just as she had been. She'd found her escape, and he'd only found additional chains.

"Why?" she whispered. She knew the answer, but she needed him to say it. She needed to know her worst nightmare had yet to be realized. "Why did you choose him? What makes him so special that he had to be the only one?"

It wasn't fair.

Vulgren beamed. "Because, dearest. There is no other like him."

He looked out at the dark male, bursting with all the pride of an honored father.

"This is Karrick Kaine. The Primordial Male."

496

Enjoyed what you read?
Please leave me a review!

Stay up to date with writing news, current and future projects, release dates, and other insights by subscribing to N.A. Walker's newsletter.

You can do so at:
www.nawalkerauthor.com

As a subscriber, you will also receive access to my novelette, *High Tide,* which is a standalone prequel to *Cloaking Fate.*

Keep reading for a sneak peek of *High Tide*.

Chapter 1

Meridia Albright slipped through the heavy door to her bed-chambers and ghosted past the sleeping guard slumped in the corridor. He'd be out for hours yet. When he woke, he'd have no memory of the sweet wine she'd spiked and had delivered to her chambers. He wouldn't recall tasting the wine to ensure it was safe for his charge's consumption.

The guard would be dismissed regardless. Her father didn't tolerate carelessness in his employ. Certainly not when it came to his only daughter's protection. Little did he know, the heir to their family name had been consorting with "riff-raff" and learning all sorts of interesting things. More recently, how to formulate undetectable elixirs. Thanks to Kallen's insatiable curiosity and his penchant for experimenting with dangerous substances, she now had about seven different ways to render someone unconscious without ever having to draw a weapon. Meridia's father, the Bladesinger of Ilistaar, would be appalled.

Remaining undetected as she navigated the seaside castle she called home required little effort. Stealth had been bred into Meridia's very bones. Excitement trilled through her as she carefully descended the eastern wall.

Getting out was the easy part. Getting down and avoiding the hundred-and-fifty foot fall off the edge of the bluff into the deadly rocks below was slightly more challenging. Meridia had navigated this cliff a handful of times, but its treachery never waned. She clung to the rocky façade like an enthusiastic barnacle. One foot. One hand. Another hand. Second foot.

A gull glided effortlessly by and screeched at her as it passed. The tireless breeze whipped a tendril of sand-colored hair free from her plait. If only the gods had given her wings. Think of all the additional grief she could have given her parents. What they *had* given her, as they'd given all shurii, was the ability to willingly shift into a second form fully equipped with claws, teeth, a tail to improve balance, increased strength and agility, and heightened senses, all of which would make her descent less perilous. Meridia, however, wasn't exactly known for playing it safe. She clambered down farther, the thrill of navigating the cliff's jagged face in her first form making her blood sing. She felt *alive*.

Thankfully, the typical morning mists were thin that day. She was skilled and, according to Kallen, had balls bigger than most males, but making this descent in a blind fog was beyond even her.

Finally, what felt like ages later, Meridia planted her boots onto the rugged path that had long ago been carved into the cliffside. She removed her gloves and rubbed her hands together as she walked, working the strain out of her aching fingers. A small, self-satisfied smile graced her lips.

Brightsea Castle stood tall and proud a hundred or so feet above her. Its northern and eastern walls were guarded by tumultuous waves, while those to the south and west rose high above the surrounding countryside, offering views of rolling hills and lush forests for miles. If she looked out the window in her father's council chamber, she would see the sprawling cluster of rooftops in the city several miles farther down the coastline. One blue-tiled roof belonged to her favorite bakery. It was seated near the beach with a small patio that overlooked the water. The sun was just rising. If she got close, she'd smell the day's fresh bread.

But the city of Brightsea wasn't her destination. Meridia was headed for a hidden cave tucked back along a recess of the bluff, about a mile down the rough-hewn path.

When she arrived, she ducked behind a thick blanket of beach vine that clung to the pale stone, obscuring the mouth of the cave. The initial entrance was dark, and Meridia crept along one wall until she reached the interior. A short distance ahead, she saw her target.

His back was turned to her, and she could just make out the thin, neatly twisted locks of coal-colored hair that fell over his broad shoulder blades. The lamp on his desk illuminated the workspace where he sat hunched over some mysterious project.

His focus made him vulnerable. Perfect.

Meridia drew a dagger, silent in the way of her family name, and crept closer. She was a ghost. Like a sigh. The muted rumble of waves crashing against the bluff outside was loud in comparison.

One more step and she'd have him.

"Hello, Meridia."

The young man spoke without turning, his voice deep and unsurprised.

She lowered her blade and straightened. "Damn it, Kallen. I was so quiet."

For someone considered 'low-born' with no formal training, he was irritatingly perceptive.

Kallen swiveled toward her, the lamplight casting amber shadows on the broad planes of his face. He grinned, and Meridia couldn't keep her gaze from snagging on his full lips.

"You were impossibly quiet."

Her cornflower gaze flicked to Kallen's. Eyes like warm, molten chocolate, a shade lighter than his skin, drank her in.

"Then how did you know?" she asked, momentarily distracted.

"I can *feel* you," he said, as if that explained everything. He pushed up from his chair.

Meridia closed the distance between them and welcomed the feel of his arms winding around her waist. She planted a kiss on his lips. "And what do you feel exactly?"

Kallen brought her hand from behind his neck to rest on his chest, over his heart. "This," he said. "I know when you are close."

A coy smile played on Meridia's lips. "And here I thought you were a man of the mind, Kallen Kaine."

He huffed a laugh. "I was until I met you."

Meridia tried to kiss him again, but he held just out of reach, finally looking at her properly. His brow furrowed as he took in her lack of claws, fur, and teeth. "How did you get here?"

"The bluff," she said, still trying to kiss him.

He evaded. "You scaled the bluff? In *first form?*"

Meridia made innocent eyes at him. "Maybe?"

Kallen stepped back and ran a hand over his clean-shaven face. The softness of youth had left him. The angles of his jaw were stronger than they had been even just last year. Sometimes, it was difficult for Meridia to believe they weren't children anymore, playing in the surf and hunting for crabs.

"Gods, Meridia," he said. "What were you thinking? It's a two-hundred-fifty-seven-foot drop to the sea."

What she'd been thinking was that she wanted to test her limits. She'd made the climb successfully in second form multiple times but never in first. It was decidedly more difficult with fingertips and booted feet instead of claws, but she'd made it.

"I wanted a challenge," she said with a shrug.

His gaze hardened, and he opened his mouth to reply.

"You asked me to come, Kallen," she said before he could lecture her further. "It sounded urgent."

He allowed the redirection, but not before pinning her with a serious look, clearly conveying their prior conversation was not over.

He sighed after a moment and slumped into the single chair. "It's my mother."

Meridia braced herself.

Kallen's mother lived in the city below Brightsea Castle and maintained what Kallen considered to be 'unsavory proclivities.' It was a polite way of saying she was a hot fucking mess.

The woman was constantly in trouble. Caught stealing, borrowing money with no means of repayment, finding her way into fights she couldn't get herself out of, experimenting with drugs. Her eighteen-year-old son was always running to her rescue, a burden he shouldn't have to shoulder and one he willingly had since he was a boy.

Lecretia's most recent risky endeavor had resulted in an unplanned pregnancy, and Kallen had been beside himself with worry over her wellbeing throughout each term. By Meridia's estimation, she was due to deliver Kallen's younger sibling any day now.

Her heart stuttered. "The baby?"

Kallen, thankfully, shook his head. "No, the baby's fine. As fine as it can be considering the poor thing's parentage anyway." He leaned back. "She's selling *kossroot*."

Meridia shook her head. Of course, she was. Lecretia couldn't just find a steady job, deliver her baby safely, raise the child in a loving environment, and allow her only other son the chance he deserved to pursue his interests without constantly having to drop everything and run to her aid.

Kallen was brilliant. An exceptional scientist and inventor. He wanted so badly to make a proper life for himself despite the unsavory aspects of his upbringing and worked tirelessly to better his standing in society.

"Who's the dealer?"

Meridia could only assume Lecretia had made a considerable mess of whatever situation she'd gotten herself into. It wouldn't be as simple as her *just* selling. The wretched woman never did anything halfway.

There were a handful of low-life dealers who peddled a number of illicit drugs along the coast. One would think the city resting in the Bladesinger's shadow would be immune to such depravity, but cockroaches found their way into even the cleanest kitchens. The good news was that roaches, elusive as they could be, were still bugs. They could be squashed. All the dealers Meridia knew of were big cowards. They'd be easy for her and Kallen to handle on their own.

"That's the problem," Kallen said with a grimace. "It wasn't a dealer she screwed over."

Meridia's face fell.

"It was Darkan Nox. The Chef."

Meridia only needed one word to adequately summarize the hundred or so thoughts that popped into her head.

"*Shit.*"

Acknowledgments

Thank you, God, for a boundless spirit, a capable body, my dear family, and so many answered prayers. This entire journey has been littered with blessings, and I cannot begin to express how deep my gratitude flows.

To my husband, Michael, thank you for your consistent willingness to sacrifice, your seemingly infinite patience, and your steadfast support. It is no easy thing for a logical man to love a whimsical woman, but you manage it with enviable success. I could not have chosen a better life partner.

Thank you, Lindsey. *Cloaking Fate* might never have found its way into existence if it weren't for your encouragement. You read every random scene, every fragment of texted dialogue, and somehow developed a genuine interest in Felíne and Kal before I truly knew who they were. Without you insisting those pieces be made whole, I don't know when I'd have found the motivation to dig into their world, unearth their spirits, and breathe life into their adventures. Thank you. Sincerely.

To my dear editor, Emma, I cannot thank you enough for your help with this story. I am so overwhelmingly appreciative of the hours you spent going line by line through this manuscript, seeing its potential, and helping me realize it. *Cloaking Fate* would not be what it is without your attention to detail and thoughtful feedback, nor would I be half as confident to share it. You corrected far more incorrectly-placed commas than was fair. I can't wait to get you the sequel.

To Paige and Rosemary, thank you for setting aside time to read all the frighteningly unpolished bones of this story and somehow envision its worth. Your feedback and reassurances meant more than you could know.

To my cover design artist, Ruxandra at Methyss Art, I don't know how, but you did it again. There aren't adequate words to express how impressed I am with this cover. You have far exceeded any expectation I could have hoped to possess. I am blown away by your talent and so thankful that our paths crossed. You have given this book a stunning shell and I am beyond proud to display it.

To the owner(s) and employees of Well Coffee Co., thank you for providing a welcoming atmosphere, warm smiles, and delectable drinks. I spent more hours than I should admit tucked away amidst your gentle greenery working on this book and sipping half-sweet lattes. Something about your little coffee shop helped to open the floodgates of my imagination.

To anyone who has offered a kind word, a congratulations, or an encouraging sentiment, *thank you*. I started this book thinking maybe only a handful of people would read it, less would like it, and only I would love it. I am so happy to have been wrong.

About the Author

N. A. Walker is an adult fantasy romance writer with a passion for weaving magic, emotion, and adventure into her stories. She holds a BA in psychology from Arizona State University and a BS in nursing from Northern Arizona University—an academic blend that allows her to suffuse her characters with both mind and heart. She works full-time as a surgical nurse, is a voracious bookworm, and prefers to hibernate during the unforgivable southwest summers. She and her husband live in Arizona with their children, dogs, and floppy cat.